PENGUIN CLASSICS

THE PORTABLE
NINETEENTH-CENTURY
AFRICAN AMERICAN
WOMEN WRITERS

HOLLIS ROBBINS, PH.D., is Director of the Center for Africana Studies at Johns Hopkins University and Chair of the Humanities Department at the Peabody Institute, where she has taught since 2006. Her work focuses on the intersection of nineteenth-century American and African American literature and the discourses of law, bureaucracy, and the press. Robbins has edited or coedited four books on nineteenth-century African American literature, including the Penguin edition of Frances E. W. Harper's 1892 novel *Iola Leroy, or Shadows Uplifted*. She is also the coeditor with Henry Louis Gates, Jr., of *The Annotated Uncle Tom's Cabin* (2006) and *In Search of Hannah Crafts* (2004). She is currently completing a monograph, *Forms of Contention: The African American Sonnet Tradition*.

HENRY LOUIS GATES, JR., is the Alphonse Fletcher University Professor and founding director of the Hutchins Center for African and African American Research at Harvard University. He is editor in chief of the Oxford African American Studies Center and TheRoot.com, and creator of the highly praised PBS documentary *The African Americans: Many Rivers to Cross*. He is general editor for a Penguin Classics series of African American works.

The Portable Nineteenth-Century African American Women Writers

Edited with an Introduction by
HOLLIS ROBBINS
and
HENRY LOUIS GATES, JR.

General Editor:
HENRY LOUIS GATES, JR.

PENGUIN BOOKS

PENGUIN BOOKS

An imprint of Penguin Random House LLC
375 Hudson Street
New York, New York 10014
penguin.com

LIBRARY OF CONGRESS CATALOGING-IN-PUBLICATION DATA
Names: Robbins, Hollis, 1963– editor. | Gates, Henry Louis, Jr., editor.
Title: The portable nineteenth-century African American women writers / edited with an introduction by Hollis Robbins and Henry Louis Gates, Jr. ; general editor, Henry Louis Gates, Jr.
Description: New York : Penguin Books, 2017. | Series: Penguin Classics
Identifiers: LCCN 2017004173 | ISBN 9780143105992 (paperback)
Subjects: LCSH: American literature—African American authors. | American literature—Women authors. | American literature—19th century. | African American women—Literary collections. | BISAC: FICTION / African American / General. | FICTION / Anthologies (multiple authors).
Classification: LCC PS508.N3 P596 2017 | DDC 810.8/0928708996073—dc23
LC record available at https://lccn.loc.gov/2017004173

Printed in the United States of America
1 3 5 7 9 10 8 6 4 2

Set in Sabon LT Std
Designed by Sabrina Bowers

Contents

THE PORTABLE
NINETEENTH-CENTURY
AFRICAN AMERICAN WOMEN WRITERS

PERSONAL ACCOUNTS OF
ABOLITION AND FREEDOM

NORTHERN WOMEN AND
THE POST-WAR SOUTH

MEMOIRS: LOOKING BACK

POETRY, DRAMA, AND FICTION

WOMEN ADDRESSING WOMEN: ADDRESSES AND ESSAYS

WOMEN MEMORIALIZING WOMEN

What Is an African American Classic?

I have long nurtured a deep and abiding affection for the Penguin Classics, at least since I was an undergraduate at Yale. I used to imagine that my attraction for these books—grouped together, as a set, in some independent bookstores when I was a student, and perhaps even in some today—stemmed from the fact that my first-grade classmates, for some reason that I can't recall, were required to dress as penguins in our annual all-school pageant, and perform a collective side-to-side motion that our misguided teacher thought she could choreograph into something meant to pass for a "dance." Piedmont, West Virginia, in 1956, was a very long way from Penguin Nation, wherever that was supposed to be! But penguins we were determined to be, and we did our level best to avoid wounding each other with our orange-colored cardboard beaks while stomping out of rhythm in our matching orange, veined webbed feet. The whole scene was madness, one never to be repeated at the Davis Free School. But I never stopped loving penguins. And I have never stopped loving the very audacity of the idea of the Penguin Classics, an affordable, accessible library of the most important and compelling texts in the history of civilization, their black-and-white spines and covers and uniform type giving each text a comfortable, familiar feel, as if we have encountered it, or its cousins, before. I think of the Penguin Classics as the very best and most compelling in human thought, an Alexandrian library in paperback, enclosed in black and white.

I still gravitate to the Penguin Classics when killing time in an airport bookstore, deferring the slow torture of the security lines. Sometimes I even purchase two or three, fantasizing that I can speed-read one of the shorter titles, then make a dent in the longer one, vainly attempting to fill the holes in the liberal arts education that our degrees suggest we have, over the course of a plane ride! Mark Twain once quipped that a classic is "something that everybody wants to have read and nobody wants to read," and perhaps that applies to my airport purchasing habits. For my generation, these titles in the Penguin Classics form the canon—the canon of the texts that a truly well-educated person should have read, and read carefully and closely, at least once. For years I rued the absence of texts by black authors in this series, and longed to be able to make even a small contribution to the diversification of this astonishingly universal list. I watched with great pleasure as titles by African American and African authors began to appear, some two dozen over the past several years. So when Elda Rotor approached me about editing a series of African American classics and collections for Penguin's Portable Series, I eagerly accepted.

Thinking about the titles appropriate for inclusion in these series led me, inevitably, to think about what, for me, constitutes a "classic." And thinking about this led me, in turn, to the wealth of reflections on what defines a work of literature or philosophy somehow speaking to the human condition beyond time and place, a work somehow endlessly compelling, generation upon generation, a work whose author we don't have to look like to identify with, to feel at one with, as we find ourselves transported through the magic of a textual time machine; a work that refracts the image of ourselves that we project onto it, regardless of our ethnicity, our gender, our time, our place. This is what centuries of scholars and writers have meant when they use the word *classic*, and—despite all that we know about the complex intersubjectivity of the production of meaning in the wondrous exchange between a reader and a text—it remains true that classic texts, even in the most conventional, conservative sense of the word *classic*, do exist, and these books will continue to be read long after the generation the text reflects and defines, the generation of readers contemporary with the text's author, is dead and gone. Classic texts speak from their authors' graves, in their names, in their voices. As Italo Calvino once remarked, "A classic is a book that has never finished saying what it has to say."

Faulkner put this idea in an interesting way: "The aim of every artist is to arrest motion, which is life, by artificial means, and hold it fixed so that a hundred years later, when a stranger looks at it, it moves again since it is life." That, I am certain, must be the desire of every writer. But what about the reader? What makes a book a classic to a reader? Here, perhaps, Hemingway said it best: "All good books are alike in that they are truer than if they had really happened and after you are finished reading one you will feel that all that happened to you, and afterward it belongs to you, the good and the bad, the ecstasy, the remorse and sorrow, the people and the places and how the weather was."

I have been reading black literature since I was fifteen, yanked into the dark discursive universe by an Episcopal priest at a church camp near my home in West Virginia in August 1965, during the terrifying days of the Watts Riots in Los Angeles. Eventually, by fits and starts, studying the literature written by black authors became my avocation; ultimately, it has become my vocation. And, in my own way, I have tried to be an evangelist for it, to a readership larger than my own people, people who, as it were, look like these texts. Here, I am reminded of something W. S. Merwin said about the books he most loved: "Perhaps a classic is a work that one imagines should be common knowledge, but more and more often isn't." I would say, of African and African American literature, that perhaps classic works by black writers are works that one imagines should be common knowledge among the broadest possible readership but that less and less are, as the teaching of reading to understand how words can create the worlds into which books can transport us yields to classroom instruction geared toward passing a state-authorized standardized exam. All literary texts suffer from this wrongheaded approach to teaching, mind you; but it especially affects texts by people of color, and texts by women—texts still struggling, despite enormous gains over the last twenty years, to gain a solid foothold in anthologies and syllabi. For every anthology, every syllabus, every publishing series such as the Penguin Classics constitutes a distinct "canon," an implicit definition of all that is essential for a truly educated person to read.

James Baldwin, who has pride of place in my personal canon

of African American authors since it was one of his books that
that Episcopal priest gave me to read in that dreadful summer
of 1965, argued that "the responsibility of a writer is to exca-
vate the experience of the people who produced him." But
surely Baldwin would have agreed with E. M. Forster that the
books that we remember, the books that have truly influenced
us, are those that "have gone a little further down our particular path than we have yet ourselves." Excavating the known is
a worthy goal of the writer as cultural archeologist; yet, at the
same time, so is unveiling the unknown, the unarticulated yet
shared experience of the colorless things that make us human:
"something we have always known (or thought we knew)," as
Calvino puts it, "but without knowing that this author said it
first." We might think of the difference between Forster and
Baldwin, on the one hand, and Calvino, on the other, as the
difference between an author representing what has happened
(Forster, Baldwin) in the history of a people whose stories,
whose very history itself, has long been suppressed, and what
could have happened (Calvino) in the atemporal realm of art.
This is an important distinction when thinking about the nature of an African American classic—rather, when thinking
about the nature of the texts that constitute the African American literary tradition or, for that matter, the texts in any
under-read tradition.

One of James Baldwin's most memorable essays, a subtle
meditation on sexual preference, race, and gender, is entitled
"Here Be Dragons." So much of traditional African American
literature, even fiction and poetry—ostensibly at least once removed from direct statement—was meant to deal a fatal blow
to the dragon of racism. For black writers since the eighteenth-
century beginnings of the tradition, literature has been one
more weapon—a very important weapon, mind you, but still
one weapon among many—in the arsenal black people have
drawn upon to fight against antiblack racism and for their
equal rights before the law. Ted Joans, the black surrealist poet,
called this sort of literature from the sixties' Black Arts Movement "hand grenade poems." Of what possible use are the nice-
ties of figuration when one must slay a dragon? I can hear you
say, give me the blunt weapon anytime! Problem is, it is more

difficult than some writers seem to think to slay a dragon with a poem or a novel. Social problems persist; literature too tied to addressing those social problems tends to enter the historical archives, leaving the realm of the literary. Let me state bluntly what should be obvious: Writers are read for how they write, not what they write about.

Frederick Douglass—for this generation of readers one of the most widely read writers—reflected on this matter even in the midst of one of his most fiery speeches addressing the ironies of the sons and daughters of slaves celebrating the Fourth of July while slavery continued unabated. In his now-classic essay "What to the Slave Is the Fourth of July?" (1852), Douglass argued that an immediate, almost transparent form of discourse was demanded of black writers by the heated temper of the times, a discourse with an immediate end in mind: "At a time like this, scorching irony, not convincing argument, is needed ... a fiery stream of biting ridicule, blasting reproach, withering sarcasm, and stern rebuke. For it is not light that is needed, but fire; it is not the gentle shower, but thunder. We need the storm, the whirlwind, and the earthquake." Above all else, Douglass concludes, the rhetoric of the literature created by African Americans must, of necessity, be a purposeful rhetoric, its ends targeted at attacking the evils that afflict black people: "The feeling of the nation must be quickened; the conscience of the nation must be roused; the propriety of the nation must be startled; the hypocrisy of the nation must be exposed; and its crimes against God and man must be proclaimed and denounced." And perhaps this was so; nevertheless, we read Douglass's writings today in literature classes not so much for their content but to understand, and marvel at, his sublime mastery of words, words—to paraphrase Calvino—that never finish saying what it is they have to say, not because of their "message" but because of the language in which that message is inextricably enfolded.

There are as many ways to define a classic in the African American tradition as there are in any other tradition, and these ways are legion. So many essays have been published entitled "What Is a Classic?" that they could fill several large anthologies. And while no one can say explicitly why generations of readers return to read certain texts, just about everyone can agree that making a best-seller list in one's lifetime is most certainly not an index of fame or influence over time; the longevity of one's readership—of books about which one says, "I am re-reading," as Calvino puts it—on the other hand, most certainly is. So, the size of one's readership (through library use, Internet access, and sales) cumulatively is an interesting factor to consider; and because of series such as the Penguin Classics, we can gain a sense, for our purposes, of those texts written by authors in previous generations that have sustained sales—mostly for classroom use—long after their authors were dead.

There can be little doubt that *Narrative of the Life of Frederick Douglass* (1845), *The Souls of Black Folk* (1903), by W. E. B. Du Bois, and *Their Eyes Were Watching God* (1937), by Zora Neale Hurston, are the three most classic of the black classics—again, as measured by consumption—while Langston Hughes's poetry, though not purchased as books in these large numbers, is accessed through the Internet as frequently as that of any other American poet, and indeed profoundly more so than most. Within Penguin's Portable Series list, the most popular individual titles, excluding Douglass's first slave narrative and Du Bois's *Souls*, are:

> *Up from Slavery* (1903), Booker T. Washington
> *The Autobiography of an Ex-Colored Man* (1912), James Weldon Johnson
> *God's Trombones* (1926), James Weldon Johnson
> *Passing* (1929), Nella Larsen
> *The Marrow of Tradition* (1898), Charles W. Chesnutt
> *Incidents in the Life of a Slave Girl* (1861), Harriet Jacobs
> *The Interesting Narrative* (1789), Olaudah Equiano
> *The House Behind the Cedars* (1900), Charles W. Chesnutt
> *My Bondage and My Freedom* (1855), Frederick Douglass
> *Quicksand* (1928), Nella Larsen

These titles form a canon of classic of African American literature, judged by classroom readership. If we add Jean Toomer's novel *Cane* (1922), arguably the first work of African American modernism, along with Douglass's first narrative, Du Bois's *The*

Souls, and Hurston's *Their Eyes*, we would most certainly have included many of the touchstones of black literature published before 1940, when Richard Wright published *Native Son*.

Every teacher's syllabus constitutes a canon of sorts, and I teach these texts and a few others as the classics of the black canon. Why these particular texts? I can think of two reasons: First, these texts signify or riff upon each other, repeating, borrowing, and extending metaphors book to book, generation to generation. To take just a few examples, Equiano's eighteenth-century use of the trope of the talking book (an image found, remarkably, in five slave narratives published between 1770 and 1811) becomes, with Frederick Douglass, the representation of the quest for freedom as, necessarily, the quest for literacy, for a freedom larger than physical manumission; we might think of this as the representation of metaphysical manumission, of freedom and literacy—the literacy of great literature—inextricably intertwined. Douglass transformed the metaphor of the talking book into the trope of chiasmus, a repetition with a stinging reversal: "You have seen how a man becomes a slave, you will see how a slave becomes a man." Du Bois, with Douglass very much on his mind, transmuted chiasmus a half century later into the metaphor of duality or double consciousness, a necessary condition of living one's life, as he memorably put it, behind a "veil."

Du Bois's metaphor has a powerful legacy in twentieth-century black fiction: James Weldon Johnson, in *Ex-Colored Man*, literalizes the trope of double consciousness by depicting as his protagonist a man who, at will, can occupy two distinct racial spaces, one black, one white, and who moves seamlessly, if ruefully, between them; Toomer's *Cane* takes Du Bois's metaphor of duality for the inevitably split consciousness that every Negro must feel living in a country in which her or his status as a citizen is liminal at best, or has been erased at worst, and makes of this the metaphor for the human condition itself under modernity, a tellingly bold rhetorical gesture—one designed to make the Negro the metaphor of the human condition. And Hurston, in *Their Eyes*, extends Toomer's revision even further, depicting a character who can gain her voice only once she can name this condition of duality or double consciousness and then glide gracefully and lyrically between her two selves, an "inside" self and an "outside" one.

More recently, Alice Walker, in *The Color Purple*, signifies upon two aspects of the narrative strategy of *Their Eyes*: First, she revisits the theme of a young black woman finding her voice, depicting a protagonist who writes herself into being through letters addressed to God and to her sister, Nettie—letters that grow ever more sophisticated in their syntax and grammar and imagery as she comes to consciousness before our very eyes, letter to letter; and second, Walker riffs on Hurston's use of a vernacular-inflected free indirect discourse to show that black English has the capacity to serve as the medium for narrating a novel through the black dialect that forms a most pliable and expansive language in Celie's letters. Ralph Ellison makes Du Bois's metaphor of the veil a trope of blindness and life underground for his protagonist in *Invisible Man*, a protagonist who, as he types the story of his life from a hole underground, writes himself into being in the first person (in contradistinction to Richard Wright's protagonist, Bigger Thomas, whose reactive tale of fear and flight is told in the third person). Walker's novel also riffs on Ellison's claim for the revolutionary possibilities of writing the self into being, whereas Hurston's protagonist, Janie, speaks herself into being. Ellison himself signified multiply upon Richard Wright's *Native Son*, from the title to the use of the first-person bildungsroman to chart the coming to consciousness of a sensitive protagonist moving from blindness and an inability to do little more than react to his environment, to the insight gained by wresting control of his identity from social forces and strong individuals that would circumscribe and confine his life choices. Toni Morrison, master supernaturalist and perhaps the greatest black novelist of all, trumps Ellison's trope of blindness by returning over and over to the possibilities and limits of insight within worlds confined or circumscribed not by supraforces (à la Wright) but by the confines of the imagination and the ironies of individual and family history, signifying upon Faulkner, Woolf, and García Márquez in the process. And Ishmael Reed, the father of black postmodernism and what we might think of as the hip-hop novel, the tradition's master parodist, signifies upon everybody and everything in the black literary tradition, from the slave narratives to the Harlem Renaissance to black nationalism and feminism.

This sort of literary signifying is what makes a literary tradition, well, a "tradition," rather than a simple list of books whose authors happen to have been born in the same country, share the same gender, or would be identified by their peers as belonging to this ethnic group or that. What makes these books special—"classic"—however, is something else. Each text has the uncanny capacity to take the seemingly mundane details of the day-to-day African American experience of its time and transmute those details and the characters' actions into something that transcends its ostensible subject's time and place, its specificity. These texts reveal the human universal through the African American particular: All true art, all classics, do this; this is what "art" is, a revelation of that which makes each of us sublimely human, rendered in the minute details of the actions and thoughts and feelings of a compelling character embedded in a time and place. But as soon as we find ourselves turning to a text for its anthropological or sociological data, we have left the realm of art; we have reduced the complexity of fiction or poetry to an essay, and this is not what imaginative literature is for. Richard Wright, at his best, did this, as did his signifying disciple Ralph Ellison; Louis Armstrong and Duke Ellington, Bessie Smith and Billie Holiday achieved this effect in music; Jacob Lawrence and Romare Bearden achieved it in the visual arts. And this is what Wole Soyinka does in his tragedies, what Toni Morrison does in her novels, what Derek Walcott did in his poetry. And while it is risky to name one's contemporaries in a list such as this, I think that Rita Dove and Jamaica Kincaid achieve this effect as well, as do Colson Whitehead and Edwidge Danticat, in a younger generation. (There are other writers whom I would include in this group had I the space.) By delving ever so deeply into the particularity of the African and African American experience, these authors manage, somehow, to come out the other side, making the race or the gender of their characters almost translucent, less important than the fact that they stand as aspects of ourselves beyond race or gender or time or place, precisely in the same magical way that Hamlet never remains for long stuck as a prince in a court in Denmark.

Each classic black text reveals to us, uncannily, subtly, how the Black Experience is inscribed, inextricably and indelibly, in the human experience, and how the human experience takes one of its myriad forms in blackface, as it were. Together, such texts also demonstrate, implicitly, that African American culture is one of the world's truly great and eternal cultures, as noble and as resplendent as any. And it is to publish such texts, written by African and African American authors, that Penguin has created this new series, which I have the pleasure of editing.

HENRY LOUIS GATES, JR.

Introduction

"The exceptional career of our women will yet stamp itself indelibly upon the thought of this country," Fannie Barrier Williams proclaimed in 1893, with a note of what we might think of as both prophetic defiance and exceptional optimism in her voice, given the mountain of sexist attitudes about the intellectual abilities of women in general, and black women in particular, that female writers had to scale. To read the work of the women in this collection is to realize that well before the dawning of the twentieth century, black women as early as the eighteenth and all through the nineteenth centuries had long embraced the social media called print culture and used print to proclaim and testify to white and black women and men—and to each other—the particularity of their identities as that rara avis, writers who were both women and of African descent. "They were phenomenal women, impressive Sojourners wielding pens of political militancy and social concern," as Gloria Wade-Gayles has rightly noted.[1] Perhaps Anna Julia Cooper put it best in 1892: "only the BLACK WOMAN can say 'when and where I enter, in the quiet, undisputed dignity of my womanhood, without violence and without suing or special patronage, then and there the whole Negro race enters with me,'" in a formulation that, for its time, was both shockingly original and so poignantly true.

This anthology spans a century that saw not only the hard-fought end to slavery but also the development of communities of free black women and men dedicated to education, political participation, and to writing themselves into full citizenship and subjectivity, within and outside of what W. E. B. Du Bois called "the Veil." During the struggle for emancipation that dominated the first two-thirds of the century, women's voices were as loud and relentless as men's voices in the clarion calls for freedom *now*. "To be free is very sweet," insisted Mary Prince, bluntly contradicting her mistress. And freedom meant, for these women, the freedom to speak their minds as women, just as surely as it meant the abolition of chattel slavery. "I am women's rights," Sojourner Truth boldly declared, calling attention to herself as the embodied truth of her statement. Maria Stewart wondered, "How long shall the fair daughters of Africa be compelled to bury their minds and talents beneath a load of iron pots and kettles?" Her response remains as inspiring today as it undoubtedly was then: "Until we begin to promote and patronize each other," she answered, calling upon black women to think of themselves as a nation within a nation within a nation, to paraphrase Martin R. Delany's famous description of black America well before the Civil War. "Can woman do this work?" Lucy Laney asks. "She can; and she must do her part, and her part is by no means small. Nothing in the present century is more noticeable than the tendency of women to enter every hopeful field of wage earning and philanthropy, and attempt to reach a place in every intellectual arena."

The fifty-two writers who appear in this anthology demonstrate a will to engage intellectually, in print, with the world, with other women generally, and with each other individually. These women writers looked at the world around them, before and after Emancipation, and resolved to speak out, to grapple with the political and social fact of their existence, and to begin to articulate the foundations of a black feminist thought, wide ranging and far seeing. Many of these women were widely read and drew on canonical literary and philosophical works to frame their own opinions on current events. Some, the children of slaves and former slaves, had no formal schooling at all and raised their voices first and foremost to express outrage in the most urgent tones. Nearly all openly acknowledged their goals and aspirations, desiring through their words to proclaim their presence, to call for social and political change, to give comfort and direction to their brothers and sisters, but also to provide context for their own goals and identities as writers.

A majority of the writers featured here constituted themselves as a defined and organized community. Most knew each other, corresponded with each other, wrote about each other's accomplishments, and supported each other's ambitions. Many rallied around each other as part of political movements or social organizations. Others thrived in relative solitude, sustained only by their own determination, writing for minimum compensation and for all the purposes that writers write. With and without the help of social networks, black women sought the power of writing and used it to express themselves poignantly, humorously, boisterously, and artistically in print. Were hashtags available, we can be certain that they would have used them brilliantly!

To be a successful writer in the nineteenth century required persistence, fearlessness, ambition, and salesmanship. Perhaps the most well-known figure in this collection, Sojourner Truth could not read or write but had an outsized flair both for self-articulation and for self-promotion. As Nell Painter describes her work, Truth "put her body and her mind to a unique task, that of physically representing women who had been enslaved."[2] Certainly there was widespread illiteracy among all the residents of the United States throughout the nineteenth century, but especially, of course, among slaves, former slaves, and the children of former slaves. But black women, just as surely as did black men, forcefully sought formal education and recorded their thoughts and reflections, their passions and fears, their aspirations and anxieties, in novels, newspaper columns, plays, poetry, letters, diaries, and scrapbooks. And perhaps not surprisingly, women fortunate enough to have experienced a formal education, such as Edmonia Highgate, strove to make a name for themselves also as advocates of modern self-determination: "Oh, how independent one feels in the saddle! One thing, I can't imagine why one needs to wear such long riding skirts. They are so inconvenient when you have to ford streams or dash through briers. Oh, fashion, will no Emancipation Proclamation free us from thee!"

As Mia Bay, Farah J. Griffin, Martha S. Jones, and Barbara D. Savage's essential recent volume *Toward an Intellectual History of Black Women* shows, when scholars continue to "put flesh on the bones" of often skeletal biographical details about these writers, the result will be "a dynamic new map of politics and culture that establishes the key relevance of black women to studies of history and literature."[3] These texts speak to the fact that feminism and women's rights were far more institutionally ingrained throughout American—and African American—life in the nineteenth century than was typically recorded either in bio-graphical sketches or literary histories. This volume builds on work such as P. Gabrielle Foreman's *Activist Sentiments: Reading Black Women in the Nineteenth Century* and Martha S. Jones's *All Bound Up Together: The Woman Question in African American Public Culture, 1830–1900*, which focus on the ways African American women in the nineteenth century worked individually and collectively for political and social change.

The strength of the various small but remarkably sustaining communities of women writers makes those who succeeded in writing and publishing without assistance or moral support from these circles all the more remarkable. Hannah Crafts's *The Bondwoman's Narrative*, we now know, gives proof of the escaped slave Hannah Bond's commitment to telling her own story of captivity, flight, and freedom, insisting on her literary kinship with—but essential difference from—the popular Victorian heroines of her day. Abby Fisher's 1881 cookbook, *What Mrs. Fisher Knows About Old Southern Cooking*, demonstrates Fisher's commitment to memorializing her life's work in print, turning a stereotype of a black woman's traditional "place in the kitchen" on its head by writing about it. Eliza Potter and Harriet Wilson chronicle their own experiences as working women in white households, turning the tables on former mistresses and employers. Collected together, these works point toward a deepening of our understanding of nineteenth-century black feminism as exemplified by both educated and wholly unlettered authors, employing the widest variety of writing styles.

As Eric Gardner remarks in his groundbreaking volume on the nineteenth-century black press, *Black Print Unbound*, "rich scholarship over the past decade that reconceptualizes African American literature" has shown the field of texts by black writers is "much more diverse in terms of genre, approach, aesthetics, venue, and language and was amazingly dynamic even as it was shaped by systemic oppression."[4] Gardner looks at the complex literary interaction between black and white writers before and after the Emancipation Proclamation, as black activists sought political influence; he offers the most thorough examination to date of the *Christian Recorder*, which published several of the authors found in our collection, notably Julia Collins's *The Curse of Caste*

(1865) and the letters of Edmonia Highgate. The black press, through the regular publication of journalism, lectures, letters to the editor, serialized novels, poetry, book reviews and literary criticism, prayers, marriage notices, and obituaries, distributed a written record of the complexities of black humanity to thousands of subscribers throughout the country.

Many of the texts collected here first appeared in one of the scores of black-owned publications launched over the course of the nineteenth century. In the pre-war period, *Freedom's Journal*, the *Colored American*, the *North Star*, and the *Elevator*, among other publications, focused primarily on the battle to end slavery. After the war, black-owned newspapers promoted community, racial pride, and economic uplift. Women's writing was essential to that success.

While most black-owned newspapers and journals were published and edited by men, an important exception is the Ontario-based *Provincial Freeman*, launched in 1853 and edited by Mary Ann Shadd Cary. Shadd Cary also published a detailed guidebook for "colored emigrants" fleeing to Canada after the Fugitive Slave Law. "Information is needed," Shadd Cary writes, and she helpfully provides it. Shadd Cary was praised by Bishop Payne, perhaps a bit condescendingly, in 1893 for her "familiarity with facts, her knowledge of men, and her fine power of discrimination." While no other black woman published a prominent newspaper until Charlotta Spears Bass bought the *California Eagle* in 1912, women were represented in the nineteenth-century black press as staff writers and columnists. Notable journalists excerpted here include Maria Stewart, who answered William Lloyd Garrison's call in 1831 for woman writers to publish in the *Liberator,* and Gertrude Bustill Mossell, who penned the first weekly column devoted to women's issues in the *New York Freeman* in 1885, to Josephine St. Pierre Ruffin, who launched the first newspaper by and for black women, *Women's Era*, in 1894.

Important recent work such as Teresa C. Zackodnik's *"We Must Be Up and Doing"* ably demonstrates the breadth of African American feminist political organization in the nineteenth and early twentieth centuries. While Zackodnik's anthology focuses on black women's social engagement, our anthology emphasizes the contours of black women's thought and personal ambition as exemplified in their own writings about themselves. The black feminist movement often aligned with but also flourished independently from movements focused on abolition, women's suffrage, temperance, and civil rights generally. While some texts are more recognizably "feminist" in a modern sense than others, all insist upon the recognition of women's intellect as essential to the history of black life in nineteenth-century America.

In total, fifty-two black women writers are collected in this volume. Their writings are organized by focus and genre and presented chronologically by publication date.

In the first section, "**Personal Accounts of Abolition and Freedom**," narratives by Mary Prince, Nancy Prince, Sojourner Truth, Hannah Crafts, Harriet Wilson, Harriet Jacobs, and Louisa Picquet testify starkly and movingly about harrowing experiences under slavery and the struggle to maintain dignity and seek escape. "I was flogged on my naked back," Mary Prince reports bluntly. "For weeks I was tormented by hundreds of little red insects, fine as a needle's point, that pierced through my skin," Harriet Jacobs describes. "If I run off, he'd blow my brains out," reports Louisa Picquet. Eliza Potter and Elizabeth Keckley write from relative privilege: Keckley, understanding her extraordinarily rare position as a former inhabitant of the White House, tells the story of how she rose to serve Mrs. Lincoln and chronicles daily life during the years of war—much, she would learn, to Mrs. Lincoln's annoyance. Potter, born free and living a life of independence and adventure as a prized hairdresser for wealthy clients, writes a tell-all book that gets her banished from her community. Her narrative is a reminder that fashion has always been in fashion. "I was never more amused in my life," she writes, describing efforts to be compensated from a train fire that burned up her clothes, "than at seeing the different railroad gentlemen pick up my list, look at and shrink from it, as if it were an impossibility for a working woman to have such a wardrobe. One of them seemed quite horrified at the very idea of my having ten silk dresses with me; but it afforded me a good deal of pleasure to let him know I had as many more at home."

"**Fugitives and Emigrants: Moving West and North**" features writers such as Mary Ann Shadd Cary, who left Pennsylvania for southern Ontario after the passage of the 1850 Fugitive Slave Act, and Mrs. John Little, who escaped with her husband to a farm in Canada. Black women made themselves at home across the country and in Canada, where Shadd Cary assured her readers that "There is no legal discrimination whatever effecting colored emigrants in Canada, nor from any cause whatever are their privileges sought to be abridged." Jennie Carter, writing from Nevada, far from the Deep South, endeavors to set the record straight about life under slavery. "I know many," she writes of slaveholders, "whose daughters in the big house were not as light as their daughters in the cabin." Abby Fisher, who moved from Mobile, Alabama, to California after the Gold Rush, made a name for herself as a cook and published her volume of recipes in San Francisco. Carter and Fisher are particularly important to the geographic breadth of this anthology; African Americans remain underrepresented in historical scholarship on the American West. It is probable that more writers like Carter will be discovered, and more research will be done on the population as a whole.

"Northern Women and the Post-War South" offers accounts of free black women determined to elevate and educate newly emancipated youths in Southern schools. After the founding of the Bureau of Refugees, Freedmen, and Abandoned Lands, known informally as the Freedmen's Bureau, on March 3, 1865, the great task of transitioning emancipated slaves into citizens required dedicated and sensitive teachers. Not surprisingly many black women, frustrated by career limitations in Northern school districts, leapt at the opportunity and promise of teaching in the South. Charlotte Forten Grimké's "Life on the Sea Islands" tells of her teaching experience in 1864, before the war was over. "It is wonderful how a people who have been so long crushed to the earth, so imbruted as these have been," Forten writes, "can have so great a desire for knowledge, and such a capability for attaining it." Edmonia Goodelle Highgate was a favorite of readers of the *Christian Recorder*, telling witty tales of culture shock in Southern towns during Reconstruction. "I don't believe in world-saving—but I do in self-making," she writes. "Create something. Aspire to leave something immortal behind you." Josephine St. Pierre Ruffin chastises white women in Georgia who did not welcome these educators from the North particularly warmly. "[O]ne of the saddest things about the sad conditions of affairs in the South has been the utter indifference which Southern women, who were guarded with unheard of fidelity during the war, have manifested to the mental and moral welfare of the children of their faithful slaves."

"Memoirs: Looking Back" offers comprehensive and organized accounts of lives in transition during the upheavals of the Civil War and its aftermath, new educational opportunities, and migrations north. Three of the writers here were preachers. Julia A. J. Foote, in *A Brand Plucked from the Fire*, describes her awakening from a life of drink to a life of religion. Jarena Lee argues that if fishermen, "ignorant of letters," were inspired to preach, why not women? Zilpha Elaw likewise takes up the task. Lucy Delaney bluntly describes the lawsuit granting her freedom in *From Darkness Cometh the Light,* and Ella Sheppard's "Historical Sketch of the Jubilee Singers," published here in its entirety, is a firsthand account of a groundbreaking cultural phenomenon, a world-famous singing group who toured the world and changed forever the music of American concert halls. "Success followed us to Washington, D.C.," Sheppard writes of their 1871 tour. "The President turned aside from pressing duties to receive us at the White House. Parson Brownlow, Tennessee's Senator, too ill to attend our concert, sent for us to visit him. He cried like a child as we sang our humble Southern slave melodies. Returning to New England we received a perfect ovation."

"Poetry, Drama, and Fiction," the central section of this volume, demonstrates the extraordinary imaginative vision of women writers in the nineteenth century. From Sarah Forten Purvis's "The Abuse of Liberty" and Ann Plato's "The Natives of America," both published in the first decades of the century, to Alice Dunbar Nelson's poem "To Madame Curie" published at the end of the century, these works testify to the sheer range of creative works that African American women produced, often in the face of harrowing obstacles. We publish here three poems from Frances Harper's long-lost first poetry collection, *Forest Leaves* (ca. 1847), recently rediscovered by Johanna Ortner. These newfound poems offer an important perspective on Harper's development as a poet and an intellectual as well as insight into Harper's Christian beliefs as the foundation for her lifelong political interventions. With *Forest Leaves*, we are given a

snapshot of Harper at age twenty, a highly literate, politically engaged, and devout young black woman in the era of slavery.
Given the contours of Harper's literary output by the end of her
career, we see how her ambitions grew and were nourished while
her subject matter remained close to that of her early poetry.

Also featured in this section are key works by Julia Collins, Pauline Hopkins, Kate Chapman Tillman, and Amelia E. Johnson, all
known to students and scholars of the era. Featured here also is
Mary E. Ashe Lee's remarkable poem "Afmerica" (1885), telling
the tale of "a child of liberty / Of independent womanhood, / The
world in wonder looks to see / If in her there is any good," here republished in its entirety. Finally, we are quite excited to include an
excerpt from the 1891 novel *True Love* by Sarah E. Farro, newly
rediscovered by Gretchen Gerzina. All together these selections delight, startle, and, most importantly, we hope, will provoke their
readers to seek out the complete works by each author.

"**Women Addressing Women**" offers addresses and essays from
the closing decades of the nineteenth century by women dedicated
to the cause of women's education and women's rights. As Mia
Bay argues, while vocal black women faced challenges and obstacles to speaking out on race prejudice, ethnology, pseudo-
scientific "race" theories, and the domestic ideal of "true
womanhood," by the 1880s and 1890s women "celebrated their
embrace of female racial self-defense as a new goal."⁵ We offer
here essays by Sarah J. Early on women in the South, and by Virginia W. Broughton, Lucy Craft Laney, and Fannie Barrier Williams on work and education. Broughton emphasizes her belief in
the moral and civilizing responsibilities women bear for keeping
men on the straight and narrow. "Those places to which he goes,
to the exclusion of women, such as saloons, club-rooms and legislative halls, are not suitable for him, and he is not safe, and we are
sure it is not good for him . . . the wreck and ruin that result from
his frequenting places of ill-repute, and the unjust and imperfect
laws he makes are substantial proof that danger and death await
those who disobey God's word." Mary V. Cook insisted upon the
importance of women writers: "Often a short article, setting forth
some digestible truth, is like seed sown in good ground, which
will bring forth a hundred fold, or like bread cast upon the water,
that may be seen and gathered after many days hence." Reframing

prevailing views of history, the optimistic Cook offers women motivation to come out of the shadows and act.

These black women wrote, it seems, about almost everything, from the most intensely personal to the broadly political, sometimes prophetically. For example, Mary Church Terrell focused not only on women's suffrage but also the convict lease system: "Those who need laborers for their farms, saw mills, brick yards, turpentine distilleries, coal or phosphate mines, or who have large contracts of various kinds, lease the misdemeanants from the county or State, which sells them to the highest bidder with merciless disregard of the fact that they are human beings, and practically gives the lessee the power of life and death over the unfortunate man or woman thus raffled off." Her scathing report exemplifies why the government, investigators, and journalists play an important role in protecting human rights even after humanitarian laws are passed. Comparisons can be drawn between Terrell's work and the work of those today who fight mass incarceration. Fighting a different but equally important battle, Williams demanded recognition for women's intellectual labor: "are we not justified in a feeling of desperation against that peculiar form of Americanism that shows respect for our women as servants and contempt for them when they become women of culture?"

We offer a separate section on **"Education and Social Reform"** to collect together essays and speeches that offer wide-ranging thoughts about the nation, race prejudice, and the role of education in envisioning a less violent and divisive future. This section includes speeches from the remarkable Fanny M. Jackson Coppin on industrial education for women. Education as a means of black advancement was Coppin's greatest concern. Her goal was to see black individuals able freely to seek the educations that best suited them. To a greater degree than her more scholarly contemporaries, Coppin strikes a balance in her addresses between higher-minded, religious discourse and practical steps that can be taken to improve the lives of African American women. Josephine J. Turpin Washington, in "Needs of Our Newspapers," offers a constructive critique of the black press, which allowed her and so many of the other voices in this anthology to be heard, demanding better quality and more

originality. Her sweeping argument takes into account economics, aesthetics, politics, and history. Washington's work
was impressively analytical. She was endlessly determined to
see the standing of the women and men of the race improve.

Notable in Julia Caldwell-Frazier's work is an interest in Darwin. She cites his theory of evolution as evidence of the inevitabil-
ity of black progress: "According to the 'survival of the fittest,' the
Negro can look cheerfully and hopefully to the future. . . .
The physical, mental, moral, and esthetic faculties of the race have
been 'weighed in the balance and not found wanting.'" Gertrude
Bustill Mossell writes on the contributions of African Americans
in musical culture, in poetry, and in political activism, giving pride
of place among her peers to the formidable champion of anti-
lynching laws: "Perhaps the greatest work of philanthropy yet accomplished by any woman of the race is that undertaken and so
successfully carried out at the present hour by Miss Ida B. Wells."

We end this section with the fiery and unforgettable work of
Wells in waking the nation to this scourge of lynching. Emphasized here too is that Wells was supported in her work by other
women who promoted her, hosted her, and comforted her.
Mossell describes Wells visiting Frances Harper in Philadelphia
and learning that her writings had provoked a violent response.
"What was her consternation to find letters pouring in upon
her from friends and correspondents at Memphis warning her
not to return to her office on pain of being lynched. She was
informed that her newspaper plant had been destroyed and the
two male editors had been forced to flee for their lives." Readers then and now, P. Gabrielle Foreman writes, "were fasci-
nated with the details of authors' lives . . . [and] the involving
trajectory of an increasingly documented race history."[6]

Finally, **"Women Memorializing Women"** offers works at the
end of the century that take stock of the contributions of African
American women writers. Lucy Wilmot Smith's "Women as Journalists: Portraits and Sketches of a Few of the Women Journalists
of the Race" anticipates the work of this anthology, and so many
that proceeded it, insisting that the work of women writers be
read, remembered, and addressed. S. Elizabeth Frazier, in "Some
Afro-American Women of Mark," a riff on Rev. William Simmons's *Men of Mark* (1887) lauds Fanny Jackson Coppin with a

tinge of sadness: "Had she been other than an American colored woman, or had she not had to struggle against the characteristic conservatism of the Society of Friends, she would have been one of the most famous of American's school reform instructors. As it is she works on modestly, indeed, too self-deprecating; eminent, but without notoriety." Frazier's touching appreciation of her intellectual sister's uphill battle for recognition provokes us to read, remember, and re-acknowledge the contributions of each of these writers whose works are gathered together in this collection.

Consider too the women never given the opportunity to seek literacy and education. What accomplishments, what writings remain of the countless black women who never became members of the publishing elite? "Historical scholarship on black women especially has yet to map the broad contours of their political and social thought in any detail," writes Mia Bay, "or to examine their distinctive intellectual tradition."[7] The range of works by the fifty-two writers featured here offers readers a glimpse of how impressively expansive the contours of the remarkably vibrant and dynamic African American woman's intellectual tradition are.

HOLLIS ROBBINS AND HENRY LOUIS GATES, JR.

NOTES

1. Gloria Wade-Gayles, "Black Women Journalists in the South, 1880–1905: An Approach to the Study of Black Women's History." *Callaloo*, no. 11–13 (February–October 1981): 138–152.
2. Nell Irvin Painter, *Sojourner Truth: A Life, A Symbol.* (New York: W. W. Norton, 1997), 3.
3. Mia Bay, Farah J. Griffin, Martha S. Jones, and Barbara D. Savage, eds., "Introduction," in *Toward an Intellectual History of Black Women* (Chapel Hill: The University of North Carolina Press, 2015), 4.
4. Eric Gardner, *Black Print Unbound: The Christian Recorder, African American Literature, and Periodical Culture* (New York: Oxford University Press, 2015), 12, 13.
5. Bay et al., *Toward an Intellectual History of Black Women*, 89.
6. P. Gabrielle Foreman, *Activist Sentiments: Reading Black Women in the Nineteenth Century* (Urbana: University of Illinois Press, 2009), 94.
7. Bay et al., *Toward an Intellectual History of Black Women*, 1.

Suggestions for Further Reading

Andrews, William L. Introduction to *Six Women's Slave Narratives.* Edited by Henry Louis Gates, Jr. New York: Oxford University Press, 1988.

Bay, Mia. Introduction to *The Light of Truth: Writings of an Anti-Lynching Crusader,* by Ida B. Wells. New York: Penguin Books, 2014.

Bay, Mia, Farah J. Griffin, Martha S. Jones, and Barbara D. Savage, eds. *Toward an Intellectual History of Black Women.* Chapel Hill: The University of North Carolina Press, 2015.

Bassard, Katherine Clay. *Spiritual Interrogations: Culture, Gender, and Community in Early African American Women's Writing.* Princeton, NJ: Princeton University Press, 1999.

Bergman, Jill. *The Motherless Child in the Novels of Pauline Hopkins.* Baton Rouge: Louisiana State University Press, 2012.

Boyd, Melba Joyce. *Discarded Legacy: Politics and Poetics in the Life of Frances E. W. Harper, 1825–1911.* Detroit, MI: Wayne State University Press, 1994.

Brown, Hallie Q. *Homespun Heroines and Other Women of Distinction.* New York: Oxford University Press, 1988.

Brown, Lois. *Pauline Elizabeth Hopkins: Black Daughter of the Revolution.* Chapel Hill: The University of North Carolina Press, 2008.

Bryant, Jacqueline K. *The Foremother Figure in Early Black Women's Literature: Clothed in My Right Mind.* New York: Garland, 1999.

Carby, Hazel V. *Reconstructing Womanhood: The Emergence of the Afro-American Woman Novelist.* New York: Oxford University Press, 1987.

Carter, Tomeiko Ashford, ed. *Virginia Broughton: The Life and Writings of a National Baptist Missionary.* Knoxville: The University of Tennessee Press, 2010.

Cobb, Jasmine Nichole. "'Forget Me Not': Free Black Women and Sentimentality." *MELUS: Multi-Ethnic Literature of the United States* 40, no. 3 (Fall 2015): 28–46.

Collins, Julia C. *The Curse of Caste; or, The Slave Bride: A Rediscovered African American Novel.* Edited by William L. Andrews and Mitch Kachun. New York: Oxford University Press, 2007.

Cooper, Valerie C. *Word, Like Fire: Maria Stewart, the Bible & the Rights of African Americans.* Charlottesville: University of Virginia Press, 2011.

Crafts, Hannah. *The Bondwoman's Narrative.* Edited by Henry Louis Gates, Jr. New Introduction and Notes by Henry Louis Gates, Jr. and Gregg Hecimovich. New York: Grand Central Publishing, Hachette Book Group, 2014.

Evans, Stephanie Y. *Black Women in the Ivory Tower, 1850–1954: An Intellectual History.* Gainesville: University Press of Florida, 2008.

Ferguson, SallyAnn H., ed. *Nineteenth-Century Black Women's Literary Emergence: Evolutionary Spirituality, Sexuality, and Identity: An Anthology.* New York: Peter Lang, 2008.

Foreman, P. Gabrielle. *Activist Sentiments: Reading Black Women in the Nineteenth Century.* Urbana: University of Illinois Press, 2009.

Foster, Frances Smith. *Written by Herself: Literary Production by African American Women, 1746–1892.* Bloomington: Indiana University Press, 1993.

Gardner, Eric. *Black Print Unbound: The* Christian Recorder, *African American Literature, and Periodical Culture.* New York: Oxford University Press, 2015.

———, ed. *Jennie Carter: A Black Journalist of the Early West.* Jackson: University Press of Mississippi, 2009.

———. "'You Have No Business to Whip Me': The Freedom Suits of Polly Wash and Lucy Ann Delaney." *African American Review* 41, no. 1 (Spring 2007): 33–50.

Gates, Henry Louis, Jr., and Hollis Robbins, eds. *In Search of Hannah Crafts: Critical Essays on* The Bondwoman's Narrative. New York: Basic Civitas Books, 2004.

Giddings, Paula J. *Ida: A Sword Among Lions: Ida B. Wells and the Campaign Against Lynching.* New York: Amistad, 2008.

Glass, Kathy L. *Courting Communities: Black Female Nationalism and "Syncre-Nationalism" in the Nineteenth-Century North.* New York: Routledge, 2006.

Grasso, Linda M. *The Artistry of Anger: Black and White Women's Literature in America, 1820–1860.* Chapel Hill: The University of North Carolina Press, 2002.

Guy-Sheftall, Beverly. "Black Feminist Studies: The Case of Anna Julia Cooper." *African American Review* 43, no. 1 (Spring 2009): 11–15.

————, ed. *Words of Fire: An Anthology of African-American Feminist Thought*. New York: The New Press, 1995.

Hall, Stephen G. *A Faithful Account of the Race: African American Historical Writing in Nineteenth-Century America*. Chapel Hill: The University of North Carolina Press, 2009.

Haynes, Rosetta R. *Radical Spiritual Motherhood: Autobiography and Empowerment in Nineteenth-Century African American Women*. Baton Rouge: Louisiana State University Press, 2011.

Higginbotham, Evelyn Brooks. *Righteous Discontent: The Women's Movement in the Black Baptist Church, 1880–1920*. Cambridge, MA: Harvard University Press, 1994.

Hopkins, Pauline. *The Magazine Novels of Pauline Hopkins: Including* Hagar's Daughter, Winona, *and* Of One Blood. Edited by Henry Louis Gates, Jr. New York: Oxford University Press, 1990.

Hubert, Susan J. "Testimony and Prophecy in *The Life and Religious Experience of Jarena Lee*," *Journal of Religious Thought* 54/55, no. 2/1 (Spring/Fall 1998): 45.

Jones, Martha S. *All Bound Up Together: The Woman Question in African American Public Culture, 1830–1900*. Chapel Hill: The University of North Carolina Press, 2009.

Kachun, Mitch. "Juneteenth, Julia Collins and Exploring History: Digging for Lost Stories from a Changing Past." *Journal of the Lycoming County Historical Society* (Winter 2010–2011): 9.

Kafka, Phillipa. *The Great White Way: African American Women Writers and American Success Mythologies*. New York: Garland, 1993.

King, Wilma. *The Essence of Liberty: Free Black Women During the Slave Era*. Columbia: University of Missouri Press, 2006.

Lawson, Ellen NicKenzie, and Marlene D. Merrill, eds. *The Three Sarahs: Documents of Antebellum Black College Women*. New York: Edwin Mellen Press, 1984.

Lee, Valerie, ed. *The Prentice Hall Anthology of African American Women's Literature*. Upper Saddle River, NJ: Pearson Prentice Hall, 2006.

Lemert, Charles, and Esme Bhan, eds. *The Voice of Anna Julia Cooper: Including "A Voice from the South" and Other Important Essays, Papers, and Letters*. Lanham, MD: Rowman & Littlefield, 1998.

Lewis, Janaka B. "Elizabeth Keckley and Freedom's Labor." *African American Review* 49, no. 1 (Spring 2016): 5–17.

Logan, Shirley Wilson. *We Are Coming: The Persuasive Discourse of Nineteenth-Century Black Women*. Carbondale: Southern Illinois University Press, 1999.

————, ed. *With Pen and Voice: A Critical Anthology of Nineteenth-Century African-American Women*. Carbondale: Southern Illinois University Press, 1995.

Maffly-Kipp, Laurie F., and Kathryn Lofton, eds. *Women's Work: An Anthology of African-American Women's Historical Writings from Antebellum America to the Harlem Renaissance*. New York: Oxford University Press, 2010.

Mance, Ajuan Maria. *Inventing Black Women: African American Women Poets and Self-Representation, 1877–2000*. Knoxville: University of Tennessee Press, 2007.

Marable, Manning, and Leith Mullings, eds. *Let Nobody Turn Us Around: Voices of Resistance, Reform, and Renewal: An African American Anthology*. Lanham, MD: Rowman & Littlefield, 2000.

May, Vivian M. *Anna Julia Cooper, Visionary Black Feminist: A Critical Introduction*. New York: Routledge, 2007.

McCluskey, Audrey Thomas. *A Forgotten Sisterhood: Pioneering Black Women Educators and Activists in the Jim Crow South*. Lanham, MD: Rowman & Littlefield, 2014.

McHenry, Elizabeth. *Forgotten Readers: Recovering the Lost History of African American Literary Societies*. Durham, NC: Duke University Press, 2002.

Mitchell, Koritha A. "Antilynching Plays: Angelina Weld Grimké, Alice Dunbar-Nelson, and the Evolution of African American Drama," in *Post-Bellum, Pre-Harlem: African American Literature and Culture 1877–1919*. Edited by Barbara McCaskill and Caroline Gebhard. New York: New York University Press, 2006, 210–230.

Moody, Joycelyn. *Sentimental Confessions: Spiritual Narratives of Nineteenth-Century African American Women*. Athens: University of Georgia Press, 2003.

Murdy, Anne-Elizabeth. *Teach the Nation: Public School, Racial Uplift, and Women's Writing in the 1890s*. New York: Routledge, 2003.

Painter, Nell Irvin. *Sojourner Truth: A Life, A Symbol*. New York: W. W. Norton, 1997.

Patton, Venetria K. *Women in Chains: The Legacy of Slavery in Black Women's Fiction*. Albany: State University of New York Press, 1999.

Pavletich, JoAnn. "Pauline Hopkins and the Death of the Tragic Mulatta." *Callaloo* 38, no. 3 (Summer 2015): 647–663.

Peterson, Carla L. *"Doers of the Word": African-American Women Speakers & Writers in the North (1830–1880)*. New York: Oxford University Press, 1995.

Potter, Eliza. *A Hairdresser's Experience in High Life.* Edited by Xio-
    mara Santamarina. Chapel Hill: The University of North Caro-
    lina Press, 2009.

Richardson, Marilyn, ed. *Maria W. Stewart, America's First Black
    Woman Political Writer: Essays and Speeches.* Bloomington: In-
    diana University Press, 1987.

Robbins, Hollis. Introduction to *Iola Leroy, or Shadows Uplifted,*
    by Frances Ellen Watkins Harper. New York: Penguin Books,
    2010.

———. "Blackening *Bleak House*: Hannah Crafts's *The Bondwom-
    an's Narrative*." *In Search of Hannah Crafts.* Eds. Gates and
    Robbins, 71–86. New York: Basic Civitas Books, 2004.

Rohrbach, Augusta. *Thinking Outside the Book.* Amherst: Univer-
    sity of Massachusetts Press, 2014.

———. *Truth Stranger Than Fiction: Race, Realism, and the U.S.
    Literary Marketplace.* New York: Palgrave Macmillan, 2002.

Samuels, Shirley, ed. *The Culture of Sentiment: Race, Gender, and
    Sentimentality in Nineteenth-Century America.* New York: Ox-
    ford University Press, 1992.

Sánchez-Eppler, Karen. "Ain't I a Symbol?" Review. *American Quar-
    terly* 50, no. 1 (1998): 149–157.

Sherman, Joan. *Invisible Poets: Afro-Americans of the Nineteenth
    Century.* Champaign: University of Illinois Press, 1989.

Sklar, Kathryn Kish, and James Brewer Stewart, eds. *Women's Rights
    and Transatlantic Antislavery in the Era of Emancipation.* New
    Haven, CT: Yale University Press, 2007.

Smith, Valerie. *Not Just Race, Not Just Gender: Black Feminist
    Readings.* New York: Routledge, 1998.

Stover, Johnnie M. *Rhetoric and Resistance in Black Women's Auto-
    biography.* Gainesville: University Press of Florida, 2003.

Streitmatter, Rodger. *Raising Her Voice: African-American Women
    Journalists Who Changed History.* Lexington: University Press
    of Kentucky, 1994.

Sumler-Lewis, Janice. "The Forten-Purvis Women of Philadelphia
    and the American Anti-Slavery Crusade." *The Journal of Negro
    History* 66, no. 4 (Winter 1981–1982): 281–288.

Tate, Claudia, ed. *The Works of Katherine Davis Chapman Tillman.*
    New York: Oxford University Press, 1991.

Wade-Gayles, Gloria. "Black Women Journalists in the South, 1880–
    1905: An Approach to the Study of Black Women's History."
    Callaloo, no. 11–13 (February–October 1981): 138–152.

Wallinger, Hanna. *Pauline E. Hopkins: A Literary Biography.* Ath-
    ens: University of Georgia Press, 2005.

Waters, Kristin, and Carol B. Conaway, eds. *Black Women's Intellectual Traditions: Speaking Their Minds*. Burlington: University of Vermont Press, 2007.

Welburn, Ron. *Hartford's Ann Plato and the Native Borders of Identity*. Albany: State University of New York Press, 2015.

White, E. Frances. *Dark Continent of Our Bodies: Black Feminism and the Politics of Respectability*. Philadelphia: Temple University Press, 2001.

Williams, Fannie Barrier. *The New Woman of Color: The Collected Writings of Fannie Barrier Williams, 1893–1918*. Edited by Mary Jo Deegan. DeKalb: Northern Illinois University Press, 2002.

Williams, Susan S. *Reclaiming Authorship: Literary Women in America, 1850–1900*. Philadelphia: University of Pennsylvania Press, 2006.

Wilson, Harriet E. *Our Nig; or, Sketches from the Life of a Free Black*. Edited by Henry Louis Gates, Jr., and Richard J. Ellis. New York: Vintage, 2011.

Yee, Shirley J. *Black Women Abolitionists: A Study in Activism, 1828–1860*. Knoxville: University of Tennessee Press, 1992.

———. "Finding a Place: Mary Ann Shadd Cary and the Dilemmas of Black Migration to Canada, 1850–1870." *Frontiers: A Journal of Women Studies* 18, no. 3 (1997): 1–16.

Yellin, Jean Fagan. *Women and Sisters: The Antislavery Feminists in American Culture*. New Haven, CT: Yale University Press, 1989.

Zackodnik, Teresa. *Press, Platform, Pulpit: Black Feminist Publics in the Era of Reform*. Knoxville: University of Tennessee Press, 2011.

———, ed. *"We Must Be Up and Doing": A Reader in Early African American Feminisms*. Peterborough, Ontario: Broadview Press, 2010.

The Portable
Nineteenth-Century
African American
Women Writers

PERSONAL ACCOUNTS OF ABOLITION AND FREEDOM

I

ANONYMOUS

(no date)

This anthology begins here, with an address by an anonymous speaker published in William Lloyd Garrison's abolitionist newspaper, the *Liberator*, to offer a sense of scope to the social and political movements behind the work in this anthology. For every woman featured in the following chapters who has been identified and recognized, there are many who are left unrecorded. This address, by a black woman to black women, insists: "We rise or fall together." Each singular, spectacular author whose work is presented here emerges out of social movements that demanded that black American women play a critical role in national politics.

"Address to the Female Literary Association of Philadelphia, on Their First Anniversary: By a Member" (1832)

SOURCE: "Address to the Female Literary Association of Philadelphia, on Their First Anniversary: By a Member," *Liberator*, October 13, 1832.

My Friends—One year has now elapsed since the formation of this association; a year filled with the most interesting events, in which friends have augmented, and the most gratifying and astonishing progress been made in intellectual improvement and in the virtues of the heart. A year fraught with blessings; for while a malignant disorder has stalked through our city, tearing asunder the most tender ties, leaving children orphans and parents childless, it has not (except in a few instances) been allowed to enter our dwellings, and in no instance has death ensued, and though neighbors and friends have fallen around us, like the chilling blasts of autumn, we have been preserved. Does not gratitude for these important blessings demand renewed exertion as our part to strict performance of duty? do not the numerous instances of sudden death we have witnessed loudly proclaim, "Be ye also ready"?

To continue this association will be one way of showing our gratitude and of aiding the cause. I presume none of you doubt this; if there is one here so skeptical, I would repeat to her a remark made by our unflinching advocate—Every effort you make in this way, said he, helps to unbind the fetters of the slave; and if she still doubts, I would tell her that as the free people of color become virtuous and intelligent, the character and condition of the slave will also improve. I would bid her, if she wishes the enfranchisement of her sisters, to sympathize in their woes, to rehearse their wrongs to her friends on every occasion, always remembering that our interests are one, that we rise or fall together, and that we can never be elevated to our proper standing while they are in bondage. Too long has it been the policy of our enemies to persuade us that we are a superior race to the slaves, and that our superiority is owing to a mixture with the whites. Away with this idea, cast it from you with the indignation it deserves, and dare to assert that the black man is equal by nature with the white, and that slavery and not his color has debased him. Yet dare to tell our enemies, that with the powerful weapons of religion and education, we will do battle with the host of prejudice which surround us, satisfied that in the end we shall be more than conquerors. My sisters, let me exhort you then to perseverance, by it great things have been effected; indeed, there are few things which perseverance, joined to a sense of duty may not accomplish. By perseverance the great Demosthenes was enabled to overcome a natural defect in his pronunciation, so great, that on his first attempt to speak in public, he was hissed: to rid himself of it, he built a vault where he might practice without disturbance. His efforts were crowned with the most brilliant success, he became the first orator of the age, and his eloquence was more dreaded by Philip than all the fleets and armies of Athens. By perseverance Hannibal passed the Alps in the depth of winter, with an army of 140,000 men. By perseverance some of you have already warred successfully with sloth, that inveterate foe to intellectual advancement. By perseverance Benjamin Franklin and a host of worthies rose superior to obscure birth and early disadvantages, and acquired lasting fame in the various departments of literature and the mechanic arts, and we may do the same.

Think that the eyes of our friends are upon us, they who have forsaken all they held dear on earth to plead our cause, are looking to us to uphold their hands, shall we disappoint them? Think of the groans, the tears of your enslaved sisters, and rouse up every slumbering energy and again go forward in the path of duty and improvement, adopting Perseverance as your motto, and the difficulties of the way will vanish like clouds before the morning sun. As often as this dear evening shall return evince, by your attendance here, that you love literature, that you love your people, and that nothing shall be wanting on your part to elevate them.

PHILADELPHIA, SEPT. 25TH, 1832.

2

SOJOURNER TRUTH

(ca. 1797–1883)

Born Isabella Baumfree in Ulster County, New York, the woman the world knows as Sojourner Truth was a slave for almost thirty years before escaping and devoting her life to the abolition movement. She rose to prominence in the 1850s, touring the North, giving speeches on the subjects of abolition and women's rights. Her first language was Dutch, she spoke with a Dutch accent, and she never learned to write. Truth was one of the few well-known abolitionists who called for all emancipated persons, men and women, to be granted equal rights. During the Civil War she worked in Washington, D.C., for the Freedman's Relief Association. After the war, she continued to give speeches and advocate for desegregation. She died in 1883.

Anthologizing Sojourner Truth poses a problem, one with which scholars such as Nell Painter, Karen Sánchez-Eppler, and many others have grappled. Truth is known to us only through the pens of other writers. The following are two versions of Truth's well-known address given at the Ohio Women's Rights Convention on May 18, 1851, in the Stone Church in Akron, Ohio. The first, from the *Anti-Slavery Bugle*, June 21, 1851, edited by *Bugle* editor Marius Robinson, Truth's close friend and secretary to the convention, does not include the phrase most associated with Truth. Frances D. Gage, who was also present, wrote the most widely known account twelve years after the fact, provoked by Harriet Beecher Stowe's account of meeting Truth, "The Libyan Sibyl," published in the April 1863 *Atlantic Monthly*. Three accounts of Truth's efforts on behalf of Western settlement are included here. The first is a petition she dictated in 1870 involving public land in the West; the second, remarks on Western settlement from the "Commemoration of the Eighth Anniversary of Negro Freedom in the United States—A Large Gathering and Eloquent Speeches in Tremont Temple, January 1, 1871." The third is a letter to the editor (dictated) from 1871.

"Speech Delivered to Women's Rights Convention in Akron Ohio" (1851)

Anti-Slavery Bugle Version (1851)

SOURCE: "Woman's Rights Convention," Salem (Ohio)
Anti-Slavery Bugle, June 21, 1851.

May I say a few words? I want to say a few words about this matter. I am a woman's rights. I have as much muscle as any man, and can do as much work as any man. I have plowed and reaped and husked and chopped and mowed, and can any man do more than that? I have heard much about the sexes being equal; I can carry as much as any man, and can eat as much too, if I can get it. I am as strong as any man that is now. As for intellect, all I can say is, if a woman have a pint and man a quart—why cant she have her little pint full? You need not be afraid to give us our rights for fear we will take too much,—for we cant take more than our pint'll hold. The poor men seem to be all in confusion, and dont know what to do. Why children, if you have woman's rights give it to her and you will feel better. You will have your own rights, and they wont be so much trouble. I cant read, but I can hear. I have heard the bible and have learned that Eve caused man to sin. Well if woman upset the world, do give her a chance to set it right side up again. The Lady has spoken about Jesus, how he never spurned woman from him, and she was right. When Lazarus died, Mary and Martha came to him with faith and love and besought him to raise their brother. And Jesus wept—and Lazarus came forth.

And how came Jesus into the world? Through God who created him and woman who bore him. Man, where is your part? But the women are coming up blessed by God and a few of the men are coming up with them. But man is in a tight place, the poor slave is on him, woman is coming on him, and he is surely between a hawk and a buzzard.

Frances D. Gage Version (1863)

SOURCE: F. D. Gage, "Sojourner Truth," *New York Independent*, April 23, 1863.

Well, chillen, whar dar's so much racket dar must be som'ting out o' kilter. I tink dat, 'twixt the niggers of de South and de women at de Norf, all ataking 'bout rights, de white men will be in a fix pretty soon. But what's all this here talking 'bout? Dat man ober dar say dat woman needs to be helped into carriages, and lifted over ditches, and to have de best place eberywhar. Nobody eber helps me into carriages, or ober mud-puddles, or gives me any best place; And ar'n't I a woman? Look at me. Look at my arm. I have plowed and planted and gathered into barns, and no man could head me—and ar'n't I a woman? I could work as much and eat as much as a man, (when I could get it,) and bear de lash as well—and ar'n't I a woman? I have borne thirteen chillen, and seen 'em mos' all sold off into slavery, and when I cried out with a mother's grief, none but Jesus heard—and ar'n't I a woman? Den dey talks 'bout dis ting in de head. What dis dey call it? ["Intellect," whispered some one near.] Dat's it, honey. What's dat got to do with woman's rights or niggers' rights? If my cup won't hold but a pint and yourn holds a quart, wouldn't ye be mean not to me have my little half-measure full? Den dat little man in black dar, he say woman can't have as much right as man 'cause Christ wa'n't a woman. Whar did your Christ come from?

Whar did your Christ come from? From God and a woman. Man had noting to do with him. That if de fust woman God ever made was strong enough to turn de world upside down all her one lone, all dese togeder, ought to be able to turn it back and git it right side up again, and now dey is asking to, de men better let 'em. 'Bleeged to ye for hearin' on me, and now old Sojourner ha'n't got nothin' more to say.

Selections on Western Settlement from
Narrative of Sojourner Truth (1875)

SOURCE: Olive Gilbert and Frances W. Titus, *Narrative of Sojourner Truth* (Salem, NH: Ayer, 1875), 199.

Petition to Congress.

"TO THE SENATE AND HOUSE OF REPRESENTATIVES, in Congress assembled:—

"*Whereas*, From the faithful and earnest representation of Sojourner Truth (who has personally investigated the matter), we believe that the freed colored people in and about Washington, dependent upon government for support, would be greatly benefited and might become useful citizens by being placed in a position to support themselves: We, the undersigned, therefore earnestly request your honorable body to set apart for them a portion of the public land in the West, and erect buildings thereon for the aged and infirm, and otherwise legislate so as to secure the desired results."

"Truths from Sojourner Truth"

"Now, here is de question dat I am here to-night to say. I been to Washin'ton, an' I fine out dis, dat do colud pepul dat is in Washin'tun libin on de gobernment dat de United Staas ort to gi' 'em lan' an' move 'em on it. Dey are libin on de gov'ment, an' dere is pepul takin' care of 'em costin' you so much, an' it don't benefit him 'tall. It degrades him wuss an' wuss. Therefo' I say dat these people, take an' put 'em in de West where you ken enrich 'em. I know de good pepul in de South can't take care of de negroes as dey ort to, case de ribils won't let 'em.

How much better will it be for to take them culud pepul an' give 'em land? We've airnt lan' enough for a home, an' it would be a benefit for you all an' God would bless de hull ob ye for doin' it. Dey say, Let 'om take keer of derselves. Why, you've taken dat all away from 'em. Ain't got nuffin lef'. Get dese culud pepul out of Washin'tun off ob de gov'ment, an' get de ole pepul out and build dem homes in de West, where dey can feed themselves, and dey would soon be abel to be a pepul among you. Dat is my commission. Now adgitate them pepul an' put 'em dere; learn 'em to read one part of de time an' learn 'em to work de udder part ob de time."

From *The N. Y. Tribune*. Sojourner Truth at Work.

"To the Editor of the Tribune:—

"SIR: Seeing an item in your paper about me, I thought I would give you the particulars of what I am trying to do, in hopes that you would print a letter about it and so help on the good cause. I am urging the people to sign petitions to Congress to have a grant of land set apart for the freed people to earn their living on, and not be dependent on the government for their bread. I have had fifty petitions printed at my own expense, and have been urging the people of the Eastern States for the past seven months. I have been crying out in the East, and now an answer comes to me from the West, as you will see from the following letter. The gentleman who writes it I have never seen or heard of before, but the Lord has raised him up to help me. Bless the Lord! I made up my mind last winter, when I saw able men and women taking dry bread from the government to keep from starving, that I would devote myself to the cause of getting land for these people, where they can work and earn their own living in the West, where the land is so plenty. Instead of going home from Washington to take rest, I am traveling around getting it before the people.

"Instead of sending these people to Liberia, why can't they have a colony in the West? This is why I am contending so in my old age. It is to teach the people that this colony can just as well be in this country as in Liberia. Everybody says this is a good work, but nobody helps. How glad I will be if you will take hold and give it a good lift. Please help me with these petitions. Yours truly,

"SOJOURNER TRUTH.

"FLORENCE, MASS., FEB. 18, 1871.

"P. S. I should have said that the Rev. Gilbert Haven of Boston is kindly aiding me in getting petitions signed, and will receive all petitions signed in Massachusetts and send them to Congress.   S. T."

3

MARY PRINCE

(ca. 1788–after 1833)

Two years after achieving her freedom, Mary Prince dictated her life story to anti-slavery activists. Her account is considered the first slave narrative by a woman. Prince tells of being born into slavery in Bermuda, purchased as an infant by a sea captain to be a gift to his granddaughter, to whom she would serve as a companion for twelve years. Prince was subsequently sold to a series of owners on other islands before returning to Bermuda. After a family named Wood brought Prince to England, the Anti-Slavery Society petitioned Parliament to demand her freedom. The family quickly left England with Prince; she subsequently became a servant to Mr. Thomas Pringle and his family. She dictated her history to anti-slavery activist Susanna Strickland; Pringle edited and published the account in 1831. This excerpt is from this popular and controversial narrative. Three editions were printed in the year of its publication; meanwhile, attacks on Prince and Pringle appeared in *Blackwood's Magazine*, in which Prince was maligned as a "despicable tool" for voicing lies invented by Pringle. Pringle was sued for libel in 1833. Prince's court appearance in these cases adds additional details to her story.

"The idea of writing Mary Prince's history was first suggested by herself," Thomas Pringle affirmed. "She wished it to be done, she said, that good people in England might hear from a slave what a slave had felt and suffered; and a letter of her late master's, which will be found in the Supplement, induced me to accede to her wish without farther delay. The more immediate object of the publication will afterwards

appear." Prince's pointed, critical voice can be dis-
cerned in her narrative, both in reports of a brutal
flogging or as she corrects the misguided views on
slavery. She withstands the rage of her master and
mistress and insists "To be free is very sweet."

Excerpt from *The History of Mary Prince, a West Indian Slave* (1831)

SOURCE: Mary Prince, *The History of Mary Prince, a West Indian Slave Narrative* (London: F. Westley and A. H. Davis, 1831).

I was also sent by Mrs. Wood to be put in the Cage one night, and was next morning flogged, by the magistrate's order, at her desire; and this all for a quarrel I had about a pig with another slave woman. I was flogged on my naked back on this occasion: although I was in no fault after all; for old Justice Dyett, when we came before him, said that I was in the right, and ordered the pig to be given to me. This was about two or three years after I came to Antigua.

When we moved from the middle of the town to the Point, I used to be in the house and do all the work and mind the children, though still very ill with the rheumatism. Every week I had to wash two large bundles of clothes, as much as a boy could help me to lift; but I could give no satisfaction. My mistress was always abusing and fretting after me. It is not possible to tell all her ill language.—One day she followed me foot after foot scolding and rating me. I bore in silence a great deal of ill words: at last my heart was quite full, and I told her that she ought not to use me so;—that when I was ill I might have lain and died for what she cared; and no one would then come near me to nurse me, because they were afraid of my mistress. This was a great affront. She called her husband and told him what I had said. He flew into a passion: but did not beat me then; he only abused and swore at me; and then gave me a note and bade me go and look for an owner. Not that he meant to sell me; but he did this to please his wife and to frighten me. I went to Adam White, a cooper, a free black, who had money, and asked him to buy me. He went directly to Mr. Wood, but was informed that I was not to be sold. The next day my master whipped me.

Another time (about five years ago) my mistress got vexed with me, because I fell sick and I could not keep on with my work. She complained to her husband, and he sent me off again to look for an owner. I went to a Mr. Burchell, showed him the note, and asked him to buy me for my own benefit; for I had saved about 100 dollars, and hoped, with a little help, to purchase my freedom. He accordingly went to my master:—"Mr. Wood," he said, "Molly has brought me a note that she wants an owner. If you intend to sell her, I may as well buy her as another." My master put him off and said that he did not mean to sell me. I was very sorry at this, for I had no comfort with Mrs. Wood, and I wished greatly to get my freedom.

The way in which I made my money was this.—When my master and mistress went from home, as they sometimes did, and left me to take care of the house and premises, I had a good deal of time to myself, and made the most of it. I took in washing, and sold coffee and yams and other provisions to the captains of ships. I did not sit still idling during the absence of my owners; for I wanted, by all honest means, to earn money to buy my freedom. Sometimes I bought a hog cheap on board ship, and sold it for double the money on shore; and I also earned a good deal by selling coffee. By this means I by degrees acquired a little cash. A gentleman also lent me some to help to buy my freedom—but when I could not get free he got it back again. His name was Captain Abbot.

My master and mistress went on one occasion into the country, to Date Hill, for change of air, and carried me with them to take charge of the children, and to do the work of the house. While I was in the country, I saw how the field negroes are worked in Antigua. They are worked very hard and fed but scantily. They are called out to work before daybreak, and come home after dark; and then each has to heave his bundle of grass for the cattle in the pen. Then, on Sunday morning, each slave has to go out and gather a large bundle of grass; and, when they bring it home, they have all to sit at the manager's door and wait till he come out: often have they to wait there till past eleven o'clock, without any breakfast. After that, those that have yams or potatoes, or fire-wood to sell, hasten to market to buy a dog's worth of salt fish, or pork, which is a great treat for them. Some of them buy a little pickle out of the shad barrels, which they call sauce, to season their yams and Indian corn. It is very wrong, I know, to work on Sunday or go to market; but will not God call the Buckra men to answer for this on the great day of judgment—since they will give the slaves no other day?

While we were at Date Hill Christmas came; and the slave woman who had the care of the place (which then belonged to Mr. Roberts the marshal), asked me to go with her to her husband's house, to a Methodist meeting for prayer, at a plantation called Winthorps. I went; and they were the first prayers I ever understood. One woman prayed; and then they all sung a hymn; then there was another prayer and another hymn; and then they all spoke by turns of their own griefs as sinners. The husband of the woman I went with was a black driver. His name was Henry. He confessed that he had treated the slaves very cruelly; but said that he was compelled to obey the orders of his master. He prayed them all to forgive him, and he prayed that God would forgive him. He said it was a horrid thing for a ranger to have sometimes to beat his own wife or sister; but he must do so if ordered by his master.

I felt sorry for my sins also. I cried the whole night, but I was too much ashamed to speak. I prayed God to forgive me. This meeting had a great impression on my mind, and led my spirit to the Moravian church; so that when I got back to town, I went and prayed to have my name put down in the Missionaries' book; and I followed the church earnestly every opportunity. I did not then tell my mistress about it; for I knew that she would not give me leave to go. But I felt I *must* go. Whenever I carried the children their lunch at school, I ran round and went to hear the teachers.

The Moravian ladies (Mrs. Richter, Mrs. Olufsen, and Mrs. Sauter) taught me to read in the class; and I got on very fast. In this class there were all sorts of people, old and young, gray headed folks and children; but most of them were free people. After we had done spelling, we tried to read in the Bible. After the reading was over, the missionary gave out a hymn for us to sing. I dearly loved to go to the church, it was so solemn. I never knew rightly that I had much sin till I went there. When I found out that I was a great sinner, I was very sorely grieved, and very much frightened. I used to pray God to pardon my sins for Christ's sake, and forgive me for every thing I had done amiss; and when I went home to my work, I always thought about what I had heard from the missionaries, and wished to be good that I might go to heaven. After a while I was admitted a candidate for the holy Communion.—I had been baptized long before this, in August 1817, by the Rev. Mr. Curtin, of the English Church, after I had been taught to repeat the Creed and the Lord's Prayer. I wished at that time to attend a Sunday School taught by Mr. Curtin, but he would not receive me without a written note from my master, granting his permission. I did not ask my owner's permission, from the belief that it would be refused; so that I got no farther instruction at that time from the English Church.

Some time after I began to attend the Moravian Church, I met with Daniel James, afterward my dear husband. He was a carpenter and cooper to his trade; an honest, hard-working, decent black man, and a widower. He had purchased his freedom of his mistress, old Mrs. Baker, with money he had earned whilst a slave. When he asked me to marry him, I took time to consider the matter over with myself, and would not say yes till he went to church with me and joined the Moravians. He was very industrious after he bought his freedom; and he had hired a comfortable house, and had convenient things about him. We were joined in marriage, about Christmas 1826, in the Moravian Chapel at Spring Gardens, by the Rev. Mr. Olufsen. We could not be married in the English Church. English marriage is not allowed to slaves; and no free man can marry a slave woman.

When Mr. Wood heard of my marriage, he flew into a great rage, and sent for Daniel, who was helping to build a house for his old mistress. Mr. Wood asked him who gave him a right to marry a slave of his? My husband said, "Sir, I am a free man, and thought I had a right to choose a wife; but if I had known Molly was not allowed to have a husband, I should not have asked her to marry me." Mrs. Wood was more vexed about my marriage than her husband. She could not forgive me for getting married, but stirred up Mr. Wood to flog me dreadfully with the horsewhip. I thought it very hard to be whipped at my time of life for getting a husband—I told her so. She said that she would not have nigger men about the yards and premises, or allow a nigger man's clothes to be washed in the same tub where hers were washed. She was fearful, I think, that I should lose her time, in order to wash and do things for my husband: but I had then no time to wash for myself; I was obliged to put out my own clothes, though I was always at the wash-tub.

I had not much happiness in my marriage, owing to my being a slave. It made my husband sad to see me so ill-treated. Mrs. Wood was always abusing me about him. She did not lick me herself, but she got her husband to do it for her, whilst she fretted the flesh off my bones. Yet for all this she would not sell me. She sold five slaves whilst I was with her; but though she was always finding fault with me, she would not part with me. However, Mr. Wood afterward allowed Daniel to have a place to live in our yard, which we were very thankful for.

After this, I fell ill again with the rheumatism, and was sick a long time; but whether sick or well, I had my work to do. About this time I asked my master and mistress to let me buy my own freedom. With the help of Mr. Burchell, I could have found the means to pay Mr. Wood; for it was agreed that I should afterward serve Mr. Burchell a while, for the cash he was to advance for me. I was earnest in the request to my owners; but their hearts were hard—too hard to consent. Mrs. Wood was very angry—she grew quite outrageous—she called me a black devil, and asked me who had put freedom into my head. "To be free is very sweet," I said: but she took good care to keep me a slave. I saw her change color, and I left the room.

About this time my master and mistress were going to England to put their son to school, and bring their daughters home; and they took me with them to take care of the child. I was willing to come to England: I thought that by going there

I should probably get cured of my rheumatism, and should return with my master and mistress, quite well, to my husband. My husband was willing for me to come away, for he had heard that my master would free me,—and I also hoped this might prove true; but it was all a false report.

The steward of the ship was very kind to me. He and my husband were in the same class in the Moravian Church. I was thankful that he was so friendly, for my mistress was not kind to me on the passage; and she told me, when she was angry, that she did not intend to treat me any better in England than in the West Indies—that I need not expect it. And she was as good as her word.

When we drew near to England, the rheumatism seized all my limbs worse than ever, and my body was dreadfully swelled. When we landed at the Tower, I shewed my flesh to my mistress, but she took no great notice of it. We were obliged to stop at the tavern till my master got a house; and a day or two after, my mistress sent me down into the wash-house to learn to wash in the English way. In the West Indies we wash with cold water—in England with hot. I told my mistress I was afraid that putting my hands first into the hot water and then into the cold, would increase the pain in my limbs. The doctor had told my mistress long before I came from the West Indies, that I was a sickly body and the washing did not agree with me. But Mrs. Wood would not release me from the tub, so I was forced to do as I could. I grew worse, and could not stand to wash. I was then forced to sit down with the tub before me, and often through pain and weakness was reduced to kneel or to sit down on the floor, to finish my task. When I complained to my mistress of this, she only got into a passion as usual, and said washing in hot water could not hurt any one;—that I was lazy and insolent, and wanted to be free of my work; but that she would make me do it. I thought her very hard on me, and my heart rose up within me. However I kept still at that time, and went down again to wash the child's things; but the English washerwomen who were at work there, when they saw that I was so ill, had pity upon me and washed them for me.

After that, when we came up to live in Leigh Street, Mrs. Wood sorted out five bags of clothes which we had used at sea, and also such as had been worn since we came on shore, for me and the cook to wash. Elizabeth the cook told her, that she did not think that I was able to stand to the tub, and that she had better hire a woman. I also said myself, that I had come over to nurse the child, and that I was sorry I had come from Antigua, since mistress would work me so hard, without compassion for my rheumatism. Mr. and Mrs. Wood, when they heard this, rose up in a passion against me. They opened the door and bade me get out. But I was a stranger, and did not know one door in the street from another, and was unwilling to go away. They made a dreadful uproar, and from that day they constantly kept cursing and abusing me. I was obliged to wash, though I was very ill. Mrs. Wood, indeed once hired a washerwoman, but she was not well treated, and would come no more.

My master quarreled with me another time, about one of our great washings, his wife having stirred him up to do so. He said he would compel me to do the whole of the washing given out to me, or if I again refused, he would take a short course with me: he would either send me down to the brig in the river, to carry me back to Antigua, or he would turn me at once out of doors, and let me provide for myself. I said I would willingly go back, if he would let me purchase my own freedom. But this enraged him more than all the rest: he cursed and swore at me dreadfully, and said he would never sell my freedom—if I wished to be free, I was free in England, and I might go and try what freedom would do for me, and be d——d. My heart was very sore with this treat-ment, but I had to go on. I continued to do my work, and did all I could to give satisfaction, but all would not do.

Shortly after, the cook left them, and then matters went on ten times worse. I always washed the child's clothes without being commanded to do it, and any thing else that was wanted in the family; though still I was very sick—very sick indeed. When the great washing came round, which was every two months, my mistress got together again a great many heavy things, such as bed-ticks, bed-coverlets, &c. for me to wash. I told her I was too ill to wash such heavy things that day. She said, she supposed I thought myself a free woman, but I was not; and if I did not do it directly I should be instantly turned out of doors. I stood a long time before I could answer, for I did not know well what to do. I knew that I was free in England, but I did not know where to go, or how to get my living; and therefore, I did not like to leave the house. But Mr. Wood said he would send for a constable to thrust me out; and at last I took courage and resolved that I would not be longer thus treated, but would go and trust to Providence. This was the fourth time they had threatened to turn me out, and, go where I might, I was determined now to take them at their word; though I thought it very hard, after I had lived with them for thirteen years, and worked for them like a horse, to be driven out in this way, like a beggar. My only fault was being sick, and therefore unable to please my mistress, who thought she never could get work enough out of her slaves; and I told them so: but they only abused me and drove me out. This took place from two to three months, I think, after we came to England.

When I came away, I went to the man (one Mash) who used to black the shoes of the family, and asked his wife to get somebody to go with me to Hatton Garden to the Moravian Missionaries: these were the only persons I knew in England. The woman sent a young girl with me to the mission house, and I saw there a gentleman called Mr. Moore. I told him my whole story, and how my owners had treated me, and asked him to take in my trunk with what few clothes I had. The missionaries were very kind to me—they were sorry for my destitute situation, and gave me leave to bring my things to be placed under their care. They were very good people, and they told me to come to the church.

When I went back to Mr. Wood's to get my trunk, I saw a lady, Mrs. Pell, who was on a visit to my mistress. When Mr. and Mrs. Wood heard me come in, they set this lady to stop me, finding that they had gone too far with me. Mrs. Pell came out to me, and said, "Are you really going to leave, Molly? Don't leave, but come into the country with me." I believe she said this because she thought Mrs. Wood would easily get me back again. I replied to her, "Ma'am, this is the fourth time my master and mistress have driven me out, or threatened to drive me—and I will give them no more occasion to bid me go. I was not willing to leave them, for I am a stranger in this country, but now I must go—I can stay no longer to be so used." Mrs. Pell then went up stairs to my mistress, and told that I would go, and that she could not stop me. Mrs. Wood was very much hurt and frightened when she found I was determined to go out that day. She said, "If she goes the people will rob her, and then turn her adrift." She did not say this to me, but she spoke it loud enough for me to hear; that it might induce me not to go, I suppose. Mr. Wood also asked me where I was going to. I told him where I had been, and that I should never have gone away had I not been driven out by my owners. He had given me a written paper some time before, which said that I had come with them to England by my own desire; and that was true. It said also that I left them of my own free will, because I was a free woman in England; and that I was idle and would not do my work—which was not true. I gave this paper afterward to a gentleman who inquired into my case.

I went into the kitchen and got my clothes out. The nurse and the servant girl were there, and I said to the man who was going to take out my trunk, "Stop, before you take up this trunk, and hear what I have to say before these people. I am going out of this house, as I was ordered; but I have done no wrong at all to my owners, neither here nor in the West Indies. I always worked very hard to please them, both by night and day; but there was no giving satisfaction, for my mistress could never be satisfied with reasonable service. I told my mistress I was sick, and yet she has ordered me out of doors. This is the fourth time; and now I am going out."

And so I came out, and went and carried my trunk to the Moravians. I then returned back to Mash the shoe-black's house, and begged his wife to take me in. I had a little West Indian money in my trunk; and they got it changed for me. This helped to support me for a little while. The man's wife was very kind to me. I was very sick, and she boiled nourishing things up for me. She also sent for a doctor to see me, and he sent me medicine, which did me good, though I was ill for a long time with the rheumatic pains. I lived a good many months with these poor people, and they nursed me, and did all that lay in their power to serve me. The man was well acquainted with my situation, as he used to go to and fro to Mr. Wood's house to clean shoes and knives; and he and his wife were sorry for me.

About this time, a woman of the name of Hill told me of the Anti-Slavery Society, and went with me to their office, to inquire if they could do any thing to get me my freedom, and send me back to the West Indies. The gentlemen of the Society took me to a lawyer, who examined very strictly into my case; but told me that the laws of England could do nothing to make me free in Antigua. However they did all they could for me: they gave me a little money from time to time to keep me from want; and some of them went to Mr. Wood to try to persuade him to let me return a free woman to my husband; but though they offered him, as I have heard, a large sum for my freedom, he was sulky and obstinate, and would not consent to let me go free.

This was the first winter I spent in England, and I suffered much from the severe cold, and from the rheumatic pains, which still at times torment me. However, Providence was very good to me, and I got many friends—especially some Quaker ladies, who hearing of my case, came and sought me out, and gave me good warm clothing and money. Thus I had great cause to bless God in my affliction.

When I got better I was anxious to get some work to do, as I was unwilling to eat the bread of idleness. Mrs. Mash, who was a laundress, recommended me to a lady for a charwoman. She paid me very handsomely for what work I did, and I divided the money with Mrs. Mash; for though very poor, they gave me food when my own money was done, and never suffered me to want.

In the spring, I got into service with a lady, who saw me at the house where I sometimes worked as a charwoman. This lady's name was Mrs. Forsyth. She had been in the West Indies, and was accustomed to Blacks, and liked them. I was with her six months, and went with her to Margate. She treated me well, and gave me a good character when she left London.

After Mrs. Forsyth went away, I was again out of place, and went to lodgings, for which I paid two shillings a week, and found coals and candle. After eleven weeks, the money I had saved in service was all gone, and I was forced to go back to the Anti-Slavery office to ask a supply, till I could get another situation. I did not like to go back—I did not like to be idle. I would rather work for my living than get it for nothing. They were very good to give me a supply, but I felt shame at being obliged to apply for relief whilst I had strength to work.

At last I went into the service of Mr. and Mrs. Pringle, where I have been ever since, and am as comfortable as I can be while separated from my dear husband, and away from my own country and all old friends and connections. My dear mistress teaches me daily to read the word of God, and takes great pains to make me understand it. I enjoy the great privilege of being enabled to attend church three times on the Sunday; and I have met with many kind friends since I have been here, both clergymen and others. The Rev. Mr. Young, who lives in the next house, has shown me much kindness, and taken much pains to instruct me, particularly while my master and mistress were absent in Scotland. Nor must I forget, among my friends, the Rev. Mr. Mortimer, the good clergyman of the parish, under whose ministry I have now sat for upward of twelve months. I trust in God I have profited by what I have heard from him. He never keeps back the truth, and I think he has been the means of opening my eyes and ears much better to understand the word of God. Mr. Mortimer tells me that he cannot open the eyes of my heart, but that I must pray to God to change my heart, and make me to know the truth, and the truth will make me free.

I still live in the hope that God will find a way to give me my liberty, and give me back to my husband. I endeavor to keep down my fretting, and to leave all to Him, for he knows what is good for me better than I know myself. Yet, I must confess, I find it a hard and heavy task to do so.

I am often much vexed, and I feel great sorrow when I hear some people in this country say, that the slaves do not need better usage, and do not want to be free. They believe the foreign people, who deceive them, and say slaves are happy. I say, Not so. How can slaves be happy when they have the halter round their neck and the whip upon their back? and are disgraced and thought no more of than beasts?—and are separated from their mothers, and husbands, and children, and sisters, just as cattle are sold and separated? Is it happiness for a driver in the field to take down his wife or sister or child, and strip them, and whip them in such a disgraceful manner?—women that have had children exposed in the open field to shame! There is no modesty or decency shown by the owner to his slaves; men, women, and children are exposed alike. Since I have been here

I have often wondered how English people can go out into the West Indies and act in such a beastly manner. But when they go to the West Indies, they forget God and all feeling of shame, I think, since they can see and do such things. They tie up slaves like hogs—moor them up like cattle, and they lick them, so as hogs, or cattle, or horses never were flogged;—and yet they come home and say, and make some good people believe, that slaves don't want to get out of slavery. But they put a cloak about the truth. It is not so. All slaves want to be free—to be free is very sweet. I will say the truth to England people who may read this history that my good friend, Miss S——, is now writing down for me. I have been a slave myself—I know what slaves feel—I can tell by myself what other slaves feel, and by what they have told me. The man that says slaves be quite happy in slavery—that they don't want to be free—that man is either ignorant or a lying person. I never heard a slave say so. I never heard a Buckra man say so, till I heard tell of it in England. Such people ought to be ashamed of themselves. They can't do without slaves, they say. What's the reason they can't do without slaves as well as in England? No slaves here—no whips—no stocks—no punishment, except for wicked people. They hire servants in England; and if they don't like them, they send them away: they can't lick them. Let them work ever so hard in England, they are far better off than slaves. If they get a bad master, they give warning and go hire to another. They have their liberty. That's just what *we* want. We don't mind hard work, if we had proper treatment, and proper wages like English servants, and proper time given in the week to keep us from breaking the Sabbath. But they won't give it: they will have work—work—work, night and day, sick or well, till we are quite done up; and we must not speak up nor look amiss, however much we be abused. And then when we are quite done up, who cares for us, more than for a lame horse? This is slavery. I tell it, to let English people know the truth; and I hope they will never leave off to pray God, and call loud to the great King of England, till all the poor blacks be given free, and slavery done up for evermore.

4

NANCY PRINCE

(1799–after 1856)

Nancy Gardner Prince rose from difficult circumstances to lead a cosmopolitan life uncharacteristic for her time. Nancy Gardner grew up in Newburyport, Massachusetts. Her father, a seaman, died when Nancy was an infant. Her mother, the daughter of slaves, remarried several times to keep the family out of poverty. Young Nancy worked as a servant for white families and became a seamstress before marrying Nero Prince, a Bostonian and founding member of the Prince Hall Freemasons, in 1824. Nancy's autobiography, *A Narrative of the Life and Travels of Mrs. Nancy Prince* (1850), focuses primarily on Nancy's married life. The couple traveled to Russia, where Nero served as a footman for the czar in St. Petersburg and Nancy operated a boardinghouse. After returning to Boston, Prince became active in the Boston Female Anti-Slavery Society and lectured widely about her travels.

The following excerpt focuses on Prince's later years, traveling to and from Jamaica. She describes an English anti-slavery society, the practices of a Jamaican Baptist Church, and a voyage from Jamaica to the United States that was troubled by poor weather and a dishonest captain.

From *A Narrative of the Life and Travels of Mrs. Nancy Prince* (1850)

SOURCE: Nancy Prince, *A Narrative of the Life and Travels of Mrs. Nancy Prince* (Boston: Published by the Author, 1850).

On the 3rd of October, 1780, there was a dreadful hurricane, which overwhelmed the little seaport town of Savannah, in Jamaica, and part of the adjacent country; very few houses were left standing, and a great number of lives were lost; much damage was done also, and many lives lost, in other parts of the island.

In January, 1823, a society was formed in London for mitigating and gradually abolishing slavery, throughout the British dominions, called the Anti-Slavery Society. His Royal Highness, the Duke of Gloucester, was President of the Society; in the list of Vice Presidents are the names of many of the most distinguished philanthropists of the day, and among them that of the never to be forgotten Mr. Wilberforce; as a bold champion, we see him going forward, pleading the cause of our down-trodden brethren. In the year 1834, it pleased God to break the chains from 800,000 human beings, that had been held in a state of personal slavery; and this great event was effected through the instrumentality of Clarkson, Wilberforce, and other philanthropists of the day.

The population of Jamaica is nearly 400,000; that of Kingston, the capital, 40,000. There are many places of worship of various denominations, namely, Church of England, and of Scotland, Wesleyan, the Baptist, and Roman Catholics, besides a Jewish Synagogue. These all differ from what I have seen in New England, and from those I have seen elsewhere. The Baptist hold what they call class-meetings. They have men and women, deacons and deaconesses in these churches; these hold separate class-meetings; some of these can read, and some cannot. Such are the persons who hold the office of judges, and go round and urge the people to come to the class, and after they come in twice or three times, they are considered candidates for baptism. Some pay fifty cents, and some more, for being baptized; they receive a ticket as a passport into the church, paying one mark a quarter, or more, and some less, but nothing short of ten pence, that is, two English shillings a year. They must attend their class once a week, and pay three pence a week, total twelve English shillings a year, besides the sums they pay once a month at communion, after service in the morning. On those occasions the minister retires, and the deacons examine the people, to ascertain if each one has brought a ticket; if not, they cannot commune; after this the minister returns, and performs the ceremony, then they give their money and depart. The churches are very large, holding from four to six thousand; many bring wood and other presents to their class-leader, as a token of their attachment; where there are so many communicants, these presents, and the money exacted, greatly enrich these establishments. Communicants are so ignorant of the ordinance, that they join the church merely to have a decent burial; for if they are not members, none will follow them to the grave, and no prayers will be said over them; these are borne through the streets by four men, the coffin a rough box; not so if they are church members; as soon as the news is spread that one is dying, all the class, with their leader, will assemble at the place, and join in singing hymns; this, they say, is to help the spirit up to glory; this exercise sometimes continues all night, in so loud a strain, that it is seldom that any of the people in the neighborhood are lost in sleep.

After leaving Jamaica, the vessel was tacked to a south-west course. I asked the Captain what this meant. He said he must take the current, as there was no wind. Without any ceremony, I told him it was not the case, and told the passengers that he had deceived us. There were two English men that were born on the island, that had never been on the water; before the third day passed, they asked the Captain why they had not seen Hayti. He told them they passed when they were asleep. I told them it was not true, he was steering south-west. The passengers in the steerage got alarmed, and every one was asking the Captain what this meant. The ninth day we made land. "By —— ," said the Captain, "this is Key West; come, passengers, let us have a vote to run over the neck, and I will go ashore and bring aboard fruit and turtle." They all agreed but myself. He soon dropped anchor. The officers from the shore came on board and congratulated him on keeping his appointment, thus proving that my suspicions were well founded. The Captain went ashore with these men, and soon came back, called for the passengers, and asked for their vote for him to remain until the next day, saying that he could, by this delay, make five or six hundred dollars, as there had been a vessel wrecked there lately. They all agreed but myself. The vessel was soon at the side of the wharf. In one hour there were twenty slaves at work to unload her; every inducement was made to persuade me to go ashore, or set my feet on the wharf. A law had just been passed there that every free colored person coming there, should be put in custody on their going ashore; there were five colored persons on board; none dared to go ashore, however uncomfortable we might be in the vessel, or however we might desire to refresh ourselves by a change of scene. We remained at Key West four days.

MARIA W. STEWART

(ca. 1803–1879)

Maria Stewart, born Maria Williams in Hartford, Connecticut, about 1803, was the first black woman to lecture publicly about slavery in the United States and was one of the earliest and most outspoken advocates for the rights of black women. Orphaned at an early age, she became an indentured domestic servant to a local clergyman's family with a large library. Stewart was exposed to books, learned to read, taught Sunday school, and, in 1826, married James W. Stewart, a successful shipping merchant and veteran of the War of 1812. After his premature death, Stewart was denied his inheritance and forced to return to domestic service. David Walker and William Lloyd Garrison inspired the outspoken Stewart to write and speak publicly.

In her forties, Stewart became a teacher in New York. In 1852 she moved to Baltimore, teaching there and in Washington, D.C., during the Civil War. Working at the Freedmen's Hospital, Stewart learned that as the widow of a veteran she was eligible to her husband's pension. Two editions of Stewart's collected works were published in her lifetime, one in 1835 by Garrison, and one before her death in 1879.

In the following address, given in the African Masonic Hall in Boston on February 27, 1833, Stewart opposes resettlement in Liberia, promoting equality in America through self-improvement. Provoking some discontent from her listeners, she cites temperance and investment in education as factors that would help raise African American social status.

"An Address Delivered at the African Masonic Hall" (1833)

SOURCE: Maria W. Stewart, "An Address, Delivered at the
African Masonic Hall in Boston, Feb. 27, 1833,"
Liberator, February 27, 1833.

African rights and liberty is a subject that ought to fire the breast of every free man of color in these United States, and excite in his bosom a lively, deep, decided and heart-felt interest. When I cast my eyes on the long list of illustrious names that are enrolled on the bright annals of fame among the whites, I turn my eyes within, and ask my thoughts, "Where are the names of *our* illustrious ones?" It must certainly have been for the want of energy on the part of the free people of color, that they have been long willing to bear the yoke of oppression. It must have been the want of ambition and force that has given the whites occasion to say, that our natural abilities are not as good, and our capacities by nature inferior to theirs. They boldly assert, that, did we possess a natural independence of soul, and feel a love for liberty within our breasts, some one of our sable race, long before this, would have testified it, notwithstanding the disadvantages under which we labor. We have made ourselves appear altogether unqualified to speak in our own defense, and are therefore looked upon as objects of pity and commiseration. We have been imposed upon, insulted and derided on every side; and now, if we complain, it is considered as the height of impertinence. We have suffered ourselves to be considered as Bastards, cowards, mean, faint-hearted wretches; and on this account, (not because of our complexion) many despise us, and would gladly spurn us from their presence.

These things have fired my soul with a holy indignation, and compelled me thus to come forward; and endeavor to turn their attention to knowledge and improvement; for knowledge is power. I would ask, is it blindness of mind, or at stupidity of soul, or the want of education, that has caused our men who are 60 to 70 years of age, never to let their voices be heard, or nor their hands be raised in behalf of their color? Or has it been for the fear of offending the whites? If it has, O ye fearful ones, throw of your fearfulness, and come forth in the name of the Lord, and in the strength of the God of Justice, and make yourselves useful and active members in society; for they admire a noble and patriotic spirit in others; and should they not admire it in us? If you are men, convince them that you possess the spirit of men; and as your day, so shall your strength be. Have the sons of Africa no souls? feel they no ambitious desires? shall the chains of ignorance forever confine them? shall the insipid appellation of "clever negroes," or "good creatures," any longer content them? Where can we find among ourselves the man of science, or a philosopher, or an able statesman, or a counsellor at law? Show me our fearless and brave, our noble and gallant ones. Where are our lecturers on natural history, and our critics in useful knowledge? There may be a few such men among us, but they are rare. It is true, our fathers bled and died in the revolutionary war, and others fought bravely under the command of Jackson, in defense of liberty. But where is the man that has distinguished himself in these modern days by acting wholly in the defense of African rights and liberty? There was one, although he sleeps, his memory lives.

I am sensible that there are many highly intelligent gentlemen of color in these United States, in the force of whose arguments, doubtless, I should discover my inferiority; but if they are blest with wit and talent, friends and fortune, why have they not made themselves men of eminence, by striving to take all the reproach that is cast upon the people of color, and in endeavoring to alleviate the woes of their brethren in bondage? Talk, without effort, is nothing; you are abundantly capable, gentlemen, of making yourselves men of distinction; and this gross neglect, on your part, causes my blood to boil within me. Here is the grand cause which hinders the rise and progress of the people of color. It is their want of laudable ambition and requisite courage.

Individuals have been distinguished according to their genius and talents, ever since the first formation of man, and will continue to be while the world stands. The different grades rise to honor and respectability as their merits may deserve. History informs us that we sprung from one of the most learned nations of the whole earth; from the seat, if not the parent of science; yes, poor, despised Africa was once the resort of sages and legislators of other nations, was esteemed the school for learning, and the most illustrious men in Greece flocked thither for instruction. But it was our gross sins and abominations that provoked the Almighty to frown thus heavily upon us, and give our glory unto others. Sin and prodigality have caused the downfall of nations, kings and emperors; and were it not that God in wrath remembers mercy; we might indeed despair; but a promise is left us; "Ethiopia shall again stretch forth her hands unto God."

But it is of no use for us to boast that we sprung from this learned and enlightened nation, for this day a thick mist of moral gloom hangs over millions of our race. Our condition as a people has been low for hundreds of years, and it will continue to be so, unless, by true piety and virtue, we strive to regain that which we have lost. White Americans, by their prudence, economy and exertions, have sprung up and become one of the most flourishing nations in the world, distinguished for their knowledge of the arts and sciences, for their polite literature. While our minds are vacant, and starving for want of knowledge, theirs are filled to overflowing. Most of our color have been taught to stand in fear of the white man, from their earliest infancy, to work as soon as they could walk, and call "master," before they scarce could lisp the name of *mother*. Continual fear and laborious servitude have in some degree lessened in us that natural force and energy which belong to man; or else, in defiance of opposition, our men, before this, would have nobly and boldly contended for their rights. But give the man of color an equal opportunity with the white from the cradle to manhood, and from manhood to the grave, and you would discover the dignified statesman, the man of science, and the philosopher. But there is no such opportunity for the sons of Africa, and I fear that our powerful one's are fully determined that there never shall be. For bid, ye Powers on high, that it should any longer be said that our men possess no force. O ye sons of Africa, when will your voices be heard in our legislative halls, in defiance of your enemies, contending for equal rights and liberty? How can you, when you reflect from what you have fallen, refrain from crying mightily unto God, to turn away from us the fierceness of his anger, and remember our transgressions against us no more forever. But a God of infinite purity will not regard the prayers of those who hold religion in one hand, and prejudice, sin and pollution in the other; he will not regard the prayers of self-righteousness and hypocrisy. Is it possible, I exclaim, that for the want of knowledge, we have labored for hundreds of years to support others, and been content to receive what they chose to give us in return? Cast your eyes about, look as far as you can see; all, all is owned by the lordly white, except here and there a lowly dwelling which the man of color, midst deprivations, fraud and opposition, has been scarce able to procure. Like King Solomon, who put neither nail nor hammer to the temple, yet received the praise; so also have the white Americans gained themselves a name, like the names of the great men that are in the earth, while in reality we have been their principal foundation and support. We have pursued the shadow, they have obtained the substance; we have performed the labor, they have received the profits; we have planted the vines, they have eaten the fruits of them.

I would implore our men, and especially our rising youth, to flee from the gambling board and the dance-hall; for we are poor, and have no money to throw away. I do not consider dancing as criminal in itself, but it is astonishing to me that our young men are so blind to their own interest and the future welfare of their children, as to spend their hard earnings for this frivolous amusement; for it has been carried on among us to such an unbecoming extent, that it has became absolutely disgusting. "Faithful are the wounds of a friend, but the kisses of an enemy are deceitful." Had those men among us, who have had an opportunity, turned their attention as assiduously to mental and moral improvement as they have to gambling and dancing, I might have remained quietly at home, and they stood contending in my place. These polite accomplishments will never enroll your names on the bright annals of tune, who admire the belle void of intellectual knowledge, or applaud the dandy that talks largely on politics, without striving to assist his fellow in the revolution, when the nerves and muscles of every other man forced him into the field of action. You have a right to rejoice, and to let your hearts cheer you in the days of your youth; yet remember that for all these things, God will bring you into judgment. Then, O ye sons of Africa, turn your mind from these perishable objects, and contend for the cause of God and the rights of man. Form yourselves into temperance societies. There are temperate men among you; then why will you any longer neglect to strive, by your example, to suppress vice in all its abhorrent forms? You have been told repeatedly of the glorious results arising from temperance, and can you bear to see the whites arising in honor and respectability, without endeavoring to grasp after that honor and respectability also?

But I forbear. Let our money, instead of being thrown away as heretofore, be appropriated for schools and seminaries of learning for our children and youth. We ought to follow the example of the whites in this respect. Nothing would raise our respectability, add to our peace and happiness, and reflect so much honor upon us, as to be ourselves the promoters of temperance, and the supporters, as far as we are able, of useful and scientific knowledge. The rays of light and knowledge have been hid from our view; we have been taught to consider ourselves as scarce superior to the brute creation; and have performed the most laborious part of American drudgery. Had we as a people received, one half the early advantages the whites have received, I would defy the government of these United States to deprive us any longer of our rights.

I am informed that the agent of the Colonization Society has recently formed an association of young men, for the purpose of influencing those of us to go to Liberia who may feel disposed. The colonizationists are blind to their own interest, for should the nations of the earth make war with America, they would find their forces much weakened by our absence; or should we remain here, can our "brave soldiers," and "fellow-citizens," as they were termed in time of calamity, condescend to defend the rights of the whites, and be again deprived of their own, or sent to Liberia in return? Or, if the colonizationists are real friends to Africa, let them expend the money which they collect, in erecting a college to educate her injured sons in this land of gospel light and liberty; for it would be most thankfully received on our part, and convince us of the truth of their professions, and save time, expense and anxiety. Let them place before us noble objects, worthy of pursuit, and see if we prove ourselves to be those unambitious negroes they term us. But ah! methinks their hearts are so frozen towards us, they had rather their money should be sunk in the ocean than to administer it to our relief; and I fear, if they dared, like Pharaoh, king of Egypt, they would order every male child among us to be drowned. But the most high God is still as able to subdue the lofty pride of these white Americans, as He was the heart of that ancient rebel. They say, though we are looked upon as things, yet we sprang from a scientific people. Had our men the requisite force and energy, they would soon convince them by their efforts both in public and private, that they were men, or things in the shape of men. Well may the colonizationists laugh us to scorn for our negligence; well may they cry, "Shame to the sons of Africa." As the burden of the Israelites was too great for Moses to bear, so also is our burden too great for Moses to bear, so also is our burden too great for our noble advocate to bear. You must feel interested, my brethren, in what he undertakes, and hold up his hands by your good works, or in spite of himself, his soul will become discouraged, and his heart will die within him; for he has, as it were, the strong bulls of Bashan to contend with.

It is of no use for us to wait any longer for a generation of well educated men to arise. We have slumbered and slept too long already; the day is far spent; the night of death approaches; and you have sound sense and good judgment sufficient to begin with, if you feel disposed to make a right use of it. Let every man of color throughout the United States, who possesses the spirit and principles of a man, sign a petition to Congress, to abolish slavery in the District of Columbia, and grant you the rights and privileges of common free citizens; for if you had had faith as a grain of mustard seed, long before this the mountains of prejudice might have been removed. We are all sensible that the Anti-Slavery Society has taken hold of the arm of our whole population, in' order to raise them out of the mire. Now all we have to do is, by a spirit of virtuous ambition to strive to raise ourselves; and I am happy to have it in my power thus publicly to say, that the colored inhabitants of this city, in some respects, are beginning to improve. Had the free people of color in these United States nobly and boldly contended for their rights, and showed a natural genius and talent, although not so brilliant as some; had they held up, encouraged and patronized each other, nothing could have hindered us from being a thriving and flourishing people. There has been a fault among us. The reason why our distinguished men have not made themselves more influential, is because they fear that the strong current of opposition through which they must pass, would cause their downfall and prove their overthrow. And what gives rise to this opposition? Envy. And what has it amounted to? Nothing. And who are the cause of it? Our whited sepulchres, who want to be great, and don't know how; who love to be called of men "Rabbi, Rabbi," who put on false sanctity, and humble themselves to their brethren, for the sake of acquiring the highest place in the synagogue, and the uppermost seats at the feast. You, dearly beloved, who are the genuine followers of our Lord Jesus Christ, the salt of the earth and the light of the world, are not so culpable. As I told you, in the very first of my writing, I tell you again, I am but as a drop in the bucket—as one particle of the small dust of the earth.

God will surely raise up those among us who will plead the cause of virtue, and the pure principles of morality, more eloquently than I am able to do.

It appears to me that America has become like the great city of Babylon, for she has boasted in her heart,—I sit a queen, and am no widow, and shall see no sorrow? She is indeed a seller of slaves and the souls of men; she has made the Africans drunk with the wine of her fornication; she has put them completely beneath her feet, and she means to keep them there; her right hand supports the reins of government, and her left hand the wheel of power, and she is determined not to let go her grasp. But many powerful sons and daughters of Africa will shortly arise, who will put down vice and immorality among us, and declare by Him that sitteth upon the throne, that they will have their rights; and if refused, I am afraid they will spread horror and devastation around. I believe that the oppression of injured

Africa has come up before the Majesty of Heaven; and when our cries shall have reached the ears of the Most High, it will be a tremendous day for the people of this land; for strong is the arm of the Lord God Almighty.

Life has almost lost its charms for me; death has lost its sting and the grave its terrors; and at times I have a strong desire to depart and dwell with Christ, which is far better. Let me entreat my white brethren to awake and save our sons from dissipation, and our daughters from ruin. Lend the hand of assistance to feeble merit, plead the cause of virtue among our sable race; so shall our curses upon you be turned into blessings; and though you should endeavor to drive us from these shores, still we will cling to you the more firmly; nor will we attempt to rise above you: we will presume to be called your equals only.

The unfriendly whites first drove the native American from his much loved home. Then they stole our fathers from their peaceful and quiet dwellings, and brought them hither, and made bond-men and bond-women of them and their little ones; they have obliged our brethren to labor, kept them in utter ignorance, nourished them in vice, and raised them in degradation; and now that we have enriched their soil, and filled their coffers, they say that we are not capable of becoming like white men, and that we never can rise to respectability in this country. They would drive us to a strange land. But before I go, the bayonet shall pierce me through. African rights and liberty is a subject that ought to fire the breast of every free man of color in these United States, and excite in his bosom a lively, deep, decided and heart-felt interest.

6

SARAH MAPPS DOUGLASS (ZILLAH)

(1806–1882)

Born into a prominent Philadelphia abolitionist family, Sarah Mapps Douglass promoted literacy and education for those less privileged than she. She founded the Female Literary Society before she was twenty years old; she became a teacher in a school founded by James Forten, grandfather of Charlotte Forten Grimké. Sarah's father was a Presbyterian minister but Sarah and her mother, Grace Bustill Douglass, joined the Society of Friends and helped found the Philadelphia Female Anti-Slavery Society in 1833. Through her abolitionist activities, she became acquainted with a wide circle of anti-slavery activists, including Sarah and Angelina Grimké. Sarah is also a cousin to Gertrude Bustill Mossell.

Under the pen name Zillah, Douglass published "A Mother's Love" in William Lloyd Garrison's *Liberator* on July 28, 1832. In it, she offers her reader a glimpse of the painful predicaments enslaved mothers found themselves in, often being forced by their masters to choose between their own well-being and the well-being of their children. The epigraph is from Hannah More's play *Moses in the Bulrushes* (1782).

"A Mother's Love" (1832)

SOURCE: Sarah Mapps Douglass, "A Mother's Love,"
Liberator, July 28, 1832.

> "All other passions change
> With changing circumstances; rise or fall,
> Dependent on their object; claim returns;
> Live on reciprocation and expire
> Unfed by hope. A mother's fondness reigns
> Without a rival, and without an end."

And dost though, poor slave, feel this holy passion? Does thy heart swell with anguish, when thy helpless infant is torn from thy arms, and carried thou knowest not whither? When thou hast no hope left that thou shalt ever see his innocent face again? Yes, I know thou dost feel all this.

I well remember conversing with a liberated slave, who told me of the many hardships she had to encounter while in a state of captivity. At one time, after having been reaping all the morning, she returned at noon to a spring near her master's house to carry water to some hired laborers. At this spring her babe was tied; she had not been allowed to come near it since sunrise, the time at which it was placed there; her heart yearned with pity and affection for her boy, and while she kneeled at the spring and dipped the water with one hand, she drew her babe to her aching bosom with the other. She would have fed it from this fountain, troubled and almost dried with grief; but, alas! This consolation was denied her. Her cruel mistress observed her from the window where she was sitting and immediately ran to her, and seizing a large stick beat her cruelly upon her neck and bosom, bidding her begone to her work. Poor creature! Rage against her mistress almost emboldened her to return the blow; she cared not for herself, but when she reflected that her child would probably be the sufferer, maternal tenderness triumphed over every other feeling, and she again tied her child, and returned to the labors of the field.

American mothers! Can you doubt that the slave feels as tenderly for her offspring as you do for yours? Do your hearts feel no throb of pity for her woes? Will you not raise your voices, and plead for her emancipation—her immediate emancipation?

At another time, when assisting her mistress to get dinner, she dropped the skin of a potato into what she was preparing. The angry woman snatched the knife from her hand, and struck her with it upon the bosom! My countenance, expressed as much horror at this account, that I believe the poor woman thought I doubted her veracity. Baring her aged bosom, "Look," said she, "my child, here is the scar"—and I looked and wept that woman should have so far forgot her gentle nature. Soon after this, she was sold to another person, and at his death freed. She then went to reside in a neighboring city. Her old mistress, after a series of misfortunes, was reduced to almost beggary, and beat her weary footsteps to the same city: and would you believe it, reader? She sent for the woman she had so cruelly wronged, to come and assist her. Her friends persuaded her not to go; but she, noble creature! woman-like, weeping that a lady should be so reduced, obeyed the call, and waited upon her as faithfully as if she had been her dearest friend.

Calumniators of my despised race, read this and blush.

ZILLAH.

PHILADELPHIA, JULY 8TH, 1832.

7

HARRIET JACOBS

(1813–1897)

Harriet Jacobs is well-known to most students of African American literature who have read her now canonical autobiography, *Incidents in the Life of a Slave Girl* (1861), the first fugitive slave narrative written by a woman in the United States, published initially under the pseudonym Linda Brent. Born into slavery in Edenton, North Carolina, Harriet escaped and lived as a fugitive slave in New York for ten years. Her narrative was immediately popular and influential among abolitionists in the United States and England.

"The Loophole of Retreat" details Jacobs's painful experience in hiding before she escaped from slavery. Confined in a small, lightless, pest-infested crawl space, Jacobs demonstrates resilience and optimism even in the midst of excruciating pain. The conversations Jacobs recalls at the end of the piece, spoken by people walking by her hiding place, indicate how precarious her position was.

"The Loophole of Retreat" from *Incidents in the Life of a Slave Girl* (1861)

SOURCE: Harriet Ann Jacobs, *Incidents in the Life of a Slave Girl* (Boston: Published for the Author, 1861).

A small shed had been added to my grandmother's house years ago. Some boards were laid across the joists at the top, and between these boards and the roof was a very small garret, never occupied by any thing but rats and mice. It was a pent roof, covered with nothing but shingles, according to the southern custom for such buildings. The garret was only nine feet long and seven wide. The highest part was three feet high, and sloped down abruptly to the loose board floor. There was no admission for either light or air. My uncle Phillip, who was a carpenter, had very skillfully made a concealed trap-door, which communicated with the storeroom. He had been doing this while I was waiting in the swamp. The storeroom opened upon a piazza. To this hole I was conveyed as soon as I entered the house. The air was stifling; the darkness total. A bed had been spread on the floor. I could sleep quite comfortably on one side; but the slope was so sudden that I could not turn on my other without hitting the roof. The rats and mice ran over my bed; but I was weary, and I slept such sleep as the wretched may, when a tempest has passed over them. Morning came. I knew it only by the noises I heard; for in my small den day and night were all the same. I suffered for air even more than for light. But I was not comfortless. I heard the voices of my children. There was joy and there was sadness in the sound. It made my tears flow. How I longed to speak to them! I was eager to look on their faces; but there was no hole, no crack, through which I could peep. This continued darkness was oppressive. It seemed horrible to sit or lie in a cramped position day after day, without one gleam of light. Yet I would have chosen this, rather than my lot as a slave, though white people considered it an easy one; and it was so compared with the fate of others. I was never cruelly overworked; I was never lacerated with the whip from head to foot; I was never so beaten and bruised that I could not turn from one side to the other; I never had my heel-strings cut to prevent my running away; I was never chained to a log and forced to drag it about, while I toiled in the fields from morning till night; I was never branded with hot iron, or torn by bloodhounds. On the contrary, I had always been kindly treated, and tenderly cared for, until I came into the hands of Dr. Flint. I had never wished for freedom till then. But though my life in slavery was comparatively devoid of hardships, God pity the woman who is compelled to lead such a life!

My food was passed up to me through the trap-door my

uncle had contrived; and my grandmother, my uncle Phillip, and aunt Nancy would seize such opportunities as they could, to mount up there and chat with me at the opening. But of course this was not safe in the daytime. It must all be done in darkness. It was impossible for me to move in an erect position, but I crawled about my den for exercise. One day I hit my head against something, and found it was a gimlet. My uncle had left it sticking there when he made the trap-door. I was as rejoiced as Robinson Crusoe could have been at finding such a treasure. It put a lucky thought into my head. I said to myself, "Now I will have some light. Now I will see my children." I did not dare to begin my work during the daytime, for fear of attracting attention. But I groped round; and having found the side next the street, where I could frequently see my children, I stuck the gimlet in and waited for evening. I bored three rows of holes, one above another; then I bored out the interstices between. I thus succeeded in making one hole about an inch long and an inch broad. I sat by it till late into the night, to enjoy the little whiff of air that floated in. In the morning I watched for my children. The first person I saw in the street was Dr. Flint. I had a shuddering, superstitious feeling that it was a bad omen. Several familiar faces passed by. At last I heard the merry laugh of children, and presently two sweet little faces were looking up at me, as though they knew I was there, and were conscious of the joy they imparted. How I longed to *tell* them I was there!

My condition was now a little improved. But for weeks I was tormented by hundreds of little red insects, fine as a needle's point, that pierced through my skin, and produced an intolerable burning. The good grandmother gave me herb teas and cooling medicines, and finally I got rid of them. The heat of my den was intense, for nothing but thin shingles protected me from the scorching summer's sun. But I had my consolations. Through my peeping-hole I could watch the children, and when they were near enough, I could hear their talk. Aunt Nancy brought me all the news she could hear at Dr. Flint's. From her I learned that the doctor had written to New York to a colored woman, who had been born and raised in our neighborhood, and had breathed his contaminating atmosphere. He offered her a reward if she could find out any thing about me. I know not what was the nature of her reply; but he soon after started for New York in haste, saying to his family that he had business of importance to transact. I peeped at him as he passed on his way to the steamboat. It was a satisfaction to have miles of land and water between us, even for a little while; and it was a still greater satisfaction to know that he believed me to be in the Free States. My little den seemed less dreary than it had done. He returned, as he did from his former journey to New York, without obtaining any satisfactory information. When he passed our house next morning, Benny was standing at the gate. He had heard them say that he had gone to find me, and he called out, "Dr. Flint, did you bring my mother home? I want to see her." The doctor stamped his foot at him in a rage, and exclaimed, "Get out of the way, you little damned rascal! If you don't, I'll cut off your head."

Benny ran terrified into the house, saying, "You can't put me in jail again. I don't belong to you now." It was well that the wind carried the words away from the doctor's ear. I told my grandmother of it, when we had our next conference at the trap-door, and begged of her not to allow the children to be impertinent to the irascible old man.

Autumn came, with a pleasant abatement of heat. My eyes had become accustomed to the dim light, and by holding my book or work in a certain position near the aperture I contrived to read and sew. That was a great relief to the tedious monotony of my life. But when winter came, the cold penetrated through the thin shingle roof, and I was dreadfully chilled. The winters there are not so long, or so severe, as in northern latitudes; but the houses are not built to shelter from cold, and my little den was peculiarly comfortless. The kind grandmother brought me bedclothes and warm drinks. Often I was obliged to lie in bed all day to keep comfortable; but with all my precautions, my shoulders and feet were frostbitten. O, those long, gloomy days, with no object for my eye to rest upon, and no thoughts to occupy my mind, except the dreary past and the uncertain future! I was thankful when there came a day sufficiently mild for me to wrap myself up and sit at the loophole to watch the passers by. Southerners have the habit of stopping and talking in the streets, and I heard many conversations not intended to meet my ears. I heard slave-hunters planning how to catch some poor fugitive. Several times I heard allusions to Dr. Flint, myself, and the history of my children, who, perhaps, were playing near the gate. One would say, "I wouldn't move my little finger to catch her, as old Flint's property." Another would say, "I'll catch *any* nigger for the reward. A man ought to have what belongs to him, if he *is* a damned brute." The opinion was often expressed that I was in the Free States. Very rarely did any one suggest that I might be in the vicinity. Had the least suspicion rested on my grandmother's house, it would have been burned to the ground. But it was the last place they thought of. Yet there was no place, where slavery existed, that could have afforded me so good a place of concealment.

Dr. Flint and his family repeatedly tried to coax and bribe my children to tell something they had heard said about me. One day the doctor took them into a shop, and offered them some bright little silver pieces and gay handkerchiefs if they would tell where their mother was. Ellen shrank away from him, and would not speak; but Benny spoke up, and said, "Dr. Flint, I don't know where my mother is. I guess she's in New York; and when you go there again, I wish you'd ask her to come home, for I want to see her; but if you put her in jail, or tell her you'll cut her head off, I'll tell her to go right back."

ELIZABETH KECKLEY

(1818–1907)

Born into slavery in Dinwiddie County, Virginia, Keckley lived as an enslaved dressmaker in St. Louis, Missouri, before buying her freedom and moving to Washington, D.C. There, she became a dressmaker for the city's growing elite, including Mary Todd Lincoln, who soon became attached to Keckley. The two forged a close, longstanding, and complicated relationship. After Abraham Lincoln's assassination, Keckley remained a supporter of his widow. Keckley published her autobiography, *Behind the Scenes, or, Thirty Years a Slave and Four Years in the White House,* in 1868, and horrified at what they saw as an invasion of privacy, Washington society and the Lincoln family turned their backs on Keckley. She lived on her income as a seamstress and after 1892 taught at Wilberforce University in the Department of Sewing and the Domestic Arts. She died in a home for the destitute that she had a role in founding.

The following excerpt from Keckley's *Behind the Scenes* shows the trust Mary Todd Lincoln put in her former dressmaker. With dwindling resources, Lincoln's widow needed to sell pieces of her wardrobe. Keckley naturally sought to help but, as the excerpt closes, race remained a harsh and inexorable barrier.

"The Secret History of Mrs. Lincoln's Wardrobe in
New York," from *Behind the Scenes, or, Thirty Years
a Slave and Four Years in the White House* (1868)

SOURCE: Elizabeth Keckley, *Behind the Scenes, or, Thirty
Years a Slave and Four Years in the White House*
(New York: G. W. Carlton and Co., 1868).

In March 1867, Mrs. Lincoln wrote to me from Chicago that, as
her income was insufficient to meet her expenses, she would be
obliged to give up her house in the city, and return to boarding.
She said that she had struggled long enough to keep up appearances, and that the mask must be thrown aside. "I have not the
means," she wrote, "to meet the expenses of even a first-class
boardinghouse, and must sell out and secure cheap rooms at
some place in the country. It will not be startling news to you, my
dear Lizzie, to learn that I must sell a portion of my wardrobe to
add to my resources, so as to enable me to live decently, for you
remember what I told you in Washington, as well as what you
understood before you left me here in Chicago. I cannot live on
seventeen hundred dollars a year, and as I have many costly
things which I shall never wear, I might as well turn them into
money, and thus add to my income, and make my circumstances
easier. It is humiliating to be placed in such a position, but as I am
in the position, I must extricate myself as best I can. Now, Lizzie,
I want to ask a favor of you. It is imperative that I should do
something for my relief. I want you to meet me in New York, between the thirtieth of August and the fifth of September next, to
assist me in disposing of a portion of my wardrobe."

I knew that Mrs. Lincoln's income was small, and also knew
that she had many valuable dresses, which could be of no value
to her, packed away in boxes and trunks. I was confident that
she would never wear the dresses again, and thought that, since
her need was urgent, it would be well enough to dispose of
them quietly, and believed that New York was the best place to
transact a delicate business of the kind. She was the wife of
Abraham Lincoln, the man who had done so much for my race,
and I could refuse nothing for her, calculated to advance her

interests. I consented to render Mrs. Lincoln all the assistance in my power, and many letters passed between us in regard to the best way to proceed. It was finally arranged that I should meet her in New York about the middle of September. While thinking over this question, I remembered an incident of the White House. When we were packing up to leave Washington for Chicago, she said to me, one morning:

"Lizzie, I may see the day when I shall be obliged to sell a portion of my wardrobe. If Congress does not do something for me, then my dresses some day may have to go to bring food into my mouth, and the mouths of my children."

I also remembered of Mrs. L. having said to me at different times, in the years of 1863 and 1864, that her expensive dresses might prove of great assistance to her some day.

"In what way, Mrs. Lincoln? I do not understand," I ejaculated, the first time she made the remark to me.

"Very simple. Mr. Lincoln is so generous that he will not save anything from his salary, and I expect that we will leave the White House poorer than when we came into it; and should such be the case, I will have no further need for an expensive wardrobe, and it will be policy to sell it off."

I thought at the time that Mrs. Lincoln was borrowing trouble from the future, and little dreamed that the event which she so dimly foreshadowed would ever come to pass.

I closed my business about the tenth of September, and made every arrangement to leave Washington on the mission proposed. On the fifteenth of September I received a letter from Mrs. Lincoln, postmarked Chicago, saying that she should leave the city so as to reach New York on the night of the seventeenth, and directing me to precede her to the metropolis, and secure rooms for her at the St. Denis Hotel in the name of Mrs. Clarke, as her visit was to be *incog.* The contents of the letter were startling to me. I had never heard of the St. Denis, and therefore presumed that it could not be a first-class house. And I could not understand why Mrs. Lincoln should travel, without protection, under an assumed name. I knew that it would be impossible for me to engage rooms at a strange hotel for a person whom the proprietors knew nothing about. I could not write to Mrs. Lincoln, since she would be on the road to

New York before a letter could possibly reach Chicago. I could not telegraph her, for the business was of too delicate a character to be trusted to the wires that would whisper the secret to every curious operator along the line. In my embarrassment, I caught at a slender thread of hope, and tried to derive consolation from it. I knew Mrs. Lincoln to be indecisive about some things, and I hoped that she might change her mind in regard to the strange program proposed, and at the last moment dispatch me to this effect. The sixteenth and then the seventeenth of September passed, and no dispatch reached me, so on the eighteenth I made all haste to take the train for New York. After an anxious ride, I reached the city in the evening, and when I stood alone in the streets of the great metropolis, my heart sank within me. I was in an embarrassing situation, and scarcely knew how to act. I did not know where the St. Denis Hotel was, and was not certain that I should find Mrs. Lincoln there after I should go to it.

I walked up to Broadway, and got into a stage going uptown, with the intention of keeping a close lookout for the hotel in question. A kind-looking gentleman occupied the seat next to me, and I ventured to inquire of him:

"If you please, sir, can you tell me where the St. Denis Hotel is?"

"Yes; we ride past it in the stage. I will point it out to you when we come to it."

"Thank you, sir."

The stage rattled up the street, and after a while the gentleman looked out of the window and said:

"This is the St. Denis. Do you wish to get out here?"

"Thank you. Yes, sir."

He pulled the strap, and the next minute I was standing on the pavement. I pulled a bell at the ladies' entrance to the hotel, and a boy coming to the door, I asked:

"Is a lady by the name of Mrs. Clarke stopping here? She came last night, I believe."

"I do not know. I will ask at the office"; and I was left alone. The boy came back and said:

"Yes, Mrs. Clarke is here. Do you want to see her?"

"Yes."

"Well, just walk round there. She is down here now."

I did not know where "round there" exactly was, but I concluded to go forward. I stopped, however, thinking that the lady might be in the parlor with some company; and pulling out a card, asked the boy to take it to her. She heard me talking, and came into the hall to see for herself.

"My dear Lizzie, I am so glad to see you," she exclaimed, coming forward and giving me her hand. "I have just received your note"—I had written her that I should join her on the eighteenth—"and have been trying to get a room for you. Your note has been here all day, but it was never delivered until to-night. Come in here, until I find out about your room"; and she led me into the office.

The clerk, like all modern hotel clerks, was exquisitely arrayed, highly perfumed, and too self-important to be obliging or even courteous.

"This is the woman I told you about. I want a good room for her," Mrs. Lincoln said to the clerk.

"We have no room for her, madam," was the pointed rejoinder.

"But she must have a room. She is a friend of mine, and I want a room for her adjoining mine."

"We have no room for her on your floor."

"That is strange, sir. I tell you that she is a friend of mine, and I am sure you could not give a room to a more worthy person."

"Friend of yours, or not, I tell you we have no room for her on your floor. I can find a place for her on the fifth floor."

"That, sir, I presume, will be a vast improvement on my room. Well, if she goes to the fifth floor, I shall go too, sir. What is good enough for her is good enough for me."

"Very well, madam. Shall I give you adjoining rooms, and send your baggage up?"

"Yes, and have it done in a hurry. Let the boy show us up. Come, Elizabeth," and Mrs. L. turned from the clerk with a haughty glance, and we commenced climbing the stairs. I thought we should never reach the top; and when we did reach the fifth story, what accommodations! little three-cornered rooms, scantily furnished. I never expected to see the widow of President Lincoln in such dingy, humble quarters.

"How provoking!" Mrs. Lincoln exclaimed, sitting down on a chair when we had reached the top, and panting from the effects of the climbing. "I declare, I never saw such unaccommodating people. Just to think of them sticking us away up here in the attic. I will give them a regular going over in the morning."

"But you forget. They do not know you. Mrs. Lincoln would be treated differently from Mrs. Clarke."

"True, I do forget. . . . Why did you not come to me yesterday, Lizzie? I was almost crazy when I reached here last night, and found you had not arrived. I sat down and wrote you a note—I felt so badly—imploring you to come to me immediately." This note was afterward sent to me from Washington:

> *St. Denis Hotel, Broadway, N. Y.*
> *Wednesday, 17 September.*
>
> MY DEAR LIZZIE: I arrived *here* last evening in utter despair *at not* finding you. I am frightened to death, being here alone. Come, I pray you, by *next* train. Inquire for
>
> Mrs. Clarke,
>
> *Room 94, 5th or 6th Story.*
>
> House so crowded could not get another spot. I wrote you especially to meet me here last evening; it makes me wild to think of being here alone. Come by *next train* without fail.
>
> YOUR FRIEND,
> MRS. LINCOLN.

> I am booked Mrs. Clarke; inquire for *no other person. Come, come, come.* I will pay your expenses when you arrive here. I shall not leave here or change my room until you come.
>
> YOUR FRIEND, M. L.

> Do not leave this house without seeing me.
> *Come!*

I transcribe the letter literally.

In reply to Mrs. Lincoln's last question I explained what has already been explained to the reader, that I was in hope she would change her mind, and knew that it would be impossible to secure the rooms requested for a person unknown to the proprietors or attachés of the hotel.

The explanation seemed to satisfy her. Turning to me suddenly, she exclaimed:

"You have not had your dinner, Lizzie, and must be hungry. I nearly forgot about it in the joy of seeing you. You must go down to the table right away."

She pulled the bell-rope, and a servant appearing, she ordered him to give me my dinner. I followed him downstairs, and he led me into the dining hall, and seated me at a table in one corner of the room. I was giving my order, when the steward came forward and gruffly said:

"You are in the wrong room."

"I was brought here by the waiter," I replied.

"It makes no difference; I will find you another place where you can eat your dinner."

9

ELIZA POTTER

(1820–after 1861)

Eliza Potter's sharp-tongued and gossipy memoir, *A Hairdresser's Experience in High Life*, is a departure from much of the serious women's writing from the era. Potter lived and worked according to her own wishes and desires, traveling from one swank holiday spot to another, always in demand as a hairdresser, able to accept clients or not as she chose. Potter traveled to the South, saw a slave auction, and was disturbed by what she saw, but these moments, while emphasized in most of the studies on Potter, do not loom large in her narrative. Rather, Potter presents herself as a recorder of the hypocrisies of her wealthy clients—their pettiness, unhappiness, and moral corruption. In contradistinction to the usual narratives of African American life under scrutiny by the white observer, Potter assumes the role of observer.

The following excerpt from Potter's memoir focuses on her experiences in New Orleans, in which she expresses disbelief about the shrewdness and scheming of members of "high society" she encounters. Potter's account reads as a witness to a corrupt and decaying aristocracy.

"New Orleans," from *A Hairdresser's Experience in High Life* (1859)

SOURCE: Eliza Potter, *A Hairdresser's Experience in High Life* (Cincinnati, OH: Published for the Author, 1859).

Did this throw a gloom over the house? No; for that very evening there was a tremendous large ball. The corpse was immediately taken away, and placed in a vault, and at the first opportunity sent to Kentucky. For my own part, the gloom did not wear off for a month; and I thought if I crossed the hall, that ghosts and hobgoblins were right behind me; and when I would go home at night, I would light three or four candles and place them in every part of the room, for the hospital was just opposite where I lived, and I knew every death that took place—man, woman, or child—by the toll of the bell. When a man would die, it would strike three times; a woman, twice, and a child, once; and never a night passed but it would toll several times. I must laugh now to think how frightened I was one day in going down the back stairs. I heard some one coming down very rapidly behind me; when I turned round I found it to be a gentleman who had just left a lady's apartment who he had been in the habit of visiting in her husband's absence, and as soon as he heard him come up the front stairs, he would rush down the back stairs. I went to the lady's room to see what was the matter, and I found her almost fainting for fear her husband had seen the man; while the husband, frightened, thinking his wife very sick, was putting back her massive curls to bathe her temples. The gentleman was frightened for fear he had been seen; and I, also, frightened on account of his haste. However, I got through that week very quietly, without seeing hobgoblins or being frightened to death.

I remember well a lady and her two daughters who, about this time, came to New Orleans. The daughters were very gay, and very pretty. The first time I saw their mother she was in the hall speculating in pianos, and the next time I saw her she was in her own room. I did not know her again, as, when I had first seen her, she had jet black hair, a profusion of curls, clear red and white complexion, and magnificent teeth; her eyes shone like diamonds; she was tall, slender, and apparently a magnificent form. On entering the room, I saw her sitting on a chair. I looked half a dozen times for the lady, when she exclaimed, "Here I am; don't you know me?" "No, madam, I did not know you." "By George, no wonder; I have not got on my pretties." Her hair was white, and her beautiful curls were all false; her complexion was *eau de beaute, blond de pearl*, and *rouge*; her teeth were the most perfect deception that ever was made, and her beautiful form was a perfect skeleton; and to hear her swear, I will acknowledge I was frightened for once by a woman.

While I was speaking to her, a handsome, amiable-looking girl stepped in, and said, "Oh, ma, why are you not dressed before this!" She replied, "Oh, don't you know I was out playing cards till near three o'clock." Hearing her speak in this manner before a stranger, her daughter shook her head, when she said, "Oh, thunder, by jingoes, there's no use shaking your head; she will soon get to know me, and like me, too." But she did not know me—for I did not like such ladies. Her daughters I became very much attached to; they were elegant, graceful and amiable girls—the eldest rather more so than the other.

In a few days I again saw this same lady in Camp-street, buying and selling bales of cotton; at another time I saw her in a wholesale store, buying sacks of coffee, and speculating on them. There was a family in the hotel, from off the coast, who had with them a very pretty maid, and a very good hair-dresser. She made her dissatisfied with her owner, that she might purchase her; she told the girl that so soon as she would earn what she paid for her, besides fixing her two daughter's heads, she would give her her freedom. The maid brought home forty dollars every month, until she had nearly paid for herself; this woman then turned round and sold her for very near as much again as she paid for her—saying nothing of what the girl had paid her. She then left the hotel and went traveling. I did not see her again for a long time, but frequently heard of her.

On one occasion I saw a very nice free girl. She proposed to this girl to sell her, and divide the money between them, and then she was to kick up a row and swear she was free. I have seen many ladies, but never one that loved money as she did.

Notwithstanding all her improper conduct, her daughters kept a fair position in society, more particularly with gentlemen.

Several seasons passed away, and I did not see or hear of this woman, till one season, on leaving Washington City, she happened to be on the same train, but not in the same car, with me. Sitting in the same seat with her, was a green, country woman. On my passing through the cars, I saw her in deep conversation with this woman, and knew immediately she was striking up some trade; so I took a seat in the same car she was in, to notice her maneuvers.

All at once I saw her jump up and, with the woman, go into a small room, called the ladies dressing-room; in a few moments she came out, laughing, and I saw she had changed her dress. I then went up to her and asked her why she changed her dress; she said, "By George, I had a good chance to sell it, and I sold it. I have worn it for a year or so, and I got as much as I gave for it. It won't be long till the cars are in Philadelphia, and I have got a waist and long sleeves under my shawl, and then the girls will have plenty of new dresses for me from the mantuamakers." She went to Philadelphia, and I did not see anything of her till about in the middle of the season, when she came to Saratoga. The salute I got from her was, "Halloo, langy!" When I turned around and saw it was her ladyship, I told her she looked very well. She said, "Yes; I come here to drink water, recruit, and get a husband." I asked her where she had been all this time; she said she had been in the New York Hotel, she and the girls, raising the devil, and having more fun than a little. "Now," says she, "I have come here, and the girls are going to be *belles* here, I can tell you that. Moreover, Pet has got a rich beau, but he is so old he can hardly stand straight," and she laughed at the top of her voice.

She made her youngest daughter make the old man believe she was desperately in love with him, and the mother pretended to give her consent. She could find no other way to speculate, so she speculated with her daughter's hand. The old man gave her a diamond ring worth several hundred dollars, an old family relic, they say. It was an expensive and elegant ring. She made him settle a large amount of property on her daughter, and got money from him herself. She went to a dress-maker's with the ring, and told her to raffle it off for three hundred dollars, at twenty-five dollars a chance. The dress-maker retained the ring for some time; but, as she did not feel very safe with it in her possession, returned it, and said she could not raffle it off. She took the ring, and there is no telling what she did with it. She then took several boxes of goods, and was going to leave them at the dress-maker's; but the dress-maker would not have anything to do with them; she knew there was something wrong, and a lady of her disposition did not care whether she got any one in trouble or not.

The season ended in Saratoga, and she, getting as much money as possible from the old man, started for Europe. The old man died, and she married her two daughters off, and remained herself in Europe, on account of the fuss about the property the old man settled on her. When I was in New York there was great confusion about the property and money the old man placed in her hands. The family grieved very much for the ring, and other pieces of jewelry belonging to the family.

I suppose that many of my readers would like to know where such a noble lady came from. She was from the South, although, when I was there, the Southerners were not proud to own her; and I am sure the North would not claim her. In the mean time my readers might ask where her husband was? A difficulty arose between a gentleman, a great gallant of hers, and her husband; the former went in her husband's office one day and shot him, and he died some time after; she ever since has been like the Wandering Jew.

A few years ago, in Louisiana, there was a family of three sons, one of them an invalid; they had a mulatto servant with them, who was, in stature, color and disposition, pretty much the same as the brothers, only a shade or so darker. This invalid brother would have no one to wait on him, he would not be taught anything, nor would he eat or drink unless he was waited on, taught and served by this mulatto. So they had to have this servant taught, to enable him to teach their brother. All this annoyed the other brothers very much.

In the course of a few years the father died. On his decease it was found that this mulatto was his son, and half-brother to those he waited on. The father dying suddenly, left him unprovided for. In a short time the sickly brother died, and then the two brothers tried to quarrel with him, and at one time tried to whip him, but he gave them a pretty good turn, and, when they were asleep, locked them in the room, and, taking as much money as he wanted, left the country.

As he was in the habit of traveling with his younger brother, there was nothing thought of it till he got to New York. He there married a white girl, and it was there I saw and conversed with him. He told me where I could find his mother, and requested me, when I went back to Louisiana, to find her, and tell her I had seen him, and all the particulars at the same time. He told me he was never struck a blow but once in his life, and that was by his brother; and he said he felt he would be willing to die to have revenge.

Some may think it strange that a white woman should marry a colored man in the North, not knowing he was colored; but it is not more so than a rich white lady of Virginia, who was a *belle* at the St. Charles, and every place she visited, marrying a man, said to be a millionaire, whose mother was a mulatto, and his father a Frenchman, who sent him to Paris and had him educated. He came back highly educated, a wealthy gentleman, and greatly sought after for his millions and his handsome appearance, and he married this great *belle*. Many knew who he was, but on account of his millions and his father, nothing was said. His mother I saw, a few years ago, in Massachusetts; she would not know him if she saw him. And there are many in the same situation; for I know two sisters now, who often visit Saratoga, from St. Louis, who married two brothers on account of their wealth. They are very nice women; but it is known by many that they were born in slavery, but raised free, and well educated. On one occasion, while in Saratoga, they were coming to the dinner-table, and some ladies, who came along, said they were not white, they looked like negroes. One of their husbands, a fine-looking man, heard the remark, and after dinner sought out the husband of the lady, who was a diminutive bit of a creature, and made him take back all his wife had said; he was glad to do so with many apologies, and the next morning he and his family were missing. All this is nothing; for, in our Queen City of the West, I know hundreds of mulattoes who are married to white men, and lawfully married.

Some of these pass for white, and some, again, are so independent they will be thought nothing but what they are.

A few years ago there was a marriage in Saratoga of a gentleman belonging to one of the best families of South Carolina. This occurred through the effects of alcohol. Several years ago a chambermaid was proved to be not respectable, and she was turned out from the hotel. She led an immoral life for some time, when Mr. —— married her. He could get no one to marry them, till at length he found out an old country parson, who performed the ceremony. There were great preparations for them to start to Charleston; but, I am told, at a certain station she was shoved off the cars, and they went on without her. Whether it was a compromise of his friends, I know not, but the apartments which he had engaged for the ensuing season were empty in Saratoga. There are a great many queer matches; one of them was a match of a gentleman of high rank and standing, with an Indian squaw. There was a camp of Indians near there, and many gentlemen chose their wives from among the squaws. This gentleman married her in the morning, and took her away with him. Several of these squaws have married men of high standing.

I knew a colored man who belonged to a family in Lexington, Ky. The children taught him to read and write, unknown to their parents. For some slight offense he was sold to a family in Bigbury; and the master found him writing passes for the servants to all parts of the city, and letters, when he was again sold, to a family living in Mississippi.

They put him to work in a cotton patch, but the head waiter in the house used to steal him newspapers to read, and at twelve o'clock they, the slaves, would go to their meals and return in a very short time, and they would lay in the grass around a tree, while he sat in the tree reading to them out of the newspaper. At last it was noticed that the slaves all hurried through their meals and it was thought so strange to see them all congregated together, that their master undertook to find out the reason. One of the young masters hid himself in one of the trees near to the one they were surrounding. They all came from their meals as usual, and he began to read the newspaper to them, he being in the tree, and they laying around. It was the time of the trouble between England and the United States on the account of McLeod, and he was explaining all the particulars, telling them England was threatening war, and what their course of conduct should be. When the master found out what they were about, he called this man to the house and questioned him; he acknowledged what he had done as he always did from the first. They then told him if he would not tell the servants, and leave the country in two hours, they would let him go; he did so, and went to Canada, I afterward saw him there at the Custom House, and we had quite a long talk.

Some will say it is very queer and they can not understand how the slaves get so enlightened; it is very easily understood. Some of them are very easily learned, and if a family has a favorite servant they will treat them as one of the family, but for the slightest offense they will sell them, and if they can, to the farthest plantation possible, and they will of course teach others.

When I commenced going down South, a widow and an overseer could, without difficulty manage a hundred slaves, now it takes three overseers and the master to rule the same number; times are fast, masters and mistresses are getting more enlightened, and so are servants. I know gentlemen and ladies who would not put on a suit of clothes without the servants say it is suitable, but if the same servants chance to offend them, they will sell them to go as far as cars and boats will carry them.

I know a widow lady who lives in Mississippi, she comes down to New Orleans every season to provide for her plantation. She is very much thought of and sought after, more particularly by merchants, on account of her immense wealth, her name is Mrs. G.; she came to the St. Charles and staid some days there. I had the pleasure of waiting on this honorable lady; she left to go home, and I went in the same boat to make a visit to a plantation further on. It seems the steward had offended her in some way, coming down, and on our going back again, when the boat stopped at her plantation, the steward came forward, expecting a dollar or so as steward's fee, she handed him a little package and told him to carry it for her; there were about fifty or so of her servants came down to see her on her arrival, and when the steward came among them, she told them that fellow had insulted her, when they all put after him like a parcel of blood-hounds, and he had to actually jump into the water to reach the plank to get on board the boat, or they would have torn him in pieces. Such devotion is from kindness. She is a kind mistress.

In the same neighborhood, a short time before, a lady was attempted to be poisoned three times by her slaves for her cruelty to them. Was this lady a Louisiana lady? No, she was not, she was from the North, and was one who had to work for her living before going South; these are always the worst of mistresses. I remember a colored woman who was raised in Cincinnati, and her parents and family now live in the midst of our city: she is now a slave-holder in the city of New Orleans: the most tyrannical, overbearing, cruel task-mistress that ever existed: so you can see color makes no difference, the propensities are the same, and those who have been oppressed themselves, are the sorest oppressors. It is a well known fact, those who are as black themselves as the ace of spades will, if they can, get mulatoes for slaves, and then the first word is "my nigger."

In the South, both whites and blacks, if they have but one garment to their back, must have a servant. I was a good deal amused one day to hear a dispute between a white and a colored woman; the colored woman was from New York, but was very wealthy, having accumulated quite a little fortune; the white woman was also from the North, and she had not been so fortunate in worldly matters: their dispute commenced on politics, and the white woman at length got so angry with some remarks of the other, that she started for the house, while in a voice quivering with passion, exclaimed, "I don't care, I have the law on my side if you have the money," while the other laughingly replied, "excuse me madam. I have both." Not withstanding there is so much hatred between the two colors, and so much enmity exists, they will associate much more so in the slave States than in the free States. There is a great deal of sociability between the free colored and the rich whites in the slave States, but when you come to the lower orders of both, there is decided enmity. I will give you a little instance that I saw with my own eyes, and I know both parties well, the white I knew when I was a little girl in New York.

A family named B——, having had some trouble in bank business, left New York and went to New Orleans. After my being in New Orleans several seasons, I found them out by visiting next door to them; the lady next door was colored, and kept elegant furnished rooms. As I told you before, there are numbers here make fortunes, and it is a common thing to have these furnished rooms, and in no mean street either, but side by side with some of the very best mansions are these furnished apartments. They are generally occupied by gentlemen, who take their meals at the St. Charles, and sleep in these apartments; and it is not thought anything if the landlady is colored; even to this day, it is very fashionable for gentlemen to take their families to these rooms.

The colored lady who kept the house I have mentioned, was very beautiful and very wealthy: she owned a great deal of property and many slaves, and kept two houses more like some of the elegant mansions of the nobility, than anything else. She inherited this property by her husband and master, he emancipated her, and then finding himself about to be involved in his business, he made all over to her—property, money and shares—a short time after, he died, leaving her in possession of all his wealth. Several gentlemen were going to see her at one time, one of these gentlemen, was a Mr. B——. They made proposals to her, not exactly of matrimony, but by them considered in the same holy light as lawful marriage; she flattered Mr. B—— for some time, making him believe she would take him for her lawful *"plaçayer."* but when the evening came on that he looked for the fulfillment of her promise, she deceived him, and took another. He went home and blew out his brains right in his father's house. Did these people treat her with contempt? No, they always treated her both before and after that as a lady, and the last time I was in New Orleans they were living beside each other, in good neighborhood and good fellowship, and she was seen daily going out to the grave-yard strewing flowers over his tomb. Such occurrences as these are frequent. I could neither find paper nor time to tell you half of such things as came under my notice.

I will now tell you of a lady I know, who was raised in high life in New York. She married a gentleman from the South, a very elegant looking man, and she thought wealthy, supposing the wealth followed the looks—as the northern ladies generally think when a man comes from the South, who is fine looking, elegantly dressed, and so forth, he must be wealthy, but it is not so, for many come to the North to pick up a rich wife, that are depending on the wages of some poor old man or woman, and it may be, had their lands to mortgage to get the money for them to flourish on. I myself, went to the house this lady's husband brought her to, a few miles from Memphis, and found it a log cabin; true she had a piano and some pieces of silver, and a great many costly things that were presented her on her leaving New York to go to her wealthy home. What a change for her from her three story brick on a fashionable street, to a little log cabin in the country, a few miles from Memphis!

Gentlemen do not think they are deceiving ladies in acting so, as they know ladies are taking them for their good looks and elegant appearance, and of course they think themselves a prize; and I know ladies who, on finding themselves so deceived, were ashamed to acknowledge it, and such often come to the North and boast of the riches and splendor of their southern home.

During the year 18—, I was in New Orleans; the season was as gay as any I had ever passed there; all was bright and brilliant. The St. Charles was crowded with people from all parts of the country; Madam Levert and Frederica Bremer were of the number. Great preparations were making for Jenny Lind, who was then in Cuba; among the rest was a gay married woman from Mississippi, whom I and numbers of others know to be a gay and fashionable lady; to my thinking she not only wore her crinoline but his pantaloons. She had at the hotel four children and several servants, and occupied two rooms, parlor and bedroom. She very seldom allowed the children to come in the parlor, but kept them with their nurse in the bedroom, unless on very particular occasions.

One day, while the children and nurse were out walking, I was in her bedroom combing her hair, when there came a knock at the door, she said, come in, and, to my surprise, a gentleman walked in and took a seat. They immediately commenced a conversation in French, when he told her to take care, as maybe I understood French, but she said, no, she is from the upper country, and does not know anything we are saying. So I combed away, and heard all their conversation. Their plan was to go to a fancy store, on the corner of Royal and St. Louis, a door opening on Royal and one on St. Louis. She was to go in at one door and a carriage was to be in waiting at the other, in which they were to drive to the Lake. The blinds were to be drawn, as if somebody was in it sick; she then told him in French, he had better go, as it was near the hour her husband come to lunch with her.

As soon as he left, I went and fastened the door, took my chair, and sat down right before her, and told her, word for word, what they had been saying, and told her never to treat any person with contempt before another because she was rich and highly educated, for there were many simple looking people, and poor people, who understood more than those who were speaking of them.

The lady became very much agitated, so much so that I feared she would faint, when I reassured her, by saying I would not expose her; I told her the circumstance I would mention, but never her name, as that should go to the grave with me; she offered me money, but I told her money never would seal my lips, nor anything except kindness. I then told her of a gentleman from Lexington, who came to me and tried to bribe me to answer just one question about some circumstance that occurred in Kentucky, which would place a lady in his power, so he offered me a seventy-five dollar silk dress if I would only answer him. She asked me if I gave him an answer. I told her no, I never did, nor I never would. She told me it was only a joke, as she was only fooling the gentleman, and did not intend to meet him; however, I had business at the St. Louis, and as it happened to be about the hour I went there to comb that she had made the appointment, I determined to see for myself, particularly as she had promised me she would not go. Shortly after I got there she came down the street, went in one door, purchased some little article, went out at the other door and into the carriage she went. I said no more to her, though I combed her for several weeks, as I had many such ladies, though their position was such no one would ever think of impeaching them.

My associate hair-dresser had a lady who, she said, was very difficult and hard to please, so she gave her over to me and I gave her one of my ladies, both of us pretending the hours would not suit. I found her very easy to get along with: after combing her for some time I found there was something wrong between her husband and herself: she was from Pittsburg and he also: they had been coming there for numbers of years. She one day asked me if I could keep a secret. I told her most assuredly I could, but I could keep it better if it was not told me. She said she for some time had her eye on me, as she thought me a bold, independent woman, and she asked me if I would go with her that afternoon our walking. I agreed, and we went out.

She took me into the French part of the city, where, after walking for several squares, we came to a little low, French built house, from appearance uninhabited, as it was all closed up, and looked as if no human being, but rats alone lived there. On going in the house she sat down and asked me if we had been seen coming there would I take the responsibility on myself. I told her that depended altogether on the nature of the case. She then told me the reason she had brought me to this strange house. She had taken a letter out of her husband's pocket the night before, from a female, saying she left the key with the hotel porter, and would meet him there, and if he could not come at that time not to come till the next day, as one of the other gentlemen would be there that day, so she got the key and determined to be there to meet her husband.

I told her if I had known such was her object in coming I would not have come with her on any account, as it might end badly, for assuredly her husband would not overlook meeting her in such a place, and I feared it would result in no good to her; however, after expostulating a long time with her I at length asked her to come to a fortune-teller's and have her fortune told and we could come back there again; she readily consented to go. Before leaving, however, we concluded to look round the place, it was certainly as curious a house as I ever saw.

The first room we went into was all lined, in place of papered ceiling and walls, with crimson oiled calico; there was a couch covered with the same, and also the chairs; there was but one mirror in the room. The next room was lined in like manner with oiled calico, but instead of crimson it was blue; the bed had a blue spread, and an elegant lace mosquito bar; a washstand was in one corner with everything on it belonging to a washstand, and in the other corner was a bureau, with everything on it a lady could require, even to paint and powder. In the third room were bottles of good old wine, bottles of champagne, dry wine, old bourbon, and every kind of liquor that could be desired; on a table spread in the middle of the floor were two or three packs of cards, with segars for both ladies and gentlemen; and on the mantlepiece were various novels. On examining some of these she declared most positively they were her books. While she sat down to look over them, panting for breath as if much agitated, I heard some one at the door trying to get in, I told her to keep quiet till I should go to the door; when I opened it I found a well known old citizen of this city and a married lady, also well known, and moving in a very high circle, who was the mother of several children. I told the gentleman, in an under tone, not to come in as there was something wrong, but to meet me at the hotel in two hours and I would explain all things to him. He and the lady went away, looking very much excited. I went back and told her it was only a man inquiring for some family who had lived there, and that it was time for us to go. We got ready and started, I slipping under my arm the books she had been looking at. When we came to the fortune-teller, I, having managed to get a moment's private conversation with the latter, told her, among other things, to say to the lady she had been looking over some books and thought they belonged to her, but she would find hers at home when she went there. I told her also to speak well of the lady's husband.

HARRIET WILSON

(1825–1900)

Harriet Wilson's semi-autobiographical novel, *Our Nig*, rediscovered by Henry Louis Gates, Jr., in 1982, is one of the first novels written by an African American woman and the first novel published by an African American in North America. Wilson was born in Milford, New Hampshire, and became an indentured servant after her father's death and her abandonment by her mother. At eighteen years old, she moved to Boston, Massachusetts, where she wrote *Our Nig*. Wilson was active in the Spiritualist Church community, giving lectures, teaching classes at the church's school, and traveling to different church branches. No evidence exists of her having produced more writing after *Our Nig*.

Included here are the Preface, Chapter I, and Chapter XII of *Our Nig*. Chapter I tells the story of the parentage of Frado, the novel's mixed-race protagonist, as "lonely" Mag Smith accepts a marriage proposal from the "African" Jim. The epigraph is from Thomas Moore's widely anthologized *Lalla Rookh* (1817).

Selections from *Our Nig* (1859)

SOURCE: Harriet E. Wilson, *Our Nig; or, Sketches from the Life of a Free Black* (Boston: G. C. Rand and Avery, 1859).

PREFACE

In offering to the public the following pages, the writer confesses her inability to minister to the refined and cultivated, the pleasure supplied by abler pens. It is not for such these crude narrations appear. Deserted by kindred, disabled by failing health, I am forced to some experiment which shall aid me in maintaining myself and child without extinguishing this feeble life. I would not from these motives even palliate slavery at the South, by disclosures of its appurtenances North. My mistress was wholly imbued with SOUTHERN principles. I do not pretend to divulge every transaction in my own life, which the unprejudiced would declare unfavorable in comparison with treatment of legal bondmen; I have purposely omitted what would most provoke shame in our good anti-slavery friends at home.

My humble position and frank confession of errors will, I hope, shield me from severe criticism. Indeed, defects are so apparent it requires no skilful hand to expose them.

I sincerely appeal to my colored brethren universally for patronage, hoping they will not condemn this attempt of their sister to be erudite, but rally around me a faithful band of supporters and defenders.

H. E. W.

CHAPTER I.

Mag Smith, My Mother.

> Oh, Grief beyond all other griefs, when fate
> First leaves the young heart lone and desolate
> In the wide world, without that only tie
> For which it loved to live or feared to die;
> Lorn as the hung-up lute, that ne'er hath spoken
> Since the sad day its master-chord was broken!
> MOORE.

Lonely Mag Smith! See her as she walks with downcast eyes and heavy heart. It was not always thus. She HAD a loving, trusting heart. Early deprived of parental guardianship, far removed from relatives, she was left to guide her tiny boat over life's surges alone and inexperienced. As she merged into womanhood, unprotected, uncherished, uncared for, there fell on her ear the music of love, awakening an intensity of emotion long dormant. It whispered of an elevation before unaspired to; of ease and plenty her simple heart had never dreamed of as hers. She knew the voice of her charmer, so ravishing, sounded far above her. It seemed like an angel's, alluring her upward and onward. She thought she could ascend to him and become an equal. She surrendered to him a priceless gem, which he proudly garnered as a trophy, with those of other victims, and left her to her fate. The world seemed full of hateful deceivers and crushing arrogance. Conscious that the great bond of union to her former companions was severed, that the disdain of others would be insupportable, she determined to leave the few friends she possessed, and seek an asylum among strangers. Her offspring came unwelcomed, and before its nativity numbered weeks, it passed from earth, ascending to a purer and better life.

"God be thanked," ejaculated Mag, as she saw its breathing cease; "no one can taunt HER with my ruin."

Blessed release! may we all respond. How many pure, innocent children not only inherit a wicked heart of their own, claiming life-long scrutiny and restraint, but are heirs also of parental disgrace and calumny, from which only long years of patient endurance in paths of rectitude can disencumber them.

Mag's new home was soon contaminated by the publicity of her fall; she had a feeling of degradation oppressing her; but she resolved to be circumspect, and try to regain in a measure what she had lost. Then some foul tongue would jest of her shame, and averted looks and cold greetings disheartened her. She saw she could not bury in forgetfulness her misdeed, so she resolved to leave her home and seek another in the place she at first fled from.

Alas, how fearful are we to be first in extending a helping hand to those who stagger in the mires of infamy; to speak the first words of hope and warning to those emerging into the sunlight of morality! Who can tell what numbers, advancing just far enough to hear a cold welcome and join in the reserved converse of professed reformers, disappointed, disheartened, have chosen to dwell in unclean places, rather than encounter these "holier-than-thou" of the great brotherhood of man!

Such was Mag's experience; and disdaining to ask favor or friendship from a sneering world, she resolved to shut herself up in a hovel she had often passed in better days, and which she knew to be untenanted. She vowed to ask no favors of familiar faces; to die neglected and forgotten before she would be dependent on any. Removed from the village, she was seldom seen except as upon your introduction, gentle reader, with downcast visage, returning her work to her employer, and thus providing herself with the means of subsistence. In two years many hands craved the same avocation; foreigners who cheapened toil and clamored for a livelihood, competed with her, and she could not thus sustain herself. She was now above no drudgery. Occasionally old acquaintances called to be favored with help of some kind, which she was glad to bestow for the sake of the money it would bring her; but the association with them was such a painful reminder of by-gones, she returned to her hut morose and revengeful, refusing all offers of a better home than she possessed. Thus she lived for years, hugging her wrongs, but making no effort to escape. She had never known plenty, scarcely competency; but the present was beyond comparison with those innocent years when the coronet of virtue was hers.

Every year her melancholy increased, her means diminished. At last no one seemed to notice her, save a kind-hearted African, who often called to inquire after her health and to see if she needed any fuel, he having the responsibility of furnishing that article, and she in return mending or making garments.

"How much you earn dis week, Mag?" asked he one Saturday evening.

"Little enough, Jim. Two or three days without any dinner. I washed for the Reeds, and did a small job for Mrs. Bellmont; that's all. I shall starve soon, unless I can get more to do. Folks seem as afraid to come here as if they expected to get some awful disease. I don't believe there is a person in the world but would be glad to have me dead and out of the way."

"No, no, Mag! don't talk so. You shan't starve so long as I have barrels to hoop. Peter Greene boards me cheap. I'll help you, if nobody else will."

A tear stood in Mag's faded eye. "I'm glad," she said, with a softer tone than before, "if there is ONE who isn't glad to see me suffer. I b'lieve all Singleton wants to see me punished, and feel as if they could tell when I've been punished long enough. It's a long day ahead they'll set it, I reckon."

After the usual supply of fuel was prepared, Jim returned home. Full of pity for Mag, he set about devising measures for her relief. "By golly!" said he to himself one day—for he had become so absorbed in Mag's interest that he had fallen into a habit of musing aloud—"By golly! I wish she'd MARRY me."

"Who?" shouted Pete Greene, suddenly starting from an unobserved corner of the rude shop.

"Where you come from, you sly nigger!" exclaimed Jim.

"Come, tell me, who is't?" said Pete; "Mag Smith, you want to marry?"

"Git out, Pete! and when you come in dis shop again, let a nigger know it. Don't steal in like a thief."

Pity and love know little severance. One attends the other. Jim acknowledged the presence of the former, and his efforts in Mag's behalf told also of a finer principle.

This sudden expedient which he had unintentionally disclosed, roused his thinking and inventive powers to study upon the best method of introducing the subject to Mag.

He belted his barrels, with many a scheme revolving in his mind, none of which quite satisfied him, or seemed, on the whole, expedient. He thought of the pleasing contrast between her fair face and his own dark skin; the smooth, straight hair, which he had once, in expression of pity, kindly stroked on her now wrinkled but once fair brow. There was a tempest gathering in his heart, and at last, to ease his pent-up passion, he exclaimed aloud, "By golly!" Recollecting his former exposure, he glanced around to see if Pete was in hearing again. Satisfied on this point, he continued: "She'd be as much of a prize to me as she'd fall short of coming up to the mark with white folks. I don't care for past things. I've done things 'fore now I's 'shamed of. She's good enough for me, any how."

One more glance about the premises to be sure Pete was away.

The next Saturday night brought Jim to the hovel again. The cold was fast coming to tarry its apportioned time. Mag was nearly despairing of meeting its rigor.

"How's the wood, Mag?" asked Jim.

"All gone; and no more to cut, any how," was the reply.

"Too bad!" Jim said. His truthful reply would have been, I'm glad.

"Anything to eat in the house?" continued he.

"No," replied Mag.

"Too bad!" again, orally, with the same INWARD gratulation as before.

"Well, Mag," said Jim, after a short pause, "you's down low enough. I don't see but I've got to take care of ye. 'Sposin' we marry!"

Mag raised her eyes, full of amazement, and uttered a sonorous "What?"

Jim felt abashed for a moment. He knew well what were her objections.

"You's had trial of white folks any how. They run off and left ye, and now none of 'em come near ye to see if you's dead or alive. I's black outside, I know, but I's got a white heart inside. Which you rather have, a black heart in a white skin, or a white heart in a black one?"

"Oh, dear!" sighed Mag; "Nobody on earth cares for ME—"

"I do," interrupted Jim.

"I can do but two things," said she, "beg my living, or get it from you."

"Take me, Mag. I can give you a better home than this, and not let you suffer so."

He prevailed; they married. You can philosophize, gentle reader, upon the impropriety of such unions, and preach dozens of sermons on the evils of amalgamation. Want is a more powerful philosopher and preacher. Poor Mag. She has sundered another bond which held her to her fellows. She has descended another step down the ladder of infamy.

CHAPTER XII.

The Winding Up of the Matter.

Nothing new under the sun.
SOLOMON.

A few years ago, within the compass of my narrative, there appeared often in some of our New England villages, professed fugitives from slavery, who recounted their personal experience in homely phrase, and awakened the indignation of non-slaveholders against brother Pro. Such a one appeared in the new home of Frado; and as people of color were rare there, was it strange she should attract her dark brother; that he should inquire her out; succeed in seeing her; feel a strange sensation in his heart towards her; that he should toy with her shining curls, feel proud to provoke her to smile and expose the ivory concealed by thin, ruby lips; that her sparkling eyes should fascinate; that he should propose; that they should marry? A short acquaintance was indeed an objection, but she saw him often, and thought she knew him. He never spoke of his enslavement to her when alone, but she felt that, like her own oppression, it was painful to disturb oftener than was needful.

He was a fine, straight negro, whose back showed no marks of the lash, erect as if it never crouched beneath a burden. There was a silent sympathy which Frado felt attracted her, and she opened her heart to the presence of love—that arbitrary and inexorable tyrant.

She removed to Singleton, her former residence, and there was married. Here were Frado's first feelings of trust and repose on human arm. She realized, for the first time, the relief of looking to another for comfortable support. Occasionally he would leave her to "lecture."

Those tours were prolonged often to weeks. Of course he had little spare money. Frado was again feeling her self-dependence, and was at last compelled to resort alone to that. Samuel was kind to her when at home, but made no provision for his absence, which was at last unprecedented.

He left her to her fate—embarked at sea, with the disclosure that he had never seen the South, and that his illiterate harangues were humbugs for hungry abolitionists. Once more alone! Yet not alone. A still newer companionship would soon force itself upon her. No one wanted her with such prospects. Herself was burden enough; who would have an additional one?

The horrors of her condition nearly prostrated her, and she was again thrown upon the public for sustenance. Then followed the birth of her child. The long absent Samuel unexpectedly returned, and rescued her from charity. Recovering from her expected illness, she once more commenced toil for herself and child, in a room obtained of a poor woman, but with better fortune. One so well known would not be wholly neglected. Kind friends watched her when Samuel was from home, prevented her from suffering, and when the cold weather pinched the warmly clad, a kind friend took them in, and thus preserved them. At last Samuel's business became very engrossing, and after long desertion, news reached his family that he had become a victim of yellow fever, in New Orleans.

So much toil as was necessary to sustain Frado, was more than she could endure. As soon as her babe could be nourished without his mother, she left him in charge of a Mrs. Capon, and procured an agency, hoping to recruit her health, and gain an easier livelihood for herself and child. This afforded her better maintenance than she had yet found. She passed into the various towns of the State she lived in, then into Massachusetts. Strange were some of her adventures. Watched by kidnappers, maltreated by professed abolitionists, who didn't want slaves at the South, nor niggers in their own houses, North. Faugh! to lodge one; to eat with one; to admit one through the front door; to sit next one; awful!

Traps slyly laid by the vicious to ensnare her, she resolutely avoided. In one of her tours, Providence favored her with a friend who, pitying her cheerless lot, kindly provided her with a valuable recipe, from which she might herself manufacture a useful article for her maintenance. This proved a more agreeable, and an easier way of sustenance.

And thus, to the present time, may you see her busily employed in preparing her merchandise; then sallying forth to encounter many frowns, but some kind friends and purchasers. Nothing turns her from her steadfast purpose of elevating herself. Reposing on God, she has thus far journeyed securely. Still an invalid, she asks your sympathy, gentle reader. Refuse not, because some part of her history is unknown, save by the Omniscient God. Enough has been unrolled to demand your sympathy and aid.

Do you ask the destiny of those connected with her EARLY history? A few years only have elapsed since Mr. and Mrs. B. passed into another world. As age increased, Mrs. B. became more irritable, so that no one, even her own children, could remain with her; and she was accompanied by her husband to the home of Lewis, where, after an agony in death unspeakable, she passed away. Only a few months since, Aunt Abby entered heaven. Jack and his wife rest in heaven, disturbed by no intruders; and Susan and her child are yet with the living. Jane has silver locks in place of auburn tresses, but she has the early love of Henry still, and has never regretted her exchange of lovers. Frado has passed from their memories, as Joseph from the butler's, but she will never cease to track them till beyond mortal vision.

HANNAH CRAFTS/BOND

(1826–after 1859)

New discoveries by Gregg Hecimovich have identified Hannah Bond as the author of *The Bondwoman's Narrative*, a fictionalized account of enslavement and escape found and republished by Henry Louis Gates, Jr., in 2002. Bond was born in 1826 on the plantation of Lewis and Catherine Pugh Bond in Bertie County, North Carolina. Bond, like the light-skinned protagonist of her story, was an enslaved house servant. In her twenties, Bond moved to the household of Esther Bond, Lewis and Catherine's daughter; in 1853, she became a maidservant to Esther's sister, Lucinda Bond Wheeler, wife of Samuel Jordan Wheeler of Murfreesboro, North Carolina. In the summer of 1856, because of various debts, Hannah became the slave of Ellen Sully Wheeler, identified as "Mrs. Wheeler" in *The Bondwoman's Narrative*.

In 1857, Hannah Bond escaped, disguised as a man, from the Wheeler plantation near Murfreesboro and made her way north. She was hidden and protected by a farmer, Horace Craft, in western New York. In return, Bond chose Crafts as her pen name. Settling in New Jersey, in a community of freed and escaped slaves, she finished her novel in 1858. After its completion, she married and became a school teacher. What she did with her manuscript, whether she ever tried to find a publisher for it, and when she died, remain unknown.

Selections from *The Bondwoman's Narrative* (ca. 1858)

SOURCE: *The Bondwoman's Narrative*. Ed. Henry Louis Gates, Jr. (New York: Warner Books 2003).

CHAPTER 1

In Childhood

It may be that I assume to[o] much responsibility in attempting to write these pages. The world will probably say so, and I am aware of my deficiencies. I am neither clever, nor learned, nor talented. When a child they used to scold and find fault with me because they said I was dull and stupid. Perhaps under other circumstances and with more encouragement I might have appeared better; for I was shy and reserved and scarce dared open my lips to any one I had none of that quickness and animation which are so much admired in children, but rather a silent unobtrusive way of observing things and events, and wishing to understand them better than I could.

I was not brought up by any body in particular that I know of. I had no training, no cultivation. The birds of the air, or beasts of the field are not freer from moral culture than I was. No one seemed to care for me till I was able to work, and then it was Hannah do this and Hannah do that, but I never complained as I found a sort of pleasure and something to divert my thoughts in employment. Of my relatives I knew nothing. No one ever spoke of my father or mother, but I soon learned what a curse was attached to my race, soon learned that the African blood in my veins would forever exclude me from the higher walks of life. That toil unremitted unpaid toil must be my lot and portion, without even the hope or expectation of any thing better. This seemed the harder to be borne, because my complexion was almost white, and the obnoxious descent could not be readily traced, though it gave a rotundity to my person, a wave and curl to my hair, and perhaps led me to fancy pictorial illustrations and flaming colors.

The busiest life has its leisure moments; it was so with mine. I had from the first an instinctive desire for knowledge and the means of mental improvement. Though neglected and a slave, I felt the immortal longings in me. In the absence of books and teachers and schools I determined to learn if not in a regular, approved, and scientific way. I was aware that this plan would meet with opposition, perhaps with punishment. My master never permitted his slaves to be taught. Education in his view tended to enlarge and expand their ideas; made them less subservient to their superiors, and besides that its blessings were destined to be conferred exclusively on the higher and nobler race. Indeed though he was generally easy and good-tempered, there was nothing liberal or democratic in his nature. Slaves were slaves to him, and nothing more. Practically he regarded them not as men and women, but in the same light as horses or other domestic animals. He ~~furnished~~ supplied their necessities of food and clothing from ~~the same~~ motives of policy, but [di]scounted the ideas of equality and fraternity as preposterous and absurd. Of course I had nothing to expect from him, yet "where there's a will there's a way."

I was employed about the house, consequently my labors were much easier than those of the field servants, and I enjoyed intervals of repose and rest unknown to them. Then, too, I was a mere child and some hours of each day were allotted to play. On such occasions, and while the other children of the house were amusing themselves I would quietly steal away from their company to ponder over the pages of some old book or newspaper that chance had thrown in [my] way. Though I knew not the meaning of a single letter, and had not the means of finding out I loved to look at them and think that some day I should probably understand them all.

My dream was destined to be realized. One day while I was sitting on a little bank, beneath the shade of some large trees, at a short distance from my playmates, when an aged woman approached me. She was white, and looked venerable with her grey hair smoothly put back beneath a plain sun bonnet, and I recollected having seen her once or twice at my master's house whither she came to sell salves and ointments, and hearing it remarked that she was the wife of a sand-digger and very poor.

She smiled benevolently and inquired why I concealed my book, and with child-like artlessness I told her all. How earnestly I desired knowledge, how our Master interdicted it, and how I was trying to teach myself. She stood for a few moments apparently buried in deep thought, but I interpreted her looks and actions favorably, and an idea struck me that perhaps she could read, and would become my teacher. She seemed to understand my wish before I expressed it.

"Child" she said "I was thinking of our Saviour's words to Peter where he commands the latter to 'feed his lambs.' I will dispense to you such knowledge as I possess. Come to me each day. I will teach you to read in the hope and trust that you will thereby be made better in this world and that to come.["] Her demeanor like her words was very grave and solemn.

"Where do you live?["] I inquired.

"In the little cottage just around the foot of the hill" she replied.

"I will come: Oh how eagerly, how joyfully" I answered "but if master finds it out his anger will be terrible; and then I have no means of paying you."

She smiled quietly, bade me fear nothing, and went her way. I returned home that evening with a light heart. Pleased, delighted, overwhelmed with my good fortune in prospective I felt like a being to whom a new world with all its mysteries and marvels was opening, and could scarcely repress my tears of joy and thankfulness.

CHAPTER 13

A Turn of the Wheel

Mrs Wheeler conceived her beauty to be on the wane. She had been a belle in youth, and the thought of her fading charms was unendurable. That very day an antiquated lady, with a large mouth filled with false teeth, a head covered with false hair, and a thin scrawny neck, beneath which swelled out a false bust, had called on my mistress with what she designated very highly important information. I supposed at first that the

President's wife was dead, or the secretary's daughter about to be married, but it was something more interesting to fashionable ladies than even that. Some great Italian chemist, a Signor with an unpronounceable name had discovered or rather invented an impalpable powder, fine, highly scented, and luxurious, that applied to the hands and face was said to produce the most marvellous effect. The skin, however sallow and unbeautiful, would immediately acquire the softness and delicacy of childhood. Tan, or freckless [freckles], or wrinkles, or other unseemly blotches would simultaneously disappear, and to render the article still more attractive it was said that only two or three boxes of it yet remained. Of course Mrs Wheeler was all impatience to obtain one of them, and her visitor was scarcely out of hearing when I was summoned, and directed to go at once to the Chemist's, and get a box of the Italian Medicated Powder. No hesitancy on account of mud or bad weather was allowable. I went, purchased the last box, and when returning passed two gentlemen, standing in a somewhat sheltered place apparently conversing on some subject of deep interest. There was something in the coat of seedy black, and the general bearing and manner of one of them, which instantly arrested my attention, but the driving mist and sleet was full in my face, with the gloom momentarily thickening, so that I failed to obtain a perfect view of his features. It was certainly very illmannered, but stimulated by curiosity I even turned back to look at them, and not minding my footing through preoccupation of mind I slipped very suddenly and came down with all my weight on the rough paving stones. The two gentlemen immediately came forward, and one of them assisting me to rise, kindly inquired if I was hurt. I looked into the face of the other I knew. ~~I knew him on the instant~~ Oh then I knew him on the instant, I could have remembered his eyes and countenance among a thousand. It was Mr Trapp[e].

Whether or not the recognition was mutual I had no means of ascertaining, but his presence to me seemed ominous of evil, and hastily murmuring my thanks I hastened home.

Mr Wheeler was in the apartment of his wife when I entered it. He was a little dapper man, very quick in his motions, and with little round piercing black eyes set far back in his head. He had the exact air and manner of a Frenchman, but was reputed to be very obstinate in his way, and to have little respect for constituted authorities in his moments of passion. Report said that he had actually quarreled with the President, and challenged a senator to fight a duel, besides laying a cowhide on a certain occasion over the broad shoulders of a member of Congress. At any rate he had been turned out of office, and now was busily engaged in hunting another. Consequently he was seldom at home, being usually to be found haunting the bureau of some department or other, and striving to engage attention by talking in sharp shrill voice, accompanied with violent gesticulation of what should be done in one place, or had been left undone in another. He knows exactly where a screw is loose, and he understands perfectly to tighten it again. On many matters he is better informed than the President. He could give instructions to the secretaries of the army and navy, but they are old, obstinate, and headstrong, and won't listen to his advice.

• • •

On the present occasion Mr Wheeler came to ask a favor of his wife. Another vacancy had occurred, but the gift was in the power of a gentleman, with whom at some time or another of his life Mr Wheeler had some disturbance, and much as he desired the office he dreaded still more the humiliation of asking for it. Could not his wife be induced to make the request? He thought with a little well-timed flattery she might. Ladies of great consideration not unfrequently petitioned for their husbands. The President had been importuned by them till he almost feared the sight of a woman. The Secretaries had fared little better; indeed all who had offices to bestow had been coaxed, and flattered, and addled by female tongues untill they scarcely knew what they were about. They said, too, that female petitioners were likeliest to succeed. Perhaps that was the reason of his frequent failure. Had he brought his wife sooner into the field, in all probability he would have secured a prize with far less trouble. The experiment is worth trying at any rate, though he is not positive that the lady will concur.

• • •

"I regret to say, my dear" continued Mr Wheeler "that I am the object of continued opposition. Men of attainment in a high position of society always have their enemies of course. I have mine. Not so with you. You, I am proud to say it, are universally admired. Then no gentleman would think for a moment of opposing a lady. Certainly not. Now a vacancy has just occurred, and Mrs Piper is intriguing to have it filled by her husband. It is a very important office, worth about two thousand a year."

"Then she expects to get it, does she?—and a failure would mortify her exceedingly. She is so haughty, vain, and conceited. Wouldn't it be pleasant to disappoint her?"

"It would, indeed."

"Who makes the appointment?"

Mr Wheeler gave the desired information.

The lady sate [sat] a few moments in profound silence, then she spoke though rather as talking to herself than any one else. "Mrs Piper, indeed, going to obtain a situation for her husband when mine has none. But I'll disappoint her, that I will. Mr Wheeler you shall have this office. I'll see to it that you do."

Mr Wheeler bowed complacently. Nothing could suit his purpose better.

"I'll go now, this very evening" continued the lady. "The weather is so bad that probably the gentleman will be at home. And then he will be more likely to be disengaged. Hannah you can prepare my toilet."

"Certainly."

"My rich antique moire, and purple velvent [velvet] mantilla. Mr Wheeler be so good as to order the carriage."

Two bows, and a two expressions of "certainly Madam" were the response to this.

Mrs Wheeler did not forget her beautifying powder.

"How lucky" she exclaimed ["]that I sent for it just when I did. Don't be sparing of it Hannah, dear, as I wish to look particularly well."

The powder was very fine, soft, and white, and certainly did add much to the beauty of her appearance. I had never seen her look better. Mr Wheeler complimented her, hoped that she would be careful of herself and not take cold, and actually kissed her hand as he assisted her into the carriage, observing to me as he stepped back on the pavement "She is a dear, good, noble woman."

The next moment I heard my voice called, and turning round beheld Mrs Wheeler leaning from the carriage window and beckoning.

"Hannah, dear" she cried on my approach. "I forgot my smelling-bottle, go and bring it, that new one I obtained purchased yesterday."

"Yes Madam" and back I went to the house, procured the smelling-bottle, Mr Wheeler advanced to meet me, took the little delicate supporter of weak nerves, and handing it to his wife, the carriage drove off.

In two hours a carriage stopped at the door; the bell was rung with a hasty jerk, and the servant admitted a lady, who came directly to Mrs Wheeler's apartment. I was greatly surprised; for though the vail, the bonnet, and the dress were those of that lady, or exactly similar, the face was black.

I stood gazing in mute amazement, when a voice not in the least languid called out "What are you gazing at me in that manner for? Am I to be insulted by my own slaves?"

Mr Wheeler just that moment stepped in. She turned towards him, and the mixture of surprise and curiosity with which he regarded her was most ludicrous.

"Are you all gone mad?" inquired the not now languid voice. "Or what is the matter?"

"You may well ask that question" exclaimed Mr Wheeler, sobbing with suppressed laughter. "Why, Madam, I didn't know you. Your face is black as Tophet.["]

"Black?" said the lady, the expression of astonishment on his countenance transferred to hers.

"Hannah bring the mirror."

I complied.

She gazed a moment, and then her mingled emotions of grief, rage, and shame were truly awful. To all Mr Wheeler's inquiries of "how did it happen, my dear?["] and ["]how came your face to turn black, my dear?" she only answered that she did not know, had no idea, and then she wept and moaned, and finally went into a fit of strong hysterics. Mr Wheeler and myself quickly flew to her assistance. To tell the truth he was now more concerned about his wife than the office now.

"Heaven help me" he said bending over her. "I fear that her beauty has gone forever. What a dreadful thing it is. I never heard of the like."

"It must have been the powder."

"The powder was white I thought."

"The powder certainly is white, and yet it may posses such chemical properties as occasion blackness. Indeed I recently saw in the newspapers some accounts of a chemist who having been jilted by a lady very liberal in the application of powder to her face had invented as a method of revenge a certain kind of smelling bottles, of which the fumes would suddenly blacken the whitest skin provided the said cosmetic had been previously applied."

"You wretch" exclaimed the lady suddenly opening her eyes. "Why didn't you tell me of this before?"

"I—I—didn't think of it, didn't know it was necessary" I stammered in extenuation.

"Oh no: you didn't think of it, you never think of anything that you ought to, and I must be insulted on account of your thoughtlessness, right before Mrs Piper, too. Get out of my sight this instant. I never want to see you again."

"My dear Madam" I said, kneeling at her feet, and attempting to kiss her hand "how should I know that those mentioned in the papers were identical with those you purchased."

Here Mr Wheeler interposed and told her that he did not see how I could be to blame.

"Of course, you don't" she replied mockingly eager to vent her spleen on somebody "of course, you don't. No: no: what husband ever could agree with his wife. Slaves generally are far preferable to wives in husbands' eyes."

Mr Wheeler's face flushed with anger. The allusion was most uncalled for, and ungenerous. However recovering his serenity in a moment he inquired who had insulted her.

"Why everybody" she replied, making another demonstration of hysterics.

"Don't have another fit, pray" said the husband, applying the camphor to her nose. "Hannah bring some water and wash off this hedious stuff."

I procured the water, brought a basin, soap, napkin, and cloth, and went to work. Gradually and by little and little the skin resumed its natural color.

• • •

Finding themselves the subjects of such unwelcome notoreity they concluded to forsake the capital and remove to their estate. The splendid mansion they occupied having been taken only temporarily could be abandoned at any time. Suddenly and without any previous intimation a certain circle was astounded with the intelligence that the Wheeler's [sic] had gone.

SARAH PARKER REMOND

(1826–1894)

Sarah Parker Remond's work stands out stylistically from the other writings in this anthology. Remond was relatively privileged: the ninth child of a wealthy free black family in Salem, Massachusetts, she had access to books and, along with other members of her abolitionist family, lectured across the Northeast and Canada. She had even greater success in London and Ireland, launching an influential tour in 1859 where she lectured and rallied support for abolition, speaking passionately on the plight of women particularly. Described as "ladylike" in the press, Remond spoke from reason rather than experience, citing facts and proofs of slavery's horrors. After the start of the Civil War, she advocated for participation of newly free blacks as soldiers. In 1868, Remond emigrated to Italy, where she lived out the rest of her life. She died in 1894 and is buried in Rome.

Remond's address presented here, "The Negroes in the United States of America," was given in London to the International Congress of Charities, Correction, and Philanthropy in 1862. African Americans, Remond argues, "desire and need the moral support of Great Britain," and the people of Great Britain have an economic incentive to support the end of slavery in America.

"The Negroes in the United States of America" (1862)

SOURCE: Sarah Parker Remond, "The Negroes in the
United States of America," *Journal of Negro History* 27,
no. 2 (April 1942): 216–18.

Amid the din of civil war, and the various and antagonistic interests arising from the internal dissensions now going on in
the United States of North America, the negroes and their descendants, whether enslaved or free, desire and need the moral
support of Great Britain, in this most important but hopeful
hour of their history. They, of all others, have the most at stake;
not only material prosperity, but "life, liberty, and the pursuit
of happiness." Almost simultaneously with the landing of the
Pilgrim Fathers in 1620, a slave-ship, a Dutch vessel, with
twenty negroes stolen from Africa, entered Chesapeake Bay,
and sailed on to Jamestown. Here the twenty negroes were
landed, and chattel slavery established in the New World; a
sad, sad hour for the African race. These twenty human souls
were landed most opportunely. The infant colony was then in a
perilous condition; many of the colonists had died from exposure and hardships; many others from incompetency to grapple
with their fate. Those who survived had become almost disheartened, when the arrival of the negroes gave new vitality to
the enfeebled colony at Virginia, and revived the sinking colonists. The negroes were received as a farmer receives a useful
and profitable animal; although, at that time, their services
were invaluable. In return for their services, they and their posterity have been doomed to a life of slavery. Then took root
chattel slavery, which has produced such physical, mental, and
moral degradation upon an unprotected and unoffending race.
It has always been exceedingly difficult to ascertain the exact
number of slaves in the Southern states; the usual estimate is
about four and a half millions. These human chattels are but
property in the estimation of slave-holders, and receive by public opinion, established custom, and law, only the protection
which is generally given to animals. From the son of a southern

slaveholder, Mr. H. R. Helper of North Carolina, we have the
number of slaves in the Southern states:—

Alabama	342,844	Brought up	1,321,767
Arkansas	47,100	Louisiana	244,809
Delaware	2,290	Maryland	90,368
Florida	39,310	Mississippi	309,878
Georgia	381,622	Missouri	87,422
Kentucky	210,981	N. Carolina	288,548
Tennessee	239,459	S. Carolina	384,984
Texas	58,161	Virginia	472,528
Carried up	1,321,767	Total	3,200,304

Free Colored Population, South 228,138
Free Colored Population, North................ 196,116
424,254

These human chattels, the property of three hundred and
forty-seven thousand slave-owners, constitute the basis of the
working class of the entire south; in fact, they are the bone and
sinew of all that makes the south prosperous, the producers of
a large proportion of the material wealth, and of some of the
most important articles of consumption produced by any working class in the world. The New Orleans *Delta* gives the
following:—"The cotton plantations in the south are about
eighty thousand, and the aggregate value of their annual product, at the present prices of cotton (before the civil war), is fully
one hundred and twenty-five millions of dollars. There are over
fifteen thousand tobacco plantations, and their annual products
may be valued at fourteen millions of dollars. There are two
thousand six hundred sugar plantations, the products of which
average annually more than twelve millions of dollars." Add to
this the domestic labor of the slaves as household servants, &c.,
and you have some conception of the material wealth produced
by the men and women termed chattels. The bulk of this money
goes to the support of the slaveholders and their families; therefore the dependence of slaveholders upon their chattels is complete. Slave labor was first applied to the cultivation of tobacco,
and afterward to that of rice; but rice is produced only in a very
limited locality; cotton is the great staple and source of prosperity and wealth, the nucleus around which gathers immense

interests. Thousands among the commercial, manufacturing, and working classes, on both sides of the Atlantic, are dependent upon cotton for all material prosperity; but the slaves who have produced two-thirds of the cotton do not own themselves; their nominal wives and their children may at any moment be sold. I call them nominal *wives*, because there is no such thing as legal marriage permitted either by custom or law. The free operatives of Britain are, in reality, brought into almost personal relations with slaves during their daily toil. They manufacture the material which the slaves have produced, and although three thousand miles of ocean roll between the producer and the manufacturer and the operatives, they should call to mind the fact, that the cause of all the present internal struggle, now going on between the northern states and the south, the civil war and its attendant evils, have resulted from the attempt to perpetuate negro slavery. In a country like England, where the manufacturer pays in wages alone £11,000,000, and the return from the cotton trade is about £80,000,000 annually—where four millions of the population are almost directly interested—where starvation threatens thousands—it is well that the only remedy which can produce desirable and lasting prosperity should receive the moral support of every class—*emancipation*.

Let no diplomacy of statesmen, no intimidation of slaveholders, no scarcity of cotton, no fear of slave insurrections, prevent the people of Great Britain from maintaining their position as the friend of the oppressed negro, which they deservedly occupied previous to the disastrous civil war. The negro, and the nominally free colored men and women, north and south, of the States, in every hour of their adversity, have ever relied upon the hope that the moral support of Britain would always be with the oppressed. The friends of the negro should recognize the fact, that the process of degradation upon this deeply injured race has been slow and constant, but effective. The real capacities of the negro race have never been thoroughly tested; and until they are placed in a position to be influenced by the civilizing influences which surround freemen, it is really unjust to apply to them the same test, or to expect them to attain the same standard of excellence, as if a fair opportunity had been given to develop their faculties. With all the demoralizing influences by which they are surrounded, they still retain far more of that which is humanizing than their masters. No such acts of cruelty have ever emanated from the victims of slavery in the Southern states as have been again and again practiced by their masters.

LOUISA PICQUET

(ca. 1829–1896)

Like Sojourner Truth and Mary Prince, Louisa Picquet did not write her narrative herself but dictated it to an abolitionist friend. Piquet was born into slavery near Columbia, South Carolina, to Elizabeth Ramsey, a fifteen-year-old mother with one black grandparent, and Ramsey's white master, John Randolph. She and her mother were sold when Randolph's wife saw Louisa's resemblance to her own infant. At the home of their new masters, the Cook family of Georgia, Elizabeth Ramsey had three more children, to Mr. Cook. At the age of thirteen, Picquet was sold away from her mother to John Williams of New Orleans. She subsequently gave birth to four children, all fathered by Williams; two survived to be emancipated, along with Picquet, after Williams died. After saving enough money to leave the south, she lived the majority of her life in Ohio. Picquet was interviewed by Hiram Mattison, a pastor, for the book *Louisa Picquet, the Octoroon: or, Inside Views of Southern Domestic Life.* The narrative is particularly remarkable for its direct discussions of the sexual exploitation female slaves experienced under slavery.

The following selection is a series of questions and answers as Louisa describes being brought to auction, separated from her mother, and sold to Mr. Williams. Picquet's matter-of-fact tone in the interview reminds readers that the abhorrent treatment she received was commonplace at the time.

"The Family Sold at Auction—Louisa Bought by a 'New Orleans Gentleman,' and What Came of It," from *The Octoroon* (1861)

SOURCE: Hiram Mattison, *Louisa Piquet, the Octoroon: or, Inside Views of Southern Domestic Life* (New York: Published by the Author, 1861).

Q.—"How did you say you come to be sold?"

A.—"Well, you see, Mr. Cook made great parties, and go off to watering-places, and get in debt, and had to break up [fail], and then he took us to Mobile, and hired the most of us out, so the men he owe should not find us, and sell us for the debt. Then, after a while, the sheriff came from Georgia after Mr. Cook's debts, and found us all, and took us to auction, and sold us. My mother and brother was sold to Texas, and I was sold to New Orleans."

Q.—"How old were you, then?"

A.—"Well, I don't know exactly, but the auctioneer said I wasn't quite fourteen. I didn't know myself."

Q.—"How old was your brother?"

A.—"I suppose he was about two months old. He was little bit of baby."

Q.—"Where were you sold?"

A.—"In the city of Mobile."

Q.—"In a yard? In the city?"

A.—"No. They put all the men in one room, and all the women in another; and then whoever want to buy come and examine, and ask you whole lot of questions. They began to take the clothes off of me, and a gentleman said they needn't do that, and told them to take me out. He said he knew I was a virtuous girl, and he'd buy me, anyhow. He didn't strip me only just under my shoulders."

Q.—"Were there any others there white like you?"

A.—"Oh yes, plenty of them. There was only Lucy of our lot, but others!"

Q.—"Were others stripped and examined?"

A.—"Well, not quite naked, but just same."

Q.—"You say the gentleman told them to 'take you out.' What did he mean by that?"

A.—"Why, take me out of the room where the women and girls were kept; where they examine them—out where the auctioneer sold us."

Q.—"Where was that? In the street, or in a yard?"

A.—"At the market, where the block is?"

Q.—"What block?"

A.—"My! don't you know? The stand, where we have to get up?"

Q.—"Did *you* get up on the stand?"

A.—"Why, of course; we all have to get up to be seen."

Q.—"What else do you remember about it?"

A.—"Well, they first begin at upward of six hundred for me, and then some bid fifty more, and some twenty-five more, and that way."

Q.—"Do you remember any thing the auctioneer said about you when he sold you?"

A.—"Well, he said he could not recommend me for any thing else only that I was a good-lookin' girl, and a good nurse, and kind and affectionate to children; but I was never used to any hard work. He told them they could see that. My hair was quite short, and the auctioneer spoke about it, but said, 'You see it good quality, and give it a little time, it will grew out again.' You see Mr. Cook had my hair cut off. My hair grew fast, and look so much better than Mr. Cook's daughter, and he fancy I had better hair than his daughter, and so he had it cut off to make a difference."

Q.—"Well, how did they sell you and your mother? that is, which was sold first?"

A.—"Mother was put up the first of our folks. She was sold for splendid cook, and Mr. Horton, from Texas, bought her and the baby, my brother. Then Henry, the carriage-driver, was put up, and Mr. Horton bought him, and then two field-hands, Jim and Mary. The women there tend mills and drive ox wagons, and plow, just like men. Then I was sold next. Mr. Horton run me up to fourteen hundred dollars. He wanted I should go with my mother. Then some one said 'fifty.' Then Mr. Williams allowed that he did not care what they bid, he was going to have me anyhow. Then he bid fifteen hundred. Mr. Horton said 'twas no use to bid any more, and I was sold to Mr. Williams. I went right to New Orleans then."

Q.—"Who was Mr. Williams?"

A.—"I didn't know then, only he lived in New Orleans. Him and his wife had parted, some way—he had three children boys. When I was going away I heard some one cryin', and prayin' the Lord to go with her only daughter, and protect me. I felt pretty bad then, but hadn't no time only to say good-bye. I wanted to go back and get the dress I bought with the half-dollars, I thought a good deal of that; but Mr. Williams would not let me go back and get it. He said he'd get me plenty of nice dresses. Then I thought mother could cut it up and make dresses for my brother, the baby. I knew she could not wear it; and I had a thought, too, that she'd have it to remember me."

Q.—"It seems like a dream, don't it?"

A.—"No; it seems fresh in my memory when I think of it—no longer than yesterday. Mother was right on her knees, with her hands up, prayin' to the Lord for me. She didn't care who saw her: the people all lookin' at her. I often thought her prayers followed me, for I never could forget her. Whenever I wanted any thing real bad after that, my mother was always sure to appear to me in a dream that night, and have plenty to give me, always."

Q.—"Have you never seen her since?"

A.—"No, never since that time. I went to New Orleans, and she went to Texas. So I understood."

Q.—"Well, how was it with you after Mr. Williams bought you?"

A.—"Well, he took me right away to New Orleans."

Q.—"How did you go?"

A.—"In a boat, down the river. Mr. Williams told me what he bought me for, soon as we started for New Orleans. He said he was getting old, and when he saw me he thought he'd buy me, and end his days with me. He said if I behave myself he'd treat me well: but, if not, he'd whip me almost to death."

Q.—"How old was he?"

A.—"He was over forty; I guess pretty near fifty. He was gray headed. That's the reason he was always so jealous. He never let me go out anywhere."

Q.—"Did you never go to church?"

A.—"No, sir; I never darken a church door from the time he bought me till after he died. I used to ask him to let me go to church. He would accuse me of some object, and said there was more rascality done there than anywhere else. He'd sometimes say, 'Go on, I guess you've made your arrangements; go on, I'll catch up with you.' But I never dare go once."

Q.—"Had you any children while in New Orleans?"

A.—"Yes; I had four."

Q.—"Who was their father?"

A.—"Mr. Williams."

Q.—"Was it known that he was living with you?"

A.—"Every body knew I was housekeeper, but he never let on that he was the father of my children. I did all the work in his house—nobody there but me and the children."

Q.—"What children?"

A.—"My children and his. You see he had three sons."

Q.—"How old were his children when you went there?"

A.—"I guess the youngest was nine years old. When he had company, gentlemen folks, he took them to the hotel. He never have no gentlemen company home. Sometimes he would come and knock, if he stay out later than usual time; and if I did not let him in in a minute, when I would be asleep, he'd come in and take the light, and look under the bed, and in the wardrobe, and all over, and then ask me why I did not let him in sooner. I did not know what it meant till I learnt his ways."

Q.—"Were your children mulattoes?"

A.—"No, sir! They were all white. They look just like him. The neighbors all see that. After a while he got so disagreeable that I told him, one day, I wished he would sell me, or 'put me in his pocket'—that's the way we say—because I had no peace at all. I rather die than live in that way. Then he got awful mad, and said nothin' but death should separate us; and, if I run off, he'd blow my brains out. Then I thought, if that be the way, all I could do was just to pray for him to die."

Q.—"Where did you learn to pray?"

A.—"I first begin to pray when I was in Georgia, about whippin'—that the Lord would make them forget it, and not whip me: and it seems if when I pray I did not get so hard whippin'."

FUGITIVES AND EMIGRANTS: MOVING WEST AND NORTH

14

MRS. JOHN LITTLE

(no date)

What we know about Mrs. John Little is gleaned from the following account, written in 1855 by Benjamin Drew (a journalist and abolitionist from Boston) during his travels through Canada to interview escaped slaves. Mrs. John Little's story is unique among fugitive slave narratives in that she and her husband escaped slavery together. Of the interactions that the Littles have with whites during their journey north, their near-capture by the Smith family is particularly interesting due to the calculated nature of the Smiths' betrayal. Once the Littles cross the border to Canada, their experience within society is remarkably different than it was in America. In Canada, Little states, "The best of the merchants and clerks pay me as much attention as though I were a white woman: I am as politely accosted as any woman would wish to be."

This text gives readers a sense of how Canadian attitudes toward fugitive slaves differed from American attitudes. It also illustrates the scope of the networks within America used to track and capture slaves escaped from bondage.

"Mrs. John Little," from *The Refugee: Narratives of Fugitive Slaves in Canada* (1856)

SOURCE: Benjamin Drew, *The Refugee: Narratives of Fugitive Slaves in Canada* (Boston: John P. Jewett and Company, 1856).

I was born in Petersburg, Va. When very young, I was taken to Montgomery county. My old master died there, and I remember that all the people were sold. My father and mother were sold together about one mile from me. After a year, they were sold a great distance, and I saw them no more. My mother came to me before she went away, and said, "Good by, be a good girl; I never expect to see you any more."

Then I belonged to Mr. T—N—, the son of my old master. He was pretty good, but his wife, my mistress, beat me like sixty. Here are three scars on my right hand and arm, and one on my forehead, all from wounds inflicted with a broken china plate. My cousin, a man, broke the plate in two pieces, and she said, "Let me see that plate." I handed up the pieces to her, and she threw them down on me: they cut four gashes, and I bled like a butcher. One piece cut into the sinew of the thumb, and made a great knot permanently. The wound had to be sewed up. This long scar over my right eye, was from a blow with a stick of wood. One day she knocked me lifeless with a pair of tongs,— when I came to, she was holding me up, through fright. Some of the neighbors said to her, "Why don't you learn Eliza to sew?" She answered, "I only want to learn her to do my housework, that's all." I can tell figures when I see them, but cannot read or write.

I belonged to them until I got married at the age of sixteen, to Mr. John Little, of Jackson. My master sold me for debt,— he was a man that would drink, and he had to sell me. I was sold to F—T—, a planter and slave-trader, who soon after, at my persuasion, bought Mr. Little.

I was employed in hoeing cotton, a new employment: my hands were badly blistered. "Oh, you must be a great lady," said the overseer, "can't handle the hoe without blistering your hands!" I told him I could not help it. My hands got hard, but I could not stand the sun. The hot sun made me so sick I could not work, and, John says if I had not come away, they would surely have sold me again. There was one weakly woman named Susan, who could not stand the work, and she was sold to Mississippi, away from her husband and son. That's one way of taking care of the sick and weak. That's the way the planters do with a weakly, sickly "nigger,"—they say "he's a dead expense to 'em," and put him off as soon as they can. After Susan was carried off, her husband went to see her: when he came back he received two hundred blows with the paddle.

I staid with T— more than a year. A little before I came away, I heard that master was going to give my husband three hundred blows with the paddle. He came home one night with an axe on his shoulder, tired with chopping timber. I had his clothes all packed up, for I knew he would have to go. He came hungry, calculating on his supper,—I told him what was going. I never heard him curse before—he cursed then. Said he, "If any man, white or black, lays his hand on me to-night, I'll put this axe clear through him—clear through him:" and he would have done it, and I would not have tried to hinder him. But there was a visitor at the house, and no one came: he ran away. Next morning, the overseer came for him. The master asked where he was; I could have told him, but would not. My husband came back no more.

When we had made arrangements for leaving, a slave told of us. Not long after, master called to me, "Come here, my girl, come here." I went to him: he tied me by the wrist with a rope. He said, "Oh, my girl, I don't blame you,—you are young, and don't know; it's that d—d infernal son of a—; if I had him here, I'd blow a ball through him this minute." But he was deceived about it: I had put John up to hurrying off.

Then master stood at the great house door, at a loss what to do. There he had Willis, who was to have run away with us, and the man who betrayed us. At last he took us all off about half a mile to a swamp, where old A— need not hear us as he was going to meeting, it being Sunday. He whipped Willis to make him tell where we were going. Willis said, "Ohio State." "What do you want to be free for? G—d— you, what do you know about freedom? Who was going with you?" "Only Jack." G—d— Jack to h—, and you too." While they were whipping Willis, he said, "Oh, master, I'll never run away." "I didn't ask you about that, you d—d son of a—, you." Then they tried to make him tell about a slave girl who had put her child aside: but he knew nothing about that. As soon as they had done whipping him, they put a plow clavis about his ankle to which they attached a chain which was secured about his neck with a horse-lock.

Then they took a rheumatic boy, who had stopped with us, whom I had charged not to tell. They whipped him with the paddle, but he said he was ignorant of it: he bore the whipping, and never betrayed us. Then they questioned him about the girl and the child, as if that boy could know any thing about it! Then came my turn; they whipped me in the same way they did the men. Oh, those slaveholders are a brutish set of people,—the master made a remark to the overseer about my shape. Before striking me, master questioned me about the girl. I denied all knowledge of the affair. I only knew that she had been with child, and that now she was not, but I did not tell them even that. I was ashamed of my situation, they remarking upon me. I had been brought up in the house, and was not used to such coarseness. Then he (master) asked, "Where is Jack?" "I don't know." Said he, "Give her h—, R—." That was his common word. Then they struck me several blows with the paddle. I kept on telling them it was of no use to whip me, as I knew nothing to tell them. No irons were ready for me, and I was put under a guard,—but I was too cunning for him, and joined my husband.

My shoes gave out before many days,—then I wore my husband's old shoes till they were used up. Then we came on barefooted all the way to Chicago. My feet were blistered and sore and my ankles swollen; but I had to keep on. There was something behind me driving me on. At the first water we came to I was frightened, as I was not used to the water. It was a swift but shallow stream: my husband crossed over, and I was obliged to follow. At the Ohio Bottoms was a great difficulty,—the water was in some places very deep,—it was black, dirty water. I was scared all but to death: but I had become somewhat used to hardship. If I had seen a white face, I would have run into the river.

By and by, we succeeded in crossing the last one. Then we struck a light at a shingle-getter's shanty, made a fire with the clapboards and dried ourselves. We were merry over our success in getting so far along, and had a good laugh as we burned the boards and part of the shanty itself. I felt afraid at getting into a boat to cross the Ohio River: I had never been in any boat whatever. Now to get on this in the night, frightened me. "John," said I, "don't you think we'll drown?" "I don't care if we do," said he. We reached Cairo well enough.

We never slept at the same time; while one slept, the other kept watch, day or night. Both of us never slept at one time,—if we had, we would not have reached Canada. One morning, as I was watching by a fire we had made, John sleeping, I saw a dog, and told John. Said he, "'t is some old white man hunting a hog,—however, we had better go from this fire." We went down into a valley and there remained. In the afternoon, an hour before sunset, a white man came suddenly upon us, while we were getting ready for a night's march. I started to run: John stood. The man said, "Stop, there!" But I kept on; his face was so white, that I wanted nothing to do with him. John said, "What did you say?" "Stop, there." John said, "I'll do no such thing." Then hard language passed between them. The man said, "I'll have a pack of hounds after you before night." John answered him with an oath to frighten him, "You had better do it, and be off yourself, or I'll blow a ball through you." The man never had heard a negro swear at him before. They are generally so cowed down, that John's swearing at him, alarmed him more than a bullet from a white man. It showed that he was desperate,—and that was the only reason why he used such language. The man struck spurs to his horse, and went off in a hurry. We followed him, as he went the same way we were going, and kept as close to him as we could: for, if the man got hounds he would start them at the place where he had seen us; and coming back over the same route with hounds, horses, and men, would kill our track, and they could not take us. But we saw no more of the man.

Soon after dark, we came to a lake. We found an old white man there in a shanty, who was caring for a slave that had been shot by his master a few days before. We went in and saw him,—he was an old, gray-headed man. His master had threatened him with a flogging, and he took to the river: just as he reached the water, his master shot him behind. But he got across. He was wounded, and without hat or shoes. In this place we were informed about our route. It was in Kentucky.

While we were stopping at the shanty, a day or two, John went out one evening with the old man, to hunt for provisions. I went to bed. By and by the dogs barked; the door opened, and by the fire I saw five white men. One said, "Who you got here?" "Only my own family." I was afraid, and crept out slyly on my hands and knees, and hid behind an ash-barrel until they were gone.

In a few days we crossed the ferry. Then we went on, and were without provisions, except some corn, which we parched. We met here a runaway slave, who knew the route of the country above us. He was returning to his master, where he had a wife and children.

At Cairo, the gallinippers were so bad, we made a smoke to keep them off. Soon after I heard a bell ring. Said I, "John, somebody's dead." It was a steamboat bell tolling. Presently there she was, a great boat full of white men. We were right on the river's bank, and our fire sent the smoke straight up into the calm. We lay flat on the ground. John read the name—Maria. No one noticed us: after the boat was gone, we had a hearty laugh at our good luck. Thinking there was no more trouble, we did not put out our fire. Presently came a yawl boat: they saw our fire, and hailed, "Boat ashore! boat ashore! runaway niggers! runaway niggers!" We lay close, and the boat kept on. We put out our fire, and went further back from the river, but the musquitoes were so bad, we made another fire. But a man with a gun then came along, looking up into the trees. I scattered the fire to put it out, but it smoked so much the worse. We at last hid in a thicket of briers, where we were almost devoured by musquitoes, for want of a little smoke.

Next day I lay down to sleep, while John kept watch. When I awoke, I told him I had dreamed about a white cow, which still seemed a white woman, and that I feared we would be caught. We were in the woods, in a low, damp place, where there was no bit of a road, and we knew not where the road was. We started to find a road, and then met with a white woman. I reminded John of my dream. "Good evening, good evening," said she. My husband asked if she would sell him some bread: this was to make conversation, so he could inquire the road. "Oh yes, just come to my house, I'll give you some bread." We went to the house, and presently her husband came in. He asked, "Have you got free papers?" John answered, "No." "Where are you travelling to?" "To the upper lakes." "We are not allowed to let a colored man go through here without free papers: if we do, we are liable to a fine of forty dollars." He allowed us to remain all

night,—but in the morning we were to go before a squire at Dorrety, and, if we were free, we would go on. This was the woman's arrangement: the man did not seem inclined to stop us. She
said, "If we stop you, we shall get fifty dollars apiece for you:
that's a—good—deal—of—money,—you know." The man
asked John if he had a pistol. John produced one. The man said
't was no harm, he would take care of it for him,—and locked it
up. They lived in a little, dirty log hut: they took the bed off the
bedstead, and lay down on it close to the door, so that it could
not be opened without disturbing him. The man took a nice
silver-mounted pistol from a cupboard, loaded it, and placed it
where he could reach it in the night. We lay on the bedstead—
they on the floor. She was the evil one: she had made the plans.
Their name was Smith.

At about three o'clock in the morning, husband aroused
me,—"I'm going away from here; I do n't value them, now
other folks are asleep." We both got up. John spoke roughly,
"Mr. Smith! Mr. Smith!" He aroused: "we are unwell, and
must pass out,—we'll be back very soon." Mr. Smith got up
very readily, and pulled the bed away a little, so we could slip
out. As John passed by the pistol, he put his hand on it, and
took it in exchange for his old one. It is a beautiful rifle pistol,
percussion lock,—John has been offered fifteen dollars for it. If
the man will come here with John's old flint lock, my husband
will exchange back, and give him boot. I am very sorry for my
friend, Mrs. Smith, that she did not get the hundred dollars to
go a shopping with in Dorrety—am much obliged to her for
our night's lodging. We went across a small stream, and waited
for daylight. Then we went on to Dorrety, and passed through
the edge of it, without calling on the squire, as we had not time.

One Sunday morning, being on a prairie where we could see
no house—about fifty miles west of Springfield—we ventured
to travel by day. We encountered an animal, which we at first
supposed to be a dog; but when he came near, we concluded it
to be a wolf. He yelped something like a dog: he did not attack
us. We went on and crossed a stream, and then we saw three
large wood-wolves, sneaking around as if waiting for darkness.
As we kept on, the three wolves kept in sight, now on one hand,
and now on the other. I felt afraid, expecting they would attack

us: but they left us. Afterward we made a fire with elder-stalks, and I undertook to make some corn bread. I got it mixed, and put it on the fire,—when I saw a party of men and boys on horseback, apparently approaching us. I put out the fire; they turned a little away, and did not appear to perceive us: I rekindled the fire, and baked our bread. John managed to keep us well supplied with pies and bread. We used to laugh to think how people would puzzle over who drank the milk and left the pitchers, and who hooked the dough.

I got to be quite hardy—quite used to water and bush-whacking; so that by the time I got to Canada, I could handle an axe, or hoe, or any thing. I felt proud to be able to do it—to help get cleared up, so that we could have a home, and plenty to live on. I now enjoy my life very well—I have nothing to complain of. We have horses and a pleasure-wagon, and I can ride out when and where I please, without a pass. The best of the merchants and clerks pay me as much attention as though I were a white woman: I am as politely accosted as any woman would wish to be.

I have lost two children by death; one little girl is all that is spared to me. She is but four years old. I intend to have her well educated, if the Lord lets us.

15

MARY ANN SHADD CARY

(1823–1893)

As the editor of the *Provincial Freeman*, Shadd Cary was the first woman at the helm of a North American newspaper. She traveled around Canada on foot, teaching, writing, and raising funds for her proposed newspaper. Her frequent encouragement of freedmen's emigration to Canada made her a controversial figure and resulted in her exclusion from the 1855 Philadelphia Colored Convention. During the Civil War she served as a Union recruiter for African American soldiers; after the war she earned a law degree and advocated on behalf of women and African Americans.

In 1861, Mary Ann Shadd Cary worked closely with Osborne P. Anderson, the only free black born in the North to participate in John Brown's raid on Harper's Ferry, in writing *A Voice from Harper's Ferry: A Narrative of Events at Harper's Ferry; with Incidents Prior and Subsequent to its Capture by Captain Brown and His Men*. Scholars disagree on the extent of Shadd Cary's assistance, but it is clear that she had an important influence on the narrative.

The selection here is a political document written by Shadd Cary that lays out some of the rules governing her Canadian settlement. Shadd Cary saw in Canada an opportunity to live free of oppression in her lifetime, an opportunity that did not exist anywhere in the United States. Similar arguments include Sojourner Truth's petition to the U.S. Government to allow impoverished blacks to settle the American West, the movement for free blacks to settle Liberia, and Maria Stewart's urging her listeners to stay put and build societies in the cities they already inhabited.

Selections from *A Plea for Emigration, or, Notes of Canada West* (1852)

SOURCE: Mary A. Shadd, *A Plea for Emigration, or, Notes of Canada West* (Detroit, MI: George W. Pattison, 1852).

Settlements,—Dawn,—Elgin,— Institution,—Fugitive Home.

Much has been said of the Canada colored settlements, and fears have been expressed by many, that by encouraging exclusive settlements, the attempt to identify colored men with degraded men of like color in the States would result, and as a consequence, estrangement, suspicion, and distrust would be induced. Such would inevitably be the result, and will be, shall they determine to have entirely proscriptive settlements. Those in existence, so far as I have been able to get at facts, do not exclude whites from their vicinity; but that settlements may not be established of that character, is not so certain. Dawn, on the Sydenham river, Elgin, or King's Settlement, as it is called, situated about ten miles from Chatham, are settlements in which there are regulations in regard to morals, the purchase of lands, etc., bearing only on the colored people; but whites are not excluded because of dislike. When purchase was made of the lands, many white families were residents,—at least, locations were not selected in which none resided. At first, a few sold out, fearing that such neighbors might not be agreeable; others, and they the majority, concluded to remain, and the result attests their superior judgment. Instead of an increase of vice, prejudice, improvidence, laziness, or a lack of energy, that many feared would characterize them, the infrequency of violations of law among so many, is unprecedented; due attention to moral and intellectual culture has been given; the former prejudices on the part of the whites, has given place to a perfect reciprocity of religious and social intercommunication. Schools are patronized equally; the gospel is common, and hospitality is shared alike by all. The school for the settlers, at Elgin, is so far superior to the one established for white children, that the latter was discontinued, and, as before said, all send together, and visit in common the Presbyterian church, there established. So of Dawn; that settlement is exceedingly flourishing, and the moral influence it exerts is good, though, owing to some recent arrangements, regulations designed to further promote its importance are being made. Land has increased in value in those settlements. Property that was worth but little, from the superior culture given by colored persons over the method before practiced, and the increasing desires for country homes, is held much higher. Another fact that is worth a passing notice, is, that a spirit of competition is active in their vicinity. Efforts are now put forth to produce more to the acre, and to have the land and tenements present a tidy appearance. That others than those designed to be benefitted by the organization, should be, is not reasonable, else might persons, not members of a society justly claim equal benefits with members. If Irishmen should subscribe to certain regulations on purchasing land, no neighboring landholders could rightfully share with them in the result of that organization. But prejudice would not be the cause of exclusion. So it is of those two settlements; it cannot be said of them, that they are caste institutions, so long as they do not express hostility to the whites; but the question of their necessity in the premises may be raised, and often is, by the settlers in Canada as well as in the States. The "Institution" is a settlement under the direction of the A. M. E. Church; it contains, at present, two hundred acres, and is sold out in ten acre farms, at one dollar and fifty cents per acre, or one shilling less than cost. They have recently opened a school, and there is a log meeting house in an unfinished state, also a burying ground. There are about fifteen families settled on the land, most of whom have cleared away a few trees, but it is not in a very prosperous condition, owing, it is said, to bad management of agents—a result to be looked for when a want of knowledge characterize them. This "Institution" bids fair to be one nucleus around which caste settlements will cluster in Canada.

The Refugees' Home is the last of the settlements of which I may speak in this place. How many others are in contemplation I do not know, though I heard of at least two others. This Society is designed to appropriate fifty thousand acres of land for fugitives from slavery, *only*, but at present the agents have in possession two hundred acres, situated about eight miles from Windsor, in the western district. The plan is to sell farms of twenty-five acres, that is, to give five acres to actual settlers, with the privilege of buying the adjoining twenty acres, at the market value—one-third of the purchase money constitutes a fund for school and other purposes; and ten years are given to pay for the twenty acres, but no interest may accumulate. This society may now be considered in operation, as they have made a purchase, though, as yet, no one has settled thereon, and the results to be looked for from it, from the extent of the field of operations, will have an important bearing on the colored people who are now settled in Canada, or who may emigrate thither. The friends of the society, actuated by benevolent feeling towards victims of American oppression and the odious Fugitive Law, are sanguine as to the success of the measure, but not so universal is the opinion in its favor, even among those designed to be benefitted; in fact, all the objections raised against previously existing settlements, hold good against these, with the additional ones of greater magnitude. It is well known that the Fugitive Bill makes insecure every northern colored man,—those *free* are alike at the risk of being sent south,—consequently, many persons, always free, will leave the United States, and settle in Canada, and other countries, who would have remained had not that law been enacted. In proslavery communities, or where colonization influence prevails, they would leave at a sacrifice; they arrive in Canada destitute, in consequence, but may not settle on the land of the Refugees' Home, from the accident of nominal freedom, when it is well known that even slaves south, from the disgrace attending manual labor when performed by whites, have opportunities, in a pecuniary way, that colored men have not in some sections north. Again, the policy of slaveholders has been to create a contempt for *free* people in the bosom of their slaves, and pretty effectually have they succeeded. Their journey to Canada for liberty has not rooted out that prejudice, quite, and reference to a man's birth, as free or slave, is generally made by colored persons, should he not be as prosperous as his better helped fugitive brethren. Thus, discord among members of the same family, is engendered; a breach made, that the exclusive use by fugitives of the society lands is not likely to mend. Again, the society, with its funds, is looked upon in the light of a powerful rival, standing in the way of poor *free* men, with its ready cash, for its lands will not all be government purchases; neither does it contemplate large blocks, exclusively, but as in the first purchase, land, wherever found, and in small parcels also. From the exclusive nature of the many settlements, (as fugitive homes,) when it shall be known for what use it is wanted, individual holders will not sell but for more than the real value, thus embarrassing poor men who would have bought on time, and as an able purchaser from government, the society must a first choice. The objections in common with other settlements, are: the individual supervision of resident agents, and the premium indirectly offered for good behavior. "We are free men," say they who advocate independent effort, "we, as other subjects, are amenable to British laws; we wish to observe and appropriate to ourselves, *ourselves*, whatever of good there is in the society around us, and by our individual efforts, to attain to a respectable position, as do the many foreigners who land on the Canada shores, as poor in purse as we were; and we do not want agents to beg for us." The accompanying are the articles in the Constitution:

Article 2. The object of this society shall be to obtain permanent homes for the refugees in Canada, and to promote their moral, social, physical, intellectual, and political elevation.

Article 11. This society shall not deed lands to any but actual settlers, who refugees from southern slavery, and who are the owners of no land.

Article 12. All lands purchased by this society, shall be divided into twenty-five acre lots, or as near as possible, and at least one-tenth of the purchase price of which shall be paid down by actual settlers before possession is given, and the balance to be paid in equal annual instalments.

Article 13. One-third of all money paid in for land by settlers, shall be used for educational purchases, for the benefit of said settlers' children, and the two-thirds for the purchase of more lands for the same object, while chattel slavery exists in the United States.

BY-LAWS.

No person shall receive more than five acres of land from this society, at less than cost.

Article 4. No person shall be allowed to remove any timber from said land until they have first made payment thereon.

These are the articles of most importance, and, as will be seen, they contemplate more than fifty thousand acres continual purchases, till slavery shall cease; and other terms, as will be seen by Art. 13 of Con., and Art. 4, By-Laws, than most fugitives just from slavery can comply with, (as destitute women with families, old men, and single women,) until after partial familiarity with their adopted country. This, say many colored Canadians, begins not to benefit until a man has proven his ability to act without aid, and is fit for political equality by his own industry, that money will get for him at any time.

Political Rights—Election Law—Oath—Currency.

There is no legal discrimination whatever effecting colored emigrants in Canada, nor from any cause whatever are their privileges sought to be abridged. On taking proper measures, the most ample redress can be obtained. The following "abstracts of acts," bearing equally on all, and observed fully by colored men qualified, will give an idea of the measures given them:

"The qualifications of voters at municipal elections in townships, are freeholders and householders of the township or ward, entered on the roll for rateable real property, in their own right or that of their wives, as proprietors or tenants, and resident at the time in the township or ward."

"In towns, freeholders and householders for rateable real property in their own names or that of their wives, as proprietors or tenants to the amount of £5 per annum or upward, resident at the time in the ward. The property qualification of town voters may consist partly of freehold and partly of leasehold."

In villages it is £3 and upward, with freehold or leasehold; in cities £8.

The laws regulating elections, and relating to electors, are not similar in the two Canadas; but colored persons are not affected by them more than others.

"No person shall be entitled to vote at county elections, who has not vested in him, by legal title, real property in said county of the clear yearly value of forty-four shillings and five pence and one farthing, currency. Title to be in fee simple or freehold under tenure of free and common soccage, or in *fief* in *rature*, or in *franc allen*, or derived from the Governor and Council of the late Province of Quebec, or Act of Parliament. Qualificatiori, to be effective, requires actual and uninterrupted possession on the part of the elector, or that he should have been in receipt of the rents and profits of said property for his own use and benefit at least six months before the date of the writ of election. But the title will be good without such anterior possession, if the property shall have come by inheritance, devise, marriage or contract of marriage, and also if the deed or patent from the Crown on which he holds to claim such estate in Upper Canada, have been registered three calendar months before the date of the writ of election. In Lower Canada, possession of the property under a written promise of sale registered, if not a notarial deed, for twelve months before the election, to be sufficient title to vote. In Upper Canada, a conveyance to wife after marriage must have been registered three calendar months, or husband have been in possession of property six months before election."

"Only British subjects of the full age of twenty-one are allowed to vote. Electors may remove objection by producing certificate, or by taking the oath."

These contain no proscriptive provisions, and there are none. Colored men comply with these provisions and vote in the administration of affairs. There is no difference made whatever; and even in the slight matter of taking the census it is impossible to get at the exact number of whites or colored, as they are not designated as such. There is, it is true, petty jealousy manifested at times by individuals, which is made use of by the designing; but impartiality and strict justice characterize proceedings at law, and the bearing of the laws. The oath, as prescribed by law, is as follows:

"I, A. B., do sincerely promise and swear, that I will bear faithful and true allegiance to Her Majesty Queen Victoria, as lawful Sovereign of the United Kingdom of Great Britain and Ireland, and of this Province of Canada, dependent on and belonging to the said United Kingdom, and that I will defend her to the uttermost of my power against all traitors, conspiracies and attempts whatever which shall be made against Her Person, Crown and Dignity, and that I will do my utmost endeavor to disclose and make known to Her Majesty, Her Heirs and Successors all treasons and traitorous conspiracies and attempts which I shall know to be against Her or any of them, and all this I do swear without any equivocation, mental evasion, or secret reservation, and, renouncing all pardons and dispensations from persons whatever, to the contrary. So help me God."

"The Deputy Returning Officer may administer oath of allegiance to persons who, according to provisions of any Act of Parliament, shall become, on taking such oath, entitled to the privileges of British birth in the Province."

"Persons knowing themselves not to be qualified, voting at elections, incur penalty of £10; and on action brought, the burden of proof shall be on the defendant. Such votes null and void."

"The qualification of Municipal Councilors are as follows:— Township Councilor must be a freeholder or householder of the township or ward, * * * as proprietor or tenant rated on the roll, in case of a freeholder for £100 or upward; householder for £200 or upward: Village Councilor, in case of a freeholder, for £10 or upward; a householder for £20 and upward: Town Councilor, in case of a freeholder £20 per annum; if a householder to the amount of £40 and upward. The property qualification of Town Councilors may be partly freehold and partly leasehold."

A tenant voter in town or city must have occupied by actual residence, as a separate tenant, a dwelling house or houses for twelve months, of the yearly value of £11 2s. 1½d. currency, and have paid a year's rent, or that amount of money for the twelve months immediately preceding the date of election writ. A person holding only a shop or place of business, but not actually residing therein, is not entitled to vote. And a voter having changed his residence within the town during the year, does not affect his right to vote, but must vote in the ward in which he resides on the day.

16

JENNIE CARTER (SEMPER FIDELIS)

(ca. 1830–1881)

Born around 1830, probably in New Orleans, Jennie Carter was among the most incisive and active social commentators of her generation. Little is known about her early life, but through her journalism, often under pen names including Semper Fidelis and Ann J. Trask, readers glimpsed a mind attuned to life as an African American woman in the West. She moved frequently and participated in political activity; she married a prominent Californian, Dennis Carter. In print, she covered topics from women's suffrage to the education of African American children to long-term strategies for racial uplift.

The two letters published in the *Elevator*, both entitled "Letter from Nevada County," September 11 and September 25, 1868 [taken from Eric Gardner, ed., *Jennie Carter: A Black Journalist of the Early West* (Jackson: University Press of Mississippi, 2009)], display Carter's sharp, unsparing critique delivered in her compelling, sensitive prose style. Here she objects forcefully to white Reconstruction-era politicians' nostalgia for the "good old days of slavery" by offering the story of one woman's monstrous treatment while enslaved.

"Letter from Nevada County: Mud Hill, September 2, 1868" (1868)

SOURCE: Jennie Carter, "Letter from Nevada County: Mud Hill, September 2, 1868," *Elevator*, September 11, 1868.

Mr. Editor:—Politicians may rant (at least some of them—the sweet sons of modern Democracy), and talk loud and strong of the good old days of slavery, when the "nigger" was in his right place, cared for by kind masters (and in those days all were kind), and regret, as I heard one of them the other day, the suffering of the colored people South since the war. I was in no mood to answer him, knowing that he, in common with other Democrats, had no use for the negro aside from servitude, and all his sympathy was the merest sham. In the company prese[n]t was a colored woman fifty years old, and she asked for the privilege of telling a story, which was readily granted.

She said she was born in the State of Alabama,—was born free, her mother being a free woman and her father a slave. The law of that State required all free born children of color to have guardians, parents counting as nothing under that most beautiful system.

When she was thirteen years of age, a noted divine, a slave owner and a near neighbor of her guardians, tendered her an invitation to accompany him to New Orleans. He had gained the consent of her guardian before asking her, and in glowing colors the trip was painted, and the fine things to be bought for her when once in the city. Girl-like she believed what was told her, and with trusting faith packed her box of clothes, and bade her weeping mother good-bye with tearless eyes for the journey of three months, as waiting-maid for the Rev. Mrs. B——m. I often wonder why there is no pitying angel standing by to stop one when men and devils conspire against them.

Six long months passed, and yet the fond mother heard not from her child.—When nearly a year had passed, home came the Rev. B——m, accompanied by his wife, but not the servant. He sent for the mother, and with a full heart told her of the happy death of her daughter—gave her her dying message, appointed a time to preach to the servants, and then with language most pathetic he told the story of the girl's conversion, sickness and triumphant death, delivering her last request to all to meet her in heaven,—and one united "I will" went up with wailing to be recorded above.

Three years went by, the mother's grief growing less as time rolled on. During the time of Mr. B.'s absence the guardian visited New Orleans, and on his return the mother asked if he had seen her child, and he replied, "No, I did not look for her." But now he had a daughter grown, and some insult was offered her by this Rev. B——m. Forthwith he started to New Orleans, and soon as possible returned with a pitiable object of humanity.

It was twilight when he arrived in F——ville. He sent a servant for the girl's mother, one for the minister, and one for those she had associated with. The beatings about the head which the girl had received, and the hardships she had endured, had destroyed her memory of former days and faces. She did not know her guardian who had brought her home— did not know her mother; but the minister who had sold her and reported her death knew her, and the sight appalled him; he fainted, and then his wife informed them how she had begged him not to sell the girl, thus convicting her husband.

The scene baffled description, and it was a long time before that girl's memory was restored to her, and what she suffered made a life impression upon her mind.—She, as a woman of fifty years, with this experience ever present, wished to impress it upon the minds of all. The sympathy the Democrats feel for the colored people at the South was the same her old guardian felt for her. He knew she was sold a slave, yet did not make any attempt for her freedom until he had hatred to gratify; and it was the hatred to the Radicals that made the Democrats so tender-hearted, so ready to weep over the poor negro.

—SEMPER FIDELIS

"Letter from Nevada County: Mud Hill, September 12, 1868" (1868)

SOURCE: Jennie Carter, "Letter from Nevada County: Mud Hill, September 12, 1868," *Elevator*, September 25, 1868.

Mr. Editor:—There is in the present political campaign less bitterness than heretofore at the North, while at the South it is increased ten-fold. A Democrat said the other day, that the feeling exhibited South was "caused by negroes seeking equality, and the people would not endure it and the despotism it brought them." They can't stand despotism. I think they ought to, for they have dealt largely in that material. Until the rebellion, who dared to express an opinion adverse to human bondage south of Mason and Dixon's line? Who dared read the first clause of the Constitution—"All men are born free and equal"—and give it a literal interpretation? And who dared preach the whole gospel—that master and servant were equal? Who dared to be seen reading the New York *Tribune*. All must put a lock on their lips, or suffer imprisonment and death. I know what I write, having spent a great portion of my life there; and often have I been told if I were a man I would be hung: and for what? Why, for saying slavery was wrong.

I recollect one time, in B—— county, Kentucky, I sat up all night with a poor slave mother, who lay in spasms, caused by the selling to a negro trader of her little boy, not three years of age. When in the morning her master came to her cabin to see how she was, I began to plead with him in humanity's name; and when that would not move him, I told him God was just, and would not suffer such things forever. He told me I had said enough to hang me.

They had better not talk of despotism and military rule now. I am sure they have more liberty than they ever allowed others. They can all speak their minds fully—even curse the Government that ought to have hung them; and now that we have the blood-bought right to speak of Christianity, humanity, morality and justice, and they cannot muzzle us, they cry "negro equality!"

We do not desire equality with them. I hope none of us are so low and so lost to all that is noble as to wish to change places with those slave owners (all Democrats), who before the war raised men and women for the market—selling their own flesh and blood, separating husband and wife, parent and child. No, we never expect to be bad enough to be their equals. As regards color, the slave-holders did all they could to produce equality. I know many of them whose daughters in the big house were not as light as their daughters in the cabin. And when I hear the Democrats say, "Want your daughter to marry a nigger?" I tell them many of your daughters have married negroes, and many more would have done it, but you choose to sell them to white men to become victims of their lust. Shame! I say. I am tired of listening to their falsehoods, and thankful that the Chinese can rest. Last year it was Chinese and Negro; this year not one word about the "moon-eyed celestials"; and next year they will be patting you on the shoulder, saying, "Come friend, give us your vote." Then should every one have the courage to say, "Depart, I never knew you, ye workers of iniquity."

—SEMPER FIDELIS.

17

ABBY FISHER

(ca. 1832–after 1881)

Abby Fisher was born, likely into slavery, in South Carolina, somewhere near 1832. Around the year 1880, she moved with her family to San Francisco where she began a successful pickling business, selling pickles, jellies, and preserves. Her business grew, and in 1881, with the help of influential friends and the San Francisco Women's Co-op Printing Office, she published the cookbook *What Mrs. Fisher Knows About Old Southern Cooking,* one of the first cookbooks to contain African American recipes. The book is credited with adding plantation-style cooking to the canon of American cuisine, allowing, for the first time, cooks not necessarily Southern or black to familiarize themselves with "Old Southern Cooking." Fisher's San Francisco catering business, which initially sparked the public's interest in her cooking style, was very successful, and her food was in demand across the bay region. Fisher's book and biography give us a glimpse into western black America, an area of history that remains neglected by most scholars of African American history and literature.

Abby Fisher was illiterate; the cookbook was compiled by friends to whom Fisher dictated her recipes. In her "Preface and Apology," Fisher credits these friends with the idea for publishing her recipes, but nonetheless expresses pride in her long experience. The recipes are notable for their simplicity and casual tone.

Selections from *What Mrs. Fisher Knows About Old Southern Cooking, Soups, Pickles, Preserves, Etc.* (1881)

SOURCE: Abby Fisher, *What Mrs. Fisher Knows About Old Southern Cooking, Soups, Pickles, Preserves, Etc.* (San Francisco: San Francisco Women's Co-op Printing Office, 1881).

Preface and Apology

The publication of a book on my knowledge and experience of Southern Cooking, Pickle and Jelly Making, has been frequently asked of me by my lady friends and patrons in San Francisco and Oakland, and also by ladies of Sacramento during the State Fair in 1879. Not being able to read or write myself, and my husband also having been without the advantages of an education—upon whom would devolve the writing of the book at my dictation—caused me to doubt whether I would be able to present a work that would give perfect satisfaction. But, after due consideration, I concluded to bring forward a book of my knowledge—based on an experience of upward of thirty-five years—in the art of cooking Soups, Gumbos, Terrapin Stews, Meat Stews, Baked and Roast Meats, Pastries, Pies and Biscuits, making Jellies, Pickles, Sauces, Ice-Creams and Jams, Preserving Fruits, etc. The book will be found a complete instructor, so that a child can understand it and learn the art of cooking.

Respectfully,

MRS. ABBY FISHER,
LATE OF MOBILE, ALA.

Jumberlie—A Creole Dish

Take one chicken and cut it up, separating every joint, and adding to it one pint of cleanly-washed rice. Take about half a dozen large tomatoes, scalding them well and taking the skins off with a knife. Cut them in small pieces and put them with the chicken in a pot or large porcelain saucepan. Then cut in small pieces two large pieces of sweet ham and add to the rest, seasoning high with pepper and salt. It will cook in twenty-five minutes. Do not put any water on it.

Oyster Gumbo Soup

Take an old chicken, cut into small pieces, salt and black pepper. Dip it well in flour, and put it on to fry, over a slow fire, till brown; don't let it burn. Cut half of a small onion very fine and sprinkle on chicken while frying. Then place chicken in soup pot, add two quarts of water and let boil to three pints. Have one quart of fresh oysters with all the liquor that belongs to them, and before dishing up soup, add oysters and let come to a boil the second time, then stir into soup one tablespoonful of gumbo [filé powder] quickly. Dish up and send to table. Have parsley chopped very fine and put in tureen on dishing up soup. Have dry boiled rice to go to table with gumbo in separate dish. Serve one tablespoonful of rice to a plate of gumbo.

Tonic Bitters—A Southern Remedy for Invalids

Take one ounce of cardamom seed, one ounce of Peruvian bark bruised, two ounces of Gentian root bruised, half ounce of dry orange peel, one ounce of aloes, and put the whole into half a gallon of best whiskey or brandy; let it come to a boil, then strain or filter it through a fine cloth or filtering paper.

Dose half wineglassfull three times a day before meals. Will strengthen and produce an appetite.

Sweet Cucumber Pickles

Take as many pickles as you want to make that have already been pickled in vinegar, and slice them in four pieces lengthwise, or cut them crosswise the thickness of a silver half-dollar, and place them in an earthen jar in layers of about three inches in thickness, covering each layer of pickles all over with granulated sugar. Keep repeating the layers three inches thick and covering them with sugar until you have placed all the pickles under sugar you have cut up. Let them remain under the sugar twenty-four hours, then take them out and put them in jars. Then make a syrup in the following way: One quart of sugar to one quart of clear water, and let it boil down to one quart. You will then have one quart of pure syrup. Add one tea-cup of wine vinegar to one pint of syrup, then add the vinegar syrup to the pickles until they are thoroughly covered. Always use granulated sugar.

Pap for Infant Diet

Take one pint of flour, sift it and tie it up in a clean cloth securely tight, so that no water can get into it; and put it in boiling water and let it boil steady for two hours, then take it out of water, and when it gets cold take outside crust from it. Whenever you are ready to nurse or feed the child, grate one tablespoonful of the boiled flour, and stir it into half a pint of boiled milk while the milk is boiling; sweeten the same with white sugar to taste. When the child has diarrhea, boil a two-inch stick of cinnamon in the pap. I have given birth to eleven children and raised them all, and nursed them with this diet. It is a Southern plantation preparation.

NORTHERN WOMEN AND THE POST-WAR SOUTH

18

CHARLOTTE FORTEN GRIMKÉ

(1837–1914)

The highly accomplished Charlotte Forten Grimké had the good fortune to be born into one prominent abolitionist family and marry into another. Her father was the scion of a distinguished and wealthy family of anti-slavery activists, while her mother, a former slave and the granddaughter of the white Governor Samuel Johnson of North Carolina, was emancipated and established in Philadelphia by her white father. The Forten family's circle of acquaintances included such figures as William Lloyd Garrison and John Greenleaf Whittier. Charlotte Forten taught both black and white students in Salem, Massachusetts, a rarity at that time. She later married Francis Grimké of the noted southern abolitionist family, continuing her work as a teacher and later as a clerk at the United States Treasury. Grimké's niece, Angelina Weld Grimké, whom Grimké helped raise, became an important figure in the Harlem Renaissance.

During the Civil War, Grimké traveled South as part of the Port Royal Experiment. Union soldiers had captured the South Carolina Sea Islands, the site of a large plantation, and established a school for the newly freed people there. Grimké was the first African American teacher to volunteer for the program. Many of her dispatches from this time, including this one, "Life on the Sea Islands," were published serially in the *Atlantic* in 1864. One of the poems included in this volume, "The Gathering of the Grand Army," was written in Boston on August 12, 1890.

"Life on the Sea Islands" (1864)

SOURCE: Charlotte Forten, "Life on the Sea Islands,"
Atlantic Monthly (May 1864).

[To THE EDITOR OF THE "ATLANTIC MONTHLY."—
The following graceful and picturesque description of the new
condition of things on the Sea Islands of South Carolina, originally written for private perusal, seems to me worthy of a place
in the "Atlantic." Its young author—herself akin to the long-
suffering race whose Exodus she so pleasantly describes—
is still engaged in her labor of love on St. Helena Island.
—J. G. W.]

Part I.

It was on the afternoon of a warm, murky day late in October
that our steamer, the United States, touched the landing at Hilton Head. A motley assemblage had collected on the wharf,—
officers, soldiers, and "contrabands" of every size and hue: black
was, however, the prevailing color. The first view of Hilton Head
is desolate enough,—a long, low, sandy point, stretching out into
the sea, with no visible dwellings upon it, except the rows of
small white-roofed houses which have lately been built for the
freed people.

After signing a paper wherein we declared ourselves loyal to
the Government, and wherein, also, were set forth fearful pen-
alties, should we ever be found guilty of treason, we were allowed to land, and immediately took General Saxton's boat,
the Flora, for Beaufort. The General was on board, and we
were presented to him. He is handsome, courteous, and affa-
ble, and looks—as he is—the gentleman and the soldier.

From Hilton Head to Beaufort the same long, low line of
sandy coast, bordered by trees; formidable gunboats in the distance, and the gray ruins of an old fort, said to have been built
by the Huguenots more than two hundred years ago. Arrived at
Beaufort, we found that we had not yet reached our journey's

end. While waiting for the boat which was to take us to our island of St. Helena, we had a little time to observe the ancient
town. The houses in the main street, which fronts the "Bay,"
are large and handsome, built of wood, in the usual Southern
style, with spacious piazzas, and surrounded by fine trees. We
noticed in one yard a magnolia, as high as some of our largest
shade—maples, with rich, dark, shining foliage. A large building which was once the Public Library is now a shelter for freed
people from Fernandina. Did the Rebels know it, they would
doubtless upturn their aristocratic noses, and exclaim in disgust, "To what base uses," etc. We confess that it was highly
satisfactory to us to see how the tables are turned, now that
"the whirligig of time has brought about its revenges." We saw
the market-place, in which slaves were sometimes sold; but we
were told that the buying and selling at auction were usually
done in Charleston. The arsenal, a large stone structure, was
guarded by cannon and sentinels. The houses in the smaller
streets had, mostly, a dismantled, desolate look. We saw no one
in the streets but soldiers and freed people. There were indica-
tions that already Northern improvements had reached this
Southern town. Among them was a wharf, a convenience that
one wonders how the Southerners could so long have existed
without. The more we know of their mode of life, the more are
we inclined to marvel at its utter shiftlessness.

Little colored children of every hue were playing about the
streets, looking as merry and happy as children ought to
look,—now that the evil shadow of Slavery no longer hangs
over them. Some of the officers we met did not impress us favorably. They talked flippantly, and sneeringly of the negroes,
whom they found we had come down to teach, using an epithet
more offensive than gentlemanly. They assured us that there
was great danger of Rebel attacks, that the yellow fever prevailed to an alarming extent, and that, indeed, the manufacture of coffins was the only business that was at all flourishing
at present. Although by no means daunted by these alarming
stories, we were glad when the announcement of our boat
relieved us from their edifying conversation. We rowed across
to Ladies Island, which adjoins St. Helena, through the splen-
dors of a grand Southern sunset. The gorgeous clouds of

crimson and gold were reflected as in a mirror in the smooth, clear waters below. As we glided along, the rich tones of the negro boatmen broke upon the evening stillness,—sweet, strange, and solemn—"Jesus make de blind to see, Jesus make de cripple walk, Jesus make de deaf to hear. Walk in, kind Jesus! No man can bender me."

It was nearly dark when we reached the island, and then we had a three-miles' drive through the lonely roads to the house of the superintendent. We thought how easy it would be for a band of guerrillas, had they chanced that way, to seize and hang us; but we were in that excited, jubilant state of mind which makes fear impossible, and sang "John Brown" with a will, as we drove through the pines and palmettos. Oh, it was good to sing that song in the very heart of Rebeldom! Harry, our driver, amused us much. He was surprised to find that we had not heard of him before. "Why, I thought eberybody at de Nort had heard o' me!" he said, very innocently. We learned afterward that Mrs. F., who made the tour of the islands last summer, had publicly mentioned Harry. Some one had told him of it, and he of course imagined that he had become quite famous. Notwithstanding this little touch of vanity, Harry is one of the best and smartest men on the island.

Gates occurred, it seemed to us, at every few yards' distance, made in the oddest fashion,—opening in the middle, like folding-doors, for the accommodation of horsemen. The little boy who accompanied us as gate-opener answered to the name of Cupid. Arrived at the headquarters of the general superintendent, Mr. S., we were kindly received by him and the ladies, and shown into a large parlor, where a cheerful wood-fire glowed in the grate. It had a home-like look; but still there was a sense of unreality about everything, and I felt that nothing less than a vigorous "shaking-up," such as Grandfather Smallweed daily experienced, would arouse me thoroughly to the fact that I was in South Carolina. The next morning L. and I were awakened by the cheerful voices of men and women, children and chickens, in the yard below. We ran to the window, and looked out. Women in bright-colored handkerchiefs, some carrying pails on their heads, were crossing the yard, busy with their morning work; children were playing, and tumbling around them. On every face there was a look of serenity and cheerfulness. My heart gave a great throb of happiness as I looked at them, and thought, "They are free! so long down-trodden, so long crushed to the earth, but now in their old homes, forever free!" And I thanked God that I had lived to see this day.

After breakfast Miss T. drove us to Oaklands, our future home. The road leading to the house was nearly choked with weeds. The house itself was in a dilapidated condition, and the yard and garden had a sadly neglected look. But there were roses in bloom; we plucked handfuls of feathery, fragrant acacia-blossoms; ivy crept along the ground and under the house. The freed people on the place seemed glad to see us. After talking with them, and giving some directions for cleaning the house, we drove to the school, in which I was to teach. It is kept in the Baptist Church,—a brick building, beautifully situated in a grove of live-oaks. These trees are the first objects that attract one's attention here: not that they are finer than our Northern oaks, but because of the singular gray moss with which every branch is heavily draped. This hanging moss grows on nearly all the trees, but on none so luxuriantly as on the live-oak. The pendants are often four or five feet long, very graceful and beautiful, but giving the trees a solemn, almost funereal look. The school was opened in September. Many of the children had, however, received instruction during the summer. It was evident that they had made very rapid improvement, and we noticed with pleasure how bright and eager to learn many of them seemed. They sang in rich, sweet tones, and with a peculiar swaying motion of the body, which made their singing the more effective. They sang "Marching Along," with great spirit, and then one of their own hymns, the air of which is beautiful and touching—

> "My sister, you want to git religion,
>   Go down in de Lonesome Valley; My brudder,
>   you want to git religion,
>   Go down in de Lonesome Valley.

CHORUS.
"Go down in de Lonesome Valley,
　　Go down in de Lonesome Valley, my Lord,
　　Go down in de Lonesome Valley,
　　To meet my Jesus dere!
"Oh, feed on milk and honey,
　　Oh, feed on milk and honey, my Lord,
　　Oh, feed on milk and honey,
　　Meet my Jesus dere!
　　Oh, John he brought a letter,
　　Oh, John he brought a letter, my Lord,
　　Oh, Mary and Marta read 'em
　　Meet my Jesus dere!

CHORUS.
"Go down in de Lonesome Valley," etc.

They repeat their hymns several times, and while singing keep
perfect time with their hands and feet. On our way homeward
we noticed that a few of the trees were beginning to turn, but we
looked in vain for the glowing autumnal hues of our Northern
forests. Some brilliant scarlet berries—the cassena—were growing along the road-side, and on every hand we saw the live-oak
with its moss-drapery. The palmettos disappointed me stiff and
ungraceful, they have a bristling, defiant look, suggestive of Rebels starting up and defying everybody. The land is low and
level,—not the slightest approach to a hill, not a rock, nor even
a stone to be seen. It would have a desolate look, were it not for
the trees, and the hanging moss and numberless vines which fes-
toon them. These vines overrun the hedges, form graceful arches
between the trees, en-circle their trunks, and sometimes climb to
the topmost branches. In February they begin to bloom, and
then through-out the spring and summer we have a succession of
beautiful flowers. First comes the yellow jessamine, with its perfect, gold-colored, and deliciously fragrant blossoms. It lights up
the hedges, and completely canopies some of the trees. Of all the
wild-flowers this seems to me the most beautiful and fragrant.
Then we have the snow-white, but scentless Cherokee rose, with

its lovely, shining leaves. Later in the season come the brilliant trumpet-flower, the passion-flower, and innumerable others.

The Sunday after our arrival we attended service at the Baptist Church. The people came in slowly for they have no way of knowing the hour, except by the sun. By eleven they had all assembled, and the church was well filled. They were neatly dressed in their Sunday attire, the women mostly wearing clean, dark frocks, with white aprons and bright-colored head-handkerchiefs. Some had attained to the dignity of straw hats with gay feathers, but these were not nearly as becoming nor as picturesque as the handkerchiefs. The day was warm, and the windows were thrown open as if it were summer, although it was the second day of November. It was very pleasant to listen to the beautiful hymns, and look from the crowd of dark, earnest faces within, upon the grove of noble oaks without. The people sang, "Roll, Jordan, roll," the grandest of all their hymns. There is a great, rolling wave of sound through it all.

"Mr. Fuller settin' on de Tree ob Life,
  Fur to hear de yen Jordan roll.
  Oh, roll, Jordan! roll, Jordan! roll, Jordan Roll!

CHORUS.
"Oh, roll, Jordan, roll! oh, roll, Jordan, roll!
My soul arise in heab'n, Lord,
Fur to hear de yen Jordan roll!

"Little chilen, learn to fear de Lord,
  And let your days be long.
  Oh, roll, Jordan! roll, Jordan! roll, Jordan, roll!

CHORUS.
"Oh, march, de angel, march! oh, march, de angel, march!
My soul arise in heah'n, Lord,
Fur to hear de yen Jordan roll!"

The "Mr. Fuller" referred to was their former minister, to whom they seem to have been much attached. He is a Southerner, but loyal, and is now, I believe, living in Baltimore. After the sermon the minister called upon one of the elders, a gray-headed old man, to pray. His manner was very fervent and impressive, but his language was so broken that to our unaccustomed ears it was quite, unintelligible. After the services the people gathered in groups outside, talking among themselves, and exchanging kindly greetings with the superintendents and teachers. In their bright handkerchiefs and white aprons they made a striking picture under the gray-mossed trees. We drove afterward a mile farther, to the Episcopal Church, in which the aristocracy of the island used to worship. It is a small white building, situated in a fine grove of live-oaks, at the junction of several roads. On one of the tombstones in the yard is the touching inscription in memory of two children,—"Blessed little lambs, and art thou gathered into the fold of the only true shepherd? Sweet lillies of the valley, and art thou removed to a more congenial soil?" The floor of the church is of stone, the pews of polished oak. It has an organ, which is not so entirely out of tune as are the pianos on the island. One of the ladies played, while the gentlemen sang,—old-fashioned New-England church-music, which it was pleasant to hear, but it did not thrill us as the singing of the people had done.

During the week we moved to Oaklands, our future home. The house was of one story, with a low-roofed piazza running the whole length. The interior had been thoroughly scrubbed and whitewashed; the exterior was guiltless of white-wash or paint. There were five rooms, all quite small, and several dark little entries, in one of which we found shelves lined with old medicine-bottles. These were a part of the possessions of the former owner, a Rebel physician, Dr. Sams by name. Some of them were still filled with his nostrums. Our furniture consisted of a bedstead, two bureaus, three small pine tables, and two chairs, one of which had a broken back. These were lent to us by the people. The masters, in their hasty flight from the islands, left nearly all their furniture; but much of it was destroyed or taken by the soldiers who came first, and what they left was removed by the people to their own houses. Certainly, they have the best right to it. We had made up our minds to dispense with all luxuries and even many conveniences; but it was rather distressing to have no fire, and nothing to eat. Mr. H.

had already appropriated a room for the store which he was going to open for the benefit of the freed people, and was superintending the removal of his goods. So L. and I were left to our
own resources. But Cupid the elder came to the rescue,—Cupid,
who, we were told, was to be our right-hand man, and who very
graciously informed us that he would take care of us; which he
at once proceeded to do by bringing in some wood, and busying
himself in making a fire in the open fireplace. While he is thus
engaged, I will try to describe him. A small, wiry figure, stock-
ingless, shoeless, out at the knees and elbows, and wearing the
remnant of an old straw hat, which looked as if it might have
done good service in scaring the crows from a cornfield. The
face nearly black, very ugly, but with the shrewdest expression I
ever saw, and the brightest, most humorous twinkle in the eyes.
One glance at Cupid's face showed that he was not a person to
be imposed upon, and that he was abundantly able to take care
of himself, as well as of us. The chimney obstinately refused to
draw, in spite of the original and very uncomplimentary epi-
thets which Cupid heaped upon it, while we stood by, listening
to him in amusement, although nearly suffocated by the smoke.
At last, perseverance conquered, and the fire began to burn
cheerily. Then Amaretta, our cook,—a neat-looking black
woman, adorned with the gayest of head-handkerchiefs, made
her appearance with some eggs and hominy, after partaking of
which we proceeded to arrange our scanty furniture, which was
soon done. In a few days we began to look civilized, having
made a table-cover of some red and yellow handkerchiefs which
we found among the store-goods,—a carpet of red and black
woollen plaid, originally intended for frocks and shirts,—a
cushion, stuffed with corn-husks and covered with calico, for a
lounge, which Ben, the carpenter, had made for us of pine
boards,—and lastly some corn-husk beds, which were an unspeakable luxury, after having endured agonies for several
nights, sleeping on the slats of a bedstead. It is true, the said
slats were covered with blankets, but these might as well have
been sheets of paper for all the good they did us. What a resting-
place it was! Compared to it, the gridiron of St. Lawrence—fire
excepted—was as a bed of roses.

The first day at school was rather trying. Most of my

children were very small, and consequently restless. Some were too young to learn the alphabet. These little ones were brought to school because the older children—in whose care their parents leave them while at work—could not come without them. We were therefore willing to have them come, although they seemed to have discovered the secret of perpetual motion, and tried one's patience sadly. But after some days of positive, though not severe treatment, order was brought out of chaos, and I found but little difficulty in managing and quieting the tiniest and most restless spirits. I never before saw children so eager to learn, although I had had several years' experience in New-England schools. Coming to school is a constant delight and recreation to them. They come here as other children go to play. The older ones, during the summer, work in the fields from early morning until eleven or twelve o'clock, and then come into school, after their hard toil in the hot sun, as bright and as anxious to learn as ever.

Of course there are some stupid ones, but these are the minority. The majority learn with wonderful rapidity. Many of the grown people are desirous of learning to read. It is wonderful how a people who have been so long crushed to the earth, so imbruted as these have been,—and they are said to be among the most degraded negroes of the South,—can have so great a desire for knowledge, and such a capability for attaining it. One cannot believe that the haughty Anglo-Saxon race, after centuries of such an experience as these people have had, would be very much superior to them. And one's indignation increases against those who, North as well as South, taunt the colored race with inferiority while they themselves use every means in their power to crush and degrade them, denying them every right and privilege, closing against them every avenue of elevation and improvement. Were they, under such circumstances, intellectual and refined, they would certainly be vastly superior to any other race that ever existed. After the lessons, we used to talk freely to the children, often giving them slight sketches of some of the great and good men. Before teaching them the "John Brown" song, which they learned to sing with great spirit, Miss T. told them the story of the brave old man who had died for them. I told them about Toussaint, thinking it well they should know what one of their own color had done for his race. They listened attentively, and seemed to understand. We found it rather hard to keep their attention in school. It is not strange, as they have been so entirely unused to intellectual concentration. It is necessary to interest them every moment, in order to keep their thoughts from wandering. Teaching here is consequently far more fatiguing than at the North. In the church, we had of course but one room in which to hear all the children; and to make one's self heard, when there were often as many as a hundred and forty reciting at once, it was necessary to tax the lungs very severely. My walk to school, of about a mile, was part of the way through a road lined with trees,— on one side stately pines, on the other noble live-oaks, hung with moss and canopied with vines. The ground was carpeted with brown, fragrant pine-leaves; and as I passed through in the morning, the woods were enlivened by the delicious songs of mocking-birds, which abound here, making one realize the truthful felicity of the description in "Evangeline,"— "The mocking-bird, wildest of singers, Shook from his little throat such floods of delirious music, That the whole air and the woods and the waves seemed silent to listen." The hedges were all aglow with the brilliant scarlet berries of the cassena, and on some of the oaks we observed the mistletoe, laden with its pure white, pearl-like berries. Out of the woods the roads are generally bad, and we found it hard work plodding through the deep sand.

Mr. H.'s store was usually crowded, and Cupid was his most valuable assistant. Gay handkerchiefs for turbans, pots and kettles, and molasses, were principally in demand, especially the last. It was necessary to keep the molasses-barrel in the yard, where Cupid presided over it, and harangued and scolded the eager, noisy crowd, collected around, to his heart's content; while up the road leading to the house came constantly processions of men, women, and children, carrying on their heads cans, jugs, pitchers, and even bottles, anything, indeed, that was capable of containing molasses. It is wonderful with what ease they carry all sorts of things on their heads,—heavy bundles of wood, hoes and rakes, everything, heavy or light that can be carried in the hands; and I have seen a woman, with a

bucketful of water on her head, stoop down and take up another in her hand, without spilling a drop from either.

We noticed that the people had much better taste in selecting
materials for dresses than we had supposed. They do not generally like gaudy colors, but prefer neat, quiet patterns. They are,
however, very fond of all kinds of jewelry. I once asked the children in school what their ears were for. "To put rings in,"
promptly replied one of the little girls. These people are exceedingly polite in their manner towards each other, each new arrival
bowing, scraping his feet, and shaking hands with the others,
while there are constant greetings, such as, "Huddy? How's yer
lady?" ("How d' ye do? How's your wife?") The hand-shaking is
performed with the greatest possible solemnity. There is never
the faintest shadow of a smile on anybody's face during this performance. The children, too, are taught to be very polite to their
elders, and it is the rarest thing to hear a disrespectful word from
a child to his parent, or to any grown person. They have really
what the New-Englanders call "beautiful manners."

We made daily visits to the "quarters," which were a few
rods from the house. The negro-houses, on this as on most of
the other plantations, were miserable little huts, with nothing
comfortable or home-like about them, consisting generally of
but two very small rooms,—the only way of lighting them, no
matter what the state of the weather, being to leave the doors
and windows open. The windows, of course, have no glass in
them. In such a place, a father and mother with a large family
of children are often obliged to live. It is almost impossible to
teach them habits of neatness and order, when they are so
crowded. We look forward anxiously to the day when better
houses shall increase their comfort and pride of appearance.

Oaklands is a very small plantation. There were not more
than eight or nine families living on it. Some of the people interested us much. Celia, one of the best, is a cripple. Her master,
she told us, was too mean to give his slaves clothes enough to
protect them, and her feet and legs were so badly frozen that
they required amputation. She has a lovely face,—well-featured
and singularly gentle. In every household where there was illness or trouble, Celia's kind, sympathizing face was the first to
be seen, and her services were always the most acceptable.

Harry, the foreman on the plantation, a man of a good deal
of natural intelligence, was most desirous of learning to read.
He came in at night to be taught, and learned very rapidly. I
never saw any one more determined to learn. We enjoyed hearing him talk about the "gun-shoot,"—so the people call the
capture of Bay Point and Hilton Head. They never weary of
telling you "how Massa run when he hear de fust gun."

"Why did n't you go with him, Harry?" I asked.

"Oh, Miss, 't was n't 'cause Massa did n't try to 'suade me. He
tell we dat de Yankees would shoot we, or would sell we to
Cuba, an' do all de wust tings to we, when dey come. 'Bery well,
Sar,' says I. 'If I go wid you, I be good as dead. If I stay here, I
can't be no wust; so if I got to dead, I might 's well dead here as
anywhere. So I'll stay here an' wait for de "dam Yankees."'Lor',
Miss, I knowed he was n't tellin' de truth all de time."

"But why did n't you believe him, Harry?"

"Dunno, Miss; somehow we hear de Yankees was our
friends, an' dat we'd be free when dey come, an' 'pears like we
believe dat."

I found this to be true of nearly all the people I talked with,
and I thought it strange they should have had so much faith in
the Northerners. Truly, for years past, they had had but little
cause to think them very friendly. Cupid told us that his master
was so daring as to come back, after he had fled from the island, at the risk of being taken prisoner by our soldiers; and
that he ordered the people to get all the furniture together and
take it to a plantation on the opposite side of the creek, and to
stay on that side themselves. "So," said Cupid, "dey could jus'
sweep us all up in a heap, an' put us in de boat. An' he telled me
to take Patience—dat's my wife—an' de chil'en down to a certain pint, an' den I could come back, if I choose. Jus' as if I was
gwine to be sich a goat!" added he, with a look and gesture of
ineffable contempt. He and the rest of the people, instead of
obeying their master, left the place and hid themselves in the
woods; and when he came to look for them, not one of all his
"faithful servants" was to be found. A few, principally house-
servants, had previously been carried away.

In the evenings, the children frequently came in to sing and
shout for us. These "shouts" are very strange,—in truth, almost

indescribable. It is necessary to hear and see in order to have any clear idea of them. The children form a ring, and move around in a kind of shuffling dance, singing all the time. Four or five stand apart, and sing very energetically, clapping their hands, stamping their feet, and rocking their bodies to and fro. These are the musicians, to whose performance the shouters keep perfect time. The grown people on this plantation did not shout, but they do on some of the other plantations. It is very comical to see little children, not more than three or four years old, entering into the performance with all their might. But the shouting of the grown people is rather solemn and impressive than otherwise. We cannot determine whether it has a religious character or not. Some of the people tell us that it has, others that it has not. But as the shouts of the grown people are always in connection with their religious meetings, it is probable that they are the barbarous expression of religion, handed down to them from their African ancestors, and destined to pass away under the influence of Christian teachings. The people on this island have no songs. They sing only hymns, and most of these are sad. Prince, a large black boy from a neighboring planta- tion, was the principal shouter among the children. It seemed impossible for him to keep still for a moment. His performances were most amusing specimens of Ethiopian gymnastics. Ama- retta the younger, a cunning, kittenish little creature of only six years old, had a remarkably sweet voice. Her favorite hymn, which we used to hear her singing to herself as she walked through the yard, is one of the oddest we have heard—

> "What makes ole Satan follow me so? Satan got
>   nuttin' 't all fur to do wid me.
>
> CHORUS.
> "Tiddy Rosa, hold your light!
> Brudder Tony, hold your light!
> All de member, hold bright light
> On Canaan's shore!"

This is one of the most spirited shouting-tunes. "Tiddy" is their word for sister.

A very queer-looking old man came into the store one day. He was dressed in a complete suit of brilliant Brussels carpeting. Probably it had been taken from his master's house after the "gun-shoot"; but he looked so very dignified that we did not like to question him about it.

The people called him Doctor Crofts,—which was, I believe, his master's name, his own being Scipio. He was very jubilant over the new state of things, and said to Mr. H.,—"Don't hab me feelins hurt now. Used to hab me feelins hurt all de time. But don't hab 'em hurt now no more." Poor old soul! We rejoiced with him that he and his brethren no longer have their "feelins" hurt, as in the old time.

On the Sunday before Thanksgiving, General Saxton's noble Proclamation was read at church. We could not listen to it without emotion. The people listened with the deepest attention, and seemed to understand and appreciate it. Whittier has said of it and its writer,—"It is the most beautiful and touching official document I ever read. God bless him! 'The bravest are the tenderest.'"

General Saxton is truly worthy of the gratitude and admiration with which the people regard him. His unfailing kindness and consideration for them—so different from the treatment they have sometimes received at the hands of other officers—have caused them to have unbounded confidence in General "Saxby," as they call him. After the service, there were six couples married. Some of the dresses were unique. One was particularly fine,—doubtless a cast-off dress of the bride's former mistress. The silk and lace, ribbons, feathers and flowers, were in a rather faded and decayed condition. But, comical as the costumes were, we were not disposed to laugh at them. We were too glad to see the poor creatures trying to lead right and virtuous lives. The legal ceremony, which was formerly scarcely known among them, is now everywhere consecrated. The constant and earnest advice of the minister and teachers has not been given in vain; nearly every Sunday there are several couples married in church. Some of them are people who have grown old together.

Thanksgiving-Day was observed as a general holiday. According to General Saxton's orders, an ox had been killed on each plantation, that the people might that day have fresh meat, which was a great luxury to them, and, indeed, to all of us. In the morning, a large number—superintendents, teachers, and freed people—assembled in the Baptist Church. It was a sight not soon to be forgotten,—that crowd of eager, happy black faces, from which the shadow of Slavery had forever passed. "Forever free! forever free!" those magical words of the Proclamation were constantly singing themselves in my soul. After an appropriate prayer and sermon by Mr. P., and singing by the people, General Saxton made a short, but spirited speech, urging the young men to enlist in the regiment then forming under Colonel Higginson. Mrs. Gage told the people how the slaves in Santa Cruz had secured their liberty. It was something entirely new and strange to them to hear a woman speak in public; but they listened with great attention, and seemed much interested. Before dispersing, they sang "Marching Along," which is an especial favorite with them. It was a very happy Thanksgiving-Day for all of us. The weather was delightful; oranges and figs were hanging on the trees; roses, oleanders, and japonicas were blooming out-of-doors; the sun was warm and bright; and over all shone gloriously the blessed light of Freedom,—Freedom forevermore!

One night, L. and I were roused from our slumbers by what seemed to us loud and most distressing shrieks, proceeding from the direction of the negro-houses. Having heard of one or two attempts which the Rebels had recently made to land on the island, our first thought was, naturally, that they had forced a landing, and were trying to carry off some of the people. Every moment we expected to hear them at our doors; and knowing that they had sworn vengeance against all the superintendents and teachers, we prepared ourselves for the worst. After a little reflection, we persuaded ourselves that it could not be the Rebels; for the people had always assured us, that, in case of a Rebel attack, they would come to us at once,— evidently thinking that we should be able to protect them. But what could the shrieks mean? They ceased; then, a few moments afterwards, began again, louder, more fearful than before; then again they ceased, and all was silent. I am ashamed to confess that we had not the courage to go out and inquire into the cause of the alarm. Mr. H.'s room was in another part of the house, too far for him to give us any aid. We hailed the dawn of day gladly enough, and eagerly sought Cupid,—who was sure. to know everything,—to obtain from him a solution of the mystery. "Why, you was n't scared at dat?" he exclaimed, in great amusement; "'t was n't nuttin' but de black sogers dat comed up to see der folks on t' oder side ob de creek. Dar was n't no boat fur 'em on dis side, so dey jus' blowed de whistle dey hab, so de folks might bring one ober fur 'em. Dat was all 't was." And Cupid laughed so heartily that we felt not a little ashamed of our fears. Nevertheless, we both maintained that we had never seen a whistle from which could be produced sounds so startling, so distressing, so perfectly like the shrieks of a human being.

Another night, while staying at a house some miles distant from ours, I was awakened by hearing, as I thought, some one trying to open the door from without. The door was locked; I lay perfectly still, and listened intently. A few moments elapsed, and the sound was repeated; whereupon I rose, and woke Miss W., who slept in the adjoining room. We lighted a candle, took our revolvers, and seated ourselves on the bed, keeping our weapons, so formidable in practised male hands, steadily pointed towards the door, and uttering dire threats against the intruders, presumed to be Rebels, of course. Having maintained this tragical position for some time, and hearing no further noise; we began to grow sleepy, and extinguished our candle, returned to bed, and slept soundly till morning. But that mystery remained unexplained. I was sure that the door had been tried, there could be no mistaking it. There was not the least probability that any of the people had entered the house, burglars are unknown on these islands, and there is nobody to be feared but the Rebels.

The last and greatest alarm we had was after we had removed from Oaklands to another plantation. I woke about two o'clock in the morning, hearing the tramp of many feet in the yard below,—the steady tramp of soldiers' feet. "The Rebels! they have come at last! all is over with us now!" I thought at once, with a desperate kind of resignation. And I lay still, waiting and listening. Soon I heard footsteps on the piazza; then the hall-door was opened, and steps were heard distinctly in the hall beneath; finally, I heard some one coming up the stairs. Then I grasped my revolver, rose, and woke the other ladies. "There are soldiers in the yard! Somebody has opened the hall-door, and is coming up-stairs!" Poor L., but half awakened, stared at me in speechless terror. The same thought filled our minds. But Mrs. B., after listening for a moment, exclaimed,—"Why, that is my husband! I know his footsteps. He is coming up-stairs to call me."

And so it proved. Her husband, who was a lieutenant in Colonel Montgomery's regiment, had come up from camp with some of his men to look after deserters. The door had been unfastened by a servant who on that night happened to sleep in the house. I shall never forget the delightful sensation of relief that came over me when the whole matter was explained. It was almost overpowering; for, although I had made up my mind to bear the worst, and bear it bravely, the thought of falling into the hands of the Rebels was horrible in the extreme. A year of intense mental suffering seemed to have been compressed into those few moments.

Part II.

A few days before Christmas, we were delighted at receiving a beautiful Christmas Hymn from Whittier, written by request, especially for our children. They learned it very easily, and enjoyed singing it. We showed them the writer's picture, and told them he was a very good friend of theirs, who felt the deepest interest in them, and had written this hymn expressly for them to sing,—which made them very proud and happy. Early Christmas morning, we were wakened by the people knocking at the doors and windows, and shouting, "Merry Christmas!" After distributing some little presents among them, we went to the church, which had been decorated with holly, pine, cassena, mistletoe, and the hanging moss, and had a very Christmas-like look. The children of our school assembled there, and we gave them the nice, comfortable clothing, and the picture-books, which had been kindly sent by some Philadelphia ladies. There were at least a hundred and fifty children present. It was very pleasant to see their happy, expectant little faces. To them, it was a wonderful Christmas-Day,—such as they had never dreamed of before. There was cheerful sunshine without, lighting up the beautiful moss-drapery of the oaks, and looking in joyously through the open windows; and there were bright faces and glad hearts within. The long, dark night of the Past, with all its sorrows and its fears, was forgotten; and for the Future,—the eyes of these freed children see no clouds in it. It is full of sunlight, they think, and they trust in it, perfectly.

After the distribution of the gifts, the children were addressed by some of the gentlemen present. They then sang Whittier's Hymn, the "John Brown" song, and several of their own hymns, among them a very singular one, commencing,—

> "I wonder where my mudder gone;
>   Sing, O graveyard!
> Graveyard ought to know me;
>   Ring, Jerusalem!
> Grass grow in de graveyard;
>   Sing, O graveyard!
> Graveyard ought to know me;
>   Ring, Jerusalem!"

They improvise many more words as they sing. It is one of the strangest, most mournful things I ever heard. It is impossible to give any idea of the deep pathos of the refrain,—

> "Sing, O graveyard!"

In this, and many other hymns, the words seem to have but little meaning; but the tones,—a whole lifetime of despairing sadness is concentrated in them. They sing, also, "Jehovyah, Hallelujah," which we like particularly:—

> "De foxes hab holes,
>   An' de birdies hab nes',
> But de Son ob Man he hab not where
>   To lay de weary head.

CHORUS.
"Jehovyah, Hallelujah! De Lord He will purvide!
Jehovyah, Hallelujah! De Lord He will purvide!"

They repeat the words many times. "De foxes hab holes,"
and the succeeding lines, are sung in the most touching, mournful tones; and then the chorus—"Jehovyah, Hallelujah"—
swells forth triumphantly, in glad contrast. Christmas night,
the children came in and had several grand shouts. They were
too happy to keep still.

"Oh, Miss, all I want to do is to sing and shout!" said our
little pet, Amaretta. And sing and shout she did, to her heart's
content.

She read nicely, and was very fond of books. The tiniest children are delighted to get a book in their hands. Many of them
already know their letters. The parents are eager to have them
learn. They sometimes said to me,—"Do, Miss, let de chil'en
learn eberyting dey can. We nebber hab no chance to learn nuttin', but we wants de chil'en to learn."

They are willing to make many sacrifices that their children
may attend school. One old woman, who had a large family of
children and grandchildren, came regularly to school in the
winter, and took her seat among the little ones. She was at least
sixty years old. Another woman—who had one of the best
faces I ever saw—came daily, and brought her baby in her
arms. It happened to be one of the best babies in the world, a
perfect little "model of deportment," and allowed its mother to
pursue her studies without interruption.

While taking charge of the store, one day, one of the men
who came in told me a story which interested me much. He was
a carpenter, living on this island, and just before the capture of
Port Royal had been taken by his master to the mainland,—
"the Main," as the people call it,—to assist in building some
houses which were to shelter the families of the Rebels in case
the "Yankees" should come. The master afterward sent him
back to the island, providing him with a pass, to bring away a
boat and some of the people. On his arrival he found that the
Union troops were in possession, and determined to remain
here with his family instead of returning to his master. Some of

his fellow-servants, who had been left on "the Main," hearing that the Federal troops had come, resolved to make their escape to the islands. They found a boat of their master's, out of which a piece six feet square had been cut. In the night they went to the boat, which had been sunk in a creek near the house, measured the hole, and, after several nights' work in the woods, made a piece large enough to fit in. They then mended and sank it again, as they had found it. The next night five of them embarked. They had a perilous journey, often passing quite near the enemy's boats. They travelled at night, and in the day ran close up to the shore out of sight. Sometimes they could hear the hounds, which had been sent in pursuit of them, baying in the woods. Their provisions gave out, and they were nearly exhausted. At last they succeeded in passing all the enemy's boats, and reached one of our gun-boats in safety. They were taken on board and kindly cared for, and then sent to this island, where their families, who had no hope of ever seeing them again, welcomed them with great rejoicing.

We were also told the story of two girls, one about ten, the other fifteen, who, having been taken by their master up into the country, on the mainland, at the time of the capture of the islands, determined to try to escape to their parents, who had been left on this island. They stole away at night, and travelled through woods and swamps for two days, without eating. Sometimes their strength gave out, and they would sink down, thinking they could go no farther; but they had brave little hearts, and got up again and struggled on, till at last they reached Port-Royal Ferry, in a state of utter exhaustion. They were seen there by a boat-load of people who were also making their escape. The boat was too full to take them in; but the people, on reaching this island, told the children's father of their whereabouts, and he immediately took a boat, and hastened to the ferry. The poor little creatures were almost wild with joy when they saw him. When they were brought to their mother, she fell down "jes' as if she was dead,"—so our informant expressed it,—overpowered with joy on beholding the "lost who were found."

New-Year's-Day—Emancipation-Day—was a glorious one to us. The morning was quite cold, the coldest we had experienced;

but we were determined to go to the celebration at Camp
Saxton,—the camp of the First Regiment South-Carolina
Volunteers,—whither the General and Colonel Higginson had
bidden us, on this, "the greatest day in the nation's history." We
enjoyed perfectly the exciting scene on board the Flora. There
was an eager, wondering crowd of the freed people in their
holiday-attire, with the gayest of head-handkerchiefs, the whitest
of aprons, and the happiest of faces. The band was playing, the
flags streaming, everybody talking merrily and feeling strangely
happy. The sun shone brightly, the very waves seemed to partake
of the universal gayety, and danced and sparkled more joyously
than ever before. Long before we reached Camp Saxton we could
see the beautiful grove, and the ruins of the old Huguenot fort
near it. Some companies of the First Regiment were drawn up in
line under the trees, near the landing, to receive us. A fine,
soldierly-looking set of men; their brilliant dress against the trees
(they were then wearing red pantaloons) invested them with a
semi-barbaric splendor. It was my good fortune to find among
the officers an old friend,—and what it was to meet a friend from
the North, in our isolated Southern life, no one can imagine who
has not experienced the pleasure. Letters were an unspeakable
luxury,—we hungered for them, we could never get enough; but
to meet old friends,—that was "too much, too much," as the people here say, when they are very much in earnest. Our friend took
us over the camp, and showed us all the arrangements. Everything looked clean and comfortable, much neater, we were told,
than in most of the white camps. An officer told us that he had
never seen a regiment in which the men were so honest. "In many
other camps," said he, "the colonel and the rest of us would find
it necessary to place a guard before our tents. We never do it here.
They are left entirely unguarded. Yet nothing has ever been
touched." We were glad to know that. It is a remarkable fact,
when we consider that these men have all their lives been slaves;
and we know what the teachings of Slavery are.

The celebration took place in the beautiful grove of live-oaks
adjoining the camp. It was the largest grove we had seen. I wish
it were possible to describe fitly the scene which met our eyes as
we sat upon the stand, and looked down on the crowd before
us. There were the black soldiers in their blue coats and scarlet

pantaloons, the officers of this and other regiments in their handsome uniforms, and crowds of lookers-on,—men, women, and children, of every complexion, grouped in various attitudes under the moss-hung trees. The faces of all wore a happy, interested look. The exercises commenced with a prayer by the chaplain of the regiment. An ode, written for the occasion by Professor Zachos, was read by him, and then sung. Colonel Higginson then introduced Dr. Brisbane, who read the President's Proclamation, which was enthusiastically cheered. Rev. Mr. French presented to the Colonel two very elegant flags, a gift to the regiment from the Church of the Puritans, accompanying them by an appropriate and enthusiastic speech. At its conclusion, before Colonel Higginson could reply, and while he still stood holding the flags in his hand, some of the colored people, of their own accord, commenced singing, "My Country, 'tis of thee." It was a touching and beautiful incident, and sent a thrill through all our hearts. The Colonel was deeply moved by it. He said that that reply was far more effective than any speech he could make. But he did make one of those stirring speeches which are "half battles." All hearts swelled with emotion as we listened to his glorious words,—"stirring the soul like the sound of a trumpet." His soldiers are warmly attached to him, and he evidently feels towards them all as if they were his children. The people speak of him as "the officer who never leaves his regiment for pleasure," but devotes himself, with all his rich gifts of mind and heart, to their interests. It is not strange that his judicious kindness, ready sympathy, and rare fascination of manner should attach them to him strongly. He is one's ideal of an officer. There is in him much of the grand, knightly spirit of the olden time,—scorn of all that is mean and ignoble, pity for the weak, chivalrous devotion to the cause of the oppressed.

General Saxton spoke also, and was received with great enthusiasm. Throughout the morning, repeated cheers were given for him by the regiment, and joined in heartily by all the people. They know him to be one of the best and noblest men in the world. His Proclamation for Emancipation-Day we thought, if possible, even more beautiful than the Thanksgiving Proclamation.

At the close of Colonel Higginson's speech he presented the flags to the color-bearers, Sergeant Rivers and Sergeant Sutton, with an earnest charge, to which they made appropriate replies. We were particularly pleased with Robert Sutton, who is a man of great natural intelligence, and whose remarks were simple, eloquent, and forcible. Mrs. Gage also uttered some earnest words; and then the regiment sang "John Brown" with much spirit. After the meeting we saw the dress-parade, a brilliant and beautiful sight. An officer told us that the men went through the drill remarkably well,—that the ease and rapidity with which they learned the movements were wonderful. To us it seemed strange as a miracle,—this black regiment, the first mustered into the service of the United States, doing itself honor in the sight of the officers of other regiments, many of whom, doubtless, "came to scoff." The men afterwards had a great feast, ten oxen having been roasted whole for their especial benefit.

We went to the landing, intending to take the next boat for Beaufort; but finding it very much crowded, waited for another. It was the softest, loveliest moonlight; we seated ourselves on the ruined wall of the old fort; and when the boat had got a short distance from the shore the band in it commenced playing "Sweet Home." The moonlight on the water, the perfect stillness around, the wildness and solitude of the ruins, all seemed to give new pathos to that ever dear and beautiful old song. It came very near to all of us,—strangers in that strange Southern land. After a while we retired to one of the tents,—for the night-air, as usual, grew dangerously damp,—and, sitting around the bright wood-fire, enjoyed the brilliant and entertaining conversation. Very unwilling were we to go home; for, besides the attractive society, we knew that the soldiers were to have grand shouts and a general jubilee that night. But the Flora was coming, and we were obliged to say a reluctant farewell to Camp Saxton and the hospitable dwellers therein, and hasten to the landing. We promenaded the deck of the steamer, sang patriotic songs, and agreed that moonlight and water had never looked so beautiful as on that night. At Beaufort we took the row-boat for St. Helena; and the boatmen, as they rowed, sang some of their sweetest, wildest hymns. It was a fitting close to such a day. Our hearts were filled with an exceeding great gladness; for, although the Government had left much undone, we knew that Freedom was surely born in our land that day. It seemed too glorious a good to realize,—this beginning of the great work we had so longed and prayed for.

L. and I had one day an interesting visit to a plantation about six miles from ours. The house is beautifully situated in the midst of noble pine-trees, on the banks of a large creek. The place was owned by a very wealthy Rebel family, and is one of the pleasantest and healthiest on the island. The vicinity of the pines makes it quite healthy. There were a hundred and fifty people on it,—one hundred of whom had come from Edisto Island at the time of its evacuation by our troops. There were not houses enough to accommodate them, and they had to take shelter in barns, out-houses, or any other place they could find. They afterwards built rude dwellings for themselves, which did not, however, afford them much protection in bad weather. The superintendent told us that they were well-behaved and industrious. One old woman interested us greatly. Her name was Daphne; she was probably more than a hundred years old; had had fifty grandchildren, sixty-five great-grandchildren, and three great-great-grandchildren. Entirely blind, she yet seemed very cheerful and happy. She told us that she was brought with her parents from Africa at the time of the Revolution. A bright, happy old face was hers, and she retained her faculties remarkably well. Fifteen of the people had escaped from the mainland in the previous spring. They were pursued, and one of them was overtaken by his master in the swamps. A fierce grapple ensued,—the master on horseback, the man on foot. The former drew a pistol and shot his slave through the arm, shattering it dreadfully. Still, the heroic man fought desperately, and at last succeeded in unhorsing his master, and beating him until he was senseless. He then made his escape, and joined the rest of the party.

One of the most interesting sights we saw was a baptism among the people. On one Sunday there were a hundred and fifty baptized in the creek near the church. They looked very picturesque in their white aprons and bright frocks and handkerchiefs. As they marched in procession down to the river's edge, and during the ceremony, the spectators, with whom the banks were crowded, sang glad, triumphant songs. The freed people on this island are all Baptists. We were much disappointed in the Southern climate. We found it much colder than we had expected,—quite cold enough for as thick winter clothing as one would wear at the North. The houses, heated only by open fires, were never comfortably warm. In the floor of our sitting-room there was a large crack through which we could see the ground beneath; and through this and the crevices of the numerous doors and windows the wind came chillingly. The church in which we taught school was particularly damp and cold. There was no chimney, and we could have no fire at all. Near the close of the winter a stove came for us, but it could not be made to draw; we were nearly suffocated with smoke, and gave it up in despair. We got so thoroughly chilled and benumbed within, that for several days we had school out-of-doors, where it was much warmer. Our school-room was a pleasant one,—for ceiling the blue sky above, for walls the grand old oaks with their beautiful moss-drapery,—but the dampness of the ground made it unsafe for us to continue the experiment.

At a later period, during a few days' visit to some friends living on the Milne Plantation, then the head-quarters of the First South-Carolina, which was on picket-duty at Port-Royal Ferry, we had an opportunity of seeing something of Port-Royal Island. We had pleasant rides through the pine barrens. Indeed, riding on horseback was our chief recreation at the South, and we enjoyed it thoroughly. The "Secesh" horses, though small, poor, and mean-looking, when compared with ours, are generally excellent for the saddle, well-trained and very easy. I remember particularly one ride that we had while on Port-Royal Island. We visited the Barnwell Plantation, one of the finest places on the island. It is situated on Broad River. The grounds are extensive, and are filled with magnificent live-oaks, magnolias, and other trees. We saw one noble old oak, said to be the largest on these islands. Some of the branches have been cut off, but the remaining ones cover an area of more than a hundred feet in circumference. We rode to a point whence the Rebels on the opposite side of the river are sometimes to be seen. But they were not visible that day; and we were disappointed in our long-cherished hope of seeing a "real live Rebel." On leaving the plantation, we rode through a long avenue of oaks,—the moss-hung branches forming a perfect arch over our heads,—and then for miles through the pine barrens. There was an Italian softness in the April air. Only a low, faint murmur—hardly "the slow song of the sea"—could be heard among the pines. The ground was thickly carpeted with ferns of a vivid green. We found large violets, purple and white, and azaleas of a deeper pink and heavier fragrance than ours. It was leaving Paradise, to emerge from the beautiful woods upon the public road,—the shell-road which runs from Beaufort to the Ferry. Then we entered a by-way leading to the plantation, where we found the Cherokee rose in all its glory. The hedges were white with it; it canopied the trees, and hung from their branches its long sprays of snowy blossoms and dark, shining leaves, forming perfect arches, and bowers which seemed fitting places for fairies to dwell in. How it gladdened our eyes and hearts! It was as if all the dark shadows that have so long hung over this Southern land had flitted away, and, in this garment of purest white, it shone forth transfigured, beautified, forevermore.

On returning to the house, we were met by the exciting news that the Rebels were bringing up pontoon-bridges, and were expected to attempt crossing over near the Ferry, which was only two or three miles from us. Couriers came in every few moments with various reports. A superintendent whose plantation was very near the Ferry had been watching through his glass the movements on the opposite side, and reported that the Rebels were gathering in large force, and evidently preparing for some kind of demonstration. A messenger was dispatched to Beaufort for reinforcements, and for some time we were in a state of expectancy, not entirely without excitement, but entirely without fear. The officers evidently enjoyed the prospect of a fight. One of them assured me that I should have the pleasure of seeing a Rebel shell during the afternoon. It was proposed that the women should be sent into Beaufort in an ambulance; against which ignoble treatment we indignantly protested, and declared our intention of remaining at our post, if the Colonel would consent; and finally, to our great joy, the best of colonels did consent that we should remain, as he considered it quite safe for us to do so. Soon a light battery arrived, and during the evening a brisk firing was kept up. We could hear the explosion of the shells. It was quite like being in the war; and as the firing was principally on our side, and the enemy was getting the worst of it, we rather enjoyed it. For a little while the Colonel read to us, in his spirited way, some of the stirring "Lays of the Old Cavaliers." It was just the time to appreciate them thoroughly, and he was of all men the fittest person to read them. But soon came a courier, "in hot haste," to make report of the doings without, and the reading was at an end. In the midst of the firing, Mrs. D. and I went to bed, and slept soundly until morning. We learned afterward that the Rebels had not intended to cross over, but were attempting to take the guns off one of our boats, which they had sunk a few days previous. The timely arrival of the battery from Beaufort prevented them from accomplishing their purpose.

In April we left Oaklands, which had always been considered a particularly unhealthy place during the summer, and came to "Seaside," a plantation on another and healthier part of the island. The place contains nearly a hundred people. The house is large and comparatively comfortable. Notwithstanding the name, we have not even a distant glimpse of the sea, although we can sometimes hear its roar. At low tide there is not a drop of water to be seen,—only dreary stretches of marsh-land, reminding us of the sad outlook of Mariana in the Moated Grange,—"The level waste and rounding gray."

But at night we have generally a good sea-breeze, and during the hottest weather the air is purer and more invigorating than in many parts of the island.

On this, as on several other large plantations, there is a "Praise-House," which is the special property of the people. Even in the old days of Slavery, they were allowed to hold meetings here; and they still keep up the custom. They assemble on several nights of the week, and on Sunday afternoons. First, they hold what is called the "Praise-Meeting," which consists of singing, praying, and preaching. We have heard some of the old negro preachers make prayers that were really beautiful and

touching. In these meetings they sing only the church-hymns
which the Northern ministers have taught them, and which are
far less suited to their voices than their own. At the close of the
Praise-Meeting they all shake hands with each other in the most
solemn manner. Afterward, as a kind of appendix, they have a
grand "shout," during which they sing their own hymns. Maurice, an old blind man, leads the singing. He has a remarkable
voice, and sings with the greatest enthusiasm. The first shout
that we witnessed in the Praise-House impressed us very much.
The large, gloomy room, with its blackened walls,—the wild,
whirling dance of the shouters,—the crowd of dark, eager faces
gathered around,—the figure of the old blind man, whose excitement could hardly be controlled, and whose attitude and
gestures while singing were very fine,—and over all, the red
glare of the burning pine-knot, which shed a circle of light
around it, but only seemed to deepen and darken the shadows
in the other parts of the room,—these all formed a wild, strange,
and deeply impressive picture, not soon to be forgotten.

Maurice's especial favorite is one of the grandest hymns that
we have yet heard:—

> "De tallest tree in Paradise
> De Christian calls de Tree ob Life,
> An' I hope dat trumpet blow me home
> To my New Jerusalem.
>
> CHORUS.
> "Blow, Gabriel! trumpet, blow louder, louder!
> An' I hope dat trumpet blow me home
> To my New Jerusalem!
>
> "Paul and Silas jail-bound
> Sing God's praise both night and day,
> An' I hope dat trumpet blow me home
> To my New Jerusalem.
>
> CHORUS.
> "Blow, Gabriel! trumpet, blow louder, louder!

An' I hope dat trumpet blow me home
To my New Jerusalem!"

The chorus has a glad, triumphal sound, and in singing it the voice of old Maurice rings out in wonderfully clear, trumpet-like tones. His blindness was caused by a blow on the head from a loaded whip. He was struck by his master in a fit of anger. "I feel great distress when I become blind," said Maurice; "but den I went to seek de Lord; and eber since I know I see in de next world, I always hab great satisfaction." We are told that the master was not a "hard man" except when in a passion, and then he seems to have been very cruel.

One of the women on the place, Old Bess, bears on her limbs many marks of the whip. Some of the scars are three and four inches long. She was used principally as a house-servant. She says, "Ebery time I lay de table I put cow-skin on one end, an' I git beatin' and thumpin' all de time. Hab all kinds o' work to do, and sich a gang [of children] to look after! One person couldn't git along wid so much work, so it go wrong, and den I git beatin'.'"

But the cruelty of Bess's master sinks into insignificance, when compared with the far-famed wickedness of another slave-holder, known all over the island as "Old Joe Eddings." There seem to have been no bounds to his cruelty and licentiousness; and the people tell tales of him which make one shudder. We were once asking some questions about him of an old, half-witted woman, a former slave of his. The look of horror and loathing which overspread her face was perfectly indescribable, as, with upraised hands, she exclaimed, "What! Old Joe Eddings? Lord, Missus, he second to none in de world but de Debil!" She had, indeed, good cause to detest him; for, some years before, her daughter, a young black girl, maddened by his persecutions, had thrown herself into the creek and been drowned, after having been severely beaten for refusing to degrade herself. Outraged, despised, and black, she yet preferred death to dishonor. But these are things too heart-sickening to dwell upon. God alone knows how many hundreds of plantations, all over the South, might furnish a similar record.

Early in June, before the summer heat had become unendurable, we made a pleasant excursion to Edisto Island. We left

St. Helena village in the morning, dined on one of the gun-boats stationed near our island, and in the afternoon proceeded to Edisto in two row-boats. There were six of us, besides an officer and the boats' crews, who were armed with guns and cutlasses. There was no actual danger; but as we were going into the enemy's country, we thought it wisest to guard against surprises. After a delightful row, we reached the island near sunset, landing at a place called Eddingsville, which was a favorite summer resort with the aristocracy of Edisto. It has a fine beach several miles in length. Along the beach there is a row of houses, which must once have been very desirable dwellings, but have now a desolate, dismantled look. The sailors explored the beach for some distance, and returned, reporting "all quiet, and nobody to be seen"; so we walked on, feeling quite safe, stopping here and there to gather the beautiful tiny shells which were buried deep in the sands.

We took supper in a room of one of the deserted houses, using for seats some old bureau-drawers turned edgewise. Afterward we sat on the piazza, watching the lightning playing from a low, black cloud over a sky flushed with sunset, and listening to the merry songs of the sailors who occupied the next house. They had built a large fire, the cheerful glow of which shone through the windows, and we could see them dancing, evidently in great glee. Later, we had another walk on the beach, in the lovely moonlight. It was very quiet then. The deep stillness was broken only by the low, musical murmur of the waves. The moon shone bright and clear over the deserted houses and gardens, and gave them a still wilder and more desolate look.

We went within-doors for the night very unwillingly. Having, of course, no beds, we made ourselves as comfortable as we could on the floor, with boat-cushions, blankets, and shawls. No fear of Rebels disturbed us. There was but one road by which they could get to us, and on that a watch was kept, and in case of their approach, we knew we should have ample time to get to the boats and make our escape. So, despite the mosquitoes, we had a sound night's sleep.

The next morning we took the boats again, and followed the course of the most winding of little creeks. In and out, in and out, the boats went. Sometimes it seemed as if we were going into the very heart of the woods; and through the deep silence we half expected to hear the sound of a Rebel rifle. The banks were overhung with a thick tangle of shrubs and bushes, which threatened to catch our boats, as we passed close beneath their branches. In some places the stream was so narrow that we ran aground, and then the men had to get out, and drag and pull with all their might before we could be got clear again. After a row full of excitement and pleasure, we reached our place of destination,—the Eddings Plantation, whither some of the freedmen had preceded us in their search for corn. It must once have been a beautiful place. The grounds were laid out with great taste, and filled with fine trees, among which we noticed particularly the oleander, laden with deep rose-hued and deliciously fragrant flowers, and the magnolia, with its wonderful, large blossoms, which shone dazzlingly white among the dark leaves. We explored the house,—after it had first been examined by our guard, to see that no foes lurked there,—but found nothing but heaps of rubbish, an old bedstead, and a bathing-tub, of which we afterward made good use. When we returned to the shore, we found that the tide had gone out, and between us and the boats lay a tract of marsh-land, which it would have been impossible to cross without a wetting. The gentlemen determined on wading. But what were we to do? In this dilemma somebody suggested the bathing-tub, a suggestion which was eagerly seized upon. We were placed in it, one at a time, borne aloft in triumph on the shoulders of four stout sailors, and safely deposited in the boat. But, through a mistake, the tub was not sent back for two of the ladies, and they were brought over on the crossed hands of two of the sailors, in the "carry-a-lady-to-London" style. Again we rowed through the windings of the creek, then out into the open sea, among the white, exhilarating breakers,—reached the gun-boat, dined again with its hospitable officers, and then returned to our island, which we reached after nightfall, feeling thoroughly tired, but well pleased with our excursion.

From what we saw of Edisto, however, we did not like it better than our own island,—except, of course, the beach; but we are told that farther in the interior it is much more beautiful. The freed people, who left it at the time of its evacuation, think it the loveliest place in the world, and long to return. When we were going, Miss T.—the much-loved and untiring friend and physician of the people—asked some whom we met if we should give their love to Edisto. "Oh, yes, yes, Miss!" they said. "Ah, Edisto a beautiful city!" And when we came back, they inquired, eagerly,—"How you like Edisto? How Edisto stan'?" Only the fear of again falling into the hands of the "Secesh" prevents them from returning to their much-loved home.

As the summer advanced, the heat became intense. We found it almost overpowering, driving to school near the middle of the day, as we were obliged to do. I gave up riding, and mounted a sulky, such as a single gentleman drives in at the North. It was exceedingly high, and I found it no small task to mount up into it. Its already very comical appearance was enhanced by the addition of a cover of black India-rubber cloth, with which a friend kindly provided me. Thus adorned, it looked like the skeleton of some strange creature surmounted by a huge bonnet, and afforded endless amusement to the soldiers we chanced to meet, who hailed its appearance with shouts of laughter, and cries of "Here comes the Calithumpian!" This unique vehicle, with several others on our island, kindred, but not quite equal to it, would create a decided sensation in the streets of a Northern city.

No description of life on these islands would be complete without a word concerning the fleas. They appeared at the opening of spring, and kept constantly "risin'," as the people said, until they reached a height the possibility of which we had never conceived. We had heard and read of fleas. We had never realized them before. Words utterly fail to describe the tortures we endured for months from these horrible little tyrants. Remembering our sufferings "through weary day and weary night," we warn everybody not gifted with extraordinary powers of endurance to beware of a summer on the Sea Islands.

Notwithstanding the heat, we determined to celebrate the Fourth of July as worthily as we could. The freed people and the children of the different schools assembled in the grove near the Baptist Church. The flag was hung across the road, between two magnificent live-oaks, and the children, being grouped under it, sang "The Star-Spangled Banner" with much spirit. Our good General could not come, but addresses were made by Mr. P.,—the noble-hearted founder of the movement for the benefit of the people here, and from first to last their stanch and much-loved friend,—by Mr. L., a young colored minister, and others. Then the people sang some of their own hymns; and the woods resounded with the grand notes of "Roll, Jordan, roll." They all afterward partook of refreshments, consisting of molasses and water,—a very great luxury to them,—and hardtack.

Among the visitors present was the noble young Colonel Shaw, whose regiment was then stationed on the island. We had met him a few nights before, when he came to our house to witness one of the people's shouts. We looked upon him with the deepest interest. There was something in his face finer, more exquisite, than one often sees in a man's face, yet it was full of courage and decision. The rare and singular charm of his manner drew all hearts to him. He was deeply interested in the singing and appearance of the people. A few days afterwards we saw his regiment on dress-parade, and admired its remarkably fine and manly appearance. After taking supper with the Colonel we sat outside the tent, while some of his men entertained us with excellent singing. Every moment we became more and more charmed with him. How full of life and hope and lofty aspirations he was that night! How eagerly he expressed his wish that they might soon be ordered to Charleston! "I do hope they will give us a chance," he said. It was the desire of his soul that his men should do themselves honor,—that they should prove themselves to an unbelieving world as brave soldiers as though their skins were white. And for himself, he was like the Chevalier of old, "without reproach or fear." After we had mounted our horses and rode away, we seemed still to feel the kind clasp of his hand,—to hear the pleasant, genial tones of his voice, as he bade us good-bye, and hoped that we might meet again. We never saw him afterward. In two short weeks came the terrible massacre at Fort Wagner, and the beautiful head of the young hero and martyr was laid low in the dust. Never shall we forget the heart-sickness with which we heard of his death. We could not realize it at first,—we, who had seen him so lately in all the strength and glory of his young manhood. For days we clung to a vain hope;

then it fell away from us, and we knew that he was gone. We knew that he died gloriously, but still it seemed very hard. Our hearts bled for the mother whom he so loved,—for the young wife, left desolate. And then we said, as we say now,—"God comfort them! He only can." During a few of the sad days which followed the attack on Fort Wagner, I was in one of the hospitals of Beaufort, occupied with the wounded soldiers of the Fifty-Fourth Massachusetts. The first morning was spent in mending the bullet-holes and rents in their clothing. What a story they told! Some of the jackets of the poor fellows were literally cut in pieces. It was pleasant to see the brave, cheerful spirit among them. Some of them were severely wounded, but they uttered no complaint; and in the letters which they dictated to their absent friends there was no word of regret, but the same cheerful tone throughout. They expressed an eager desire to get well, that they might "go at it again." Their attachment to their young colonel was beautiful to see. They felt his death deeply. One and all united in the warmest and most enthusiastic praise of him. He was, indeed, exactly the person to inspire the most loyal devotion in the hearts of his men. And with everything to live for, he had given up his life for them. Heaven's best gifts had been showered upon him, but for them he had laid them all down. I think they truly appreciated the greatness of the sacrifice. May they ever prove worthy of such a leader! Already, they, and the regiments of freedmen here, as well, have shown that true manhood has no limitations of color.

Daily the long-oppressed people of these islands are demonstrating their capacity for improvement in learning and labor. What they have accomplished in one short year exceeds our utmost expectations. Still the sky is dark; but through the darkness we can discern a brighter future. We cannot but feel that the day of final and entire deliverance, so long and often so hopelessly prayed for, has at length begun to dawn upon this much-enduring race. An old freedman said to me one day, "De Lord make me suffer long time, Miss. 'Peared like we nebber was gwine to git troo. But now we's free. He bring us all out right at las'." In their darkest hours they have clung to Him, and we know He will not forsake them.

"The poor among men shall rejoice,
For the terrible one is brought to nought."

While writing these pages I am once more nearing Port
Royal. The Fortunate Isles of Freedom are before me. I shall
again tread the flower-skirted wood-paths of St. Helena, and
the somber pines and bearded oaks shall whisper in the sea-
wind their grave welcome. I shall dwell again among "mine
own people." I shall gather my scholars about me, and see
smiles of greeting break over their dusk faces. My heart sings a
song of thanksgiving, at the thought that even I am permitted
to do something for a long-abused race, and aid in promoting
a higher, holier, and happier life on the Sea Islands.

"Charles Sumner, On Seeing Some Pictures of the Interior of His House" (1874)

SOURCE: *The Dunbar Speaker and Entertainer: Containing
the Best Prose and Poetic Selections by and about
the Negro Race.* Ed. Alice Dunbar-Nelson.
(J. J. Nichols & Co., 1920).

Only the casket left, the jewel gone
Whose noble presence filled these stately rooms,
And made this spot a shrine where pilgrims came—
Stranger and friend—to bend in reverence
Before the great, pure soul that knew no guile;
To listen to the wise and gracious words
That fell from lips whose rare, exquisite smile
Gave tender beauty to the grand, grave face.

Upon these pictured walls we see thy peers,—
Poet, and saint, and sage, painter, and king,—
A glorious band;—they shine upon us still;
Still gleam in marble the enchanting forms
Whereupon thy artist eye delighted dwelt;

Thy favorite Psyche droops her matchless face,
Listening, methinks, for the beloved voice
Which nevermore on earth shall sound her praise.

All these remain,—the beautiful, the brave,
The gifted, silent ones; but thou art gone!
Fair is the world that smiles upon us now;
Blue are the skies of June, balmy the air
That soothes with touches soft the weary brow;
And perfect days glide into perfect nights,—
Moonlit and calm; but still our grateful hearts
Are sad, and faint with fear,—for thou art gone!

Oh friend beloved, with longing, tear-filled eyes
We look up, up to the unclouded blue,
And seek in vain some answering sign from thee.
Look down upon us, guide and cheer us still
From the serene height where thou dwellest now;
Dark is the way without the beacon light
Which long and steadfastly thy hand upheld.
Oh, nerve with courage new the stricken hearts
Whose dearest hopes seem lost in losing thee!
　　　　　　　　　—Charlotte F. Grimké,
　　　　　　　　　Columbia, S.C.,
　　　　　　　　　June 1874.

"The Gathering of the Grand Army" (1890)

SOURCE: *The Life and Writings of the Grimké Family.* Ed.
　Anna Julia Haywood Cooper. N.p. 1951. 2: 25–26.

Through all the city's streets there poured a flood,
　A flood of human souls, eager, intent;
One thought, one purpose stirred the people's blood,
　And through their veins its quickening current sent.

The flags waved gayly in the summer air,
　　O'er patient watchers 'neath the clouded skies;
Old age, and youth, and infancy were there,
　　The glad light shining in expectant eyes.

And when at last our country's saviors came,—
　　In proud procession down the crowded street,
Still brighter burned the patriotic flame,
　　And loud acclaims leaped forth their steps to greet.

And now the veterans scarred and maimed appear,
　　And now the tattered battle-flags uprise;
A silence deep one moment fills the air,
　　Then shout on shout ascends unto the skies.

Oh, brothers, ye have borne the battle strain,
　　And ye have felt it through the ling'ring years;
For all your valiant deeds, your hours of pain,
　　We can but give to you our grateful tears!

And now, with heads bowed low, and tear-filled eyes
　　We see a Silent Army passing slow;
For it no music swells, no shouts arise,
　　But silent blessings from our full hearts flow.

The dead, the living,—All,—a glorious host,
　　A "cloud of witnesses,"—around us press—
Shall we, like them, stand faithful at our post,
　　Or weakly yield, unequal to the stress?

Shall it be said the land they fought to save,
　　Ungrateful now, proves faithless to her trust?
Shall it be said the sons of sires so brave
　　Now trail her sacred banner in the dust?

Ah, no! again shall rise the people's voice
　　As once it rose in accents clear and high—

"Oh, outraged brother, lift your head, rejoice!
   Justice shall reign,—Insult and Wrong shall die!"

So shall this day the joyous promise be
   Of golden days for our fair land in store;
When Freedom's flag shall float above the free,
   And Love and Peace prevail from shore to shore.
                                   —Charlotte F. Grimké,
                                              Boston,
                                   August 12, 1890

JOSEPHINE ST. PIERRE RUFFIN

(1842–1924)

Born into a wealthy, biracial family in Boston, Josephine St. Pierre Ruffin used her relatively privileged position to advocate for racial equality and women's suffrage. Among the organizations that she helped found were the American Women's Suffrage Association, the National Federation of Afro-American Women, the National Association of Colored Women's Clubs, the Women's Era Club, the League of Women for Community Service, and the NAACP. As a writer, Ruffin wrote for the Boston weekly, the *Courant*, and founded *Women's Era*, the first newspaper in the United States published by and for black women. She used her newspaper as a platform to promote an image of black women as members of society, active beyond the confines of the home.

The following pieces speak directly to the disappointment Ruffin felt in the resistance of white Southern women during Reconstruction to recognizing the humanity of African Americans. Why, Ruffin asks, do black southern children still lack access to a quality education? Why do southern women's clubs still forbid blacks from joining? Ruffin refutes white southern women's view of themselves as exemplary, claiming that if southern white women were truly the pinnacles of class they believed themselves to be, they wouldn't need to seek the North's help when racially integrating their society. Ruffin's "An Open Letter to the Educational League of Georgia" (1889) was featured in Alice Moore Dunbar's 1914 anthology, *Masterpieces of Negro Eloquence*.

"Address to the First National Conference of Colored Women" (1895)

SOURCE: Josephine St. Pierre Ruffin, "Address to the First National Conference of Colored Women," *Women's Era* (1895).

It is with especial joy and pride that I welcome you all to this, our first conference. It is only recently that women have waked up to the importance of meeting in council, and great as has been the advantage to women generally, and important as it is and has been that they should confer, the necessity has not been nearly so great, matters at stake not nearly so vital, as that we, bearing peculiar blunders, suffering under especial hardships, enduring peculiar privations, should meet for a "good talk" among ourselves. Although rather hastily called, you as well as I can testify how long and how earnestly a conference has been thought of and hoped for and even prepared for.

These women's clubs, which have sprung up all over the country, built and run upon broad and strong lines, have all been a preparation, small conferences in themselves, and their spontaneous birth and enthusiastic support have been little less than inspiration on the part of our women and a general preparation for a large union such as it is hoped this conference will lead to. Five years ago we had no colored women's club outside of those formed for the special work; to-day, with little over a month's notice, we are able to call representatives from more than twenty clubs. It is a good showing, it stands for much, it shows that we are truly American women, with all the adaptability, readiness to seize and possess our opportunities, willingness to do our part for good as other American women.

The reasons why we should confer are so apparent that it would seem hardly necessary to enumerate them, and yet there is none of them but demand our serious consideration. In the first place we need to feel the cheer and inspiration of meeting each other; we need to gain the courage and fresh life that comes from the mingling of congenial souls, of those working for the same ends. Next we need to talk over not only those things which are of vital importance to us as women, but also the things that are of special interest to us as colored women, the training of our children, openings for boys and girls, how they can be prepared for occupations and occupations may be found or opened for them, what we especially can do in the moral education of the race with which we are identified, our mental elevation and physical development, the home training it is necessary to give our children in order to prepare them to meet the peculiar conditions in which they shall find themselves, how to make the most of our own, to some extent, limited opportunities, these are some of our own peculiar questions to be discussed. Besides these are the general questions of the day, which we cannot afford to be indifferent to: temperance, morality, the higher education, hygiene and domestic questions. If these things need the serious consideration of women more advantageously placed by reason of all the aid to right thinking and living with which they are surrounded, surely we, with everything to pull us back, to hinder us in developing, need to take every opportunity and means for the thoughtful consideration which shall lead to wise action.

I have left the strongest reason for our conferring together until the last. All over America there is to be found a large and growing class of earnest, intelligent, progressive colored women, women who, if not leading full useful lives, are only waiting for the opportunity to do so, many of them warped and cramped for lack of opportunity, not only to do more but to be more; and yet, if an estimate of the colored women of American is called for, the inevitable reply, glibly given is: "For the most past ignorant and immoral, some exceptions, of course, but these don't count." Now for the sake of the thousands of self-sacrificing young women teaching and preaching in lonely southern backwoods for the noble army of mothers who has given birth to these girls, mothers whose intelligence is only limited by their opportunity to get at books, for the sake of the fine cultured women who have carried off the honors in school here and often abroad, for the sake of our own dignity, the dignity of our race and the future good name of our children, it is "mete, right and our bounded duty" to stand forth and declare ourselves and principles, to teach an ignorant and suspicious world that our aims and interests are identical with those of all good aspiring women.

Too long have we been silent under unjust and unholy charges; we cannot expect to have them removed until we disprove them through ourselves. It is not enough to try and disprove unjust charges through individual effort that never goes any further. Year after year southern women have protested against the admission of colored women into any national organization on the ground of the immorality of these women, and because all refutation has only been tried by individual work the charge has never been crushed, as it could and should have been at the first. Now with an army of organized women standing for purity and mental worth, we in ourselves deny the charge and open the eyes of the world to a state of affairs to which they have been blind, often willfully so, and the very fact that the charges, audaciously and flippantly made, as they often are, are of so humiliating and delicate a nature, serves to protect the accuser by driving the helpless accused into mortified silence. It is to break this silence, not by noisy protestations of what we are not, but by a dignified showing of what we are and hope to become that we are impelled to take this step, to make of this gathering an object lesson to the world.

For many and apparent reasons it is especially fitting that the women of the race take the lead in this movement, but for all this we recognize the necessity of the sympathy of our husbands, brothers and fathers. Our women's movement is woman's movement in that it is led and directed by women for the good of women and men, for the benefit of all humanity, which is more than any one branch or section of it. We want, we ask the active interest of our men, and, too, we are not drawing the color line; we are women, American women, as intensely interested in all that pertains to us as such as all other American women: we are not alienating or withdrawing, we are only coming to the front, willing to join any others in the same work and cordially inviting and welcoming any others to join us. If there is any one thing I would especially enjoin upon this conference it is union and earnestness. The questions that are to come before us are of too much import to be weakened by any trivialities or personalities. If any differences arise, let them be quickly settled, with the feeling that we are all workers to the same end, to elevate and dignify colored American womanhood.

This conference will not be what I expect if it does not show the wisdom, indeed the absolute necessity of a national organization of our women. Every year new questions coming up will prove it to us. This hurried, almost informal convention does not begin to meet our needs, it is only a beginning, made here in dear old Boston, where the scales of justice and generosity hang evenly balanced, and where the people "dare be true" to their best instincts and stand ready to lend aid and sympathy to worthy strugglers. It is hoped and believed that from this will spring an organization that will in truth bring in a new era to the colored women of America.

"An Open Letter to the Educational League of Georgia" (1889)

SOURCE: Josephine St. Pierre Ruffin, "An Open Letter to the Educational League of Georgia (1889)," in *Masterpieces of Negro Eloquence*. Ed. Alice Moore Dunbar (New York: The Bookery Publishing Company, 1914), 173–177.

Ladies of the Georgia Educational League:

The telegram which you sent to Governor Northen to read to his audience, informing the people of the North of your willingness to undertake the moral training of the colored children of Georgia, merits more than a passing notice. It is the first time, we believe, in the history of the South where a body of representative Southern white women have shown such interest in the moral welfare of the children of their former slaves as to be willing to undertake to make them more worthy the duties and responsibilities of citizenship. True, there have been individual cases where courageous women have felt their moral responsibility, and have nobly met it, but one of the saddest things about the sad condition of affairs in the South has been the utter indifference which Southern women, who were guarded with unheard of fidelity during the war, have manifested to the mental and moral welfare of the children of their faithful slaves, who, in the language of Henry Grady, placed a black mass of loyalty between them and dishonor. This was a rare opportunity for you to have shown your gratitude to your slaves and your interest in their future welfare.

The children would have grown up in utter ignorance had not the North sent thousands of her noblest daughters to the South on this mission of heroic love and mercy; and it is worthy of remark of those fair daughters of the North, that, often eating with Negroes, and in the earlier days sleeping in their humble cabins, and always surrounded by thousands of them, there is not one recorded instance where one has been the victim of violence or insult. If because of the bitterness of your feelings, of your deep poverty at the close of the war, conditions were such that you could not do this work yourselves, you might have give a Christian's welcome to the women who came a thousand miles to do the work, that, in all gratitude and obligation belonged to you,—but instead, these women were often persecuted, always they have been ruthlessly ostracised, even until this day; often they were lonely, often longed for a word of sympathy, often craved association with their own race, but for thirty years they have been treated by the Christian white women of the South,—simply because they were doing your work,—the work committed to you by your Saviour, when he said, "Inasmuch as you did it to one of the least of these my brethren, you did it unto me,"—with a contempt that would serve to justify a suspicion that instead of being the most cultured women, the purest, bravest missionaries in America, they were outcasts and lepers.

But at last a change has come. And so you have "decided to take up the work of moral and industrial training of the Negroes," as you "have been doing this work among the whites with splendid results." This is one of the most hopeful stars that have shot through the darkness of the Southern sky. What untold blessings might not the educated Christian women of the

South prove to the Negro groping blindly in the darkness of the swamps and bogs of prejudice for a highway out of servitude, oppression, ignorance, and immorality!

• • •

The leading women of Georgia should not ask Northern charity to do what they certainly must have the means for making a beginning of themselves. If your heart is really in this work—and we do not question it—the very best way for you to atone for your negligence in the past is to make a start yourselves. Surely if the conditions are as serious as you represent them to be, your husbands, who are men of large means, who are able to run great expositions and big peace celebrations, will be willing to provide you with the means to protect your virtue and that of your daughters by the moral training you propose to give in the kindergartens.

There is much you might do without the contribution of a dollar from any pocket, Northern or Southern. On every plantation there are scores, if not hundreds, of little colored children who could be gathered about you on a Sabbath afternoon and given many helpful inspiring lessons in morals and good conduct.

• • •

It is a good augury of better days, let us hope, when the intelligent, broad-minded women of Georgia, spurning the incendiary advice of that human firebrand who would lynch a thousand Negroes a month, are willing to join in this great altruistic movement of the age and endeavor to lift up the degraded and ignorant, rather than to exterminate them. Your proposition implies that they may be uplifted and further, imports a tacit confession that if you had done your duty to them at the close of the war, which both gratitude and prudence should have prompted you to do, you would not now be confronted with a condition which you feel it necessary to check, in obedience to the great first law of nature—self-protection. If you enter upon this work you will doubtless be criticised by a class of your own people who think you are lowering your own dignity, but the

South has suffered too much already from that kind of false pride to let it longer keep her recreant to the spirit of the age.

If, when you have entered upon it, you need the co-operation, either by advice or other assistance, of the colored women of the North, we beg to assure you that they will not be lacking,— until then, the earnest hope goes out that you will bravely face and sternly conquer your former prejudices and quickly undertake this missionary work which belongs to you.

20

EDMONIA GOODELLE HIGHGATE

(1844–1870)

Born and raised in Syracuse, New York, Edmonia Goodelle Highgate spent most of her short life traveling throughout the South with her sister, Caroline. Their father, a barber, died when Edmonia and Caroline were in their teens. At Syracuse High School, Edmonia graduated with honors and received a teaching certificate. She started work at a black school in Montrose, Pennsylvania, the only job available to her at the time; from there she moved to a larger school in Binghamton, New York. In 1863, energized by the American Missionary Society's effort to set up makeshift schools for emancipated and fugitive slaves, Edmonia asked to take part in the effort to educate freedmen. While teaching in the South, both Edmonia and Caroline became romantically attached to white men who abandoned them. Edmonia died after a botched abortion; Caroline struggled alone, raising six children.

The following four pieces, all originally published in 1865 and 1866 in the *Christian Recorder*, give the reader a sense of the enthusiasm Highgate had for her work. She pours herself into her writing before sprinting off to partake in the next task ("Oh! It is time for my night school."). The black press as a whole was optimistic during Reconstruction. Her pieces are enthusiastic rallying cries for self-improvement, educational equality, and a vision of the United States in which possibilities were open to all.

"A Spring Day Up the James" (1865)

SOURCE: Edmonia Goodelle Highgate, "A Spring Day Up
the James," *Christian Recorder*, May 27, 1865.

DEAR RECORDER:—Bright, joyous April, yet tearful enough to
be in sympathy with the national sorrow, will ever be memorable
to your scribbler. The recent trophies and grand victories placed
us in the king's gallery of delightful enthusiasm; but to how many,
many hearts, they brought mourning in their train, because of the
sacrifice of the first born or dearest one? How many mothers,
wives and sisters read telegrams or letters saying: "He fell on the
field making a desperate charge," or, "terribly wounded in five
places!" "Oh, Christ of the seven wounds, comfort the hearts of
the national mothers whose sons die with faces turned away, and
no last word to say!" Our pangs in this freedom birth of America
are agonizing, yet we rejoice, for the cost endears the end.

Reader, did you ever go to the front to search for your beloved
wounded? If you have, you can sympathize, if not, you can learn
how trying it is to spend long hours on government transports,
moving slowly and lazily along. Then after you have got within
five hours' sail of some desired place, to be ordered back to Point
Lookout, or somewhere else to be overhauled? Or worse, to be
detained by such examination as to have to wait a day and night
in such agony that two nights come together, then to miss entirely what you hoped to gain, and then looking vainly upward
to see the hand of God in these delays.

We started up the James on a half-fare ticket, owing to the
kindness of that most Christ-like body, the "Christian Commission," with several delegates, whose kind attention tended to as-
suage the grief that burdened our heart. A young lady, unattended,
going to the front is something unusual, but still she is protected
on her sad mission by the better part in the hearts of the roughest.

We anchored first at Newport News, very important in the
first days of the war. Then at Grove's landing. Again we paused
as if by consent at Jamestown, so famous in the history of American Slavery, which is a most miserable, unimportant dilapidated
little town, but ever notable as being the birth-place of the

monster which has swallowed our brothers, ay! and spoiled our maidens, and beaten our mothers, robbed and killed their babes. Thank God for the privilege of telling it! Next we moored our bark at Fort Powhattan, a name interwoven with the romantic legendary of Virginia. Then at Harrison's Landing, where diminutive Mac found a retreat. Again we stop, and find ourselves at Wilson's Wharf, where one black regiment defeated the chivalry under Fitz Hugh Lee. After nine hours' ride we reached City Point, or rather, the city of tents and hospitals, cheering members of the Christian Commission bade us welcome, and gave us some refreshments. Then we walked on for over a mile, looking for the Fifth Corps hospital, fear and hope in conflict at every step. At last we looked into the schooled face and calm eyes of a delegate who visited the corps and knew the whole story that we wanted to hear. There in the darkness of that night, the rain pouring down in torrents, we searched with great patience clerks, hospital records with a very reasonable amount of "red tape." Oh, how they hated to say that "your brother died of his wounds two weeks ago." But we felt it to be the truth, and their pale lips confirmed it. We then knew how sublime a thought it is to suffer and be strong.

So feelingly they led us back to a rough tent, where three other women were lamenting similar losses. With a soldier's blanket about us we stretched upon a board to watch through the long, long, weary night. Two of these women were southerners who grumbled about being out of the union, yet grew livid because their husband's property had been taken from them. Who knew that they might be true to their confederate instincts, and attempt our lives! One sweet young wife smiling so pleasantly—and with kindly hands she tried to comfort us— was on her way to the front to find her husband, who she said was sounded, little dreaming of the real truth.

Next morning we sat down with about fifty noble representatives of the Christian Commission to a rude fare, but our masticating powers were paralyzed with grief, and refused to do their work. Then we went in an ambulance to follow the body of our hero. His comrades in the fight and playmates from his youth up, have sent his body home to his mother.

We left those kind friends who had wept with us for our bereavement, and as we together listened to the groans of the dying, martial-music sounded in the distant, which heralded the
execution of some convalescent rebel, who rewarded the Gov-
ernmental nursing by tearing up a portion of the Railroad.
There was a large concourse of southern female friends on the
boat back to Fortress Monroe, who sneered at the Yankee flag,
while receiving favors from the very source which they spurned
in their apologies for souls. Would that every confederate
female could be turned, lest they meet eternal retribution.

Waiting for the transport to B. Oh! God, thou art past finding on tin the afflictions with which thou visitest on thy children. Waiting, weeping, hoping, yet,

> "I praise Thee while my days go on,
> I love Thee while my days go on,
> Through dark and death, through fire and frost,
> With emptied arms and treasures lost,
> I thank Thee while my days go on."

"Rainy-Day Ink Drops" (1865)

SOURCE: Edmonia Goodelle Highgate, "Rainy-Day Ink
Drops," *Christian Recorder*, September 30, 1865.

A debit and credit side you will find all through nature and life.
They do pay,—perhaps not the price we put upon them, but
undoubtedly all they are worth. If man can't wring compensation out of snarled matters, God can.

Didn't it pay England, even though Charles the First was so
bad, that she had to behead him, to have him for her king, when,
if she had had a better man, the English people never would have
got the degree of liberty which they now enjoy. Didn't it pay
England, in 1216, to have the imbecile John for her monarch, for

if a better man had ruled the British Isles, would they have obtained the Habeas Corpus Act, which was to the Magna Charta, as the marriage certificate is to the betrothal ring?

Didn't it pay to have McClellan, Scott, and Halleck make the war drag its slow length along when it gave us the assurance that four millions of our race are forever free, even though they have not yet the right of suffrage—the safeguard of liberty? Don't it pay to humble the South and secure something like a balance of power in this country, even at the cost of millions of dollars and streams of blood? Don't it pay to make soldiers of slaves—to teach chattels the sublime act of taking life scientifically, and the sublimer one of reading and writing. I tell you, it does.

But I am afraid it will appear not to pay, if the wives and daughters of our colored soldiers, who can't read, do not know as much as these blue-coated ones, when they come marching home. This inequality, which too often exists in the domestic circle, will be the ten percentage some families must pay, if our sisters,—fond women though they have been,—don't embrace every opportunity to be equal, in that respect, to their returned or returning soldiers husbands. It don't pay to get some one to write your letters in the long run. Our nice, trim, blue coat, who learned so much from some camp teacher or chaplain, won't be content to remain at home at nights, after the first flush of joy is over, unless his home is neat and attractive. Don't it pay to dress to please a pair of brown or black masculine eyes? Maybe a clean collar and a nicely combed head don't inspire the right sort of pride, but you will find they pay. Don't it pay to love prayerfully and steadily one who is almost entirely lost to you? I tell you a woman who grasps tight hold of the Savior, and goes nobly, blamelessly, on her quiet way, can save a man, if he be a man. If not, she can inspire to noble deeds, mere masculine clay. It pays to love a bad, faithless husband, with a reforming love. It pays to bear and forbear with a good husband. Mothers, it pays to work your fingers off to educate that bright-eyed, high-browed boy or that sweet, thoughtful girl. It will pay when you are in the grave. It will pay you, teacher, to study the nature of that wayward pupil. It will always pay to be true to yourself and every body else.

There is no humbug about that "casting your bread upon the

waters." You will gather it up some day, ten loaves for one. Bright smiles pay—they may be benedictions. Kind words pay,—"they never die." It pays to get a good article, if you have to pay more for it than a cheap one. It pays to trust God in the human or in the abstract. "Trust is truer than our fears," sings Whittier, and he has got the right tune. It pays to work off, mentally or physically, the blues. The rain has ceased to fall.

Louisville, Sept. 1st, 1865.

"Neglected Opportunities" (1866)

SOURCE: Edmonia Goodelle Highgate, "Neglected Opportunities," *Christian Recorder,* July 14, 1866.

In the sober light of reason, one is often led to wonder what punishment the great Dealer of justice has in store for that class of persons who have amber-hued opportunities, and never develop in their lives—a purpose—never make themselves felt in their own State, County, town, village or ward.

Some girls and boys at twenty-two or five,—good-rate, graduate from an academic course, possibly before thirty, from a collegiate course—come out into the earnest, hard-working world of realities, without ever feeling that they have a role to enact. Without realizing that their advantages have made them liable to be the grand starter in some move that could draw thousands with them. Too many males and females, with an ambition equal to Caesar's, or Napoleon's, or Margaret Fuller's, or Frederick Douglass's, never make any thing of themselves. Do not even become energetic tradesmen. Why is it? Some of our elaborately educated young men dash all their energy upon some love-sick penchant for some imperious, handsome-faced, brainless girl, who for want of other avenues, uses efforts at passing cupid darts through their gizzards. Excuse me, "embryo hearts" I meant. Some of our men that might have been good physicians, lawyers, orators, professors and essayists,

have been lost to the higher cause of literature or sacred manhood, by this dashing against Charybdis. Too many friends spoil
this, and give abortive developments of their own personal ruin.
A rich father has made too many earth-encumbering sons, or
useless lady shadows.

All things alternately will be tried by the test of ability, and I
would not have it otherwise. It is more than a fancy that many of
these people, who have been like good gardens, which contain
weeds and nothing else, all their fifty or sixty years of earth—
death will have exquisite tantales hereafter in punishment for
lost opportunities. A real man or woman makes circumstances
and controls them. They be deterred from doing what duty calls
them to! Never! They control their destiny and observe every
weaker mind within the square of the distance. I find it easier to
coalesce with a person who has been guilty of ennui, and whose
lives are proof of their repentance, than these good-for-nothing
aspirants! Any thing which you young pump-strutters earnestly
wish to be, you can be. God gives every key to a sober demander.
All that you ought to be, pretty beau-catcher wearer, you can be,
if you have to wait till you are thirty-five to attain your goal, and
do without Mr. Exquisite for your partner in an aimless non-
existence. I hate a weak man or woman. I fling them from me as
I do half-drowned, clinging cats. Yet no one sooner than I would
be a strong friend to one who has determined to reform—to be
definitely something.

I don't believe in world-saving—but I do in self-making—
No—I am no shining light; but I have a reverence for a real every-
inch-man, or a whole woman, who earnestly is a definite
something besides a fawning husband—liver and corset lacer,
and liver and dier by this eternal "style." Come out into the glory
of God's world of functions and uses—Create something. Aspire
to leave something immortal behind you. That's the life test at
last. The monument you leave—I don't mean granite or marble—
but something that will stand the corruption of the ages. A principle well developed will in science or ethics—A cause will—An
immortal healthy soul. Ah! the gods would any of these! Have I
said too much? Is it inelegant? Does it not breath balm of a thousand flowers? Opopinax, excuse me,—but I never wear perfumed

kids, especially when I have to touch wads. Up! work, make something out of yourself, even if it is like getting blood from a turnip. Try! The race needs living, working demonstrations—the world does. Young man, the master in world-reconstruction has called; is calling, but will not enact, for you and your sister.

New Orleans, June 21st.

"On Horse Back—Saddle Dash, No. 1" (1866)

SOURCE: Edmonia Goodelle Highgate, "On Horse Back—
Saddle Dash, No. 1," *Christian Recorder*,
November 3, 1866.

Who that has taught school, the elementary branches year in and year out, don't know what teacher's *ennui* is? I always thought I did, but find that I have just found out. Here I am in the western interior of Louisiana trying with my might to instruct these very French, little and large Creoles, in the simplest English, and in morals. But for my roan, I would break down as a harp unstrung; but as soon as day-school is out I am on his back, and off on a quick gallop for these grand old October woods. I took my first ride of six miles to a famous old spring, at which the rebel General Morton drank with his wretchedly demoralized command in their retreat after the battle of Shiloh. My horse, like everything else here, was Creole, and I am afraid rather *confederate* in his tendencies; for when I was feeling lost, almost to my surroundings in some meditations of an intensely union cast, he had the bad taste to get into a fence leaping mood. Of course I conquered, and made myself mistress of the situation. Then I plunged into the thickest of the oak tree forest with its exquisite drapery of array hanging moss. The old dame must have anticipated some children visitors, for she had swings ready made, formed of the thick inter-lapping vine-like branches, reaching from treetop to treetop all through these woods. What delightful order! Oh, if dear Henry D. Thoreau were here, wouldn't he go into a rhapsody! But he is here in spirit.

Natures admiring children, who perseveringly labor to know her secrets while in earth form, only learn more after they "cross the river Jordan," and they hover around beautiful retreats. Yes, they are "ministering spirits." Then don't imagine me a modern spiritualist after the "affinity-seeking," "wife and husband leaving" strife. No, I detest "table rapping's and crockery breaking," especially the last; for I have broken so much. But those who are of the same mind do coalesce whether in the spirit or out. Oh, what a cluster of scarlet blossoms! All negroes like red; so pash on, pony, I must have those flowers! How I wish my Philadelphia friends had these! Why they are handsomer than either "fuchsia's or bleeding heart." But I have left my botany in the city; so I can't trace their genera.

Oh, how independent one feels in the saddle! One thing, I can't imagine why one needs to wear such long riding skirts. They are so inconvenient when you have to ford streams or dash through briers. Oh, fashion, will no Emancipation Proclamation free us from thee!

My . . .

Now for the matter in this saddle-dash. I had to keep off horse back several days in order to recover from extreme fatigue and soreness, but my bay is at the door this glorious Saturday morning, and I am off till noon. Some rebel equestrians just passed, and fired four times almost in my face. But who is going to let grape keep them off horse back or off duty? Hasn't He promised to keep His workers? "Then to doubt would be disloyal; to falter would be sin."

Oh! I forgot to say my roan did not understand English any better than my scholars do. When I said, "Whoa, pony," he would gallop.

Au revoir.

I am home again from my canter. We passed through several cotton and cornfields worked on shares. The former owners are giving half what the crops yield to the hands in payment. Besides, there is five per cent tax levied to pay for the school privilege for the children of the hands. These men work well. Their employers say; "better than slaves did." But they work all day Sunday of their own accord on land they have rented; so anxious are they to get places of their own. Cotton is worth from 40 to 50 cents per pound here. One would soon get rich with one of these plantations. Oh! It is time for my night school. Believe me, *Vetre Amie des Chevauz.*

Oct. 13th, Vermillionville, Lafayette Parish, La.

MEMOIRS:
LOOKING BACK

21

JULIA A. J. FOOTE

(1823–1900)

Julia A. J. Foote was the first female to be ordained as a deacon in the African Methodist Episcopal Zion Church. She grew up in upstate New York, the daughter of former slaves. At the age of sixteen she married George Foote, and she spent the entirety of her adult life traveling and preaching. Though her race and gender made it initially hard for her to gain a following, she eventually grew popular among both black and white audiences. Her autobiography, *A Brand Plucked from the Fire* (1879), is excerpted on the following pages. Foote died in 1900 and was buried in Cypress Hill Cemetery in Brooklyn, New York.

The first two chapters excerpted here contain stories from Foote's childhood, including a near poisoning at age five and the execution of a teacher. The second two chapters describe the challenges Foote faced as a woman fighting for her dignity and reputation, while insisting on her right to preach. She fights to reconcile her devotion to Christianity with the relentless opposition to her desire to preach.

Selections from *A Brand Plucked from the Fire* (1879)

SOURCE: Julia A. J. Foote, *A Brand Plucked from the Fire* (Cleveland, OH: Printed for the Author by Lauer and Yost, 1879).

CHAPTER I.

Birth and Parentage

I was born in 1828, in Schenectady, N.Y. I was my mother's fourth child. My father was born free, but was stolen, when a child, and enslaved. My mother was born a slave, in the State of New York. She had one very cruel master and mistress. This man, whom she was obliged to call master, tied her up and whipped her because she refused to submit herself to him, and reported his conduct to her mistress. After the whipping, he himself washed her quivering back with strong salt water: At the expiration of a week she was sent to change her clothing, which stuck fast to her back. Her mistress, seeing that she could not remove it, took hold of the rough tow-linen under-garment and pulled it off over her head with a jerk, which took the skin with it, leaving her back all raw and sore.

This cruel master soon sold my mother, and she passed from one person's hands to another's, until she found a comparatively kind master and mistress in Mr. and Mrs. Cheeseman, who kept a public house.

My father endured many hardships in slavery, the worst of which was his constant exposure to all sorts of weather. There being no railroads at that time, all goods and merchandise were moved from place to place with teams, one of which my father drove.

My father bought himself, and then his wife and their first child, at that time an infant. That infant is now a woman, more than seventy years old, and an invalid, dependent upon the bounty of her poor relatives.

I remember hearing my parents tell what first led them to think seriously of their sinful course. One night, as they were on their way home from a dance, they came to a stream of water, which, owing to rain the night previous, had risen and carried away the log crossing. In their endeavor to ford the stream, my mother made a misstep, and came very nearly being drowned, with her babe in her arms. This nearly fatal accident made such an impression upon their minds that they said, "We'll go to no more dances;" and they kept their word. Soon after, they made a public profession of religion and united with the M.E. Church.

They were not treated as Christian believers, but as poor lepers. They were obliged to occupy certain seats in one corner of the gallery, and dared not come down to partake of the Holy Communion until the last white communicant had left the table.

One day my mother and another colored sister waited until all the white people had, as they thought, been served, when they started for the communion table. Just as they reached the lower door, two of the poorer class of white folks arose to go to the table. At this, a mother in Israel caught hold of my mother's dress and said to her, "Don't you know better than to go to the table when white folks are there?" Ah! she did know better than to do such a thing purposely.

This was one of the fruits of slavery. Although professing to love the same God, members of the same church, and expecting to find the same heaven at last, they could not partake of the Lord's Supper until the lowest of the whites had been served. Were they led by the Holy Spirit? Who shall say? The Spirit of Truth can never be mistaken, nor can he inspire anything unholy. How many at the present day profess great spirituality, and even holiness, and yet are deluded by a spirit of error, which leads them to say to the poor and the colored ones among them, "Stand back a little—I am holier than thou."

My parents continued to attend to the ordinances of God as instructed, but knew little of the power of Christ to save; for their spiritual guides were as blind as those they led.

It was the custom, at that time, for all to drink freely of wine, brandy and gin. I can remember when it was customary at funerals, as well as at weddings, to pass around the decanter and glasses, and sometimes it happened that the pall-bearers could scarcely move out with the coffin. When not handed round, one after another would go to the closet and drink as much as they chose of the liquors they were sure to find there. The officiating clergyman would imbibe as freely as any one. My parents kept liquor in the house constantly, and every morning sling was made, and the children were given the bottom of the cup, where the sugar and a little of the liquor was left, on purpose for them. It is no wonder, is it, that every one of my mother's children loved the taste of liquor?

One day, when I was but five years of age, I found the blue chest, where the black bottle was kept, unlocked—an unusual thing. Raising the lid, I took the bottle, put it to my mouth, and drained it to the bottom. Soon after, the rest of the children becoming frightened at my actions, ran and told aunt Giney—an old colored lady living in a part of our house—who sent at once for my mother, who was away working. She came in great haste, and at once pronounced me DRUNK. And so I was—stupidly drunk. They walked with me, and blew tobacco smoke into my face, to bring me to. Sickness almost unto death followed, but my life was spared. I was like a "brand plucked from the burning."

Dear reader, have you innocent children, given you from the hand of God? Children, whose purity rouses all that is holy and good in your nature? Do not, I pray, give to these little ones of God the accursed cup which will send them down to misery and death. Listen to the voice of conscience, the woes of the drunkard, the wailing of poverty-stricken women and children, and touch not the accursed cup. From Sinai come the awful words of Jehovah, "No drunkard shall inherit the kingdom of heaven."

CHAPTER IV.

My Teacher Hung for Crime

My great anxiety to read the Testament caused me to learn to spell quite rapidly, and I was just commencing to read when a great calamity came upon us. Our teacher's name was John Van Paten. He was keeping company with a young lady, who repeated to him a remark made by a lady friend of hers, to the effect that John Van Paten was not very smart, and she didn't see why this young lady should wish to marry him. He became very angry, and, armed with a shotgun, proceeded to the lady's house, and shot her dead. She fell, surrounded by her five weeping children. He then started for town, to give himself up to the authorities. On the way he met the woman's husband and told him what he had done. The poor husband found, on reaching home, that John's words were but too true; his wife had died almost instantly.

After the funeral, the bereaved man went to the prison and talked with John and prayed for his conversion until his prayers were answered, and John Van Paten, the murderer, professed faith in Christ.

Finally the day came for the condemned to be publicly hung (they did not plead emotional insanity in those days). Everybody went to the execution, and I with the rest. Such a sight!

Never shall I forget the execution of my first school-teacher. On the scaffold he made a speech, which I cannot remember, only that he said he was happy, and ready to die. He sang a hymn, the chorus of which was,

> "I am bound for the kingdom;
> Will you go to glory with me?"

clasping his hands, and rejoicing all the while.

The remembrance of this scene left such an impression upon my mind that I could not sleep for many a night. As soon as I fell into a doze, I could see my teacher's head tumbling about the room as fast as it could go; I would waken with a scream, and could not be quieted until some one came and staid with me.

Never since that day have I heard of a person being hung, but a shudder runs through my whole frame, and a trembling seizes me. Oh, what a barbarous thing is the taking of human life, even though it be "a life for a life," as many believe God commands. That was the old dispensation. Jesus said: "A new commandment I give unto you, that ye love one another." Again: "Resist not evil; but whosoever shall smite thee on thy right cheek, turn to him the other also." Living as we do in the Gospel dispensation, may God help us to follow the precepts and example of Him, who, when he was reviled, reviled not again, and in the agony of death prayed: "Father, forgive them, for they know not what they do." Christian men, vote as you pray, that the legalized traffic in ardent spirits may be abolished, and God grant that capital punishment may be banished from our land.

CHAPTER XIX.

Public Effort—Excommunication

From this time the opposition to my life work commenced, instigated by the minister, Mr. Beman.

Many in the church were anxious to have me preach in the hall, where our meetings were held at that time, and were not a little astonished at the minister's cool treatment of me. At length two of the trustees got some of the elder sisters to call on the minister and ask him to let me preach. His answer was: "No; she can't preach her holiness stuff here, and I am astonished that you should ask it of me." The sisters said he seemed to be in quite a rage, although he said he was not angry.

There being no meeting of the society on Monday evening, a brother in the church opened his house to me, that I might preach, which displeased Mr. Beman very much. He appointed a committee to wait upon the brother and sister who had opened their doors to me, to tell them they must not allow any more meetings of that kind, and that they must abide by the rules of the church, making them believe they would be excommunicated if they disobeyed him. I happened to be present at this interview, and the committee remonstrated with me for the course I had taken. I told them my business was with the Lord, and wherever I found a door opened intended to go in and work for my Master.

There was another meeting appointed at the same place, which I, of course, attended; after which the meetings were stopped for that time, though I held many more there after these people had withdrawn from Mr. Beman's church.

I then held meetings in my own house; whereas the minister told the members that if they attended them he would deal with them, for they were breaking the rules of the church. When he found that I continued the meetings, and that the Lord was blessing my feeble efforts, he sent a committee of two to ask me if I considered myself a member of his church. I told them I did, and should continue to do so until I had done something worthy of dismemberment.

At this, Mr. Beman sent another committee with a note, asking me to meet him with the committee, which I did. He asked me a number of questions, nearly all of which I have forgotten.

One, however, I do remember: he asked if I was willing to comply with the rules of the discipline. To this I answered: "Not if the discipline prohibits me from doing what God has bidden me to do; I fear God more than man." Similar questions were asked and answered in the same manner. The committee said what they wished to say, and then told me I could go home. When I reached the door, I turned and said: "I now shake off the dust of my feet as a witness against you. See to it that this meeting does not rise in judgment against you."

The next evening, one of the committee came to me and told me that I was no longer a member of the church, because I had violated the rules of the discipline by preaching.

When this action became known, the people wondered how any one could be excommunicated for trying to do good. I did not say much, and my friends simply said I had done nothing but hold meetings. Others, anxious to know the particulars, asked the minister what the trouble was. He told them he had given me the privilege of speaking or preaching as long as I chose, but that he could not give me the right to use the pulpit, and that I was not satisfied with any other place. Also, that I had appointed meeting on the evening of his meetings, which was a thing no member had a right to do. For these reasons he said he had turned me out of the church.

Now, if the people who repeated this to me told the truth— and I have no doubt but they did—Mr. Beman told an actual falsehood. I had never asked for his pulpit, but had told him and others, repeatedly, that I did not care where I stood—any corner of the hall would do. To which Mr. Beman had answered: "You cannot have any place in the hall." Then I said: "I'll preach in a private house." He answered me: "No, not in this place; I am stationed over all Boston." He was determined I should not preach in the city of Boston. To cover up his deceptive, unrighteous course toward me, he told the above falsehoods.

From his statements, many erroneous stories concerning me gained credence with a large number of people. At that time, I thought it my duty as well as privilege to address a letter to the

Conference, which I took to them in person, stating all the facts. At the same time I told them it was not in the power of Mr. Beman, or any one else, to truthfully bring anything against my moral or religious character—that my only offense was in trying to preach the Gospel of Christ—and that I cherished no ill feelings toward Mr. Beman or anyone else, but that I desired the Conference to give the case an impartial hearing, and then give me a written statement expressive of their opinion. I also said I considered myself a member of the Conference, and should do so until they said I was not, and gave me their reasons, that I might let the world know what my offense had been.

My letter was slightingly noticed, and then thrown under the table. Why should they notice it? It was only the grievance of a woman, and there was no justice meted out to women in those days. Even ministers of Christ did not feel that women had any rights which they were bound to respect.

CHAPTER XXII.

A Visit to My Parents—Further Labors

Some of the dear sisters accompanied me to Flatbush, where I assisted in a bush meeting. The Lord met the people in great power, and I doubt not there are many souls in glory to-day praising God for that meeting.

From that place I went home to my father's house in Binghamton, N.Y. They were filled with joy to have me with them once more, after an absence of six years. As my mother embraced me, she exclaimed: "So you are a preacher, are you?" I replied: "So they say." "Well, Julia," said she, "when I first heard that you were a preacher, I said that I would rather hear you were dead." These words, coming so unexpectedly from my mother, filled me with anguish. Was I to meet opposition here, too? But my mother, with streaming eyes, continued: "My dear daughter, it is all past now. I have heard from those who have attended your meetings what the Lord has done for you, and I am satisfied."

My stay in Binghamton was protracted several months. I held meetings in and around the town, to the acceptance of the people, and, I trust, to the glory of God. I felt perfectly satisfied, when the time came for me to leave, that my work was all for the Lord, and my soul was filled with joy and thankfulness for salvation. Before leaving, my parents decided to move to Boston, which they did soon after.

I left Binghamton the first of February, 1855, in company with the Rev. Henry Johnson and his wife, for Ithaca, N.Y., where I labored a short time. I met with some opposition from one of the A.M.E. Church trustees. He said a woman should not preach in the church. Beloved, the God we serve fights all our battles, and before I left the place that trustee was one of the most faithful at my meetings, and was very kind to assist me on my journey when I left Ithaca. I stopped one night at Owego, at Brother Loyd's and I also stopped for a short time at Onondaga, returned to Ithaca on the 14th of February, and staid until the 7th of March, during which time the work of grace was greatly revived. Some believed and entered into the rest of full salvation, many were converted, and a number of backsliders were reclaimed. I held prayer meetings from house to house. The sisters formed a woman's prayer-meeting, and the whole church seemed to be working in unison for Christ.

March 7th I took the stage for Geneva, and, arriving late at night, went to a hotel. In the morning Brother Rosel Jeffrey took me to his house and left me with his wife. He was a zealous Christian, but she scoffed at religion, and laughed and made sport during family worship. I do not know, but hope that long ere this she has ceased to ridicule the cause or the followers of Christ. In the latter part of the day Brother Condell came and invited me to his house. I found his wife a pleasant Christian woman. Sabbath afternoon I held a meeting in Brother Condell's house. The colored people had a church which the whites had given them. It was a union church, to be occupied on alternate Sundays by the Methodists and Baptists.

According to arrangement, this Sunday evening was the time for the Methodists to occupy the church. The Rev. Dawsey, of Canandaigua, came to fill his appointment, but, when we arrived at the church, the Baptist minister, William Monroe, objected to our holding a meeting in the house that evening, and his members joined with him in his unchristian course. Rather than have any trouble, we returned to Brother Condell's house. The minister preached and I followed with a short exhortation. The Lord was present to bless. They made an appointment for me to preach at the union meeting-house on the following Tuesday evening.

Monday evening I went with some of the sisters to the church, where there was a meeting for the purpose of forming a moral reform society.

After the meeting, Brother Condell asked the trustees if they had any objection to having me speak in the church the next evening. To this, Minister Monroe and another man—I had almost said a fiend in human shape—answered that they did not believe in women's preaching, and would not admit one in the church, striving hard to justify themselves from the Bible, which one of them held in his unholy hands.

I arose to speak, when Mr. Monroe interrupted me. After a few words I left the house.

The next afternoon, while taking tea at the house of one of the sisters, Minister Monroe came in to tell me he heard that our brethren had said they would have the church for me if they had to "shed blood." He asked me if I wanted to have anything to do with a fight of that kind. I replied: "The weapons with which I fight are not carnal, and, if I go to a place and am invited to use the weapons God has given me, I must use them to his glory."

"Well," said he, "I shall be in the pulpit at an early hour, and will not leave it though they break my head."

"Mr. Monroe," said I, "God can take you from the pulpit without breaking your head." At this he became very much excited, and raved as if he were a madman. For two hours he walked the floor, talking and reading all the time. I made him no reply and tried not to notice him, and finally he left me.

At the proper time we went to the church. It was full, but everything was in confusion. Mr. Monroe was in the pulpit. I saw at once that God could not be glorified in the midst of such a pandemonium; so I withdrew at once. I was told they kept up the contention until after ten o'clock. Mr. Monroe tried hard to get our trustees to state I should not preach in the place, but they would give him no such promise.

As I was obliged to leave in a few days, to meet other appointments, our men procured a large house, where I held a meeting the next evening. All that attended were quiet and orderly; one man arose for prayers.

Dear sisters, who are in the evangelistic work now, you may think you have hard times; but let me tell you, I feel that the lion and lamb are lying down together, as compared with the state of things twenty-five or thirty years ago. Yes, yes; our God is marching on. Glory to his name!

JARENA LEE

(1783–1855)

Most of what is known about Jarena Lee's life is gleaned from her autobiographical account, *The Life and Religious Experience of Jarena Lee* (1836), and an expanded version, *Religious Experience and Journal of Mrs. Jarena Lee,* (1849). Lee tells of being born to free black parents in Cape May, New Jersey, in 1783 but sent out to work at age seven. She describes her struggles with sin, a conversion in 1804 at age twenty-one, and her unusual request of the Rev. Richard Allen, head of the A.M.E. Church, for an opportunity to preach her own sermon. Allen denied Lee at first, but, eight years later, after seeing Lee reinvigorate another preacher's failing sermon, he allowed Lee to preach, making her the church's first authorized female preacher. For the rest of her life, Lee worked tirelessly, giving hundreds of sermons each year and promoting abolitionism in the United States and Canada. Lee's work, like that of Sojourner Truth and Phillis Wheatley, broke down the initial barriers between black men and black women and set the stage for later, post–Civil War, black women's movements.

In the following excerpt from *Religious Experience and Journal of Mrs. Jarena Lee, Giving an Account of Her Call to Preach the Gospel,* Lee describes her reasons for wanting to be a preacher. To Lee, the act of preaching is no more complicated than the retelling of Christ's story. She writes, "Did not Mary *first* preach the risen Savior, and is not the doctrine of the resurrection the very climax of Christianity . . . ?" Lee insists that men and women are equals in the eyes of God. "If a man may preach, because the Savior died for him, why not the woman? . . . Is he not a whole Savior, instead of a half one?" Like the other female preachers whose work is featured in this anthology, Julia A. J. Foote and Zilpha Elaw, Lee answers to a higher authority than the rule of any man on earth.

Selection from *Religious Experience and Journal of Mrs. Jarena Lee, Giving an Account of Her Call to Preach the Gospel* (1849)

SOURCE: Jarena Lee, *Religious Experience and Journal of Mrs. Jarena Lee, Giving an Account of Her Call to Preach the Gospel* (Philadelphia: Printed and Published for the Author, 1849).

By the increasing light of the Spirit, I had found there yet remained the root of pride, anger, self-will, with many evils, the result of fallen nature. I now became alarmed at this discovery, and began to fear that I had been deceived in my experience. I was now greatly alarmed, lest I should fall away from what I knew I had enjoyed; and to guard against this I prayed almost incessantly, without acting faith on the power and promises of God to keep me from falling. I had not yet learned how to war against temptation of this kind. Satan well knew that if he could succeed in making me disbelieve my conversion, that he would catch me either on the ground of complete despair, or on the ground of infidelity. For if all I had passed through was to go for nothing, and was but a fiction, the mere ravings of a disordered mind, then I would naturally be led to believe that there is nothing in religion at all.

From this snare I was mercifully preserved, and led to believe that there was yet a greater work than that of pardon to be wrought in me. I retired to a secret place (after having sought this blessing, as well as I could, for nearly three months, from the time brother Scott had instructed me respecting it) for prayer, about four o'clock in the afternoon. I had struggled long and hard, but found not the desire of my heart. When I rose from my knees, there seemed a voice speaking to me, as I yet stood in a leaning posture—"Ask for sanctification." When to my surprise, I recollected that I had not even thought of it in my whole prayer. It would seem Satan had hidden the very object from my mind, for which I had purposely kneeled to pray. But when this voice whispered in my heart, saying, "Pray for sanctification," I again bowed in the same place, at the same time, and said, "Lord *sanctify* my soul for Christ's sake?" That very instant, as if lightning had darted through me, I sprang to my feet, and cried, "The Lord has sanctified my soul!" There was none to hear this but the angels who stood around to witness my joy—and Satan, whose malice raged the more. That Satan was there, I knew; for no sooner had I cried out, "The Lord has sanctified my soul," than there seemed another voice behind me, saying, "No, it is too great a work to be done." But another spirit said, "Bow down for the witness—I received it— *thou art sanctified!*" The first I knew of myself after that, I was standing in the yard with my hands spread out, and looking with my face toward heaven.

I now ran into the house and told them what had happened to me, when, as it were, a new rush of the same ecstasy came upon me, and caused me to feel as if I were in an ocean of light and bliss.

During this, I stood perfectly still, the tears rolling in a flood from my eyes. So great was the joy, that it is past description. There is no language that can describe it, except that which was heard by St. Paul, when he was caught up to the third heaven, and heard words which it was not lawful to utter.

My Call to Preach the Gospel.

Between four and five years after my sanctification, on a certain time, an impressive silence fell upon me, and I stood as if some one was about to speak to me, yet I had no such thought in my heart. But to my utter surprise there seemed to sound a voice which I thought I distinctly heard, and most certainly understood, which said to me, "Go preach the Gospel!" I immediately replied aloud, "No one will believe me." Again I listened, and again the same voice seemed to say, "Preach the Gospel; I will put words in your mouth, and will turn your enemies to become your friends."

At first I supposed that Satan had spoken to me, for I had read that he could transform himself into an angel of light, for the purpose of deception. Immediately I went into a secret place, and called upon the Lord to know if he had called me to preach, and whether I was deceived or not; when there appeared to my view the form and figure of a pulpit, with a Bible lying thereon, the back of which was presented to me as plainly as if it had been a literal fact.

In consequence of this, my mind became so exercised that during the night following, I took a text, and preached in my sleep. I thought there stood before me a great multitude, while I expounded to them the things of religion. So violent were my exertions, and so loud were my exclamations, that I awoke from the sound of my own voice, which also awoke the family of the house where I resided. Two days after, I went to see the preacher in charge of the African Society, who was the Rev. Richard Allen, the same before named in these pages, to tell him that I felt it my duty to preach the gospel. But as I drew near the street in which his house was, which was in the city of Philadelphia, my courage began to fail me; so terrible did the cross appear, it seemed that I should not be able to bear it. Previous to my setting out to go to see him, so agitated was my mind, that my appetite for my daily food failed me entirely. Several times on my way there, I turned back again; but as often I felt my strength again renewed, and I soon found that the nearer I approached to the house of the minister, the less was my fear. Accordingly, as soon as I came to the door, my fears subsided, the cross was removed, all things appeared pleasant— I was tranquil.

I now told him, that the Lord had revealed it to me, that I must preach the gospel. He replied by asking, in what sphere I wished to move in? I said, among the Methodists. He then replied, that a Mrs. Cook, a Methodist lady, had also some time before requested the same privilege; who it was believed, had done much good in the way of exhortation, and holding prayer meetings; and who had been permitted to do so by the verbal license of the preacher in charge at the time. But as to women preaching, he said that our Discipline knew nothing at all about it—that it did not call for women preachers. This I was glad to hear, because it removed the fear of the cross—but no sooner did this feeling cross my mind, than I found that a love of souls had in a measure departed from me; that holy energy which burned within me, as a fire, began to be smothered. This I soon perceived.

O how careful ought we to be, lest through our by-laws of church government and discipline, we bring into disrepute even the word of life. For as unseemly as it may appear now-a-days for a woman to preach, it should be remembered that nothing is impossible with God. And why should it be thought impossible, heterodox, or improper, for a woman to preach? seeing the Savior died for the woman as well as the man.

If a man may preach, because the Savior died for him, why not the woman? seeing he died for her also. Is he not a whole Savior, instead of a half one? as those who hold it wrong for a woman to preach, would seem to make it appear.

Did not Mary *first* preach the risen Savior, and is not the doctrine of the resurrection the very climax of Christianity— hangs not all our hope on this, as argued by St. Paul? Then did not Mary, a woman, preach the gospel? for she preached the resurrection of the crucified Son of God.

But some will say, that Mary did not expound the Scripture, therefore, she did not preach, in the proper sense of the term. To this I reply, it may be that the term *preach*, in those primitive times, did not mean exactly what it is now *made* to mean; perhaps it was a great deal more simple then, than it is now:—if it were not, the unlearned fishermen could not have preached the gospel at all, as they had no learning.

To this it may be replied, by those who are determined not to believe that it is right for a woman to preach, that the disciples, though they were fishermen, and ignorant of letters too, were inspired so to do. To which I would reply, that though they were inspired, yet that inspiration did not save them from showing their ignorance of letters, and of man's wisdom; this the multitude soon found out, by listening to the remarks of the envious Jewish priests. If then, to preach the gospel, by the gift of heaven, comes by inspiration solely, is God straitened; must he take the man exclusively? May he not, did he not, and can he not inspire a female to preach the simple story of the birth, life, death, and resurrection of our Lord, and accompany it too, with power to the sinner's heart. As for me, I am fully persuaded that the Lord called me to labor according to what I have received, in his vineyard. If he has not, how could he consistently bear testimony in favor of my poor labors, in awakening and converting sinners?

In my wanderings up and down among men, preaching according to my ability, I have frequently found families who told me that they had not for several years been to a meeting, and yet, while listening to hear what God would say by his poor colored female instrument, have believed with trembling—tears rolling down their cheeks, the signs of contrition and repentance toward God. I firmly believe that I have sown seed, in the name of the Lord, which shall appear with its increase at the great day of accounts, when Christ shall come to make up his jewels.

At a certain time, I was beset with the idea, that soon or late I should fall from grace, and lose my soul at last. I was frequently called to the throne of grace about this matter, but found no relief; the temptation pursued me still. Being more and more afflicted with it, till at a certain time when the spirit strongly impressed it on my mind to enter into my closet, and carry my case once more to the Lord; the Lord enabled me to draw nigh to him, and to his mercy seat, at this time, in an extraordinary manner; for while I wrestled with him for the victory over this disposition to doubt whether I should persevere, there appeared a form of fire, about the size of a man's hand, as I was on my knees; at the same moment, there appeared to the eye of faith a man robed in a white garment, from the shoulders down to the feet; from him a voice proceeded, saying: "Thou shalt never return from the cross." Since that time I have never doubted, but believe that God will keep me until the day of redemption. Now I could adopt the very language of St. Paul, and say that nothing could have separated my soul from the love of God, which is in Christ Jesus. From that time, 1807, until the present, 1833, I have not yet doubted the power and goodness of God to keep me from falling, through sanctification of the spirit and belief of the truth.

23

ZILPHA ELAW

(1790–after 1845)

Zilpha Elaw, like Jarena Lee, was a groundbreaking black female preacher in the United States. Lee was born in Pennsylvania to free black parents and, at the age of fourteen, joined the Methodist Church. Much of what we know about her is taken from her autobiography, *Memoirs of the Life, Religious Experience, Ministerial Travels and Labours of Mrs. Zilpha Elaw, An American Female of Color: Together with Some Account of the Great Religious Revivals of America* (1846).

In the following excerpt, Elaw describes the series of events that led her to become a preacher, starting with a public prayer at a campground and ending with her sister's dying wishes. Elaw cites Satan as the cause of her hesitance to devote her life to preaching. Unlike Jarena Lee and Julia A. J. Foote, Elaw's difficulties on her path to becoming a preacher are described as coming from within her soul rather than without, from family or friends.

Selection from *Memoirs of the Life, Religious Experience, Ministerial Travels and Labours of Mrs. Zilpha Elaw, an American Female of Colour* (1846)

SOURCE: Zilpha Elaw, *Memoirs of the Religious Experience, Ministerial Travels and Labours of Ms. Zilpha Elaw, an American Female of Colour; Together with Some Account of the Great Religious Revivals in America [Written by Herself]* (London: Published by the Authoress, 1846).

Truly I durst not move, because God was so powerfully near to me; for the space of several hours I appeared not to be on earth, but far above all earthly things. I had not at this time offered up public prayer on the camp ground; but when the prayer meeting afterward commenced, the Lord opened my mouth in public prayer; and while I was thus engaged, it seemed as if I heard my God rustling in the tops of the mulberry-trees. Oh, how precious was this day to my soul! I was after this very frequently requested to present my petitions to the throne of grace in the public meetings at the camp; and to my astonishment, during one of the services, an old gentleman and his wife, whose heads were blanched by the frost of time, came to me, fell upon their knees, and desired me to pray for them, as also many others whom I expect to meet in a happier world: and before the meeting at this camp closed, it was revealed to me by the Holy Spirit, that like another Phœbe, or the matrons of the apostolic societies, I must employ myself in visiting families, and in speaking personally to the members thereof, of the salvation and eternal interests of their souls, visit the sick, and attend upon other of the errands and services of the Lord; which I afterward cheerfully did, not confining my visits to the poor only, but extending them to the rich also, and even to those who sit in high places in the state; and the Lord was with me in the work to own and bless my labors. Like Enoch, I walked and talked with God: nor did a single cloud intervene betwixt God and my soul for many months after.

But Satan at length succeeded in producing a cloud over my mind, and in damping the delightful ardors of my soul in these blessed labors, by suggesting, that I ought not to make so bold a profession of an entire sanctification and holiness of spirit, lest I should be unable at all times to maintain it; and to this evil suggestion I sinfully acceded, and dilated chiefly in my visits on the goodness of God; and much ceased to enforce that high attainment, and to witness to the indwelling presence and superintending sway of the Holy Spirit in a clean and obedient heart, which I had so powerfully experienced; but alas! I soon proved that to God must be cheerfully ascribed the glory, or he will not vouchsafe to us a continuance of the happy enjoyment.

I write this as a warning to others who may be attacked with the same temptation, that they may be careful not thus to grieve the Holy Spirit of God: but ever remember, that we are witnesses of that gracious passage of Scripture, "This is the will of God, even your sanctification." "For this the Savior prayed on behalf of his disciples, 'Sanctify them by thy truth, Thy word is truth'": and Peter says, "Ye have purified your souls in obeying the truth through the Spirit": and "As he which hath called you is holy, so be ye holy in all manner of conversation." As, therefore, this blessed doctrine is most certainly believed by us Methodists, it is both our high privilege and bounden duty to manifest it to those around us; and, in default thereof, we shall bring clouds of darkness upon our souls.

I shall here narrate a very extraordinary circumstance which occurred in the family of Mr. Boudinot, one of the richest gentlemen in the city of Burlington. The Lord bade me repair to this gentleman's residence, and deliver a gospel message to him. I was astounded at the idea of going to such a man, to talk to him of the condition of his soul; and began to reason with myself as to the propriety thereof. Satan also suggested that a man of his rank and dignity would not listen to such a poor, ignorant creature as myself. I therefore concluded, that possibly I might be mistaken about this message, and that it might have arisen in my imagination merely, and not have come from God. I accordingly decided in my mind that I would not go to him. But oh! how soon did my heavenly Master show me that I had disobeyed his high commands, given me by the impression of his Spirit upon my heart; for I habitually enjoyed so clear an illumination of the divine presence and glory upon my soul, a conscience so pure, and an eye so single, that the slightest omission would produce the intervention of a cloud and an obscuration of the divine ray upon my spirit; and thus I felt on this occasion, being deprived of the divine ray, and of the peculiar zest and nearness of divine intercourse I had hitherto enjoyed with my heavenly Father. I endeavored to search out and ascertain the reason, why the luster of my Father's countenance was obscured upon my soul; for so manifest was the gloom on my spirit, that even my class leader said, "Why, how is this Zilpha, that you appear less lively than you did a week or two since?" yet I still remained ignorant of the cause thereof; but on the next class evening, one of the itinerating ministers presided, and he gave forth the following lines to be sung—

> "Jesus, the hindrance show,
>   Which I have feared to see;
> And let me now consent to know,
>   What keeps me back from Thee."

While singing these lines, I was led to discover that I had not obeyed the call of the Lord, by refusing to go to Mr. Boudinot's, as I had been directed.

> "In me is all the bar,
>   Which God would fain remove:
> Remove it; and I shall declare,
>   That God is only love."

I then laid open my case before my dear minister; and I shall never forget the kind and excellent advice he gave me upon that occasion. I never durst take any important step without first consulting my superiors; and having informed him of the painful exercises of mind I had passed through, and of the disregard I had paid to my heavenly direction, he advised me, by all means, to go whither I had been directed, and no more confer with flesh and blood; but proceed in the course of duty and obedience, leaving the event to God, before whose judgment-seat we shall all stand to give an account of our stewardship. Upon this, I again sought my heavenly Father at the throne of grace, promising that I would go in His name, whither he had sent me, if He would be pleased to restore to me the light of his countenance and Spirit; and He graciously favored me with the request of my heart.

I then went to the residence of Mr. Elias Boudinot, and had access to all who were in his house; and it was a day for ever to be remembered; for such an outpouring of divine unction took place, as I never witnessed in all my life. All other matters were laid aside but that of religion; and little was to be seen but weeping and mourning. Some of us were occupied in praising the Lord, but most of the household were weeping the penitential tear for their sins. There were company visiting at the house at the time, and when dinner was ready, there were none to come and partake of it; we had quite a search to find, and some trouble to induce them to come to dinner. One lady, who was then on a visit there, had shut herself up in her apartment to read the New Testament; another was shut up in another apartment; one of the servants had locked himself up in the pantry, and there he cried aloud upon God for mercy. It was a day of wonders, indeed! Oh, that so gracious a visitation might come upon thousands of families in England! How sweet is the path of obedience! God will bless while man obeys; "for what his mouth hath said, his own almighty hand will do." I again enjoyed a full measure of the Holy Spirit, and kept that sacred, hallowed fire alive in my soul; to God be all the praise!

I thus attended to my Master's business in this and similar spheres of effort for the space of five years; during which period, much good resulted from the attempts of so simple and weak an instrument as myself; because directed by the wisdom, and sustained by the mighty power of God. Five happy years, on the whole, were they indeed to me; notwithstanding that I had many sorrows and grievous trials to endure and contend with.

> "Trials must and will befal;
>   But with humble faith to see,
> Love inscribed upon them all,
>   This is happiness to me."

The bitters of my cup were continually sweetened by the smiles of Jesus; and all things went on easy, because my heavenly Father took the heaviest end of the cross and bore it with me: thus the crooked was made straight, and the rough became smooth.

In 1816, I had a presentiment on my mind of a speedy dissolution; and felt so confident in this expectation, that, when in the class-meeting, I could not forbear from speaking in a strain which implied my speedy departure. My leader inquired if I was about to leave Burlington? Upon which, I opened my mind to him, and the train of my feelings; he made no comment upon it at the time; and in the week following, I accidentally met with a severe fall, by which I was so injured internally, as to allow no presage of recovery; my medical attendant pronounced it impossible that I could live, and my friends for many days looked to see me breathe my last; but God ordered it otherwise to every expectation.

While I was thus lying with but one step betwixt me and death, a dear lady, who was a preaching Quakeress, came to see me, and take a last farewell, not expecting to see me again in this life, as she was about taking a religious tour in the country. She affectionately told me she hoped that all would be well with me, and that we should again meet in a better world, though we might meet no more in the flesh. But though my recovery was very gradual indeed, yet it pleased God to raise me up again; and then, with what renewed pleasure did I sit under the sound of the glorious gospel of our Lord and Savior Jesus Christ, and resume the work of my heavenly Master, going forth in his great name from day to day, and holding sweet converse with my God, as a man converses with his friend. This family or household ministry, as I may call it, was a particular duty, a special calling, which I received from the Lord to discharge for the space of five years; at the expiration of which, it was taken from me, and consigned to another sister in the same class with myself. How wonderful are the works of the Almighty, and his ways past finding out by the children of men! I was often so happy in this work as to be quite unable to contain myself; sometimes I cried out, "Lord, what wilt thou have me to do?" for it seemed as if the Lord had yet something more in reserve for me to undertake.

I had at this time but one sister living, who resided in

Philadelphia, about twenty miles distant from Burlington; she was the only sister, who with myself arrived at years of maturity; a very pious woman, and she conducted herself very strictly and exemplarily in all her movements: she was so sanctified and devoted a Christian, that some persons have informed me, that they have sat with her in their meetings, and received much edification from beholding the earnest devotedness of mind she manifested in the house of God; thus, "as iron sharpeneth iron, so doth the countenance of a man his friend."

This dear sister of mine was at length attacked with a mortal disease, and intelligence of her illness was communicated to me. I therefore repaired to Philadelphia; and. on entering the room, I found her so emaciated and altered in appearance, that I scarcely knew her; but in so happy a frame of mind, that the body seemed almost unable to detain so heavenly a spirit. As I stood by her bed-side weeping, she said,

> "I'll take my sister by the hand,
> And lead her to the promised land."

Thus I found her; and after staying with her a few days, thus I left her, and returned home to Burlington. But being pressed with concern for her, I could not long rest at home; I therefore arranged my affairs there, and taking my little daughter with me, set off again for Philadelphia. When I arrived at the house of my brother-in-law, I went directly into the chamber where my sister was lying; and the first thing she said to me was, "My dear sister, I am going to hell." I had not either spoken or sat down in the house; but upon hearing this, I kneeled down and tried to pray; but she instantly exclaimed, "Oh, do not pray, for you will only send me the sooner to judgment!" My astonishment was immense at finding her in such an altered condition of mind; for only a fortnight previously she was exulting in the high praises of God, completely weaned from all things of an earthly nature, and longing to depart to the world of spirits. Many kind brethren and sisters visited her, and prayer was made day and night unto God for her, that her soul might be released from the bonds of darkness; but she remained in this horrible state for nearly a week after my arrival. Some of the ministers bade me not to be discouraged on her account; saying that for they had witnessed others who had been in a similar condition, and had afterward experienced a most powerful deliverance. I had never before heard of such a case, much less witnessed one; and it was equally as surprising as it was afflictive to me; but the Spirit of God at times whispered in my heart, "Be of good cheer, thou shalt yet see the glory of God." My faith and hope were thereby strengthened; yet the sorrowful sight of my poor dear sister opposing every effort of the friends to pray with and for her, did not a little, at intervals, deject and cast me down. Thanks be unto God, the hour at last arrived when he was pleased to burst through the gloom, and set the captive free. A number of the friends had assembled in the house, and we joined in prayer together; after several friends had prayed, in a moment such a spirit of prayer came upon me, as seemed to shake the whole place, as at the memorable apostolic prayer-meeting. Acts v. 31. I immediately commenced praying; and while thus engaged, my dear sister exclaimed aloud, "Look up, children, the Master is coming!" and she shouted, "Glory to God in the highest, and on the earth peace; for I again have found Jesus, the chiefest among ten thousand. Honor and glory, and majesty and power, be given to Him for ever and ever." "Now," said she, "turn me round, and let me die in the arms of Jesus; for I shall soon be with Him in glory." We then turned her over on her other side, as she requested, and awaited the event; she then swooned away, and lay for some time to all appearance dead.

What will infidelity say to this? It surely will not attempt to charge a sincere and godly Christian on her death-bed with hypocrisy; nor can it be consistently attributed to fanaticism. The antagonizing conflicts of Christian faith, and its triumphs through the aids of the Holy Spirit over the powers of darkness, as exemplified on such occasions, are very remote from the whimsical vagaries of an over-heated and incoherent imagination; such experience, under certain circumstances, is the natural cause and effect of exercise of Christian faith, in collision with forces asserted by the gospel to be engaged in hostile action to it; and it is a fact worthy of extensive observation, that the vast variety of mental exercises and religious experiences of all true and lively Christians, in every grade of society, in all ages, and in all denominations and sections of the Christian Church, are of too uniform and definite a character to be ascribed to the wild and fluctuating uncertainties of fanaticism: so widely spread an uniformity as that which exists in the genuine pilgrim's progress of Christian experience, can never be philosophically shewn to be an attribute of fanaticism; an uniformity, like that of the human constitution, admitting of the greatest variety of individual features, yet all governed by the same laws; and it may be retorted also, that stubborn facts continually prove, in other countries as well as in modern Gaul, that no fanaticism is more luxuriant, bewitching, and arrogant, than that which inscribes on its ensign—"The Age of Reason," and roots itself in the soil of infidelity.

After my dear sister had laid in a swoon for some time, she revived, and said, among other things which I could not remember, "I have overcome the world by the kingdom of heaven"; she then began singing, and appeared to sing several verses; but the language in which she sung was too wonderful for me, and I could not understand it. We all sat or stood around her with great astonishment, for her voice was as clear, musical, and strong, as if nothing had ailed her; and when she had finished her song of praise, (for it was indeed a song of praise, and the place was full of glory,) she addressed herself to me, and informed me, that she had seen Jesus, and had been in the society of angels; and that an angel came to her, and bade her tell Zilpha that she must preach the gospel; and also, that I must go to a lady named Fisher, a Quakeress, and she would tell me further what I should do. It was then betwixt one and two o'clock in the morning, and she wished me to go directly to visit this lady, and also to commence my ministry of preaching, by delivering an address to the people then in the house. I cannot describe my feelings at this juncture; I knew not what to do, nor where to go: and my dear sister was pressingly urgent for me to begin and preach directly; and then to go and see the above-named lady. I was utterly at a loss what to say, or how to move; dear heart, she waited in silence for my commencing, and I stood in silence quite overwhelmed by my feelings. At length, she raised her head up, and said, "Oh, Zilpha!

why do you not begin?" I then tried to say something as I stood occupied in mental prayer; but she said, "Oh! do not pray, you must preach." I then addressed a few words to those around me, and she was very much pleased with the attempt: two of the sisters then took me by the arm, and led me into another room; they there informed me they expected to see me sink down upon the floor, and that they thought my sister was perhaps a little delirious. The next day when I was alone with her, she asked me if that hymn which she had sung on the previous night was not beautiful; adding, "Ah, Zilpha! angels gave it me to sing; and I was told that you must be a preacher; and oh! how you hurt me last night by not going where I told you; but as soon as you moved, I was released." She continued in this happy frame of mind until her soul fell asleep in Jesus. The whole of this sick-bed scene, until its termination in death, was as surpassingly wonderful to me, as a Christian, for its depths of religious experience and power, as it was afflictively interesting to me as a relative. I have, however, since learnt that some other Christians have occasionally been known, when in the very arms of death, to break forth and sing with a melodious and heavenly voice, several verses in a language unknown to mortals. A pure language, unalloyed by the fulsome compliment, the hyperbole, the tautology and circumlocution, the insinuation, double meaning and vagueness, the weakness and poverty, the impurity, bombast, and other defects, with which all human languages are clogged, seems to be essential for the associations of glorified spirits and the elevated devotions of heaven, are, doubtless, in use among the holy angels, and seems to be a matter of gracious promise on the part of Jehovah, on behalf of his redeemed people. Zephaniah iii. 9.

I have been very careful, and the more minute in narrating the experience of my dear sister during her illness and death, in hope that it may possibly meet the cases of others tempted in a similar manner; that they may take encouragement from her happy and triumphant end. She had evidently grieved the Holy Spirit in some way or other, and He had withdrawn from her His comforting presence for a time; but He returned to her again with abundant mercy and comforting grace. After receiving a little refreshment, the last words she spoke were, "Now I want a good prayer"; her husband then commenced prayer; and during the exercise, her happy spirit bade adieu to the frailties and sorrows of this mortal life, prepared for, and assured of, her title to a jointure in the ever-blooming glories of the inheritance of the saints in light.

Notwithstanding the plain and pointed declaration of my sister, and though the Scriptures assert that not many wise, rich, and noble are called; but God hath chosen the foolish things of this world to confound the wise, and the weak things of the world to confound the mighty, I could not at the time imagine it possible that God should select and appoint so poor and ignorant a creature as myself to be his messenger, to bear the good tidings of the gospel to the children of men. Soon after this, I received a visit from a female who was employed in the work of the ministry, who asked me if I did not think that I was called by the Lord to that work? to which I replied in the negative; she then said, "I think you are; now tell me, do not passages of Scripture often open to thy mind as subjects for public speaking and exposition? Weigh well this matter and see; for I believe that God has provided a great work for thy employment."

24

LUCY DELANEY

(ca. 1830–after 1891)

Lucy Ann Delaney (born Polly Crockett and also known as Polly Wash) was born into slavery to a woman named Polly Berry, who had been born free but was kidnapped and enslaved. Delaney's father's name is unknown. New information uncovered by scholars, notably Eric Gardner and Robert Moore, Jr., have filled out the details known previously only from her 1891 memoir, *From Darkness Cometh the Light, or, Struggles for Freedom*, one of the few slave narratives published after the Civil War and one of the few first-person accounts of a slave suing for freedom.

In these excerpts describing her long imprisonment during her freedom suit, Delaney writes as a participant-historian, expressing her outrage even while offering helpful biographical and professional details about her jailors, her lawyers, and the presiding judge. Psychologically astute, she describes her terror as an out-of-body experience, feeling sorry for the young girl she was, awaiting her fate. After winning her suit, she acknowledges the kindnesses shown her in prison, the gesture of an individual who ought not to have been imprisoned, which is her point.

Selections from *From Darkness Cometh the Light* (1891)

SOURCE: Lucy Delaney, *From Darkness Cometh the Light, or, Struggles for Freedom* (St. Louis, MO: J. T. Smith, 1891).

CHAPTER IV.

On the morning of the 8th of September, 1842, my mother sued Mr. D. D. Mitchell for the possession of her child, Lucy Ann Berry. My mother, accompanied by the sheriff, took me from my hiding-place and conveyed me to the jail, which was located on Sixth Street, between Chestnut and Market, where the Laclede Hotel now stands, and there met Mr. Mitchell, with Mr. H. S. Cox, his brother in-law.

Judge Bryant Mullanphy read the law to Mr. Mitchell, which stated that if Mr. Mitchell took me back to his house, he must give bond and security to the amount of two thousand dollars, and furthermore, I should not be taken out of the State of Missouri until I had a chance to prove my freedom. Mr. H. S. Cox became his security and Mr. Mitchell gave bond accordingly, and then demanded that I should be put in jail.

"Why do you want to put that poor young girl in jail?" demanded my lawyer. "Because," he retorted, "her mother or some of her crew might run her off, just to make me pay the two thousand dollars; and I would like to see her lawyer, or any other man, in jail, that would take up a d— nigger case like that."

"You need not think, Mr. Mitchell," calmly replied Mr. Murdock, "because my client is colored that she has no rights, and can be cheated out of her freedom. She is just as free as you are, and the Court will so decide it, as you will see."

However, I was put in a cell, under lock and key, and there remained for seventeen long and dreary months, listening to the

> "—foreign echoes from the street,
> Faint sounds of revel, traffic, conflict keen—
> And, thinking that man's reiterated feet

Have gone such ways since e'er the world has been,
I wondered how each oft-used tone and glance
Retains its might and old significance."

My only crime was seeking for that freedom which was my
birthright! I heard Mr. Mitchell tell his wife that he did not believe in slavery, yet, through his instrumentality, I was shut
away from the sunlight, because he was determined to prove
me a slave, and thus keep me in bondage. Consistency, thou art
a jewel!

At the time my mother entered suit for her freedom, she was
not instructed to mention her two children, Nancy and Lucy,
so the white people took advantage of this flaw, and showed a
determination to use every means in their power to prove that
I was not her child.

This gave my mother an immense amount of trouble, but she
had girded up her loins for the fight, and, knowing that she was
right, was resolved, by the help of God and a good lawyer, to
win my case against all opposition.

After advice by competent persons, mother went to Judge
Edward Bates and begged him to plead the case, and, after
fully considering the proofs and learning that my mother was a
poor woman, he consented to undertake the case and make his
charges only sufficient to cover his expenses. It would be well
here to give a brief sketch of Judge Bates, as many people wondered that such a distinguished statesman would take up the
case of an obscure negro girl.

Edward Bates was born in Belmont, Goochland county, Va.,
September, 1793. He was of Quaker descent, and inherited all
the virtues of that peace-loving people. In 1812, he received a
midshipman's warrant, and was only prevented from following
the sea by the influence of his mother, to whom he was greatly
attached. Edward emigrated to Missouri in 1814, and entered
upon the practice of law, and, in 1816, was appointed prosecuting lawyer for the St. Louis Circuit. Toward the close of the
same year, he was appointed Attorney General for the new
State of Missouri, and in 1826, while yet a young man, was
elected representative to congress as an anti-Democrat, and
served one term. For the following twenty-five years, he

devoted himself to his profession, in which he was a shining light. His probity and uprightness attracted to him a class of people who were in the right and only sought justice, while he repelled, by his virtues, those who traffic in the miseries or mistakes of unfortunate people, for they dared not come to him and seek counsel to aid them in their villainy.

In 1847, Mr. Bates was delegate to the Convention for Internal Improvement, held in Chicago, and by his action he came prominently before the whole country. In 1850, President Fillmore offered him the portfolio of Secretary of War, which he declined. Three years later, he accepted the office of Judge of St. Louis Land Court.

When the question of the repeal of the Missouri Compromise was agitated, he earnestly opposed it, and thus became identified with the "free labor" party in Missouri, and united with it, in opposition to the admission of Kansas under the Lecompton Constitution. He afterwards became a prominent antislavery man, and in 1859 was mentioned as a candidate for the presidency. He was warmly supported by his own State, and for a time it seemed that the opposition to Governor Seward might concentrate on him. In the National Republican Convention, 1860, he received forty-eight votes on the first ballot, but when it became apparent that Abraham Lincoln was the favorite, Mr. Bates withdrew his name. Mr. Lincoln appointed Judge Bates Attorney General, and while in the Cabinet he acted a dignified, safe and faithful part. In 1864, he resigned his office and returned to his home in St. Louis, where he died in 1869, surrounded by his weeping family.

> "—loved at home, revered abroad.
> Princes and lords are but the breath of kings;
> 'An honest man's the noblest work of God.'"

On the 7th of February, 1844, the suit for my freedom began. A bright, sunny day, a day which the happy and care-free would drink in with a keen sense of enjoyment. But my heart was full of bitterness; I could see only gloom which seemed to deepen and gather closer to me as I neared the courtroom. The jailer's sister-in-law, Mrs. Lacy, spoke to me of submission and patience; but I could not feel anything but rebellion against my lot. I could not see one gleam of brightness in my future, as I was hurried on to hear my fate decided.

Among the most important witnesses were Judge Robert Wash and Mr. Harry Douglas, who had been an overseer on Judge Wash's farm, and also Mr. MacKeon, who bought my mother from H. S. Cox, just previous to her running away.

Judge Wash testified that "the defendant, Lucy A. Berry, was a mere infant when he came in possession of Mrs. Fannie Berry's estate, and that he often saw the child in the care of its reputed mother, Polly, and to his best knowledge and belief, he thought Lucy A. Berry was Polly's own child."

Mr. Douglas and Mr. MacKeon corroborated Judge Wash's statement. After the evidence from both sides was all in, Mr. Mitchell's lawyer, Thomas Hutchinson, commenced to plead. For one hour, he talked so bitterly against me and against my being in possession of my liberty that I was trembling, as if with ague, for I certainly thought everybody must believe him; indeed I almost believed the dreadful things he said, myself, and as I listened I closed my eyes with sickening dread, for I could just see myself floating down the river, and my heart-throbs seemed to be the throbs of the mighty engine which propelled me from my mother and freedom forever!

Oh! what a relief it was to me when he finally finished his harangue and resumed his seat! As I never heard anyone plead before, I was very much alarmed, although I knew in my heart that every word he uttered was a lie! Yet, how was I to make people believe? It seemed a puzzling question!

Judge Bates arose, and his soulful eloquence and earnest pleading made such an impression on my sore heart, I listened with renewed hope. I felt the black storm clouds of doubt and despair were fading away, and that I was drifting into the safe harbor of the realms of truth. I felt as if everybody must believe him, for he clung to the truth, and I wondered how Mr. Hutchinson could so lie about a poor defenseless girl like me.

Judge Bates chained his hearers with the graphic history of my mother's life, from the time she played on Illinois banks, through her trials in slavery, her separation from her husband, her efforts to become free, her voluntary return to slavery for the sake of her child, Lucy, and her subsequent efforts in securing her own freedom. All these incidents he lingered over step by step, and concluding, he said:

"Gentlemen of the jury, I am a slave-holder myself, but, thanks to the Almighty God. I am above the base principle of holding any a slave that has as good right to her freedom as this girl has been proven to have; she was free before she was born; her mother was free, but kidnapped in her youth, and sacrificed to the greed of negro traders, and no free woman can give birth to a slave child, as it is in direct violation of the laws of God and man!"

At this juncture he read the affidavit of Mr. A. Posey, with whom my mother lived at the time of her abduction; also affidavits of Mr. and Mrs. Woods, in corroboration of the previous facts duly set forth. Judge Bates then said:

"Gentleman of the jury, here I rest this case, as I would not want any better evidence for one of my own children. The testimony of Judge Wash is alone sufficient to substantiate the claim of Polly Crockett Berry to the defendant as being her own child."

The case was then submitted to the jury, about 8 o'clock in the evening, and I was returned to the jail and locked in the cell which I had occupied for seventeen months, filled with the most intense anguish.

CHAPTER V.

"There's a joy in every sorrow,
  There's a relief from every pain;
  Though to-day 'tis dark to-morrow
  HE will turn all bright again."

Before the sheriff bade me good night he told me to be in readiness at nine o'clock on the following morning to accompany him back to court to hear the verdict. My mother was not at the trial. She had lingered many days about the jail expecting my case would be called, and finally when called to trial the dear, faithful heart was not present to sustain me during that dreadful speech of Mr. Hutchinson. All night long I suffered agonies of fright, the suspense was something awful, and could only be comprehended by those who have gone through some similar ordeal.

I had missed the consolation of my mother's presence, and I felt so hopeless and alone! Blessed mother! how she clung and fought for me. No work was too hard for her to undertake. Others would have flinched before the obstacles which confronted her, but undauntedly she pursued her way, until my freedom was established by every right and without a questioning doubt!

On the morning of my return to Court, I was utterly unable to help myself. I was so overcome with fright and emotion,—with the alternating feelings of despair and hope—that I could not stand still long enough to dress myself. I trembled like an aspen leaf; so I sent a message to Mrs. Lacy to request permission for me to go to her room, that she might assist me in dressing. I had done a great deal of sewing for Mrs. Lacy, for she had showed me much kindness, and was a good Christian. She gladly assisted me, and under her willing hands I was soon made ready, and, promptly at nine o'clock, the sheriff called and escorted me to the courthouse.

On our way thither, Judge Bates overtook us. He lived out a short distance in the country, and was riding on horseback. He tipped his hat to me as politely as if I were the finest lady in the land, and cried out, "Good morning Miss Lucy, I suppose you had pleasant dreams last night!" He seemed so bright and smiling that I was inbued with renewed hope; and when he addressed the sheriff with "Good morning Sir. I don't suppose the jury was out twenty minutes were they?" and the sheriff replied "oh! no, sir," my heart gave a leap, for I was sure that my fate was decided for weal or woe.

I watched the judge until he turned the corner and desiring to be relieved of suspense from my pent-up anxiety, I eagerly asked the sheriff if I were free, but he gruffly answered that "he didn't know." I was sure he did know, but was too mean to tell me. How could he have been so flinty, when he must have seen how worried I was.

At last the courthouse was reached and I had taken my seat in such a condition of helpless terror that I could not tell one person from another. Friends and foes were as one, and vainly did I try to distinguish them. My long confinement, burdened with harrowing anxiety, the sleepless night I had just spent, the unaccountable absence of my mother, had brought me to an indescribable condition. I felt dazed, as if I were no longer myself. I seemed to be another person—an on looker—and in my heart dwelt a pity for the poor, lonely girl, with down-cast face, sitting on the bench apart from anyone else in that noisy room. I found myself wondering where Lucy's mother was, and how she would feel if the trial went against her; I seemed to have lost all feeling about it, but was speculating what Lucy would do, and what her mother would do, if the hand of Fate was raised against poor Lucy! Oh! how sorry I did feel for myself!

At the sound of a gentle voice, I gathered courage to look upward, and caught the kindly gleam of Judge Bates' eyes, as he bent his gaze upon me and smilingly said, "I will have you discharged in a few minutes, Miss Lucy!"

Some other business occupied the attention of the Court, and when I had begun to think they had forgotten all about me, Judge Bates arose and said calmly, "Your Honor, I desire to have this girl, Lucy A. Berry, discharged before going into any other business."

Judge Mullanphy answered "Certainly!" Then the verdict was called for and rendered, and the jurymen resumed their places. Mr. Mitchell's lawyer jumped up and exclaimed:

"Your Honor, my client demands that this girl be remanded to jail. He does not consider that the case has had a fair trial, I am not informed as to what course he intends to pursue, but I am now expressing his present wishes?"

Judge Bates was on his feet in a second and cried: "For shame! is it not enough that this girl has been deprived of her liberty for a year and a half, that you must still pursue her after a fair and impartial trial before a jury, in which it was clearly proven and decided that she had every right to freedom? I demand that she be set at liberty at once!"

"I agree with Judge Bates," responded Judge Mullanphy, "and the girl may go!"

Oh! the overflowing thankfulness of my grateful heart at that moment, who could picture it? None but the good God above us! I could have kissed the feet of my deliverers, but I was too full to express my thanks, but with a voice trembling with tears I tried to thank Judge Bates for all his kindness.

As soon as possible, I returned to the jail to bid them all good-bye and thank them for their good treatment of me while under their care. They rejoiced with me in my good fortune and wished me much success and happiness in years to come.

I was much concerned at my mother's prolonged absence, and was deeply anxious to meet her and sob out my joy on her faithful bosom. Surely it was the hands of God which prevented mother's presence at the trial, for broken down with anxiety and loss of sleep on my account, the revulsion of feeling would have been greater than her over-wrought heart could have sustained.

As soon as she heard of the result, she hurried to meet me, and hand in hand we gazed into each other's eyes and saw the light of freedom there, and we felt in our hearts that we could with one accord cry out: "Glory to God in the highest, and peace and good will towards men."

Dear, dear mother! how solemnly I invoke your spirit as I review these trying scenes of my girlhood, so long agone! Your patient face and neatly-dressed figure stands ever in the foreground of that checkered time; a figure showing naught to an on-looker but the common place virtues of an honest woman! Never would an ordinary observer connect those virtues with aught of heroism or greatness, but to me they are as bright rays as ever emanated from the lives of the great ones of earth, which are portrayed on historic pages—to me, the qualities of her true, steadfast heart and noble soul become "a constellation, and is tracked in Heaven straightway."

25

ELLA SHEPPARD

(1851–1914)

Samuella (Ella) Sheppard was born into slavery on Andrew Jackson's plantation, Hermitage, in Nashville, Tennessee. Her father purchased his freedom and moved the family to Cincinnati, where young Ella began taking lessons from a well-known vocal coach. After her father's death, Ella Sheppard supported her mother and sisters by working as a teacher. After the Civil War, she moved back to Nashville to attend the Fisk Free Colored School. George White, Fisk's treasurer, noted Sheppard's skill as a pianist and invited her to join the Fisk Jubilee Singers on a concert tour. Sheppard went on to lead the group to great fame across North America and Europe; the group's popularity abroad indicates the pro–African American attitudes of many Europeans. White disbanded the group in 1882. After retiring from music, Sheppard married Rev. George Washington Moore, a well-known minister, devoting the rest of her life to teaching and political reform.

In her memoir, Sheppard demonstrates the financial, historical, and cultural importance of the Fisk Jubilee Singers across the country and in Europe. In the United States, "everywhere the experience was the same. Hotels refused us, and families of the highest social prestige received us into their homes. We sang in halls where Negroes had never been allowed upon the platform." In Europe, concerts often brought in $1,000 per night; the Singers met royalty and stayed in the best hotels without mishap. Sheppard closes by noting the important role that the Fisk Jubilee Singers played in keeping Fisk University financially stable.

"Historical Sketch of the Jubilee Singers" (1911)

SOURCE: Ella Sheppard, "Historical Sketch of the Jubilee Singers," *Fisk University News: The Jubilee Singers* (October 1911).

Part I. Personal

Forty-five years ago the sudden death of my father in Cincinnati, Ohio, brought me to extreme poverty, without protection and with no chance to finish my education or to prepare myself for life's duties and responsibilities. Besides, I had been an invalid for nearly two years. Although frail, I tried every honorable opportunity to make a living. I took in washing and ironing, worked in a family, and had a few music pupils who paid me poorly. Finally I left Cincinnati and taught school in Gallatin, Tennessee. In five months I realized my deficiencies and came to Fisk School in September, 1868, with all my possessions in a trunk (which was not full) so small that the boys immediately called it [a] "Pie Box." I had six dollars, and when Mr. White, the Treasurer, said that this amount would keep me a little over three weeks, I asked for work. He said there were already many others waiting for a chance to work. I decided to stay until my money ran out.

Exceptional musical advantages then very rare for colored girls in the South secured me three pupils, who paid me four dollars each per month. Wednesdays and Saturdays I went to the city and taught each pupil one hour, which made it impossible for me, running all the way, over the rough, rocky hills and roads, to get back in time for the last tap of the bell for supper: so I went without supper those days and waited on the table one day and washed dishes the other day. The school was very poor and food was scarce, yet it filled one. . . .

There were no helpful "mission barrels" in those days; so many of us shivered through that first winter with not an inch of flannel upon our bodies. In spite of our poverty and hardships we were a jolly set of natural girlish girls, and when we had a chance romped and played with all the abandon of children. Once a month we were allowed to go to the city to church and once a month to an entertainment, usually at Baptist College (afterward Roger Williams University), occupying the oldest part of what is now Knowles Public School Building. Our girls and boys labored as strenuously then for the favorite ones to accompany them over the rough, muddy roads and hills, as now to entertainments.

Organizing the Company

We were especially fond of music and gladly gave half of our noon hour and all spare time to study under Mr. George L. White. We made rapid progress, and soon began to help our school by sometimes going Fridays and Saturdays to neighboring towns and cities to give concerts. We always succeeded financially and left behind a thirst for education. Those were the days of the Ku Klux Klan and the Civil Rights Bill. The latter bill prevented our being put out of a ladies coach if we once got in. Our trips often led into many hardships and real dangers. Sometimes after a concert we received private notice of such a nature that we wisely took the first train away.

A Sample Trip

Once we were *enroute* to a large city to give the "Cantata of Queen Esther," which we had already given most successfully in our own city. An accident ahead of us compelled us to stop all day at a station in the woods to await the night train. The only visible house was the hotel. It was election time. All day men gathered from far and near drinking at the hotel bar. Our presence attracted their attention, and seeing Mr. White among us and discovering our mission, word soon traveled that he was a "Yankee nigger school teacher."

Threatenings began near evening. Mr. White, anxious and fearful for us, had us stroll to the railway platform, and sitting on a pile of shingles we prayed through song for deliverance and protection. Mr. White stood between us and the men directing our singing. One by one the riotous crowd left off their jeering and swearing and slunk back, until only the leader stood near Mr. White, and finally took off his hat. Our hearts were fearful and tender and darkness was falling. We were softly finishing the last verse of "Beyond the smiling and the weeping I shall be soon," when we saw the bull's eye of the coming engine and knew that we were saved. The leader begged us with tears falling to sing the hymn again, which we did. As the train passed slowly by I heard him repeating, "Love, rest and home, sweet, sweet home."

Slave Songs Not in Repertoire

The slave songs were never used by us then in public. They were associated with slavery and the dark past, and represented the things to be forgotten. Then, too, they were sacred to our parents, who used them in their religious worship and shouted over them. We finally grew willing to sing them privately, usually in Professor Spence's sitting-room, and sitting upon the floor (there were but few chairs) we practiced softly, learning from each other the songs of our fathers. We did not dream of ever using them in public. Had Mr. White or Professor Spence suggested such a thing, we certainly [would have] rebelled. It was only after many months that gradually our hearts were opened to the influence of these friends and we began to appreciate the wonderful beauty and power of our songs; but we continued to sing in public the usual choruses, duets, solos, etc., learned at school.

Falling Buildings and Resources

The time came when the old hospital buildings must either be greatly repaired or torn down. Many a night in '68 and '69, while some of the girls occupied rooms in the back row of buildings, the wind whistled around and groaned so fearfully that we trembled in horror in our beds, thinking the sounds were the cries of lost spirits of the soldiers who had died in them. We dared not sleep for fear a ghost would grab us, and one night we were sure that a ghost cried out, "O Lordy. O Lordy." Our screams aroused the neighborhood as we fled in terror.

Our privations and limited food began to tell on the vitality of the students and some of our best pupils were sacrificed. There was no money even for food, much less for repairs. Many a time [a] special prayer was offered for the next meal. The American Missionary Association decided that the school must be given up. Teachers, pupils, and citizens felt that this would be an irreparable mistake and calamity, but no one could see how nor where to get the money even for our necessities, and our needs were growing.

When Mr. White proposed to take a company of students to the North to sing for the money, there was consternation at Fisk, and the city people began to object. Everywhere such a plan was looked upon as "a wild goose chase." Opposition developed and grew into vicious criticisms. Prayers for light, guidance and patience went up daily. His peace fell upon us, and while we waited for guidance Mr. White called for volunteers from his singing class and choir. More than enough volunteered and he selected eleven voices. He rehearsed us daily.

The American Missionary Association officers, having heard of Mr. White's plans and of the criticisms, and feeling no doubt the responsibility was too great to assume such a quixotic agency for raising funds, said we must not go. Mr. White wrote to a leading member of the Board and requested a loan to defray our expenses. He not only refused, but protested. Mr. White telegraphed him. "'Tis root, hog, or die: I'm depending on God, not you." Our teachers caught the vision and enthusiasm of Mr. White, and, although fearful of failure, set to and helped to get us ready, dividing their clothing with us. Our company's clothing represented Joseph's coat of many colors and styles. Not one of us had an overcoat or wrap. Mr. White had an old gray shawl.

The Singers Go Forth

Taking every cent he had, all the school treasury could spare
and all he could borrow, and leaving his invalid wife and two
small children in the care of a faithful colored nurse, Mr. White
started, in God's strength, October 6, 1871, with his little band
of singers to sing the money out of the hearts and pockets of
the people.

On our reaching Cincinnati, two Congregational ministers,
the Reverend Messrs. Moore and Halley, opened their churches
for us for praise meetings. On Sunday these meetings were
crowded. On Monday we sang at Chillicothe, Ohio, realizing
nearly $50.00. It was the Sunday and Monday of Chicago's aw-
ful fire. We gladly donated our first proceeds to the Chicago
Relief Fund and left our needs and debts in God's hands. The
mayor and citizens of Chillicothe took notice of our gift and in
a public card cordially commended our cause. The two concerts which followed were well attended. In this city began the
operation of caste prejudice which was to follow us, and which
it was to be a part of our mission if not to remove at least to
ameliorate.

There was no room for us at two leading hotels. A humane
landlord of a third hotel took us in, serving our meals before
the usual hour. Dense audiences met in Cincinnati on Sunday
at Reverend Mr. Moore's church, but a slim audience greeted
our paid concert in Mozart Hall. Evidently the concert was
enjoyed and the morning papers said "the sweetness of the
voices, the accuracy of the execution and the precision of the
time carried the mind back to the early concerts of the Hutchin-
sons, the Gibsons and other famous families, who years ago
delighted audiences and taught them with sentiment while they
pleased them with melody."

Our appearance before the National Council of Congregations Churches at Oberlin, Ohio, brought our cause before the
ministers and laymen, representatives of a large part of the
constituency of the American Missionary Association. They
were deeply impressed with our singing; they endorsed our
cause and helped us by good collection. Two officers of the
American Missionary Association who were present realized

that Mr. White was greatly overtaxed and arranged for an assistant as advance agent. A hearing before the Presbyterian Synod at Springfield, Ohio, brought our cause prominently before the Presbyterians. At first we were welcomed in the Sunday Schools and churches. The collections were small and the concerts poorly attended.

On the Road

Burdens grew and our strength was failing under the ill treatment at hotels, on railroads, poorly attended concerts, and ridicule; besides we were too thinly clad for the increasing cold of a northern climate. Moreover our teachers at school constantly wrote of their limitations and appealed to us to send them money. A less trusting, less brave heart than Mr. J. White's had broken; yet, he pushed on, doing the advance work which later it required five men to do. Often he left us at railway stations while he and some other man of the troupe waded through sleet or snow or rain from hotel to hotel seeking shelter for us. Many a time our audiences in large halls were discouragingly slim, except for the bootblacks and their kith, who crowded in and often joined in the chorus of "John Brown," with voices, feet and bootjacks. On such occasions Mr. White, after thanking those present for coming, explained our mission and appealed for help, saying, "If there are any of the Lord's people present with any of His treasure, will you not help us pay our honest debts and railroad fare to our next appointment?" Always enough money came to do just that and no more, and we went day by day on prayer and faith.

The Name "Jubilee Singers"

Realizing that we must have a name, we held a prayer meeting at Columbus, Ohio. Our Fisk pastor, Reverend H. S. Bennett, was present. Next morning Mr. White met us with a glowing face. He had remained in prayer all night alone with God. "Children," he said, "it shall be Jubilee Singers in memory of the Jewish year of

Jubilee." The dignity of the name appealed to us. At our usual family worship that morning there was great rejoicing.

Programs

At first our programs had been made up wholly of what we called the white man's music. Occasionally two or three slave songs were sung at the close of the concert.

The following is a sample program sung at Mansfield, Ohio. November 29, 1871:

1. Holy Lord God of Sabaoth.
2. Friends, We Come with Hearts of Gladness.
3. There's Moonlight on the Lake.
4. Irish Ballad. Patrick McCuishla.
5. Recitation. Sheridan's Ride.
6. Gipsey Chorus.
7. Solo. The Loving Heart that Won Me.
8. Songs of Summer.
9. Temperance Medley.
10. Wine is a Mocker.

1. Hail America.
2. Merrily o'er the Calm Blue Sea.
3. Old Folks at Home.
4. Away to the Meadows.
5. Comin' Through the Rye.
6. Roll, *Jording* [Jordan], Roll.
7. Turn Back Pharaoh's Army.
8. Vocal Medley.
9. Home, Sweet Home.

But very soon our sufferings and the demand of the public changed this order. A program of nineteen numbers, only two or three of which were slave songs, was inverted. To recall and to learn of each other the slave songs demanded much mental labor, and to prepare them for public singing required much rehearsing. . . .

Our experiences repeated themselves from place to place on our journey toward New York. As the slave song says, "We were sometimes up and sometimes down, but still our souls kept heavenly bound." Arriving in New York we found "no room in the inn" and three of our American Missionary Association secretaries, the Reverends Cravath, Smith, and Pike, took us to their home in Brooklyn, where we remained for six weeks.

Through the interest and co-operation of the leading ministers of New York, led by that noble man, Henry Ward Beecher, our cause was soon before the public and we were received with the wildest enthusiasm. Our concerts were crowded. In each city where we appeared, a perfect furore of excitement prevailed. Varied and favorable criticisms filled the dailies of our ability as musicians, of the wonderful spiritual effect of the slave songs, now called Jubilee songs. We visited many of the principal cities and towns of New York, Pennsylvania and New Jersey. We went into New England, and everywhere the experience was the same. Hotels refused us, and families of the highest social prestige received us into their homes. We sang in halls where Negroes had never been allowed upon the platform. . . .

Success followed us to Washington, D.C. The President turned aside from pressing duties to receive us at the White House. Parson Brownlow, Tennessee's Senator, too ill to attend our concert, sent for us to visit him. He cried like a child as we sang our humble Southern slave melodies. Returning to New England we received a perfect ovation. Extra excursions were often run to our concerts. Our songs, which had been taken down by Professor Theodore F. Seward and published, were sold at our concerts during the intermission. Soon the land rang with our slave songs, sung in the homes of the people.

Our first campaign closed at Poughkeepsie. New York. We not only had paid the debts at home of nearly $1,500 and furnished other money for support of Fisk; but we carried home $20,000, with which was purchased the present site of twenty-five acres for our new school. At Louisville we were roughly turned out of the sitting-room at the railway station amid the jeers of about two thousand roughs, but the railroad superintendent put us in a first-class coach, in which we returned to Fisk amid great rejoicing.

Part II. At the World's Peace Jubilee

Remaining at home only one week we again took the road. That we might meet the greater demands for concerts, and also visit smaller places where it would be too expensive to go with a full company, our number had been increased. We had been invited to sing at the second World's Peace Jubilee in June. After a few concerts *enroute*, we stopped at Boston to rehearse and rest.

Mr. White had unusual taste and gifts. For weeks he trained our voices to sing the Battle Hymn of the Republic. He reasoned that the thousands of instruments to be used in the great building would very likely play it in E flat, the one key in which the various instruments could harmonize. Hence, in order to be heard satisfactorily by the vast audience, we must be able to enunciate with perfect accuracy of pitch and purity of tone every word and every part of a word in a key three half steps higher than usual. So, little by little, each day or two going a bit higher, using his violin, he trained us on those words from C to E flat until he was satisfied.

The day came when the Battle Hymn was to be sung. Two colored girls, sisters and beautiful singers, too, were to sing the first two verses, and we the last, "He hath sounded forth the trumpet." Evidently the sisters had not anticipated the change of key, and to their chagrin they found themselves obliged greatly to strain their voices and unable to sing their parts satisfactorily. The conductor told us to sing on the choruses, but we preferred to hold all our force in reserve until the time came for us to sing, though trembling like spirited race horses in our excitement to begin. Then with apparently one voice, pure, clear and distinct, we sang out.

> *He hath sounded forth the trumpet.*
> *Which shall never call retreat.*

The audience of forty thousand people was electrified. Men and women arose in their wild cheering, waving and throwing up handkerchiefs and hats. The twenty thousand musicians and singers behind us did likewise. One German raised his violincello and thwacked its back with the bow, crying. "Bravo, bravo!" and Strauss, the great composer, waved his violin excitedly. It was a triumph not to be forgotten. For days we sang: the people seemed never to tire of listening.

Another Campaign

The summer was spent in rest and rehearsals at Acton, Mass., a very busy and successful campaign followed during the next three months. Our double (or two) companies were reorganized into one company of eleven singers. Again we battled with prejudice in the City of Brotherly Love. Only one hotel, The Continental, would receive us. At Princeton, New Jersey, the color line was drawn for the first and only time in our concerts, in that the colored people of the audience were obliged to sit by themselves. The singers would have refused to sing had it not been that so many of their friends had come a long distance to hear them.

Since a visit to England was planned for the early spring, the closing weeks were used to giving farewell concerts. Most cordial and complimentary letters of introduction were given us by leading ministers and people of the highest rank and attainment in the United States to a similar class of citizens abroad, which happily brought [us] once before the choicest spirits among the religious, philanthropic and social classes. An evidence of civic and social prejudice was shown through the refusal of one after another of the ocean steamship lines to take us as cabin passengers. Finally, the Cunard Line received us on the good ship, "Batavia." The kindness of the captain and crew we shall never forget.

The Singers in England

We had our first hearing in Great Britain [May 6, 1873] in [Willis] Rooms. Cards of invitation issued in the name of his Lordship, the Earl of Shaftsbury, and the committee of the Freedman's Mission Aid Society were sent to the nobility, members of Parliament, leading clergymen of different denominations, editors and others of influence. The house was packed. We carried everything before us. Congratulations and invitations were abundant. One of those which we accepted was from the Duke and Duchess of Argyle to Argyle Lodge, their city home. The next day all the leading dailies had favorable criticisms. This introduction to the British public paved the way to countless invitations for concerts and social functions among Great Britain's distinguished people. At Argyle Lodge we met many of the elite of society, with whom we conversed freely and pleasantly, often amusingly. Our many shades of brown and black got us mixed up at times and, too, their English accent was so different from ours that at first we could not easily understand each other.

To our great surprise and delight Her Majesty, Queen Victoria, drove over to meet us and we sang for her. She expressed pleasure and said we comforted her. The Ducess of Argyle presented each of us with a gift. Another social invitation which we accepted was to the Deanery at Westminster Abbey, from Dean and Lady Stanley. For three months we were kept busy filling engagements. At Mr. Samuel Gur[n]ey's we were introduced to the great Quaker circle, who are known the world over for their friendship for the oppressed. George McDonald, the author, a relative of our Professor Spence, invited us to his annual garden party for London's poor, held at his beautiful home on the Thames.

The most distinguished attentions we received were from England's premier, Mr. Gladstone. Three times this great man invited us to his home, first to Carlton Terrace, his London home, to sing at a luncheon given to the Prince and Princess of Wales and her sister, the Czarina of Russia, members of the Diplomatic Corps, John Bright, the Bishop of Manchester (son of the great Wilberforce), Jenny Lind, and others. The second time, soon after the first, we went as their guests and were seated at a table among other guests as distinguished as those on the previous occasion and were royally entertained as guests. The third time we were invited to Mr. Gladstone's home in North Wales. We spent the day in their lovely home, mingling freely with the family, enjoying and examining not only art treasures in the drawing-rooms, but especially his table of axes collected from all over the world in his study. He shows us his favorite ax. It is said that Mr. Gladstone felled a tree every morning before breakfast. At dinner the servants were dismissed and Mr. Gladstone explained to us that he and Mrs. Gladstone wanted the honor of serving us to show us how greatly we and our mission were esteemed. Later he sent a valuable collection of books in the library of Fisk University.

A [. . .] of visits to the many national societies, religious and secular [. . .] us actively before all the people. We met many dignitaries, among them the venerable Dr. Robert Moffatt fifty years a missionary to Africa, father-in-law of David Livingstone, also the daughter of Livingstone, the sweet "Nannie," of whom he wrote so tenderly. Temperance societies adopted us throughout the kingdom because we did not use strong drink. We had it understood at social events that our glasses must be turned down. Churches which had never opened their doors for paid entertainments opened to us. Rev. Charles Spurgeon's Tabernacle was one of many to welcome us.

Our whole journey to and through Scotland, Ireland and Wales was like that experienced in England. In Scotland our concerts in large cities very frequently were presided over by the Lord Provost. Indeed, Lord Shaftsbury's letters preceded us everywhere and led even Edinburgh, Glasgow and other cities officially to invite us to visit them. Social invitations greeted us everywhere and abundant opportunities were given us to assist in the Christian efforts of uplifting the needy. Our concerts were successful, sometimes more than crowded. Some Sabbaths we sang at six services. In Edinburgh and Glasgow we sang at the 6 a.m. breakfast to thousands of the poor: at nine at the Sunday Schools: in the afternoons to working people: later to the outcasts, often in Guild Halls, where people stood shoulder to shoulder to hear God's word: the women came at one hour and the men at another. We sang in the open air to thousands, in the hospitals, prisons, beside sick bed, everywhere. One invalid of forty years in Dundee, Scotland, had prayed for a year that the Lord would send us to sing just one

song to him. Gifts for our school continued to come and sometimes we received personal gifts. At Paisley, Scotland, Sir Peter
Coats (the thread manufacturer) presided at our concert, entertained us in his home, and invited us to his factory, where he
gave each of us a shawl, a real "Paisley."

Often we came across Messrs. Moody and Sankey and had
the privilege of assisting them. Once we surprised them. We arrived late and had to go into the small fifth gallery. During a
pause following an earnest appeal to sinners we softly sang,

> "There are Angels hovering round
>   To carry the tidings home."

The effect was wonderful and most impressive. Some people
said they really thought for a moment that the music came
from an angelic band. Mr. Moody looked as though he would
not have been more surprised had his Lord appeared. He afterward spoke of it.

Our concerts often brought as much as $1,000 a night, and
we were kept in a whirl of work and excitement. We daily had
to turn away from worthy causes which appealed to us. The
correspondence alone was very taxing upon our management,
who were already falling in strength while attempting to keep
up the routine of duties incident to the business side of the
work. Miss Gilbert, our chaperon who mothered us for ten
years, became very ill and had to rest. Mr. Pike, our business
manager, broke down and others had to be laid off. Poor Mr.
White, while on the verge of prostration, was suddenly called
to Glasgow, where his family lived, to see his loved wife die of
typhoid fever, leaving three little children in the care of her
friend and companion, Dr. Addie Williams, who had gone with
them from America. With so many of the management ill and
absent, the singers, with volunteer help, carried on the work to
the close of the season, ending our first campaign in Great Britain at the Exeter Hall, London, Lord Shaftsbury presiding. The
doxology was sung by the entire audience and we bade farewell
to our friends and soon sailed for America. The proceeds of the
last concert were the largest received in Great Britain. The total
receipts of this campaign were nearly $50,000.

Second Campaign Abroad

The year 1875 was noted for important events; Fisk received its first President, Rev. E. M. Cravath; completed its first decade; graduated its first college class, and entered Jubilee Hall, the historic building which will ever stand as a memorial, not only to the labors of George L. White and his Jubilee Singers, but also to those who remained at home and kept up the work for Christ's neglected, needy race of children.

Larger and growing needs as the work developed required greater funds to insure permanency, so after the singers had rested a while, another campaign abroad was planned for them. A few concerts in the North brought to our notice the fact that many other companies had entered the field, each claiming to be the original company from Fisk University. Some of the them appropriated our testimonials and impersonated our singers, reaping unharvested fields, much to our loss. Much of their work was a discredit and disgrace to the good work which we had done only a few months before.

On May 15th our reorganized company of eleven members, with Mr. White and Miss Gilbert, our loved chaperon, again sailed for England. It was gratifying to find that more than one steamship line which had before refused us cabin passage, now offered it to us at reduced rates, but we turned to the Cunard steamship, "Algeria." We were accompanied by Prof. Theodore F. Seward, our new director of music, and his family. President Cravath came later as business manager. May 31st found us at the annual meeting of the Freedmen's Mission Aid Society held in City Temple, London. Our friends had heard that we would be there and packed both upper and lower halls, the corridors and streets so solidly that Lord Shaftsbury had difficulty in reaching the rostrum. His Lordship welcomed our return "in behalf of thousands and tens of thousands of British citizens, with joy." Dr. Joseph Parker reiterated the same in an address which followed, and we received a most cordial ovation.

In less than an hour after our arrival a request came from D. L. Moody for us to help him in his service that afternoon at the Haymarket Opera House. The next day also we sat beside him and sang "Steal Away," after a touching sermon to an audience representing the wealth and rank of London, some one said, "The effect could not have been happier had the song been written for the sermon or the sermon for the song." It seemed our duty to turn aside from concerts to help win souls. We took summer quarters for the purpose of rest in East London, near Bow Road Hall, where Messrs. Moody and Sankey were laboring. We gave a month singing at the services daily to an audience of ten or twelve thousand souls. At the close of the meetings, we received the grateful thanks of our friends and Mr. Moody gave each of us a Baxter Bible containing his autograph. Thousands were converted during the meetings. One man who died soon after said that he went to hear the preaching, but the singing had saved his soul.

After a few successful concerts in Wales and England we again entered Scotland. Applications for concerts poured in from all parts of the kingdom and full houses greeted us. One concert in Glasgow netted $1,700. A similar work to that of the first campaign was carried on in concerts, extra Christian efforts and social functions. It was impossible to respond to all the invitations that came to us.

We went to Ireland and our work there was a repetition of that in other countries, only our Irish friends, in their enthusiasm, seemed even more demonstrative than other people in expressing their appreciation. Before meeting Hon. Horatius Gates Jones in Philadelphia, an Irish friend, and these friends in Dublin, we had always supposed that the Irish were our natural enemies, because of experiences in both the North and South. We rejoiced at the discovery of our mistake. At our first concert fifteen hundred applicants for tickets were turned away. Opportunities for Sabbath services and social functions were more than we could fill. We found that Ireland, too, had received letters from our good friend, Lord Shaftsbury.

After a flying trip to several cities in Northern and Southern Ireland we turned to Geneva, Switzerland, to rest for the summer. During the summer gave a concert in Geneva, at which Pere Hyacinth presided. Although he and the audience could not understand English they applauded, wept or smiled at the same places as an English audience. They said, "We feel it," and were very cordial in their looks and handshakes.

In Holland

We went to Holland by invitation of a Dutch friend of Rotterman, G. P. Ittman, Esq., who had heard us in London. Our "Story With Songs," was translated into Dutch, the programs containing both English and Dutch side by side. Local committees of leading citizens were formed in almost every place we visited. These committees met us at stations and escorted us to our hotels and assumed all the responsibilities of the campaign. Where suitable halls could not be found, their churches or [Domes] were opened to us. Great as had been the attentions show us, none had equaled the dazzling splendor of the reception given us at the palatial home of Baron Von Wassenaer de Catwick at the Hague. The Queen of the Netherlands, wearing a diamond coronet, and other members of the royal family, were present in court dress, and a hundred or more of the nobility and diplomatic corps were present in all their splendor. Our hotel was just across the street, but court etiquette required that we drive across to their door. We wore our usual simple dresses, but our reception was most cordial and enthusiastic. The scene was beyond description in brilliancy and magnificence. Even the liveried servants who ushered guests to cloak rooms or salons and files of soldiers that lined the path to the door, reminded us that we were in the midst of royalty. Even the Queen conversed freely and directly with us. Later we met the King at his palace, [the Lon], where we met other distinguished guests. He gave us a large contribution. We were grateful for the $10,000 which our two months' work in Holland had netted us, but even more grateful for the hospitality which we had enjoyed.

Among the several friends whom we learned to love was the Van Heemstra family. Baroness Cornelia Van Heemstra became my personal friend and later, when I became ill in Germany, she sent for me to come to the Hague, and sent me, as her friend, to a hospital reserved for the nobility, where I remained for six weeks. I was treated like a sister beloved. Amusing incidents occurred in the smaller towns and cities of Holland, where no colored person had ever been before. Our arrival created a greater sensation than a circus in the United

States. We could not go walking or shopping on foot because
crowds of children in wooden shoes surrounded us so closely
that we could not get on. In hotels and at every social event we
were treated royally.

In Germany

In October, 1877, we entered Germany. Again we found that
Lord Shaftsbury's generous letters had acquainted the philanthropic, religious and musical circles with our coming and mission. At once we received invitations to dinners, receptions, etc.
where we met many of the elite of Germany. Rare and special
favors in beautiful homes greeted us, the most significant being
an invitation from the Crown Prince to New Palace, Potsdam,
to meet the royal family. The imperial carriages met us. Arriving at the palace we were soon ushered into the presence of the
royal family, the crown prince Frederick and Crown Princess,
daughter of Queen Victoria, and their children; also the aged
Emperor or Kaiser. A delightful time was spent in familiar and
cordial conversation and we sang a number of our sweetest
slave songs, to the delight of all. Queen Victoria had written
her daughter three years before of her enjoyment of our songs
and how they comforted her, which had made the Crown Princess anxious to meet us. Lunch was served us in the palace, after which the good-bye's were said and we entered the carriages
and returned to Berlin. The Crown Prince begged a copy of our
songs, that he might sing them with his family. As Mr. Marsh
had well said, "It was a delightful glimpse of the home life of
today in the palace of Frederick the Great."

At one of the grand receptions I felt so keenly that a certain
Countess' eyes were constantly fixed upon me that I could not
help asking her in broken German, "What is the matter?" She,
in equally broken English, replied: "Oh, I so astonished you
speak English—beautifully, and oh, you dress like we." I replied, "Why what did you expect me to have on?" She replied,
"Oh, Africani Africani." I suppose she expected us to have on
only five yards of calico wrapped around us, à l'Africaines.

We felt that out first concert, which was to be given in the

The Final Word by President Gates

The account of the striking success in raising money by the original Jubilee Singers, which money was used in the purchase of a good part of the campus on which the university now stands and for the erection of Jubilee Hall, may suggest the impression that at this time, 1911, the University still has adequate financial support. Such an impression would be as unfortunate as it would be untrue. The University has come now upon a second crisis. Its expenses have been running ahead of its income for some years. The demands for enlargement have been so imperative as to be nothing less than a command to take some steps in the line of progress.

But the time has come now for a change in this respect. The Trustees have determined to raise at least $300,000 which they hope to make $300,000, in the immediate future, for endowment. A member of the Board of Trustees, Mr. H. L. Simmons, is devoting his whole time and strength to the work of raising this fund which we must have.

Meantime there are heavy annual expenses which must be provided for outside the few sources of modest revenue that can be depended upon. These sources are Fees from the students, an annual grant for the Slater Board and an annual appropriation from the American Missionary Association. It is a time when Fisk University needs the stalwart help of all its old friends and a large number of new ones. In this great work of putting the institution anew on its feet we must succeed.

POETRY, DRAMA,
AND FICTION

26

SARAH FORTEN PURVIS (MAGAWISCA)

(1814–1884)

Sarah Louisa Forten Purvis, the third daughter of James Forten and Charlotte Vandine Forten, was yet another member of Philadelphia's prominent abolitionist Forten family whose writing is featured in this anthology. Like her niece, Charlotte Forten Grimké, Sarah Forten Purvis considered herself an abolitionist first and foremost, but was celebrated for her literary work. Her poem "The Grave of the Slave" (1831) was set to music by bugler and bandleader Francis "Frank" Johnson. In 1839, she married Joseph Purvis, a member of another prominent Philadelphia family.

The following poems, "The Slave Girl's Address to Her Mother" and "Lines," along with the essay, "The Abuse of Liberty," were all featured in the *Liberator*, William Lloyd Garrison's abolitionist newspaper; she was a frequent contributor under the pen names Ada and Magawisca. Her work offers a glimpse into the robust women's abolitionist movement, centered around the Philadelphia-based Forten family before the Civil War. Her writings for the *Liberator* emerged from her devotion to organizations like the Underground Railroad and the Philadelphia Anti-Slavery Society. These are political works written by a staunch activist at a time when political consequences could not be more dire for the writer and for the nation.

"The Slave Girl's Address to Her Mother" (1831)

SOURCE: Sarah Forten Purvis, "The Slave Girl's Address to
Her Mother," *Liberator*, January 29, 1831.

Oh! mother, weep not, though our lot be hard,
And we are helpless—God will be our guard:
For He our heavenly guardian doth not sleep;
He watches o'er us—mother, do not weep.

And grieve not for that dear loved home no more
Our sufferings and our wrongs, ah! why deplore?
For though we feel the stern oppressor's rod,
Yet he must yield, as well as we, to God.

Torn from our home, our kindred and our friends,
And in a stranger's land our days to end,
No heart feels for the poor, the bleeding slave;
No arm is stretched to rescue, and to save.

Oh! ye who boast of Freedom's sacred claims,
Do ye not blush to see our galling chains;
To hear that sounding word—"that all are free"—
When thousands groan in hopeless *slavery?*

Upon your land it is a cruel stain—
Freedom, what art thou?—nothing but a name.
No more, no more! Oh God, this cannot be;
Thou to thy children's aid wilt surely flee:
In thine own time deliverance thou wilt give,
And bid us rise from slavery, and live.
   Philadelphia.   ADA.

"The Abuse of Liberty" (1831)

SOURCE: Sarah Forten Purvis, "The Abuse of Liberty,"
Liberator, March 26, 1831.

I know no evil under the wide-spread canopy of Heaven, so
great as the abuse of man's liberty; and no where has this vice
a more extensive sway, than in this boasted land of Philanthropy, that offers to every white man the right to enjoy life,
liberty, and happiness. I say every white man, because those
who cannot shew a fair exterior, (no matter what be the noble
qualities of their mind,) are to be robbed of the rights by which
they were endowed by an all-wise and merciful Creator, who,
in his great wisdom, cast a sable hue over some of the "lords of
creation." And does it follow, that those are to be loaded with
ignominy, crushed by the galling chain of slavery, and degraded
even to the level of the brute? Is it because their skins are black,
that they are to be deprived of every tender tie that binds the
heart of man to earth? Is it for this unalterable cause, that they
are to bow beneath the lash, and with a broken, bleeding heart,
enrich the soil of the pale faces? Yet it is no less true than infamous, that this monstrous vice has been suffered to pursue its
course in the breasts of so many of our noble countrymen. It is a
lamentable fact, that they can with remorseless hearts rush like
fiends into the retirement of a happy, unsuspecting family, and
with an unshaken hand, tear the unconscious husband from his
tender wife, and the helpless babe from its mother's breast. And
is *he* a happy man, who can thus, without a shudder,—yes, without a sigh, plant the thorn of misery where once contentment
reigned? No—there is no state of life so anxious as his; he lives
contrary to the dictates of conscience; he is in constant dread lest
they, whom be unjustly condemns to bondage, will burst their
fellers, and become oppressors in their turn.—And is it the insa-
tiable thirst for mammon that has blinded our countrymen? and
the glitter of paltry gold that has made them so callous to their
immortal safety?

Oh, that the scales of error might fall from their eyes, that
they might clearly behold with what rapidity that little stream

they first introduced into their country, has spread itself! It will soon expand into a mighty river, that will ere long overwhelm them in its dark abyss. Awake from your lethargy; exert every nerve; cast off the yoke from the oppressed; let the bondmen go free; and cry unto your offended God to send freedom with its strong battlements to impede the progress of this raging flood;—I say, cry unto Him for aid; for can you think He, thee Great Spirit, who created all men free and equal—He, who made the sun to shine on the black man as well as on the white, will always allow you to rest tranquil on your downy couches? No,—He is just, and his anger will not always slumber. He will wipe the tear from Ethiopia's eye; He will shake the tree of liberty, and its blossoms shall spread over the earth.

MAGAWISCA

PHILADELPHIA, MARCH 14, 1831

"Lines" (1838)

SOURCE: Sarah Forten Purvis, "Lines,"
Liberator, October 5, 1838.

On the suppression, by a portion of our public journals, of the intelligence of the Abolition of Slavery in the British West Indies.

From fair Jamaica's fertile plains,
    Where joyous summer smiles,
To where eternal winter reigns,
    On Greenland's naked isles;
Or, from Barbado's, eastward borne,
    Upon the fresh'ning breeze,
To every sunny isle that decks
    The Atlantic seas;

Wherever mild Religion's light
  Has shed its cheering ray,
Or where the gloom of heathen night
  Excludes the Gospel day—
Where e'er the poor down-trodden slave
  In weary bondage pines,
From proud Columbia's fair domain,
  "To Sibir's dreary mines"—

Truth shall prevail, and Freedom's light
  Shall speed its onward course,
Impeded by no human might,
  Quelled by no human force.
Vain, then, the endeavor to suppress,
  In this enlightened land,
Those tiding which create such joy
  Upon West Indies' strand

No sword was drawn, no blood was spilt
  Upon the verdant sod,
Yet man, enfranchised, stands erect,
  The image of his God
Then let the joyful news be given
  To every human ear,
Which e'en the Angels, high in Heaven,
  Might lean to earth to hear.

ANN PLATO

(ca. 1820–after 1841)

Ann Plato was born free in Hartford, Connecticut, the daughter of a farmer and a seamstress. Most of what is known about her was written by her mentor, Rev. James W. C. Pennington, in the introduction to her book, *Essays: Including Biographies and Miscellaneous Pieces, in Prose and Poetry*, which Plato published at the age of sixteen. Plato was an educator, working at the Free African Schools in Hartford. Her writings stress the importance of education and promote New England Puritan values. Plato's date of death is unknown.

Ann Plato's writings might be characterized by an unshakable sense of belonging to the broader American political project, not a racial project. Her community and her audience is the nation, not fellow African Americans. Her essay "Education" argues that education is the key to national greatness and that any person, through education, is capable of making a mark upon history. Her only published poem, "The Natives of America," is framed as a lesson taught by a Native father to a daughter, describing the oppression of their ancestors by European colonizers.

"Education" (1841)

SOURCE: Ann Plato, *Essays: Including Biographies and Miscellaneous Pieces, in Prose and Poetry* (Hartford, CT: Printed by the Author, 1841).

This appears to be the great source from which nations have become civilized, industrious, respectable and happy. A society or people are always considered as advancing, when they are found paying proper respect to education. The observer will find them erecting buildings for the establishment of schools, in various sections of their country, on different systems, where their children may at an early age commence learning, and having their habits fixed for higher attainments. Too much attention, then, can not be given to it by people, nation, society or individual. History tells us that the first settlers of our country soon made themselves conspicuous by establishing a character for the improvement, and diffusing of knowledge among them.

We hear of their inquiry, how shall our children be educated? and upon what terms or basis shall it be placed? We find their questions soon answered to that important part; and by attending to this in every stage of their advancement, with proper respect, we find them one of the most enlightened and happy nations on the globe.

It is, therefore, an unspeakable blessing to be born in those parts where wisdom and knowledge flourish; though it must be confessed there are even in these parts several poor, uninstructed persons who are but little above the late inhabitants of this country, who knew no modes of the civilized life, but wandered to and fro, over the parts of the then unknown world.

We are, some of us, very fond of knowledge, and apt to value ourselves upon any proficiency in the sciences; one science, however, there is, worth more than all the rest, and that is the science of living well—which shall remain "when tongues shall cease," and "knowledge shall vanish away."

It is owing to the preservation of books, that we are led to embrace their contents. Oral instructions can benefit but one age and one set of hearers; but these silent teachers address all ages and all nations. They may sleep for a while and be neglected; but whenever the desire of information springs up in the human breast, there they are with mild wisdom ready to instruct and please us.

No person can be considered as possessing a good education without religion. A good education is that which prepares us for our future sphere of action and makes us contented with that situation in life in which God, in his infinite mercy, has seen fit to place us, to be perfectly resigned to our lot in life, whatever it may be. Religion has been decreed as the passion of weak persons; but the Bible tells us "to seek first the kingdom of heaven, and His righteousness, and all other things shall be added unto us." This world is only a place to prepare for another and a better.

If it were not for education, how would our heathen be taught therefrom? While science and the arts boast so many illustrious names; there is another and more extended sphere of action where illustrious names and individual effort has been exerted with the happiest results, and their authors, by their deeds of charity, have won bright and imperishable crowns in the realms of bliss. Was it the united effort of nations, or of priestly synods that first sent the oracles of eternal truth to the inhospitable shores of Greenland— or placed the lamp of life in the hut of the Esquemaux—or carried a message of love to the burning climes of Africa—or that directed the deluded votaries of idolatry in that benighted land where the Ganges rolls its consecrated waters, to Calvary's Sacrifice, a sacrifice that sprinkled with blood the throne of justice, rendering it accessible to ruined, degraded man.

In proportion to the education of a nation, it is rich and powerful. To behold the wealth and power of Great Britain, and compare it with China;

America with Mexico; how confused are the ideas of the latter, how narrow their conceptions, and are, as it were in an unknown world.

Education is a system which the bravest men have followed. What said Alexander about this? Said he: "I am more indebted to my tutor, Aristotle, than to my father Philip; for Philip gives me my living, but Aristotle teaches me how to live." It was Newton that threw aside the dimness of uncertainty which shrouded for so many centuries the science of astronomy; penetrated the arena of nature, and soared in his eagle-flight far, far beyond the wildest dreams of all former ages, defining with certainty the motions of those flaming worlds, and assigning laws to the fartherest star that lies on the confines of creation—that glimmers on the verge of immensity.

Knowledge is the very foundation of wealth, and of nations. Aristotle held unlimited control over the opinions of men for fifteen centuries, and governed the empire of mind where ever he was known. For knowledge, men brave every danger, they explore the sandy regions of Africa, and diminish the arena of contention and bloodshed. Where ever ignorance holds unlimited sway, the light of science, and the splendor of the gospel of truth is obscure and nearly obliterated by the gloom of monkish superstition, merged in the sable hues of idolatry and popish cruelty; no ray of glory shines on those degraded minds; "darkness covers the earth, and gross darkness the people."

Man is the noblest work in the universe of God. His excellence does not consist in the beautiful symmetry of his form, or in the exquisite structure of his complicated physical machinery; capable of intellectual and moral powers. What have been the conquests of men in the field of general science? What scholastic intrenchment is there which man would not have wished to carry—what height is there which he would not have wished to survey—what depth that he would not like to explore?—even the mountains and the earth—hidden minerals—and all that rest on the borders of creation he would like to overpower.

But shall these splendid conquests be subverted? Egypt, that once shot over the world brilliant rays of genius, is sunk in darkness. The dust of ages sleeps on the besom of Roman warriors, poets, and orators. The glory of Greece has departed, and leaves no Demosthenes to thunder with his eloquence, or Homer to soar and sing.

It is certainly true that many dull and unpromising scholars have become the most distinguished men; as Milton, Newton, Walter Scott, Adam Clarke. Newton stated of himself, that his superiority to common minds was not natural, but acquired by mental discipline. Hence, we perceive that the mind is capable of wonderful improvement. The mother of Sir William Jones said to him when a child: "If you wish to understand, read;" how true, that "education forms the mind."

How altogether important, then, is education; it is our guide in youth, and it will walk with us in the vale of our declining years. This knowledge we ought ever to pursue with all diligence. Our whole life is but one great school; from the cradle to the grave we are all learners; nor will our education be finished until we die.

A good education is another name for happiness. Shall we not devote time and toil to learn how to be happy? It is a science which the youngest child may begin, and the wisest man is never weary of. No one should be satisfied with present attainments; we should aim high, and bend all our energies to reach the point aimed at.

We ought not to fail to combine with our clear convictions of what is right, a firmness and moral courage sufficient to enable us to "forsake every false way," and our course will be like that of the just—"brighter and brighter unto the perfect day."

"The Natives of America" (1841)

Tell me a story, father please,
And then I sat upon his knees.
Then answer'd he,—"what speech make known,
Or tell the words of native tone,
Of how my Indian fathers dwelt,
And, of sore oppression felt;
And how they mourned a land serene,
It was an ever mournful theme."
Yes, I replied,—I like to hear,
And bring my father's spirit near;
Of every pain they did forego,
Oh, please to tell me all you know.
In history often I do read,
Of pain which none but they did heed.

He thus began. "We were a happy race,
When we no tongue but ours did trace,
We were in ever peace,
We sold, we did release—
Our brethren, far remote, and far unknown,
And spake to them in silent, tender tone.
We all were then as in one band,
We join'd and took each others hand;
Our dress was suited to the clime,
Our food was such as roam'd that time,
Our houses were of sticks compos'd;
No matter,—for they us enclos'd.

But then discover'd was this land indeed
By European men; who then had need
Of this far country. Columbus came afar,
And thus before we could say Ah!
What meaneth this?—we fell in cruel hands.
Though some were kind, yet others then held bands
Of cruel oppression. Then too, foretold our chief,—
Beggars you will become—is my belief.
We sold, then some bought lands,
We altogether moved in foreign hands.

Wars ensued. They knew the handling of fire-arms.
Mothers spoke,—no fear this breast alarms,
They will not cruelly us oppress,
Or thus our lands possess.
Alas! it was a cruel day; we were crush'd:
Into the dark, dark woods we rush'd
To seek a refuge.

My daughter, we are now diminish'd, unknown,
Unfelt! Alas! no tender tone
To cheer us when the hunt is done;
Fathers sleep,—we're silent every one.

Oh! silent the horror, and fierce the fight,
When my brothers were shrouded in night;

Strangers did us invade—strangers destroy'd
The fields, which were by us enjoy'd.

Our country is cultur'd, and looks all sublime,
Our fathers are sleeping who lived in the time
That I tell. Oh! could I tell them my grief
In its flow, that in roaming, we find no relief.

I love my country; and shall, until death
Shall cease my breath.

Now daughter dear I've done,
Seal this upon thy memory; until the morrow's sun
Shall sink, to rise no more;
And if my years should score,
Remember this, though I tell no more."

JULIA COLLINS

(unknown–1865)

We know very little for certain about Julia Collins beyond what appears in the *Christian Recorder*, the A.M.E. Church publication in which Collins published her works. It is known that Julia worked as a teacher in Williamsport, Pennsylvania, in the 1850s. She was married to Stephen Carlisle Collins, a veteran and barber, with whom she may have had two daughters. Her novel, *The Curse of Caste; or the Slave Bride*, which is excerpted on the following pages, is unfinished because of Collins's death from consumption in 1865. *The Curse of Caste* is among the first novels written by African American women.

The following are five chapters from *The Curse of Caste*. Throughout them, Collins engages with the tragic predicament of being a child born of a slave and master. Slavery's wide social reach ruins the Tracy family and prevents Richard Tracy from living a free life even though his marriage to Lina, a slave, is legal in New England. The repercussions of their marriage are felt for several generations and provoke the reader to wonder if their relationship was worth the ideal that it stood for.

Selections from *The Curse of Caste;* or *The Slave Bride* (1865)

SOURCE: Julia Collins, *The Curse of Caste; or the Slave Bride*, serialized in *Christian Recorder* ("Chapter VI," April 1, 1865; "Chapter VIII," April 15, 1865; "Chapter

X," April 29, 1865; "Chapter XXVII," August 26, 1865;
"Chapter XXIX," September 9, 1865).

CHAPTER VI.

Richard was warmly greeted by his parents, and the negroes
were jubilant over massa's return. Mrs. Tracy felt proud of the
great, tall, noble-looking youth, who stooped to kiss her still
blooming cheek. And well might she feel proud, for never was
a nobler, better son given to gladden a mother's heart.

Col. Tracy took especial pride in introducing his son to all
his acquaintances, but was horrified and dismayed to hear
Richard give expression to many anti-slavery principles, which
he had imbibed while at the north. He tried to reason with him
about the absurdity of entertaining such notions as social
equality between races so widely divergent, in every respect, as
the white and black. But Richard stoutly adhered to his belief
that it was wrong for one man to enslave another, and keep in
bondage a human being, having a mind and soul susceptible of
improvement and cultivation.

Col. Tracy found too much of his own spirit infused into his
son's character, to think of eradicating these sentiments by argument, but trusted to time, and the influence of Southern
principles and society, to effect the desired change. Thus the
subject was dropped, and both father and son avoided alluding
to it again.

Richard, while at a party made in honor of his return,
formed the acquaintance of a young man, by the name of
George Manville. Young Manville was a gay, good-looking fellow, good-natured and perfectly well acquainted with the city
and the circle in which Richard moved. They soon became fast
friends. Manville was rich and handsome, and much sought after by those who failed in reading his true character, as did
Richard Tracy. But Manville was a villain—the beautiful casket enshrined a heart black as the shadows of Hades, and dead
to all the finer feelings, those minor chords which render the
life of man replete with living beauty.

Richard sometimes felt the subtle influence that this Manville exerted over him without understanding it, however; for candid and honorable himself, he did not readily doubt others. These two men were fated to be connected in a degree, through life.

One morning, at breakfast, Col. Tracy declared his intention of going up to the plantation for a few days, on business. We will here state that Col. Tracy had moved to the city of New Orleans, the old homestead being occupied by his overseer's family.

During his father's absence, Richard usually spent the mornings with his mother and little Lloyd. He told her of his love for the beautiful Lina, of their betrothal, and her singular presentiment of evil. Mrs. Tracy was interested in the unknown girl, whose cause her son pleaded so eloquently.

"You would only need see her, to love her," he said, persuasively.

Mrs. Tracy did not doubt that Lina was all Richard's fond imagination painted; but she asked:

"Do you know any thing of this family of Hartleys? You know your father's prejudice against persons marrying with those beneath them in rank and fortune, no matter what their qualities may be."

"I know, mother," said the young man, "but should Lina become poor by any untoward circumstance, that is no reason why I should seek to absolve the vows registered in the sight of Heaven. Of Lina's family I know nothing. I only know she is good and pure. I hope, for my father's sake, she may be rich, and her family such as he would desire my alliance with. But, my gentle mother, whatever misfortune may befall Lina, I will marry her just the same."

"God bless you, my noble son," said Nellie Tracy, with deep feeling. "I trust all may be well."

That same morning Richard's portrait was sent home. It had been painted by a celebrated artist, who had succeeded admirably in giving the picture a true and life-like expression. Before they had finished hanging the picture, Manville was announced, and with the freedom of a privileged friend, came into the room.

When at last the picture was hung in a proper position, with just enough light to give a good effect, all stood back to take a full view of it. Mrs. Tracy remembered, years after, the feelings she experienced when that picture was hung. All were pleased and expressed their satisfaction.

When Col. Tracy returned from his visit to the plantation, he told Richard, in the presence of Manville and Mrs. Tracy, that he had made a very foolish investment. All looked inquiringly at him.

"I attended a sale of slaves, the property of old Hartley, who resides about fifty miles up the river, and was formerly a man of considerable wealth, but being of a wild, reckless disposition, has, in a few years, squandered his fortune, and degenerated into a confirmed drunkard and gambler. I purchased several plantation and house servants, among whom is a beautiful quadroon, who is the daughter of old Hartley's, I understand, and has been educated at a Catholic school, in Canada, and believed herself his lawful child.

The young girl is beautiful, and I think, well educated. Her distress was really affecting, and, out of pity for the young thing, I bought her with the lot, but what I am to do with the baggage, I cannot conceive, for slaves educated at the North, are not just the thing to be introduced into a Southern household. So, I guess I will sell this bit of humanity at the first offer. Why, she had the audacity to faint, when, by accident, she learned the name of her future master was Col. Tracy. I must say, although I claim to be a kind and indulgent master, I have no use for this sensitive class of negroes."

Col. Tracy, at this juncture, noticed the effect of his language upon his wife and son, which seemed to him as singular as it was inexplicable. Mrs. Tracy looked pale and horrified, while Richard's pale and almost defiant expression, betokened a fixed resolution, although he uttered not a word, and soon left the house, accompanied by Manville. Mrs. Tracy soon left the room also, and Col. Tracy was the sole occupant, and was at liberty to digest his astonishment as best he might.

A few hours later, Manville returned, and, after a long conference with Col. Tracy, departed with the document in his pocket, which pronounced him lawful owner of the young quadroon.

Richard returned at tea time with seeming composure, but his mother's eye penetrated the veil. She alone read his feelings, and felt the resolution he had taken. Her heart was too full for utterance, when, after tea, Richard motioned her to follow him. He led the way to the library. A long time elapsed ere they appeared again. Mrs. Tracy was deeply agitated, while Richard's face still wore the same determined expression. What passed during that strange conference, none ever knew. Richard followed his mother to the parlor, when he kissed her gently, saying fervently:

"Mother, pray for me. I hope all may yet be well. Pray for Lina, too. Poor child! God knows she needs your prayers."

A moment more, and Mrs. Tracy was alone. Richard had gone. Where this would all end, she could not tell.

One beautiful morning, in a quiet New England village, far from their own home, Richard Tracy and the beautiful quadroon, Lina, were united for life. It was a quiet bridal, witnessed only by Manville and Richard's aunt, whom we have known as Col. Tracy's sister, Laura, while Laura's husband performed the rite, which united this ill-fated couple.

We will here state that all correspondence had ceased, long years ago, between Laura Tracy and her brother. Her marriage with a poor minister, Alfred Hays, had incurred his lasting displeasure. Laura had several times sought to conciliate her brother, but without success. Alfred Hays was good and noble, and with his lovely wife, joined his efforts to make the young bride happy.

Richard was happy, and soon the shadows left Lina's fair brow. They were happy, but it was as the calm that precedes the raging storm. Did Richard—did Lina feel its dread coming? Had they no warning of the shadow, that would soon fall, crushing the life from their young hearts?

CHAPTER VIII.

The Flower Fadeth.

Time passed slowly with the inmates of Rose Cottage, until the first letter would be received from Richard. Lina wandered about he cottage and garden with a listless air, and Juno seemed more quiet and thoughtful. She knew more of the real state of affairs than the young wife supposed. Juno had lived so long with Laura Hays that she was well acquainted with the history of the Tracys. She also knew much of the character and disposition of Colonel Frank Tracy; she was about twelve years old when Frank was married to pretty Nellie Thornton. She was then living with Laura's aunt. Juno saw Frank Tracy once after that; it was when he came to forbid Laura's marriage with the young minister, Alfred Hays. She knew well his overweening family pride, and love of wealth and position. Alfred Hays was one of nature's noblemen, but wealth and position he had not. Juno was not likely to forget the terrible family quarrel that ensued, when Laura, who possessed much of her brother's spirit and resolution, persisted in marrying the poor minister, declaring that she had the right and was capable of choosing her own husband, and was prepared to follow the dictates of her own heart. Frank, finding that Laura would not be persuaded to give Alfred up, said, angrily:

"Laura, if you persist in marrying that beggar, that mere fortune hunter, you are no longer a sister of mine; so reflect well ere you decide. I will never receive him as a brother."

He was about leaving the room when his sister's voice arrested him. She said, in a low firm tone, "I need not time for reflection, my decision is already made; I will marry Alfred. If he is poor, he is good and noble, while your interference is unnatural and cruelly unjust, and—"

"Enough," cried Frank, impatiently interrupting and pushing her from him. "I will say no more; you have taken your own course, and must abide by the consequences." And he strode from the room, leaving his sister heart-stricken and aghast.

Poor Laura had not quite expected this unhappy turn affairs had taken, yet she was not prepared to sacrifice her life's happiness to her brother's selfish demands.

Frank sought his aunt, and told her the result of his interview with his sister. Laura need not indulge the hope that he would relent his cruel decision, it was unalterable. He departed without seeing Laura again, and from that time all communication between them ceased.

Not until after their marriage did Alfred Hays learn the bitter sacrifice his gentle wife had made, when she fulfilled her plighted troth with him. Miss Tracy then went to reside with her niece, taking Juno with her. A few years later she died, leaving her entire fortune, with the exception of a legacy of ten thousand dollars, to her niece, Laura. The above legacy was willed to Frank Tracy's little son, Richard, to be placed in the care of Alfred Hays, until the young heir should become of age, the interest of which was payable on or after his nineteenth birthday. What had induced Miss Tracy to leave this legacy to little Richard, whom she had never seen, would be impossible to say, but future events proved the wisdom of her last act of kindness.

Juno knew all this, she also knew that all was not satisfactory in relation to Richard's marriage. She knew that some trouble was expected, though the exact nature of it she did not know, but her suspicions were very nearly correct.

Juno always had her "suspicions," and the remarkable part of it is, they were nearly always right. At last a letter came from Richard—a kind and hopeful letter—which did much towards reviving Lina's spirits. It was soon followed by others, all written in the same hopeful, happy style, from various points on the route, and, finally, one written immediately upon his arrival in New Orleans. "Manville," he said," was at present out of the city. I shall go home this evening. You need not look for a letter again for some time, as I shall not write until I know the final result of my visit."

Several weeks elapsed and yet no other letter came. In vain it was that Juno went to the village post-office every day, after the Ruthford stage came in; she failed to bring the white-winged messenger that would have won back the lost smile to Lina's sad face. Truly "hope deferred maketh the heart sick," for Lina's face grew more pale and sad and her step more languid, as week after week sped by, and she received no tidings from the absent one.

Every day, when it drew near the time for Juno's return from the village, she would walk down to the little gate, and wait anxiously for her coming, with eager and expectant face, but when Juno reported her ill success, she would turn away with such a look of keen disappointment, such hopeless despair as to make Juno shed tears of sympathy with the fragile creature that leaned heavily upon her arm.

At last Lina ceased to look for a letter. She never complained, but that quiet despairing look was pitiful to behold. It was in vain Juno taxed her brain in the manufacture of choice delicacies to tempt the palate of the gentle invalid, who invariably thanked her faithful friend with a sweet smile, but failed to do justice to the dainties she prepared. The golden autumn days had passed, and dreary November, with its leaden sky, made all without seem cheerless. The wind moaned dismally through the branches of the Tamaracs at the door, and played at "hide and seek" among the leafless rose bushes. One day, after Lina had been more despondent than ever, and Juno, having finished her household duties, was sitting with folded hands, seemingly intent upon the gambols of a playful kitten; but in reality thinking of Lina, and considering what she had best do, her mistress said:

"Juno, I wish to have a long talk with you."

This was just what Juno had long been wishing for, and she arose with alacrity and followed Lina into the little parlor, where a cheerful fire was burning on the hearth, which, with the heavy red curtains, served to give the room a cheerful appearance. The piano stood open, but no light fingers called forth its lively notes. Juno would open it every morning, saying, apologetically, "that it made the room look more pleasant-like, and more as if master Richard was home."

Lina seated herself in a large easy chair, while Juno took a seat on a low ottoman at her feet.

"Juno, I have never confided to you my early history. I have been thinking much of late, and have concluded to tell you all about myself." Whereupon she told Juno all the reader already knows, together with other facts which it is not our purpose at present to disclose.

"Juno," she continued, after a long silence, during which she had been toying with a beautiful ring on her third finger—it was Richard's gift, "I sometimes think I shall not live long, and, indeed, I should not wish to, if Richard never returns, for I could not live without him."

"Oh, my dear mistress Lina, don't talk that way! Master will come back! You must not talk of dying!" cried Juno, striving to keep back the tears that would fall in spite of all effort to restrain them.

"No, Juno, you cannot deceive me. I know that I cannot get well. You know my situation, and it is not best that you should be with me any longer alone. I wish you to engage the services of some competent old lady immediately. My marriage certificate and letters you will find in a little rose-wood box in my work-stand drawer. When I am gone, Juno, put this ring with the other things, and keep them carefully for my sake. If Richard ever comes home, you may give them to him. Tell him that though my heart was breaking, I loved him to the last. That is all, now I am tired and wish to sleep. You may stop at the post-office as you come through the village."

Juno was successful in finding an old lady of suitable qualifications. Old Mrs. Butterworth had just arrived by the Ruthford stage, and was one of those fat, motherly, smiling, rosy-cheeked old ladies that straightway win one's confidence. So home she went with Juno, who, though delighted with her success, did not forget to stop at the post-office.

The postmaster, from Juno's frequent visits and disappointed face, had learned to know her, and on this occasion hastened to produce and hand to the astonished woman a letter bearing the New Orleans post-mark, and address to Mrs. Lina H. Tracy. Juno gave an exclamation of delight, as she thought of the joyful tidings she hoped to convey to the anxious, weary wife.

Lina was standing by the window when Juno and Mrs. Butterworth came up the walk, the former holding the letter triumphantly aloft. Lina sank nervous and trembling into a seat, as Juno rushed tumultuously into the room, exclaiming, "a letter from master Richard!" and could only articulate faintly, "Give it to me, Juno." She glanced at the well-known superscription, and, with trembling hand, opened the fatal letter, to read the cruel words which would freeze the life from her young heart, and extinguish the life of the rapidly fading flower. Once, twice she read, with staring eyes, the words that closed her brief dream of happiness, when she fell heavily to the floor in a death-like swoon.

CHAPTER X.

Richard in New Orleans.

Soon after Richard's arrival in New Orleans he wended his way home. It was late in the afternoon. Colonel Tracy was seated on the verandah, reading, when Richard came up. "Good afternoon, father," he said, cheerfully, extending his hand at the same time, Colonel Tracy took no notice of the proffered hand, but exclaimed, angrily, "So sir, you have come to insult me with your presence! But follow me to the library, I wish not to quarrel with you here!"

Richard followed the choleric old gentleman, as requested, into the library. Colonel Tracy closed and locked the door, to secure them from intrusion; then confronting his son, with threatening mien, said: "Now, sir, give an account of your proceedings; I want no evasion whatever, but a clear and concise statement of facts."

Richard related all that had transpired, from his first acquaintance with Lina to the present time. His betrothal on the Alhambra—the scene at the dinner table, after Colonel Tracy's return from the plantation. Manville's purchase of the slave girl Lina, which was only a ruse, as Manville merely acted for his friend. The departure of the trio for the north, the quiet bridal at the little New England parsonage, Alfred Hays' departure, the purchase of Rose Cottage, and subsequent experiences for the Colonel's benefit, in his usual characteristic manner.

The Colonel's rage was without bounds, and he wrathfully exclaimed, "Oh! that a son of mine should thus disgrace himself and family, as to marry a negress—a slave—the illegitimate offspring of a spendthrift, a drunkard, and a libertine; a being sunk so low in the scale of humanity as to be unworthy the name of a man. It's awful! 'Tis abominable! Fool, that you are, to allow yourself to be thus entrapped by a pretty face; and, no doubt, by this time you have wearied of your toy. If you have, it will be well, for as you are under age, your marriage is illegal, and, with the assistance of a trusty lawyer, its validity may be annulled. You can visit Europe a year or two, until the memory of this disgraceful affair has died out. I will settle an annuity on your—" he could not add the word *wife*, it would have choked him, so he corrected himself by saying, "on the girl, which will be sufficient to support her decently; and that is much better than she deserves, the artful wench, to palm herself off for a lady. Our society is getting into a pretty state, when the sons of the best families stoop to marry their fathers' slaves. You have imbibed the pernicious sentiments of northern demagogues until they have encompassed your ruin. What is to become of our institution, if we take our slaves upon an equality with ourselves? What slave on the plantation would properly respect you as their master, while they knew your wife was a negro slave— yes, worse than a slave? But to return to the point in question, will you renounce that girl? The way is perfectly clear, and the desired result may be arrived at with little difficulty. Of course it will cause some commotion in the 'upper circles,' and give your name an unpleasant notoriety for a season, but in the course of time that will wear away. As I said before, visit Europe a year or two, and when you return, there is not a young lady in New Orleans that would not accept your hand and fortune."

Colonel Tracy stopped abruptly, and turned to his son, who sat erect, with livid face and flashing eyes, and with an air of such resolute determination, that he felt very uncertain as to the impression produced by his reasoning, and he imperatively asked: "Well, sir, what is your decision?"

Richard possessed extraordinary power of self-control, and replied, in those calm, measured tones, which always give such an advantage in an exciting discussion, and voluntarily win the respect of an opponent, "Father, as much as I love and respect you, I cannot accede to a proposal that would so deeply involve my honor and integrity. I cannot forsake my wife. I did not win Lina's affections to basely deceive her, nor did I marry her to cruelly desert her. I would submit to any fate rather than become a party to such a degrading proceeding. I see no honorable avenue of escape, if I desired one; and I earnestly assure you I do not. Those pernicious sentiments, as you are pleased to term them, which I have imbibed at the north only teach me to respect the rights of my fellow-citizens. Lina is not responsible for her unfortunate birth and surroundings. She is pure, refined, and good, has been educated far from the contaminating influence which southern society exerts over its followers. All else I can well overlook. I would not own a slave if I possessed the wealth of a Croesus. The institution of slavery is of itself accursed, and will yet prove the fatal Nemesis of the South, for do not think that a just God will allow any people so deeply wronged to go unavenged."

Colonel Tracy sat speechless with rage and astonishment, while Richard was speaking, and when he had finished he rose from his chair and confronting his son said: "Richard, if you persist in carrying out this unexampled piece of folly, I shall disinherit you. Not a penny of mine shall go to you or yours, and my doors shall ever be closed against you. Your mother and brother shall never acknowledge you as son and brother, and your name shall be as that of one who has slept a century in his tomb, uncared for and forgotten; so you can make your choice; you know the conditions."

"I cannot forsake my wife," was the firm, unfaltering reply. "Your judgment is severe, and—perhaps, it is just, but I will abide by it without murmuring."

"You dare to defy me!" yelled the Colonel, his face black with rage. "But I will conquer you yet! For I will see you die at my feet before you shall return to the arms of that accursed wife! Yes, I will kill you, and suffer hanging for it!" and drawing a pistol from his pocket took deliberate aim and fired.

Richard, having risen from his chair, exclaimed:

"Father, would you murder your own son!" and fell heavily to the floor, writhing in his own blood, the ball having entered his right side.

Hurrying feet were heard traversing the wide halls—the door was burst open, and Mrs. Tracy rushed into the library, closely followed by Manville, who had just returned, and hearing of Richard's arrival, had come direct to Colonel Tracy's, while groups of frightened negroes crowded the door and thronged the hall, presenting a weird scene, as the twilight shadows were now gathering.

Nellie Tracy gazed from the insensible form of her son to her husband, exclaiming, "Frank, O! Frank! May God forgive you! You have killed my child!" and then sunk fainting to the floor.

Colonel Tracy stood gazing upon the forms of his wife and son, with wild, glaring eyes. Manville alone possessed some presence of mind. He directed the negroes to take charge of their mistress, while he turned his attention to Colonel Tracy. "Come, my friend," he said, attempting to lead him from the library.

"Manville, I am perfectly sane; I know what I have done. Take that boy away, any where, out of my sight and hearing, for I care not whether he lives or dies."

Manville knew that the Colonel was in earnest, so he hailed a passing hack, and, with the assistance of the driver and several of the slaves, the wounded man was carefully placed in it, and driven slowly to a quiet private boarding-house, in a retired part of the city, while others were dispatched in quest of medical aid.

It would be impossible to attempt a description of Colonel Tracy's feelings. Indignation against Richard, and apprehension for his delicate wife, were the predominant workings of his soul. Mrs. Tracy was indeed in a critical state, and well might her passionate husband tremble for her safety. Through the long watches of the night great was the anxiety of that wretched man, for the life of his loved one hung, as it were, by a thread.

CHAPTER XXVII.

Mrs. Butterworth's Revelation.

"Her last words were when asked if she had no word to leave for her husband, for she avoided speaking of him, 'Tell him I loved and—,' but the sentence was never finished. Poor, young thing! It was well she died as soon as she did," continued the matter of fact Mrs. Butterworth, who had thus far failed to notice the extreme agitation of her questioners, "for her husband was a villain, and she escaped a great many trials, by passing from the earth thus early."

Richard was deeply agitated, and motioning Monsieur Sayvord to proceed with questioning their fellow-traveler, he prepared to await further developments. Monsieur Sayvord proceeded to question the old lady with his usual abruptness.

"So the child did not die, you say?"

"No, sir; it lived, and was as fine and healthy a child as you could wish to see."

"What was the colored nurse's name?"

"Juno Hays."

"And what induced you to think that Mrs. Tracy's husband was a villain?"

"Why," replied the old lady, her round, honest eyes flashing with indignation, "if he had been a good and honorable man, he would have written to his poor little heart-broken wife, as a husband ought. He would never have gone to Europe without her knowledge, leaving her among strangers, to die alone. May God forgive the wicked man, wherever he may be!"

"How do you know he went to Europe? And what became of the child and nurse?"

Mrs. Butterworth then related the particulars of Manville's visit, the sale of Rose Cottage, and subsequent removal of Juno and baby Claire to the eastern part of the State. That was all she knew, and since that time she had lost all trace of them.

"But," suggested Mrs. Butterworth, seeing how deeply interested the gentlemen were, "I think Dr. Murdoch could tell you more concerning them. Maybe you're a relation?" she said inquiringly.

Without answering her question directly, Monsieur Sayvord replied:

"We are very much interested in any thing that relates to Mrs. Tracy, and thank you for the information you have given. And I wish to disabuse your mind of false opinions concerning Richard Tracy. I know him well. He is a true and noble man, and mourns yet the early death of his young and gentle wife, who, with himself, was the victim of that designing villain, Manville. Through his representations, Richard has believed, until very recently, that the child had died immediately after birth, and was buried with is mother."

Mrs. Butterworth was very much astonished at this view of the case, but readily transferred her indignation from Richard to Manville. And our friend possessed her sympathy as he has always had ours.

Arriving at the end of their journey, they parted company with the old nurse, and repaired to the best hotel the village afforded. After Richard had partially regained his composure, and they had partaken of a genuine New England dinner, they started in quest of Dr. Murdoch, the old village physician, whose professional business was now carried on by Dr. Murdoch, Jr. The old gentleman was pleased with their visit, and cheerfully related what he knew of the inmates of Rose Cottage. It wrung Richard's heart to hear him talk so touchingly about Lina.

"Mr. Villars owns the cottage now. he bought it, furniture and all, when that dashing young Southerner came and took away Juno and the little baby, which was fast becoming a great favorite with me. I suppose she is a young lady now," said the old doctor, thoughtfully. "Ah, me! how time flies. Why, it is eighteen years ago, and I was an old man *then*."

"Do you know to what town or village they moved?"

"Somewhere in the vicinity of the town of L—, but that you know, was so long ago, they may have moved again."

Thus learning all they could, they took leave of Dr. Murdoch, and returned to the hotel, when they determined, much to the discomfiture of the landlord, who did not like the idea of losing two such distinguished guests, to take the night express for Danbury, and so be enabled to take the first eastern train, the following day. It was their intention to seek out Juno before starting for New Orleans. They knew Claire was ill,—perhaps dying, but Richard felt that he must see Juno first. And impatient as was Monsieur Sayvord, he thought it best to go to L— and make inquiry concerning the old nurse.

Taking the night express they arrived at Danbury at 4 A.M., and taking the train for the east at 11 A.M., they reached L— at 7 o'clock on the morning of the following day. After a fresh toilet, and a hasty breakfast, they started out upon their tour of inquiry. For a long time they could learn nothing. It was very evident Juno did not live in L—.

"She may be living in the country, some where," suggested

Monsieur, as he noticed his friend's despairing look. "Here comes a nice looking colored man, let us ask him."

This colored man proved to be none other than Thomas, Miss Ellwood's hired man, who built fires, and did chores about the Seminary. In answer to their inquiry, Thomas replied:

"Yes, sir, there is such a woman living a few miles from this place. I do not know much about her myself, but the lady I live with can tell you; for she often comes to the Seminary, to see Miss Ellwood, and before Miss Claire left school, Juno used to visit her sometimes."

"Well, my man, I think we have been very fortunate in meeting you, and you will further oblige us by leading the way to the Seminary."

Miss Ellwood was quite astonished when she learned that one of her unexpected guests was the son of Col. Tracy, and more astonished when he declared himself to be the father of her favorite pupil, Claire Neville.

She told him how Manville had placed Claire in the Seminary, six years before, with the understanding that she (Miss Ellwood) was to spare neither pains nor expense upon the child's education. The bills were always regularly paid, one year in advance. She told Richard much of Claire's disposition and habits, and related many little incidents of her school life.

Thomas had returned from the post-office in the mean time, bringing various letters for Miss Ellwood, one of which was from Col. Tracy, acknowledging the receipt of her package. Richard waited with ill-concealed impatience, until she had finished reading the somewhat lengthy epistle. Miss Ellwood turned to him with a smile when she had finished the letter and said, gently—

CHAPTER XXIX.

Convalescent.

Claire was convalescent, and an air of cheerfulness reigned throughout the household of the Tracys. Mrs. Tracy spent the most of her time by the couch upon which the invalid reclined—she whose cheeks and short raven locks formed a beautiful contrast with the crimson pillows. Every one, from the stern old Colonel down to the youngest urchin about the establishment, seemed desirous of doing something to show their love for the young creature, who received their smallest attention with heartfelt gratitude. The Colonel was always thinking of something that would add to her comfort. It was either a new easy chair, a rare painting, or choice engraving— always something new and diverting. Lloyd would drop in and while away an hour in pleasant chat. The Count brought her favorite authors, and read to her for hours, sometimes stealing a stealthy glance at the rose which deepened upon the white cheek for one short moment, and then faded. Laura and Nellie robbed the gardens and conservatories of their choicest treasures, which were laid as an offering of love before Claire, who repaid each with a sweet kiss. Jim and the cook did their part also. Never were choicer delicacies prepared to tempt the palate of an invalid than those which found their way to Claire's room. And Isabella, who seldom visited the sick-room, now asked, in a cold, formal manner, each morning, after Claire's health. Drs. Singleton and Thorne called each day, more from force of habit than that Claire required their professional services.

Count Sayvord watched Dr. Singleton with interest. Reason as he would, he could not divest himself of the thought that the Doctor knew something of Claire's parents. Times without number he had determined to seek the old gentleman's confidence, and as many times gave it up, from the fear that his intentions might be misconstrued.

Dr. Singleton regarded young Sayvord with a friendly eye, and thought he should like to know more of him. "Who knows," thought the Doctor, "but he may have met Richard Tracy somewhere during his years of travel, or may know some one that has seen him! And I may be enabled to get race of him; for at this rate, the confession of Manville is likely to lie in my private drawer for a century to come." An opportunity soon presented itself, which was improved by the Doctor.

During a pause in the conversation, he asked the Count if he had ever met an American gentleman by the name of Tracy during his lengthy travels.

"Years ago," replied the young man, "I met a gentleman of that name at my Uncle Sayvord's country-seat. Richard Tracy was the name, I remember well. He was a thoughtful, sad-browed man, over whose life a shadow seemed to have fallen."

"The same! The same!" exclaimed the Doctor, excitedly. "Have you heard any thing of him since—or do you know where he is now?"

"I received a letter from him about six weeks ago, and am expecting another by every mail. He is at present at my Uncle Clayburn Sayvord's, in the southern part of France."

"Can it be possible!" ejaculated the Doctor. "Will you allow me to see the letter you received from Richard?"

"Certainly," replied the Count, passing him the letter.

"The same clear, manly hand," said the Doctor, glancing at the superscription, as he proceeded to read the contents of the letter. When finished, he again turned to the young man, saying:

"So you too had a suspicion of the truth; for Claire Neville is indeed the daughter of Richard Tracy, and grand-daughter of the Colonel."

"Let there be full confidence between us, Doctor," said the Count. "Tell me of her mother; for there is a secret somewhere which I have failed to ferret out."

Dr. Singleton looked very thoughtful for a moment, and then replied, very gravely:

"Count Sayvord, if you will first answer truthfully two questions, which I shall ask, I will cheerfully tell you all I know."

The Count readily assured him that he would answer to the best of his ability any question he might ask. The Doctor hesitated a moment, and then abruptly asked:

"Do you love Claire Neville? Do you wish to make her your wife? Or—"

"Enough, sir!" angrily interrupted Sayvord. "I did not expect this. Such questions are intrusive."

"I beg your pardon, if I have offended you," replied the Doctor, courteously; "but, believe me, I was actuated by no idle curiosity."

The Count, somewhat mollified, felt a little ashamed of his

hasty temper. The truth was, he had never analyzed his feelings toward Claire. But the Doctor's question told him that he did love her with the whole depths of his ardent nature.

"I do love Claire—and if she will accept me, I will make her my wife, beloved and honored above woman." The Doctor grasped the young man's hand and shook it warmly.

"That is the right kind of talk. None of your sentimental nonsense for me. I am a plain man, and always express my thoughts in the plainest phrases. I have foreseen all this for some time, and have thus seemingly interfered with your private business, to prevent trouble hereafter, and, perhaps, a great deal of unhappiness to both parties. Caste has proved the bane of Richard Tracy's life. It may prove the bane of yours."

Sayvord was somewhat mystified by the Doctor's language. The old man continued:

"Richard Tracy's wife, the mother of Claire Neville, was a *quadroon*, and once a *slave*, owned by her own *father*, and sold by him to Colonel Tracy."

Sayvord was greatly excited at this revelation, and exclaimed: "Impossible, Doctor! You are laboring under some mistake!"

"Not a bit of it!" was the emphatic reply; and he related the entire history of Richard's life. when concluded, he remarked, "I have told you these facts, that you may accustom yourself to thinking of them—and if you marry Claire Neville, you do so with a full knowledge of her origin; and, knowing these facts, if you give her up, you alone are the sufferer, and she is spared the bitter knowledge that caste is the bane of her life's happiness."

The Count had been swayed by various emotions during the Doctor's narrative. He now sat thoughtful and silent. He as last said slowly:

"I must think of this, Doctor. It is best to accustom one's self to look unpleasant facts steadily in the face; and I thank you for your forethought."

"And now," said Dr. Singleton, "let us talk of Richard Tracy. He is, or was, when last heard from, with your uncle, in France."

"Yes," replied the Count; "but if he is not already, he soon will be, on his way to America; for I have written him to come without delay."

"All the better. I hope he will come—"

The sentence remained unfinished; for at this moment Jim entered the room, and said, with an overwhelming bow:

"A letter for de Count Sayvord."

The Count hastily broke the seal, and read the almost unintelligible scrawl, exclaiming, as he roughly shook the Doctor's arm:

"My uncle and Richard Tracy are in New Orleans at this moment."

FRANCES ELLEN WATKINS HARPER

(1825–1911)

At her most active as a public speaker for the Maine Anti-Slavery Society and the Pennsylvania Anti-Slavery Society, Frances Harper addressed lecture halls as many as three times a day to advocate for emancipation and citizenship. Harper, as photographs attest, was small in stature, but reviews suggest a commanding presence on stage: lively but dignified, vital and demanding; magnificent. Harper's poetry might be described as advocacy bordering on propaganda. Harper's work, as Joan Sherman has said, "is the most valuable single poetic record we have of the mind and heart of the race whose fortunes shaped the tumultuous years of her career, 1850–1900."

In the following works, Harper engages with subjects both intimate and grand. Her writing is most notable for its passionate portrayal of love from within the institution of slavery, and the authoritative voice in which it is written almost predicts the poet's own historical importance. Here, also, anthologized for the first time, is a version of Harper's poem "Bible Defence of Slavery," [sic] originally published in her first book, *Forest Leaves*. The volume of poetry was thought lost until 2015, when a copy was discovered in Baltimore by scholar Johanna Ortner at the Maryland Historical Society.

"Enlightened Motherhood: An Address Before the Brooklyn Literary Society, November 15, 1892"

SOURCE: Frances Ellen Watkins Harper, "Enlightened
Motherhood: An Address by Mrs. Frances E. W. Harper
Before the Brooklyn Literary Society, November 15th, 1892."

It is nearly thirty years since an emancipated people stood on the threshold of a new era, facing an uncertain future—a legally unmarried race, to be taught the sacredness of the marriage relations; an ignorant people, to be taught to read of the Christian law and to learn to comprehend more fully the claims of the gospel of the Christ of Calvary. A homeless race, to be gathered into homes of peaceful security and to be instructed how to plant around their firesides the strongest batteries against sins that degrade and the race vices that demoralize. A race unversed in the science of government and unskilled in the just administration of law, to be translated from the old oligarchy of slavery into the new common-wealth of freedom, and to whose men came the right to exchange the fetters on their wrists for the ballots in their right hands—a ballot which, if not vitiated by fraud or restrained by intimidation, counts just as much as that of the most talented and influential man in the land.

While politicians may stumble on the barren mountain of fretful controversy, and men, lacking faith in God and the invisible forces which make for righteousness, may shrink from the unsolved problems of the hour, into the hands of Christian women comes the opportunity of serving the ever blessed Christ, by ministering to His little ones and striving to make their homes the brightest spots on earth and the fairest types of heaven. The school may instruct and the church may teach, but the home is an institution older than the church and antedates schools, and that is the place where children should be trained for useful citizenship on earth and a hope of holy companionship in heaven.

Every mother should endeavor to be a true artist. I do not mean by this that every woman should be a painter, sculptor, musician, poet, or writer, but the artist who will write on the table of childish innocence thoughts she will not blush to see read in the light of eternity and printed amid the archives of heaven, that the young may learn to wear them as amulets around their hearts and throw them as bulwarks around their lives, and that in the hour of temptation and trial the voices from home may linger around their paths as angels of guidance, around their steps, and be incentives to deeds of high and holy worth.

The home may be a humble spot, where there are no velvet carpets to hush your tread, no magnificence to surround your way, nor costly creations of painter's art or sculptor's skill to please your conceptions or gratify your tastes; but what are the costliest gifts of fortune when placed in the balance with the confiding love of dear children or the devotion of a noble and manly husband whose heart can safely trust in his wife? You may place upon the brow of a true wife and mother the greenest laurels; you may crowd her hands with civic honors; but, after all, to her there will be no place like home, and the crown of her motherhood will be more precious than the diadem of a queen.

As marriage is the mother of homes, it is important that the duties and responsibilities of this relation should be understood before it is entered on. A mistake made here may run through every avenue of the future, cast its shadow over all our coming years, and enter the lives of those whom we should shield with our love and defend with our care.

We may be versed in ancient lore and modern learning, may be able to trace the path of worlds that roll in light and power on high, and to tell when comets shall cast their trail over our evening skies. We may understand the laws of stratification well enough to judge where lies the vein of silver and where nature has hidden her virgin gold. We may be able to tell the story of departed nations and conquering chieftains who have added pages of tears and blood to the world's history; but our education is deficient if we are perfectly ignorant how to guide the little feet that are springing up so gladly in our path, and to see in undeveloped possibilities gold more fine than the pavements of heaven and gems more precious than the foundations of the holy city. Marriage should not be a blind rushing together of tastes and fancies, a mere union of fortunes or an affair of convenience. It should be "a tie that only love and truth should weave and nothing but death should part."

Marriage between two youthful and loving hearts means the laying the foundation stones of a new home, and the woman who helps erect that home should be careful not to build it above the reeling brain of a drunkard or the weakened fiber of a debauchee. If it be folly for a merchant to send an argosy, laden with the richest treasures, at midnight on a moonless sea, without a rudder, compass, or guide, is it not madness for a woman to trust her future happiness, and the welfare of the dear children who may yet nestle in her arms and make music and sunshine around her fireside, in the unsteady hands of a characterless man, too lacking in self-respect and self-control to hold the helm and rudder of his own life; who drifts where he ought to steer, and only lasts when he ought to live?

The moment the crown of motherhood falls on the brow of a young wife, God gives her a new interest in the welfare of the home and the good of society. If hitherto she had been content to trip through life a lighthearted girl, or to tread amid the halls of wealth and fashion the gayest of the gay, life holds for her now a high and noble service. She must be more than the child of plea-sure or the devotee of fashion. Her work is grandly constructive. A helpless and ignorant babe lies smiling in her arms. God has trusted her with a child, and it is her privilege to help that child develop the most precious thing a man or woman can possess on earth, and that is a good character. Moth may devour our finest garments, fire may consume and floods destroy our fairest homes, rust may gather on our silver and tarnish our gold, but there is an asbestos that no fire can destroy, a treasure which shall be richer for its service and better for its use, and that is a good character.

But the question arises, What constitutes an enlightened motherhood? I do not pretend that I will give you an exhaustive analysis of all that a mother should learn and of all she should teach. In the Christian scriptures the story is told of a mother of whom it was said: "From henceforth all nations shall call her blessed." While, in these days of religious unrest, criticism, and investigation, numbers are ready to relegate this story to the limbo of myth and fiction; whether that story be regarded as fact or fiction, there are lessons in it which we could not take into our lives without its making life higher, better, and more grandly significant. It is the teaching of a divine overshadowing and a touching self-surrender which still floats down the ages, fragrant with the aroma of a sweet submission. "The hand-maid of the Lord, be it done unto me according to Thy word."

We read that Christ left us an example that we should tread in His footsteps; but does not the majority of the Christian world hold it as a sacred creed that the first print of His feet in the flesh began in the days of His antenatal life; and is not the same spirit in the world now which was there when our Lord made His advent among us, bone of our bone and flesh of our flesh; and do we not need the incarnation of God's love and light in our hearts as much now as it was ever needed in any preceding generation? Do we not need to hold it as a sacred thing, amid sorrow, pain, and wrong, that only through the love of God are human hearts made strong? And has not every prospective mother the right to ask for the overshadowing of the same spirit, that her child may be one of whom it may be truly said, "Of such is the kingdom of heaven," and all his life he shall be lent to the Lord? Had all the mothers of this present generation dwelt beneath the shadow of the Almighty, would it have been possible for slavery to have cursed us with its crimes, or intemperance degraded us with its vices? Would the social evil still have power to send to our streets women whose laughter is sadder than their tears, and over whose wasted lives death draws the curtains of the grave and silently hides their sin and shame? Are there not women, respectable women, who feel that it would wring their hearts with untold anguish, and bring their gray hairs in sorrow to the grave, if their daughters should trail the robes of their womanhood in the dust, yet who would say of their sons, if they were trampling their manhood down and fettering their souls with cords of vice, "O, well, boys will be boys, and young men will sow their wild oats."

I hold that no woman loves social purity as it deserves to be loved and valued, if she cares for the purity of her daughters and not her sons; who would gather her dainty robes from contact with the fallen woman and yet greet with smiling lips and clasp with warm and welcoming hands the author of her wrong and ruin. How many mothers to-day shrink from a double standard for society which can ostracize the woman and condone the offense of the man? How many mothers say within their hearts, "I intend to teach my boy to be as pure in his life, as chaste in his conversation, as the young girl who sits at my side encircled in the warm clasp of loving arms?" How many mothers strive to have their boys shun the gilded saloon as they would the den of a deadly serpent? Not the mother who thoughtlessly sends her child to the saloon for a beverage to make merry with her friends. How many mothers teach their boys to shrink in horror from the fascinations of women, not as God made them, but as sin has degraded them?

To-night, if you and I could walk through the wards of various hospitals at home and abroad, perhaps we would find hundreds, it may be thousands, of young men awaiting death as physical wrecks, having burned the candle of their lives at both ends. Were we to bend over their dying couches with pitying glances, and question them of their lives, perhaps numbers of them could tell you sad stories of careless words from thoughtless lips, that tainted their imaginations and sent their virus through their lives; of young eyes, above which God has made the heavens so eloquent with His praise, and the earth around so poetic with His ideas, turning from the splendor of the magnificent sunsets or glorious early dawns, and finding allurement in the dreadful fascinations of sin, or learning to gloat over impure pictures and vile literature. Then, later on, perhaps many of them could say, "The first time I went to a house where there were revelry and song, and the dead were there and I knew it not, I went with men who were older than myself; men, who should have showed me how to avoid the pitfalls which lie in the path of the young, the tempted, and inexperienced, taught me to gather the flowers of sin that blossom around the borders of hell."

Suppose we dared to question a little further, not from idle curiosity, but for the sake of getting, from the dying, object lessons for the living, and say, "God gave you, an ignorant child, into the hands of a mother. Did she never warn you of your dangers and teach you how to avoid them?" How many could truthfully say, "My mother was wise enough to teach me and faithful enough to warn me." If the cholera or yellow-fever were raging in any part of this city, and to enter that section meant peril to health and life, what mother would permit her child to walk carelessly through a district where pestilence was breathing its bane upon the morning air and distilling its poison upon the midnight dews? And yet, when boys go from the fireside into the arena of life, how many ever go there forewarned and forearmed against the soft seductions of vice, against moral conditions which are worse than "fever, plague and palsy, and madness *all* combined?"

Among the things I would present for the enlightenment of mothers are attention to the laws of heredity and environment. Mrs. Winslow, in a paper on social purity, speaks of a package of letters she had received from a young man of talent, good education, and a strong desire to live a pure and useful life. In boyhood he ignorantly ruined his health, and, when he resolved to rise above his depressed condition, his own folly, his heredity and environment, weighed him down like an incubus. His appeals, she says, are most touching. He says: "If you cannot help me, what can I do? My mother cursed me with illegitimacy and hereditary insanity. I have left only the alternative of suicide or madness." A fearful legacy! For stolen money and slandered character we may make reparation, but the opportunity of putting the right stamp on an antenatal life, if once gone, is gone forever; and there never was an angel of God, however bright, terrible, or strong he may be, who was ever strong enough to roll away the stone from the grave of a dead opportunity.

In the annals of this State may be found a record of six generations of debased manhood and womanhood, and prominent among them stands the name of Margaret, the mother of criminals. She is reported as having five sisters, the greater number of whom trailed the robes of their womanhood in the dust, and became fallen women. Some time since, their posterity was traced out, and five hundred and forty persons are represented as sharing the blood of these unfortunate women; and it is remarkable, as well as very sad, to see the lines of debasement and weakness, vice and crime, which are displayed in their record. In the generation of Margaret, fifty per cent of the women were placed among the fallen, and in all the generations succeeding, including only those of twelve years of age and over, to the extent of fifty per cent; and of this trail of weakness there were three families in the sixth generation who had six children sent to the house of refuge. Out of seven hundred and nine members of this family, nearly one-ninth have been criminals, and nearly one-tenth paupers; twenty-two had acquired property, and eight had lost property; nearly one-seventh were illegitimate, and one sister was the mother of distinctively pauperized lines.

Or, take another line of thought. Would it not be well for us women to introduce into all of our literary circles, for the purpose of gaining knowledge, topics on this subject of heredity and the influence of good and bad conditions upon the home life of the race, and study this subject in the light of science for our own and the benefit of others? For instance, may we not seriously ask the question, Can a mother or father be an habitual tippler, or break God's law of social purity, and yet impart to their children, at the same time, abundant physical vitality and strong moral fibre? Can a father dash away the reins of moral restraint, and, at the same time, impart strong willpower to his offspring?

A generation since, there lived in a Western city a wealthy English gentleman who was what is called a high liver. He drank his toddy in the morning, washed down his lunch with champagne, and finished a bottle of port for dinner, though he complained that the heavy wines here did not agree with him, owing to the climate. He died of gout at fifty years, leaving four sons. One of them became an epileptic, two died from drinking. Called good fellows, generous, witty, honorable young men, but before middle age miserable sots. The oldest of the brothers was a man of fixed habits, occupying a leading place in the community, from his keen intelligence, integrity, and irreproachable morals. He watched over his brothers, laid them in their graves, and never ceased to denounce the vice which had ruined them; and when he was long past middle age, financial trouble threw him into a low, nervous condition, for which wine was prescribed. He drank but one bottle. Shortly after, his affairs were righted and his health and spirits returned, but it was observed that once or twice a year he mysteriously disappeared for a month or six weeks. Nor wife, nor children, nor even his partner, knew where he went; but at last, when he was old and gray headed, his wife was telegraphed from an obscure neighboring village, where she found him dying of *mania a potu*. He had been in the habit of hiding there when the desire for liquor became maddening, and when there he drank like a brute.

May Wright Sewall, president of the Woman's National Council, writing of disinherited children, tells of a country school where health and joyousness and purity were the rule, vulgarity and coarseness the exception, and morbid and mysterious manners quite unknown. There came one morning, in her childhood, two little girls, sisters, of ten and twelve years. They were comfortably dressed. At the noonday meal their baskets opened to an abundant and appetizing lunch. But they were not like other children. They had thin, pinched faces, with vulgar mouths, and a sidelong look from their always downcast eyes which made her shudder; and skin, so wrinkled and yellow, that her childish fears fancied them to be witches' children. They held themselves aloof from all the rest. For two or three years they sat in the same places in that quiet school doing very little work, but, not being disorderly, they were allowed to stay. One day, when my father had visited the school, as we walked home together, I questioned him as to what made Annie and Minnie so different from all the other little girls at the school, and the grave man answered: Before they were born their father sold their birthright, and they must feed on pottage all their lives. She felt that an undefined mystery hovered around their blighted lives. She knew, she says, that they were blighted, as the simplest child knows the withered leaf of November from the glowing green of May, and she questioned no more, half conscious that the mystery was sin and that knowledge of it would be sinful too.

But we turn from these sad pictures to brighter pages in the great books of human life. To Benjamin West saying: "My mother's kiss made me a painter." To John Randolph saying: "I should have been an atheist, or it had not been for one recollection, and that was the memory of the time when my departed mother used to take my little hands in hers and sank me on my knees to say: 'Our Father, who art in heaven.'" Amid the cold of an Arctic expedition, Adam Isles found sickness had settled on part of his comrades, and the request came to him, I think from one of the officers of the ship, saying: "Isles, for God's sake, take some spirits, or we will be lost." Then the memory of the dear mother came back, and looking the entreaty in the face, he said, "I promised my mother I would not do it, and I wouldn't do it if I die in the ice."

I would ask, in conclusion, is there a branch of the human race in the Western Hemisphere which has greater need of the inspiring and uplifting influence that can flow out of the lives and examples of the truly enlightened than ourselves? Mothers who can teach their sons not to love pleasure or fear death; mothers who can teach their children to embrace every opportunity, employ every power, and use every means to build up a future to contrast with the old sad past. Men may boast of the aristocracy of blood; they may glory in the aristocracy of the talent, and be proud of the aristocracy of wealth, but there is an aristocracy which must ever outrank them all, and that is the aristocracy of character.

The work of the mothers of our race is grandly constructive. It is for us to build above the wreck and ruin of the past more stately temples of thought and action. Some races have been overthrown, dashed in pieces, and destroyed; but to-day the world is needing, fainting, for something better than the results of arrogance, aggressiveness, and indomitable power. We need mothers who are capable of being character builders, patient, loving, strong, and true, whose homes will be uplifting power in the race. This is one of the greatest needs of the hour. No race can afford to neglect the enlightenment of its mothers. If you would have a clergy without virtue or morality, a manhood without honor, and a womanhood frivolous, mocking, and ignorant, neglect the education of your daughters. But if, on the other hand, you would have strong men, virtuous women, and good homes, then enlighten your women, so that they may be able to bless their homes by the purity of their lives, the tenderness of their hearts, and the strength of their intellects. From schools and colleges your children may come well versed in ancient lore and modern learning, but it is for us to learn and teach, within the shadow of our own homes, the highest and best of all sciences, the science of a true life. When the last lay of the minstrel shall die upon his ashy lips, and the sweetest numbers of the poet cease to charm his death-dulled ear; when the eye of the astronomer shall be too dim to mark the path of worlds that roll in light and power on high; and when all our

earthly knowledge has performed for us its mission, and we are
ready to lay aside our environments garments we have outworn
and outgrown: if we have learned that science of a true life, we
may rest assured that this acquirement will go with us through
the valley and shadow of death, only to grow lighter and
brighter through the eternities.

Newfound Poems from *Forest Leaves* (ca. 1840)

SOURCE: Frances Ellen Watkins Harper, "Haman and
Mordecai," "A Dream," "The Felon's Dream," *Forest
Leaves* (Baltimore: James Young, ca. 1840).

"Haman and Mordecai"

He stood at Persia's Palace gate
And vassal round him bow'd,
Upon his brow was written hate
And he heeded not the crowd.

He heeded not the vassal throng
Whose praises rent the air,
His bosom shook with rage and scorn
For Mordecai stood there.

When ev'ry satrap bow'd
To him of noble blood,
Amid that servile crowd
One form unbending stood.

And as he gaz'd upon that form,
Dark flash'd his angry eye,
'Twas as the light'ning ere the storm
Hath swept in fury by.

On noble Mordecai alone,
He scorn'd to lay his land;
But sought an edict from the throne
'Gainst all the captive band.

For full of pride and wrath
To his fell purpose true,
He vow'd that from his path
Should perish ev'ry Jew.

Then woman's voice arose
In deep impassion'd prayer,
Her fragile heart grew strong
'Twas the nervings of despair.

The king in mercy heard
Her pleading and her prayer,
His heart with pity stirr'd,
And he resolved to spare.

And Haman met the fate
He'd for Mordecai decreed,
And from his cruel hate
The captive Jews are freed.

"A Dream"

I had a dream, a varied dream,
A dream of joy and dread;
Before me rose the judgment scene
For God had raised the dead.

Oh for an angel's hand to paint
The glories of that day,
When God did gather home each saint
And wipe their tears away.

Each waiting one lifted his head
Rejoic'd to see him nigh,
And earth cast out her sainted dead
To meet him in the sky.

Before his white and burning throne
A countless throng did stand;
Whilst Christ confess'd his own,
Whose names were on his hand.

I had a dream, a varied dream,
A dream of joy and dread;
Before me rose the judgment scene
For God had rais'd the dead.

Oh for an angel's hand to paint
The terrors of that day,
When God in vengeance for his saints
Girded himself with wrath to slay.

But, oh the terror, grief, and dread,
Tongue can't describe or pen portray;
When from their graves arose the dead,
Guilty to meet the judgment day.

As sudden as the lightning's flash
Across the sky doth sweep,
Earth's kingdom's were in pieces dash'd,
And waken'd from their guilty sleep.

I heard the agonizing cry,
Ye rocks and mountains on us fall,
And hide us from the Judge's eye,
But rocks and mounts fled from the call.

I saw the guilty ruin'd host
Standing before the burning throne,
The ruin'd, lost forever lost,
Whom God in wrath refus'd to own.

"The Felon's Dream"

He slept, but oh, it was not calm,
As in the days of infancy;
When sleep is nature's tender balm
To hearts from sorrow free.

He dream'd that fetters bound him fast,
He pin'd for liberty;
It seem'd deliverance came at last
And he from bonds were free.

In thought he journey'd where
Familiar voices rose,
Where not a brow was dim with care,
Or bosom heav'd with woes.

Around him press'd a happy band;
His wife and child drew near;
He felt the pressure of her hand,
And dried each falling tear.

His tender mother cast aside
The tears that dim'd her eye;
His father saw him as the pride
Of brighter days gone by.

He saw his wife around him cling,
He heard her breathe his name;
Oh! woman's love 's a precious thing,
A pure undying flame.

His brethren wept for manly pride,
May bend to woman's tears;
Then welcom'd round their fireside
The playmate of departed years.

His gentle sister fair and mild
Around him closely press'd,

She clasp'd his hand and smil'd
Then wept upon his breast.

All, all were glad around that hearth,
They hop'd his wanderings o'er;
That weary of the strange cold earth
He'd roam from them no more.

'Twas but a dream, 'twas fancy's flight
It mock'd his yearning heart;
It made his bosom feel its blight,
It probed him like a dart.

A prison held his fettered limbs,
Confinement was his lot,
No kindred voice rose to cheer,
He seem'd by friends and all forgot.

Later Poems

SOURCE: Frances Ellen Watkins Harper, "Eliza Harris,"
"The Slave Auction," "The Drunkard's Child," "The
Revel," "Ethiopia," "The Fugitive's Wife," *Poems
on Miscellaneous Subjects* (Boston: J. B. Yerrinton
& Son, 1855).

"Eliza Harris"

Like a fawn from the arrow, startled and wild,
A woman swept by us, bearing a child;
In her eye was the night of a settled despair,
And her brow was o'ershaded with anguish and care.

She was nearing the river—in reaching the brink,
She heeded no danger, she paused not to think!

For she is a mother—her child is a slave—
And she'll give him his freedom, or find him a grave!

'Twas a vision to haunt us, that innocent face—
So pale in its aspect, so fair in its grace;
As the tramp of the horse and the bay of the hound,
With the fetters that gall, were trailing the ground!

She was nerved by despair, and strengthen'd by woe,
As she leap'd o'er the chasms that yawn'd from below;
Death howl'd in the tempest, and rav'd in the blast,
But she heard not the sound till the danger was past.

Oh! how shall I speak of my proud country's shame?
Of the stains on her glory, how give them their name?
How say that her banner in mockery waves—
Her "star-spangled banner"—o'er millions of slaves?

How say that the lawless may torture and chase
A woman whose crime is the hue of her face?
How the depths of forest may echo around
With the shrieks of despair, and the bay of the hound?

With her step on the ice, and her arm on her child,
The danger was fearful, the pathway was wild;
But, aided by Heaven, she gained a free shore,
Where the friends of humanity open'd their door.

So fragile and lovely, so fearfully pale,
Like a lily that bends to the breath of the gale,
Save the heave of her breast, and the sway of her hair,
You'd have thought her a statue of fear and despair.

In agony close to her bosom she press'd
The life of her heart, the child of her breast:—
Oh! love from its tenderness gathering might,
Had strengthen'd her soul for the dangers of flight.

But she's free!—yes, free from the land where the slave
From the hand of oppression must rest in the grave;
Where bondage and torture, where scourges and chains
Have plac'd on our banner indelible stains.

The bloodhounds have miss'd the scent of her way;
The hunter is rifled and foil'd of his prey;
Fierce jargon and cursing, with clanking of chains,
Make sounds of strange discord on Liberty's plains.

With the rapture of love and fullness of bliss,
She plac'd on his brow a mother's fond kiss:—
Oh! poverty, danger and death she can brave,
For the child of her love is no longer a slave!

"The Slave Auction"

The sale began—young girls were there,
   Defenseless in their wretchedness,
Whose stifled sobs of deep despair
   Revealed their anguish and distress.

And mothers stood, with streaming eyes,
   And saw their dearest children sold;
Unheeded rose their bitter cries,
   While tyrants bartered them for gold.

And woman, with her love and truth—
   For these in sable forms may dwell—
Gazed on the husband of her youth,
   With anguish none may paint or tell.

And men, whose sole crime was their hue,
   The impress of their Maker's hand,
And frail and shrinking children too,
   Were gathered in that mournful band.

Ye who have laid your loved to rest,
    And wept above their lifeless clay,
Know not the anguish of that breast,
    Whose loved are rudely torn away.

Ye may not know how desolate
    Are bosoms rudely forced to part,
And how a dull and heavy weight
    Will press the life-drops from the heart.

"Lines"

SOURCE: Frances Ellen Watkins Harper, "Lines," *National Anti-Slavery Standard*, November 29, 1856.

At the Portals of the Future,
    Full of madness, guilt and gloom,
Stood the hateful form of Slavery,
    Crying, Give, Oh! give me room—

Room to smite the earth with cursing,
    Room to scatter, rend and slay,
From the trembling mother's bosom
    Room to tear her child away;

Room to trample on the manhood
    Of the country far and wide;
Room to spread o'er every Eden
    Slavery's scorching lava-tide.

Pale and trembling stood the Future,
    Quailing 'neath his frown of hate,
As he grasped with bloody clutches
    The great keys of Doom and Fate.

In his hand he held a banner
    All festooned with blood and tears:

'Twas a fearful ensign, woven
   With the grief and wrong of years.

On his brow he wore a helmet
   Decked with strange and cruel art;
Every jewel was a life-drop
   Wrung from some poor broken heart.

Though her cheek was pale and anxious,
   Yet, with look and brow sublime,
By the pale and trembling Future
   Stood the Crisis of our time.

And from many a throbbing bosom
   Came the words in fear and gloom,
Tell us, Oh! thou coming Crisis,
   What shall be our country's doom?

Shall the wings of dark destruction
   Brood and hover o'er our land,
Till we trace the steps of ruin
   By their blight, from strand to strand?

"Bible Defence of Slavery"

Version 1

SOURCE: Frances Ellen Watkins Harper, *Forest Leaves*
   (Baltimore: James Young, ca. 1840).

Take sackcloth of the darkest dye,
   And shroud the pulpits round!
Servants of Him that cannot lie,
   Sit mourning on the ground.

Let holy horror blanch each cheek,
   Pale every brow with fears;
And rocks and stones, if ye could speak,
   Ye well might melt to tears!

Let sorrow breathe in every tone,
    In every strain ye raise;
Insult not God's majestic throne
    With th' mockery of praise.

A "reverend" man, whose light should be
    The guide of age and youth,
Brings to the shrine of Slavery
    The sacrifice of truth!

For the direst wrong by man imposed,
    Since Sodom's fearful cry,
The word of life has been unclos'd,
    To give your God the lie.

Oh! When ye pray for heathen lands,
    And plead for their dark shores,
Remember Slavery's cruel hands
    Make heathens at your doors!

Version 2

SOURCE: Frances Ellen Watkins Harper, *Poems on Miscellaneous Subjects* (Boston: J. B. Yerrinton & Son, 1855).

Take sackcloth of the darkest dye
And shroud the pulpits round,
Servants of him that cannot lie
Sit mourning on the ground.

Let holy horror blanche each cheek,
Pale ev'ry brow with fears,
And rocks and stones if ye could speak
Ye well might melt to tears.

Let sorrow breathe in ev'ry tone
And grief in ev'ry strain ye raise,
Insult not heaven's majestic throne
With the mockery of praise.

A man whose light should be
The guide of age and youth,
Brings to the shrine of slavery
The sacrifice of truth.

For the fiercest wrong that ever rose
Since Sodom's fearful cry,
The word of life has been unclos'd
To give your God the lie.

An infidel could do no more
To hide his country's guilty blot,
Than spread God's holy record o'er
The loathesome leprous spot.

Oh, when ye pray for heathen lands,
And plead for dark benighted shores,
Remember slavery's cruel hands
Make heathens at your doors.

"The Drunkard's Child"

He stood beside his dying child,
  With a dim and bloodshot eye;
They'd won him from the haunts of vice
  To see his first-born die.
He came with a slow and staggering tread,
  A vague, unmeaning stare,
And, reeling, clasped the clammy hand,
  So deathly pale and fair.

In a dark and gloomy chamber,
  Life ebbing fast away,
On a coarse and wretched pallet,
  The dying sufferer lay:
A smile of recognition
  Lit up the glazing eye;

"I'm very glad," it seemed to say,
 "You've come to see me die."

That smile reached to his callous heart,
 It sealed fountains stirred;
He tried to speak, but on his lips
 Faltered and died each word.
And burning tears like rain
 Poured down his bloated face,
Where guilt, remorse and shame
 Had scathed, and left their trace.

"My father!" said the dying child,
 (His voice was faint and low,)
"Oh! clasp me closely to your heart,
 And kiss me ere I go.
Bright angels beckon me away,
 To the holy city fair—
Oh! tell me, Father, ere I go,
 Say, will you meet me there?"

He clasped him to his throbbing heart,
 "I will! I will!" he said;
His pleading ceased—the father held
 His first-born and his dead!
The marble brow, with golden curls,
 Lay lifeless on his breast;
Like sunbeams on the distant clouds
 Which line the gorgeous west.

"The Revel"

"HE KNOWETH NOT THAT THE DEAD ARE THERE."

In yonder halls reclining
 Are forms surpassing fair,
And brilliant lights are shining,
 But, oh! the dead are there!

There's music, song and dance,
　　There's banishment of care,
And mirth in every glance,
　　But, oh! the dead are there!

The wine cup's sparkling glow
　　Blends with the viands rare,
There's revelry and show,
　　But still, the dead are there!

'Neath that flow of song and mirth
　　Runs the current of despair,
But the simple sons of earth
　　Know not the dead are there!

They'll shudder start and tremble,
　　They'll weep in wild despair
When the solemn truth breaks on them,
　　That the dead, the dead are there!

"Ethiopia"

Yes! Ethiopia yet shall stretch
　　Her bleeding hands abroad;
Her cry of agony shall reach
　　The burning throne of God.

The tyrant's yoke from off her neck,
　　His fetters from her soul,
The mighty hand of God shall break,
　　And spurn the base control.

Redeemed from dust and freed from chains,
　　Her sons shall lift their eyes;
From cloud-capt hills and verdant plains
　　Shall shouts of triumph rise.

Upon her dark, despairing brow,
　　Shall play a smile of peace;
For God shall bend unto her wo,
　　And bid her sorrows cease.

'Neath sheltering vines and stately palms
　　Shall laughing children play,
And aged sires with joyous psalms
　　Shall gladden every day.

Secure by night, and blest by day,
　　Shall pass her happy hours;
Nor human tigers hunt for prey
　　Within her peaceful bowers.

Then, Ethiopia! stretch, oh! stretch
　　Thy bleeding hands abroad;
Thy cry of agony shall reach
　　And find redress from God.

"To Mrs. Harriet Beecher Stowe"

SOURCE: Frances Ellen Watkins Harper, "To
Mrs. Harriet Beecher Stowe," *Frederick Douglass' Paper,*
February 3, 1854.

I thank thee for thy pleading
　　For the helpless of our race
Long as our hearts are beating
　　In them thou hast a place.

I thank thee for thy pleading
　　For the fetter'd and the dumb
The blessing of the perishing
　　Around thy path shall come.

I thank thee for the kindly words
　　That grac'd thy pen of fire,

And thrilled upon the living chords
   Of many a heart's deep lyre.

For the sisters of our race
   Thou'st nobly done thy part
Thou hast won thy self a place
   In every human heart.

The halo that surrounds thy name
   Hath reached from shore to shore
But thy best and brightest fame
   Is the blessing of the poor.

"The Fugitive's Wife"

It was my sad and weary lot
   To toil in slavery;
But one thing cheered my lowly cot—
   My husband was with me.

One evening, as our children played
   Around our cabin door,
I noticed on his brow a shade
   I'd never seen before;

And in his eyes a gloomy night
   Of anguish and despair;—
I gazed upon their troubled light,
   To read the meaning there.

He strained me to his heaving heart—
   My own beat wild with fear;
I knew not, but I sadly felt
   There must be evil near.

He vainly strove to cast aside
   The tears that fell like rain:—

Too frail, indeed, is manly pride,
   To strive with grief and pain.

Again he clasped me to his breast,
   And said that we must part:
I tried to speak—but, oh! it seemed
   An arrow reached my heart.

"Bear not," I cried, "unto your grave,
   The yoke you've borne from birth;
No longer live a helpless slave,
   The meanest thing on earth!"

"An Appeal to My Countrywomen"

SOURCE: Frances Ellen Watkins Harper, "An Appeal
to My Countrywomen," *Poems* (Philadelphia: 1006
Bainbridge Street, 1896).

You can sigh o'er the sad-eyed Armenian
   Who weeps in her desolate home.
You can mourn o'er the exile of Russia
   From kindred and friends doomed to roam.

You can pity the men who have woven
   From passion and appetite chains
To coil with a terrible tension
   Around their heartstrings and brains.

You can sorrow o'er little children
   Disinherited from their birth,
The wee waifs and toddlers neglected,
   Robbed of sunshine, music and mirth.

For beasts you have gentle compassion;
   Your mercy and pity they share.
For the wretched, outcast and fallen
   You have tenderness, love and care.

But hark! from our Southland are floating
   Sobs of anguish, murmurs of pain,
And women heart-stricken are weeping
   Over their tortured and their slain.

On their brows the sun has left traces;
   Shrink not from their sorrow in scorn.
When they entered the threshold of being
   The children of a King were born.

Each comes as a guest to the table
   The hand of our God has outspread,
To fountains that ever leap upward,
   To share in the soil we all tread.

When ye plead for the wrecked and fallen,
   The exile from far-distant shores,
Remember that men are still wasting
   Life's crimson around your own doors.

Have ye not, oh, my favored sisters,
   Just a plea, a prayer or a tear,
For mothers who dwell 'neath the shadows
   Of agony, hatred and fear?

Men may tread down the poor and lowly,
   May crush them in anger and hate,
But surely the mills of God's justice
   Will grind out the grist of their fate.

Oh, people sin-laden and guilty,
   So lusty and proud in your prime,
The sharp sickles of God's retribution
   Will gather your harvest of crime.

Weep not, oh my well-sheltered sisters,
   Weep not for the Negro alone,
But weep for your sons who must gather
   The crops which their fathers have sown.

Go read on the tombstones of nations
  Of chieftains who masterful trod,
The sentence which time has engraven,
  That they had forgotten their God.

'Tis the judgment of God that men reap
  The tares which in madness they sow,
Sorrow follows the footsteps of crime,
  And Sin is the consort of Woe.

30

PAULINE HOPKINS

(1859–1930)

Pauline Elizabeth Hopkins was born in Portland, Maine, and lived the majority of her life in Boston. A celebrated writer and magazine editor, Hopkins wrote novels, journalism, pamphlets, and musical plays, and had key roles in the founding and editing of the black magazines *Colored American Magazine*, *Voice of the Negro*, and *New Era Magazine*. Her creative breadth and the force of her prose made Hopkins one of the prominent black intellectuals of her time.

The following excerpts show Hopkins's range: the first from her successful musical, or "ballad opera," *Peculiar Sam* and the second, a mystery story, "Talma Gordon." In *Peculiar Sam*, written when Hopkins was only twenty, comic dialect gives way to "proper" speech for successful characters in freedom. "Talma Gordon" is a gothic mystery involving race, inheritance, and romance.

Selections from *Peculiar Sam, or, the Underground Railroad*, a Musical Drama in Four Acts (1879)

SOURCE: Pauline Elizabeth Hopkins, *Peculiar Sam, or, the Underground Railroad* (Boston: Hopkins' Colored Troubadors, 1879). Electronic edition by Alexander Street Press, L.L.C., 2017.

ACT III

(Time, night. Banks of a river. River at back. Trees and shrubbery along banks. Enter party led by SAM*)*

SAM: *(looks around)* See hyar Mammy, I hope nuthin' aint happened to Jinny, kase when I was on de top ob dat las' hill we crossed 'pears like I seed a lot ob white folks comin'.

MAMMY: It's only through de blessin' ob de Lor', we haint been tooken long 'go. I don't neber see wha's got inter Marser's dogs.

SAM: Mammy dar aint a dog widin' ten mile roun' Marser's place, dat aint so sick he kan't hol' his head up. 'Deed Mammy a chile could play wif 'em.

MAMMY: *(holds up her hands in astonishment)* Wha! Wha' you been doin' to Marser's dogs? Why boy he'll kill us.

SAM: He will sho nuff Mammy ef he ketches us. Marse he hab plenty ob money an' I thought I'd done nuff to 'sarve some ob it, an' I jes helped mysel' to a pocket full. An' wif some ob it I bought de stuff wha' fixed dem dogs; 'deed I did, kase dis chile am no fool.

MAMMY: *(more surprised)* Been stealin' too. *(groans)* I neber 'spected dat ob you Sam.

SAM: No use Mammy, we mus' hab money, de 'litioners am good frien's to us, but money's ebery man's frien', an'll neber 'tray eben a forsook coon.

JUNO: *(has been looking anxiously up the road)* Dey's comin Mammy! Here's Jinny Sam.

> *(All rush to look up road.* VIRGINIA *sings solo, all join in chorus. At close enter* CAESAR, VIRGINIA, *and* PETE, *throw down bundles, embrace)*

CAESAR: Well my chillern, we's almos' free de dark valley, le's sing one mo' hymn 'fo' we bids good-bye to de sunny Souf.

CHORUS: "Old Kentucky Home"

SAM: *(as they close picks up bundle)* Come on Mammy, come on Jinny, le's git on board de raf'. I tell you chillern I feels so happy I doesn't kno' mysel'. Jes feel dis air, it smells like freedom; jes see dose trees, dey look like freedom. *(points across river)* an' look ober yonder chillern, look dar good, dat ar am ol' freedom himsel'. *(gets happy, begins to sing)* "Dar's only one mo' riber to cross."

(All join in song, shake hands, laugh and shout, exit. Singing grows fainter, but louder as raft shoots into sight. JIM rushes panting on the stage, peers after raft. Tableau, music growing fainter)

(Curtain)

ACT IV

(The time is after the war in Canada. The place is an old fashioned kitchen with a fireplace. There is a door at back and a window at the right with closed inside blinds. Mammy sits at table knitting, Caesar, her husband now, sits before fireplace.)

CAESAR: Ol' 'ooman it are a long time sense we an' de chillern lef' de ol' home, seems to me de Lor' has blessed us all. Hyars you an' me married, Jinny a singist, Juno a school marm; an' las' but not leas', dat boy, dat pecoolar Sam, eddicated an' gwine to de United States Congress. I tell you ol' 'ooman de ways ob de Lor' am pas' findin' out.

MAMMY: Yas ol' man, an' hyar we is dis blessed Christmas evenin', a settin' hyar like kings an' queens, waitin', fer dat blessed boy o' ours to come home to us. Tell you ol' man, it's 'mazin' how dat boy has 'scaped de gins an' sneers ob de worl', an' to-day am runnin' fer Congress dar in Cincinattie, it am 'mazin. D' ye s'pose he'll git it ol' man?

CAESAR: I don't spec' nothin' else, kase dat boy allers gits what he goes fer. But it's 'mos' time fer de train, wonder whar dem gals is.

(song by VIRGINIA, *behind scenes, after style of "Swanee River")*

MAMMY: *(at close)* Ol' man, Ise totable 'tented hyar till I hears dat dear chile sing dem ol' songs, in dat angel voice ob hers, an' den I feels so bad, kase dey carries me way bact to dem good ol' times dat'll neber return. De ol' plantation, an' Mistis an' ol' Marser, an' de dear little lily chillern; thar I kin seem to see de fiel's ob cotton, an' I kin seem to smell de orange blossoms dat growed on de trees down de carriage drive. *(wipes her eyes)* Ise been totable 'tented hyar, but I boun' to trabble back 'gin 'fo I die.

CAESAR: *(wiping his eyes)* An' ol' 'ooman, ef de ol' man dies firs', bury me at ol' Marser's feet, under de 'Nolia tree. *(Clocks strikes seven. Enter* VIRGINIA *and* JUNO*)*

VIRGINIA: O, Mammy isn't it time for the train yet? It seems as if the hours would never pass *(Throws open the blinds, disclosing moonlight on the snow. She stands looking out)*

JUNO: Virginia you're not the only anxious one. How I do long to see my dear old fellow, my own old Sam. I tell you Mammy I could dance. *(places her hands in her apron pockets, and takes two or three steps of a jig)*

MAMMY: *(interrupts her)* Quit dat, you Juno, quit dat. 'Deed I neber seed sech a crazy head as you has got.

CAESAR: Mammy do lef' dat gal 'lone, let her 'joy herself, fer I does like to see young people spirited.

JUNO: Of course you do Poppy. *(hugs him with one arm around the neck)* And just to think, if Sam's elected you'll be poppy to a representative, and Mammy'll be mother to one, and I'll be sister to one. *(to* VIRGINIA*)* And what'll you be to him, Jinny?

VIRGINIA: Don't talk about that Juno; there can be nothing done until Jim is found. *(turns to come from window)*

MAMMY: *(listens)* Shh! I thought I hyard sleigh bells!

(All listen. Tableau. Sleigh bells outside)

SAM: *(outside)* Whoa!

ALL: It's Sam! *(rush to door. Enter* SAM*, all surround him, and advance to footlights followed by* PETE *and* POMP*)*

SAM: *(throws off wraps,* JUNO *carries them off, returns immediately)* Yes, it is I, and I cannot tell you how happy I am to be at home once more.

PETE: Jes tell us one thing cap'n, 'fore you goes eny farther, is you 'lected?

VIRGINIA: Yes, Sam do relieve our anxiety.

SAM: I think you may safely congratulate me, on a successful election. My friends in Cincinnati have stood by me nobly.

MAMMY: Praise de Lord! Chillern I hasn't nuthin' lef' to lib fer.

PETE: *(he and* POMP *shake hands with* SAM *in congratulation)* Ol' fellar Ise glad of it. Now I'll jes step out an' put up dat annimal, an' then return. *(exit door)*

CAESAR: *(goes up to* SAM*)* Lef' me look at you, I wants to see ef you's changed eny. *(shakes his head solemnly)* No, you's all dar jes de same. *(to* MAMMY*)* Ol' 'ooman, I allers knowed dat boy neber growed dat high fer nuthin'. *(Reenter* PETE. *Company seat themselves)*

JUNO: If things don't stop happening I shall have to get someone to hold me. Virginia, imagine you and me at Washington leading the colored bong tongs. O my! *(fans herself, laughter)*

SAM: *(to* VIRGINIA*)* Haven't you one word for me, Virginia?

VIRGINIA: Find Jim, and we will be happy.

SAM: Well, then sing for me. Surely you cannot refuse this request.

(Solos, quartets, and chorus. Mr. [Sam] Lucas introduces any of his songs that have not been sung elsewhere. At close loud knocking at door)

MAMMY: Wonder who dat is? *(all rise)*

SAM: *(hurries to door, opens it.* JIM *rushes past him into room)* Whom do you wish to see sir? I think you have made a mistake.

CAESAR: *(aside)* 'Pears like I know dat fellar.

JIM: *(looks smilingly around)* Don't you know me? Well I don't reckon you do, bein's Ise changed so. There's my card. *(gives immense card to* SAM*)*

SAM: *(reads)* "Mr. James Peters, Esq., D.D., attorney at law, at the Massachusetts bar, and declined overseer of the Magnolia plantation."

(all astonished, VIRGINIA *shrinks behind* MAMMY*)*

JIM: *(bows profoundly)* Dat's me. Declined overseer ob de 'Nolia plantation.

JUNO: Overseer Jim, as I live, turned monkey! *(exits hurriedly)*

SAM: If you have come here to create a disturbance, sir, I warn you to go out the way you came in, or I'll throw you out.

JUNO: *(reenters on a run, with pistol; rushes at JIM)* Did you wink, did you dare to wink?

JIM: *(frightened, stumbles over two or three chairs. Groans)* O Lord no! *(to company)* Don't let her shoot me, Ise oly called hyar to 'stantiate myself an' be frien's 'long wif you. *(JUNO lays pistol aside, laughing)*

SAM: Well sir, state your business, and be quick about it.

JIM: *(goes toward VIRGINIA followed by SAM)* Virginie, you needn't be 'fraid on me, kase I isn't hyar to mislest you. Chile, I kno's dat warnt no weddin', de law wouldn't 'low it nohow. *(to all)* An' den you see, I has no free distution ob mysel' at all, kase Ise got a truly wife, an' Ise got twins, a boy an' gal; one's nam'd Jinny an' de tother one Sam.

(laughter)

SAM: Mr. Peters I congratulate you, you have certainly made the most of your freedom.

JIM: *(strutting up and down)* Fac'! An' you's all hyar. Mammy and Caesar, an' the Virginie rose-bird, an' Juno, and Pete, and Pomp. *(slaps SAM on arm)* Ol' ol' Sam himself. *(SAM shrinks)* O, I know you feel big, but I can't forgit dem ol' times, an' what a chase I had after you, an' then jes missed of you.

MAMMY: Well tell us Jim, wha' ol' Marse done, when he foun' we was gone? *(all gather around JIM)*

JIM: Fus' place you see, I had to walk clean back home, kase dat pecoolar rascal thar, stole all my money. *(laughter)* An' when I had done got back, Marse he nigh took all de skin off this ol' back o' mine; an' I declar, I wished I'd gone 'long wif you. Well arter that ol' Lincoln sent his sogers down dar, an' Marse he runned 'way an' seein' he didn't stop for his valuables, I propitiated 'em to my private uses. Then I started North, got as far as Massatoosetts, found the eddicational devantages were 'ery perfectible, an' hyar I is, one ob de pillows ob de Massatoosetts bar.

SAM: Well Jim, I forgive you freely for all that's past, and here's my hand on it. (JIM *shakes hands all around to* VIRGINIA) And now Virginia I await your answer, when shall our wedding take place?

MAMMY: Gals neber know nothin' 'bout sech things; an' seein's tomorror's Christmas, we'll celebrate it wif a weddin', whether Jinny's willin' or not. What dyo say ol' man?

CAESAR: Den is jes' my senimens ol' 'ooman, we'll has a weddin'. (SAM *and* VIRGINIA *talk at one side*)

JUNO: Somebody hold me, or I shall bust. I'm so full. *(to company)* Come on boys and girls, let's have an ol' Virginia, it's the only safe exit for surplus steam.

CAESAR: *(rising)* Dat's jes the thing, I feel mysel' growin' twenty-five years younger dis blessed minute, aint dat so ol' 'ooman?

MAMMY: Dat's jes so ol' man.

JUNO: But Lor', I forgot, we can't dance anything but hightoned dances, we must remember that ther's the dignity of an M.C. to be upheld. But anyhow, you fellows have out the chairs and things, an' we'll have a quadrille.

(Stage cleared. Lively music. Each one selects partner, PETE *with* JUNO, JIM *with* POMP. SAM *as caller. Go through three or four figures lively,* JUNO, MAMMY, *and* CAESAR *begin to get happy. Suddenly* SAM *stops calling, rushes to footlights)*

SAM: Ladies and gentlemen, I hope you will excuse me for laying aside the dignity of an elected M.C., and allow me to appear before you once more as peculiar Sam of the old underground railroad.

(Plantation chorus, SAM *dancing to "Golden Slippers," remainder happy)*

(Curtain)

"Talma Gordon" (1900)

SOURCE: Pauline Hopkins, "Talma Gordon," *Colored
American Magazine* 1, no. 5 (October 1900): 272–3.

The Canterbury Club of Boston was holding its regular
monthly meeting at the palatial Beacon Street residence of Dr.
William Thornton, expert medical practitioner and specialist.
All the members were present, because some rare opinions
were to be aired by men of profound thought on a question of
vital importance to the life of the Republic, and because the
club celebrated its anniversary in a home usually closed to society. The Doctor's winters, since his marriage, were passed at
his summer home near his celebrated sanitarium. This winter
found him in town with his wife and two boys. We had heard
much of the beauty of the former, who was entirely unknown
to social life, and about whose life and marriage we felt sure a
romantic interest attached. The Doctor himself was too bright
a luminary of the professional world to remain long hidden
without creating comment. We had accepted the invitation to
dine with alacrity, knowing that we should be welcomed to a
banquet that would feast both eye and palate; but we had not
been favored by even a glimpse of the hostess. The subject for
discussion was "Expansion: Its Effect Upon the Future Development of the Anglo-Saxon Throughout the World."

Dinner was over, but we still sat about the social board
discussing the question of the hour. The Hon. Herbert Clapp,
eminent jurist and politician, had painted in glowing colors the
advantages to be gained by the increase of wealth and the exalted position which expansion would give the United States in
the councils of the great governments of the world. In smoothly
flowing sentences marshaled in rhetorical order, with compact
ideas, and incisive argument, he drew an effective picture with
all the persuasive eloquence of the trained orator.

Joseph Whitman, the theologian of worldwide fame, accepted the arguments of Mr. Clapp, but subordinated all to the
great opportunity which expansion would give to the religious
enthusiast. None could doubt the sincerity of this man, who

looked once into the idealized face on which heaven had set the seal of consecration.

Various opinions were advanced by the twenty-five men present, but the host said nothing; he glanced from one to another with a look of amusement in his shrewd gray-blue eyes. "Wonderful eyes," said his patients who came under their magic spell. "A wonderful man and a wonderful mind," agreed his contemporaries, as they heard in amazement of some great cure of chronic or malignant disease which approached the supernatural.

"What do you think of this question, Doctor?" finally asked the president, turning to the silent host.

"Your arguments are good; they would convince almost anyone."

"But not Doctor Thornton," laughed the theologian.

"I acquiesce whichever way the result turns. Still, I like to view both sides of a question. We have considered but one tonight. Did you ever think that in spite of our prejudices against amalgamation, some of our descendants, indeed many of them, will inevitably intermarry among those far-off tribes of dark-skinned peoples, if they become a part of this great Union?"

"Among the lower classes that may occur, but not to any great extent," remarked a college president.

"My experience teaches me that it will occur among all classes, and to an appalling extent," replied the doctor.

"You don't believe in intermarriage with other races?"

"Yes, most emphatically, when they possess decent moral development and physical perfection, for then we develop a superior being in the progeny born of the intermarriage. But if we are not ready to receive and assimilate the new material which will be brought to mingle with our pure Anglo-Saxon stream, we should call a halt in our expansion policy."

"I must confess, Doctor, that in the idea of amalgamation you present a new thought to my mind. Will you not favor us with a few of your main points?" asked the president of the club, breaking the silence which followed the Doctor's remarks.

"Yes, Doctor, give us your theories on the subject. We may not agree with you, but we are all open to conviction."

The Doctor removed the half-consumed cigar from his lips,

drank what remained in his glass of the choice Burgundy, and leaning back in his chair contemplated the earnest faces before him.

"We may make laws, but laws are but straws in the hands of Omnipotence.

> There's a divinity that shapes our ends,
> Rough-hew them how we will.

And no man may combat fate. Given a man, propinquity, opportunity, fascinating femininity, and there you are. Black, white, green, yellow—nothing will prevent intermarriage. Position, wealth, family, friends—all sink into insignificance before the God-implanted instinct that made Adam, awakening from a deep sleep and finding the woman beside him, accept Eve as bone of his bone; he cared not nor questioned whence she came. So it is with the sons of Adam ever since, through the law of heredity which makes us all one common family. And so it will be with us in our re-formation of this old Republic. Perhaps I can make my meaning clearer by illustration, and with your permission I will tell you a story which came under my observation as a practitioner.

"Doubtless all of you heard of the terrible tragedy which occurred at Gordonville, Mass., some years ago, when Capt. Jonathan Gordon, his wife, and little son were murdered. I suppose that I am the only man on this side of the Atlantic, outside of the police, who can tell you the true story of that crime.

"I knew Captain Gordon well; it was through his persuasions that I bought a place in Gordonville and settled down to spending my summers in that charming rural neighborhood. I had rendered the Captain what he was pleased to call valuable medical help, and I became his family physician. Captain Gordon was a retired sea captain, formerly engaged in the East India trade. All his ancestors had been such; but when the bottom fell out of that business he established the Gordonville Mills with his first wife's money, and settled down as a money-making manufacturer of cotton cloth. The Gordons were old New England Puritans who had come over in the *Mayflower*, they had owned Gordon Hall for more than a hundred years. It was a baronial-like pile of granite with towers, standing on a hill which commanded a superb view of Massachusetts Bay and the surrounding country. I imagine the Gordon star was under a cloud about the time Captain Jonathan married his first wife, Miss Isabel Franklin of Boston, who brought to him the money which mended the broken fortunes of the Gordon house, and restored this old Puritan stock to its rightful position. In the person of Captain Gordon the austerity of manner and indomitable willpower that he had inherited were combined with a temper that brooked no contradiction.

"The first wife died at the birth of her third child, leaving him two daughters, Jeannette and Talma. Very soon after her death the Captain married again. I have heard it rumored that the Gordon girls did not get on very well with their stepmother. She was a woman with no fortune of her own, and envied the large portion left by the first Mrs. Gordon to her daughters.

"Jeannette was tall, dark, and stern like her father; Talma was like her dead mother, and possessed of great talent, so great that her father sent her to the American Academy at Rome, to develop the gift. It was the hottest of July days when her friends were bidden to an afternoon party on the lawn and a dance in the evening, to welcome Talma Gordon among them again. I watched her as she moved about among her guests, a fairylike blonde in floating white draperies, her face a study in delicate changing tints, like the heart of a flower, sparkling in smiles about the mouth to end in merry laughter in the clear blue eyes. There were all the subtle allurements of birth, wealth, and culture about the exquisite creature:

> 'Smiling, frowning evermore,
> Thou art perfect in love-lore,
> Ever varying Madeline,'

quoted a celebrated writer as he stood apart with me, gazing upon the scene before us. He sighed as he looked at the girl.

"'Doctor, there is genius and passion in her face. Sometime our little friend will do wonderful things. But is it desirable to be singled out for special blessings by the gods? Genius always carries with it intense capacity for suffering: "Whom the gods love die young."'

"'Ah,' I replied, 'do not name death and Talma Gordon together. Cease your dismal croakings; such talk is rank heresy.'

"The dazzling daylight dropped slowly into summer twilight. The merriment continued; more guests arrived; the great dancing pagoda built for the occasion was lighted by myriads of Japanese lanterns. The strains from the band grew sweeter and sweeter, and 'all went merry as a marriage bell.' It was a rare treat to have this party at Gordon Hall, for Captain Jonathan was not given to hospitality. We broke up shortly before midnight, with expressions of delight from all the guests.

"I was a bachelor then, without ties. Captain Gordon insisted upon my having a bed at the Hall. I did not fall asleep readily; there seemed to be something in the air that forbade it. I was still awake when a distant clock struck the second hour of the morning. Suddenly the heavens were lighted by a sheet of ghastly light; a terrific midsummer thunderstorm was breaking over the sleeping town. A lurid flash lit up all the landscape, painting the trees in grotesque shapes against the murky sky, and defining clearly the sullen blackness of the waters of the bay breaking in grandeur against the rocky coast. I had arisen and put back the draperies from the windows, to have an unobstructed view of the grand scene. A low muttering coming nearer and nearer, a terrific roar, and then a tremendous downpour. The storm had burst.

31

KATHERINE DAVIS CHAPMAN TILLMAN

(1870–after 1922)

Katherine Davis Chapman Tillman published variously under the names Kate D. Chapman, Katie D. C. Davis Tillman (in 1893), and Katherine Davis Tillman (in 1898). She was born in Mound City, Illinois, into a poor family and did not attend school until the age of twelve, when the family moved to Yankton, South Dakota. She finished high school and took classes at State University in Louisville, Kentucky, and Wilberforce University in Wilberforce, Ohio. While at Wilberforce, she married George M. Tillman, an A.M.E. minister from Pennsylvania. His first assignment had been in Yankton, where they likely met. Tillman was known as a literary prodigy: she published poems, short fiction, and journalism in many of the black publications of the time and edited the *Women's Missionary Recorder*. She was also socially active, serving as an officer in the National Association of Colored Women. After 1922, and a long illness, she stopped publishing.

The following three poems are concerned with history and the idea of black progress within American society. They take the stance of looking back from a future imagined by Tillman in which African Americans can pursue greatness. Tillman, in her work, highlights historical figures, singling them out from within important American moments as if to preempt future attempts at hiding black progress behind a greater theme of American progress. These extraordinary individuals, Tillman argues, lived violently, apart from, and often at odds with the history of their own nation.

"A Question of To-day" (1889)

SOURCE: Kate D. Chapman, "A Question of To-day,"
Freeman (June 8, 1889).

"Human we are, of blood as good;
  As rich the crimson stream;
  God-planned, ere creation stood.
  However it may seem.

"Oh! sit not tamely by and see
  Thy brother bleeding sore;
  For is there not much work for thee,
  While they for help implore?

"From Wahalak came the news,
  Our men are lying dead.
  Did it not hatred rank infuse
  When word like this was read?

"And now White Caps, with hearts as black
  As hell,—of Ku-Klux fame,
  Still ply the lash on freedman's back;
  And must he bear the same?"

Thus said a woman, old and gray,
  To me, while at her door,
  Speaking of what so heavy lay
  And made her heart so sore.

"What, woman! dost thou speak of war.
  The weaker, 'gainst the strong?
  That, surely, would our future mar.
  Nor stop the tide of wrong.

"We must be patient, longer wait.
  We'll get our cherished rights.—"
"Yes, when within the pearly gate.
  And done with earthly sights,—"

Replied the woman, with a sneer
Upon her countenance.
"You men do hold your lives too dear
To risk with spear or lance."

"Naomi, at Fort Pillow fell
Three hundred blacks one day;
The cannon's roar their only knell,
In one deep grave they lay.

"Our men have bravely fought, and will,
Whene'er the time shall come;
Bat now we hear His 'Peace, be still!'
And stay within our home.

"Let but our people once unite,
Stand firmly as a race,
Prejudice, error, strong to fight,
Each hero in his place,—

"And not a favored few demand
Bribes of gold, position,
While many freemen in our land
Bewail their hard condition,—

"Liberty, truly, ours will be,
And error pass away;
And then no longer shall we see
Injustice hold her sway.

"As Americans we shall stand.
Respected by all men;
An honored race in this fair land,
So praised by word and pen.

"And those to come will never know
The pain we suffered here;
In peace shall vow, in peace shall plow,
With naught to stay or fear."

Said Naomi: "You may be right;
God grant it as you say.
I've often heard the darkest night
Gives way to brightest day."

"Lines to Ida B. Wells" (1894)

SOURCE: Kate D. Chapman, "Lines to Ida B. Wells,"
Christian Recorder (July 5, 1894).

Thank God, there are hearts in England
    That feel for the Negro's distress,
And gladly give of their substance
    To seek for his wrongs a redress!

Speed on the day when the lynchers
    No more shall exist in our land,
When even the poorest Negro
    Protected by justice shall stand.

When no more the cries of terror
    Shall break on the midnight air,
While poor and defenseless Negroes
    Surrender their lives in despair.

When the spirit of our inspired Lincoln,
    Wendell Phillips and Summer brave
Shall enkindle a spirit of justice
    And our race from oppression save.

When loyal hearts of the Southland
    With those of the North, tried and true,
Shall give to the struggling Negro
    That which is by nature his due.

And the cloud that threatens our land
   Shall pale beneath Liberty's sun,
And in a prosperous future
   Be atoned the wrongs to us done.

Go on, thou brave woman leader,
   Spread our wrongs from shore to shore,
Until clothed with his rights is the Negro,
   And lynchings are heard of no more.

And centuries hence the children
   Sprung up from the Hamitic race
On history's unwritten pages
   Thy daring deeds shall trace.

And the Afro-American mother
   Who of Negro history tells
Shall speak in words of grateful praise
   Of the noble Ida B. Wells!

"A Tribute to Negro Regiments" (1898)

SOURCE: Kate D. Chapman, "A Tribute to Negro
Regiments," *Christian Recorder* (June 9, 1898).

Watch as they march from the West to the Sea,
Cavalry brave and armed infantry:
Men who have fought, so the records say,
Like lions, on the frontiers far away.

"Black Buffaloes," the Indians called them first,
   But when in the fight they got the worst
Of the awful burst of shot and shell,
   They turned and rushed away pell-mell.

There were Negroes fighting at Bunker Hill;
In 1812 they were at it still,
And when they were called in '61,
Thousands shouldered the government gun.

Loyal? I guess so—game till death;
Braver soldiers never drew breath.
Just treat them like men 'tis all they ask,
And then they are ripe for the sternest task.

They fight, not as Negroes, they fight like men;
As men with rights they gladly maintain.
They fight for a land that's theirs by birth,
And die for a cause, the grandest on earth.

32

AMELIA E. JOHNSON

(ca. 1858–1922)

Amelia E. Johnson was born Amelia Etta Hall in Toronto, Canada; she lived most of her life in Baltimore, where she married the Baptist pastor Harvey Johnson. She was the founder of the eight-page monthly publication *Joy* and published poetry, fiction, and journalism in various periodicals throughout her lifetime. She is most well known for her three novels—*Clarence and Corinne*, *The Hazeley Family*, and *What is My Motive?*—published by the American Baptist Publication Society of Philadelphia, one of the largest publishing houses of the time. She was the first African American and the first woman to publish Sunday School fiction for the publisher.

The following is an excerpt from Johnson's 1890 novel, *Clarence and Corinne*. The tragic subject matter of the book points toward the moralistic and religious beliefs that much of the black American population preached in the years following the Civil War. Black intellectuals of the time and many of the authors featured in this collection believed temperance and religious movements held the key to lifting blacks out of rural poverty and into the upper echelons of society. Throughout this excerpt, characters are punished for making decisions that the author considers immoral.

Selections from *Clarence and Corinne,*
or God's Way (1890)

SOURCE: A. E. Johnson, *Clarence and Corinne,*
or God's Way (Philadelphia: American Baptist
Publications Society, 1890).

CHAPTER I.

Discouraged.

On the outskirts of the pretty town of N——, among neat vine-covered homes, like a blot upon a beautiful picture, there stood a weather-beaten, tumble-down cottage.

Its windows possessed but few unbroken panes, and rags took the place of glass. The rough door hung on a single hinge, which was so rusty as almost to refuse to perform its duty for the paintless boards that hung upon it for support. There was a little garden plot in front, separated from the street by broken palings, and a gate that was never closed. The brick walk that led to the house was uneven and grass-grown; while weeds grew unmolested in the hard, dry soil which had been intended for fairer and more fragrant occupants.

Dismal as was the outside of this wretched abode, still more so was the inside. The floor, devoid of carpet, and unacquainted with soap and water, creaked under foot, and in places was badly broken.

The two or three rickety chairs, a rough pine table and crazy bedstead could hardly be dignified with the name of furniture. Some chipped plates and handleless cups were piled in confusion on the table, and had evidently been left there since noon.

A rickety stove, that was propped up on bricks, which did duty for legs, was littered with greasy pots and pans. Ashes strewed the hearth, and the few unbroken lights in the windows were so begrimed with dust as to be of little use, so far as letting in the daylight was concerned.

So much for the dwelling; now for the inmates.

In an old rocking chair sat the mistress of all this misery. In her hands she held a tattered garment, bearing but small semblance to either male or female attire. She had been engaged, apparently, in attempting to draw together some of the many rents into which it had been torn; but whether the task had seemed a hopeless one, or whether her thoughts were far away from her occupation, I cannot say. At any rate, her hands were resting listlessly in her lap, where they had dropped, with the work still unfinished between her fingers.

Aside from the fact that her appearance partook of the general aspect of her surroundings, she was a comely woman, but one upon whose countenance was stamped despair, and, judging from her swollen eye, one also who was the victim of ill-usage.

She was the sole occupant of the room at the time our story opens, but she did not remain so long, for presently the half-open door was pushed back on its unwilling hinge, and a boy of twelve years entered, followed by a little girl of nine. They were both attractive children, notwithstanding the fact that they bore in their appearance and faces the stamp of neglect and scanty fare.

The boy advanced to his mother's side, and throwing himself down on the floor, resting his elbow on her knee and his head upon his hand, burst out impetuously: "Oh, how I wish we could dress decently, and go to school again like other children!"

The mother roused herself from her apathy and looked at him, half curiously, half sadly.

"What now, Clarence? What's the good of wishing for what can't be?" she said, wearily.

"But why can't it be? It drives me just wild to see the boys coming from school, and to know that they have been there learning, while we're just running around every day; and I'm getting so big too. Now, there's Tom and Lizzie Greene; we met them to-day going to school, looking decent and clean, and, of course, Mr. Tom had to holler 'ragamuffin' at me; but I didn't give it to him, did I?" And the boy chuckled with satisfaction at the way he had served his tormentor.

"Yes; but, Clarence, I was real sorry for poor Lizzie, she was so frightened; besides, I like her: she don't call names, and always speaks to me."

This came from Corinne, Clarence's sister, who had seated herself on the edge of the ragged bed.

"Come, come, my boy," said Mrs. Burton, taking up her mending again, in a disheartened way, and beginning to draw the needle and thread slowly back and forth. "There's no use talking, and there's no use trying to be decent when your father is likely to come home drunk at any time, and knock and beat a body about as he does. I tell you it's no use talking." And her voice rang out sharp and harsh. "Take the basket," she continued, after a moment's pause, "and go and get some chips to start a fire to get some supper, if your father should bring anything home to eat."

Silenced, but not satisfied, the boy obeyed and left the room, followed closely by his sister. He knew that what his mother said was true, and he felt that there was but little benefit to be gained by talking.

Corinne was devotedly fond of her brother, whom she considered a miracle of wisdom; and indeed the lad did have a fund of information about things in general, acquired after the manner usual to observant boys. To this was added an ardent desire to possess an education. Then he was honest and truthful; in fact, he was a boy who might become a useful man; but, as he said to his sister, as he walked slowly along, "he'd no chance."

"Corrie," he exclaimed, suddenly coming to a standstill, and flinging the old basket away from him savagely, "I'm going to run away; so there, now!"

The little girl looked at him in amazement, for a moment, too surprised to say anything. Then the tears gathered in her black eyes, and she said, reproachfully:

"Oh, Clarence! Will you go away and leave me?"

The boy was not proof against the pleading look in the sad little face, for if there was one person in the world whom he really loved, it was his sister. And now, as he looked at her, the fierce hard look slowly died out of his face.

"Now that's just it, Corinne," he said, "if it wasn't for you, I'd go to-morrow; but I do hate to leave you. Never mind, don't cry; maybe something will turn up some day. Here, wipe your eyes on my silk handkerchief."

This had the effect he desired on the little girl, for a smile spread over her face, like sunshine after rain, and she laughed merrily; for the "silk handkerchief" of which her brother spoke was an old bandanna which was so comically dilapidated as to make it a matter of doubt as to whether she would find sufficient handkerchief with which to dry her tears.

While the children were thus engaged with each other a lady approached. The boy and his sister moved aside so that she might pass; but instead of doing this, she came to a stop in front of them.

They looked up into her face in surprise. A very pleasant face it was that they saw, lighted by a pair of very dark and very bright eyes. Clarence knew the face; it was that of a teacher in the school, the very same school that he was so anxious to attend. Yes, he knew her well enough, for he had met her often, and once or twice she had smiled at him, but had never spoken before.

"Your name is Clarence Burton, is it not?" she asked, pleasantly, after surveying the boy from head to foot.

"Yes'm," he answered, looking down at the ground.

"And is the little girl your sister?"

"Yes'm," he said again, "she's Corrie."

"Well, Clarence, why don't you and Corrie come to school?"

"I've nothing fit to come in; neither has Corrie."

"But you would like to come, wouldn't you?"

"Yes, ma'am; it's what I'd like to do more'n anything."

"Won't your mother let you come?"

"Don't know as she'd care, but we ain't going anywhere to be called names, we ain't." And the old hard look came again into the boy's eyes, and he picked up his basket, and was moving away unceremoniously. But it wasn't a part of Miss Gray's plan to have him go yet.

"Clarence," she said, "don't you know that it isn't just polite to do that?"

Something in her voice made Clarence halt, in spite of himself, although he felt as if he would like very much to run away as fast as he could.

He looked up again in the lady's face, expecting to see the "school ma'am" in it, but there was the same kindly expression in the dark eyes that he had seen before.

Again he dropped his to the ground, and twisted a bit of the poor ill-used basket between his uneasy fingers, but he said not a word.

"Clarence," began Miss Gray again, "I have been noticing you for a long time, and I have passed by your home a great many times; and, my poor boy, I know all about it and I'm so sorry for you." And she reached out her neatly gloved hand and took the boy's grimy one and gave it a squeeze.

This was altogether more than Clarence could stand, especially in his present state of mind, and he snatched his band away and hid his face with it. Of course, he wouldn't have any one think that he was crying—oh, no, not for a moment; but however that may be, there was a tremulousness in his voice when he answered Miss Gray's kind "good-bye." "I'm coming to see your mother soon, Clarence," she added, with a parting smile at Corinne, who had done nothing but gaze at the pleasant face of their new acquaintance.

The children watched her for a while after she left them, and then they slowly turned and resumed their interrupted walk. They were going to a new house that was being built, some blocks distant from their home.

Not one word did either of them say until they had reached the building, and were busily engaged in filling their basket with the bits of wood and shavings that had been left by the workmen. When the basket would hold no more they sat down to rest.

"Clarence," said Corinne, looking about her, curiously, "who do you s'pose will live in this house when it's finished?"

"How should I know," returned her brother, rather tartly.

"It's going to be a nice house, Clarence," she went on, without heeding the curtness of the answer to her former question, "and I guess the people that'll live in it will have all sorts of nice things. It must be fine to have all the nice things you want." And the little girl sighed wistfully, as she thought how barren of "nice things" her own poor little life was.

"Don't you fret, Corrie," said her brother, comfortingly; "one of these days you shall have nice things too."

"Where will they come from, Clarence?" asked the child, opening her brown eyes wide.

"Oh, you'll see," was Clarence's answer, given with a wise shake of the head, as he arose to go; and bidding Corinne "come on," he added that the new house was nothing to them, "and never would be." Ah, Clarence, how little we know what the future contains for us!

CHAPTER IV.

Provided For.

Clarence was quite as determined that he would not wear Tom Greene's clothes to his mother's funeral as he had been that he would not go to Tom Greene's home the day before; so, leaving his sister and Mrs. Greene together, he climbed up to his attic, and having succeeded in finding materials, proceeded to draw together, as best he could, the rents in the garments his poor mother had been attempting to mend on the last sad day of her life. The articles consisted of a jacket and trousers; and he was working away industriously, if not skillfully, when Corinne, who had missed him, stole quietly upon him.

"Whatever are you doing, Clarence?" she asked.

"Oh, nothing much," he answered; "only fixing these things to put on."

"But you won't need them, Clarence. Mrs. Greene has brought a nice suit of her Tom's for you to wear. Why, you know that!"

"Yes, I know it well enough. I shan't wear it, though."

"Not wear the clothes Mrs. Greene brought!"

"No; I'd rather wear the worst kind of rags than put on Tom Greene's things and have him throw it in my face afterward."

"Oh, but, Clarence, Mrs. Greene will be angry! And she has been so good to us! I am to wear a dress of Lizzie's."

"Oh, it's all right about you; they wouldn't bother you. Just let me do as I want to about this, Corrie, there's a good girl. I'll make it all right with Mrs. Greene. She needn't know why I don't want to wear the clothes she brought. Run away down, now, won't you?"

Corrie did as she was told; and her brother, finishing his mending, put on the garments and went down.

"Why, Clarence, I thought you were putting on the suit I brought for you. Hurry, now, and get it on," cried Mrs. Greene.

"I'd rather wear these things, Mrs. Greene, please," stammered the boy.

"Why, what on earth——" began the puzzled woman impatiently. But she was interrupted by a knock on the door.

There was no further time to spend in talking, for the hearse was waiting for its burden. The mother, in her rough coffin, was placed within, and the two children followed it to the burial place, where a short service was read; and then the earth was thrown in upon all that was mortal that remained of their parent. The two children had cried so much that they could do nothing now but stand and look on in a dazed sort of way. When all was over they turned sadly and walked away.

Mrs. Greene was waiting for them at the door of the little cottage. She had determined not to notice any further the boy's refusal to wear the clothes. She told the children that she was waiting to take them home with her to pass the night. To her astonishment, Clarence said, quietly:

"You have been very kind to us, Mrs. Greene, and we're very thankful to you for all you have done for us; but, if you please, ma'am, I am going to stay here to-night. Corrie can do as she likes; she can go if she wants to."

"No, no, Clarence; I'll stay with you," whispered his sister, although the vision of Mrs. Greene's cozy, neat rooms was a great deal more inviting than the dingy, dreary cottage. But she was unwilling to leave her brother alone. He was all she had to look up to, and she wanted to be near him.

"Well, Clarence Burton," said Mrs. Greene, when she had recovered enough to say anything, "I didn't think you were such an ungrateful, headstrong boy. But there; that's all one has a right to expect from such people." And she walked away with an angry air.

"Oh, Clarence! I thought she would be angry," said Corinne, regretfully.

"Well, I can't help it," answered her brother. "Of course, I'm thankful for what she has done; but that doesn't make me want to go to her house. I couldn't go there, and that's all about it." He turned and entered the house, and Corinne followed.

The night seemed very long and dreary, especially to the little girl, who was a timid, nervous child; and daylight was a welcome sight. Good Mrs. Greene, although she was angry at the boy's persistent refusal to come to her home, could not bring herself to forget the forlorn children entirely; so she sent Lizzie over with some breakfast, which they were glad to receive, and for which they thanked her warmly.

Early that morning, their friend, Miss Gray, came to deliver her message to Clarence, who received it with real pleasure. Having done this, she was about to tell Corinne to get ready to go home with her for the day, when Miss Rachel Penrose unceremoniously entered.

As I have already said, Miss Rachel was the owner of the wretched old cottage; and she had come to tell the children that it would be no longer their home. When she heard that the boy had been offered a situation she nodded her head approvingly, and said that, "seein' as the boy's provided for, I guess I'll take the girl. She's likely to be of service to run errands and wash dishes and such."

And so it was settled, and the cottage was closed. Corinne went to her new home with Miss Rachel, and Clarence went with Miss Gray, who was to show him the way to Dr. Barrett's office. He found that good gentleman just getting ready to go out.

"Oh, so you're 'the boy,' are you?" he said, adjusting his gold-rimmed spectacles to get a better view of him. "What is your name?"

"Clarence Burton, sir."

"Clarence, is it, eh? Well, that's a good name. Now, Clarence, I've got to go out for a while. Just turn about in here, and rub things up generally: for everything is at sixes and sevens as the saying goes. I had a good smart boy, but he was taken sick and compelled to go home, and I haven't been able to find another to suit me, until I heard about you"

Clarence, much pleased at his hearty reception, promised to do his best to please the good doctor.

After giving directions as to how he wanted things "rubbed up," and charging him to be careful, he went out, leaving the boy feeling very strange and queer. He set to work, however—clumsily enough, to be sure, at first, but with the determination to do his best to give satisfaction.

Meanwhile, Corinne had gone with Miss Penrose. "Miss Rachel Penrose, Seamstress," was the announcement the plate on her door made to the passers-by. Miss Rachel was a spinster who supported herself by her needle. Not that she was wholly dependent upon it for a living; for besides owning the house in which she lived and the cottage in which the Burtons had lived, she had a snug sum of money in the savings bank. As she was a good seamstress, she had a large run of custom and was well paid for her work.

But Miss Rachel was stingy. "Saving" was her besetting sin. Now the habit of saving, when exercised wisely and properly, is a virtue; but when saving means depriving one's self, and others, of the actual necessities of life, in order to lay away money for the sake of simply *possessing*, then it becomes a vice.

It had become so with Miss Rachel. Every cent she spent was parted with as though it were a drop of blood, without which she could not possibly survive. She counted her coals, she counted the potatoes, she meted out everything with the smallest measurement possible. A bright fire, in her opinion, was a waste, and enough to eat entirely unnecessary.

Such was the woman with whom our little friend Corinne had found a home. The child had led an idle, useless life. Her mother had made no effort whatever to train her in any way. Indeed, she had paid but little attention to her children since their earliest years. She had given way altogether to despondency, and had lost all energy and ambition, doing hardly anything, save to sit and brood bitterly and rebelliously over the fate that had shut out from her the light of happiness. Had Mrs. Burton been a Christian she would not have done so, but would have sought to rear her boy and girl properly, and would have striven to accept her lot at least cheerfully. But she was not a Christian, and, therefore, lived as one without hope. She had been born and reared in the country, but had been early deprived of her parents. She had been cared for by strangers, and had grown to be a giddy, thoughtless girl. She had met and formed the acquaintance of James Burton; and although she well knew that he was given to hard drinking, she married him. There had been friendly people who had advised her to do otherwise, and had warned her of the dangers before her; but she was headstrong, and so chose her own way and found it full of thorns. She had thought she knew best, and cherished many bright hopes for a happy future. But alas! like the man in the Lord's sermon, she had built upon the sand. And the rain descended, and the floods came, and the winds blew, and beat upon her house; and it fell, and great was the fall of it.

When she could, she would not hear; and when she saw her bright prospects slipping from her she had nothing to cling to—no hope in this world nor in the world to come. Was it any wonder, then, that she had drifted into the wretched creature she became? With their two little children, the unhappy couple left their country home and came to N——to live in the old cottage, which was only fit to be torn down. For this they paid but little, but more than the place was worth; its owner saw to that. Proud and mortified, Mrs. Burton had shut herself up, alone with her wretchedness, and had repelled all attempts on the part of her neighbors to befriend her. To pay the bit of house rent was now pretty much the extent of James Burton's provision for his family; and so it was but a short while before the abused and despondent wife lost all care as to whether things were kept in order or not. The children went to school as long as their clothes lasted; and, be it said to her credit, their mother did mend and fix over their scanty wardrobe as long as it could be done, and some of the hottest battles between the wretched pair were fought that she might obtain decent clothing for them. But she wearied of the struggle at last, and the garments had become so worn that they were no longer fit to wear to school, especially as the more favored but cruelly thoughtless children had taken advantage of this to nickname the brother and sister "ragamuffins"; and so they went to school no more. Clarence did odd jobs whenever he could get them to do, and but for this the lot of his mother and Corinne would have been even harder than it was.

These were the surroundings amid which Corinne Burton had passed her young life. It is but natural to conclude that it was a sudden change from such a home as I have already described to one where everything was as prim and orderly as its prim mistress.

Miss Rachel Penrose had had a girl to do her housework, but

she had been taken ill, and had gone to her home just previous
to the death of Mrs. Burton. It was on the day when Miss Rachel had gone to the cottage at the request of Mrs. Greene, that
she conceived the idea of supplying the place of her former
maid-of-all-work with the homeless little Corinne, persuading
herself into the belief that she was very benevolent and charitable to take a motherless child and provide her with a home
and food, which she would pay for by the help she would render in her home.

33

MARY E. ASHE LEE

(1850–1932)

Mary E. Ashe Lee was born in Mobile, Alabama, and moved to Wilberforce, Ohio, in 1858. Her work was widely read and praised in its time; Gertrude Mossell, for example, wrote that Ashe Lee "has, by her intelligence and sympathy, done much to inspire the students of that University with a love for the broad culture, true refinement and high moral aims . . . and by her contributions of verse."

Ashe Lee's poem *Afmerica* recounts the historical experience of the archetypal African American woman. Like Katherine Tillman's poetry, *Afmerica* carves a space in American history that is distinctly black and female. Ashe Lee looks back to her ancestors from a position of triumph, urging readers to never forget that blacks suffered for centuries at the hands of their countrymen in order to achieve their present circumstances.

"Afmerica" (1885)

SOURCE: Mary E. Ashe Lee, "Afmerica," *A.M.E. Church Review* (July 1885).

> Hang—up the harp! I hear them say,
> Nor sing again an Afric lay,
> The time has passed; we would forget—
> And sadly now do we regret
> There still remains a single trace
> Of that dark shadow of disgrace,

Which tarnished long a race's fame
Until she blushed at her own name;
And now she stands unbound and free,
In that full light of liberty.
"Sing not her past!" cries out a host,
"Nor of her future stand and boast.
Oblivion be her aimed-for goal,
In which to cleanse her ethnic soul,
And coming out a creature new,
On life's arena stand in view."
But stand with no identity?
All robbed of personality
Perhaps, this is the nobler way
To teach that wished-for brighter day.
Yet shall the good which she has done
Be silenced all and never sung?
And shall she have no inspirations
To elevate her expectations?
From singing I cannot refrain.
Please pardon this my humble strain.

With cheeks as soft as roses are,
And yet as brown as chestnuts dark;
And eyes that borrow from a star
A tranquil, yet a brilliant spark;
Or face of olive, with a glow
Of carmine on the lip and cheek;
The hair in wavelets falling low,
With jet or hazel eyes, that speak;
Or brow of pure Caucasian hue,
With auburn or with flaxen hair;
And eyes that beam in liquid blue,
A perfect type of Saxon fair,—
Behold this strange, this well-known maid,
Of every hue, of every shade!

We find this maiden everywhere,—
From wild and sun-kissed Mexico
To where the Rocky Mountains rear

Their snow-peaked heads in Idaho.
From East to West, she makes her home;
From Carolina's pine-clad State,
Across the plains, she still doth roam
To California's golden gate.
Yet roaming not as gypsy maid,
Nor as the savage red-man's child,
But seeking e'er the loving shade
Of home and civil habits mild.
A daughter of futurity,
The problem of the age is she.

And why should she be strange to-day?
Why called the problem of the age?
Not so when slavery held its sway,
And she was like a bird in cage.
She was a normal creature then,
And in her true allotted place;
Giving her life to fellow-men,
A proud and avaricious race.
But now, a child of liberty,
Of independent womanhood,
The world in wonder looks to see
If in her there is any good;
If this new child, Afmerica,
Can dwell in free Columbia.

"'Twas mercy brought me here," said one,
E'en Phillis Wheatly, child of song,
Who, born beneath an Afric sun,
In her kind mistress found no wrong.
Though maid and mistress, they were true
Companions, both in mind and heart,
No sad impression Phillis knew,
She was content to play her part,
In her is found the purest type
of Afric intellectual might,
Which fast will grow and soon will ripe,
When nourished by the Christian light.

'Tis like Egyptian wheat that slept
In mummy graves, while ages crept.

When first America began
To give the world a nation new,
Then this strange child, called African,
Began to make her history, too,
In New York's Knickerbocker days,
As she would in the corner sit,
She sang with glee her cheerful lays,
And joined the family's mirth and wit.
New England even took her in
As servile at her own fireside;
But when convinced that it was sin,
And wounding to a Christian's pride,
To hold a fellow-man in chains,
She washed her hands from slavery's stains.

The warm affections of her heart,
Her patience and fidelity,
Adapted her in every part
A Washington's fit nurse to be.
And other children, too, of state
Were nurtured on her trustful breast;
Their wants she would alleviate
And solace them when in distress.
Full well she filled her humble sphere
As cook or drudge or ladies' maid;
For all the varied household care
Was on her docile shoulders laid;
While in *ennui* her mistress fair
Was burdened with herself to bear.

Her lot grew harder year by year;
For she was called from household care,
And forced within the fields t'appear,
The labor of the men to share.
In purple fields of sugarcane,
At early morn, her task began

In regions of the Pontchartrain,
She did the hardy work of men
From Florida to Maryland,
In cotton, rice, and fields of corn.
Such work as calls for masculine hands,
All weary, overtasked, and worn,
Subdued, she was compelled to do.
She helped in clearing forests, too.

The cultivation through her toil,
The literal labor of her hands,
Brought to perfection Southern soil
And swelled the commerce of those lands.
But as she toiled she prayed and longed
For freedom and for womanhood.
No Jewess, when in Goshen wronged,
In trusting God e'er firmer stood
Than sad Afmerica, who, through
The thick'ning of the midnight gloom,
Looked steadfast on the North Star true,
And knew Jehovah held her doom.
So thus for twice a century
She sang the song of jubilee.

Nor did she wait on God in vain.
No disappointment comes to those
Who ever strong in faith remain
And in God's confidence repose.
At last, a signal crisis came.
When on the first of sixty three
Brave Lincoln made the bold proclaim:
'Twas but a war necessity,
Which Heaven did potentiate,
That he on that day did decree
In every fighting Southern State
Afmerica forever free.
God wrought this glorious victory,
Triumphant swelled the Jubilee.

Well did she use her chances few,
Each opportunity she prized
As silvery drops of falling dew,
Sent to her from benignant skies.
So freedom found her not without
Fair education in the North.
In Southern cities, too, no doubt
Her acquisitions proved her worth.
In many of her homes were found
Refinement true, and some degree
Of culture there, too, did abound,
Ere she was absolutely free.
Her small one talent was not hid,
Whate'er she found to do she did.

O turbulent America!
So mixed and intermixed, until
Throughout this great Columbia
All nationalities at will
Become thine own, thy legal heirs,—
Behold, this colored child is thine!
Deny it, if there's one who dares,
Amid these glaring facts that shine
Upon the face of this ripe age.
As history doth record thy good,
We trace these facts on every page,—
These facts cry out like Abel's blood;
And "I am vengeance," saith the Lord;
"I will repay." Here his own word.

This hardest of all problems hard,
Which baffles wit of every school
And further progress doth retard,
Is solved but by the Golden rule.
Be calm and think, sublimity—
Have ye not learned, America?—
Is only sweet simplicity.
Cease *working out* Afmerica;
Most simple and sublime is truth.

A truth divine points out to you
The duty owed e'en from thy youth;
One which you need not *solve*, but do.
Acknowledge and protect thy child,
Regard her not as strange or wild.

Afmerica! her home is here;
She wants or knows no other home;
No other lands, nor far nor near,
Can charm or tempt her thence to roam.
Her destiny is marked out here.
Her ancestors, like all the rest,
Came from the eastern hemisphere:
But *she* is native of the *west*.
She'll lend a hand to Africa,
And in her elevation aid.
But here in brave America
Her home, her only home, is made.
No one has power to send her hence;
This home was planned by Providence.

Whatever other women do
In any sphere of busy life,
We find her, though in numbers few,
Engaged heroic in the strife.
In song and music, she can soar;
She writes, she paints and sculptures well:
The fine arts seem to smile on her.
In elocution, she'll excel;
In medicine, she has much skill.
She is an educator, too;
She lifts her voice against the *still*.
To Christ she tries man's soul to woo.
In love and patience, she is seen
In her own home, a blessed queen.

O ye, her brothers, husbands, friends,
Be brave, be true, be pure and strong!
For on your manly strength depends

Her firm security from wrong.
Oh, let her strong right arm be bold!
And don that lovely courtesy
Which marked the chevaliers of old.
Buttress her home with love and care;
Secure her those Amenities
Which make a woman's life most dear;
Give her your warmest sympathies:
Thus high her aspirations raise
For nobler deeds in coming days.

34

H. CORDELIA RAY

(1849–1916)

Henrietta Cordelia Ray was born in New York City into a prominent abolitionist family: her father, Charles B. Ray, was editor and publisher of the *Colored American*; her mother, Henrietta Green Ray, was the first president of the New York Female Literary Society and co-founder of the African Dorcas Association, which provided supplies to students in the African Free Schools in New York City. Cordelia (her preferred name) graduated from the City University of New York in 1891 and taught in the New York City public school system. She first came to national attention when her poem "Lincoln" was read at the unveiling of the Freedmen's Monument to Abraham Lincoln in Washington, D.C., on April 14, 1876, just before an address by Frederick Douglass. Less well known today, she was praised by Elizabeth Frazier in "Some Afro-American Women of Mark" (1892) as "a woman full of *savoir-faire*, [who] stands among our able women writers, not only in poetry, but in prose, excelling in poetry in the sonnet, in prose critical literature." Gertrude Mossell said of Ray that she "has won for herself a place in the front rank of our literary workers."

In the following poems, "Lincoln," "To My Father," "Shakespeare," "In Memoriam (Frederick Douglass)," and "William Lloyd Garrison," Cordelia Ray celebrates figures to whom she feels indebted. In ecstatic language, she conjures complex images while nodding to work of English Romantic poets. Ray's poetry pays homage to the black experience of her time while also attempting to transcend it.

"Lincoln" (1876)

SOURCE: H. Cordelia Ray. "Lincoln." *Emancipation: Its Course and Progress*. (Normal School Steam Power Press Print, 1882)

To-day, O martyred chief, beneath the sun
We would unveil thy form; to thee who won
Th'applause of nations for thy soul sincere,
A loving tribute we would offer here.
'Twas thine not worlds to conquer, but men's hearts;
To change to balm the sting of slavery's darts;
In lowly charity thy joy to find,
And open "gates of mercy on mankind."
And so they come, the freed, with grateful gift,
From whose sad path the shadows thou didst lift.

Eleven years have rolled their seasons round,
Since its most tragic close thy life-work found.
Yet through the vistas of the vanished days
We see thee still, responsive to our gaze,
As ever to thy country's solemn needs.
Not regal coronets, but princely deeds
Were thy chaste diadem; of truer worth
Thy modest virtues than the gems of earth.
Stanch, honest, fervent in the purest cause,
Truth was thy guide; her mandates were thy laws.

Rare heroism, spirit-purity,
The storied Spartan's stern simplicity,
Such moral strength as gleams like burnished gold
Amid the doubt of men of weaker mold,
Were thine. Called in thy country's sorest hour,
When brother knew not brother—mad for power—
To guide the helm through bloody deeps of war,
While distant nations gazed in anxious awe,
Unflinching in the task, thou didst fulfill
Thy mighty mission with a deathless will.

Born to a destiny the most sublime,
Thou wert, O Lincoln! in the march of time,
God bade thee pause and bid the oppressed go free—
Most glorious boon giv'n to humanity.
While slavery ruled the land, what deeds were done?
What tragedies enacted 'neath the sun!
Her page is blurred with records of defeat,
Of lives heroic lived in silence, meet
For the world's praise; of woe, despair and tears,
The speechless agony of weary years.

Thou utteredst the word, and Freedom fair
Rang her sweet bells on the clear winter air;
She waved her magic wand, and lo! from far
A long procession came. With many a scar
Their brows were wrinkled, in the bitter strife,
Full many had said their sad farewell to life
But on they hastened, free, their shackles gone;
The aged, young,—e'en infancy was borne
To offer unto thee loud paeans of praise,—
Their happy tribute after saddest days.

A race set free! The deed brought joy and light!
It bade calm Justice from her sacred height,
When faith and hope and courage slowly waned,
Unfurl the stars and stripes, at last unstained!
The nations rolled acclaim from sea to sea,
And Heaven's vault rang with Freedom's harmony.
The angels 'mid the amaranths must have hushed
Their chanted cadences, as upward rushed
The hymn sublime: and as the echoes pealed,
God's ceaseless benison the action sealed.

As now we dedicate this shaft to thee,
True champion! in all humility
And solemn earnestness, we would erect
A monument invisible, undecked,
Save by our allied purpose to be true
To Freedom's loftiest precepts, so that through

The fiercest contests we may walk secure,
Fixed on foundations that may still endure,
When granite shall have crumbled to decay,
And generations passed from earth away.

Exalted patriot! illustrious chief!
Thy life's immortal work compels belief.
To-day in radiance thy virtues shine,
And how can we a fitting garland twine?
Thy crown most glorious to a ransomed race!
High on our country's scroll we fondly trace,
In lines of fadeless light that softly blend,
Emancipator, hero, martyr, friend!
While Freedom may her holy sceptre claim,
The world shall echo with Our Lincoln's name.

"To My Father" (1893)

SOURCE: H. Cordelia Ray, "To My Father," "Shakespeare,"
Sonnets (New York: J. J. Little and Co., 1893).

A leaf from Freedom's golden chaplet fair,
We bring to thee, dear father! Near her shrine
None came with holier purpose, nor was thine
Alone the soul's mute sanction; every prayer
Thy captive brother uttered found a share
In thy wide sympathy; to every sign
That told the bondman's need thou didst incline
No thought of guerdon hadst thou but to bear
A loving part in Freedom's strife. To see
Sad lives illumined, fetters rent in twain,
Tears dried in eyes that wept for length of days—
Ah! was not that a recompense for thee?
And now where all life's mystery is plain,
Divine approval is thy sweetest praise

"Shakespeare" (1893)

We wonder what the horoscope did show
When Shakespeare came to earth. Were planets there,
Grouped in unique arrangement? Unaware
His age of aught so marvelous, when lo!
He speaks! men listen! what of joy or woe
Is not revealed! love, hatred, marking care,
All quivering 'neath his magic touch. The air
Is thick with beauteous elves, a dainty row,
Anon, with droning witches, and e'en now
Stalks gloomy Hamlet, bent on vengeance dread.
One after one they come, smiling or scarred,
Wrought by that mind prismatic to which bow
All lesser minds. They by thee would be fed,
Poet incomparable! Avon's Bard!

"In Memoriam (Frederick Douglass)" (1897)

SOURCE: H. Cordelia Ray, "In Memoriam (Frederick
Douglass)" in *In Memoriam: Frederick Douglass*. Ed. Helen
Douglass. (Philadelphia: John. C. Yorston & Co.
Publishers, 1897).

One whose majestic presence ever here
Was as an inspiration held so dear
Will greet us nevermore upon the earth.
The funeral bells have rung; there was no dearth
Of sorrow as the solemn cortege passed;
But ours is a grief that will outlast
The civic splendor. Say, among all men,
Who was this hero that they buried then,
With saddest plaint and sorrow-stricken face?
Ay! 'twas a princely leader of his race!

And for a leader well equipped was he;
Nature had given him most regally

E'en of her choicest gifts. What matter then
That he in chains was held, what matter when
He could uplift himself to noblest heights.
E'en with his native greatness, neither slights
Nor wrongs could harm him; and a solemn wrath
Burned in his soul. He well saw duty's path;
His days heroic purposes did know,
And could he then his chosen work forego?

Born to a fate most wretched, most forlorn!
A slave! alas! of benefits all shorn
Upon his entrance into life, what lot
More destitute of hope! Yet e'en that blot
Could not suffice to dim the glowing page
He leaves to History; for he could wage
Against oppression's deadliest blows a war
That knew no ending, until nevermore
Should any man be called a bondman. Ay!
Such was a conflict for which one could die!

Panting for freedom early, he did dare
To throw aside his shackles, for the air
Of slavery is poison unto men
Molded as Douglass was; they suffer, then
Manhood asserts itself; they are too brave,
Such souls as his, to die content a slave.
So being free, one path alone he trod,
To bring to liberty—sweet boon from God—
His deeply injured race; his tireless zeal
Was consecrated to the bondman's weal.

He thought of children sobbing round the knees
Of hopeless mothers, where the summer breeze
Blew o'er the dank savannas. What of woe
In their sad story that he did not know!
He was a valiant leader in a cause
Than none less noble, though the nation's laws
Did seem to spurn it; and his matchless speech
To Britain's sea-girt island shores did reach.

Our Cicero, and yet our warrior knight,
Striving to show mankind might is not right!

He saw the slave uplifted from the dust,
A freeman! Loyal to the sacred trust
He gave himself in youth, with voice and pen,
He had been to the end. And now again
The grandest efforts of that brain and heart
In ev'ry human sorrow bore a part.
His regnant intellect, his dignity,
Did make him honored among all to be;
And public trusts his country gladly gave
Unto this princely leader, born a slave!

Shall the race falter in its courage now
That the great chief is fallen? Shall it bow
Tamely to aught of injury? Ah, nay!
For daring souls are needed e'en to-day.
Let his example be a shining light,
Leading through duty's paths to some far height
Of undreamed victory. All honored be
The silv'ry head of him we no more see!
Children unborn will venerate his name,
And History keep spotless his fair fame.

The Romans wove bright leafy crowns for those
Who saved a life in battle with their foes;
And shall not we as rare a chaplet weave
To that great master-soul for whom we grieve?
Yea! Since not always on the battle-field
Are the best vict'ries won; for they who yield
Themselves to conquer in a losing cause,
Because 'tis right in God's eternal laws,
Do noblest battle; therefore fitly we
Upon their brows a victor's crown would see.

Yes! our great chief has fallen as might fall
Some veteran warrior, answering the call
Of duty. With the old serenity,

His heart still strung with tender sympathy,
He passed beyond our ken; he'll come no more
To give us stately greeting as of yore.
We cannot fail to miss him. When we stand
In sudden helplessness, as through the land
Rings echo of some wrong he could not brook,
Then vainly for our leader will we look.

But courage! no great influence can die.
While he is doing grander work on high,
Shall not his deeds an inspiration be
To us left in life's struggle? May not we
Do aught to emulate him whom we mourn?
We are a people now, no more forlorn
And hopeless. We must gather courage then,
Rememb'ring that he stood man among men.
So let us give, now he has journeyed hence,
To our great chieftain's memory, reverence!

"William Lloyd Garrison" (1905)

SOURCE: H. Cordelia Ray, "William Lloyd Garrison,"
Poems (New York: Grafton Press, 1910).

Some names there are that win the best applause
Of noble souls; then whose shall more than thine
All honored be? Thou heardst the Voice Divine
Tell thee to gird thyself in Freedom's cause,
And cam'st in life's first bloom. No laggard laws
Could quench thy zeal until no slave should pine
In galling chains, caged in the free sunshine.
Till all the shackles fell, thou wouldst not pause.
So to thee who hast climbed heroic heights,
And led the way to where chaste Justice reigns,
An anthem,—tears and gratitude and praise,
Its swelling chords,—uprises and invites
A nation e'en to join the jubilant strains,
Which celebrate thy consecrated days.

35

SARAH E. FARRO

(1859–after 1937)

Sarah Farro's novel, *True Love* (1891), was only recently rediscovered in the course of research by scholar Gretchen Gerzina. Unlike writers in this anthology who write about experiences in America, Farro situated her novel in Victorian England and populated it with white characters, in the model of her favorite writers, Charles Dickens and William Thackeray. Farro's work was widely publicized and sold well. The *Washington Post* of May 8, 1892, announced, "The first negro novelist has appeared, Miss Sarah E. Farro, of Chicago, a woman of good education, aged about 26. The melancholy story "True Love" is not a book of especial promise, but the first edition is nearly exhausted, and the author is writing another story." There is no record of a second work and Farro's novel faded from view even as earlier novels published by black women, such as *Our Nig*, were rediscovered. *True Love* was most likely neglected by scholars and anthologizers in the twentieth century because it contains no black characters and does not engage with issues of race.

Chapter 1, "Mrs. Brewster's Daughters," introduces the novel's main characters and sets the stage for the romance to follow. Note the use of dollars, rather than pounds, signaling the author's American sensibilities.

Chapter 1 from *True Love: A Story of English Domestic Life* (1891)

SOURCE: Sarah E. Farro, *True Love: A Story of English Domestic Life* (Chicago: Donohue & Henneberry, 1891).

Mrs. Brewster's Daughters.

A fine old door of oak, a heavy door standing deep within a portico inside of which you might have driven a coach, brings you to the residence of Mrs. Brewster. The hall was dark and small, the only light admitted to it being from windows of stained glass; numberless passages branched off from the hall, one peculiarity being that you could scarcely enter a single room in it but you must first go down a passage, short or long, to get to it; had the house been designed by an architect with a head upon his shoulders and a little common sense within it, he might have made a respectable house to say the least; as it was, the rooms were cramped and narrow, cornered and confined, and the good space was taken up by these worthless passages; a plat of ground before it was crowded with flowers, far too crowded for good taste, as the old gardener would point out to her, but Mrs. Brewster loved flowers and would not part with one of them. Being the daughter of a carpenter and the wife of a merchant tailor, she had scrambled through life amidst bustle and poverty, moving from one house to another, never settled anywhere for long. It was an existence not to be envied, although it is the lot of many. She was Mrs. Brewster and her husband was not a very good husband to her; he was rather too fond of amusing himself, and threw all the care upon her shoulders; she spent her time nursing her sickly children and endeavoring to make one dollar go as far as two. One day, to her unspeakable embarrassment, she found herself changed from a poor woman in moderate circumstances to an heiress to a certain degree, her father having received a legacy from a relative, and upon his death it was willed to her. She had much sorrow, having lost one child after another, until she had but two left. Then she lost her husband and father; then settled at

Bellville near her husband's native place, upon her limited means. All she possessed was the interest upon this sum her father had left her, the whole not exceeding $2,000. She had two daughters, Mary Ann and Janey; the contrast between them was great, you could see it most remarkably as they sat together, and her love for them was as contrasted as light is with darkness. Mary Ann she regarded with an inordinate affection amounting almost to a passion; for Janey she did not care; what could be the reason of this; what is the reason that parents, many such may be found, will love some of their children and dislike others they cannot tell any more than she could; ask them and they will be unable to give you an answer. It does not lie in the children; it often happens that those obtaining the least love will be the most deserving of it. Such was the case here. Mary Ann Brewster was a pale, sickly, fretful girl, full of whims, full of complaints, giving trouble to everybody about her. Janey, with her sweet countenance and her merry heart, made the sunshine of her home; she bore with her sister's exacting moods, she bore with her mother's want of love, she loved them both and waited on them, and carrolled forth her snatches of song as she moved around the house, and was as happy as the day was long. Ask the servants—they kept only two—and they would tell you that Mrs. Brewster was cross and selfish, but Miss Janey was worth her weight in gold; the gold was soon to be transplanted to a home where it would be appreciated and cherished, for Janey was the affianced wife of Charles Taylor. For nearly a mile beyond Bellville lived Charles Taylor, a quiet, refined gentleman, and the son of a wealthy capitalist; his father had not only made a fortune of his own, but had several bestowed upon him; he had died several years before this time, and his wife survived him one year. There were three sisters, a cousin and two servants that had lived in this family for a number of years.

The beams of the setting sun streamed into the dining-room of the Taylor mansion; it was a room of fine proportions, not dull and heavy as it is the custom of some dining-rooms, but light and graceful as could be wished. Charles Taylor, with his fine beauty, sat at one end of the room, Miss Mary Taylor, a maiden lady of mature years, good looking also in her peculiar style, sat opposite him, she wore a white dress, its make remarkably young, and her hair fell in ringlets, young also; at her right-hand sat Matilda, singularly attractive in her quiet loveliness, with her silver dotted muslin dress trimmed with white ribbons; at her left sat Martha, quiet in manner, plain in features; she had large gray eyes, reflective strangely deep, with a circle of darker gray around them, when they were cast upon you it was not at you they looked, but at what was within you, at your mind, your thoughts; at least such was the impression they carried. Thus sat this worthy group, deep in thought, for they had been conversing about the weather, that had been so damp, for it had been raining for months, and the result was a malarial fever, visiting the residents of Belleville, and it was very dangerous, for the sufferer would soon lapse into unconsciousness and all was over; and it was generally believed that the fever was abated. A rap at the door brought Charles Taylor to his feet, it was George, the old gardener, he had come to tell them the fever had broken out again. "What!" exclaimed Charles. "The fever broken out again?" "Yes, it have," said George, who had the build of a Dutchman, and was taciturn upon most subjects; in manner he was most surly and would hold his own opinion, especially if it touched upon his occupation, against the world.

The news fell upon Charles' heart like a knell; he fully believed the danger to have passed, though not yet the sickness. "Are you sure that the fever has broken out again, George?" he asked, after a pause. "I ain't no surer than I was told," returned George. "I met Doctor Brown, and he said as he passed, that the fever had broken out again." "Do you know where?" asked Charles. "He said, I believe, but I didn't catch it; if I stopped to listen to the talk of fevers where would my work be?" George moved on ere he had done speaking, possibly from the impression that the present talk was not forwarding his work. Taking his black silk hat Charles said, "I shall go out and see if I can glean any news; I hope it may be a false report." He was just outside the walks when he saw Doctor Brown, the most popular doctor in the village, coming along quickly in his buggy; Charles motioned his hand, and the driver pulled up. "It is true, this fresh report of fever?" "Too true, I fear," replied the doctor. "I am on my way now, just summoned." "Who's attacked?" "Mary

Ann Brewster." The name appeared to startle Charles. "Mary Ann Brewster," he uttered, "she will never pull through it." The doctor raised his eye-brows as if he thought it doubtful, and motioned to his driver to move on. On the morning in question Mary Ann Brewster awoke sick; in her impatient, fretful way she called out to Janey, who slept in an adjoining room. Janey was fast asleep, but she was used to being aroused out of her sleep at unreasonable hours by Mary Ann and she threw on her dressing-gown and hastened to her. "I want some tea," began Mary Ann, "I am as sick and thirsty as I can be." She was really of a sickly constitution and to hear her complain of being "sick and thirsty" was nothing unusual. Janey in her loving nature, her sweet patience, received the information with as much concern as though she had never heard it before. She bent over Mary Ann and spoke tenderly, "where do you feel pain, dear, in your head or chest, where is it?" "I told you that I was sick and thirsty, and that's enough," peevishly answered Mary Ann. "Go and get me some tea." "As soon as I can," said Janey, soothingly. "There is no fire yet, the girls are not up, I do not think it can be later than four, by the look of the morning." "Very well," cried Mary Ann, the sobs being contrived by the catching up of her breath in temper not by tears, "you can't call the maids I suppose, and you can't put yourself the least out of the way to alleviate my suffering; you want to go to bed again and sleep till nine o'clock; when I am dead you will wish you were more like a sister; you possess great, rude health yourself, and you feel no compassion for those who do not." An assertion unjust and untrue like many others made by Mary Ann. Janey did not possess rude health, though she was not like her sister always complaining, and she had more compassion for Mary Ann than she deserved. "I will see what I can do," she gently said, "you shall soon have some tea." Passing into her own room Janey hastily dressed herself. When Mary Ann was in one of her exacting moods there could be no more sleep for Janey.

"I wonder," she said to herself, "whether I could not make the fire without waking the girls, they had such a hard day's work yesterday cleaning house; yes, if I can get some chips I will make a fire." She went down to the kitchen, hunted up what was required, laid the fire and lighted it; it did not burn quickly, she thought the chips might be damp and she got the bellows; there she was on her knees blowing at the chips and sending the blaze amid the coals, when some one entered the kitchen. "Miss Janey!" It was one of the girls, Eliza; she had heard a noise in the kitchen and had arisen. Janey explained that her sister was sick and tea was wanted. "Why did you not call us?" "You went to bed so late and had worked so hard, I thought that I would not disturb you." "But it is not lady's work, Miss." "I think ladies should put on gloves when they undertake it," gayly laughed Janey: "look at my black hands." "What would Mr. Taylor say if he saw you on your knees lighting a fire?" "He would say I was doing right, Eliza," replied Janey, a shade of reproof in her firm tones, though the allusion caused the color to crimson her cheeks; the girl had been with them some time and assumed more privilege than a less respected servant would have been allowed to do. The tea ready Janey carried a cup of it to her sister, with a slice of toast that she had made. Mary Ann drank the tea at a draft, but she turned with a shiver from the toast, she seemed to be shivering much. "Who was so stupid as to make that? you might know I could not eat it, I am too sick." Janey began to think she looked very sick, her face was flushed shivering though she was, her lips were dry, her bright eyes were unnaturally heavy; she gently laid her hands, cleanly washed, upon her sister's brow; it felt burning, and Mary Ann screamed out, "Do keep your hands away, my head is splitting with pain." All at once Janey thought of the fever, the danger from which they had been reckoning to have passed. "Would you like me to bathe your forehead with water, Mary Ann?" asked Janey, kindly. "I would like you to stop until things are asked for and not to worry me," replied Mary Ann. Janey sighed, not for the cross temper, Mary Ann was always cross in sickness, but for the suffering she thought she saw and the half-doubt, half-dread which had arisen within her. I think I had better call mamma, she thought to herself, though if she sees nothing unusual the matter with Mary Ann she will only be angry with me; proceeding to her mother's chamber Janey knocked gently, her mother slept still, but the entrance aroused her. "Mamma, I do not like to disturb you, but Mary Ann is sick." "Sick again, and only last week she was in bed three days, poor, dear sufferer; is it her chest?"

"Mamma she seems unusually ill, otherwise I should not have disturbed you, I feared, I thought you will be angry with me, if I say, perhaps"; "say what, don't stand like a statue, Janey." Janey dropped her voice, "dear mamma, suppose it should be the fever?" For one startling moment Mrs. Brewster felt as if a dagger was piercing her heart; the next she turned upon Janey. "Fever for Mary Ann! How dared she prophesy it, a low common fever confined to the poor and the town and which had gone away or all but; was it likely to turn itself back again and come up here to attack her darling child?" Janey, the tears in her eyes, said she hoped it would prove to be only a common headache; that it was her love for Mary Ann which awoke her fears. The mother proceeded to the sick-chamber and Janey followed. Mrs. Brewster was not accustomed to observe caution and she spoke freely of the "fever" before Mary Ann; seemingly for the purpose of casting blame upon Janey. Mary Ann did not catch the fear, she ridiculed Janey as her mother had done; for several hours Mrs. Brewster did not catch it either, she would have summoned medical aid at first, but Mary Ann in her fretfulness protested that she would not have a doctor; later she grew worse and Doctor Brown was sent for, you saw him in his buggy going to the house.

Mrs. Brewster came forward to meet him, Janey, full of anxiety, near her. Mrs. Brewster was a thin woman, with a shriveled face and a sharp red nose, her gray hair banded closely under a white cap, her style of headdress never varied, it consisted always of a plain cap with a quilled border trimmed with purple ribbon, her black dresses she had not laid aside since the death of her husband and intended never to do so. She grasped the arm of the doctor, "You must save my child!" "Higher aid permitting me," answered the surgeon. "What makes you think it's the fever? For months I have been summoned by timid parents to any number of fever cases and when I have arrived in haste they have turned out to be no fever at all." "This is the fever," Mrs. Brewster replied; "had I been more willing to admit that it was, you would have been sent for hours ago, it was Janey's fault; she suggested at day-break that it might be the fever, and it made my darling girl so angry that she forbade my sending for advice; but she is worse now, come and see her."

The doctor laid his hand upon Janey's head with a fond gesture as he followed Mrs. Brewster; all the neighbors of Bellville loved Janey Brewster. Tossing upon her uneasy bed, her face crimson, her hair floating untidily around it, lay Mary Ann, still shivering; the doctor gave one glance at her, it was quite enough to satisfy him that the mother was not mistaken.

"Is it the fever," impatiently asked Mary Ann, un-closing her hot eyelids; "if it is we must drive it away," said the doctor cheerfully. "Why should the fever have come to me?" she rejoined in a tone of rebellion. "Why was I thrown from my buggy last year and my back sprained? Such unpleasant things do come to us." "To sprain your back is nothing compared with this fever; you got well again." "And we will get you well if you will be quiet and reasonable." "I am so hot, my head is so heavy." The doctor, who had called for water and a glass, was mixing up a brown powder which he had produced from his pocket; she drank it without opposition, and then he lessened the weight of the bedclothes, and afterward turned his attention to the bedroom. It was close and hot, and the sun which had just burst forth brightly from the gray sky shone full upon it. "You have got the chimney stuffed up," he exclaimed. "Mary Ann will not allow it to be open," said Mrs. Brewster; "she is sensitive to cold, and feels the slightest draft." The doctor walked to the chimney, turned up his coat cuff and wristband and pulled down a bag filled with shavings; some soot came with it and covered his hand, but he did not mind that; he was as little given to ceremony as Mrs. Brewster was to caution, and he walked leisurely up to the wash-stand to wash it off. "Now, if I catch that bag or any other bag up there obstructing the air, I shall pull down the bricks and make a good big hole that the sky can be seen through; of that I give you notice, madam." He next pulled the window down at the top behind the blind, but the room at its best did not find favor with him. "It is not airy; it is not cool," he said. "Is there not a better ventilated room in the house? if so, she shall be moved to it." "My room is a cool one," interposed Janey eagerly; "the sun never shines upon it, doctor." It appears that Janey, thus speaking, must have reminded the doctor that she was present for in the same unceremonious fashion that he had laid his hands upon the chimney bag, he now laid them upon her shoulder and walked her out of the room. "You go down stairs, Miss Janey, and do not come within a mile of this room again until I give you notice." During this time Mary Ann was talking imperiously and fretfully. "I will not be moved into Janey's room; it is not furnished with half the comforts of mine; it has only a little bed-side carpet; I will not go there, doctor." "Now, see here, Mary Ann," said the doctor firmly, "I am responsible for getting you well, and I shall take my own way to do it. If I am to be contradicted at every suggestion, your mother can summon some one else to attend you, I will not undertake it."

"My dear you shall not be moved to Janey's room"; said her mother coaxingly; "you shall be moved to mine, it is larger than this, you know, doctor, with a draft through it, if you wish to open the door and windows."

"Very well," replied the doctor, "let me find her in it when I come again this evening, and if there's a carpet on the floor take it up, carpets were never intended for bed-rooms." He went into one of the sitting-rooms with Mrs. Brewster as he descended; "What do you think of the case," she earnestly inquired. "There will be some difficulty with it," was his candid reply. "Her hair must be cut off." "Her hair cut off!" screamed Mrs. Brewster, "that it never shall! She has the most beautiful hair, what is Janey's compared to her's?"

"You heard what I said," he positively replied.

"But Mary Ann will not allow it to be done," she returned, shifting the ground of remonstrance from her own shoulders, "and to do it in opposition would be enough to kill her." "It will not be done in opposition," he answered, "she will be unconscious before it is attempted." Mrs. Brewster's heart sank within her. "You anticipate she will be dangerously ill?" "In such cases there is always danger, but worse cases than, as I believe hers will be, are curable." "If I lose her I shall die myself"; she exclaimed, "and if she is to have it badly she will die! Remember, doctor, how weak she has always been." "We sometimes find that the weak of constitution battle best with an epidemic," he replied, "many a hearty one is stricken down with it and taken off, many a sickly one has pulled through it and been the better afterward."

"Everything shall be done as you wish," said Mrs. Brewster humbly in her great fear. "Very well. There is one caution I would earnestly impress upon you, that of keeping Janey from the sick-room." "But there is no one to whom Mary Ann is so accustomed as a nurse," objected Mrs. Brewster. "Madam," burst forth the doctor angrily, "would you subject Janey to the risk of taking the infection in deference to Mary Ann's selfishness or to yours, better lose all the treasures your house contains than lose Janey, she is the greatest treasure." "I know how remarkably prejudiced you have always been in Janey's favor," spitefully spoke Mrs. Brewster. "If I disliked her as much as I like her, I should be equally solicitous to guard her from the danger of infection," said Doctor Brown. "If you chose to put Janey out of consideration you cannot put Charles Taylor; in justice to him she must be taken care of."

Mrs. Brewster opened her mouth to reply, but closed it again; strange words had been hovering upon her lips. "If Charles Taylor had not been blind his choice would have fallen upon Mary Ann, not upon Janey." In her heart there was a sore topic of resentment; for she fully appreciated the advantages of a union with the Taylors. Those words were swallowed down to give utterance to others. "Janey is in the house, and therefore must be liable to take the fever; whether she takes the infection or not, I cannot fence her around with an air-tight wall so that not a breath of tainted atmosphere shall touch her, I would if I could, but I cannot." "I would send her from the house, Mrs. Brewster; at any rate, I would forbid her to go near her sister; I don't want two patients on my hands instead of one," he added in his quaint fashion as he took his departure. He was about to step into his buggy when he saw Charles Taylor advancing with a quick step. "Which of them is it that is seized?" he inquired as he came up. "Not Janey, thank goodness," replied the doctor. "It is Mary Ann; I have been persuading the madam to send Janey from home; I should send her were she a daughter of mine." "Is Mary Ann likely to have it dangerously?" "I think she will. Is there any necessity for you going to the house just now, Mr. Taylor?" Charles Taylor smiled. "There is no necessity for my keeping away; I do not fear the fever any more than you do." He passed into the garden as he spoke, and the doctor drove on. Janey saw him and came running out. "Oh! Charles, don't come in; do not come." His only answer was to take her upon his arm and enter. He raised the drawing-room window, that as much air might circulate through the house as was possible, and stood at it with her holding her before him. "Janey, what am I to do with you?" "To do with me? What should you do with me, Charles?" "Do you know, my dear, that I cannot afford to let this danger touch you?" "I am not afraid," she gently said. He knew that she had a brave unselfish heart, but he was afraid for her, for he loved her with a jealous love, jealous of any evil that might come too near her. "I should like to take you out of the house with me now, Janey. I should like to take you far from this fever-tainted town; will you come?" She looked up at him with a smile, the color coming into her cheeks. "How could I, Charles?" Anxious thoughts were passing through the mind of Charles Taylor. We cannot put aside the conventionalities of life, though there are times when they press upon us as an iron weight; he would have given his own life almost to have taken Janey from that house, but how was he to do it? No friend would be likely to receive her; not even his own sisters; they would have too much dread of the infection she might bring. He would fain have carried her to some sea-breezed town and watch over her and guard her there until the danger should be over. None would have protected her more honorably than Charles Taylor. But those conventionalities the world has to bow down to, how would the step have accorded with them? Another thought passed through his mind. "Listen, Janey," he said, "suppose we get a license and drive to the parson's house; it could all be done in a few hours, and you could be away with me before night." As the meaning dawned upon her, she bent her head, and her blushing face, laughing at the wild improbability. "Oh! Charles, you are only joking; what would people say?" "Would it make any difference to us what they said?" "It could not be, Charles; it is a vision impossible," she replied seriously. "Were all other things meet, how could I run away from my sister on her bed of dangerous illness to marry you?"

Janey was right and Charles Taylor felt that she was; the conventionalities must be observed no matter at what cost. He held her fondly against his heart, "if aught of ill should arise to you from your remaining here I should never forgive myself." Charles could not remain longer, he must be at his office, for business was urging. His cousin, George Gay, was in the private room alone when he entered, he appeared to be buried five feet deep in business, though he would have preferred to be five feet deep in pleasure. "Are you going home to supper this evening," inquired Charles? "The fates permitting," replied Mr. Gay, "You tell my sisters that I will not return until after tea, Mary will not thank me for running from Mrs. Brewster's house to hers, just now." "Charles," warmly spoke George in an impulse of kindly feeling, "I do hope the fever will not extend itself to Janey." "I hope not," fervently breathed Charles Taylor.

36

ALICE RUTH MOORE DUNBAR-NELSON

(1875–1935)

Alice Ruth Moore Dunbar-Nelson was born in New Orleans, Louisiana, into a mixed-race family. After graduating from Straight University, she worked as a teacher in the New Orleans public school system, and in 1895 she published *Violets and Other Tales*, her first collection of short stories and poems. She married the poet Paul Laurence Dunbar in 1898; the marriage was violent. They separated in 1902 and she moved to Wilmington, Delaware, where she taught at several schools including Howard High School. She married Robert Nelson, an activist, in 1912.

The following selection consists of an essay, "The Woman," and five poems, "I Sit and Sew," "Sonnet," "To Madame Curie," "To the Negro Farmers of the United States," and "Amid the Roses." In "The Woman," Dunbar-Nelson asks, "Why should well-salaried women marry?" Marriage, for her, is "based on a desire to possess the physical attractions of the woman by the man, pretty much as a child desires a toy, and an innate love of man, a wild desire not to be ridiculed by the foolish as an 'old maid,' and a certain delicate shrinking from the work of the world—laziness is a good name for it—by the woman." Why should women sacrifice their space in the professional world for the sake of their families (especially husbands)? Alice Dunbar-Nelson's poetry, seemingly frank and personal, contains all of the power of her prose. The short poems offered here alternate between celebrating their subjects, as "To Madame Curie" and "To the Negro Farmers of the United States" do, and voicing anxieties and desires.

"The Woman" (1895)

SOURCE: Alice Moore Dunbar-Nelson, "The Woman,"
Violets and Other Tales (Boston:
The Monthly Review, 1895).

The literary manager of the club arose, cleared his throat, adjusted his cravat, fixed his eyes sternly upon the young man, and in a sonorous voice, a little marred by his habitual lisp, asked: "Mr. ——, will you please tell us your opinion upon the question, whether woman's chances for matrimony are increased or decreased when she becomes man's equal as a wage earner?"

The secretary adjusted her eyeglass, and held her pencil alertly poised above her book, ready to note which side Mr. —— took. Mr. —— fidgeted, pulled himself together with a violent jerk, and finally spoke his mind. Someone else did likewise, also someone else, then the women interposed, and jumped on the men, the men retaliated, a wordy war ensued, and the whole matter ended by nothing being decided, pro or con—generally the case in wordy discussions. *Moi?* Well, I sawed wood and said nothing, but all the while there was forming in my mind, no, I won't say forming, it was there already. It was this, *Why should well-salaried women marry?* Take the average working-woman of today. She works from five to ten hours a day, doing extra night work, sometimes, of course. Her work over, she goes home or to her boarding-house, as the case may be. Her meals are prepared for her, she has no household cares upon her shoulders, no troublesome dinners to prepare for a fault-finding husband, no fretful children to try her patience, no petty bread and meat economies to adjust. She has her cares, her money-troubles, her debts, and her scrimpings, it is true, but they only make her independent, instead of reducing her to a dead level of despair. Her day's work ends at the office, school, factory or store; the rest of the time is hers, undisturbed by the restless going to and fro of housewifely cares, and she can employ it in mental or social diversions. She does not incessantly rely upon the whims of a cross man to take her to such amusements as she desires. In this nineteenth century she is free to go

"I Sit and Sew" (1918)

SOURCE: Alice Moore Dunbar-Nelson, "I Sit and Sew,"
A.M.E. Church Review (1918).

I sit and sew—a useless task it seems,
My hands grown tired, my head weighed down with dreams—
The panoply of war, the martial tred of men,
Grim-faced, stern-eyed, gazing beyond the ken
Of lesser souls, whose eyes have not seen Death,
Nor learned to hold their lives but as a breath—
But—I must sit and sew.

I sit and sew—my heart aches with desire—
That pageant terrible, that fiercely pouring fire
On wasted fields, and writhing grotesque things
Once men. My soul in pity flings
Appealing cries, yearning only to go
There in that holocaust of hell, those fields of woe—
But—I must sit and sew.

The little useless seam, the idle patch;
Why dream I here beneath my homely thatch,
When there they lie in sodden mud and rain,
Pitifully calling me, the quick ones and the slain?
You need me, Christ! It is no roseate dream
That beckons me—this pretty futile seam,
It stifles me—God, must I sit and sew?

where she pleases—provided it be in a moral atmosphere—without comment. Theatres, concerts, lectures, and the lighter amusements of social affairs among her associates, are open to her, and there she can go, see, and be seen, admire and be admired, enjoy and be enjoyed, without a single harrowing thought of the baby's milk or the husband's coffee.

Her earnings are her own, indisputably, unreservedly, undividedly. She knows to a certainty just how much she can spend, how well she can dress, how far her earnings will go. If there is a dress, a book, a bit of music, a bunch of flowers, or a bit of furniture that she wants, she can get it, and there is no need of asking anyone's advice, or gently hinting to John that Mrs. So and So has a lovely new hat, and there is one ever so much prettier and cheaper down at Thus & Co.'s. To an independent spirit there is a certain sense of humiliation and wounded pride in asking for money, be it five cents or five hundred dollars. The working woman knows no such pang; she has but to question her account and all is over. In the summer she takes her savings of the winter, packs her trunk and takes a trip more or less extensive, and there is none to say her nay,—nothing to bother her save the accumulation of her own baggage. There is an independent, happy, free-and-easy swing about the motion of her life. Her mind is constantly being broadened by contact with the world in its working clothes; in her leisure moments by the better thoughts of dead and living men which she meets in her applications to books and periodicals; in her vacations, by her studies of nature, or it may be other communities than her own. The freedom which she enjoys she does not trespass upon, for if she did not learn at school she has acquired since habits of strong self-reliance, self-support, earnest thinking, deep discriminations, and firmly believes that the most perfect liberty is that state in which humanity conforms itself to and obeys strictly, without deviation, those laws which are best fitted for their mutual self-advancement.

And so your independent working woman of to day comes as near being ideal in her equable self poise as can be imagined. So why should she hasten to give this liberty up in exchange for a serfdom, sweet sometimes, it is true, but which too often becomes galling and unendurable.

It is not marriage that I decry, for I don't think any really sane person would do this, but it is this wholesale marrying of girls in their teens, this rushing into an unknown plane of life to avoid work. Avoid work! What housewife dares call a moment her own?

Marriages might be made in Heaven, but too often they are consummated right here on earth, based on a desire to possess the physical attractions of the woman by the man, pretty much as a child desires a toy, and an innate love of man, a wild desire not to be ridiculed by the foolish as an "old maid," and a certain delicate shrinking from the work of the world—laziness is a good name for it—by the woman. The attraction of mind to mind, the ability of one to compliment the lights and shadows in the other, the capacity of either to fulfil the duties of wife or husband—these do not enter into the contract. That is why we have divorce courts.

And so our independent woman in every year of her full, rich, well-rounded life, gaining fresh knowledge and experience, learning humanity, and particularly that portion of it which is the other gender, so well as to avoid clay-footed idols, and finally when she does consent to bear the yoke upon her shoulders, does so with perhaps less romance and glamor than her younger scoffing sisters, but with an assurance of solid and more lasting happiness. Why should she have hastened this; was aught lost by the delay?

"They say" that men don't admire this type of woman, that they prefer the soft, dainty, winning, mindless creature who cuddles into men's arms, agrees to everything they say, and looks upon them as a race of gods turned loose upon this earth for the edification of womankind. Well, may be so, but there is one thing positive, they certainly respect the independent one, and admire her, too, even if it is at a distance, and that in itself is something. As to the other part, no matter how sensible a woman is on other questions, when she falls in love she is fool enough to believe her adored one a veritable Solomon. Cuddling? Well, she may preside over conventions, brandish her umbrella at board meetings, tramp the streets soliciting subscriptions, wield the blue pencil in an editorial sanctum, hammer a typewriter, smear her nose with ink from a galley full of pied type, lead infant ideas through the tortuous mazes of c-a-t and r-a-t, plead at the bar, or wield the scalpel in a dissecting room, yet when the right moment comes, she will sink as gracefully into his manly embrace, throw her arms as lovingly around his neck, and cuddle as warmly and sweetly to his bosom as her little sister who has done nothing else but think, dream, and practice for that hour. It comes natural, you see.

"Amid the Roses" (1895)

SOURCE: Alice Moore Dunbar-Nelson, "Amid the Roses," *Violets and Other Tales* (Boston: The Monthly Review, 1895).

There is tropical warmth and languorous life
Where the roses lie
In a tempting drift
Of pink and red and golden light
Untouched as yet by the pruning knife.
And the still, warm life of the roses fair
That whisper "Come,"
With promises
Of sweet caresses, close and pure
Has a thorny whiff in the perfumed air.
There are thorns and love in the roses' bed,
And Satan too
Must linger there;
So Satan's wiles and the conscience stings,
Must now abide—the roses are dead.

"Sonnet" (1919)

SOURCE: Alice Moore Dunbar-Nelson, "Sonnet," *Crisis*
(August 1919).

I had not thought of violets late,
The wild, shy kind that spring beneath your feet
In wistful April days, when lovers mate
And wander through the fields in raptures sweet.
The thought of violets meant florists' shops,
And bows and pins, and perfumed papers fine;
And garish lights, and mincing little fops
And cabarets and soaps, and deadening wines.
So far from sweet real things my thoughts had strayed,
I had forgot wide fields; and clear brown streams;
The perfect loveliness that God has made,—
Wild violets shy and Heaven-mounting dreams.
And now—unwittingly, you've made me dream
Of violets, and my soul's forgotten gleam.

"To the Negro Farmers of the United States" (1920)

SOURCE: Alice Moore Dunbar-Nelson, "To the Negro
Farmers of the United States," *Dunbar Speaker and
Entertainer* (Naperville, IL: J. L. Nichols, 1920).

God washes clean the souls and hearts of you,
His favored ones, whose backs bend o'er the soil,
Which grudging gives to them requite for toil
In sober graces and in vision true.
God places in your hands the pow'r to do
A service sweet. Your gift supreme to foil
The bare-fanged wolves of hunger in the moil
Of Life's activities. Yet all too few
Your glorious band, clean sprung from Nature's heart;
The hope of hungry thousands, in whose breast

Dwells fear that you should fail. God placed no dart
Of war within your hands, but pow'r to start
Tears, praise, love, joy, enwoven in a crest
To crown you glorious, brave ones of the soil.

"To Madame Curie" (1921)

SOURCE: Alice Moore Dunbar-Nelson, "To Madame
Curie," Philadelphia *Public Ledger* (August 21, 1921).

Oft have I thrilled at deeds of high emprise,
And yearned to venture into realms unknown,
Thrice blessed she, I deemed, whom God had shown
How to achieve great deeds in woman's guise.
Yet what discov'ry by expectant eyes
Of foreign shores, could vision half the throne
Full gained by her, whose power fully grown
Exceeds the conquerors of th' uncharted skies?
So would I be this woman whom the world
Avows its benefactor; nobler far,
Than Sybil, Joan, Sappho, or Egypt's queen.
In the alembic forged her shafts and hurled
At pain, diseases, waging a humane war;
Greater than this achievement, none, I ween.

WOMEN ADDRESSING WOMEN: ADDRESSES AND ESSAYS

37

SARAH J. EARLY

(1825–1907)

Sara Jane Early was born Sarah Jane Woodson in Chillicothe, Ohio, into the family that founded the first black Methodist Church west of the Alleghenies. After graduating from Oberlin College, she joined the faculty at Wilberforce University and became its first black female college instructor. In her later life, she was a lecturer, author, and the superintendent of the black division of the Women's Christian Temperance Movement.

In the following address, Early notes the importance of the women's club movement, which organized groups of black women throughout the United States in the years after the Civil War, promoting education, temperance, women's rights, and Christianity. Many of the writers featured in this anthology were central figures in their city's or region's women's clubs and wrote for their local newspapers. Mixing Christian, inspirational language with tangible measures of women's club's growth, Early argues in this detailed and passionate essay that the progress already made by black women is evidence that black culture and society will thrive.

"The Organized Efforts of the Colored Women of the South to Improve Their Condition" (1894)

SOURCE: Sarah J. Early, "The Organized Efforts of the
Colored Women of the South to Improve Their Condition,"
World's Congress of Representative Women, Vol. 2. Ed.
Mary Wright Sewall (Chicago: Rand McNally, 1894).

In this age of development and advancement all the forces which have been accumulating for centuries past seem to be concentrated in one grand effort to raise mankind to that degree of intellectual and moral excellence which a wise and beneficent Creator designed that he should enjoy. No class of persons is exempt from this great impulse. The most unlettered, the most remote and obscure, as well as the most refined and erudite seem to have felt the touch of an unseen power, and to have heard a mysterious voice calling them to ascend higher in the scale of being. It is not a strange coincidence, then, that in this period of restlessness and activity the women of all lands should simultaneously see the necessity of taking a more exalted position, and of seeking a more effective way of ascending to the same plane, and assuming the more responsible duties of life with her favored brother.

In organization is found all the elements of success in any enterprise, and by this method alone are developed the force and ability that have reared the grand structure of human society. God intended that man should be a social being, for he has given to no one individual the genius to construct by his efforts alone the complex edifice.

Step by step, as the dark cloud of ignorance and superstition is dispelled by the penetrating rays of the light of eternal truth, men begin to think, and thought brings revolution, and revolution changes the condition of men and leads them into a happier and brighter existence. So have the great revolutions of the age affected the condition of the colored people of the Southern States, and brought them into a more hopeful relation to the world. When they emerged from the long night of oppression, which shrouded their minds in darkness, crushed the energies of their soul, robbed them of every inheritance save their trust in God, they found themselves penniless, homeless, destitute, with thousands of aged and infirm and helpless left on their hands to support, and poverty and inexperience prevailing everywhere. To improve their social condition was the first impulse of their nature. For this purpose they began immediately to organize themselves into mutual aid societies, the object of which was to assist the more destitute, to provide for the sick, to bury the dead, to provide a fund for orphans and widows. These societies were the beginning of their strength, the groundwork of their future advancement and permanent elevation. They were constructed with admirable skill and harmony. Excellent charters were secured, and the constitution and by-laws were adhered to with remarkable fidelity. The membership increased rapidly, and the funds in the treasuries grew daily. The women, being organized separately, conducted their societies with wonderful wisdom and forethought. Their influence for good was felt in every community, and they found themselves drawn together by a friendly interest which greatly enhanced the blessings of life. Their sick and dead and orphans have been properly cared for. Thus our people have shown a self-dependence scarcely equaled by any other people, a refined sensibility in denying themselves the necessities of life to save thousands of children from want and adults from public charity; in screening them from the stinging arrows of the tongue of slander and the carping criticisms of a relentless foe.

These organizations number at least five thousand and carry a membership of at least a half-million women. They have widened into State societies, and some of the stronger bodies into national organizations, meeting in annual assemblies to transact business and to discuss their future well-being. They have in some States built and sustained orphans' homes, and in others purchased their own cemeteries. They have built commodious halls for renting purposes; they have assisted in building churches and other benevolent institutions. They have granted large death benefits, and thus provided homes for many orphan children, and have deposited large sums in savings banks for future use. Should the question be asked what benefit has accrued from these organized efforts, we answer, much in every way.

Their organizations have bound the women together in a common interest so strong that no earthly force can sever it. Organization has taught them the art of self-government, and has prepared the way for future and grander organizations. By their frequent convocations and discussions their intellectual powers have been expanded and their judgment has been enlightened. Organization has given hope for a better future by revealing to colored women their own executive ability. It has stimulated them to acquire wealth by teaching them to husband their means properly. It has intensified their religion by giving them a more exalted idea of God through a constant survey of his goodness and mercies toward them. It has refined their morality through adherence to their most excellent constitutions and by-laws. It has assisted in raising them from a condition of helplessness and destitution to a state of self-dependence and prosperity; and now they stand a grand sisterhood, nearly one million strong, bound together by the strongest ties of which the human mind can conceive, being loyal to their race, loyal to the government, and loyal to their God.

Having thus provided for their future well-being, their attention was turned to the spread of the gospel. With hearts glowing with the love of God, they longed to assist in building up his kingdom on earth. Many devout women joined themselves into missionary societies to obtain means with which to send the gospel to other parts of the world more destitute than their own. They were auxiliary to the churches of various denominations, and multiplied until their scanty donations amounted to sums sufficient to accomplish much good in the Master's cause. On the women's part in the African Methodist Episcopal church they have donated the sum of thirty thousand dollars, and a like amount in each of the five other leading denominations. The Presbyterian Home and Foreign Missionary Society sustains missions in West Africa, the West Indies, the Bermuda Islands, South America, and the islands of Hayti and St. Thomas. The home missions of the various denominations occupy the time of more than one thousand ministers. About the year 1890 the women of the African Methodist Episcopal church formed a mite missionary society, which has its auxiliary branches all over the Union. They now labor assiduously for the advancement of the foreign missions they had prayed for. They believe in him who blessed the widow's mite, and who pronounced a divine benediction on the modest disciple who had done what she could.

This organization raises two thousand dollars annually, sustaining two or three missionaries in Hayti, and assists in the Bermuda and West African missions. The aggregate of all the money raised annually by the colored churches amounts to over half a million of dollars, and by far the greater share is raised by the women.

Many a benighted heathen has heard the gospel through their instrumentalities. By their efforts they themselves have become better informed concerning the gospel, and better acquainted with the world and its inhabitants. In trying to raise others they have learned to look up from their toilsome and abject present to a brighter and more glorious future. They have learned to exalt the goodness of God as manifest in the sanctification of their work to his honor and glory. This has raised in them a holy ambition to accomplish greater good for their fellow-men.

The colored women of the Southern States have not been indifferent to the necessity of guarding their homes against the pernicious influences of the drinking system. They have begun to fortify themselves against the most powerful of all enemies—strong drink. Woman's Christian temperance unions have been formed in all Southern States, into which many hundreds have gathered, who work with much patience and diligence. Hospital work, prison work, social purity, and flower mission work, and the distribution of literature among all classes of persons have been performed faithfully, and many erring and destitute souls have felt the tenderness and shared the bounty of the benevolent hearts and ready hands of the colored women of the Woman's Christian Temperance Unions.

These organizations have accomplished much in forming temperance sentiment among the people and in the churches, and have helped materially in changing votes at the polls for prohibition.

Again, when this fair land was distracted by contending factions, and military forces left desolation and ruin in their pathway, while enemies met in deadly conflict on the fields of battle, the expiring soldier longed for the soothing touch of woman's hand, and his heart yearned for the consoling words of woman's prayer. It was then on the blood-drenched field that the colored women showed the deepest sympathy for suffering humanity and the highest valor and loyalty by stanching the bleeding wounds, and cooling the parched lips with water, and raising the fainting head, and fanning the fevered brow, and with tender solicitude watching by the dying couch, and breathing the last prayer with him who had laid down his life for his country. The colored men often endangered their lives by passing the line of the enemy to carry messages to the officers of the Union army, so that a part of the army was saved not once nor twice but often by their daring valor. And when her loyal and chivalric brothers, of whose loyalty and valor she was justly proud, returned from the conflict with halting limbs and shattered frames, and victory perched on their banners, they were content to lie down and die, and leave their widows and orphans to the care of a merciful God and their brave comrades. When the women of the nation proposed to form relief corps to assist the needy comrades of the Grand Army of the Republic and care for their orphans and widows, the colored women did not hesitate, but when opportunity offered they organized, and they have many active and industrious corps accomplishing much noble work, in assisting the needy, decorating graves, presenting flags to schools, and in many ways instilling patriotism.

If we compare the present condition of the colored people of the South with their condition twenty-eight years ago, we shall see how the organized efforts of their women have contributed to the elevation of the race and their marvelous advancement in so short a time. When they emerged from oppression they were homeless and destitute; now they are legal owners of real estate to the value of two hundred and sixty-three millions of dollars. Then they were penniless, but now they have more than two millions in bank. In several States they have banks of their own in successful operation, in which the women furnish the greater number of deposits. Then they had no schools, and but few of the people were able to read; now more than four millions of their women can read. Then they had no high schools, but now they have two hundred colleges, twenty-seven of which are owned and conducted by their own race.

These feeble efforts at organization to improve our condition seem insignificant to the world, but this beginning, insignificant as it may seem, portends a brighter and nobler future. If we in the midst of poverty and proscription can aspire to a noble destiny to which God is leading all his rational creatures, what may we not accomplish in the day of prosperity?

Hark! I hear the tramp of a million feet, and the sound of a million voices answer, we are coming to the front ranks of civilization and refinement.

Five hundred thousand girls and young women are now crowding our schools and colleges; they are forming literary societies, Young Women's Christian Associations, Christian Endeavor Societies, bands of King's Daughters, and with all the appliances of modern civilization which have a tendency to enlighten the mind and cultivate the heart, they will emerge into society, with all their acquired ability, to perfect that system of organization among their race of which they themselves are the first fruits.

38

LUCY CRAFT LANEY

(1854–1933)

Lucy Craft Laney was born in Macon, Georgia. After graduating from the Normal School at Atlanta University, she taught in several Georgia towns before founding the Haines Institute in Augusta where she served as principal for fifty years. Laney, Dr. Martin Luther King, Jr., and Reverend Henry McNeal Turner were the first African Americans to have their pictures hung in the Georgia State Capitol.

In the following piece, Laney cites familial instability during slavery, poverty, and high levels of incarceration as causes of black women's low social and economic standing. She encourages women to pursue work and education as a means of gaining status and influence. Laney hews to the practical. She claims cash as a force that can uplift, and she turns to numbers and statistics while making her argument. As educators, Laney states, black women can make a dramatic impact on the world. Her view of education is holistic, reaching beyond the schoolhouse to the home and the public lectern.

"The Burden of the Educated Colored Woman" (1899)

SOURCE: Lucy Craft Laney, "The Burden of the Educated Colored Woman," *Report of the Hampton Negro Conference*, no. III (1899): 37–42.

If the educated colored woman has a burden—and we believe she has—what is that burden? How can it be lightened, how may it be lifted? What it is can be readily seen perhaps better than told, for it constantly annoys to irritation; it bulges out as did the load of Bunyan's Christian—ignorance—with its inseparable companions, shame and crime and prejudice.

That our position may be more readily understood, let us refer to the past; and it will suffice for our purpose to begin with our coming to America in 1620, since prior to that time, we claim only heathenism. During the days of training in our first mission school—slavery—that which is the foundation of right training and good government, the basic rock of all true culture—the home, with its fire side training, mother's molding, woman's care, was not only neglected but utterly disregarded. There was no time in the institution for such teaching. We know that there were, even in the first days of that school, isolated cases of men and women of high moral character and great intellectual worth, as Phillis Wheatley, Sojourner Truth, and John Chavis, whose work and lives should have taught, or at least suggested to their instructors, the capabilities and possibilities of their dusky slave pupils. The progress and the struggles of these for noble things should have led their instructors to see how the souls and minds of this people then yearned for light— the real life. But alas! these dull teachers, like many modern pedagogues and school keepers, failed to know their pupils—to find out their real needs, and hence had no cause to study methods of better and best development of the boys and girls under their care. What other result could come from such training or want of training than a conditioned race such as we now have?

For two hundred and fifty years they married, or were given in marriage. Oft times marriage ceremonies were performed for them by the learned minister of the master's church; more often there was simply a consorting by the master's consent, but it was always understood that these unions for cause, or without cause, might be more easily broken, than a divorce can be obtained in Indiana or Dakota. Without going so long a distance as from New York to Connecticut, the separated could take other companions for life, for a long or short time; for during those two hundred and fifty years there was not a single marriage legalized in a single southern state, where dwelt the mass of this people. There was something of the philosopher in the plantation preacher, who, at the close of the marriage ceremony, had the dusky couple join their right hands, and then called upon the assembled congregation to sing, as he lined it out, "Plunged in a gulf of dark despair," for well he knew the sequel of many such unions. If it so happened that a husband and wife were parted by those who owned them, such owners often consoled those thus parted with the fact that he could get another wife; she, another husband. Such was the sanctity of the marriage vow that was taught and held for over two hundred and fifty years.

Habit is indeed second nature. This is the race inheritance. I thank God not of all, for we know, each of us, of instances, of holding most sacred the plighted love and keeping faithfully and sacredly the marriage vows. We know of pure homes and of growing old together. Blessed heritage! If we only had the gold there might be many "Golden Weddings." Despair not; the crushing burden of immorality which has its root in the disregard of the marriage vow, can be lightened. It must be, and the educated colored woman can and will do her part in lifting this burden.

In the old institution there was no attention given to homes and to home making. Homes were only places in which to sleep, father had neither responsibility nor authority; mother, neither cares nor duties. She wielded no gentle sway nor influence. The character of their children was a matter of no concern to them; surroundings were not considered. It is true, house cleaning was sometimes enforced as a protection to property, but this was done at stated times and when ordered. There is no greater enemy of the race than these untidy and filthy homes; they bring not only physical disease and death, but they are very incubators of sin; they bring intellectual and moral death. The burden of giving knowledge and bringing about the practice of the laws of hygiene among a people ignorant of the laws of nature and common decency, is not a slight one. But this, too, the intelligent women can and must help to carry.

The large number of young men in the state prison is by no means the least of the heavy burdens. It is true that many of these are unjustly sentenced; that longer terms of imprisonment are given Negroes than white persons for the same offences; it is true that white criminals by the help of attorneys, money, and influence, oftener escape the prison, thus keeping small the number of prisoners recorded, for figures never lie. It is true that many are tried and imprisoned for trivial causes, such as the following, clipped from the *Tribune*, of Elberton, Ga.: "Seven or eight Negroes were arrested and tried for stealing two fish hooks last week. When the time of our courts is wasted in such a manner as this, it is high time to stop and consider whither we are driving. Such picayunish cases reflect on the intelligence of a community. It is fair to say the courts are not to blame in this matter." Commenting on this *The South Daily* says: "We are glad to note that the sentiment of the paper is against the injustice. Nevertheless these statistics will form the basis of some lecturer's discourse."

This fact remains, that many of our youth are in prison, that large numbers of our young men are serving out long terms of imprisonment, and this is a very sore burden. Five years ago while attending a Teacher's Institute at Thomasville, Ga., I saw working on the streets in the chain gang, with rude men and ruder women, with ignorant, wicked, almost naked men, criminals, guilty of all the sins named in the decalogue, a large number of boys from ten to fifteen years of age, and two young girls between the ages of twelve and sixteen. It is not necessary that prison statistics be quoted, for we know too well the story, and we feel most sensibly this burden, the weight of which will sink us unless it is at once made lighter and finally lifted.

Last, but not least, is the burden of prejudice, heavier in that it is imposed by the strong, those from whom help, not hindrance, should come. They are making the already heavy burden of their victims heavier to bear, and yet they are commanded by One who is even the Master of all: "Bear ye one another's burdens, and thus fulfill the law." This is met with and must be borne everywhere. In the South, in public conveyances, and at all points of race contact; in the North, in hotels, at the baptismal pool, in cemeteries; everywhere, in some shape or form, it is to be borne. No one suffers under the weight of this burden as the educated Negro woman does; and she must help to lift it.

Ignorance and immorality, if they are not the prime causes,

have certainly intensified prejudice. The forces to lighten and finally to lift this and all of these burdens are true culture and
character, linked with that most substantial coupler, cash. We
said in the beginning that the past can serve no further purpose
than to give us our present bearings. It is a condition that con-
fronts us. With this we must deal, it is this we must change. The
physician of today inquires into the history of his patient, but
he has to do especially with diagnosis and cure. We know the
history; we think a correct diagnosis has often been made—let
us attempt a cure. We would prescribe: homes—better homes,
clean homes, pure homes; schools—better schools; more culture; more thrift; and work in large doses; put the patient at
once on this treatment and continue through life. Can woman
do this work? She can; and she must do her part, and her part
is by no means small.

Nothing in the present century is more noticeable than the
tendency of women to enter every hopeful field of wage-earning
and philanthropy, and attempt to reach a place in every intellectual arena. Women are by nature fitted for teaching very
young children; their maternal instinct makes them patient and
sympathetic with their charges. Negro women of culture, as
kindergartners and primary teachers have a rare opportunity to
lend a hand to the lifting of these burdens, for here they may
instill lessons of cleanliness, truthfulness, loving kindness, love
for nature, and love for Nature's God. Here they may daily start
aright hundreds of our children; here, too, they may save years
of time in the education of the child; and may save many lives
from shame and crime by applying the law of prevention. In the
kindergarten and primary school is the salvation of the race.

For children of both sexes from six to fifteen years of age,
women are more successful as teachers than men. This fact is
proven by their employment. Two-thirds of the teachers in the
public schools of the United States are women. It is the glory of
the United States that good order and peace are maintained not
by a large, standing army of well trained soldiers, but by the
sentiment of her citizens, sentiments implanted and nourished
by her well trained army of four hundred thousand school
teachers, two-thirds of whom are women.

The educated Negro woman, the woman of character and

culture, is needed in the schoolroom not only in the kindergarten, and in the primary and the secondary school; but she is
needed in high school, the academy, and the college. Only those
of character and culture can do successful lifting, for she who
would mould character must herself possess it. Not alone in the
schoolroom can the intelligent woman lend a lifting hand, but as
a public lecturer she may give advice, helpful suggestions, and
important knowledge that will change a whole community and
start its people on the upward way. To be convinced of the good
that can be done for humanity by this means one need only recall the names of Lucy Stone, Mary Livermore, Frances Harper,
Frances Willard and Julie Ward Howe. The refined and noble
Negro woman may lift much with this lever. Women may also
be most helpful as teachers of sewing schools and cooking
classes, not simply in the public schools and private institutions,
but in classes formed in neighborhoods that sorely need this
knowledge. Through these classes girls who are not in school
may be reached; and through them something may be done to
better their homes, and inculcate habits of neatness and thrift.
To bring the influence of the schools to bear upon these homes is
the most needful thing of the hour. Often teachers who have labored most arduously, conscientiously, and intelligently have become discouraged on seeing that society had not been benefited,
but sometimes positively injured by the conduct of their pupils.

The work of the schoolroom has been completely neutralized
by the training of the home. Then we must have better homes,
and better homes mean better mothers, better fathers, better
born children. Emerson says, "To the well-born child all the virtues are natural, not painfully acquired."

But "The temporal life which is not allowed to open into the
eternal life becomes corrupt and feeble even in its temporal-
ness." As a teacher in the Sabbath school, as a leader in young
people's meetings and missionary societies, in women's societies
and Bible classes our cultured women are needed to do a great
and blessed work. Here they may cause many budding lives to
open into eternal life. Froebel urged teachers and parents to see
to the blending of the temporal and divine life when he said,
"God created man in his own image; therefore man should create and bring forth like God." The young people are ready and

anxiously await intelligent leadership in Christian work. The less fortunate women already assembled in churches, are ready for work. Work they do and work they will; that it may be effective work, they need the help and leadership of their more favored sisters.

A few weeks ago this country was startled by the following telegram of southern women of culture sent to Ex-Governor Northen of Georgia, just before he made his Boston speech: "You are authorized to say in your address tonight that the women of Georgia, realizing the great importance to both races of early moral training of the Negro race, stand ready to undertake this work when means are supplied." But more startled was the world the next day, after cultured Boston had supplied a part of the means, $20,000, to read the glaring head lines of the southern press, "Who Will Teach the Black Babies?" because some of the cultured women who had signed the telegram had declared when interviewed, that Negro women fitted for the work could not be found, and no self-respecting southern white woman would teach a colored kindergarten. Yet already in Atlanta, Georgia, and in Athens, Georgia, southern women are at work among Negroes. There is plenty of work for all who have the proper conception of the teacher's office, who know that all men are brothers, God being their common father. But the educated Negro woman *must* teach the "Black Babies;" she must come forward and inspire our men and boys to make a successful onslaught upon sin, shame, and crime.

The burden of the educated colored woman is not diminished by the terrible crimes and outrages that we daily hear of, but by these very outrages and lawlessness her burdens are greatly increased.

Somewhere I read a story, that in one of those western cities built in a day, the half-dozen men of the town labored to pull a heavy piece of timber to the top of a building. They pushed and pulled hard to no purpose, when one of the men on the top shouted to those below: "Call the women." They called the women; the women came; they pushed; soon the timber was seen to move, and ere long it was in the desired place. Today not only the men on top call, but a needy race,—the whole world, calls loudly to the cultured Negro women to come to the rescue. Do they hear? Are they coming? Will they push?

39

FANNIE BARRIER WILLIAMS

(1855–1944)

In 1870, at the age of fifteen, Fannie Barrier was the first African American to graduate from the Brockport State Normal School (now State University of New York, Brockport). She moved to Washington, D.C., as did many young, educated blacks, but became disillusioned by the rampant racism there. She moved to Boston and began studying piano at the New England Conservatory until white students complained about her presence. Barrier returned to Washington, D.C., and at age thirty-two married lawyer Samuel Laing Williams, a close friend of Booker T. Washington. The couple moved to Chicago. Barrier Williams spoke at the World's Columbian Exposition, famously attended by Frederick Douglass and Paul Laurence Dunbar. The National Association of Colored Women, the National League of Colored Women, and, later, the National Association for the Advancement of Colored People were among the organizations that Williams helped found.

Williams's essay could serve as a guidebook to the authors in this anthology who did the majority of their writing after emancipation. Williams's writing both celebrates the rapid progress that black American women made in the second half of the nineteenth century and laments broader society's hesitation to accept black women as social and economic equals. She expresses particular frustration with employers who, on principle, do not hire black women, and she sees American society as operating under a hypocritical system of chivalry. Ever optimistic, Williams saw social and economic equality for black Americans as inevitable.

"The Intellectual Progress of the Colored Woman of the United States Since the Emancipation Proclamation" (1893)

SOURCE: Fannie Barrier Williams, "The Intellectual
Progress of the Colored Women of the United States Since
the Emancipation Proclamation," *World's Congress of
Representative Women* 2 (1893).

Less than thirty years ago the term progress as applied to colored women of African descent in the United States would have been an anomaly. The recognition of that term to-day as appropriate is a fact full of interesting significance. That the discussion of progressive womanhood in this great assemblage of the representative women of the world is considered incomplete without some account of the colored women's status is a most noteworthy evidence that we have not failed to impress ourselves on the higher side of American life.

Less is known of our women than of any other class of Americans.

No organization of far-reaching influence for their special advancement, no conventions of women to take note of their progress, and no special literature reciting the incidents, the events, and all things interesting and instructive concerning them are to be found among the agencies directing their career. There has been no special interest in their peculiar condition as native-born American women. Their power to affect the social life of America, either for good or for ill, has excited not even a speculative interest.

Though there is much that is sorrowful, much that is wonderfully heroic, and much that is romantic in a peculiar way in their history, none of it has as yet been told as evidence of what is possible for these women. How few of the happy, prosperous, and eager living Americans can appreciate what it all means to be suddenly changed from irresponsible bondage to the responsibility of freedom and citizenship!

The distress of it all can never be told, and the pain of it all can never be felt except by the victims, and by those saintly women of the white race who for thirty years have been consecrated to the uplifting of a whole race of women from a long-enforced degradation.

The American people have always been impatient of ignorance and poverty. They believe with Emerson that "America is another word for opportunity," and for that reason success is a virtue and poverty and ignorance are inexcusable. This may account for the fact that our women have excited no general sympathy in the struggle to emancipate themselves from the demoralization of slavery. This new life of freedom, with its far-reaching responsibilities, had to be learned by these children of darkness mostly without a guide, a teacher, or a friend. In the mean vocabulary of slavery there was no definition of any of the virtues of life. The meaning of such precious terms as marriage, wife, family, and home could not be learned in a school-house. The blue-back speller, the arithmetic, and the copy-book contain no magical cures for inherited inaptitudes for the moralities. Yet it must ever be counted as one of the most wonderful things in human history how promptly and eagerly these suddenly liberated women tried to lay hold upon all that there is in human excellence. There is a touching pathos in the eagerness of these millions of new home-makers to taste the blessedness of intelligent womanhood. The path of progress in the picture is enlarged so as to bring to view these trustful and zealous students of freedom and civilization striving to overtake and keep pace with women whose emancipation has been a slow and painful process for a thousand years. The longing to be something better than they were when freedom found them has been the most notable characteristic in the development of these women. This constant striving for equality has given an upward direction to all the activities of colored women.

Freedom at once widened their vision beyond the mean cabin life of their bondage. Their native gentleness, good cheer, and hopefulness made them susceptible to those teachings that make for intelligence and righteousness. Sullenness of disposition, hatefulness, and revenge against the master class because of two centuries of ill-treatment are not in the nature of our women.

But a better view of what our women are doing and what their present status is may be had by noticing some lines of progress that are easily verifiable.

First it should be noticed that separate facts and figures relative to colored women are not easily obtainable. Among the white women of the country independence, progressive intelligence, and definite interests have done so much that nearly every fact and item illustrative of their progress and status is classified and easily accessible. Our women, on the contrary, have had no advantage of interests peculiar and distinct and separable from those of men that have yet excited public attention and kindly recognition.

In their religious life, however, our women show a progressiveness parallel in every important particular to that of white women in all Christian churches. . . .

While there has been but little progress toward the growing rationalism in the Christian creeds, there has been a marked advance toward a greater refinement of conception, good taste, and the proprieties. It is our young women coming out of the schools and academies that have been insisting upon a more godly and cultivated ministry. It is the young women of a new generation and new inspirations that are making tramps of the ministers who once dominated the colored church, and whose intelligence and piety were mostly in their lungs. . . .

Another evidence of growing intelligence is a sense of religious discrimination among our women. Like the nineteenth century woman generally, our women find congeniality in all the creeds, from the Catholic creed to the no-creed of Emerson. There is a constant increase of this interesting variety in the religious life of our women.

Closely allied to this religious development is their progress in the work of education in schools and colleges. For thirty years education has been the magic word among the colored people of this country. That their greatest need was education in its broadest sense was understood by these people more strongly than it could be taught to them. It is the unvarying testimony of every teacher in the South that the mental development of the colored women as well as men has been little less than phenomenal. In twenty-five years, and under conditions discouraging in the extreme, thousands of our women have been educated as teachers. They have adapted themselves to the work of mentally lifting a whole race of people so eagerly and readily that they afford an apt illustration of the power of self-help. Not only have these women become good teachers in less than twenty-five years, but many of them are the prize teachers in the mixed schools of nearly every Northern city.

These women have also so fired the hearts of the race for education that colleges, normal schools, industrial schools, and universities have been reared by a generous public to meet the requirements of these eager students of intelligent citizenship. As American women generally are fighting against the nine-teenth century narrowness that still keeps women out of the higher institutions of learning, so our women are eagerly de-manding the best of education open to their race. They con-tinually verify what President Rankin of Howard University recently said, "Any theory of educating the Afro-American that does not throw open the golden gates of the highest culture will fail on the ethical and spiritual side."

It is thus seen that our women have the same spirit and met-tle that characterize the best of American women. Everywhere they are following in the tracks of those women who are swift-est in the race for higher knowledge.

To-day they feel strong enough to ask for but one thing, and that is the same opportunity for the acquisition of all kinds of knowledge that may be accorded to other women. This granted, in the next generation these progressive women will be found successfully occupying every field where the highest intelli-gence alone is admissible. In less than another generation American literature, American art, and American music will be enriched by productions having new and peculiar features of interest and excellence.

The exceptional career of our women will yet stamp itself indelibly upon the thought of this country.

American literature needs for its greater variety and its deeper soundings that which will be written into it out of the hearts of these self-emancipating women.

The great problems of social reform that are now so engag-ing the highest intelligence of American women will soon need for their solution the reinforcement of that new intelligence which our women are developing. In short, our women are ambitious to be contributors to all the great moral and intellectual forces that make for the greater weal of our common country.

If this hope seems too extravagant to those of you who know these women only in their humbler capacities, I would remind you that all that we hope for and will certainly achieve in authorship and practical intelligence is more than prophesied by what has already been done, and more that can be done, by hundreds of Afro-American women whose talents are now being expended in the struggle against race resistance.

The power of organized womanhood is one of the most interesting studies of modern sociology. Formerly women knew so little of each other mentally, their common interests were so sentimental and gossipy, and their knowledge of all the larger affairs of human society was so meager that organization among them, in the modern sense, was impossible. Now their liberal intelligence, their contact in all the great interests of education, and their increasing influence for good in all the great reformatory movements of the age has created in them a greater respect for each other, and furnished the elements of organization for large and splendid purposes. The highest ascendancy of woman's development has been reached when they have become mentally strong enough to find bonds of association interwoven with sympathy, loyalty, and mutual trustfulness. To-day union is the watch-word of woman's onward march.

If it be a fact that this spirit of organization among women generally is the distinguishing mark of the nineteenth century woman, dare we ask if the colored women of the United States have made any progress in this respect? . . .

Benevolence is the essence of most of the colored women's organizations. The humane side of their natures has been cultivated to recognize the duties they owe to the sick, the indigent and ill-fortuned. No church, school, or charitable institution for the special use of colored people has been allowed to languish or fail when the associated efforts of the women could save it. . . .

The hearts of Afro-American women are too warm and too large for race hatred. Long suffering has so chastened them that they are developing a special sense of sympathy for all who suffer and fail of justice. All the associated interests of church, temperance, and social reform in which American women are winning distinction can be wonderfully advanced when our women shall be welcomed as co-workers, and estimated solely by what they are worth to the moral elevation of all the people.

I regret the necessity of speaking to the question of the moral progress of our women, because the morality of our home life has been commented upon so disparagingly and meanly that we are placed in the unfortunate position of being defenders of our name.

It is proper to state, with as much emphasis as possible, that all questions relative to the moral progress of the colored women of American are impertinent and unjustly suggestive when they relate to the thousands of colored women in the North who were free from the vicious influences of slavery. They are also meanly suggestive as regards thousands of our women in the South whose force of character enabled them to escape the slavery taints of immorality. The question of the moral progress of colored women in the United States has force and meaning in this discussion only so far as it tells the story of how the once-enslaved women have been struggling for twenty-five years to emancipate themselves from the demoralization of their enslavement.

While I duly appreciate the offensiveness of all references to American slavery, it is unavoidable to charge to that system every moral imperfection that mars the character of the colored American. The whole life and power of slavery depended upon an enforced degradation of everything human in the slaves. The slave code recognized only animal distinctions between the sexes, and ruthlessly ignored those ordinary separations that belong to the social state.

It is a great wonder that two centuries of such demoralization did not work a complete extinction of all the moral instincts. But the recuperative power of these women to regain their moral instincts and to establish a respectable relationship to American womanhood is among the earlier evidences of their moral ability to rise above their conditions. In spite of a cursed heredity that bound them to the lowest social level, in spite of everything that is unfortunate and unfavorable, these women have continually shown an increasing degree of teach-ableness as to the meaning of women's relationship to man.

Out of this social purification and moral uplift have come a chivalric sentiment and regard from the young men of the race that give to the young women a new sense of protection. I do not wish to disturb the serenity of this conference by suggesting why this protection is needed and the kind of men against whom it is needed.

It is sufficient for us to know that the daughters of women who thirty years ago were not allowed to be modest, not allowed to follow the instincts of moral rectitude, who could cry for protection to no living man, have so elevated the moral tone of their social life that new and purer standards of personal worth have been created, and new ideals of womanhood, instinct with grace and delicacy, are everywhere recognized and emulated.

This moral regeneration of a whole race of women is no idle sentiment—it is a serious business; and everywhere there is witnessed a feverish anxiety to be free from the mean suspicions that have so long underestimated the character strength of our women.

These women are not satisfied with the unmistakable fact that moral progress has been made, but they are fervently impatient and stirred by a sense of outrage under the vile imputations of a diseased public opinion. . . .

It may now perhaps be fittingly asked, What mean all these evidences of mental, social, and moral progress of a class of American women of whom you know so little? Certainly you can not be indifferent to the growing needs and importance of women who are demonstrating their intelligence and capacity for the highest privileges of freedom.

The most important thing to be noted is the fact that the colored people of America have reached a distinctly new era in their career so quickly that the American mind has scarcely had time to recognize the fact, and adjust itself to the new requirements of the people in all things that pertain to citizenship. . . .

It seems to daze the understanding of the ordinary citizen that there are thousands of men and women everywhere among us who in twenty-five years have progressed as far away from the non-progressive peasants of the "black belt" of the South as the highest social life in New England is above the lowest levels of American civilization.

This general failure of the American people to know the new generation of colored people, and to recognize this important change in them, is the cause of more injustice to our women than can well be estimated. Further progress is everywhere seriously hindered by this ignoring of their improvement.

Our exclusion from the benefits of the fair play sentiment of the country is little less than a crime against the ambitions and aspirations of a whole race of women. The American people are but repeating the common folly of history in thus attempting to repress the yearnings of progressive humanity.

In the item of employment colored women bear a distressing burden of mean and unreasonable discrimination. . . .

It is almost literally true that, except teaching in colored schools and menial work, colored women can find no employment in this free America. They are the only women in the country for whom real ability, virtue, and special talents count for nothing when they become applicants for respectable employment. Taught everywhere in ethics and social economy that merit always wins, colored women carefully prepare themselves for all kinds of occupation only to meet with stern refusal, rebuff, and disappointment. One of countless instances will show how the best as well as the meanest of American society are responsible for the special injustice to our women.

Not long ago I presented the case of a bright young woman to a well-known bank president of Chicago, who was in need of a thoroughly competent stenographer and typewriter. The president was fully satisfied with the young woman as exceptionally qualified for the position, and manifested much pleasure in commending her to the directors for appointment, and at the same time disclaimed that there could be any opposition on account of the slight tinge of African blood that identified her as a colored woman. Yet, when the matter was brought before the directors for action, these mighty men of money and business, these men whose prominence in all the great interest of the city would seem to lift them above all narrowness and foolishness, scented the African taint, and at once bravely came to the rescue of the bank and of society by dashing the hopes of this capable yet helpless young woman. . . .

Can the people of this country afford to single out the women of a whole race of people as objects of their special contempt? Do these women not belong to a race that has never faltered in its support of the country's flag in every war since Attucks fell in Boston's streets?

Are they not the daughters of men who have always been true as steel against treason to everything fundamental and splendid in the republic? In short, are these women not as thoroughly American in all the circumstances of citizenship as the best citizens of our country?

If it be so, are we not justified in a feeling of desperation against that peculiar form of Americanism that shows respect for our women as servants and contempt for them when they become women of culture? We have never been taught to understand why the unwritten law of chivalry, protection, and fair play that are everywhere the conservators of women's welfare must exclude every woman of a dark complexion.

We believe that the world always needs the influence of every good and capable woman, and this rule recognizes no exceptions based on complexion. In their complaint against hindrances to their employment colored women ask for no special favors. . . .

Another, and perhaps more serious, hindrance to our women is that nightmare known as "social equality." The term equality is the most inspiring word in the vocabulary of citizenship. It expresses the leveling quality in all the splendid possibilities of American life. It is this idea of equality that has made room in this country for all kinds and conditions of men, and made personal merit the supreme requisite for all kinds of achievement.

When the colored people became citizens, and found it written deep in the organic law of the land that they too had the right to life, liberty, and the pursuit of happiness, they were at once suspected of wishing to interpret this maxim of equality as meaning social equality.

Everywhere the public mind has been filled with constant

alarm lest in some way our women shall approach the social sphere of the dominant race in this country. Men and women, wise and perfectly sane in all things else, become instantly unwise and foolish at the remotest suggestion of social contact with colored men and women. At every turn in our lives we meet this fear, and are humiliated by its aggressiveness and meanness. If we seek the sanctities of religion, the enlightenment of the university, the honors of politics, and the natural recreations of our common country, the social equality alarm is instantly given, and our aspirations are insulted. "Beware of social equality with the colored American" is thus written on all places, sacred or profane, in this blessed land of liberty. The most discouraging and demoralizing effect of this false sentiment concerning us is that it utterly ignores individual merit and discredits the sensibilities of intelligent womanhood. The sorrows and heartaches of a whole race of women seem to be matters of no concern to the people who so dread the social possibilities of these colored women.

On the other hand, our women have been wonderfully indifferent and unconcerned about the matter. The dread inspired by the growing intelligence of colored women has interested us almost to the point of amusement. It has given to colored women a new sense of importance to witness how easily their emancipation and steady advancement is disturbing all classes of American people. It may not be a discouraging circumstance that colored women can command some sort of attention, even though they be misunderstood. We believe in the law of reaction, and it is reasonably certain that the forces of intelligence and character being developed in our women will yet change mistrustfulness into confidence and contempt into sympathy and respect. It will soon appear to those who are not hopelessly monomaniacs on the subject that the colored people are in no way responsible for the social equality nonsense. We shall yet be credited with knowing better than our enemies that social equality can neither be enforced by law nor prevented by oppression. Though not philosophers, we long since learned that equality before the law, equality in the best sense of that term under our institutions, is totally different from social equality. We know, without being exceptional students of history, that the social relationship of the two races will be adjusted equitably in spite of all fear and injustice, and that there is a social gravitation in human affairs that eventually overwhelms and crushes into nothingness all resistance based on prejudice and selfishness.

Our chief concern in this false social sentiment is that it attempts to hinder our further progress toward the higher spheres of womanhood. On account of it, young colored women of ambition and means are compelled in many instances to leave the country for training and education in the salons and studios of Europe. On many of the railroads of this country women of refinement and culture are driven like cattle into human cattle-cars lest the occupying of an individual seat paid for in a first-class car may result in social equality. This social quarantine on all means of travel in certain parts of the country is guarded and enforced more rigidly against us than the quarantine regulations against cholera.

Without further particularizing as to how this social question opposes our advancement, it may be stated that the contentions of colored women are in kind like those of other American women for greater freedom of development. Liberty to be all that we can be, without artificial hindrances, is a thing no less precious to us than to women generally.

We come before this assemblage of women feeling confident that our progress has been along high levels and rooted deeply in the essentials of intelligent humanity. We are so essentially American in speech, in instincts, in sentiments and destiny that the things that interest you equally interest us.

We believe that social evils are dangerously contagious. The fixed policy of persecution and injustice against a class of women who are weak and defenseless will be necessarily hurtful to the cause of all women. Colored women are becoming more and more a part of the social forces that must help to determine the questions that so concern women generally. In this Congress we ask to be known and recognized for what we are worth. If it be the high purpose of these deliberations to lessen the resistance to woman's progress, you can not fail to be interested in our struggles against the many oppositions that harass us.

Women who are tender enough in heart to be active in humane societies, to be foremost in all charitable activities, who are loving enough to unite Christian womanhood everywhere against the sin of intemperance, ought to be instantly concerned in the plea of colored women for justice and humane treatment. Women of the dominant race can not afford to be responsible for the wrongs we suffer, since those who do injustice can not escape a certain penalty.

But there is no wish to overstate the obstacles to colored women or to picture their status as hopeless. There is no disposition to take our place in this Congress as faultfinders or suppliants for mercy. As women of a common country, with common interests, and a destiny that will certainly bring us closer to each other, we come to this altar with our contribution of hopefulness as well as with our complaints. . . .

If the love of humanity more than the love of races and sex shall pulsate throughout all the grand results that shall issue to the world from this parliament of women, women of African descent in the United States will for the first time begin to feel the sweet release from the blighting thrall of prejudice.

The colored women, as well as all women, will realize that the inalienable right to life, liberty, and the pursuit of happiness is a maxim that will become more blessed in its significance when the hand of woman shall take it from its sepulture in books and make it the gospel of every-day life and the unerring guide in the relations of all men, women, and children.

40

VIRGINIA W. BROUGHTON

(1856–1934)

Virginia W. Broughton was born to enslaved parents Nelson Walker and Eliza Smart Walker in Nashville, Tennessee; her father worked to purchase freedom for the family. The transition from slavery to economic self-sufficiency and membership in an educated middle class was possible in more populated areas of the South, such as Nashville, where there were schools and libraries. The Walkers succeeded. Nelson became a businessman and attorney; Eliza, a seamstress and homemaker. They had eight children. Young Virginia Walker spent much of her childhood on the grounds of what would become Fisk University, which began as a grammar school in 1866. She was among the first decades of graduates of the University, receiving her BA in 1875 and her MA in 1878. Broughton worked primarily as a teacher. She was also known for being a devout Baptist missionary. Her progressive stance toward women's roles in the Baptist Church made her a leading women's rights advocate of the time. She is best known for her work "Woman's Work, as Gleaned from the Women of the Bible."

Her sixteen-page autobiography was only recently discovered: "A Brief Sketch of the Life and Labors of Mrs. V. W. Broughton, Bible Band Missionary, for Middle and West Tennessee" (1895), written for the 1894 Atlanta International and Cotton States Exposition, a fair devoted to the achievement of black men and women.

In the following address, "Woman's Work," Broughton draws from the Bible to argue that, in God's eyes, women deserve to stand alongside men in America's institutions. She stresses that women, through mothering, hold the bulk of the responsibility for inspiring American citizens to act with good character. Men, when acting alone, make decisions that are dangerous to women's well-being, she asserts.

"Woman's Work" (1894)

SOURCE: Virginia Broughton, "Woman's Work" (delivered at the National Baptist Educational and Foreign Mission Convention, Washington, D.C., September 14, 1893), *National Baptist Magazine* 1, no. 1 (January 1894): 30–35.

I come to you rejoicing in the fullness of the gospel, rejoicing for what God has wrought for the world, and above all, for what he has done for woman through the gospel of his dear Son. "Known unto God are all his works from the beginning of the world."—(Acts xv. 13.) And gradually has his works been made manifest to the world.

> "How firm a foundation, ye saints of the Lord,
> Is laid for your faith in his excellent word!
> What more can he say, than to you he has said,
> To you, who for refuge to Jesus hath fled."

To-day, with holy awe and reverence, we are to consider the gospel message which says, "There is neither Jew nor Greek; there is neither bond nor free; there is neither male nor female; for ye are all one in Christ Jesus."

In the beginning God created the heavens and the earth, and the earth was without form and void; and darkness was upon the face of the deep. Emerging from this state of chaos and darkness, God presented man, for his habitation, a beautiful garden fragrant with the perfume of flowers; resonant with the carol of birds, and supplied with all that was necessary for the well-being of man, and then said: "It is not good that the man be alone, I will make an help-meet for him." Beginning with creation we find that woman has figured conspicuously, by proving herself a desirable help to man in every important dispensation of God's providence. As woman was instrumental in the fall, God also used her in redeeming fallen humanity. He gave us this, assurance in the first promise—"The seed of the woman shall bruise the serpent's head."

When God called out a peculiar people for himself, he made CHOICE of the MOTHER of Israel; thereby instituting the holy ordinance of matrimony and directing his children how to enter into it. But alas! as in other things, so in this all-important matter, we've left the commandment of God, and followed the doctrines of men—to the ruin and havoc of social blessedness. The following poetical strain applies to matrimonial bliss, as well as our Christian relation; in fact, Christ likens his love for his church to that which should exist between husband and wife:

"Blest be the tie that binds
  Our hearts in mutual love,
  The fellowship of kindred minds
  Is like to that above."

No union, based upon anything than true love, as a result of real worth of character of the contracting parties, can be happy and productive of the great good God destined by the holy ordinance. In the deliverance of Israel from Egyptian bondage, it was the love and wisdom of woman that preserved, nourished and trained the man child that God called to be the leader, judge and priest for his people. Just here, as the care and training of children is preeminently the work of woman, we pause to say a few words concerning the influence and duty of women to children.

The fondest love and strongest ties of earth exist between mother and child.

"At home or away, in alley or street,
  Wherever I chance in this wide world to meet
  A girl that is thoughtless or boy that is wild,
  My heart echoes softly, 't'is somebody's child.'

No matter how far from the right she has strayed;
No matter what inroads dishonor has made;
No matter that sin and pain has tarnished the pearl;
Though tarnished and sullied, she is some mother's girl.

No matter how wayward his footsteps have been;
No matter how deeply he has sunken in sin;
No matter how low is his standard of joy;
Though guilty and loathsome, he is some mother's boy."

The mother transmits her virtues or her vices to her children; in fact, she reproduces herself in her children, and she is exerting an influence for good or ill, in spite of her will, from the time the child is sensible of anything until it leaves the world. Oh, how careful ought she to be to make the most of herself, physically, mentally and morally, that her children might be a power in the world for good, and rise up and call her blessed! If there was no other reason favoring the higher education of women than the fact that they are to be the mothers of the nation, that one alone is all-sufficient; for the mother has almost the entire care of the child in early life. She is its first God-given teacher, and wields an influence no one else can. Let women see to it that they use every opportunity for development of all their powers.

A more important position is filled by no one than that held by the mothers of our country, not even the executive head of the government, for it is what the mothers make the boys that will give us a good or bad government; and the mothers control their children, while the executive head of this government is the servant of the people, since it is a government of the people, for the people and by the people.

We are learning now that we are responsible for the well-being of our children, and our neighbors' children, as to their bodies, minds and spirits, and feel the weight of this responsibility to the extent that we are trying by organized effort to prepare ourselves to meet it; that we may help on the onward march of all that is grand and glorious.

The story of Hannah leads us to understand how soon we should begin the training of our children. When the child was weaned, she carried him to the temple and gave him to the

Lord, and God used Samuel as a powerful agency to reprove the wrong and defend the right.

In union there is strength, so the organizations of Christian women are giving them strength of character, and preparing them for effective service—such organization as the W. C. T. U., Missionary Circles, King's Daughters, Bible Bands and Fireside Schools—the last named organization is a plan God has recently given our beloved sister J. P. Moore. It is so comprehensive that every woman in the land can enjoy its blessings. It is an organization for the improvement of the home life; the development of the women and the training of children. As the name indicates, it is a school around the fireside, and though it is of recent birth, God has wondrously blessed it, and there is already a host of women in the South-land as witnesses of its effectiveness in the elevation of our homes. Brethren and sisters, let me entreat you to encourage and foster the Fireside School, and as this sainted mother of Israel, who has given her life for our people, declines in strength, and step by step walks out of labor to reward, a halo of glory may crown her efforts, and she may go home rejoicing with the laurels of a victorious conqueror.

We believe that God meant what he said in Gen. ii. 18, as in Mark xvi. 16; and I'm sure you all agree that woman is a help along the line I've spoken; but we advance further, and affirm that it is not good for man to be alone anywhere. Those places to which he goes, to the exclusion of women, such as saloons, club-rooms and legislative halls, are not suitable for him, and he is not safe, and we are sure it is not good for him, because God says that it is not good for man to be alone; and the wreck and ruin that result from his frequenting places of ill-repute, and the unjust and imperfect laws he makes are substantial proof that danger and death await those who disobey God's word. But what about man going alone to war? We answer by asking who was it that drove the nail into Sisera's temple? and what of the heroism of Joan of Arc? War is one of man's inventions; it is not good in itself, neither is it good for man to go to war alone, most especially in the Lord's work. "Neither is the man without the woman, neither the woman without the man in the Lord." I Cor. xi. II. In the Lord we must be together.

Esther and her people laboring together with God saved her nation. Anna and Simeon together welcomed Jesus when he was brought to the temple for the first time after his birth. In these perilous times, when our men's hearts are failing, and there are distress and perplexities of various kinds, there is the same need of the prayers of earnest Christian women that there was when Peter was in prison.

The power of prayer can not be over-estimated. "If ye abide in me and my words abide in you, ye shall ask what ye will, and it shall be done unto you." Many a husband, father, brother and son have been saved in answer to the faithful prayer of woman, and God has given you this evidence of woman's worth, that you might encourage her, and recognize her as your help-meet in evangelizing the world. We still have the poor and neglected, the widows and orphans, and hence Dorcas' work needs to be continued; the traveling servant of God are to be administered unto, and Lydias are in demand to entertain them, especially at such times as this; and since others need to be instructed in the way of the Lord more perfectly, Pricillas can find work to do.

We praise God that we all have the same blessed Savior, and Master, who has given us all the same blessed Gospel that he gave the Samaritan woman at the well, and Mary at the Sepulchre; and he is calling now; loudly calling you and me; calling by the lightning; by the storm and tempest; by persecution, famine, pestilence and death, and by the Gospel of his dear Son, ever from the mouths of women and children, do we hear this pleading voice, take the Cross and follow on.

We claim for woman her God-given name, help-meet, and insist that man needs her help in every department of life. He cannot be right to put woman in one corner and man in another. All of our church work stands greatly in need of the united effort of its members, and since the majority of the membership is women, unless they work, very little can be accomplished.

Isn't it strange, men will suffer women to do all the drudgery work, plow, plant, cultivate and gather the crop, draw water and split rails, and all other kinds of drudgery; but when it comes to mental or spiritual work, men wish to exclude women; as if they thought women had all the muscular strength and they had the brains and thinking powers.

Friends, we must come to the acknowledgment of this truth, "That it is not good for man to be alone," and our church work needs the wisdom of both sexes to carry it on as God ordains it.

The President has a Cabinet and an errand boy that stands by his side; both are his helpers; he needs both, but could better dispense with his errand boy than with his Cabinet. Now, we would like to whisper to man that he needs woman's help more in his cabinet than as an errand girl.

Did I say woman more needed in your cabinet than as an errand girl? Yes, brethren, you will find her of service upon your Executive Boards, both State and National. She'll do you good everywhere, all the days of your life; for God has said, "It is not good that man should be alone."

God help us to examine this subject in the light of his Word! Do it for the sake of the children, who need the united wisdom of men and women to guard their wayward feet in the path of righteousness; do it for the sake of our homes, where we want love, order, peace and purity; but know we cannot have them unless husband and wife work and plan together. Let us do it for the sake of our country, where good and just laws are so much needed for the protection and encouragement of both man and woman; and above all for the sake of the Lord Jesus, who has prayed the Father that we might be one even as he and his Father were one; that the World might believe he was sent of the Father.

What a glory shall follow in the wake of the acceptance of this glorious truth. God's Church will awake, Jews and Greeks; bond and free, male and female, and when awakened, a mighty host will be in action—stalwart men, women and children—and the Gospel Message shall soon extend throughout the earth, and we shall say no longer, one to the other, "know ye the Lord," but all shall know him, and

> "From Greenland's icy mountains,
> From India's coral stand;
> And Afric's sunny fountains,"

shall ascend songs of praise to the Lamb that was slain.

> "And Jesus shall reign, where'er the sun
> Doth his successive journeys run;
> His kingdom, spread from shore to shore,
> Till moons shall wax and wane no more."

In closing my thoughts on woman's work, as presented in God's word, Mr. Moody's four words necessary to the study of God's word are very suggestive, "ADMIT, SUBMIT, COMMIT, TRANSMIT." Admit—believe it all, from Genesis to Revelation; don't stop at the Jordan, but grow in grace and in the knowledge of the Lord Jesus Christ. Submit—yield to its requirements. Commit—learn it, treasure it—"Thy words have I hid in my heart." Transmit—"give it to others," (Deut. vi. 6–9.)—that we may all take heed thereto, and go forward as laborers together with God, seeking to save this lost world!

41

ANNA JULIA COOPER

(1860–1964)

Anna Julia Cooper was born in Raleigh, North Carolina, to Hannah Stanley, a slave, and most likely her master, Dr. Fabius J. Haywood, or his brother, George Washington Haywood. Both Anna and her mother were freed by the Emancipation Proclamation. In 1868, Anna enrolled in St. Augustine's Normal School and Collegiate Institute where she soon demanded to take courses available only to men. In 1877 she married George Cooper, an Episcopal priest from the West Indies, who died within two years. She enrolled at Oberlin College and graduated in 1884 along with Mary Church Terrell and another African American woman, Ida Gibbs Hunt. Cooper received her MA in mathematics from Oberlin three years later and began teaching at Wilberforce University, St. Augustine's, and the M Street High School. She enrolled at the University of Paris-Sorbonne and received her PhD in 1925, becoming the fourth black woman in American history to earn a doctorate (the first three were Sadie Tanner Mossell Alexander, niece of Nathaniel Mosell; Eva B. Dykes; and Georgiana Rose Simpson).

In her paper "Womanhood a Vital Element," Cooper urges the black clergy of the Protestant Episcopal Church to expand their perceptions of black prosperity. The average black American woman, Cooper argues, should serve as the barometer of her race's well-being, not the highest achieving black men. We note Cooper's knowledge of Islam was somewhat limited. In 1894, Cooper, representing the Washington Negro Folk-Lore Society, delivered a paper to the

Folklore Conference at Hampton Normal School, arguing that artists need to free themselves from white
aesthetic models.

"Womanhood a Vital Element in the Regeneration and Progress of a Race" (1886)

SOURCE: Anna Julia Cooper, "Womanhood a Vital
Element in the Regeneration and Progress of a Race" (read
before the convocation of colored clergy of the Protestant
Episcopal Church at Washington D.C., 1886), *A Voice
from the South: By A Woman from the South* (Xenia, Oh.:
Aldine Printing House, 1892).

The two sources from which, perhaps, modern civilization has
derived its noble and ennobling ideal of woman are Christianity and the Feudal System.

In Oriental countries woman has been uniformly devoted to
a life of ignorance, infamy, and complete stagnation. The Chinese shoe of to-day does not more entirely dwarf, cramp, and
destroy her physical powers, than have the customs, laws, and
social instincts, which from remotest ages have governed our
Sister of the East, enervated and blighted her mental and moral
life.

Mahomet makes no account of woman whatever in his pol-
ity. The Koran, which, unlike our Bible, was a product and not
a growth, tried to address itself to the needs of Arabian civilization as Mahomet with his circumscribed powers saw them. The
Arab was a nomad. Home to him meant his present camping
place. That deity who, according to our western ideals, makes
and sanctifies the home, was to him a transient bauble to be
toyed with so long as it gave pleasure and then to be thrown
aside for a new one. As a personality, an individual soul, capable of eternal growth and unlimited development, and

destined to mould and shape the civilization of the future to an incalculable extent, Mahomet did not know woman. There was no hereafter, no paradise for her. The heaven of the Mussulman is peopled and made gladsome not by the departed wife, or sister, or mother, but by *houri*—a figment of Mahomet's brain, partaking of the ethereal qualities of angels, yet imbued with all the vices and inanity of Oriental women. The harem here, and—"dust to dust" hereafter, this was the hope, the inspiration, the *summum bonum* of the Eastern woman's life! With what result on the life of the nation, the "Unspeakable Turk," the "sick man" of modern Europe can to-day exemplify.

Says a certain writer: "The private life of the Turk is vilest of the vile, unprogressive, unambitious, and inconceivably low." And yet Turkey is not without her great men. She has produced most brilliant minds; men skilled in all the intricacies of diplomacy and statesmanship; men whose intellects could grapple with the deep problems of empire and manipulate the subtle agencies which check-mate kings. But these minds were not the normal outgrowth of a healthy trunk. They seemed rather ephemeral excrescencies which shoot far out with all the vigor and promise, apparently, of strong branches; but soon alas fall into decay and ugliness because there is no soundness in the root, no life-giving sap, permeating, strengthening and perpetuating the whole. There is a worm at the core! The homelife is impure! and when we look for fruit, like apples of Sodom, it crumbles within our grasp into dust and ashes.

It is pleasing to turn from this effete and immobile civilization to a society still fresh and vigorous, whose seed is in itself, and whose very name is synonymous with all that is progressive, elevating and inspiring, viz., the European bud and the American flower of modern civilization.

And here let me say parenthetically that our satisfaction in American institutions rests not on the fruition we now enjoy, but springs rather from the possibilities and promise that are inherent in the system, though as yet, perhaps, far in the future.

"Happiness," says Madame de Stael, "consists not in perfections attained, but in a sense of progress, the result of our own endeavor under conspiring circumstances *toward* a goal which continually advances and broadens and deepens till it is swallowed up in the Infinite." Such conditions in embryo are all that we claim for the land of the West. We have not yet reached our ideal in American civilization. The pessimists even declare that we are not marching in that direction. But there can be no doubt that here in America is the arena in which the next triumph of civilization is to be won; and here too we find promise abundant and possibilities infinite.

Now let us see on what basis this hope for our country primarily and fundamentally rests. Can any one doubt that it is chiefly on the homelife and on the influence of good women in those homes? Says Macaulay: "You may judge a nation's rank in the scale of civilization from the way they treat their women." And Emerson, "I have thought that a sufficient measure of civilization is the influence of good women." Now this high regard for woman, this germ of a prolific idea which in our own day is bearing such rich and varied fruit, was ingrafted into European civilization, we have said, from two sources, the Christian Church and the Feudal System. For although the Feudal System can in no sense be said to have originated the idea, yet there can be no doubt that the habits of life and modes of thought to which Feudalism gave rise, materially fostered and developed it; for they gave us chivalry, than which no institution has more sensibly magnified and elevated woman's position in society.

Tacitus dwells on the tender regard for woman entertained by these rugged barbarians before they left their northern homes to overrun Europe. Old Norse legends too, and primitive poems, all breathe the same spirit of love of home and veneration for the pure and noble influence there presiding—the wife, the sister, the mother.

And when later on we see the settled life of the Middle Ages "oozing out," as M. Guizot expresses it, from the plundering and pillaging life of barbarism and crystallizing into the Feudal System, the tiger of the field is brought once more within the charmed circle of the goddesses of his castle, and his imagination weaves around them a halo whose reflection possibly has not yet altogether vanished.

It is true the spirit of Christianity had not yet put the seal of catholicity on this sentiment. Chivalry, according to Bascom, was but the toning down and softening of a rough and lawless period. It gave a roseate glow to a bitter winter's day. Those who looked out from castle windows revelled in its "amethyst tints." But God's poor, the weak, the unlovely, the commonplace were still freezing and starving none the less, in unpitied, unrelieved loneliness.

Respect for woman, the much lauded chivalry of the Middle Ages, meant what I fear it still means to some men in our own day—respect for the elect few among whom they expect to consort.

The idea of the radical amelioration of womankind, reverence for woman as woman regardless of rank, wealth, or culture, was to come from that rich and bounteous fountain from which flow all our liberal and universal ideas—the Gospel of Jesus Christ.

And yet the Christian Church at the time of which we have been speaking would seem to have been doing even less to protect and elevate woman than the little done by secular society. The Church as an organization committed a double offense against woman in the Middle Ages. Making of marriage a sacrament and at the same time insisting on the celibacy of the clergy and other religious orders, she gave an inferior if not an impure character to the marriage relation, especially fitted to reflect discredit on woman. Would this were all or the worst! but the Church by the licentiousness of its chosen servants invaded the household and established too often as vicious connections those relations which it forbade to assume openly and in good faith. "Thus," to use the words of our authority, "the religious corps became as numerous, as searching, and as unclean as the frogs of Egypt, which penetrated into all quarters, into the ovens and kneading troughs, leaving their filthy trail wherever they went." Says Chaucer with characteristic satire, speaking of the Friars:

> 'Women may now go safely up and doun,
> In every bush, and under every tree,
> Ther is non other incubus but he,
> And he ne will don hem no dishonour.'

Henry, Bishop of Liege, could unblushingly boast the birth of twenty-two children in fourteen years.

It may help us under some of the perplexities which beset our way in "the one Catholic and Apostolic Church" to-day, to recall some of the corruptions and incongruities against which the Bride of Christ has had to struggle in her past history and in spite of which she has kept, through many vicissitudes, the faith once delivered to the saints. Individuals, organizations, whole sections of the Church militant may outrage the Christ whom they profess, may ruthlessly trample under foot both the spirit and the letter of his precepts, yet not till we hear the voices audibly saying "Come let us depart hence," shall we cease to believe and cling to the promise, "*I am with you to the end of the world.*"

> "Yet saints their watch are keeping,
> The cry goes up 'How long!'
> And soon the night of weeping
> Shall be the morn of song."

However much then the facts of any particular period of history may seem to deny it, I for one do not doubt that the source of the vitalizing principle of woman's development and amelioration is the Christian Church, so far as that church is coincident with Christianity.

Christ gave ideals not formulæ. The Gospel is a germ requiring millennia for its growth and ripening. It needs and at the same time helps to form around itself a soil enriched in civilization, and perfected in culture and insight without which the embryo can neither be unfolded or comprehended. With all the strides our civilization has made from the first to the nineteenth century, we can boast not an idea, not a principle of action, not a progressive social force but was already mutely foreshadowed, or directly enjoined in that simple tale of a meek and lowly life. The quiet face of the Nazarene is ever seen a little way ahead, never too far to come down to and touch the life of the lowest in days the darkest, yet ever leading onward, still onward, the tottering childish feet of our strangely boastful civilization.

By laying down for woman the same code of morality, the same standard of purity, as for man; by refusing to countenance the shameless and equally guilty monsters who were gloating over her fall—graciously stooping in all the majesty of his own spotlessness to wipe away the filth and grime of her guilty past and bid her go in peace and sin no more; and again in the moments of his own careworn and footsore dejection, turning trustfully and lovingly, away from the heartless snubbing and sneers, away from the cruel malignity of mobs and prelates in the dusty marts of Jerusalem to the ready sympathy, loving appreciation and unfaltering friendship of that quiet home at Bethany; and even at the last, by his dying bequest to the disciple whom he loved, signifying the protection and tender regard to be extended to that sorrowing mother and ever afterward to the sex she represented;—throughout his life and in his death he has given to men a rule and guide for the estimation of woman as an equal, as a helper, as a friend, and as a sacred charge to be sheltered and cared for with a brother's love and sympathy, lessons which nineteen centuries' gigantic strides in knowledge, arts, and sciences, in social and ethical principles have not been able to probe to their depth or to exhaust in practice.

It seems not too much to say then of the vitalizing, regenerating, and progressive influence of womanhood on the civilization of today, that, while it was foreshadowed among Germanic nations in the far away dawn of their history as a narrow, sickly and stunted growth, it yet owes its catholicity and power, the deepening of its roots and broadening of its branches to Christianity.

The union of these two forces, the Barbaric and the Christian, was not long delayed after the Fall of the Empire. The Church, which fell with Rome, finding herself in danger of being swallowed up by barbarism, with characteristic vigor and fertility of resources, addressed herself immediately to the task of conquering her conquerers. The means chosen does credit to her power of penetration and adaptability, as well as to her profound, unerring, all-compassing diplomacy; and makes us even now wonder if aught human can successfully and ultimately withstand her far-seeing designs and brilliant policy, or gainsay her well-earned claim to the word *Catholic*.

She saw the barbarian, little more developed than a wild beast. She forbore to antagonize and mystify his warlike nature by a full blaze of the heartsearching and humanizing tenets of her great

Head. She said little of the rule "If thy brother smite thee on one cheek, turn to him the other also"; but thought it sufficient for the needs of those times, to establish the so-called "Truce of God" under which men were bound to abstain from butchering one another for three days of each week and on Church festivals. In other words, she respected their individuality: non-resistance pure and simple being for them an utter impossibility, she contented herself with less radical measures calculated to lead up finally to the full measure of the benevolence of Christ.

Next she took advantage of the barbarian's sensuous love of gaudy display and put all her magnificent garments on. She could not capture him by physical force, she would dazzle him by gorgeous spectacles. It is said that Romanism gained more in pomp and ritual during this trying period of the Dark Ages than throughout all her former history.

The result was she carried her point. Once more Rome laid her ambitious hand on the temporal power, and allied with Charlemagne, aspired to rule the world through a civilization dominated by Christianity and permeated by the traditions and instincts of those sturdy barbarians.

Here was the confluence of the two streams we have been tracing, which, united now, stretch before us as a broad majestic river. In regard to woman it was the meeting of two noble and ennobling forces, two kindred ideas the resultant of which, we doubt not, is destined to be a potent force in the betterment of the world.

Now after our appeal to history comparing nations destitute of this force and so destitute also of the principle of progress, with other nations among whom the influence of woman is prominent coupled with a brisk, progressive, satisfying civilization,—if in addition we find this strong presumptive evidence corroborated by reason and experience, we may conclude that these two equally varying concomitants are linked as cause and effect; in other words, that the position of woman in society determines the vital elements of its regeneration and progress.

Now that this is so on *a priori* grounds all must admit. And this not because woman is better or stronger or wiser than man, but from the nature of the case, because it is she who must first form the man by directing the earliest impulses of his character.

Byron and Wordsworth were both geniuses and would have stamped themselves on the thought of their age under any circumstances; and yet we find the one a savor of life unto life, the other of death unto death. "Byron, like a rocket, shot his way upward with scorn and repulsion, flamed out in wild, explosive, brilliant excesses and disappeared in darkness made all the more palpable."

Wordsworth lent of his gifts to reinforce that "power in the Universe which makes for righteousness" by taking the harp handed him from Heaven and using it to swell the strains of angelic choirs. Two locomotives equally mighty stand facing opposite tracks; the one to rush headlong to destruction with all its precious freight, the other to toil grandly and gloriously up the steep embattlements to Heaven and to God. Who—who can say what a world of consequences hung on the first placing and starting of these enormous forces!

Woman, Mother,—your responsibility is one that might make angels tremble and fear to take hold! To trifle with it, to ignore or misuse it, is to treat lightly the most sacred and solemn trust ever confided by God to human kind. The training of children is a task on which an infinity of weal or woe depends. Who does not covet it? Yet who does not stand awe-struck before its momentous issues! It is a matter of small moment, it seems to me, whether that lovely girl in whose accomplishments you take such pride and delight, can enter the gay and crowded salon with the ease and elegance of this or that French or English gentlewoman, compared with the decision as to whether her individuality is going to reinforce the good or the evil elements of the world. The lace and the diamonds, the dance and the theater, gain a new significance when scanned in their bearings on such issues. Their influence on the individual personality, and through her on the society and civilization which she vitalizes and inspires—all this and more must be weighed in the balance before the jury can return a just and intelligent verdict as to the innocence or banefulness of these apparently simple amusements.

Now the fact of woman's influence on society being granted, what are its practical bearings on the work which brought together this conference of colored clergy and laymen in

Washington? "We come not here to talk." Life is too busy, too pregnant with meaning and far reaching consequences to allow you to come this far for mere intellectual entertainment.

The vital agency of womanhood in the regeneration and progress of a race, as a general question, is conceded almost before it is fairly stated. I confess one of the difficulties for me in the subject assigned lay in its obviousness. The plea is taken away by the opposite attorney's granting the whole question.

"Woman's influence on social progress"—who in Christendom doubts or questions it? One may as well be called on to prove that the sun is the source of light and heat and energy to this many-sided little world.

Nor, on the other hand, could it have been intended that I should apply the position when taken and proven, to the needs and responsibilities of the women of our race in the South. For is it not written, "Cursed is he that cometh after the king?" and has not the King already preceded me in "The Black Woman of the South"?

They have had both Moses and the Prophets in Dr. Crummell and if they hear not him, neither would they be persuaded though one came up from the South.

I would beg, however, with the Doctor's permission, to add my plea for the *Colored Girls* of the South:—that large, bright, promising fatally beautiful class that stand shivering like a delicate plantlet before the fury of tempestuous elements, so full of promise and possibilities, yet so sure of destruction; often without a father to whom they dare apply the loving term, often without a stronger brother to espouse their cause and defend their honor with his life's blood; in the midst of pitfalls and snares, waylaid by the lower classes of white men, with no shelter, no protection nearer than the great blue vault above, which half conceals and half reveals the one Care-Taker they know so little of. Oh, save them, help them, shield, train, develop, teach, inspire them! Snatch them, in God's name, as brands from the burning! There is material in them well worth your while, the hope in germ of a staunch, helpful, regenerating womanhood on which, primarily, rests the foundation stones of our future as a race.

It is absurd to quote statistics showing the Negro's bank account and rent rolls, to point to the hundreds of newspapers edited by colored men and lists of lawyers, doctors, professors, D. D's, LL D's, etc., etc., etc., while the source from which the life-blood of the race is to flow is subject to taint and corruption in the enemy's camp.

True progress is never made by spasms. Real progress is growth. It must begin in the seed. Then, "first the blade, then the ear, after that the full corn in the ear." There is something to encourage and inspire us in the advancement of individuals since their emancipation from slavery. It at least proves that there is nothing irretrievably wrong in the shape of the black man's skull, and that under given circumstances his development, downward or upward, will be similar to that of other average human beings.

But there is no time to be wasted in mere felicitation. That the Negro has his niche in the infinite purposes of the Eternal, no one who has studied the history of the last fifty years in America will deny. That much depends on his own right comprehension of his responsibility and rising to the demands of the hour, it will be good for him to see; and how best to use his present so that the structure of the future shall be stronger and higher and brighter and nobler and holier than that of the past, is a question to be decided each day by every one of us.

The race is just twenty-one years removed from the conception and experience of a chattel, just at the age of ruddy manhood. It is well enough to pause a moment for retrospection, introspection, and prospection. We look back, not to become inflated with conceit because of the depths from which we have arisen, but that we may learn wisdom from experience. We look within that we may gather together once more our forces, and, by improved and more practical methods, address ourselves to the tasks before us. We look forward with hope and trust that the same God whose guiding hand led our fathers through and out of the gall and bitterness of oppression, will still lead and direct their children, to the honor of His name, and for their ultimate salvation.

But this survey of the failures or achievments of the past, the difficulties and embarrassments of the present, and the mingled hopes and fears for the future, must not degenerate into mere dreaming nor consume the time which belongs to the practical and effective handling of the crucial questions of the hour; and there can be no issue more vital and momentous than this of the womanhood of the race.

Here is the vulnerable point, not in the heel, but at the heart of the young Achilles; and here must the defenses be strengthened and the watch redoubled.

We are the heirs of a past which was not our fathers' moulding. "Every man the arbiter of his own destiny" was not true for the American Negro of the past: and it is no fault of his that he finds himself to-day the inheritor of a manhood and womanhood impoverished and debased by two centuries and more of compression and degradation.

But weaknesses and malformations, which to-day are attributable to a vicious schoolmaster and a pernicious system, will a century hence be rightly regarded as proofs of innate corruptness and radical incurability.

Now the fundamental agency under God in the regeneration, the re-training of the race, as well as the ground work and starting point of its progress upward, must be the *black woman*.

With all the wrongs and neglects of her past, with all the weakness, the debasement, the moral thralldom of her present, the black woman of to-day stands mute and wondering at the Herculean task devolving around her. But the cycles wait for her. No other hand can move the lever. She must be loosed from her bands and set to work.

Our meager and superficial results from past efforts prove their futility; and every attempt to elevate the Negro, whether undertaken by himself or through the philanthropy of others, cannot but prove abortive unless so directed as to utilize the indispensable agency of an elevated and trained womanhood.

A race cannot be purified from without. Preachers and teachers are helps, and stimulants and conditions as necessary as the gracious rain and sunshine are to plant growth. But what are rain and dew and sunshine and cloud if there be no life in the plant germ? We must go to the root and see that it is sound and healthy and vigorous; and not deceive ourselves with waxen flowers and painted leaves of mock chlorophyll.

We too often mistake individuals' honor for race development and so are ready to substitute pretty accomplishments for sound sense and earnest purpose.

A stream cannot rise higher than its source. The atmosphere of homes is no rarer and purer and sweeter than are the mothers in those homes. A race is but a total of families. The nation is the aggregate of its homes. As the whole is sum of all its parts, so the character of the parts will determine the characteristics of the whole. These are all axioms and so evident that it seems gratuitous to remark it; and yet, unless I am greatly mistaken, most of the unsatisfaction from our past results arises from just such a radical and palpable error, as much almost on our own part as on that of our benevolent white friends.

The Negro is constitutionally hopeful and proverbially irrepressible; and naturally stands in danger of being dazzled by the shimmer and tinsel of superficials. We often mistake foliage for fruit and overestimate or wrongly estimate brilliant results.

The late Martin R. Delany, who was an unadulterated black man, used to say when honors of state fell upon him, that when he entered the council of kings the black race entered with him; meaning, I suppose, that there was no discounting his race identity and attributing his achievements to some admixture of Saxon blood. But our present record of eminent men, when placed beside the actual status of the race in America to-day, proves that no man can represent the race. Whatever the attainments of the individual may be, unless his home has moved on *pari passu*, he can never be regarded as identical with or representative of the whole.

Not by pointing to sun-bathed mountain tops do we prove that Phoebus warms the valleys. We must point to homes, average homes, homes of the rank and file of horny handed toiling men and women of the South (where the masses are) lighted and cheered by the good, the beautiful, and the true,—then and not till then will the whole plateau be lifted into the sunlight.

Only the BLACK WOMAN can say "when and where I enter, in the quiet, undisputed dignity of my womanhood, without violence and without suing or special patronage, then and there the whole *Negro race enters with me*." Is it not evident then that as individual workers for this race we must address ourselves with no half-hearted zeal to this feature of our mission. The need is felt and must be recognized by all. There is a call for workers, for missionaries, for men and women with the double consecration of a fundamental love of humanity and a desire for its melioration through the Gospel; but superadded to this we demand an intelligent and sympathetic comprehension of the interests and special needs of the Negro.

I see not why there should not be an organized effort for the protection and elevation of our girls such as the White Cross League in England. English women are strengthened and protected by more than twelve centuries of Christian influences, freedom and civilization; English girls are dispirited and crushed down by no such all-levelling prejudice as that supercilious caste spirit in America which cynically assumes "A Negro woman cannot be a lady." English womanhood is beset by no such snares and traps as betray the unprotected, untrained colored girl of the South, whose only crime and dire destruction often is her unconscious and marvelous beauty. Surely then if English indignation is aroused and English manhood thrilled under the leadership of a Bishop of the English church to build up bulwarks around their wronged sisters, Negro sentiment cannot remain callous and Negro effort nerveless in view of the imminent peril of the mothers of the next generation. "*I am my Sister's keeper!*" should be the hearty response of every man and woman of the race, and this conviction should purify and exalt the narrow, selfish and petty personal aims of life into a noble and sacred purpose.

We need men who can let their interest and gallantry extend outside the circle of their aesthetic appreciation; men who can be a father, a brother, a friend to every weak, struggling unshielded girl. We need women who are so sure of their own social footing that they need not fear leaning to lend a hand to a fallen or falling sister. We need men and women who do not exhaust their genius splitting hairs on aristocratic distinctions and thanking God they are not as others; but earnest, unselfish souls, who can go into the highways and byways, lifting up and leading, advising and encouraging with the truly catholic benevolence of the Gospel of Christ.

As Church workers we must confess our path of duty is less obvious; or rather our ability to adapt our machinery to our conception of the peculiar exigencies of this work as taught by experience and our own consciousness of the needs of the Negro, is as yet not demonstrable. Flexibility and aggressiveness are not such strong characteristics of the Church to-day as in the Dark Ages.

As a Mission field for the Church the Southern Negro is in some aspects most promising; in others, perplexing. Aliens neither in language and customs, nor in associations and sympathies, naturally of deeply rooted religious instincts and taking most readily and kindly to the worship and teachings of the Church, surely the task of proselytizing the American Negro is infinitely less formidable than that which confronted the Church in the Barbarians of Europe. Besides, this people already look to the Church as the hope of their race. Thinking colored men almost uniformly admit that the Protestant Episcopal Church with its quiet, chaste dignity and decorous solemnity, its instructive and elevating ritual, its bright chanting and joyous hymning, is eminently fitted to correct the peculiar faults of worship—the rank exuberance and often ludicrous demonstrativeness of their people. Yet, strange to say, the Church, claiming to be missionary and Catholic, urging that schism is sin and denominationalism inexcusable, has made in all these years almost no inroads upon this semi-civilized religionism.

• • •

After all the Southern slave owners were right: either the very alphabet of intellectual growth must be forbidden and the Negro dealt with absolutely as a chattel having neither rights nor sensibilities; or else the clamps and irons of mental and moral, as well as civil compression must be riven asunder and the truly enfranchised soul led to the entrance of that boundless vista through which it is to toil upwards to its beckoning God as the buried seed germ, to meet the sun.

A perpetual colored diaconate, carefully and kindly superintended by the white clergy; congregations of shiny faced peasants with their clean white aprons and sunbonnets catechised at regular intervals and taught to recite the creed, the Lord's prayer and the ten commandments—duty towards God and duty towards neighbor, surely such well tended sheep ought to be grateful to their shepherds and content in that station of life to which it pleased God to call them. True, like the old professor lecturing to his solitary student, we make no provision here for irregularities. "Questions must be kept till after class," or dispensed with altogether. That some do ask questions and insist on answers, in class too, must be both impertinent and annoying. Let not our spiritual pastors and masters however be grieved at such self-assertion as merely signifies we have a destiny to fulfill and as men and women we must *be about our Father's business.*

It is a mistake to suppose that the Negro is prejudiced against a white ministry. Naturally there is not a more kindly and implicit follower of a white man's guidance than the average colored peasant. What would to others be an ordinary act of friendly or pastoral interest he would be more inclined to regard gratefully as a condescension. And he never forgets such kindness. Could the Negro be brought near to his white priest or bishop, he is not suspicious. He is not only willing but often longs to unburden his soul to this intelligent guide. There are no reservations when he is convinced that you are his friend. It is a saddening satire on American history and manners that it takes something to convince him.

That our people are not "drawn" to a Church whose chief dignitaries they see only in the chancel, and whom they reverence as they would a painting or an angel, whose life never comes down to and touches theirs with the inspiration of an objective reality, may be "perplexing" truly (American caste and American Christianity both being facts) but it need not be surprising. There must be something of human nature in it, the same as that which brought about that "the Word was made flesh and dwelt among us" that He might "draw" us towards God.

Men are not "drawn" by abstractions. Only sympathy and love can draw, and until our Church in America realizes this and provides a clergy that can come in touch with our life and have a fellow feeling for our woes, without being imbedded and frozen up in their "Gothic antipathies," the good bishops are likely to continue "perplexed" by the sparsity of colored Episcopalians.

A colored priest of my acquaintance recently related to me, with tears in his eyes, how his reverend Father in God, the

Bishop who had ordained him, had met him on the cars on his way to the diocesan convention and warned him, not unkindly, not to take a seat in the body of the convention with the white clergy. To avoid disturbance of their godly placidity he would of cource please sit back and somewhat apart. I do not imagine that that clergyman had very much heart for the Christly (!) deliberations of that convention.

To return, however, it is not on this broader view of Church work, which I mentioned as a primary cause of its halting progress with the colored people, that I am to speak. My proper theme is the second oversight of which in my judgment our Christian propagandists have been guilty: or, the necessity of church training, protecting and uplifting our colored womanhood as indispensable to the evangelization of the race.

Apelles did not disdain even that criticism of his lofty art which came from an uncouth cobbler; and may I not hope that the writer's oneness with her subject both in feeling and in being may palliate undue obtrusiveness of opinions here. That the race cannot be effectually lifted up till its women are truly elevated we take as proven. It is not for us to dwell on the needs, the neglects, and the ways of succor, pertaining to the black woman of the South. The ground has been ably discussed and an admirable and practical plan proposed by the oldest Negro priest in America, advising and urging that special organizations such as Church Sisterhoods and industrial schools be devised to meet her pressing needs in the Southland. That some such movements are vital to the life of this people and the extension of the Church among them, is not hard to see. Yet the pamphlet fell still-born from the press. So far as I am informed the Church has made no motion towards carrying out Dr. Crummell's suggestion.

The denomination which comes next our own in opposing the proverbial emotionalism of Negro worship in the South, and which in consequence like ours receives the cold shoulder from the old heads, resting as we do under the charge of not "having religion" and not believing in conversion—the Congregationalists—have quietly gone to work on the young, have established industrial and training schools, and now almost every community in the South is yearly enriched by a fresh infusion of vigorous young hearts, cultivated heads, and helpful hands that have been trained at Fisk, at Hampton, in Atlanta University, and in Tuskegee, Alabama.

These young people are missionaries actual or virtual both here and in Africa. They have learned to love the methods and doctrines of the Church which trained and educated them; and so Congregationalism surely and steadily progresses.

Need I compare these well known facts with results shown by the Church in the same field and during the same or even a longer time.

The institution of the Church in the South to which she mainly looks for the training of her colored clergy and for the help of the "Black Woman" and "Colored Girl" of the South, has graduated since the year 1868, when the school was founded, *five young women*; and while yearly numerous young men have been kept and trained for the ministry by the charities of the Church, the number of indigent females who have here been supported, sheltered and trained, is phenomenally small. Indeed, to my mind, the attitude of the Church toward this feature of her work, is as if the solution of the problem of Negro missions depended solely on sending a quota of deacons and priests into the field, girls being a sort of *tertium quid* whose development may be promoted if they can pay their way and fall in with the plans mapped out for the training of the other sex.

Now I would ask in all earnestness, does not this force potential deserve by education and stimulus to be made dynamic? Is it not a solemn duty incumbent on all colored churchmen to make it so? Will not the aid of the Church be given to prepare our girls in head, heart, and hand for the duties and responsibilities that await the intelligent wife, the Christian mother, the earnest, virtuous, helpful woman, at once both the lever and the fulcrum for uplifting the race.

As Negroes and churchmen we cannot be indifferent to these questions. They touch us most vitally on both sides. We believe in the Holy Catholic Church. We believe that however gigantic and apparently remote the consummation, the Church will go on conquering and to conquer till the kingdoms of this world, not excepting the black man and the black woman of the South, shall have become the kingdoms of the Lord and of his Christ.

That past work in this direction has been unsatisfactory we must admit. That without a change of policy results in the future will be as meagre, we greatly fear. Our life as a race is at stake. The dearest interests of our hearts are in the scales. We must either break away from dear old landmarks and plunge out in any line and every line that enables us to meet the pressing need of our people, or we must ask the Church to allow and help us, untrammelled by the prejudices and theories of individuals, to work agressively under her direction as we alone can, with God's help, for the salvation of our people.

The time is ripe for action. Self-seeking and ambition must be laid on the altar. The battle is one of sacrifice and hardship, but our duty is plain. We have been recipients of missionary bounty in some sort for twenty-one years. Not even the senseless vegetable is content to be a mere reservoir. Receiving without giving is an anomaly in nature. Nature's cells are all little workshops for manufacturing sunbeams, the product to be *given out* to earth's inhabitants in warmth, energy, thought, action. Inanimate creation always pays back an equivalent.

Now, *How much owest thou my Lord?* Will his account be overdrawn if he call for singleness of purpose and self-sacrificing labor for your brethren? Having passed through your drill school, will you refuse a general's commission even if it entail responsibility, risk and anxiety, with possibly some adverse criticism? Is it too much to ask you to step forward and direct the work for your race along those lines which you know to be of first and vital importance?

Will you allow these words of Ralph Waldo Emerson? "In ordinary," says he, "we have a snappish criticism which watches and contradicts the opposite party. We want the will which advances and dictates [acts]. Nature has made up her mind that what cannot defend itself, shall not be defended. Complaining never so loud and with never so much reason, is of no use. What cannot stand must fall; *and the measure of our sincerity and therefore of the respect of men is the amount of health and wealth we will hazard in the defense of our right.*"

"Paper by Mrs. Anna J. Cooper" (1894)

SOURCE: Anna Julia Cooper, "Paper by Mrs. Anna J. Cooper," delivered to the Folklore Conference at Hampton Normal School, *Southern Workman* 23, no. 7 (1894): 133.

Folk-Lore and Ethnology.

On Friday evening, May 25th, a Folk-Lore Conference was held at the Hampton Normal School under the auspices of the Hampton Folk-Lore Society. Mr. Wm. Wells Newell of the American Folk-Lore Society, and Mrs. Anna Julia Cooper of the Washington Negro Folk-Lore Society had been invited to deliver addresses. The meeting was held in the large Assembly room of Academic Hall, and the audience was composed mainly of trustees, teachers, officers and graduates of the school, Mr. F. D. Wheelock, President of the Hampton Folk-Lore Society, introduced Mr. Newell who delivered the following address.

Paper By Mrs. Anna J. Cooper.

In the direction of original productiveness, the American Negro is confronted by a peculiar danger. In the first place he is essentially imitative. This in itself is not a defect. The imitative instinct is the main spring of civilization and in this aptitude the Negro is linked with the most progressive nations of the world's history. The Phœnecians imitated the Egyptians, the Greeks borrowed from the Phœnecians, the Romans unblushingly appropriated from the Greeks whatever they could beg or steal. The Norman who became the brain and nerve of the Anglo Saxon race, who contributed the most vigorous and energetic elements in modern civilization, was above all men an imitator. "Whenever," says one, "his neighbor invented or possessed anything worthy of admiration, the sharp, inquisitive Norman poked his long aquiline nose," and the same writer adds, "wherever what we now call the march of intellect advanced, there was the sharp eager face of the Norman in the van." It is not then where or how a man or race gets his ideas but what use does he make of them that settles his claim to originality. "He has seen some of my work," said the great Michael Angelo of the young Raphael when he noticed an adroit appropriation of some of his own touches. But Raphel was no copyist. Shakespeare was a veritable freebooter in the realm of literature, but Shakespeare was no plagiarist.

I heard recently of a certain great painter, who before taking his brush always knelt down and prayed to be delivered from his model, and just here as it seems to me is the real need of deliverance for the American black man. His "model" is a civilization which to his childlike admiration must seem overpowering. Its steam servants thread the globe. It has put the harness on God's lightening which is now made to pull, push, pump, lift, write, talk, sing, light, kill, cure. It seems once more to have realized the possession of Aladdin's wonderful lamp for securing with magic speed and dexterity fabulous wealth, honor, ease, luxury, beauty, art, power. What more can be done? What more can be desired? And as the Queen of Sheba sunk under the stupendousness of Solmon's greatness, the children of Africa in America are in danger of paralysis before the splendor of Anglo Saxon achievements. Anglo Saxon ideas. Anglo Saxon standards, Anglo Saxon art, Anglo Saxon literature, Anglo Saxon music— surely this must be to him the measure of perfection. The whispered little longings of his own soul for utterance must be all a mistake. The simple little croonings that rocked his own cradle must be forgotten and outgrown and only the lullabies after the approved style affected. Nothing else is grammatical, nothing else is orthodox. To write as a white man, to sing as a white man, to swagger as a white man, to bully as a white man— this is achievement, this is success.

And, as in all imitations that means mere copying, the ridiculous mannerisms and ugly defects of the model are appropriated more successfully than the life and inner spirit which alone gave beauty or meaning to the original. Emancipation from the model is what is needed. Servile copying foredooms mediocrity: it cuts the nerve of soul expression. The American Negro cannot produce an original utterance until he realizes the sanctity of his homely inheritance. It is the simple, common, everyday things of man that God has cleansed. And it is the untaught, spontaneous lispings of the child heart that are fullest of poetry and mystery.

Correggio once wandered from his little provincial home and found his way to Rome where all the wonder of the great art world for the first time stood revealed before him. He drank deep and long of the rich inspiration and felt the quickening of his own self consciousness as he gazed on the marvelous canvasses of the masters.

"*I too am a painter*," he cried and the world has vindicated the assertion. Now it is just such a quickening as this that must come to the black man in America, to stimulate his original activities. The creative instinct must be aroused by a wholesome respect for the thoughts that lie nearest. And this to my mind is the vital importance for him of the study of his own folk-lore. His songs, superstitions, customs, tales are the legacy left from the imagery of the past. These must catch and hold and work up into the pictures he paints. The poems of Homer are valued today chiefly because they are the simple unstudied view of the far away life of the Greeks—its homely custom and superstitions as well as its more heroic achievements and activities. The Canterbury Tales do the same thing for the England of the 14th century.

The Negro too is a painter. And he who can turn his camera on the fast receding views of this people and catch their simple truth and their sympathetic meaning before it is all too late will no less deserve the credit of having revealed a characteristic page in history and of having made an interesting study.

42

MARY CHURCH TERRELL

(1863–1954)

Mary Church Terrell was born Mary Eliza Church in Memphis, Tennessee, the daughter of two former slaves. After graduating from Oberlin College, she earned a master's degree in teaching and married Robert Herberton Terrell, who went on to become the first black municipal judge in Washington, D.C. Mary Church Terrell was politically active throughout her life, fighting for women's suffrage and civil rights. She was the first president of the National Association of Colored Women, and she was chosen by W. E. B. Du-Bois as a charter member of the National Association for the Advancement of Colored People.

In the following two pieces, Terrell strikes two distinct tones. "The Progress of Colored Women" is an optimistic essay on the accomplishments of colored women in the United States since the signing of the Emancipation Proclamation. Like other such essays in this anthology, Terrell's notes black women's devotion to church, charity, and chastity. She also accounts for the financial and educational resources under black women's control, claiming that 80 percent of black teachers are women, and that black women donated over $500,000 in support of the cause of education. In "Peonage in the United States," Terrell investigates a corrupt prison system that replicates slavery. Under the convict lease system, unlike on plantations, there is no financial interest in keeping workers healthy.

"The Progress of Colored Women" (1898)

SOURCE: Mary Church Terrell, "The Progress of Colored
Women," delivered before the National American Women's
Suffrage Association, Cong. Rooms, 1898.

When one considers the obstacles encountered by colored
women in their effort to educate and cultivate themselves, since
they became free, the work they have accomplished and the
progress they have made will bear favorable comparison, at
least with that of their more fortunate sisters, from whom the
opportunity of acquiring knowledge and the means of self-
culture have never been entirely withheld. Not only are colored
women with ambition and aspiration handicapped on account
of their sex, but they are almost everywhere baffled and mocked
because of their race. Not only because they are women, but
because they are colored women, are discouragement and disappointment meeting them at every turn. But in spite of the obstacles encountered, the progress made by colored women
along many lines appears like a veritable miracle of modern
times. Forty years ago for the great masses of colored women,
there was no such thing as home. Today in each and every section of the country there are hundreds of homes among colored
people, the mental and moral tone of which is as high and as
pure as can be found among the best people of any land.

To the women of the race may be attributed in large measure
the refinement and purity of the colored home. The immorality
of colored women is a theme upon which those who know little
about them or those who maliciously misrepresent them love to
descant. Foul aspersions upon the character of colored women
are assiduously circulated by the press of certain sections and
especially by the direct descendants of those who in years past
were responsible for the moral degradation of their female
slaves. And yet, in spite of the fateful heritage of slavery, even
though the safeguards usually thrown around maidenly youth
and innocence are in some sections entirely withheld from colored girls, statistics compiled by men not inclined to falsify in

favor of my race show that immorality among the colored women of the United States is not so great as among women with similar environment and temptations in Italy, Germany, Sweden and France.

Scandals in the best colored society are exceedingly rare, while the progressive game of divorce and remarriage is practically unknown.

The intellectual progress of colored women has been marvelous. So great has been their thirst for knowledge and so Herculean their efforts to acquire it that there are few colleges, universities, high and normal schools in the North, East and West from which colored girls have not graduated with honor. In Wellesley, Vassar, Ann Arbor, Cornell and in Oberlin, my dear alma mater, whose name will always be loved and whose praise will always be sung as the first college in the country broad, just and generous enough to extend a cordial welcome to the Negro and to open its doors to women on an equal footing with the men, colored girls by their splendid records have forever settled the question of their capacity and worth. The instructors in these and other institutions cheerfully bear testimony to their intelligence, their diligence and their success.

As the brains of colored women expanded, their hearts began to grow. No sooner had the heads of a favored few been filled with knowledge than their hearts yearned to dispense blessings to the less fortunate of their race. With tireless energy and eager zeal, colored women have worked in every conceivable way to elevate their race. Of the colored teachers engaged in instructing our youth it is probably no exaggeration to say that fully eighty percent are women. In the backwoods, remote from the civilization and comforts of the city and town, colored women may be found courageously battling with those evils which such conditions always entail. Many a heroine of whom the world will never hear has thus sacrificed her life to her race amid surroundings and in the face of privations which only martyrs can bear.

Through the medium of their societies in the church, beneficial organizations out of it and clubs of various kinds, colored women are doing a vast amount of good. It is almost impossible to ascertain exactly what the Negro is doing in any field, for the records are so poorly kept. This is particularly true in the case of the women of the race. During the past forty years there is no doubt that colored women in their poverty have contributed large sums of money to charitable and educational institutions as well as to the foreign and home missionary work. Within the twenty-five years in which the educational work of the African Methodist Episcopal Church has been systematized, the women of that organization have contributed at least five hundred thousand dollars to the cause of education. Dotted all over the country are charitable institutions for the aged, orphaned and poor which have been established by colored women. Just how many it is difficult to state, owing to the lack of statistics bearing on the progress, possessions and prowess of colored women.

Up to date, politics have been religiously eschewed by colored women, although questions affecting our legal status as a race are sometimes agitated by the most progressive class. In Louisiana and Tennessee colored women have several times petitioned the legislatures of their respective states to repel the obnoxious Jim-Crow laws. Against the convict-lease system, whose atrocities have been so frequently exposed of late, colored women here and there in the South are waging a ceaseless war. So long as hundreds of their brothers and sisters, many of whom have committed no crime or misdemeanor whatever, are thrown into cells whose cubic contents are less than those of a good size grave, to be overworked, underfed and only partially covered with vermin infested rags, and so long as children are born to the women in these camps who breathe the polluted atmosphere of these dens of horror and vice from the time they utter their first cry in the world till they are released from their suffering by death, colored women who are working for the emancipation and elevation of their race know where their duty lies. By constant agitation of this painful and hideous subject, they hope to touch the conscience of the country, so that this stain upon its escutcheon shall be forever wiped away.

Alarmed at the rapidity with which the Negro is losing ground in the world of trade, some of the farsighted women are trying to solve the labor question, so far as it concerns the women at least, by urging the establishment of schools of domestic science wherever means therefore can be secured. Those who are interested in this particular work hope and believe that if colored women and girls are thoroughly trained in domestic service, the boycott which has undoubtedly been placed upon them in many sections of the country will be removed. With so few vocations open to the Negro and with the labor organizations increasingly hostile to him, the future of the boys and girls of the race appears to some of our women very foreboding and dark.

The cause of temperance has been eloquently espoused by two women, each of whom has been appointed national superintendent of work among colored people by the Woman's Christian Temperance Union. In business, colored women have had signal success. There is in Alabama a large milling and cotton business belonging to and controlled by a colored woman, who has sometimes as many as seventy-five men in her employ. Until a few years ago the principal ice plant of Nova Scotia was owned and managed by a colored woman, who sold it for a large amount. In the professions there are dentists and doctors whose practice is lucrative and large. Ever since a book was published in 1773 entitled "Poems on Various Subjects, Religious and Moral by Phillis Wheatley, Negro Servant of Mr. John Wheatley," of Boston, colored women have given abundant evidence of literary ability. In sculpture we were represented by a woman upon whose chisel Italy has set her seal of approval; in painting by one of Bouguereau's pupils and in music by young women holding diplomas from the best conservatories in the land. In short, to use a thought of the illustrious Frederick Douglass, if judged by the depths from which they have come, rather than by the heights to which those blessed with centuries of opportunities have attained, colored women need not hang their heads in shame. They are slowly but surely making their way up to the heights, wherever they can be scaled. In spite of handicaps and discouragements they are not losing heart. In a variety of ways they are rendering valiant service to their race. Lifting as they climb, onward and upward they go struggling and striving and hoping that the buds and blossoms of their desires may burst into glorious fruition ere long. Seeking no favors because of their color nor charity because of their needs they knock at the door of Justice and ask for an equal chance.

"The Convict Lease System and the Chain Gangs" (1907)

SOURCE: Mary Church Terrell, "Peonage in the United States: The Convict Lease System and the Chain Gangs," *The Nineteenth Century and After: A Monthly Review* 57 (July–December 1907).

IN the chain gangs and convict lease camps of the South to-day are thousands of colored people, men, women, and children, who are enduring a bondage, in some respects more cruel and more crushing than that from which their parents were emancipated forty years ago. Under this modern *régime* of slavery thousands of colored people, frequently upon trumped-up charges or for offences which in a civilized community would hardly land them in gaol, are thrown into dark, damp, disease-breeding cells, whose cubic contents are less than those of a good-sized grave, are overworked, underfed, and only partially covered with vermin-infested rags. As the chain gangs and the convict lease system are operated in the South to-day they violate the law against peonage, the constitutionality of which was affirmed by the Supreme Court two years ago. In the famous case of Clyatt *versus* the United States, Attorney-General Moody, recently placed upon the bench of the Supreme Court, represented the Government, while Senator Bacon and others appeared for Clyatt, a resident of Georgia, who had been convicted in the Federal Courts of that State and sentenced to four years' hard labor on the charge of having held two colored men in peonage on account of debt, in violation of the law. In his brief, Attorney Moody declared that the executive arm of the law, so far as the enforcement of the statute against peonage was concerned, has been practically paralyzed.

"Notwithstanding the fact that several United States Courts have held this law to be constitutional" [said Judge Moody], "the Government is powerless to compel its enforcement or observance, even in the most typical and flagrant cases. We think we may truthfully say" [continues Judge Moody], "that upon the decision of this case (Clyatt v. the United States) hangs the liberty of thousands of persons, mostly colored, it is true, who are now being held in a condition of involuntary servitude, in many cases worse than slavery itself, by the unlawful acts of individuals, not only in violation of the thirteenth amendment to the constitution, but in violation of the law which we have under consideration."

With one or two exceptions, perhaps, no case decided by the Supreme Court within recent years involved graver considerations than were presented by the questions raised in the Clyatt case, for the constitutionality of the law against peonage was thereby affirmed.

If anybody is inclined to attach little importance to Judge Moody's description of the conditions under which thousands of peons are living in the South to-day, on the ground that they may be simply the exaggerated statement of a Northerner who, at best, has received his information second hand, let him listen to the words of a man, born and reared in the South, who was commissioned a few years ago to investigate the convict camps of his own State. After Colonel Byrd, of Rome, Ga., had inspected every county camp in the State which it was possible for him to discover, he addressed himself to Governor Atkinson, who for years had been trying to improve existing conditions, as follows:

"Your Excellency never did a more noble deed nor one that has been more far reaching in good or beneficent results to a helpless and friendless class of unfortunates than when you sent Special Inspector Wright into the misdemeanor camps of Georgia two years ago. His one visit did valiant service for human beings that were serving a bondage worse than slavery. True they were lawbreakers and deserved punishment at the hands of the State, but surely the State has no right to make helpless by law and then to forsake the helpless to the mercies of men who have no mercy. Surely there can be no genuine civilization when man's inhumanity to man is so possible, so plainly in evidence."

Immediately after the constitutionality of the law against peonage was affirmed by the Supreme Court in March 1904, Judge Emory Speer, of Savannah, Georgia, one of the most eminent jurists in the country, began to attack the chain gangs of the South on the ground that they violate both the thirteenth amendment and the law against peonage. Since the thirteenth amendment declares that "involuntary servitude except as punishment for crime, whereof the party shall have been duly convicted, shall not exist in the United States," Judge Speer attacked the chain gangs, because men, women, and children by the hundreds are forced into involuntary servitude by being sentenced to work upon them, who are not even charged with crime, but are accused of some petty offence, such as walking on the grass, expectorating upon the side walk, going to sleep in a depot, loitering on the streets, or other similar misdemeanors which could not by any stretch of the imagination be called a crime. Judge Speer also declared it to be his opinion that even those who sentence these helpless and friendless people to the chain gangs, and thus force them into involuntary servitude, are guilty of violating the law and are liable to punishment therefore; since it was explicitly stated in the decision rendered by the Supreme Court that even though "there might be in the language of the court either a municipal ordinance or State law sanctioning the holding of persons in involuntary servitude, Congress has power to punish those who thus violate the thirteenth amendment" and the law against peonage at one and the same time.

In spite, however, of the overwhelming weight of evidence showing that atrocities are daily being perpetrated upon American citizens in almost every State of the South, with the connivance of those who administer the law, which are as shocking and unprintable as those endured by the Russian Jew, in spite of the power which the Supreme Court asserts is possessed by Congress, but feeble efforts are being put forth to suppress the chain gangs and the convict lease camps of the South. It is surprising how few there are among even intelligent people in this country who seem to have anything but a hazy idea of what the convict lease system means.

The plan of hiring out short term convicts to an individual or a company of individuals who needed laborers was adopted by the southern States shortly after the war, not from choice, it is claimed, but because there was neither a sufficient number of jails nor money enough to build them. Those who need laborers for their farms, saw mills, brick yards, turpentine distilleries, coal or phosphate mines, or who have large contracts of various kinds, lease the misdemeanants from the county or State, which sells them to the highest bidder with merciless disregard of the fact that they are human beings, and practically gives the lessee the power of life and death over the unfortunate man or woman thus raffled off. The more work the lessee gets out of the convict, the more money goes into his gaping purse. Doctors cannot be employed without the expenditure of money, while fresh victims may be secured by the outlay of little cash when convicts succumb to disease and neglect. From a purely business standpoint, therefore, it is much more profitable to get as much work out of a convict as can be wrung from him at the smallest possible expense, and then lay in a fresh supply, when necessary, than it is to clothe, and shelter, and feed him properly, and spend money trying to preserve his health. It is perfectly clear, therefore, that it is no exaggeration to say that in some respects the convict lease system, as it is operated in certain southern States, is less humane than was the bondage endured by slaves fifty years ago. For, under the old *régime*, it was to the master's interest to clothe and shelter and feed his slaves properly, even if he were not moved to do so by considerations of mercy and humanity, because the death of a slave meant an actual loss in dollars and cents, whereas the death of a convict to-day involves no loss whatsoever either to the lessee or to the State.

Speaking of this system a few years ago, a governor of Kentucky said:

"I cannot but regard the present system under which the State penitentiary is leased and managed as a reproach to the commonwealth. It is the *system* itself and not the officer acting under it with which I find fault. Possession of the convict's person is an opportunity for the State to make money—the amount to be made is whatever can be wrung from him without regard to moral or mortal consequences. The penitentiary which shows the largest cash balance paid into the State treasury is the best penitentiary. In the main the notion is clearly set forth and followed that a convict, whether pilferer or murderer, man, woman, or child, has almost no human right that the State is bound to be at any expense to protect."

Again, at a meeting of the National Prison Association which was held in New Orleans a few years ago, a speaker who had carefully studied the convict lease system declared that the convicts in the South, most of whom are negroes, are in many cases worse off than they were in the days of slavery. "They are bought as truly," said he, "are more completely separated from their families, are irretrievably demoralized by constant evil association and are invariably worse off when they leave the camps than when they entered." "Over certain places where the convicts of Alabama are employed," said an authority on penology, "should be written the words 'All hope abandon, ye who enter here,' so utterly demoralizing is the entire management." And so it would be possible to quote indefinitely from men all over the country in every station of life, from judges, governors of States, prison experts, and private citizens, whose testimony without a single exception proves conclusively that the convict lease system in particular, and the chain gang on general principles, are an insult to the intelligence and humanity of an enlightened community.

It is frequently asserted that the convict lease camps and other forms of peonage are dying out in the south. First one State and then another passes laws against leasing convicts to private individuals or attempts to pass such a law, or, if it still adheres to the convict lease system, it tries to provide for the inspection of the camps by men appointed to do this work by the State. But facts which have been brought to light during the last year or two show that those who extract comfort from the reports which announce the disappearance of the convict camps and the chain gangs build their hope upon a foundation of sand. During the year 1906 allegations of the existence of slavery in Florida were made to the department of justice, and evidence was produced to show that hundreds of men, the majority of whom were colored, but a few among the number white, were virtually reduced to the condition of slaves.

Facts were produced which showed that the officers of the law, the sheriffs themselves, were parties to reducing to a condition of slavery the colored people who work in the phosphate and coal mines, in the lumber mills or on the turpentine farms of Florida, for instance. These camps were inspected by a woman who was commissioned, it is said, by those high in authority to secure the facts. Only last September a government detective disguised as a man anxious to purchase timber lands, visited the railroad camps of Blount Co., Tenn., and secured evidence against some of the most prominent contractors in that section, which showed that hundreds of colored men have systematically been deprived of their liberty, while it is impossible to state how many of them lost their lives.

Before the grand jury the victims of this barbarous system of peonage, many of whom had been brought to Tennessee from North and South Carolina, told pitiable tales of their suffering and maltreatment and related stories of seeing men killed, dragged to the river in blankets, weighted, and then sunk into the water, which are too horrible to believe. As a result of this trial one of the largest railroad contractors of Knoxville, Tenn., was indicted by the grand jury on the charge of peonage, the indictment containing twenty-five counts.

Upon the evidence of a colored soldier who was with President Roosevelt in Cuba, and who sawed his way to freedom through the floor of the shack in which he was confined at night, together with a large number of peons, the man who thus held him in bondage in Missouri was sentenced to three and a half years in the penitentiary of Fort Leavenworth, Kansas, in addition to paying a fine of five thousand dollars and costs. Several others who were engaged in conducting this particular camp, among them the son of the chief offender, were also sentenced to the penitentiary, fined, and obliged to pay the costs. Last spring six colored people filed suits against a family by whom they had been held in a state of peonage in Ashley Co., Ark. Their complaint set forth inhuman treatment, imprisonment in jails in various places, that they were bound like beasts, paraded through public streets, and then imprisoned on plantations, where they were compelled to do the hardest kind of labor without receiving a single cent.

While colored people were originally the only ones affected to any great extent by the practice of peonage in the southern States, in recent years white people in increasingly large numbers have been doomed to the same fate. For instance, only last July the chairman of the Board of Commissioners of Bradford Co.,

Florida, was arrested for holding in a state of peonage an orphan white girl sixteen years old. The girl declares that she was so brutally treated, she started to walk to Jacksonville, Fla. When she had gone six miles, she was overtaken, she says, by her hard task-master and forced to walk back by a road covered with water in places, so that she was obliged to wade knee deep. When she returned, she declared her master beat her with a hickory stick and showed bruises to substantiate the charge. Last October a wealthy family, living in Arkansaw, was convicted of holding two white girls from St. Louis, Mo., in peonage, and was forced to pay one of the white slaves one thousand dollars damages, and the other 625 dollars. The farmer had induced the girls to come from Missouri to Arkansaw, and then promptly reduced them to the condition of slaves. In the same month of October came the startling announcement that one thousand white girls, who are rightful heiresses to valuable timber lands in the wilds of the Florida pine woods, wear men's clothing and work side by side with colored men who are held in slavery as well as the girls. Stories of the treatment accorded these white slave girls of Florida, which reached the ears of the Washington officials, equal in cruelty some of the tales related in *Uncle Tom's Cabin* by Harriet Beecher Stowe. In the black depths of pine woods, living in huts never seen by civilized white men other than the bosses of the turpentine camps, girls are said to have grown old in servitude. These girls are said to be the daughters of crackers who, like fathers in pre-historic times, little value the birth of a girl, and sell the best years of their daughters' lives to the turpentine or sulfur miners and to the lumber men for a mere song. To be discharged from one of these camps means death to an *employé*. Since they receive nothing for their services, their dismissal is no revenge for an angered foreman or boss. The slaves are too numerous to be beaten, and it is said to be a part of the system never to whip an *employé*, but invariably to shoot the doomed man or woman upon the slightest provocation, so that the others might be kept in constant subjection.

Two white men of Seymour, Indiana, went to Vance, Mississippi, not very long ago, to work for a large stave company, as they supposed; but when they reached Vance, they were told they must go to the swamp and cut timber. When they demurred, the foreman had them arrested for securing their transportation money "on false pretenses." The squire before whom they were taken fined each of them 45 dollars and costs. They were then obliged to ride twenty-three miles on horseback to Belen, the county seat, where they were kept three days and given one meal. Then they were taken to Essex, Mississippi, turned over to the owner of a plantation, placed in a stockade at night and forced to work under an armed guard. They were ordered to work out their fine at *fifteen cents a day*, such a contract being made by the *court officers themselves*. These Indiana men learned during the nine days they were in this Mississippi stockade that there were men on the plantation who had been there for ten years trying to work out their fines. Before one fine could be worked out a new charge would be trumped up to hold them. Only last August a young white man who had lived in New York returned to his home, half starved, his body covered with bruises, resulting from unmerciful beatings he had received in a State camp in North Carolina, and related a story which was horrifying in its revelations of the atrocities perpetrated upon the men confined in it. This young white man claimed that at the time he escaped there were no less than twenty other youths from New York unable to return to their homes, and enduring the torture to which he was subjected by inhuman bosses every day. According to this young New Yorker's story, there were about one thousand men at work in this camp, each of whom was obliged to contribute 50 cents a week toward the support of a physician.

"On one occasion" [said he] "the foreman threw heavy stones at me, one of which struck me on the head, knocking me senseless, because I sat down to rest. For hours I lay on the cot in my shack without medical aid, and I bear the mark of that stone to-day. For refusing to work because of lack of nourishment, for our meals consisted only of a slice of bread and a glass of water, I saw the foreman take a revolver, shoot a young negro through the leg and walk away, leaving him for dead. This fellow lay for days without medical aid and was finally taken away, nobody knows where. Three Italians were killed and two others were severely injured in a fight between the foreman and laborers, and yet not one of these men was arrested. Since the post office was under the control of the men running the camp, the letters written by the New York boys to their friends and relatives never reached their destination."

The cases just cited prove conclusively that not only does peonage still rage violently in the southern States and in a variety of forms, but that while it formerly affected only colored people, it now attacks white men and women as well.

From renting or buying colored men, women, and children, who had really fallen under the ban of the law, to actually trapping and stealing them was a very short step indeed, when labor was scarce and the need of additional hands pressed sore. Very recently, incredible as it may appear to many, colored men have been captured by white men, torn from their homes and forced to work on plantations or in camps of various kinds, just as truly as their fathers before them were snatched violently by slave catchers from their native African shores. Only last February (1906) two cotton planters of Houston Co., Texas, were arrested for a kind of peonage which is by no means uncommon in the South to-day. The planters needed extra help, so they captured two strong, able-bodied negroes, whom they charged with being indebted to them, and with having violated their contracts. Without resort to law they manacled the negroes and removed them to their plantations, where they forced them to work from twelve to sixteen hours a day without paying them a cent. The sheriff who arrested the planters admitted that this practice of capturing negroes when labor is needed on the plantations has prevailed for a long time in Madison Co., Texas, where the population is mainly negro. The captured men are worked during the cotton-planting season, are then released with empty pockets and allowed to return to their homes as best they can, where they remain until they are needed again, when they are recaptured.

But the methods generally used by the men who run the convict camps of the South or who own large plantations, when they need colored laborers, are much more skillful and less likely to involve them in trouble than those which the Texans just mentioned employ. Colored men are convicted in magistrates' courts of trivial offences, such as alleged violation of contract or something of the kind, and are given purposely heavy sentences with alternate fines. Plantation owners and others in search of labor, who have already given their orders to the officers of the law, are promptly notified that some available laborers are theirs to command and immediately appear to pay the fine and release the convict from jail only to make him a slave. If the negro dares to leave the premises of his employer, the same magistrate who convicted him originally is ready to pounce down upon him and send him back to gaol. Invariably poor and ignorant, he is unable to employ counsel or to assert his rights (it is treason to presume he has any) and he finds all the machinery of the law, so far as he can understand, against him. There is no doubt whatever that there are scores, hundreds perhaps, of colored men in the South to-day who are vainly trying to repay fines and sentences imposed upon them five, six, or even ten years ago. The horror of ball and chain is ever before them, and their future is bright with no hope.

In the annual report of the "Georgia State Prison Commission," which appeared only last June, the secretary shows that during the year 1905–06, there was a decrease of fully 10 per cent in the number of misdemeanor convicts on the county chain gangs in Georgia, notwithstanding the fact that there has been an increase among the felony convicts. This decrease in the number of misdemeanants is explained as follows: "Owing to the scarcity of labor, farmers who are able to do so pay the fines of able-bodied prisoners and put them on their plantations to work them out." "Had it not been for the fact that many farmers have paid the fines of the men convicted," explains the prison commission, "in order to get their labor, there is no doubt that there would be an increase instead of a decrease in the number on the misdemeanor gangs." This very frank admission of the open manner in which the law against peonage is deliberately broken by the farmers of Georgia is refreshing, to say the least. Surely they cannot be accused by prudish and unreasonable persons of violating the thirteenth amendment by mysterious methods hard to detect and transgressing the peonage law in secret, when the decrease in the number of misdemeanants of a sovereign State is attributed in a printed report to the fact that the farmers are buying up able-bodied negroes a bit more briskly than usual.

While the convict lease camps of no State in the South have presented conditions more shocking and cruel than have those in Georgia, it is also true that in no State have more determined and conscientious efforts to improve conditions been put forth by a portion of its citizens than in that State. In spite of this fact it is well known that some of the wealthiest men in the State have accumulated their fortunes by literally buying colored men, women, and children, and working them nearly, if not quite, to death. Reference has already been made to the report submitted to the Georgia legislature a few years ago by Colonel Byrd, who was appointed special commissioner to investigate the convict lease camps of his State. In reviewing this report the *Atlanta Constitution* summed up the charges against the convict lease system as follows: "Colonel Byrd's report was not written by a Northerner, who does not understand conditions in the South, or the people living in that section" (as is so frequently asserted, when one who does not live in the sunny south dares to comment on anything which takes place below Mason's and Dixon's line); "but it is written by one of the South's most distinguished citizens who did not deal in glittering generalities, but in facts." Colonel Byrd gave a truthful account of his trips to the camps, of his visits in the day time and at night, when none knew of his coming. He made it a rule, he said, to arrive at each camp unannounced, and he has told us exactly what he saw with his eyes and heard with his ears. Of the fifty-one chain gangs visited, Colonel Byrd discovered that at least half were operated exclusively by private individuals who had practically the power of life and death over the convicts. Seldom was provision made for the separation of the sexes, either during work by day or sleep by night. Little or no attention was given to the comfort or sanitary condition of the sleeping quarters, and women were forced to do men's work in men's attire. The murder of the men and the outrage of the women in these camps, the political pulls by which men occupying lofty positions in the State were shielded and saved from indictment by grand juries, formed the subjects of many indignant editorials in the *Atlanta Constitution*.

Briefly summed up, the specific charges preferred by one of the South's most distinguished sons who had made a most painstaking and exhaustive investigation of the convict lease camps of Georgia are as follow:

(1) Robbing convicts of their time allowances for good behavior. According to Colonel Byrd, there were not five camps in the State that had complied with the law requiring them to keep a book in which the good or bad conduct of each convict shall be entered daily. In the event of good conduct the law provides that a prisoner's term of confinement shall be shortened four days during each month of service. In fifteen out of twenty-four private camps the contractors did not give the convicts a single day off for good service, nor did they even make pretense of doing so.

(2) Forcing convicts to work from fourteen to twenty hours a day.

(3) Providing them no clothes, no shoes, no beds, no heat in winter, and no ventilation whatever in single rooms in summer in which sixty convicts slept in chains.

(4) Giving them rotten food.

(5) Allowing them to die, when sick, for lack of medical attention.

(6) Outraging the women.

(7) Beating to death old men too feeble to work.

(8) Killing young men for the mere sake of killing.

(9) Suborning jurors and county officers, whose sworn duty it is to avenge the wrongdoing of guards.

It is when he struck the convicts leased to private individuals that Colonel Byrd took off his gloves, as the *Atlanta Constitution* well said, and dipped his pen in red ink. In these private camps Colonel Byrd found the convicts, men committed at the most for some trivial offence or perhaps none at all, had no clothes except greasy, grimy garments, which in many cases were worn to threads and were worthless as protection. These men, women, and children, for there were children only eight years old in the camps inspected by Colonel Byrd a few years ago, were badly shod and in the majority of cases went barefoot the year round. In many of the pine belt gangs, where the convicts were buried in the fastness of mighty pine forests, they went from year's end to year's end without a taste of vegetables. Usually after the convicts returned from their fourteen hours' work they were given raw chunks of meat to prepare for their own dinner. In the matter of buildings the report was no less severe. In a camp owned by a well-known Georgian, Colonel Byrd found eleven men sleeping in a room ten feet square and but seven feet from floor to ceiling, with no window at all, but one door which opened into another room. In another camp the convicts slept in tents which had no bunks, no mattresses, and not even a floor. Fully thirteen of the camps out of twenty-four contained neither bunks nor mattresses, and the convicts were compelled to sleep in filthy, vermin-ridden blankets on the ground. And the men were obliged to sleep chained together.

Many of the camps had no arrangements and scarcely miserable excuses for means of warming the barn-like buildings in which the convicts were confined during stormy days and wintry nights. The suffering the helpless inmates were forced to endure in winter, according to Colonel Byrd's description, must have been terrible, while in the summer they were locked into the sweat boxes without ventilation, in order that the lessee might save the expense of employing night guards.

"In two instances," said Colonel Byrd, "I found by the bedside of sick convicts tubs that had been used for days without having been emptied and in a condition that would kill anything but a misdemeanor convict." But Colonel Byrd's description of the insanitary condition of some of the camps and the horrors of convict life are unprintable. He calls attention to the fact that the death rate in the private camps is double that of the county camps. In one of the camps one out of every four convicts died during their incarceration. In another camp one out of every six unfortunates who had committed some slight infraction of the law, if he were guilty at all, was thrust into a camp which he never left alive. In twenty-one out of twenty-four private camps there were neither hospital buildings nor arrangements of any kind for the sick. After describing the lack of bathing facilities, which Colonel Byrd says gave the convicts a mangy appearance, he refers to the inhuman beatings inflicted upon the convicts. A leather strop was the instrument of punishment found by the commissioner in all the camps, "and my observation has been," said he, "that where the strap has been used the least the best camps exist and the best work is turned out by the convicts."

In the camp in which the negroes looked worst the commissioner found very few reported dead. On the very date of inspection, however, there were three men, all new arrivals, locked in the filthy building, sick. They said they had been there a week, and two of them looked as though they could not recover. In another camp there was not even a stove, and the negroes had to cook on skillets over log fires in the open air. There were no beds at all and the few blankets were reeking with filth, as they were scattered about over a dirty floor.

In his report Colonel Byrd called particular attention to a few of the many cases of brutality, inhumanity, and even murder which came under his own personal observation. In the banner camp for heavy mortality the commissioner found two men with broken legs, so terribly surrounded as practically to make it impossible for them to recover. Both in this camp and in others there were numerous instances of sudden deaths among convicts, which were attributed to brain trouble and other diseases. On reliable authority Colonel Byrd learned that the guards in one of the camps visited had just a short while before his arrival literally beaten one of the convicts to death and then burned his remains in his convict suit with his shackles on. "A reputable citizen," said Colonel Byrd, "told me that he had seen the guards beating this convict, and that in their anger they had caught him by the shackles and run through the woods, dragging him along feet foremost." He stated he had gone before the grand jury of Pulaski Co., where the camp was situated, and had sworn to these facts, but that Mr. Allison, who ran this camp, had friends on the jury and that other citizens had thought it would be best to hush the whole deplorable affair up, so as to keep it out of the newspapers and courts. The superintendent of the camp simply claimed that the murdered negro had died of dropsy and was buried in his stripes and shackles to save time.

The camp of W. H. and J. H. Griffin in Wilkes Co. was described as being "very tough." It was in that camp that Bob Cannon, a camp guard, beat to death an aged negro named

Frank McRay. The condition in this camp was too horrible to describe. The prison was an abandoned kitchen or outhouse in the yard of a large *ante bellum* residence. Every window in it had been removed and the openings closely boarded up and sealed. It was a small square box with not even an augur hole for air or light.

"When the door was opened" [said Colonel Byrd], "and I had recovered from the shock caused by the rush of foul air, I noticed a sick negro sitting in the room. How human beings could consign a fellow being to such an existence I cannot understand any more than I can understand how a human being could survive a night of confinement in such a den. There was an open can in the center of the room and it looked as if it had not been emptied in a fortnight. A small bit of cornbread lay on a blanket near the negro, and that poor victim, guilty of a misdemeanor only, while sick, confined in this sweat-box dungeon, humbly asked to be furnished with a drink of water.

"It was in this gang that I found Lizzie Boatwright, a nineteen-year-old negress sent up from Thomas, Ga., for larceny. She was clad in men's clothing, was working side by side with male convicts under a guard, cutting a ditch through a meadow. The girl was small of stature and pleasant of address, and her life in this camp must have been one of long drawn out agony, horror, and suffering. She told me she had been whipped twice, each time by the brutal white guard who had beaten McRay to death, and who prostituted his legal right to whip into a most revolting and disgusting outrage. This girl and another woman were stripped and beaten unmercifully in plain view of the men convicts, because they stopped on the side of the road to bind a rag about their sore feet."

Be as sanguine as one may, he cannot extract much comfort from the hope that conditions at present are much better, if any, than they were when Col. Byrd made this startling, shocking revelation, as the result of a careful investigation of these camps several years ago, since camps for misdemeanor convicts are being conducted by private individuals to-day just as they were then. The eighth annual report of the Prison Commission, issued May 1905, shows that thirteen of the misdemeanor convict camps in the State of Georgia are worked for and in some cases by private individuals, contrary to law, who hire them directly from the authorities having them in charge after conviction with no legal warrant from the county authorities in those counties where they are worked. These convicts, according to the last year's report from Georgia, are entirely in the custody and control of private individuals. The officials hire them in remote counties, never seeing them after delivery, and the county authorities where they are worked never exercise supervision over or control of them.

The law explicitly states that the Prison Commission of Georgia shall have general supervision of the misdemeanor convicts of the State.

> "It shall be the duty of one of the Commissioners, or, in case of emergency, an officer designated by them, to visit from time to time, at least quarterly, the various camps where misdemeanor convicts are at work, and shall advise with the county or municipal authorities working them, in making and altering the rules for the government control and management of said convicts. . . . And if the county or municipal authorities fail to comply with such rules, or the law governing misdemeanor chain gangs [reads the statute], then the Governor with the Commission shall take such convicts from said county or municipal authorities. Or the Governor and Commission in their discretion may impose a fine upon each of the said county or municipal authorities failing to comply with such rules or the law."

But this law is easily evaded, because the county authorities where the convict is sentenced have established no chain gang, and the county authorities where the convict is worked none, so that neither can be proceeded against by the Commission. "The Prison Commission of Georgia has repeatedly called the attention of the General Assembly to this condition," says the report, and cannot refrain from again doing so, hoping that some means may be devised by which this violation of the law may be prevented.

Again and again efforts put forth by humane people, both in

Georgia and in other southern States, to correct abuses in the camps have been frustrated by men high in authority, who belong to the State legislatures and who make large fortunes out of the wretches they abuse. Colonel Byrd called attention to the fact that the whole political machinery of the State and county stood in with the lessees, because the first money earned by the poor victims paid the cost of trial and conviction. Not a dollar of the rental for the convicts reached the county treasury, he declared, till sheriff, deputy sheriff, county solicitor, bailiffs, court clerks, justice of the peace, constables and other officials who aided to put the convict in the chain gang were paid their fees in full. "It is not to be supposed," said Colonel Byrd, "that these people would be in favor of destroying a system profitable to themselves." The following incident throws some light on this point. A colored man was convicted of larceny and sentenced to twelve months on the chain gang. The county solicitor personally took charge of him, carried him to a private camp, where the contractor gave him 100 dollars in cash for this prisoner. A few months later it was discovered that the man was innocent of the crime. Both the judge and the jury before whom he was convicted signed a petition to the Governor praying for the prisoner's release. The county solicitor refused to sign it, however, because he had received his 100 dollars in advance and distributed it among the other court officials and did not want to pay it back.

There are in Georgia at the present time 1,500 men who were sold to the highest bidder the 1st of April, 1904, for a period of five years. The Durham Coal and Coke Co. leased 150 convicts, paying for them from 228 dollars to 252 dollars apiece per annum. The Flower Brothers Lumber Co. leased one hundred and paid 240 dollars a piece for them for a year. Hamby and Toomer leased five hundred, paying 221 dollars a head. The Lookout Mountain Coal and Coke Co. took 100 at 223.75 dollars a head.

The Chattahoochee Brick Co. secured 175 men at 223.75 dollars apiece per annum. E. J. McRee took one hundred men and paid 220.75 dollars for each. In its report the Prison Commission points with great pride to the fact that for five years, from the 1st of April, 1904, to the 1st of April, 1909, this batch of prisoners alone will pour annually into the State coffers the gross sum of 340,000 dollars with a net of 225,000 dollars, which will be distributed proportionately among the various counties for school purposes.

In 1903 a man whose barbarous treatment of convicts leased to him by Tallapoosa and Coosa Counties, Alabama, had been thoroughly exposed, and who had been indicted a number of times in the State courts, succeeded in leasing more convicts for a term of three years without the slightest difficulty, in spite of his record. The grand jury for the May term, 1903, of the District Court of the middle of Alabama returned ninety-nine indictments for peonage and conspiring to hold parties in a condition of peonage. In these ninety-nine true bills only eighteen persons were involved. Under the convict lease system of Alabama the State Board of Convicts then had no control whatever over the County convicts, and if they were leased to an inhuman man there was absolutely nothing to prevent him from doing with them what he wished. During the trial of the cases in Alabama to which reference has been made, a well-known journalist declared over his signature that when the chief of the State Convict Inspecting Bureau, who had been sent to Tallapoosa Co. to investigate conditions obtaining in the penal camps there, reported that some of the largest land-owners and planters in the State were engaged in the traffic of selling negroes into involuntary servitude, the Governor took no further steps to bring about the conviction of the guilty parties.

In Alabama a justice of the peace in criminal cases has power to sentence a convicted prisoner to hard labor for a term not exceeding twelve months. He is required under law to make a report of such cases to the Judge of Probate of his respective county, and to file a mittimus with the jailer of each man who is tried before him who has been convicted and fails to give bond. As soon as a man was convicted in Tallapoosa and Coosa counties by a Justice of the Peace, who was in collusion with the party or parties who had a contract with the county for leasing the county convicts, he would turn each of them over to the lessee without committing them to the county jail, and without filing a certificate of these convictions with the

Judge of Probate. Since there was no public examiner to go over the books of the Justice of the Peace, it was easy, when they were examined by order of the grand jury, to explain away as a mistake any discrepancies upon the docket. Since there was nothing on the docket of the Justice of the Peace to show the length of time the man was to serve, he was held by the lessee, until he broke down or managed to escape. Moreover, the prosecution of the cases mentioned showed that trumped-up charges would be frequently made against negroes in the two counties mentioned for the most trivial offences, such as happened in the case of one convict who was arrested for letting one man's mule bite another man's corn. It also came out in the trial that when the sentence of two convicts expired at the same time they were often provoked into a difficulty with each other and then each man would be taken down before a Justice of the Peace without the knowledge of the other, and persuaded to make an affidavit against the other man for an affray. Both would then be tried before a Justice, convicted and sentenced to imprisonment at hard labor for six months, and this would go on indefinitely. It was also developed at this Alabama trial that there was often no trial at all. An affidavit would be sworn out, but never entered upon the docket, and after a mock trial the man would be sentenced for three months or six and the judgment never entered up.

If there was an examination by the grand jury of the county, there would be no way for it to secure the facts, and no one in the community seemed to think it was his duty to make any charges. Between A and B, both of whom were convicted of peonage in Alabama in 1903, it is said that there was an understanding that the men arrested in A's neighborhood were to be tried before C, one of B's brothers-in-law, while those whom B wanted would be tried before one of the A's, who was Justice of the Peace. If material ran short, the men held by the A's were taken down and tried before B's brother-in-law and turned over to B and *vice versa*. It can easily be seen that negroes—friendless, illiterate, and penniless—had no salvation at all except when the strong arm of the United States Government took them under its protection. Although the grand jury at the May term in 1903 declared that Tallapoosa and Coosa counties were the only localities in the State where peonage existed, subsequent arrests of persons who were bound over by a United States Commissioner to await the action of the United States grand jury at the December term of 1903 proved conclusively that there were many cases of peonage in Covington, Crenshaw, Pike, Coffee, Houston, and other counties in the State of Alabama.

Describing the convict lease system, as it is operated in Mississippi, one of the best attorneys in that State said:

> "This institution is operated for no other purpose than to make money, and I can compare it with nothing but Dante's Inferno. Hades is a paradise compared with the convict camps of Mississippi. If an able-bodied young man sent to one of these camps for sixty or ninety days lives to return home, he is fit for nothing the rest of his natural life, for he is a physical wreck at the expiration of his term."

As in other States, the convict camps of Mississippi are operated by planters or others who have secured a contract from the County Board to work all prisoners sent up by the magistrates or other courts. A stipulated sum per capita is paid for the prisoners, who have to work out their fines, costs, and living expenses, receiving practically nothing for their labor. As spring comes on, officers of the law become exceedingly busy looking up cases of vagrancy or misdemeanor, so as to supply their regular patrons.

It is interesting and illuminating to see what class of men have been indicted for holding their fellows in bondage in the stockades of the South. A few years ago a leading member of the Georgia legislature, together with his brothers, operated an extensive camp in Lowndes Co. Witnesses testified before the grand jury that in this camp, owned by a member of the legislature, the brutalities practiced were too revolting to describe. It is also interesting to know that a member of that same family was awarded 100 convicts on the 1st of April 1904, and this lease is good for five years. Witnesses testified that this member of the Georgia legislature operated a camp in which prisoners were stripped and unmercifully lashed by the whipping bosses for the slightest offence. It was also alleged that this lawmaker for a sovereign State and his brothers were accustomed to go into counties adjoining Lowndes, pay the fines of the misdemeanor convicts, carry them into their Ware county camp and there keep them indefinitely.

The grand jury claimed that at least twenty citizens of Ware Co. were held as slaves in the camp owned by the brothers to whom reference has been made, long after their terms had expired. An ex-sheriff of Ware Co. and a well-known attorney of Georgia pleaded guilty not very long ago to the charge of holding citizens in a condition of peonage, and were each fined 1,000 dollars (500 dollars of which was remitted) by Judge Emory Speer. A sheriff in Alabama was recently indicted for peonage. Manufacturers of Georgia and railroad contractors in Tennessee have recently been indicted for holding men and women in involuntary servitude. The chairman of the Board of Commissioners of Bradford Co., Fla., was indicted not long ago for the same offence. In March 1905 the Federal Grand Jury indicted the city of Louisville and the superintendent of the workhouse for violating the federal statute against peonage.

There is no doubt whatever that every misdemeanor convict in the chain gangs and convict lease camps in the South operated by private individuals could appeal to the courts and secure release. Incarceration of misdemeanor convicts in these camps is as much disobedience of the laws as the original offence which led to conviction. There is no doubt that every misdemeanor camp in the southern States which is controlled by private individuals is a nest of illegality. Every man employing misdemeanor convicts for private gain is a law-breaker. Every county official who leases or permits to be leased a misdemeanor convict for other than public work transgresses one of the plainest statutes on the law books of some of the States in which the offence is committed, and violates an amendment to the constitution of the United States besides. There is no lack of law by which to punish the guilty, but they are permitted to perpetrate fearful atrocities upon the unfortunate and helpless, because there are thousands of just and humane people in this country who know little or nothing about the methods pursued in the chain gangs, the convict lease system and the contract labor system, which are all children of one wicked and hideous mother, peonage.

The negro was armed with the suffrage by just and humane men, because soon after the War of the Rebellion the legislatures of the southern States began to enact vagrant or peonage laws, the intent of which was to reduce the newly emancipated slaves to a bondage almost as cruel, if not quite as cruel, as that from which they had just been delivered. After the vote had been given the negro, so that he might use it in self-defense, the peonage laws became a dead letter for a time and lay dormant, so to speak, until disfranchisement laws were enacted in nearly every State of the South. The connection between disfranchisement and peonage is intimate and close. The planter sees the negro robbed of his suffrage with impunity, with the silent consent of the whole country, and he knows that political preferment and great power are the fruits of this outrage upon a handicapped and persecuted race. He is encouraged, therefore, to apply the same principle for profit's sake to his business affairs. The politician declares that the negro is unfit for citizenship and violently snatches from him his rights. The planter declares the negro is lazy and forces him into involuntary servitude contrary to the law. Each tyrant employs the same process of reasoning to justify his course.

43

MARY V. COOK

(1863–1945)

Mary Virginia Cook Parish was a lifelong activist for the rights of black women. She was born in Bowling Green, Kentucky, and despite limited academic opportunities, Cook progressed through school and graduated at the head of her class, going on to become a professor and principal at the normal department at Simmons University. Throughout her career, Cook lectured and wrote as means of fighting for educational equality between the races. She spoke at many Baptist Conventions, and her columns appeared in the *South Carolina Tribune*, *American Baptist*, *Our Women and Children*, and *Hope*. Cook was one of the founders of the National Association of Colored Women (1896) and the National Baptist Women's Convention (1900). In 1898 Cook married George Henry Parrish, a pastor and president of the Eckstein Norton Foundation. The couple moved to Louisville, where Cook took on leadership roles in Louisville's National Association of Colored Women, the Thirteenth Annual Convention of the National Association in Louisville, the Parent Teacher Association, and the YWCA. She also was the first president of the Colored Republicans Women's Club in Louisville and served as an alternative delegate to the 1932 National Republican Convention in Chicago.

Cook argues here for women's historical importance through a Christian lens, recalling women from scripture who were important to the development of Christianity. Cook draws on her own experience in the Baptist Church to inspire Christian women to be more aware of their importance in their own communities. She argues, essentially, that behind every good

Christian man is a good Christian woman. One of the most notable sections of this essay, "The Newspaper Work of the Denomination," encourages women to write and edit publications.

"Women's Place in the Work of the Denomination" (1887)

SOURCE: Mary V. Cook, "Women's Place in the Work of the Denomination," American National Baptist Convention, *Journals and Lectures*, 45–56, 1887.

How pleasant it is to wander over, and enjoy this beautiful world God has made. Its green meadows, its beautiful fields, its dense forests with wild flowers and rippling streams, its wide expanse of water and lofty mountains all delight us. But while charmed with its beauty, our joy is greater if we can comprehend that it "was without form and void" and contrast its present beauty with the roughness of its former state. So in viewing the wonders of divine grace, we need to note its results in connection with what might have been, and before attempting to describe woman's work in the denomination and the great blessings God has bestowed upon her, we will first consider her condition when His gospel found her, that we may better appreciate the grace which wrought the change. Among all nations woman was degraded. Besides being bartered or sold as a thing of merchandise, there were barbarous laws and customs among the Phoenicians, Armenians, Carthaginians, Medes and Persians, and all too revolting and indecent to be mentioned. Greece, whose land abounded in scholars, heroes, and sages where the sun of intellect illumined the world, looked upon her as an object "without a soul." Gibbon says; "the Romans married without love, or loved without delicacy or respect."

In China, Japan and Africa the condition is the same except where christianity has emancipated her. And wherever the religion of the true Messiah has spread its snowy white pinions and lighted up the deep dark recesses of man's heart, woman has been loved adored respected. I will not affirm that all virtue and joy were unknown: There are some fertile spots in the most arid deserts; there is light in the darkest places amid all this wickedness and infidelity. God has preserved the spark of faith, purity, and love. Though we live in the Nineteenth century, and have it in its beauty and strength, our own beloved America is not free from the curse. Modern Athens is not totally unlike ancient Athens.

The leaven of infidelity is infesting this land. Immoralities, indecencies and crimes as revolting as ever withered and blighted a nation are of usual occurrence. They fearlessly maintain their hold and flaunt their wicked banners in the face of the government which is either too corrupt to care, or to timid to oppose. Who is to wipe these iniquities from our land if it be not christian women? A reform in these things can not be effected by the ballot, by political station, or by mere supremacy of civil law.

It must come by woman's unswerving devotion to a pure and undefiled christianity, for to that alone, woman owes her influence, her power and all she is. To establish this truth we will recount history as its light comes to us from the pages of the Bible. Fortunately the records of the past present an array of heroic and saintly women whose virtues have made the world more tolerable, and chief among these are the wives, mothers and daughters of the Holy Scriptures.

In the formation of the world when the beasts of the field, the fowls of the air, the fish of the sea and the beautiful garden of Paradise were made for the happiness of man, and when man himself was made in the image of his Creator, God plucked Eve from the side of Adam "without childhood or growth" to be "a helpmeet for him." When Adam first looked upon her he was enraptured with the perfectness of her form, the splendor of her beauty, the purity of her countenance and in this excess of joy he exclaimed: "bone of my bone, flesh of my flesh, therefore shall a man leave his father and mother and shall cleave unto his wife." They knew naught but divine happiness. Their hearts were filled with pure love unsullied by sin, but alas! in a short time the scene was changed—Eve was tempted—partook of the forbidden fruit and gave to Adam and he did eat. In this fallen state they were driven from the garden, yet she proved still a helpmeet for her husband, sharing his sorrow as she had shared his joy. Many have been the reproaches uttered against her—few have been her defenders. Dr. Pendleton says: "Eve acting under a mistake and a delusion was by no means excusable, but Adam was far more inexcusable than she for he acted intelligently as well as voluntarily. He knew what he was doing." There is much to admire in the character of Sarah, wife of Abraham, her reverence for her husband; her devotion to her son; her faithfulness to duty; her willingness in its performance. She was beautiful, chaste, modest and industrious—all these she sacrificed for the good and welfare of those around her. It was in this family God preserved the seed of righteousness. Also we find Miriam cheering on the hosts of Israel with her timbrel in her hands as she uttered the songs of praise "Sing, sing ye to the Lord, for he has triumphed gloriously, the horse and his rider hath he thrown into the sea." God's thought and appreciation of woman's work appears when he appoints Deborah to be a warrior, judge and prophet. Her work was distinct from her husband's who, it seems took no part whatever in the work of God while Deborah was inspired by the Eternal expressly to do His will and to testify to her countrymen that He recognizes in His followers neither male nor female, heeding neither the "weakness" of one, nor the strength of the other, but strictly calling those who are perfect at heart and willing to do his bidding. She was a woman of much meekness and humility, but of great force of character. Her song of praise, when Israel overcame the enemy, has only been excelled by the Psalms of David: "and Israel had rest forty years." Mention might also be made of Huldah, wife of Shallum, who dwelt in Jerusalem in a college, to whom went Hilkiah, the priest, and Ahikam, and Achbor and Shapham and Asaiah to enquire concerning the words of the book that was found in the house of the Lord. It was a woman whom God had chosen as a medium between Him and His people who would faithfully report all that he desired. Huldah's dwelling in college shows that she was anxious to become familiar with the law—to better prepare herself for the work of Him Who had called her. Woman's faith and devotion are beautifully illustrated by the touching scene between Ruth and Naomi, when Naomi besought Ruth to return to the home of her birth, thinking that the pleasure of childhood days had endeared it to her, and when Ruth with that pathos of devotion, and fairness said: "Entreat me not to leave thee, or to return from following after thee: For whither thou goest, I will go; and where thou lodgest, I will lodge; thy people shall be my people and thy God my God; where thou diest I will die, and there will I be buried; the Lord do so to me and more too if aught but death part thee and me." We cannot forget the maternal tenderness of Hagar, the well kept promise of Hannah, the filial devotion of Jephthah's daughter, nor the queenly patriotism of Esther. But no woman bore such recognition as Mary the mother of Jesus, who was chosen to bear a prominent part in human regeneration. After the fall of our first parents, God promised that a virgin should bear a son who should be the Redeemer of the human race. The memory of this promise was preserved through all nations, and each was desirous of the honor. The story of the birth of Romulus and Remus coincides with the miraculous birth of Jesus Christ. Silvia became their mother by the God Mars, even as Christ was the son of the Holy Ghost. An effort was made to take the life of these boys by throwing the cradle which contained them into the river Arno, whence it was carried into the Tiber. The cradle was stranded at the foot of Palatine and the infants were carried by a she-wolf into her den where they were tenderly cared for. This escape is likened to the flight into Egypt, and while this story has become a myth, the birth of Christ becomes more and more a reality. There are others who claim this mysterious birth. The most revered goddess of the Chinese sprung from the contact of a flower. Buddha was claimed to have been borne by a virgin named Maha-Mahai, but none realized the power of the words spoken by the angel, *"Hail full of grace, the Lord is with thee! Blessed are thou among women*, save Mary." History and tradition tell us she excelled all her young companions in her intelligence and skill. Denis, the Areopagite says: "She was a dazzling beauty." St. Epiphanius, writing in the fourth century, from traditions and manuscripts says: "In stature she was above the medium, her hair was blonde; her face oval; her eyes bright and slightly olive in color; her eyebrows perfectly arched, her nose equaline and of irreproachable perfection and her lips were ruby red. The ardent sun of her country had slightly bronzed her complexion; her hands were long, her fingers were slender" as a virgin she honored one of the most beautiful virtues of woman; as a mother she nourished a Redeemer. She gave the world an example of non-excelled maternal devotion; of the most magnificent grief which history affords. The life of Christ furnishes many examples of woman's work, love and devotion. They took part in the Savior's work, followed Him on His journeys, believed on Him and loved Him. They were "last at the cross and first at the grave." Christ did certainly atone for the sins of man, but His mission to woman was a great deal more; for He has not only saved her soul, but actually brought out and cultivated her intellect for the good of His cause. He was her friend, her counselor and her Savior. She bathed His feet with her tears and wiped them with the hairs of her head. He found comfort in the home of Mary and Martha when burdened, or tired from a day's journey. At the well of Samaria He converses with a woman which was unlawful for a man of respect to do, but He not only talked with her but permitted her to do good for mankind and the advancement of His cause. Filled with enthusiasm she leaves her water pot and hastens to proclaim her loyalty to One Who had won her heart and spoken to her of "living water." She testified that she had seen the true Messiah and invites others to see Him for themselves. To Mary Magdalene was the commission given to bear the joyful intelligence that Jesus had risen. It was the women more than men whose faith ventured to show Jesus those personal kindnesses which our Lord ever appreciated. In the lives and acts of the Apostles women are discovered praying, prophesying and spreading the gospel. Prominent for good works and alms deeds which she did was Dorcas. Like the Savior she went about doing good, but in the midst of this usefulness she died and so great was the grief of the widows unto whom she had ministered that the Lord again restored her to them. Paul placed much value on the work of Phebe and commends her to the churches as "our sister." Phebe was a deaconess of the church of Cenchrea and was, no doubt a great helper of Paul's "in the gospel." In the letter she carries to Rome, mention is made of quite a number of women who had been co-workers with the apostle. One of the first on the list was Priscilla, the wife of Aquilla who had with her husband laid down her neck for him. She possessed high qualities and did active work in the cause which she espoused. Lydia was the first European convert—after she received the word into her heart; at once opens her house and offers a home to the apostle who had been instrumental in her conversion. At Thessalonica we find "the chief women not a few" among the workers of the church. The church today wants more Priscillas, Phebes, Chloes, Elizabeths, Marys, Annas, Tryphenas, Tryphosas, Julias and Joannas to labor in the gospel, to give of their substance; to follow Jesus; to be willing to sacrifice their substance; to follow Jesus; to be willing to sacrifice their lives for the love they bear their Lord. It is not christianity which disparages the intellect of woman and scorns her ability for doing good, for its records are filled with her marvelous successes. Emancipate woman from the chains that now restrain her and who can estimate the part she will play in the work of denomination? In the Baptist denomination women have more freedom than in any other denomination on the face of the earth. I am not unmindful of the kindness you noble brethren have exhibited in not barring us from your platforms and deliberations. All honor I say to such men.

Every woman in the world ought to be a Baptist, for in this blessed denomination men are even freer than elsewhere. Free men cannot conscientiously shut the doors against those whom custom has limited in privileges and benefits. As the vitalizing principles of the Baptists expand and permeate the religious principles of the world women will become free. As the Bible is an iconoclastic weapon—it is bound to break down images of error that have been raised. As no one studies it so closely as the Baptists their women shall take the lead. History gives a host of women who have achieved and now enjoy distinction as writers, linguists, poets, physicians, lecturers, editors, teachers and missionaries. Visit the temples of the living God and there you will find them kneeling at His shrine as ready now as in centuries past, to attest their faith by their suffering and if need be by the sacrifice of life. As they by their numbers, who followed Christ up Calvary's rugged road, caused the cowardice of man to blush, so in the crowds of worshippers who do Him honor to-day put to shame the indifference and the coldness of man's allegiance to God. But to the limited subject,

What is Denominational Work?

I deem it to be the most honorable, the most exalted and the most enviable. It strengthens the link between the church militant and the church triumphant—between man and his Creator. All Woman who are truly christians are candidates in this broad field of labor. It calls for valiant hearted women who will enlist for life. None whose soul is not overflowing with love for Christ and whose chief aim is not to save souls need apply. Success need not necessarily depend on learning, genius, taste, style, elegant language, nor a rapid use of the tongue, but it is the earnestness of the soul, the simplicity of the Word accompanied by the Spirit of the living God. The Maker of all has wisely distributed these talents and whatever characterizes the individual He has commanded to "to occupy till I come" and to use well the talent entrusted to your care. It often happens that some humble woman bent on her staff full of fervor yet unlettered, does more by her upright living, her words of counsel, her ardent prayers "that go up to God as a sweet smelling savor" than many who pick their words and try to appear learned. This denominational work demands active labor in and for the churches. It does not demand that every woman shall be a Deborah, a Huldah, a Dorcas, or a Phebe—It simply asks that every woman be a woman—a christian woman who is willing to consecrate all for the cause of Christ. A story is told of a woman who when she was unable to express intelligently and satisfactorily what the Lord had done for her and when the anxious crowd was about to turn away disappointed she exclaimed: "I cannot talk for Him, but I can die for Him." "Whosoever will lose his life for my sake, the same shall save it." To serve the church we must die daily to selfishness, pride, vanity, a lying tongue, a deceitful heart and walk worthy of the calling in Christ Jesus. We are to pray without ceasing—to be fervent in season and out of season—"to present our bodies a living sacrifice, holy and acceptable before God which is our reasonable service." We are to speak as the spirit shall give utterance, that He may work in us to will and to do His good pleasure. I know Paul said "Let the woman keep silence in the churches" but because he addressed this to a few Grecian and Asiatic woman who were wholly given up to idolatry and the fashion of the day is no reason why it should be quoted to the pious women of the present. A woman may suffer martyrdom, she may lift her voice in song, she may sacrifice modesty to collect money from the church, for her work in this particular is considered essential and it matters not how prominent a place she occupies in fairs, festivals, sociables, tea parties, concerts and tableaux, but to take part in the business meeting of the church is wholly out of place because Paul said so. We are apt to quote Paul and shut our eyes and ears to the recognition and privilege Christ, his Master, gave us, and not only did the Apostle appreciate the labors of women, and show towards them the greatest care and tenderest affection, but we find him in some places greatly dependent upon them, for co-operation in the foundation of the churches. But a change is coming; it has already commenced, and God is shaking up the church—He is going to bring it up to something better and that, too, greatly through the work of the women. Already the harvest is great. Can ye not discern the signs of the time? Do you not see how wickedness and crime are flooding our country—how tares are growing up in the midst of the wheat? See the foothold the Catholics are getting in our christian land. They are taking our children putting clothes on their backs, food in their mouths and educating them that they must swell their number and represent their claim. See how nations, every where, are opening to the reception of the gospel. Listen to the cry of Africa's heathen sons—note the rush of other denominations to offer their faith, their belief, to satisfy the hunger of their souls and quench the thirst of their spirits. Can ye not discern the signs? It is quite time christian soldiers were taking the field for Christ. The doctrines of our denomination must be so thoroughly diffused that a man though he be a fool need not err. A good pastor should have a good wife. He should find in her rest from care; comfort when distressed; his depressed spirits must be lifted by her consoling words; she must be his wisdom; his courage; his strength; his hope; his endurance. She is to beautify his home and make it a place of peace and cheerfulness—she is to be an example worthy of pattern for the neighborhood in which she lives—she is to take the lead in all worthy causes. Women are to look after the spiritual interest of the church as well as the men. Let them be punctual at services and make the prayer meeting interesting. Woman's power of song, her heartfelt prayer, her ability to go into the highways and hedges and compel singers to come in, have marked her as proficient in revivals. A praying mother exerts more influence over the minds of the youth than all else. The recollections of such seasons when the tender plants were garnered in can never be effaced. The voice of that sainted mother still lingers upon them, and memory can never relinquish the priceless treasure she holds. Some of our best men owe their conversion and all that they are to the influence of a sainted mother, a devoted sister or some dear female friend. For money raising woman has no equals.

Our churches are largely supported by her financial efforts, but she should discountenance many of the plans to which she and her daughters are subjected—they are gates of vice that lead to destruction—this begging money from any and every body only invites and encourages insults and it must be stopped. Our churches must have some system in money raising and thereby save the girls. Many a girl with good intent got her start downward by this very act of soliciting money. A woman's place is to assist the pastor, work in the Sabbath school, visit the sick, to care for the sick and lift up the fallen. She has a conspicuous place in

The Newspaper Work of the Denomination

which is a powerful weapon for breaking down vice, establishing virtue, spreading the gospel and disseminating a general knowledge of the work of the denomination. Here she can command the attention of thousands. She can thunder from the editor's chair and make the people hear. It has a wider circulation and as has been said "penetrates the most remote corners of the country." In this field we need strong intellectual women. We need women of courage, who dare defend the faith and make the truth felt. As an editor a woman can better reach the mothers, daughters and sisters. Let her be a regular correspondent. Let the articles be strong and vigorous, let them show thought, learning and an earnestness for the cause represented. If she cannot be a regular correspondent she should write occasionally such articles as will give the people something to think and talk about. She should make them so plain and attractive that children will read them with eagerness and let some be especially to them; make them feel that some one else is interested in them besides mother and father and endeavor to impress them with upright living. Assist the editor in getting subscribers and see that a Baptist paper is in every home. See that the Baptist family reads your denominational paper.

The field of juvenile literature is open. I said recently before the National Press Convention, held in Louisville Ky. there are now published 24 secular papers and magazines in the United States for the children with a circulation of 775,934. The largest of which is the "Youth's Companion" with a circulation of 385,251. Of the religious journals there are 47 with 678,346 circulation. Sunday School Journal (Methodist) claim 81,090: "The Sunday School Times" 77,500 and "Our Young People" 47,000. Of this number, 71 secular and religious papers, there is not one so far as I know, edited especially for colored children. There is a little paper whose name does not appear on the list that is written for the colored youth, being edited and controlled by Miss J. P. Moore of Louisiana. It is known as "Hope" and though of humble pretentions, in its silent way it is sowing seed from which shall spring an abundant harvest.

The educational work of the denomination belongs principally to woman. Three centuries ago women were almost universally uneducated and a half century ago found American women shut out from all places of learning. Ignorance seemed a bliss while wisdom a foolish idea. A young girl in Italy and a young widow in France almost simultaneously conceived the idea of educating young girls. It was the beginning of an institution that was destined to reform the world and this they comprehended, for they said "This regeneration of this corrupt world must be accomplished by children, for children will reform the families, families will reform the provinces and the provinces will reform the world." Mademoiselle de Sainte-Beuve, foundress of the "Ursilines" of France, purchased a house at the Faubourg St. Jacques where she had two hundred pupils. It was her delight to watch them in their sport and as she looked upon them with maternal gaze she charmingly said "They sprung not from her loins, but from her heart." At her death her portrait represented her before a window, her eyes fixed with intent devotion upon a garden full of beehives, with the legend "Mother of Bees." Mary Lyons, in our own century, opened the way, and established Mount Holly Seminary, the first institution established for girls. This is what woman has done, and may not our women do ever more for the denomination with the surrounding advantages? May they not found more "Spelman" and "Hartshorn" seminaries, more "Vassars?" The women have been promoted from mere kitchen drudgery, household duties, and gossiping from house to house—they can teach not as subordinates merely, but as principals, as professors. Woman has not only the art of inspiring the affections in her pupils, but also in keeping them interested in the tasks to be performed. I think the duty of our women is to impressibly teach the Scriptures and the doctrines of our denomination to the young under their care. I think we talk and preach baptism, "The Lord's Supper," and the "Final Perseverance of the Saints," too little. Not one-half of the members of our churches can give a doctrinal reason why they are Baptists. We are too fearful of feelings, when we have the Bible that makes the Baptist churches on our side. They should instill in the child's mind love toward God, his Creator, his Benefactor, his Saviour, and respect for all mankind.

As an author, woman has shown rare talents. The profession of mind affords the strongest evidence that God created her for society. As the fragrance which is in the bud will, when the bud expands, escape from its confinement and diffuse itself through the surrounding atmosphere, so if forms of beauty and sublimity are in the mind, they will exhibit themselves, and operate on other minds. The genius of woman was long hidden. Greece had a Sappho and a Carina; Israel had a Miriam. Antiquity turned a deaf ear to the cultivation of woman's talent. The home of Cicero and Virgil neglected her intellect, but the revolution of ages and the progress of the present century have wrought a new change of affairs, and now woman has the pen, and participates in the discussion of the times. It was when Christianity and infidelity were wrestling in Europe, that Hannah More came from retirement to take part in the contest. It was when slavery was at its highest, that Phillis Wheatly, Francis Ellen Harper, and Harriet Beecher Stowe, gave vent to their fullness of their souls in beautiful lines of poetry and prose. The human voice is fast receding, the written voice predominates. Since this is true, let the women see that the best and purest literature comes from them. Let them feel that they are called upon to consecrate all to truth and piety. Lecturers address the people through the sense of hearing; writing through the sense of sight. Many persons will pay goodly sums to hear a good talk on some subject, rather than spend the time investigating books. As public lecturers women have been successful, and have secured good audiences. Rev. Mr. Higginson says: "Among the Spanish Arabs women were public lecturers and secretaries of kings, while Christian Europe was sunk in darkness. In Italy, from the fifteenth to the nineteenth century, it was not esteemed unfeminine for women to give lectures in public to crowded and admiring audiences. They were freely admitted members of learned societies, and were consulted by men of prominent scientific attainments as their equals in scholarship."

All good causes owe their success to the push of woman. The temperance cause had its origin in her, and to-day finds noble advocates in the persons of Frances E. Harper and Frances E. Willard. Indeed, the place of woman is broad, and of the vocations of life none are so grand, so inspiring, as that of being a missionary. Long before the organization of any general missionary society of our denomination in this country, Christian women were actively engaged in prosecuting the work of home missions. Little bands of women organized in the churches to help the pastors in the poor churches, by sending clothing and other supplies needed. When the Foreign Mission Enterprise was begun, it found in these women ready and powerful allies—they sent up contributions annually for both Home and Foreign work. The first missionary society ever organized in the country was by the women in 1800. It was composed of fourteen women. From this many branches sprang. The women of to-day are realizing that in the homes among the degraded there is a great work to be done. It belongs to woman's tender nature, sympathy, and love, to uplift the fallen. A home can not be raised above the mother, nor the race above the type of womanhood, and no women are more ready to respond to the call than the women of the Baptist Church. They feel the necessity of meeting the responsibility with organized forces in the field. Many have been effected, and great has been the result.

This work is not exclusively confined to the churches, but to orphans, asylums, hospitals, prisons, alms-houses, on the street, in the home, up the alley, and in all places where human souls are found, have woman, with her love for Christ and fallen humanity, found her way, amid the jeers and scorn of those who were too foolish to care for any other save self and household.

Woman sways a mighty influence. It began with Eve in the Garden of Eden, and is felt even now. It has not been exaggerated nor exhausted. She exalts man to the skies, or casts him beneath the brutes. She makes him strong or she makes him weak. Under her influence nations rise or fall. In the dark days of Rome, when woman received her most cruel treatment from the hand of her lord, Cato said: "Even then the Romans governed the world, but the women governed the Romans."

Bad women sometimes have great power with men. It was Phryne who inspired the chisel of Praxiteles. Cotytto had her altars at Athens and Corinth under the title of "Popular Venus." Aspasia decided peace or war, directing the counsel of Pericles. Demosthenes, the great orator, cast himself at the feet of Lais, and history gives scores of instances where women governed the passions of men for good or evil. It was Delilah who, by her words, persuaded Sampson to tell wherein his strength lay, and which Milton has so beautifully portrayed in these words:

> "Of what I suffer, she was not the prime cause, but I myself,
> Who vanquished with a peal of words (Oh, weakness)!
> Gave up my forte of silence to a woman."

It came to pass when Solomon was old, that his wives turned away his heart after other gods, and his heart was not perfect with the Lord his God, as was the heart of his father, David. There was none like unto Ahab, who did sell himself to work wickedness in the sight of God, whom Jezebel, his wife, stirred up. There are good women like Volumna, the mother of Coriolanus, who saved Rome by her influence over her son. The women of this country inspired the fathers and sons on to battle, and in all the affairs of life woman has encouraged or discouraged men; he is moved by her faintest smile, her lightest whisper. The Duke of Halifax says: "She has more strength in her looks than we have in our laws, and more power by hers than we have in our arguments." Though woman is a mixture of good and evil, be it said to her credit, that history has never recorded a single instance where she denied her Saviour. Her influence is entwined with every religion, and diffuses itself through every circle where there is mind to act upon. It gives tone to religion and morals and forms the character of man. Every woman is the center around which others move. She may send forth healthy, purifying streams, which will enlighten the heart and nourish the seeds of virtue; or cast a dim shadow, which will enshroud those upon whom it falls in moral darkness. Woman should consecrate her beauty, her wit, her learning, and her all, to the cause of Christ. She should put aside selfishness, for a selfish person is not only hideous, but fiendish, and destructive. She should not rest at ease, heedless of the perishing souls who need her prayers, her songs of praise, her words of counsel, her interpretations of the Scriptures for their salvation. Many a conversion has been attributed to some soul-stirring song; indeed, there is no music so penetrating, so effective as that produced by the human voice.

Much good has been accomplished by a well written tract commending some word of God, which has certainly not returned unto Him void, but has prospered in the thing whereunto God sent it. Often a short article, setting forth some digestible truth, is like seed sown in good ground, which will bring forth a hundred fold, or like bread cast upon the water, that may be seen and gathered after many days hence.

Perhaps the most important place of woman in the denomination is to teach the children at home, and wherever she can reach them, to love God, to reverence His holy name, and to love the Baptist Church. The moral training of the youth is the highest kind, and it is of vast importance that the first opportunity be seized for installing into the minds of children the sentiment of morality and religion, and the principles of the Baptist doctrine. The future of the denomination depends on the rising generation, and too much care can not be taken in the development of their characters. It requires constant, anxious watching to realize the embryo. Though the seed be long buried in dust, it shall not deceive your hopes—"the precious gain shall never be lost, for grace insures the crop."

The only foundation for all Christian graces is humility. Practice, as far as possible, Christ's meekness, his benevolence, his forgiveness of injuries, and his zeal for doing good. Woman is the hope of the Church, the hope of the world. God is slowly but surely working out the great problem of woman's place and position in life. Virtue will never reign supreme, and vice will never be wiped from the land, until woman's work of head, heart, and hand is recognized and accepted. No great institution has flourished without her support, neither has man succeeded without her, but the two must be unified. The work is not confined within the narrow limits of the church walls, not to the prayers sent forth or the songs sung. It extends far beyond this. Her work is in every cause, place, and institution where Christianity is required. The platform is broad, and upon it she must stand. Although the responsibilities to be met are great, the position is to be maintained. China, with her degraded million, India, with her ignorance and idolatry, dark and benighted Africa, yea, the world, with its sin and wickedness, all have just and imperative claims on woman, such as she can and must meet.

Dear women, the cry comes to us from afar to bring the light of love, and to lead into the paths of peace and righteousness. From your ranks, as mother, wife, daughter, sister, friend, little as you have hitherto thought of it, are to come the women of all professions, from the humble Christian to the expounder of His word; from the obedient citizen to the ruler of the land. This may be objectionable to many, but no profession should be recognized that fails to recognize Christ, and all the Christians have a legal right where He is, for "with Him there is neither Jew nor Greek, there is neither bond nor free, there is neither male nor female, for ye are all one in Christ Jesus." There is no necessity for a woman to step over the bounds of propriety, or to lay aside modesty, to further the work, and she will not, if God be her guide. If, indeed, the King of all the Universe chooses a woman to kill a man who had opposed Israel for twenty years, it is all right, and who dare question God's right, if he raise up a woman who shall become a judge, and a leader of his people? God, at one time, used a dumb brute to do His service, and that alone is sufficient to convince any one that He can use whom He will, and glorify himself by whatever means he pleases to employ. Should woman be silent in this busy, restless world of missions and vast church enterprises? No! A long, loud No! Give place for her, brethren. Be ready to accept her praying heart, her nimble fingers, her willing hands, her swift feet, her quick eye, her charming voice, the superintendent's chair, the Sunday School teacher's place, the Bible student, the prayer circle, the sick bed, the house of mourning, the foreign mission field, all these are her place.

Dear brethren, point them out, direct my sisters, and help them to work for Christ. My dear sisters, wherever you are, and wherever this paper may be mentioned, remember that there is no department of your life that you can not bend your influence to the benefit of our blessed denomination. Let us take sharpness out of our tongues and put in our pens; take the beauty from our face and put it into our lives; let us love ourselves less and God more; work less for self-aggrandizement, and more for the Church of Christ.

"Do not then stand idly waiting,
    For some greater work to do,
Fortune is a lazy goddess—
    She will never come to you.

"Go, and toil in any vineyard,
    Do not fear to do and dare;
If you want a field of labor,
    You can find it anywhere."

EDUCATION AND
SOCIAL REFORM

44

JULIA CALDWELL-FRAZIER

(1863–1929)

The name of Julia Caldwell-Frazier is well known to the campus of Howard University—Frazier Hall, the first residence hall for women at Howard, was named for her, one of the first women to receive an AB in literature from Howard, in 1887. Julia Caldwell was born in Alabama, raised in Columbus, Georgia, and taught for a brief period before enrolling at Howard. After graduation, she taught at Morris Brown College in Atlanta, Georgia. She moved to Dallas, Texas, in 1892 and founded the Ladies Reading Circle. In 1908, she married fellow schoolteacher W. W. Frazier. Throughout her life, she continued her education, earning certificates in English, Latin, and German, as well as in pedagogy and psychology.

In the following piece, "The Decisions of Time," published in the *A.M.E. Church Review* (April 1889), Frazier argues that social progress, particularly for women and American blacks, is inevitable given the relationship between time and human achievement. She situates the struggle amidst the contentious moments along the way toward enlightenment and Christianity, encompassing human history since Ancient Greece, to argue that American society will, with time, become more inclusive and just. The scale and intellectual strength of this grand scheme is remarkable.

"The Decisions of Time" (1889)

SOURCE: Julia L. Cadd Caldwell, "The Decisions of Time,"
A.M.E. Church Review (April 1889).

THERE is an old adage which says: "Time cures all ills." This means that truth always triumphs ultimately over error; that

> "Truth is mighty, truth is sure,
> Truth is strong and must endure,"

and that at last it vindicates and establishes character.

The history of the world is the record of alternate triumphs and depressions. Greece and Rome furnish examples of such vicissitudes. Men make use of the Past's decisions as preventives of evil in approaching times. We know too well what was the condition of affairs in Rome and Greece when, by the priesthood, black and dreary despotism covered the land; when the rulers in religion and politics grew more corrupt and dark-eyed. Oppression preyed on every subject. Notwithstanding all the conservative power of the past, the progressive force of on-coming time has prevailed, and the papal throne is now tottering in its decrepitude. It may be asked, what are the general agencies preventing at once the establishment of truth and right? We answer, Ignorance, Prejudice, Despotism, Priestcraft and Socialism involving caste. In the course of time, ignorance will be blotted out; the black garb of prejudice, despotism and socialism will be laid aside, and Benevolence, looking upon every man as one of a vast brotherhood, shall open wide the doors of her spacious halls and invite all to freedom's feast.

We notice first the decisions of time politically. We remember that the first form of government was the patriarchal, of which so beautiful a picture is given in the Holy Scriptures; we find it developed as the tribe, but as time went on this evolved into the clan, a larger body. Feudalism came a step higher; this in turn, developed into the monarchy; and, lastly, we have the *republic*—the form of government upon which time has set its approving seal. During these different changes and stages many good and illustrious men suffered.

Greece had her Pericles, and during his age she acknowledged no rival and feared none. Regardless of the motives of honor and fame, the remembrance of the great actions of their ancestors, the grateful titles of the sovereigns of Greece—which motives Pericles employed to animate the Athenians, and by which they had always been successful—they had such inimical feelings toward him, that his mere sight and presence became insupportable to them. They deprived him of his high office and sentenced him to pay a heavy fine. However, this public disgrace of Pericles was not to be lasting. The anger of the people was appeased by this first effort, and had spent itself in this injurious treatment of him, as the bee leaves its sting in the wound; and we see his death-bed surrounded by his friends and admirers, who recited the many illustrious exploits of his glorious life. Pericles has passed away, and Greece has been sitting in sackcloth for ages, gazing at the scattered fragments of her former glory.

However, with these several changes of government, knowledge increased, men took different views of matters and profited by past experiences.

What have been the decisions of time intellectually? Literature, the arts and sciences were, of necessity, crude and imperfect in their infancy. Time molded and refined them. But the pathway of their perfection was not smooth and pleasant. There was a period when philosophy was ignored; when the temple of Nature was denounced as no less Godless than the shrines of Greece; and to look from Nature up to Nature's God was regarded as impious idolatry. The greatest scientific reformers the world ever produced were, in their day, stigmatized as "idle dreamers," "seditious persons," and many suffered death for promulgating their new ideas.

Socrates, the wisest of mankind, the first to conceive the thought of bringing down philosophy from heaven, was accused by the Athenians of holding bad opinions concerning the gods, and of corrupting their youth, because he endeavored to unmask the vices and discredit the false eloquence of the sophists. He

experienced the most malignant envy, the most envenomed hatred, and was condemned to drink the fatal hemlock. The people
of Athens did not see their mistake until after his death. *Time*
having given them opportunity for reflection, the injustice of the
notorious sentence appeared in all its horrors. Then they punished his accusers, and erected a brazen statue to him.

Aristotle, the prince of philosophy, was accused and ostracized by the Athenians, and yet no philosopher has exerted so
large an influence through so many centuries and on the ideas
of so many nations as this illustrious Stagyrite.

What disgraceful treatment the venerable philosopher Galileo received for teaching a new and sublime theory of nature
and astronomy, a theory that finally proved true.

What obstacles and failures Prof. Morse encountered when
he completed his rough model of the recording electro-magnetic
telegraph; but see of what inestimable value his invention has
been to mankind! Was not public opinion opposed to the telephone?—styled it "a useless thing." But within a decade the
telephone has become the most patronized means of urban intercommunication. Through all the innumerable obstacles and
oppositions, we see, by the decisions of time, science tracing
the wild comet in its vast eccentric course through the heavens;
we see science bringing down the very lightning from the
clouds, making it a remedial agent and a messenger, quick as
light, to carry our thoughts. What denunciations have been
made against the principles of evolution—not as yet fully
established—still science is more and more tending that way,
and Darwin's views have been adopted by some of the most scientific men, such as Huxley, Spencer and Gray.

Milton's works were not well received at first, while some
other authors were welcomed with world-wide applause. The
latter have sunk into oblivion, and Milton's writings have become an indestructible monument of his fame—a sublime
structure well proportioned in all its parts.

Society has been greatly changed by the decisions of time.
There was a period when the ideas of superiority and aristocracy
prevailed, and the chosen few monopolized all the advantages of
life. During that age darkness grew more dense, the star of science had set, and the night was waxing blacker and blacker. But

the star of Reformation arose, and light began to spread. Science and Freedom awoke from their sleep of ages, and, like twin sisters, unitedly advanced, dispelling the gloom and bringing "peace out of confusion." Turn to hoary and imbecile India and view its iron-walled castes, offering liberty to one class and slavery to the rest. Once we could discern nothing of that brotherhood of man, but gradually the walls are being battered down. In France and England, the broad lines of demarkation, which anciently separated one class of men and one profession from another, have been erased or filled up by an increasing refinement and extension of personal liberty.

America, the so-called "land of the free and home of the brave," has had its share of caste and race prejudice; but the ethnic principle is being overcome, and as time moves on there will be no distinction either in regard "to race, color or previous condition of servitude," but there will be a grand intermingling and absorption of races as in the case of the Normans and Saxons.

What have been the decisions of time for Christianity? The patriarchal, the Jewish and the Christian dispensations have been but the unfolding of one general plan. In the first we see the folded bud, in the second the expanded leaf, and in the third the blossom and the fruit. But Christianity has not always been without opposition; the religious elements have been perverted and abused. The Crusades and the Inquisition are historical monuments of the infatuation of the human heart, operated upon by ignorance and false zeal for the service and glory of God. Christianity slowly made its way among the lowly and the unpretending; soon the number of followers increased and extended from the lower to the higher walks in life. Then heathenism took alarm, and the priests feared for their livelihood. Bitter hatred arose, and biting persecutions visited those Christians who could not and would not renounce their glorious faith. The secular arm was outstretched, not to *save*, but to *strike*, and numerous, worthy and devoted, were its victims. Everywhere combined powers of Church and State resisted a pure Christianity.

Persecution kindled its fires, brought forth its wild beasts. Blood flowed like water; and the blood of such martyrs as Polycarp, Justin, Latimer and Ridley became the seed of the

Church. Notwithstanding all its oppositions, Christianity has banished idolatry and ended the bloody gladiatorial contests; has crushed that infamous institution, slavery; raised the general standard of morality, and introduced the great principle of benevolence.

What have been the decisions of time for woman? Anciently, she was looked upon as an inferior being, as either man's slave or plaything. She had little part in the world's history. But since the memorable age of chivalry and spread of Christianity her position has been defined, and she has been raised to her true level. We see women graduating from many of our colleges; they are in all the professions, are journalists, authors in poetry, romance, philosophy and general literature. They as reformers are at the head of great moral movements.

What is the prevailing sentiment concerning the Women's Congress which convened in Washington last spring? Did they not show that they were keeping pace with the times?

If women have made such progress in the last fifty years, what will be the decisions of time for the next half century? If such decisions have been made for particular classes, what may we expect for the entire human race? What may we not expect for that race which, in this land, has been so long held down by ignorance, prejudice and the iron heel of caste? From its late history the Negro race has made most rapid progress in education, wealth and culture; it has done much to elevate itself, and, considering the short period of its enfranchisement, it has made more marked progress than any other race on the globe. Since wealth and knowledge have done so much for other races, who can tell but that if wealth and intelligence shall prevail with this race, the Negro will be the equal of any, socially and politically, and sovereigns with them all. It is a conceded fact that race prejudice is bound to give way before the potent influences of character, education and wealth; and these are the necessary conditions for the growth of a people. Without wealth there can be no leisure; without leisure there can be no thought; and without thought there can be no progress.

According to the "survival of the fittest," the Negro can look cheerfully and hopefully to the future. Is he not endowed with those salient qualities of manhood that must insure success in the end? The physical, mental, moral and esthetic faculties of the race have been "weighed in the balance and not found wanting." We are rising upon the inflooding wave which has been steadily advancing, and we know that as "there is a tide in the affairs of men which, taken at the flood, leads on to fortune," so there is in the affairs of races and nations.

Shall the Negro race be content with its present attainments? Shall it only gaze with complacency upon the silver dawn of its success? Nay, rather let it be the rising sun, and with undaunted courage and happy hope await the glorious coming of the golden noon. When we take a retrospective view of the decisions of time—when we see the papal power tottering in its decrepitude; see the floods of despotism abating; see the mob of ignorance and superstition quelled; see the progress of government; see the sun of literature and science moving from east to west around the globe; see the hydra-headed monsters, caste and race prejudice, cut down and Christianity reigning supremely, we can only echo Priestley's words: "What has been achieved tells us that the greater lies before us." According to the signs of the times, the day is not far distant when the men of all races will be educated where they will be mutually engaged in the search of truth, and will avail themselves of every means of advancement. Together will they follow the intricacies of science and explore its *arcana* and philosophy. They will roam through the elysian fields of literature, search out its richest treasures, pluck its fairest flowers, gather its brightest gems, and in the realms of classic art they will fill the mind with images of beauty and the soul with lofty conceptions. There will be no antagonisms of views—all shall see eye to eye. There will be no distinction of wealth and none of station. True manhood will be recognized and respected, whether it be presented by a Negro or an Anglo-Saxon; and the idea of Burns will prevail, that "rank is but the guinea's stamp," and that "a man is a man for a' that and a' that."

Then, and not until then, will the universal brotherhood of men be fully realized.

45

FANNIE M. JACKSON COPPIN

(1837–1913)

The heroic educator for whom Coppin State University in Baltimore is named was born a slave in Washington, D.C., and orphaned at a young age. Fannie M. Jackson's freedom was purchased by an aunt who ensured young Fannie would be well educated. Coppin attended Oberlin College, where she excelled in the men's course of study and established a night school to teach freed slaves. Coppin subsequently taught at the Institute for Colored Youth in Philadelphia, where she became principal and the first African American woman to rise to the position. Of commanding stature and dignified bearing, Coppin founded homes for impoverished women, wrote columns in Philadelphia newspapers promoting education and equal rights, and became an active missionary. In 1881, she married Levi Jackson Coppin, a Reverend in the A.M.E. Church. After her death in 1913, Fanny Jackson Coppin Normal School (Now Coppin State University) was built in her honor.

The excerpts here speak to Jackson Coppin's political range and optimism. She dances between registers in her writing, touching on the spirituality of her audience while, at the same time, reminding them of the remaining social and economic legacies of slavery. "A Plea for Industrial Opportunity" focuses on practical matters, encouraging blacks, in down-to-earth language that stands out from most other pieces in this anthology, to seek economic prosperity.

"Commencement Address" (1876)

SOURCE: Fannie M. Jackson Coppin, "A Race's Progress. Its
Twenty-Second Annual Commencement—A Rare Event—
Addresses by the Graduates—Essays on the Best Order—
Miss Fanny M. Jackson, The Principal, to the Scholars—A
Noble Effort," *Christian Recorder* 29 (June 1876).

A Race's Progress.

Its Twenty-Second Annual Commencement— A Rare Event—Addresses by the Graduates—Essays on the Best Order Miss—Fanny M. Jackson, the Principal, to the Scholars—A Noble Effort.

Yesterday afternoon the twenty-second annual commencement
of this renowned institution took place at Horticultural Hall
before the managers, the graduates, and scholars, and in the
presence of an immense audience, among whom were a large
number of the representative Friends, including the venerable Lucretia Mott. This great establishment, maintained by the
generosity of the Society of Friends, and founded long before
slavery was abolished, has grown into larger proportions under
the splendid management of the executive, officer, or principal,
Miss Fanny M. Jackson. There were fourteen graduates, each of
whom spoke or read a treatise; but the crowded state of our columns will not allow us to refer to each in detail. All of them
were excellent, and several of them extraordinary, especially
that of Miss Florence A. Lewis, who spoke the salutatory in
Latin with the ease and correctness of a practiced linguist and
orator; also "Trades and Professions," by Morris H. Layton,
full of philosophy. The "Augustan Age of English Literature,"
by Miss Bassett, was an essay of exquisite skill and deep study.
The address on "The Study of the Natural Sciences," by Thomas
H. Murray a young black man with all the marked characteristics of his race, was a production so natural, nervous, and

original as to stamp it all his own; and crowned as it was by his valedictory, including short speeches to his teacher, school-mates, classmates and managers, proved Mr. Murray to be sure of a brilliant future. But the gem of the evening was the beautiful closing counsel of Miss Jackson to her graduates, which we print entire. It was spoken without notes, and with a dignity, pathos, and tact that went to every heart in the vast audience. It is a pattern of womanly eloquence and culture:

This occasion furnishes an apt illustration of the rapidity with which time passes, than which a more impressive lesson could not be given you, nor one more worthy your attention at the outset of your career. Four years ago how far off this day appeared, but it seems now a few months since you entered school. And so it will be with the years of your life; see to it that you faithfully improve and wisely use them. It remains to be seen how much of the instruction you have received has been digested, assimilated, and has become your own. Some persons study because it is respectable to do so, and some that they may obtain a smattering of learning and huckster it for their daily bread. Such persons cannot be expected to continue their studies when they are no longer under the restraint of a task-master. But I am unwilling to believe that you have studied for either of these reasons. The infinite capabilities of a liberal education to ennoble your lives and to serve you in our highest needs you will only upon the condition that you warmly and devotedly continue your pursuit of learning. Many of you intend to be teachers. The profession of which Dr. Arnold was a member cannot be altogether without honor; but it also carried with it the grave responsibilities which you cannot escape.

Without speaking of matters in touching upon which we may justly congratulate ourselves, I will speak of certain problems which appear difficult of solution; of certain respects in which the education which we aim to give appears to fall short of its high purpose. We aim to discipline, develop, and strengthen the powers of the mind; but we too often fail to produce persons of judgment, thought, and mental power. We aim, by refining and cultivating the taste, to put our student in high fellowship with what is pure, and beautiful, and true, and to shut off just so many avenues of mere animal enjoyment; but we do not end by making the conversation, the manners, and the intercourse of the lower levels sharply offensive to them.

We aim to inflame them with some high purpose in living to show them the possibilities of [ ] life. But many of them live aimlessly and drift downward. The [ ] of these cases is irresistible—either because we failed to understand their disposition and mental resources, or because when they came to us to be instructed the ground was already occupied, we failed to educate them. There is a wise indirectness in teaching, particularly ethic and aesthetic studies, which is of more value than years of direct teaching from books; such as bringing your pupils within the range of elevating and refining it [ ] and in contact with persons of superior mind and character.

Many of you will probably teach in obscure towns and villages, where you will be surrounded by persons who make no pretense to "book-learning." You will not, I feel assured, on this account overrate your own ability or acquirements; you will preserve a teachable spirit, and defer to the opinions of worthy persons older than yourselves, whose knowledge, gained from observation and experience and ripened by age, will excellently supplement what you have learned from books. Goethe has said that no man is so commonplace that something may not be learned from him, and I would add that no one is so unlettered but that he may teach the learned something. And now I cannot be indifferent to the fact that you are being graduated at an important period in the history of this country. Said Mr. Phillips a few days ago in Boston: "Once, a hundred years ago, our fathers announced this sublime and, as it seemed then, the audacious, declaration—that God intended all men to be free and equal; all men, without restriction, without qualification, without limit. A hundred years have rolled away almost since that great announcement, and today, with a territory that makes ocean kiss ocean, with forty millions of people, with two wars behind her, with the sublime achievement of having grappled the great faith that threatened its central life, and put every fetter under its foot, the great Republic launches into the second century of its existence. Between this event and your graduation there is now merely a similarity of dates; it is possible for you to make it an auspicious coincidence. The founders of this Government, the heroes of the past, and the historic Republic of the Old World seem to stand about us as solemn spectators of this Centennial Celebration and by their eloquent and imperishable memories they charge this generation to see to it that in the second century of her existence the Republic shall receive no detriment. Her future is not menaced by millions of savage and revengeful foes, nor by famine, nor by isolation. Her own splendid prosperity is more carefully to be guarded against than the invasion of hostile armies or the thunders of foreign fleets.

Rich and powerful, she becomes a tempting prey to dishonest and unprincipled men. Her bulwark of protection for the future must be intelligent, down rightly honest, and high minded men and women. There is no absurdity in saying that the little rill of influence issuing from this Institution, broadening and deepening in the years to come may play a part not altogether without honor or importance in the future history of this country. The sources of beneficient and majestic rivers may be traced to very insignificant beginnings in obscure places. Dare to stand by your own convictions of what is right, dare to champion a weak and despised cause if you believe it to be a worthy one, and remember that: "Nullum theatrum virtuti conscientia majus est." May your lives be made luminous by daily acts of self denial and of high endeavor in worthy causes. Your only reliance is upon Divine Wisdom and the Grace of God. Our tender interest and our benedictions shall follow you wherever you go. Farewell.

"Christmas Eve Story" (1880)

SOURCE: Fannie M. Jackson Coppin, "Christmas Eve Story," *Christian Recorder* 23 (December 1880).

Once upon a time, there was a little girl named Maggie Devins, and she had a brother named Johnny, just one year older than she. Here they both are. Now if they could they would get up and make you a bow. But dear me! We all get so fastened down in pictures that we have to keep as quiet as mice, or we'd tear the paper all to pieces. I'm going to tell you something about this little boy and girl, and perhaps some little reader will remember it. You see how very clean and neat both of them look. Well, if you had seen them when Grandma Devins first found them you never would have thought that they could be made to look as nice as this. Now hear their story:

Last Christmas eve while Grandma Devins was sitting by her bright fire, there was a loud knock at the door, and upon opening it, she found a policeman who had in his arms two children that were nearly dead. "I come, mum," he said, "to ask you if you will let these poor little young ones stay here tonight in your kitchen; their mother has just died from the fever. She lived in an old hovel around in Acorn Alley, and I'm afraid to leave the young ones there tonight, for they're half starved and half frozen to death now. God pity the poor, mum, God pity the poor, for it's hard upon them, such weather as this." Meanwhile, Grandma Devins had pulled her big sofa up to the fire and was standing looking down upon the dirty and pinched little faces before her. She didn't say anything, but she just kept looking at the children and wiping her eyes and blowing her nose. All at once she turned around as if she had been shot; she flew to the pantry and brought out some milk which she put on the fire to boil. And very soon she had two streaming cups of hot milk with nice biscuit broken into it, and with this she fed the poor little creatures until a little color came into their faces, and she knew that she had given them enough for that time. The policeman said he would call for the children in the morning and take them to the almshouse. The fact is the policeman was a kind-hearted man, and he secretly hoped that he could get some one to take the children and be kind to them.

As soon as Maggie and Johnny had had their nice warm milk they began to talk. Johnny asked Grandma Devins if she had anybody to give her Christmas presents and Grandma said, "no." but Maggie spoke up and said her mamma told her before she died that God always gave Christmas presents to those who had no one to give them any. And throwing her arms around Grandma's neck she said, "God will not forget you, dear lady, for you've been so good to us." Like a flash of light it passed through Grandma Devins' mind that God had sent her these children as her Christmas gift. So she said at once:

"Children, I made a mistake. I have had a Christmas present."

"There," said Maggie, "I knew you would get one; I knew it." When the policeman came in the morning his heart was overjoyed to see the "young ones," as he called them, nicely washed and sitting by the fire bundled up in some of Grandma Devins' dresses. She had burnt every stitch of the few dirty rags which they had on the night before so that accounted for their being muffled up so.

"You can go right away, policeman; these children are my Christmas gift, and please God I'll be mother and father both, to the poor little orphans."

A year has passed since then, and she says that Johnny and Maggie are the best Christmas gifts that any old woman ever had. She has taught Maggie to darn and sew neatly, and one of these days she will be able to earn money as a seamstress. Have you noticed her little needle-case hanging against the wall? Do you see the basket of apples on one side? Johnny was paring them when Maggie asked him to show her about her arithmetic, for Johnny goes to school, but Maggie stay sat home and helps Grandma. Now as soon as Grandma comes back she is going to make them some mince pies for Christmas. Johnny will finish paring the apples while Maggie is stoning the raisins. Oh! What a happy time they will have tomorrow. For I will whisper in your ear, little reader, that Grandma Devins is going to bring home something else with her than raisins. The same kind-hearted policeman that I told you about in the beginning, has made Johnny a beautiful sled, and painted the name "Hero" on it. Grandma has bought for Maggie the nicest little hood and cloak that ever you saw. Is not that nice? I guess if they knew what they're going to get they wouldn't sit so quietly as we see them; they'd jump up and dance about the floor, even if they tore the paper all to pieces. Oh! Let every little boy and girl thank our loving heavenly Father for the blessed gift of His dear Son on the first Christmas day, eighteen hundred and eighty years ago.

"A Plea for the Mission School" (1891)

SOURCE: Fannie M. Jackson Coppin, "A Plea for the Mission School," *Christian Recorder* (August 13, 1891).

The history of missionary effort, the world over, shows that the NATIVE helpers are ten to one in all permanent missionary fields and we shall never have our work of evangelization securely planted in foreign lands until we raise up the natives and train them on their own soil under the watchful care of our missionaries. We must establish the mission seminary by the side of the mission church. Here native young people who have accepted the truth of the gospel and who give promise of future usefulness receive elementary instruction in Bible truths and in Christian principles. They must be lifted for a little time out of their heathen life and associations and be brought near to the missionary, where they can be easily nourished in Christian living until they are strong enough to go out and be helpers of the missionary. Speaking the language, they have at once powerful advantage over one who does not speak it. All missionaries admit that the gospel ought to be preached to foreign natives in their own tongue, and that their work is much hindered until they can learn the language of the country.

Secondly; Understanding the disposition and habits of their own people, the natives know best how to approach them.

Thirdly; Being well acquainted with the country they can penetrate into the interior, where a stranger could find no way of entrance.

Fourthly; They are acclimated and can defy the scorching tropical sun and the African fever.

It is easy to see then, that the native helpers, trained in the mission school, become the more powerful allies and helpers of the missionaries, and without some well organized effort of this kind to constantly keep up and increase the supply of laborers, the work stops when our missionaries stop; languishes when they languish; dies when they die.

Our work in Hayti flames up, pales and then keeps up a gasping existence because there is no steady supply of trained material to nourish it. Well do I remember the imploring letters of that noble and self-sacrificing woman—Mrs. Mossell—who wrote to our society, begging that we would send her young women to assist her and help carry forward the splendid mission school, which she and her husband had established. And now Brother Frederick writes that his health requires that he should come home, but into whose hand, can he entrust the work which he has founded with much labor and prayer and self-sacrificing effort.

Now, the question arises, how is the mission school provided with its teachers and its evangelists? for the missionary only has general charge.

First; There must be a seed sent from this country. We must earnestly pray that there may be an outpouring of the missionary spirit, which will inspire the hearts of more of our young men and women to consecrate their lives and talents to the works of carrying the gospel to the lands now lying in darkness.

Secondly; We must bring to this country some of the best and most promising young people from Africa and Hayti and have them prepared to go back to carry the light which they have received. They must not be kept here long enough to lose the love of their home; to forget the great purpose for which they were brought here and to imbibe the vanities and vices of our modern civilization. I have heard of one who was educated in this country and, of course, had to be put through the long collegiate course of Latin and Greek, etc. Upon his return to Africa he was so disgusted that he would not even go up into the interior to see his poor old heathen mother. Do you think that a true woman would ever have done that? Why have so few NATIVE WOMEN been trained for the missionary field? Many native young men are being so trained in this country and in England. Yet, women have continuity of purpose, they have capacity to endure hardships, they have self-sacrificing love and they have natural adaptation for teaching and for evangelistic work.

The history of missions proves, that there is excellent stock in women for missionary labor. Can we only have one Mrs. Mossell, one Amanda Smith? "Is the arm of the Lord shortened!" There is a little namesake of Amanda Smith, in Africa and if our mission school has been established, her foster mother might have had the joy of leaving her there to be educated for mission work. I understand that the girls belonging to the very same tribe are very intelligent and tractable. From the Rev. Solomon Porter Hood, our present missionary to Hayti, we have received the names of some very promising A.M.E. girls, who speak both the French and the Spanish language, and their parents are willing that they should come to this country and be trained for mission work in Hayti, but while a few must be educated in this country, the greater number must be trained in the mission school in their own land.

The Catholics are wise in their day and generation. They bid for the children, and we can get the men and women, if we can. The most hopeful evangelization begins with childhood, when the little one is around the mother's skirts. If we take no care to instruct in christian training, the girls, the future wives and mothers, then we leave our christian young men to marry with heathen women. And if Solomon, the wisest man that ever lived, was led astray by his heathen wives, and the strongest man that ever lived was utterly ruined by his fascinating heathen, Delilah, what may be expected of ordinary young men of the present day? Therefore, I am strong in the belief that a great mistake has been made in not preparing native women in this country and on their own soil for the missionary work.

The W.P.M.M. Society has given a great deal of thought to this subject and they believe that their ideas will commend themselves to the intelligent judgment of workers in the missionary cause both at home and abroad. When the prison doors of slavery were thrown open, and the A.M.E. denomination entered the South, it carried the bible in one hand and the spelling book in the other. Religion without christian instruction is heat without light. Surely when this land is dotted with schools and colleges, we can afford at least one mission school in Hayti, and one in Africa, where some of the most promising of the native young people may be instructed in the bible, in christian principles, and in elementary knowledge and may go forth as allies and coworkers with our missionaries to carry out the light of gospel truth, into the darkest regions of the country.

"A Plea for Industrial Opportunity" (1879)

SOURCE: Fannie M. Jackson Coppin, "A Plea for Industrial
Opportunity," *Masterpieces of Negro Eloquence*. Ed. Alice
Moore Dunbar (New York: The Bookery Publishing
Company, 1914).

The great lesson to be taught by this Fair is the value of co-
operative effort to make our cents dollars, and to show us what
help there is for ourselves in ourselves. That the colored people
of this country have enough money to materially alter their financial condition, was clearly demonstrated by the millions of
dollars deposited in the Freedmen's Bank; that they have the
good sense, and the unanimity to use this power, are now
proved by this industrial exhibition and fair.

It strikes me that much of the recent talk about the exodus
has proceeded upon the high-handed assumption that, owing
largely to the credit system of the South, the colored people
there are forced to the alternative, to "curse God, and die," or
else "go West." Not a bit of it. The people of the South, it is
true, cannot at this time produce hundreds of dollars, but they
have millions of pennies; and millions of pennies make tens of
thousands of dollars. By clubbing together and lumping their
pennies, a fund might be raised in the cities of the South that the
poorer classes might fall back upon while their crops are growing; or else, by the opening of co-operative stores, become their
own creditors and so effectually rid themselves of their merciless extortioners. "Oh, they won't do anything; you can't get
them united on anything!" is frequently expressed. The best
way for a man to prove that he can do a thing is to do it, and
that is what we have shown we can do. This fair, participated in
by twenty four States in the Union, and gotten up for a purpose
which is of no pecuniary benefit to those concerned in it, effectually silences all slanders about "we won't or we can't do," and
teaches its own instructive and greatly needed lessons of self-
help,—the best help that any man can have, next to God's.

Those in charge, who have completed the arrangement of the
Fair, have studiously avoided preceding it with noisy and

demonstrative babblings, which are so often the vapid precursors of promises as empty as those who make them; therefore, in some quarters, our Fair has been overlooked. It is not, we think, a presumptuous interpretation of this great movement, to say, that the voice of God now seems to utter "Speak to the people that they go forward." "Go forward" in what respect? Teach the millions of poor colored laborers of the South how much power they have in themselves, by co-operation of effort, and by a combination of their small means, to change the despairing poverty which now drives them from their homes, and makes them a mill-stone around the neck of any community, South or West. Secondly, that we shall go forward in asking to enter the same employments which other people enter. Within the past ten years we have made almost no advance in getting our youth into industrial and business occupations. It is just as hard for instance, to get a boy into a printing-office now as it was ten years ago. It is simply astonishing when we consider how many of the common vocations of life colored people are shut out of. Colored men are not admitted to the printers' trade-union, nor, with very rare exceptions are they employed in any city of the United States in a paid capacity as printers or writers; one of the rare exceptions being the employment of H. Price Williams, on the *Sunday Press* of this city. We are not employed as salesmen or pharmacists, or saleswomen, or bank clerks, or merchants' clerks, or tradesmen, or mechanics, or telegraph operators, or to any degree as State or government officials, and I could keep on with the string of "ors" until to-morrow morning, but the patience of an audience has its limit.

Slavery made us poor, and its gloomy, malicious shadow tends to keep us so. I beg to say, kind hearers, that this is not spoken in a spirit of recrimination. We have no quarrel with our fate, and we leave your Christianity to yourselves. Our faith is firmly fixed in that "Eternal Providence," that in its own good time will "justify the ways of God to man." But, believing that to get the right men into the right places is a "consummation most devoutly to be wished," it is a matter of serious concern to us to see our youth with just as decided diversity of talent as any other people, herded together into but three or four occupations.

It is cruel to make a teacher or a preacher of a man who ought to be a printer or a blacksmith, and that is exactly the condition we are now obliged to submit to. The greatest advance that has been made since the War has been effected by political parties, and it is precisely the political positions that we think it least desirable our youth should fill. We have our choice of the professions, it is true, but, as we have not been endowed with an overwhelming abundance of brains, it is not probable that we can contribute to the bar a great lawyer except once in a great while. The same may be said of medicine; nor are we able to tide over the "starving time," between the reception of a diploma and the time that a man's profession becomes a paying one.

Being determined to know whether this industrial and business ostracism lay in ourselves or "in our stars," we have from time to time, knocked, shaken, and kicked, at these closed doors of employment. A cold, metallic voice from within replies, "We do not employ colored people." Ours not to make reply, ours not to question why. Thank heaven, we are not obliged to do and die; having the preference to do or die, we naturally prefer to do.

But we cannot help wondering if some ignorant or faithless steward of God's work and God's money hasn't blundered. It seems necessary that we should make known to the good men and women who are so solicitous about our souls, and our minds, that we haven't quite got rid of our bodies yet, and until we do, we must feed and clothe them; and this attitude of keeping us out of work forces us back upon charity.

That distinguished thinker, Mr. Henry C. Carey, in his valuable works on political economy, has shown by the truthful and forceful logic of history, that the elevation of all peoples to a higher moral and intellectual plane, and to a fuller investiture of their civil rights, has always steadily kept pace with the improvement in their physical condition. Therefore we feel that resolutely and in unmistakable language, yet in the dignity of moderation, we should strive to make known to all men the justice of our claims to the same employments as other's under the same conditions. We do not ask that anyone of our people shall be put into a position because he is a colored person, but we do most emphatically ask that he shall not be kept out of a position because he is a colored person. "An open field and no favors" is all that is requested. The time was when to put a colored girl or boy behind a counter would have been to decrease custom; it would have been a tax upon the employer, and a charity that we were too proud to accept; but public sentiment has changed. I am satisfied that the employment of a colored clerk or a colored saleswoman wouldn't even be a "nine days' wonder." It is easy of accomplishment, and yet it is not. To thoughtless and headstrong people who meet duty with impertinent dictation I do not now address myself; but to those who wish the most gracious of all blessings, a fuller enlightment as to their duty,—to those I beg to say, think of what is suggested in this appeal.

46

VICTORIA EARLE MATTHEWS

(1861–1907)

Victoria Earle Matthews was born into slavery in Fort Valley, Georgia. After escaping to New York and working as a housekeeper, she began a career in journalism and wrote for three New York newspapers, the *Times*, the *Herald*, and the *Sunday Mercury*, and contributed to African American newspapers such as the Boston *Advocate* and the *New York Globe*. She also wrote the novel *Aunt Lindy* and delivered lectures, such as "The Value of Race Literature" and "The Awakening of the Afro-American Woman." Matthews founded the Woman's Loyal Union and the National Federation of Afro-American Women and served as the first national organizer of the combined National Colored Women's League and National Association of Colored Women.

As Gertrude Mossell writes, "'Aunt Lindy,' by (Victoria Earle) Mrs. W. E. Matthews . . . is a beautiful little story and is deserving of careful study, emanating as it does from the pen of a representative of the race, and giving a vivid and truthful aspect of one phase of Negro character. It shows most conclusively the need of the race to produce its own delineators of Negro life."

"The Value of Race Literature" (1895)

SOURCE: Victoria Earle Matthews, "The Value of Race
Literature: An Address Delivered at the First Congress of
Colored Women of the United States at Boston, Mass., July
30th, 1895."

"If the black man carries in his bosom an indispensable element of a new and coming civilization, for the sake of that
element, no money, nor strength, nor circumstance can hurt
him; he will survive and play his part. . . . If you have *man*,
black or white is an insignificance. The intellect—that is miraculous! who has it, has the talisman. His skin and bones,
though they were the color of night, are transparent, and the
everlasting stars shine through with attractive beams."
                                        —RALPH WALDO EMERSON.

By Race Literature, we mean ordinarily all the writings emanating from a distinct class—not necessarily race matter; but a general collection of what has been written by the men and women
of that Race: History, Biographies, Scientific Treatises, Sermons,
Addresses, Novels, Poems, Books of Travel, miscellaneous essays
and the contributions to magazines and newspapers.

Literature, according to Webster, is learning; acquaintance
with books or letters: the collective body of literary productions, embracing the entire results of knowledge and fancy, preserved in writing, *also the whole body of literature*, productions
or writings upon any given subject, or in reference to a particular science, a branch of knowledge, as the Literature of Biblical
Customs, the Literature of Chemistry, Etc.

In the light of this definition, many persons may object to the
term, Race Literature, questioning seriously the need, doubting
if there be any, or indeed whether there can be a Race Literature in a country like ours apart from the general American
Literature. Others may question the correctness of the term
American Literature, since our civilization in its essential features is a reproduction of all that is most desirable in the

civilizations of the Old World. English being the language of America, they argue in favor of the general term, English Literature.

While I have great respect for the projectors of this theory, yet it is a limited definition; it does not express the idea in terms sufficiently clear.

The conditions which govern the people of African descent in the United States have been and still are, such as create a very marked difference in the limitations, characteristics, aspirations and ambitions of this class of people, in decidedly strong contrast with the more or less powerful races which dominate it.

Laws were enacted denying and restricting their mental development in such pursuits, which engendered servility and begot ox-like endurance; and though statutes were carefully, painstakingly prepared by the most advanced and learned American jurists to perpetuate ignorance, yet they were powerless to keep all the race out from the Temple of Learning. Many though in chains mastered the common rudiments and others possessing talent of higher order—like the gifted Phyllis Wheatley, who dared to express her meditations in poetic elegance which won recognition in England and America, from persons distinguished in letters and statesmanship—dared to seek the sources of knowledge and wield a pen.

While oppressive legislation, aided by grossly inhuman customs, successfully retarded all general efforts toward improvement, the race suffered physically and mentally under a great wrong, an appalling evil, in contrast with which the religious caste prejudice of India appears as a glimmering torch to a vast consuming flame.

The prejudice of color! Not condition, not character, not capacity for artistic development, not the possibility of emerging from savagery into Christianity, not these, but the "Prejudice of Color." Washington Irving's Life of Columbus contains a translation from the contemporaries of Las Casas, in which this prejudice is plainly evident. Since our reception on this continent, men have cried out against this inhuman prejudice; granting that, a man may improve his condition, accumulate wealth, become wise and upright, merciful and just as an infidel or

Christian, but they despair because he can not change his color, as if it were possible for the victim to change his organic structure, and impossible for the oppressor to change his wicked heart.

But all this impious wrong has made a Race Literature a possibility, even a necessity to dissipate the odium conjured up by the term "colored" persons, not originally perhaps designed to humiliate, but unfortunately still used to express not only an inferior order, but to accentuate and call unfavorable attention to the most ineradicable difference between the races.

So well was this understood and deplored by liberal minded men, regardless of affiliation, that the editor of "Freedom's Journal," published in New York City in 1827, the first paper published in this country by Americans of African descent, calls special attention to this prejudice by quoting from the great Clarkson, where he speaks of a master not only looking with disdain upon a slave's features, but hating his very color.

The effect of this unchristian disposition was like the merciless scalpel about the very heart of the people, a sword of Damocles, at all times hanging above and threatening all that makes life worth living. Why they should not develop and transmit stealthy, vicious and barbaric natures under such conditions, is a question that able metaphysicians, ethnologists and scientists will, most probably in the future, investigate with a view of solving what to-day is considered in all quarters a profound mystery, the Negro's many-sided, happy, hopeful, enduring character.

Future investigations may lead to the discovery of what to-day seems lacking, what has deformed the manhood and womanhood in the Negro. What is bright, hopeful and encouraging is in reality the source of an original school of race literature, of racial psychology, of potent possibilities, an amalgam needed for this great American race of the future.

Dr. Dvorak claims this for the original Negro melodies of the South, as every student of music is well aware. On this subject he says, "I am now satisfied that the future music of this continent must be founded upon what are called the Negro melodies. This can be the foundation of a serious and original school of composition to be developed in the United States.

"When I first came here, I was impressed with this idea, and it has developed into a settled conviction. The beautiful and varied themes are the product of the soil. *They are American, they are the folk songs of America, and our composers must turn to them.* All of the great musicians have borrowed from the songs of the common people.

"Beethoven's most charming *scherzo* is based upon what might now be considered a skillfully handled Negro melody. I have myself gone to the simple half-forgotten tunes of the Bohemian peasants for hints in my most serious work. Only in this way can a musician express the true sentiment of a people. He gets into touch with common humanity of the country.

"*In the Negro melodies of America I discover all that is needed for a great and noble school of music. They are pathetic, tender, passionate and melancholy, solemn, religious, bold, merry, gay, gracious, or what you will. It is music that suits itself to any work or any purpose. There is nothing in the whole range of composition that cannot find a thematic source here.*"

When the literature of our race is developed, it will of necessity be different in all essential points of greatness, true heroism and real Christianity from what we may at the present time, for convenience, call American Literature. When some master hand writes the stories as Dr. Dvorak has caught the melodies, when, amid the hearts of the people, there shall live a George Eliot, moving this human world by the simple portrayal of the scenes of our ordinary existence; or when the pure, ennobling touch of a black Hannah More shall rightly interpret our unappreciated contribution to Christianity and make it into universal literature, such writers will attain and hold imperishable fame.

The novelists most read at the present time in this country find a remunerative source for their doubtful literary productions based upon the wrongly interpreted and too often grossly exaggerated frailties. This is patent to all intelligent people. The Negro need not envy such reputation, nor feel lost at not reveling in its ill-gotten wealth or repute. We are the only people most distinctive from those who have civilized and governed this country, who have become typical Americans, and we rank next to the Indians in originality of soil, and yet remain a distinct people.

In this connection, Joseph Wilson, in the Black Phalanx, says:

"The Negro race is the only race that has ever come in contact with the European race that has proved itself able to withstand its atrocities and oppression. All others like the Indians whom they could not make subservient to their use they have destroyed."

Prof. Sampson in his "Mixed Races" says, "The American Negro is a new race, and is not the direct descent of any people that has ever flourished."

On this supposition, and relying upon finely developed, native imaginative powers, and humane tendencies, I base my expectation that our Race Literature when developed will not only compare favorably with many, but will stand out preeminent, not only in the limited history of colored people, but in the broader field of universal literature.

Though Race Literature be founded upon the traditionary history of a people, yet its fullest and largest development ought not to be circumscribed by the narrow limits of race or creed, for the simple reason that literature in its loftiest development reaches out to the utmost limits of soul enlargement and outstrips all earthly limitations. Our history and individuality as a people, not only provides material for masterly treatment; but would seem to make a Race Literature a necessity as an outlet for the unnaturally suppressed inner lives which our people have been compelled to lead.

The literature of any people of varied nationality who have won a place in the literature of the world, presents certain cardinal points. French literature for instance, is said to be "not the wisest, not the weightiest, not certainly the purest and loftiest, but by odds the most brilliant and the most interesting literature in the world."

Ours, when brought out, and we must admit in reverence to truth that, as yet, we have done nothing distinctive, but may when we have built upon our own individuality, win a place by the simplicity of the story, thrown into strong relief by the multiplicity of its dramatic situations; the spirit of romance, and even tragedy, shadowy and as yet ill-defined, but from which our race on this continent can never be disassociated.

When the foundations of such a literature shall have been properly laid, the benefit to be derived will be at once apparent. There will be a revelation to our people, and it will enlarge our scope, make us better known wherever real lasting culture exists, will undermine and utterly drive out the traditional Negro in dialect,—the subordinate, the servant as the type representing a race whose numbers are now far into the millions. It would suggest to the world the wrong and contempt with which the lion viewed the picture that the hunter and a famous painter besides, had drawn of the King of the Forest.

As a matter of history, the only high-type Negro that has been put before the American people by a famous writer, is the character Dred founded upon the deeds of Nat Turner, in Mrs. Stowe's novel.

Except the characters sketched by the writers of folk-lore, I know of none more representative of the spirit of the writers of to-day, wherein is infiltrated in the public mind that false sense of the Negro's meaning of inalienable rights, so far as actual practice is concerned, than is found in a story in "Harper's Magazine" some years ago. Here a pathetic picture is drawn of a character generally known as the typical "Darkey."

The man, old and decrepit, had labored through long years to pay for an humble cabin and garden patch; in fact, he had paid double and treble the original price, but dashing "Marse Wilyum" quieted his own conscience by believing, so the writer claimed, that the old Darkey should be left free to pay him all he felt the cabin was worth to him. The old man looked up to him, trusted him implicitly, and when he found at last he had been deceived, the moment he acknowledged to himself that "Marse Wilyum" had cheated him, a dejected listlessness settled upon him, an expression weak and vacant came in his dull eyes and hung around his capacious but characterless mouth, an exasperatingly meek smile trembled upon his features, and casting a helpless look around the cabin that he thought his own, nay, knew it was, with dragging steps he left the place! "Why did you not stand out for your rights?" a sympathizing friend questioned some years afterward. To this the writer makes the old man say:

"Wid white folks dat's de way, but wid niggers its dif'unt."

Here the reader is left to infer whatever his or her predilection will incline to accept, as to the meaning of the old man's words. The most general view is that the old man had no manhood, not the sense, nothing to even suggest to his inner conscience aught that could awaken a comprehension of the word man, much less its rightful price; no moral responsibility, no spirit or, as the Negro-hating Mark Twain would say, no capacity of kicking at real or imaginary wrongs, which in his estimation makes the superior clan. In a word, there was nothing within the old man's range of understanding to make him feel his inalienable rights.

We know the true analysis of the old man's words was that faith, once destroyed, can never be regained, and the blow to his faith in the individual and the wound to his honest esteem so overwhelming, rendered it out of the question to engage further with a fallen idol.

With one sweep of mind he had seen the utter futility of even hoping for justice from a people who would take advantage of an aged honest man. That is the point, and this reveals a neglected subject for analytical writers to dissect in the interest of truth the real meaning of the so-called cowardice, self-negation and lack of responsibility so freely referred to by those in positions calculated to make lasting impressions on the public, that by custom scoffs at the meaning introduced in Mrs. Stowe's burning words, when she repeated a question before answering;—"What can any individual do?" "There is one thing every individual can do. They can see to it that they feel right—an atmosphere of sympathetic influence encircles every human being; and the man or woman who feels strongly, healthily and justly on the great interests of humanity, is a constant benefactor to the human race."

Think of the moral status of the Negro, that Mr. Ridpath in his history degrades before the world. Consider the political outline of the Negro, sketched with extreme care in "Bryce's Commonwealth," and the diatribes of Mr. Froude. From these, turn to the play, where impressions are made upon a heterogeneous assemblage—Mark Twain's "Pudd'n Head Wilson," which

Beaumount Fletcher claims as "among the very best of those productions which gives us hope for a distinctive American drama."

In this story we have education and fair environment attended by the most deplorable results, an educated octoroon is
made out to be a most despicable, cowardly villain. "The one
compensation for all this," my friend, Professor Greener wittily
remarks, "is that the 'white nigger' in the story though actually
a pure white man, is indescribably worse in all his characteristics than the 'real nigger,' using the vernacular of the play, was
ever known to be, and just here Mark Twain unconsciously
avenges the Negro while trying his best to disparage him."

In "Imperative Duty," Mr. Howells, laboriously establishes
for certain minds, the belief that the Negro possesses an
Othello like charm in his ignorance which education and refinement destroys, or at best makes repulsive.

In explaining why Dr. Olney loves Rhoda, whose training
was imparted by good taste, refined by wealth, and polished by
foreign travel, he says: "It was the elder world, the beauty of
antiquity which appealed to him in the luster and sparkle of
this girl, and *the remote taint* of her servile and savage origin,
gave her a fascination which refuses to let itself be put in words,
it was the grace of a limp, the occult, indefinable, lovableness
of deformity, but transcending these by its allurements, in indefinite degree, and going for the reason of its effect deep into
the mysterious places of being, where the spirit and animal
meet and part in us.

"The mood was of his emotional nature alone, it sought and
could have won no justification from the moral sense which indeed it simply submerged, and blotted out for all time."

All this tergiversation and labored explanation of how a
white man came to love a girl with a remote tinge of Negro
blood! But he must have recourse to this tortuous jugglery of
words, because one of his characters in the story had taken
pains to assert, "That so far as society in the society sense is
concerned we have frankly simplified the matter, and no more
consort with the Negroes than we do with lower animals, so
that one would be quite as likely to meet a cow or a horse in an
American drawing-room, as a person of color." This is the

height of enlightenment! and from Dean Howells too, littérateur, diplomat, journalist, altruist!

Art, goodness, and beauty are assaulted in order to stimulate or apologize for prejudice against the educated Negro!

In Dr. Huguet, we have as a type a man pitifully trying to be self-conscious, struggling to feel within himself, what prejudice and custom demand that he feel.

In "A Question of Color" the type is a man of splendid English training, that of an English gentleman, surrounded from his birth by wealth, and accepted in the most polished society, married to a white girl, who sells herself for money, and after the ceremony like an angelic Sunday-school child, shudders and admits the truth, that she can never forget that he is a Negro, and he is cad enough to say, so says the writer, that he will say his prayers at her feet night and morning not withstanding!

We all know, no man, negro or other, ever enacted such a part; it is wholly inconsistent with anything short of a natural born idiot! And yet a reputable house offers this trash to the public, but thanks to a sensible public, it has been received with jeers. And so stuff like this comes apace, influencing the reading-world, not indeed thinkers and scholars; but the indiscriminate reading-world, upon whom rests, unfortunately, the bulk of senseless prejudice.

Conan Doyle, like Howells, also pays his thoughtful attention to the educated negro—making him in this case more blood-thirsty and treacherous and savage than the Seminole. One more, and these are mentioned only to show the kind of types of Negro characters eminent writers have taken exceeding care to place before the world as representing us.

In the "Condition of Women in the United States," Mme. Blanc, in a volume of 285 pages, devotes less than 100 words to negro women; after telling ironically of a "Black Damsel" in New Orleans engaged in teaching Latin, she describes her attire, the arrangement of her hair, and concludes, "I also saw a class of little Negro girls with faces like monkeys studying Greek, and the disgust expressed by their former masters seemed quite justified."

Her knowledge of history is as imperfect so far as veracity

goes, as her avowal in the same book of her freedom from prejudice against the Negro. The "little girls" must have been over thirty years old to have had any former masters even at their birth! And all this is the outcome in the nineteenth century of the highest expressions of Anglo-Saxon acumen, criticism and understanding of the powers of Negroes of America!

The point of all this, is the indubitable evidence of the need of thoughtful, well-defined and intelligently placed efforts on our part, to serve as counter-irritants against all such writing that shall stand, having as an aim the supplying of influential and accurate information, on all subjects relating to the Negro and his environments, to inform the American mind at least, for literary purposes.

We cannot afford any more than any other people to be indifferent to the fact, that the surest road to real fame is through literature. Who is so well known and appreciated by the cultured minds as Dumas of France, and Pushkin of Russia? I need not say to this thoughtful and intelligent gathering that, any people without a literature is valued lightly the world round. Who knows or can judge of our intrinsic worth, without actual evidences of our breadth of mind, our boundless humanity. Appearing well and weighted with many degrees of titles, will not raise us in our own estimation while color is the white elephant in America. Yet, America is but a patch on the universe: if she ever produces a race out of her cosmopolitan population, that can look beyond mere money-getting to more permanent qualities of true greatness as a nation, it will call this age her unbalanced stage.

No one thinks of mere color when looking upon the Chinese, but the dignified character of the literature of his race, and he for monotony of expression, color and undesirable individual habits is far inferior in these points to the ever-varying American Negro. So our people must awaken to the fact, that our task is a conquest for a place for ourselves, and is a legitimate ground for action for us, if we shall resolve to conquer it.

While we of to-day view with increasing dissatisfaction the trend of the literary productions of this country, concerning us, yet are we standing squarely on the foundation laid for us by our immediate predecessors?

This is the question I would bring to your minds. Are we adding to the structure planned for us by our pioneers? Do we know our dwelling and those who under many hardships, at least, gathered the material for its upbuilding? Knowing them do we honor—do we love them—what have they done that we should love? Your own Emerson says—"To judge the production of a people you must transplant the spirit of the times in which they lived."

In the ten volumes of American Literature edited by H. L. Stoddard only Phyllis Wheatley and George W. Williams find a place. This does not show that we have done nothing in literature; far from it, but it does show that we have done nothing so brilliant, so effective, so startling as to attract the attention of these editors. Now it is a fact that thoughtful, scholarly white people do not look for literature in its highest sense, from us any more than they look for high scholarship, profound and critical learning on any one point, nor for any eminent judicial acumen or profound insight into causes and effects.

These are properly regarded as the results only of matured intellectual growth or abundant leisure and opportunity, when united with exceptional talents, and this is the world's view, and it is in the main a correct one. Even the instances of precocious geniuses and the rare examples of extraordinary talent appearing from humble and unpromising parentage and unfortuitous surroundings, are always recognized as brilliant, sporadic cases, exceptions.

Consequently our success in Race Literature will be looked upon with curiosity and only a series of projected enterprises in various directions—history, poetry, novel writing, speeches, orations, forensic effort, sermons, and so on, will have the result of gaining for us recognition.

You recall Poteghine's remark in Turgenev's novel of "Smoke." How well it applies to us.

"For heaven's sake do not spread the idea in Russia that we can achieve success without preparation. No, if your brow be seven spans in width *study*, begin with the alphabet or *else remain quiet* and say nothing. Oh! it excites me to think of these things."

Dr. Blyden's essays, Dr. Crummell's sermons and addresses, and Professor Greener's orations, all are high specimens of sustained English, good enough for any one to read, and able to bear critical examination, and reflect the highest credit on the race.

Your good city of Boston deserves well for having given us our first real historian, William C. Nell—his history of "The Colored Patriots of the Revolution"—not sufficiently read nowadays or appreciated by the present generation; a scholarly, able, accurate book, second to none written by any other colored man.

William Wells Brown's "Black Man" was a worthy tribute in its day, the precursor of more elaborate books, and should be carefully studied now; his "Sights and Scenes Abroad" was probably the first book of travel written by an American Negro. The same is doubtless true of his novel, *Clotel*. The "Anglo-African" magazine published in New York City in 1859, is adjudged by competent authority to be the highest, best, most scholarly written of all the literature published by us in fifty years.

We have but to read the graphic descriptions and eloquent passages in the first edition of the "Life and Times" of Frederick Douglass to see the high literary qualities of which the race is capable. "Light and Truth," a valuable volume published many years ago; Dr. Perry's "Cushite!" "Bond and Free, or Under the Yoke," by John S. Ladue; "The Life of William Lloyd Garrison," by Archibald Grimké; Joseph Wilson's "Black Phalanx"; and "Men of Mark," by Rev. W. J. Simmons; "Noted Women," by Dr. Scruggs; "The Negro Press and Its Editors', by I. Garland Penn"; "Paul Dunbar's Dialect Poems," which have lately received high praise from the Hoosier Poet, James Whitcomb Reilly, "Johnson's School History"; "From a Virginia Cabin to the Capitol," by Hon. J. M. Langston; "Iola Leroy," by Mrs. F. E. W. Harper; "Music and Some Highly Musical People," by James M. Trotter, are specimen books within easy reach of the public, that will increase in interest with time.

Professor R. T. Greener as a metaphysician, logician, orator, and prize essayist, holds an undisputed position in the annals of our literature second to none. His defense of the Negro in the "National Quarterly Review," 1880, in reply to Mr. Parton's strictures, has been an arsenal from which many have since supplied their armor. It was quoted extensively in this country and England.

And it is not generally known that one of the most valuable contributions to Race Literature, has appeared in the form of a scientific treatise on "Incandescent Lighting" published by Van Nostrand of New York, and thus another tribute is laid to Boston's credit by Lewis H. Latimer.

In the ecclesiastical line we have besides those already mentioned, the writings of the learned Dr. Pennington, Bishops Payne and Tanner of the A. M. E. Church.

The poems, songs and addresses by our veteran literary women F. E. W. Harper, Charlotte Forten Grimké, H. Cordelia Ray, Gertrude Mossell, "Clarence and Corinne," "The Hazeltone Family" by Mrs. G. E. Johnson, and "Appointed" by W. H. Stowers, and W. H. Anderson are a few of the publications on similar subjects; all should be read and placed in our libraries, as first beginnings it is true, but they compare favorably with similar work of the most advanced people.

Our journalism has accomplished more than can now be estimated; in fact not until careful biographers make special studies drawn from the lives of the pioneer journalists, shall we or those contemporary with them ever know the actual meed of good work accomplished by them under almost insurmountable difficulties.

Beginning with the editors of the first newspapers published in this country by colored men, we New Yorkers take pride in the fact that Messrs. Cornish and Russwurm of "Freedom's Journal," New York City, 1827, edited the first paper in this country devoted to the upbuilding of the Negro. Philip A. Bell of the "Weekly Advocate," 1837, named by contemporaries "the Nestor of African American journalists." The gifted Dr. James McCune Smith was associated with him. The "Weekly Advocate" later became the "Colored American." And in 1839, on Mr. Bell's retirement Dr. Charles Ray assumed the editorial chair, continued until 1842, making an enviable record for zeal on all matters of race interest. These men were in very truth the Pioneers of Race Journalism.

Their lives and record should be zealously guarded for the future use of our children, for they familiarized the public with the idea of the Negro owning and doing the brain work of a newspaper. The people of other sections became active in establishing journals, which did good work all along the line. Even the superficial mind must accept the modest claim that "These journals proved a powerful lever in diverting public opinion, public sympathy, and public support toward the liberation of the slave."

Papers were edited by such men as Dr. H. H. Garnet, David Ruggles, W. A. Hodges, and T. Van Rensselaer, of the "Ram's Horn." In 1847 our beloved and lofty minded Frederick Douglass edited his own paper "The North Star," in the City of Rochester, where his mortal remains now peacefully rest. His paper was noted for its high class matter—and it had the effect of raising the plane of journalism thereafter. About this time Samuel Ringold Ward of the "Impartial Citizen," published in Syracuse, N. Y., "forged to the front," winning in after years from Mr. Douglass a most flattering tribute. "Samuel Ringold Ward," the sage of Anacostia once said to the writer, "was one of the smartest men I ever knew if not the smartest."

The prevailing sentiment at that time was sympathy for the ambitious Negro. At a most opportune time, "The Anglo African," the finest effort in the way of a newspaper made by the race up to that time, was established in January of 1859 in New York City, with Thomas Hamilton as editor and proprietor. The columns were opened to the most experienced writers of the day. Martin R. Delany contributed many important papers on astronomy, among which was one on "Comets," another on "The Attraction of the Planets." George B. Vashon wrote "The Successive Advances of Astronomy," James McCune Smith wrote his comments "On the Fourteenth Query of Thomas Jefferson's Notes on Virginia" and his "German Invasion"—every number contained gems that to-day are beyond price. In these pages also appeared "Afric-American Picture Gallery," by "Ethiope"—Wm. J. Wilson; Robert Gordon's "Personality of the First Cause"; Dr. Pennington on "The Self-Redeeming Power of the Colored Races of the World"; Dr. Blyden on "The Slave Traffic"; and on the current questions of the day, such brave minds as Frederick Douglass, William C. Nell, John Mercer Langston, Theodore Holly, J. Sella Martin, Frances

Ellen Watkins, Jane Rustic, Sarah M. Douglass, and Grace A. Mapps! What a galaxy! The result was a genuine race newspaper, one that had the courage to eliminate everything of personal interest, and battle for the rights of the whole people, and while its history, like many other laudable enterprises, may be little known beyond the journalistic fraternity, to such men as Wendell Phillips and William Lloyd Garrison, the paper and staff were well known and appreciated. In those days, the Negro in literature was looked upon as a prodigy; he was encouraged in many ways by white people particularly, as he was useful in serving the cause of philanthropic agitators for the liberation of the slave. The earnest, upright character and thoughtful minds of the early pioneers acted as a standing argument in favor of the cause for which the abolitionists were then bending every nerve when the slave was liberated and the Civil War brought to a close. The spirit of Mr. Lincoln's interview with a committee of colored citizens of the District of Columbia, in August, 1862, as told by William Wells Brown, in which Mr. Lincoln said, "But for your people among us, there would be no war," reacted upon the public, and from that time until the present, a vigorous system of oppression, under the name of natural prejudice, has succeeded immeasurably in retarding our progress.

As a matter of history, we have nothing to compare with the weekly publications of 25 or 30 years ago. The unequal contest waged between Negro journals and their white contemporaries is lost sight of by the people, as only those connected with various publications are aware of the condition and difficulties surrounding the managements of such journals.

Our struggling journalists not only find themselves on the losing side, but as if to add to their thankless labor, they often times receive the contemptuous regard of the people who should enthusiastically rally to their support. The journalist is spurred with the common sense idea that every enterprise undertaken and carried on by members of the race is making a point in history for that entire race, and the historians of the future will not stop to consider our discontented and sentimental whys and wherefores, when they critically examine our race enterprises; but they will simply record their estimate of what the men and women journalists of to-day not only represented, but actually accomplished.

It is so often claimed that colored newspapers do not amount to anything. People even who boast of superior attainments, voice such sentiments with the most ill-placed indifference; the most discreditable phase of race disloyalty imaginable—one that future historians will have no alternative but to censure.

If our newspapers and magazines do not amount to anything, it is because our people do not demand anything of better quality from their own. It is because they strain their purses supporting those white papers that are and always will be independent of any income derived from us. Our contributions to such journals are spasmodic and uncertain, like fluctuating stocks, and are but an excess of surplus. It is hard for the bulk of our people to see this; it is even hard to prove to them that in supporting such journals, published by the dominant class, we often pay for what are not only vehicles of insult to our manhood and womanhood, but we assist in propagating or supporting false impressions of ourselves or our less fortunate brothers.

Our journalistic leader is unquestionably T. Thomas Fortune, Editor of "The New York Age," and a regular contributor of signed articles to the "New York Sun," one of the oldest and ablest daily newspapers in the United States, noted on two continents for its rare excellence.

For many years Mr. Fortune has given his best efforts to the cause of race advancement, and the splendid opportunities now opening to him on the great journals of the day, attest the esteem in which he is held by men who create public opinion in this country.

If John E. Bruce, "Bruce-Grit," "John Mitchell, Jr." W. H. A. Moore, Augustus M. Hodge "B Square," were members of any other race, they would be famous the country over. Joe Howard or "Bill Nye" have in reality done no more for their respective clientage than these bright minds and corresponding wits have done for theirs.

T. T. Fortune of "The Age," Ida Wells-Barnett of the "Free Speech," and John Mitchell of the "Richmond Planet," have made a nobler fight than the brilliant Parnell in his championship of Ireland's cause, for the reason that the people for whom he battled, better knew and utilized more the strength obtained only by systematic organization, not so is the case with the constituents of the distinguished journalists I have mentioned.

Depressing as this fact is, it should not deter those who know that Race Literature should be cultivated for the sake of the formation of habits. First efforts are always crude, each succeeding one becomes better or should be so. Each generation by the law of heredity receives the impulse or impression for good or ill from its predecessors, and since this is the law, we must begin to form habits of observation and commence to build a plan for posterity by synthesis, analysis, ourselves aiming and striving after the highest, whether we attain it or not. Such are the attempts of our journalists of to-day, and they shall reap if they faint not.

Race Literature does not mean things uttered in praise, thoughtless praise of ourselves, wherein each goose thinks her gosling a swan. We have had too much of this, too much that is crude, rude, pompous, and literary nothings, which ought to have been strangled before they were written much less printed; and this does not only apply to us; for it is safe to say that, only an infinitesimal percentage of the so-called literature filling the book shelves to-day, will survive a half century.

In the words of a distinguished critic, "It is simply amazing' how little of all that is written and printed in these days that makes for literature; how small a part is permanent, how much purely ephemeral, famous to-day on account of judicious advertising, forgotten to-morrow. We should clear away the under-brush of self-deception which makes the novice think because sentences are strung together and ordinary ideas evolved, dilated upon and printed, that such trash is literature." If this is claimed for the more favored class, it should have a tendency with us to encourage our work, even though the results do not appear at once.

It should serve the student by guarding him against the fulsome praise of "great men," "great writers," "great lawyers," "great ministers," who in reality have never done one really great or meritorious thing.

Rather should the student contemplate the success of such as

Prof. Du Bois who won the traveling fellowship at Harvard on metaphysical studies, and has just received his Ph. D., at the last commencement, on account of his work. For such facts demonstrate that it is the character of the work we do, rather than the quantity of it, which counts for real Race Literature.

Race Literature does mean though the preserving of all the records of a Race, and thus cherishing the materials saving from destruction and obliteration what is good, helpful and stimulating. But for our Race Literature, how will future generations know of the pioneers in Literature, our statesmen, soldiers, divines, musicians, artists, lawyers, critics, and scholars? True culture in Race Literature will enable us to discriminate and not to write hasty thoughts and unjust and ungenerous criticism often of our superiors in knowledge and judgment.

And now comes the question, What part shall we women play in the Race Literature of the future? I shall best answer that question by calling your attention to the glorious part which they have already performed in the columns of the "Woman's Era," edited by Josephine St. P. Ruffin.

Here within the compass of one small journal we have struck out a new line of departure—a journal, a record of Race interests gathered from all parts of the United States, carefully selected, moistened, winnowed and garnered by the ablest intellects of educated colored women, shrinking at no lofty theme, shirking no serious duty, aiming at every possible excellence, and determined to do their part in the future uplifting of the race.

If twenty women, by their concentrated efforts in one literary movement, can meet with such success as has engendered, planned out, and so successfully consummated this convention, what much more glorious results, what wider spread success, what grander diffusion of mental light will not come forth at the bidding of the enlarged hosts of women writers, already called into being by the stimulus of your efforts?

And here let me speak one word for my journalistic sisters who have already entered the broad arena of journalism. Before the "Woman's Era" had come into existence, no one except themselves can appreciate the bitter experience and sore disappointments under which they have at all times been compelled to pursue their chosen vocations.

If their brothers of the press have had their difficulties to contend with, I am here as a sister journalist to state, from the fullness of knowledge, that their task has been an easy one compared with that of the colored woman in journalism.

Woman's part in Race Literature, as in Race building, is the most important part and has been so in all ages. It is for her to receive impressions and transmit them. All through the most remote epochs she has done her share in literature. When not an active singer like Sappho, she has been the means of producing poets, statesmen, and historians, understandingly as Napoleon's mother worked on Homeric tapestry while bearing the future conqueror of the world.

When living up to her highest development, woman has done much to make lasting history, by her stimulating influence and there can be no greater responsibility than that, and this is the highest privilege granted to her by the Creator of the Universe.

Such are some brief outlines of the vast problem of Race Literature. Never was the outlook for Race Literature brighter. Questions of vast importance to succeeding generations on all lines are now looming up to be dissected and elucidated.

Among the students of the occult, certain powers are said to be fully developed innately in certain types of the Negro, powers that when understood and properly directed will rival if not transcend those of Du Maurier's Svengali.

The medical world recognizes this especially when investigating the science of neurology,—by the merest chance it was discovered that certain types of our nurses—male and female—possessed invaluable qualities for quieting and controlling patients afflicted with the self-destructive mania. This should lead our physicians to explore and investigate so promising a field.

American artists find it easy to carricature the Negro, but find themselves baffled when striving to depict the highest characteristics of a Sojourner Truth. If he lacks the required temperament, there is thus offered a field for the race-loving Negro artist to compete with his elder brother in art, and succeed where the other has failed.

American and even European historians have often proved themselves much enchained by narrow local prejudice, hence there is a field for the unbiased historian of this closing century.

The advance made during the last fifteen or twenty years in mechanical science is of the most encouraging nature possible for our own ever-increasing class of scientific students.

The scholars of the race, linguists and masters of the dead languages have a wide field before them, which when fully explored, will be of incalculable interest to the whole people—I mean particularly the translators of the writings of the ancient world, on all that pertains to the exact estimate in which our African ancestors were held by contemporaries. This will be of interest to all classes, and especially to our own.

Until our scholars shall apply themselves to these greatly neglected fields, we must accept the perverted and indifferent translations of those prejudiced against us.

Dr. Le Plongeon, an eminent explorer and archeologist, in his Central American studies, has made startling discoveries, which, if he succeeds in proving, will mean that the cradle of man's primitive condition is situated in Yucatan, and the primitive race was the ancestor of the Negro.

The "Review of Reviews," of July has this to say: "That such a tradition should have been handed down to the modern Negro is not so improbable in view of the fact that the inhabitants of Africa appear certainly to have had communication with the people of the Western world up to the destruction of the Island of Atlanta, concerning which events Dr. Le Plongeon has much to tell us."

Think of it! What a scope for our scholars not only in archeology, but in everything that goes to make up literature!

Another avenue of research that commands dignified attention is the possibility that Negroes were among those who embarked with Columbus. Prominent educators are giving serious attention to this. Prof. Wright, of Georgia, lately sailed to England with the express purpose of investigating the subject, during his vacation, in some of the famous old libraries of Europe.

The lesson to be drawn from this cursory glance at what I may call the past, present and future of our Race Literature apart from its value as first beginnings, not only to us as a people but literature in general, is that unless earnest and systematic effort be made to procure and preserve for transmission to our successors, the records, books and various publications already produced by us, not only will the sturdy pioneers who paved the way and laid the foundation for our Race Literature, be robbed of their just due, but an irretrievable wrong will be inflicted upon the generations that shall come after us.

47

GERTRUDE BUSTILL MOSSELL

(1855–1948)

Gertrude Bustill Mossell was born in Philadelphia in 1855 to a prominent free black family; her great grandfather served as a baker for George Washington during the Revolution; her sister, Maria Louisa Bustill, was the mother of Paul Robeson. Henry McNeal Turner, editor of the *Christian Recorder*, recognized Gertrude's literary gifts and invited her to contribute poems and essays. While working as a teacher, she wrote for several black newspapers in Philadelphia and New York. After marrying the physician Nathaniel F. Mossell in 1883, she pursued political activism and journalism, becoming the women's editor for the *New York Age* and the Indianapolis *World* and encouraging women to become writers and play an active role in politics. Her niece, Sadie Tanner Mossell Alexander, earned her PhD from the University of Pennsylvania in 1921, becoming the first African American to obtain a PhD in Economics in the United States, the first African American woman to receive a law degree from the University of Pennsylvania's Law School, and the first African American woman to be admitted to the Pennsylvania Bar.

In the eyes of many of the later writers featured in this anthology, Christianity, temperance, and racial equality were linked causes ushering a new era of social progress into American society. Mossell advocates for the expansion of the A.M.E. Church into Africa and extols the value of temperance within the American family. Mossell's eloquence and social stature made her an important figure around whom many women could rally. She represented a national black progressive movement to unify the regional clubs and churches organized during and after Reconstruction.

"Baby Bertha's Temperance Lesson" (1885)

SOURCE: Gertrude Bustill Mossell, "Baby Bertha's
Temperance Lesson," *Christian Recorder* (January 8, 1885).

Baby Bertha in the doorway,
Stands with slow, reluctant feet,
Wide the blue eyes still are open,
Hushed the cheek so fair and sweet.

She has listened to her mother
Pitying poor drunken Lynn,
Heard her pray for his salvation
From his downward path of sin.

Heard her Auntie say, "Lets offer
Him a glass of water cool,
As he passes to the tavern,
Every noon, as in his rule."

But Mamma says, "No, I think not,
It would only do us harm,
He might offer blow or insult."
Thus she spoke in quick alarm.

Then they sighed, and soon forgot him;
Passed the time in quiet talk,
Bade goodbye, and then they parted,
Each one for her homeward.

But our Baby Bertha listened,
And the firm resolve was made;
"For a little child shall lead them,"
Gospel truth that will not fade.

So next noon as Lynn was passing,
In his path the child's form stood
With her little cup and pitcher
And a plate of wholesome food.

"Please don't go to drink to-day sir,
  Have some of this water, cool,
  Have some of my bread and cheese, sir,
  I will hold your hat and rule."

Quick, the thirsty man took from her,
  Drained the goblet at one draught;
  Then he stopped and smiled and kissed her,
  And would then have onward passed,

But to him the child was clinging,
"I will give my little cup,
  You may take it, have and keep it,
  If you'll give the drinking up."

Then he understood her nature,
  And his cheek was flushed with shame,
  But he made and kept that promise
  In the strength of Jesus' name.

Thus the mother learned a lesson,
  That the faith though small indeed,
  Joined unto prayer of Christians
  Shall the wanderer homeward lead.

PHILADELPHIA, PA.

"Will the Negro Share the Glory That Awaits Africa?" (1893)

SOURCE: Gertrude Bustill Mossell, "Will the Negro Share
the Glory that Awaits Africa?," *Christian Recorder*
(January 5, 1893).

Mr. Editor:

Under the above title there appeared in your last issue an appeal from J. M. Henderson one of the most forcible writers for the columns of the RECORDER. This appeal closed with the following thought: "There is wisdom, deep wisdom in Bishop Turner's ceaseless appeal for the evangelization of Africa. It is disheartening to see that it is musunderstood and unresponded to."

These words went straight to my heart. I am not a member of the A.M.E. Church, nor do I favor the Negroes leaving America in a body and colonizing in Africa, but several years ago I was present at Lincoln University, when President Rendall brought on the stage ten native African boys. It was my first sight of a native African. I loved those children from that day. Year after year I met them, went to their graduations until the last one bade the college farewell. It was a marvel to witness their ability, their eloquence.

One of the noblest souls that it has ever been my lot to meet—Thomas H. Roberts—was among that number. Some of these men remained in this country, some are still laboring efficiently. Knowing these ten, I feel that I know the capabilities in ten tribes at least. My heart is in the work. I believe with Dr. Decker Johnson, that Bishop Turner with his influence, his boundless enthusiasm, could, if one more Bishop would unite with him, carry the work to a successful issue. What grander work to close an already memorable career. If our people will rally to the support of the effort, those in the A.M.E. Church and out of it, make it our work in this new century about to open, we will make for ourselves a glorious place in history. To become one of the first and most successful agencies in the redemption of Africa, in the evangelization of its unconverted human souls, to establish firmly commercial relations (through the agency of this church) between Africa and America would be to us like the discovering of a new world.

The A.M.E. Church has gone on conquering and to conquer, North, South, East and West, and the Islands of the sea; why not Africa? Every great effort towards progress has first been cradled in the boundless enthusiasm of one individual, but others must come to their aid, must encourage their drooping spirits by words of sympathy, by the assistance that lies in their power.

At this present hour Bishop Turner seems by his appointment for this quadrennium to mission work, and his known stand upon the question, best able to lead the forces. Why not rally to his support? We hope to live to see the work and accomplished fact.

The "Voice of Missions" will certainly aid in the accomplishment of this work, bring it near us. Let each Sabbath School in the Church take one little native boy or girl under its wing; show them each others pictures; let them write to each other. Let Kings Daughters and Sons Circles take a man or woman and do the same. Let all take a share in the Steamship Co. Let us for once UNITE in favor of a great object. To the women and children it would be but a widening of the loving influences they throw around their own home circle.

To the men but one more responsibility that would strengthen the developing manhood of the race. Let it be one of our New Year resolutions to co-operate with this work of uniting America and Africa. Let us lay the foundation with Our Father and "the times that are in his hands" remaineth the harvest.

48

AMELIA L. TILGHMAN

(1856–1931)

Amelia L. Tilghman was born in the free black community of Washington, D.C.; her mother was a laundress and her father was a servant. After graduating with honors from the Normal program at Howard University in 1871, she taught at public schools in Washington, D.C., and pursued a career in singing. While traveling the country directing and performing in choral works, such as William Bradbury's *Esther the Beautiful Queen* (1856), Tilghman befriended scores of African American musicians and writers. In 1886 Tilghman founded the *Musical Messenger*, the first periodical dedicated to African American music and musicians.

Tilghman's "Dedicated to Her Gracious Majesty, Queen Victoria, of England" unabashedly praises Queen Victoria, a figure held in high esteem by many women of the era, notably Ida B. Wells and Ella Sheppard. Victoria represented female power. Moreover, English royalty's pro-abolition stance gave nineteenth-century African American women overseas allies in their fight for justice. She was a role model, and England had long been a haven for African Americans seeking refuge from race violence at home.

"Dedicated to Her Gracious Majesty, Queen Victoria, of England" (1892)

SOURCE: Amelia L. Tilghman, "Dedicated to Her Gracious Majesty, Queen Victoria, of England," *Women of*

Distinction: Remarkable in Works and Invincible in Character. Ed. Lawson A. Scruggs (Raleigh, NC: L. A. Scruggs, 1893).

Reign on! most glorious Queen!
  And let thy sceptre sway,
Till Ireland's people are redeemed,
  Their darkness turned to day.

Reign on! till right shall rule,
  And wrong shall buried be,
Reign on! most generous, noble soul!
  The world needs such as thee.

Reign on! ne'er let thy power
  Be ever rent in twain,
Thy life so noble, good and pure,
  Be tarnished with one stain.

Reign on! for God doth guide
  Thy sovereigns at His will,
And He who stills the raging tide
  Will bid thy foes be still.

Reign on! unequaled Queen,
  Till man to man is free,
Till not one shackle shall be seen,
  And nowhere slaves shall be.

Reign on! reign ever on!
  Not in this world alone,
But may thy pure and holy life
  Be echoed at God's throne.

Reign on! till Heaven is gained,
  And thou with the redeemed
Shall there receive the victor's crown,
  Most noble, glorious Queen!

49

JOSEPHINE J. TURPIN WASHINGTON

(1861–1949)

Josephine J. Turpin Washington was born in Gooch-land County, Virginia. She attended Howard University and worked as a typist for Frederick Douglass during her summer vacations. After graduating in 1886, she taught at Richmond Theological Seminary, Howard University, and Selma University. Washington was a prolific writer from the time she was a teenager. She is most well known for her essays, which were published widely in periodicals of her time.

The selections here begin with "A Great Danger," a thorough dismantling of the racist views of a white woman, Annie Porter, published in the *Independent* under the headline "A Few More Plain Words." On a gentler note, Washington argues, in "The Province of Poetry," that in poetry "[o]ur most indefinite yearnings for higher things, our half unconscious longings and aspirations are recognized and expressed." In "Needs of Our Newspapers," Washington offers a constructive critique of the black press. She returns to her biting tone in "Anglo Saxon Supremacy," excoriating white Northerners "who came South and out-Herod Herod himself in injustice to the Negro."

"A Great Danger" (1884)

SOURCE: Josephine J. Turpin Washington, "A Great Danger," *New York Globe* 2 (February 1884).

Annie Porter Excoriated.

A Vehement Onslaught Against the Negro
Replied to by a Female Representative
of the Race

To the Editor of The Globe:—In the *Independent* of December 27, appeared an article bearing the title quoted above and written by one who signed herself Annie Porter. The communication is a vehement onslaught against the Negro, who is held up and denounced as "a great danger" to Louisiana in particular and the United States in general. The falsity of some of the statements is apparent from the very nature of things, and the contradictions running through many of the others attest their untruthfulness.

The writer opens with a bitter bewailing of the "extraordinary relapse into barbarism which is going on among the Negroes in Louisiana at this moment;" and shows how dangerous it is to this country that a "large and increasing population of savages should be established in its borders." What does Annie Porter mean by the Negro's relapse into barbarism? A relapse is a falling back into a former state. The use of this term then implies that the Negro was at some subsequent period in a state of barbarism, that he rose above it into some degree of civilization and that he is now falling back or "relapsing," into his former degradation. Is this true? That the Negro in the United States has been in an ignorant and debased condition bordering on barbarism, he, together with his friends and his enemies, is ready to admit. That he has during any time in the country been more advanced in civilization than now, is not conceded. When was this period of pristine wisdom and goodness? Annie Porter cannot mean that it was in the "good old times of slavery;" for, in her own words, she "never approved of slavery" but "always considered it a curse to the people and the country." If then she does think the race a "large and increasing populations of savages," she certainly uses the wrong word when she speaks of their "relapse into barbarism." Without saying anything in regard to the improvement that has been made—an improvement which thousands of honest men and women are ready and glad to declare, these past twenty years has undoubtedly witnessesed no relapse.

Speaking of the majority of Negroes in the village in which she resides, it is remarked that the "Negroes' tendency to leave country homes and drift together in centers either of towns or hamlets is inveterate." Is this social inclination peculiar to the Negro, so that it is worthy of being the subject of special comment? And even if it were, would the fact be in any wise discreditable? Why, Annie Porter herself, in applying the remedies for manifold Negro ills, descants on the advantages of having them together in "industrial centers."

We are entertained (?) with a graphic and extended description of a Negro applicant for the situation of cook. Is Annie Porter as deeply impressed by the dress and manners and conversation of all the unlettered and uncultured characters with whom she comes into contact? Can she not find hundreds of women who differ materially in no respect, save perhaps in color, from the one depicted? Would like ignorance of an Irish woman be attributed to the fact that she is Irish, or of a Dutch that she is Dutch, or of any Anglo-Saxon to the fact of her race? Is it just to Judge the Negro by a standard altogether different from that according to which other people are judged?

That "Negro men are sunk in sloth," is information as unique as it is startling. It seems rather strange, to say the least, that the men who for, lo, these many years have worked the great plantations of the South have hoed the corn, picked the cotton, cultivated the rice; the men who are the very bone and sinew of the South, should be spoken of as "sank in sloth."

How one believes in the power and efficacy of the gospel can think a people possessing any knowledge whatever of it "worse of than if they had never heard of Christianity," I cannot divine. Yet this is what Annie Porter says of the Negroes, concerning whom she further asserts: "Their idea of God is of the most material and at the same time the most superstitious description. Of Jesus they only know as a sort of charm, though common belief prevails among them that he was a black man." They are, in the language of the writer, "given up to the wildest, most extraordinary ideas and superstitions." Superstition exists to a greater or less degree among any ignorant people. The proud Anglo-Saxon will find this exemplified in tracing back the history of his race to the early days of their barbarous and savage state. There are ignorant classes of white people, and as a natural consequence of the ignorance there is superstition among them; but that their idea of God is of the kind declared and their knowledge of Christ as limited as is affirmed, I most emphatically deny. I am of these people; and I know them better than one who stands afar off and fears to have her dainty robes touch their rough and toil-stained garments.

An account is given of a young man "born and brought up a mule-driver," who wanted to become a minister. (Rather strange idea, that of being "born a mule-driver!") A better plan of action than to deride his desire because of his unfitness, would have been to attempt to impress him with the importance of due preparation for the accomplishment of his mission. The fact that she had "tried faithfully to teach him," but that he still had "no knowledge of anything except his trade," signifies nothing. Annie Porter shows her lack of faith in the Negro's capacity, when she declares him "entirely unable to take in geographical and political distinctions." That teacher who has no belief in the existence of the very powers which it is her office to draw out, is calculated to do harm rather than good. Had the young man referred to studied this trade under this fair instructress he would probably have known nothing of that.

And now I quote the foulest aspersion against the women of the race: "I firmly believe that no Negro woman brought up in a former slave state and among those who have been slaves knows the meaning of the word chastity, or grasps the idea of physical morality in the slightest degree." Is a Negress less than a woman, that any condition could rob her of all natural modesty and delicacy? It is false; I repeat it, it is false. Slavery has much for which to render an account; it invaded the sanctity of homes, it nullified the marriage bond, it exposed the temptation and induced to immorality, it prostrated virtue at the foot of vice; it did all this and more; it was a huge blot upon the face of society, a great ulcer upon the body politic, a burning shame to the American people; but it did not, because it could not, take from the women of the oppressed race that innate regard for purity and chastity which remained theirs by right of their womanhood. The instance of a well-taught and well-trained girl falling from virtue and then making excuses for her wrong-doing, is not an uncommon one and is by no means restricted to the Negro race.

If Annie Porter is to write next of murder and bloodshed in the South, she might gain some information by conning matter relative to the late Danville massacre. She might, too, study the art of lynching, prevalent among her white brethren of the south; and might, also, with profit examine into the history of the Ku-Klux. For a Negro to appear as midnight assassin and cut-throat would be an entirely new role. When he had ample opportunities for gratifying any such propensity it did not disclose itself. When the strong and brave among his enemies were away fighting to keep him in bondage and those near and dear to them were at his mercy, instead of rising up to kill and to slay he watched over, worked for, cared for, and harmed not a hair in their heads. Was this the manifestation of a violent and vindictive spirit?

Annie Porter thinks school and churches though "excellent things," do the Negro "little or no good;" but recommends industrial centers and a separate system of local government as their salvation. Industrial pursuits do more than has been accredited to them, if they train head and heart as well as hand, and churches and schools do less than they are intended to do, if they cannot spread the gospel and diffuse knowledge among any people. How the inhabitants of the ideal Negro village painted are to profit by that "higher and better civic training," if they are—as the writer maintains—"entirely unable to take in political and geographic distinctions," and unable to learn the teachings of school or church, I cannot determine. This is but another instance of contradictory views and statements.

Annie Porter observes that a marked feature of the race is their distrust of white people. If this be true, can it not be easily accounted for? Trust or distrust originates from some knowledge of past action. The black man's terrible experience in the hands of white men may, in many cases, have his mind against them, not because they are white but because they have so wronged him. Every such article as Annie Porter's serves to strengthen this feeling. We have, however, too many friends among the white people for this distrust to be general. We can discriminate between our friends and enemies; between those who would do us justice and those who themselves neither regard us aright, nor would have others do so; between those who, actuated by broad and noble principles, would help and encourage struggling humanity and those who, controlled by blind and ignoble prejudices, would use their strength and influence against the Negro's elevation.

JOSEPHINE J. TURPIN.

HOWARD UNIVERSITY, WASHINGTON, D.C.

"The Province of Poetry" (1889)

SOURCE: Josephine J. Turpin Washington, "The Province of Poetry," *A.M.E. Church Review*, no. 6 (1889): 139–141.

What is poetry? Of what does its essence consist? What is its distinguishing principle?

Perhaps in this instance it is easier to give a negative than a positive definition. The language of Shelley, in his "Hymn to the Spirit of Nature," might appropriately be applied to the genius of poetry:

"All feel, yet see thee never";

and two other lines, taken from the same, may fittingly be added:

"Lamp of Earth, where'er thou movest,
Its dim shapes are clad with brightness."

It is agreed that all verse is not poetry. We read perchance a newspaper or magazine effusion and throw it down in disgust, exclaiming, "There is no poetry in that." Why? Probably not one in a hundred could tell, and yet the judgment of the whole hundred might be correct. The want is one easily felt, but difficult to express. Of the explanations attempted, some might approach the truth after this wise: "Oh, there is no soul in it," or "It does not make me feel," or "It deals altogether with the trivial and superficial."

Poets and critics have responded to this inquiry with answers variously worded; but, beneath the outer garb of diverse language, we catch the glimpse of a common meaning. Webster defines poetry as "Modes of expressing thought and feeling which are suitable to the imagination when excited or elevated, and characterized usually by a measured form of one sort or another." Emerson says, "Poetry is the perpetual endeavor to express the spirit of the thing; to pass the brute body, and search the life and reason which cause it to exist." Ruskin calls poetry "the suggestion, by the imagination, of noble grounds for the noble emotions." Charles James Fox characterizes it as "The great refreshment of the human mind, the only thing after all." Aristotle terms it imitation. Bacon says that "It was ever thought to have some participation of divineness, because it doth raise and erect the mind by submitting the show of things to the desires of the mind, whereas reason doth buckle and bow the mind unto the nature of things." Shelley calls it "The best and happiest thoughts of the best and happiest minds," and Poe declares that "A poem deserves its title only inasmuch as it excites by elevating the soul." Matthew Arnold thinks poetry "Simply the most beautiful, impressive and widely effective mode of saying things," and Macauley says, "By poetry we mean the art of employing words in such a manner as to produce an illusion on the imagination; the art of doing by means of words what the painter does by means of color."

If we dared to essay a definition, not discarding and yet not wholly accepting any of the above, but combining with the substance of each the popular idea, which generally has its foundation in truth, we might say that poetry is a species of composition, usually metrical in form, addressed especially to the imagination, and tending to please, instruct and inspire.

There are people who pride themselves upon being what they call "practical," and who look with contempt upon anything verging on sentiment. By the term "practical" they mean that which directly contributes to worldly success, business prosperity, the accumulation of wealth—in short, whatever primarily aids in the solution of the problem what we shall eat, what we shall drink, and wherewithal we shall be clothed. The talk of such a character is of stocks and bonds, of the state of the market, of buying and selling, his highest aspiration to be a "good liver," to dress his wife in silks and furs, to be spoken of as a prosperous businessman, one who knows how to get along in the world. For him Nature has no charm, save as a contributor to his physical wants; literature no allurement, unless it teaches him how to turn what he touches to gold. He could see nothing in Niagara but wasted water-power, and would consider Homer to have been better employed casting up accounts in a ledger than writing the Iliad. The deepest and most tender affections are beyond his comprehension, and he goes through life maimed in soul, dwarfed and incomplete.

What thinks such a man of poetry? All bosh, nonsense, as some think of religion, fit food for women and children. What of poets and their devotees? Fools, simpletons, crack-brained folks, worthy only of commiseration.

> "A primrose by the river's brim
> A yellow primrose is to him,
> And it is nothing more."

There are Mr. Gradgrinds outside of Dickens' pages, and the young lives of many a Tom and Louise have been sadly wrecked by their blundering stupidity. Only the weak are afraid of being tender; only the fool cultivates one part of his nature at the expense of the other. A great brain and a great heart are usually found conjoined.

Sentiment may be termed the true sense of things. It is the underlying thought of being, the soul of phenomena, the reason for the existence of external manifestations. In the words of Madame De Stael, "What a world, when animated by sentiment, without which the world itself were but a desert!" There is a closer connection between what is entitled sentiment and what is classed in the category of the practical than most people think. What teacher has not had pupils who "couldn't see any use in the study of the classics and the higher mathematics?" I have even known a young man, and one too who aspired to pulpit oratory, to say that he "Didn't think he needed to take history and literature—they would be of no practical service to him." There are older and more experienced people in the world quite as narrow in their views as this simple youth. Everybody is familiar with the arguments for the study of sciences of which we do not make direct use in common, everyday life. Similar reasons, though these not the most worthy which can be given, might be advanced for the cultivation of sentiment and its hand-maiden, poetry.

Let it be observed here that there is a distinction between sentiment and the weak mawkishness known as sentimentality. The one is genuine coin, the other spurious imitation; the one alive to all honest, active endeavor for humanity; the other, "dabbling in the fount of tears, divorces the feeling from her mate the deed." The one is affected to tears by the woes of the imaginary hero of stage or novel, yet indifferent to the misery of real men and women; the other, while perhaps no less moved by the distresses of fictitious beings, is touched by the actual suffering about him, and labors for its relief.

While sentiment, feeling, the cultivation of an inner, a soul life, does not directly contribute to the bread-winning process, it sweetens and strengthens and ennobles man's whole nature, and so fits him for the better performance of any duty; arms him more effectually for any conflict, whether with difficulty or temptation, and makes him more of a man, abler to do a man's work in the world.

> "Whatever elevates,
> Inspires, refreshes any human soul,
> Is useful to that soul."

Mr. G. J. Goshen, an English banker and political economist, declares that the cultivation of the imagination is essential to the highest success in politics, in learning, and in the commercial business of life. He who lacks a poetic taste lacks imagination, without which are wanting clearness of vision, comprehensiveness of understanding, and the subtle tact which is as oil to the machinery of both public and private life. To the cultivation of this faculty all who are deficient therein should assiduously address themselves. How this may be done Pres. Porter states: "The study and reading of poetry exercise and cultivate the imagination, and in this way impart intellectual power. It is impossible to read the products of any poet's imagination without using our own. To reach what he creates is to recreate in our own minds the images and pictures which he first conceived and then expressed in language." One who cannot like poetry may be said to have been born into the world mentally blind and deaf—a misfortune as much greater than the deprivation of the corresponding natural senses as spiritual things are superior to material.

Poets are seers, divining and revealing hidden truths; interpreters of beauty and inspirers to a life of a loftier type. In these choice and gifted spirits the great heart of humanity finds its voice; through them all that is best in man speaks from soul to soul. Sentiments we hold sacred are clothed in worthy language. That we have long thought or felt vaguely is expressed in fitting phrases:

> "As imagination bodies forth
> The forms of things unknown, the poet's pen
> Turns them to shapes, and gives to airy nothing
> A local habitation and a name."

Our most indefinite yearnings for higher things, our half-unconscious longings and aspirations are recognized and addressed. Each finds passages that seem meant specially for himself, so fully are the varied needs of the soul understood and supplied. The poet's is

> "The gift, the vision of the unsealed eye,
> To pierce the mist o'er life's deep meanings spread,
> To reach the hidden fountain-urns that lie
> Far in man's heart."

Poetry has a particular charm for the lover of nature. It knows his favorites, paints them lovingly, descries new beauties, points out hidden relations, unveils the thought behind their creation, and sends him back to the woods more humble and reverent of spirit, and yet filled with new delight in what was before his pleasure. The green of the grass is fresher, the glitter of the dew-drop more brilliant, the carol of the birds a divine pean. It is as if he has had his eyes touched with holy spittle: he no longer sees "men as trees walking," but looks forth with clear and perfect vision. To him who has hitherto been dull to the glories of nature, it may be said to add a sense. The world takes on a new aspect for him. Nothing is any longer commonplace or ordinary. He can find beauty, melody, sweetness everywhere. He rejoices in the scent of new-mown hay, the sheen of leaves, the waving of branches, the smell of damp fresh earth, the coloring and grouping of clouds. Solitude no longer means loneliness, nor leisure ennui. He now hath

> "The child's sight in his breast,
>   And sees all *new*,
> What oftenest he has viewed,
> He views with the first glory.
>   Fair and good
>   Pall never on him."

The poet

> "Finds tongues in trees, books in the running brooks,
>   Sermons in stones, and good in everything."

> "The violet by the mossy stone,
>   Half hidden from the eye,"

is to him not merely a bit of vegetable beauty, but a symbol of modesty and sweet retirement. He considers "The lilies of the field, how they toil not, neither do they spin," and from them learns a lesson of quiet trust and restfulness in the sustaining power of a gracious Providence. The great ethical truths which Nature "half reveals and half conceals" are presented by the poet; yet we do not feel that he aims to "point a moral," but rather that his heart is full, and he needs must speak what is. His is the surest fame. He writes for no one time or country. With him anachronisms are impossible. He addresses himself to the heart, and by the heart; the same in every age and clime, he will always be understood. He portrays the beauty of Nature, perennial in its charm and constant in its attraction for the sons of men.

Poetry is closely allied to our best affections. Home, wife, mother, country, are themes ever dear to the poet. He recognizes that "The heart has needs above the head," and seeks to supply it with food fit for its use. By the study of poetry the affections are strengthened, purified and refined, divested of earthy dross and rendered more ethereal in their nature. We are taught to accord the sensibility its proper prominence in life and to keep the heart child-like, tender and susceptible of holy emotions.

The whole aim of poetry, working within her God-given sphere, is to spiritualize the nature. Even when perverted and debased, divorced from her rightful function, she yet shows some signs of her original calling. Perhaps no great poet has so misapplied his powers as Byron; yet what lofty and soul-inspiring strains are found in his works. As illustrative of his higher and better self, the following stanza may be quoted:

"There is a pleasure in the pathless woods,
    There is a rapture on the lonely shore,
There is society where none intrudes,
    By the deep sea, and music in its roar;
I love not man the less, but Nature more,
    From these interviews, in which I steal
From all I may be, or have been before,
    To mingle with the Universe, and feel
What I can ne'er express, yet cannot all conceal."

Even Don Juan contains occasional passages of purity and delicacy. What can be finer than this?

"'Tis sweet to hear the watch-dog's honest bark
    Bay deep-mouthed welcome as we draw near home;
'Tis sweet to know there is an eye will mark
    Our coming, and look brighter when we come;

'Tis sweet to be awakened by the lark,
   Or lulled by falling waters; sweet the hum
Of bees, the voice of girls, the song of birds,
The lisp of children, and their earliest words."

Poetry takes us out of ourselves; it carries us into a new world, the world presided over by

"The glorious faculty assigned
To elevate the more than reasoning mind,
And color life's dark cloud with orient rays.

• • •

Imagination lofty and refined."

What delight to escape for a while from the cares, the vexations and annoyances of the common life and spend an hour with creations of divinely inspired origin. Irving says of Chaucer's "Flower and Leaf": "It brings into our closets all the freshness and fragrance of the dewy landscape." Poetry rejuvenates the old, imparts to the world-worn a relish for simple pleasures, and converts even the cynic to sympathy with the innocent gladness of childhood, the bright hopefulness of youth, the rapture of first love, the smile of woman, the fond pride of the young mother. It is not true that the poet paints a life which does not exist. He paints the best of the life which is, a life opposed to the worldly and artificial, "hidden from the wise and prudent and revealed unto babes." All children are poets, for in them the believing predominates over the examining state of mind.

Poetry is the divinest of all arts. So thought Milton, who wrote with the conscious dignity of a prophet. In the words of Poe, it produces "An elevating excitement of the soul quite independent of that passion which is the intoxication of the heart, or of that truth which is the satisfaction of the reason." Carlyle, in his "Life of Burns," calls "A true poet a man in whose heart resides some effluence of wisdom, some tone of the 'eternal melodies,'" and declares that he is "The most precious gift that can be bestowed on a generation." That is not true poetry which cannot uplift and inspire. It may be rhyme or verse, but it lacks the divine fire without which the draft is flat and vapid. "The poet is born, not made." He writes because he must, not because he will. Pope says of himself:

> "As yet a child, nor yet a fool to fame,
>   I lisped in numbers, for the numbers came."

What is more ludicrous than the pretentions and affectations of would-be poets—jugglers in the divine art? Some of these are poor self-deluded creatures who persist in believing themselves inspired, the verdict of all mankind to the contrary not withstanding; others, because they think it a "fine thing" to be a poet, turn to poetry with a deliberateness they would carry into watch or cabinetmaking, not realizing that their needs must be filled with an inflatus from on high. They ape the style and manner of Apollo's favorites, adopt Byronic collars and flowing locks, assume an air sometimes wild and frenzied, sometimes dreamy and abstracted; disregard the simple things of life, and strain after what is high and mighty. With such individuals sense is

> "sacrificed to sound,
> And truth cut short to make the period round."

While there is much written for poetry which does not deserve the name, there are poems that are never penned. There are "mute, inglorious Miltons who die with all their music in them." To these has been given the poet-soul, but not the poet's power of expression. They have somewhat of that "divine madness," of that "fine frenzy" which characterizes the poet, and are those who best understand and appreciate him.

All true poets are "touched with a coal from heaven," but all do not burn with the same intensity; all are not poets of the same order. We would not have it otherwise. Tennyson is best suited to some minds, Longfellow to others. To-day we may enjoy the sublime eloquence of Milton; to-morrow prefer the calm beauty of Wordsworth. The mountains uplift the sensitive soul to an exaltation of delight, but stay too long among them and the feeling of awe becomes oppressive.

The poet is his own benefactor as well as ours. There are many who put on their singing robes when sad and weary, many who strike the lyre when their hearts are torn with grief, and are comforted by the strains they themselves evoke. When the real world was shut out from James the First of Scotland, he consoled himself with the world of imagination. Tasso relieved the gloom of his lonely cell with the splendid scenes of his Jerusalem. A poet, describing the pleasure derived from exercising the imaginative faculty, exclaims, "Oh! to create within the soul is bliss!" Tennyson, in his "Memoriam," a poem which is the product of a great grief, speaks of even "The sad mechanic exercise" of verse-making "like dull narcotics, numbing pain." Many an overtaxed heart or brain, which otherwise might have succumbed to the burden imposed upon it, has found vent for itself in song. Who knows what relief the writing of Samson Agonistes, whose hero was afflicted with the poet's own sad malady, may have been to Milton; or the "Raven" to Poe, with whom poetry was "not a purpose, but a passion?" Even Byron's egotism may be viewed leniently when we consider that probably he wrote for the relief of a life which, however erring, was much wronged and most unfortunate.

In this age, when, with the advancement of civilization and the greater cultivation of the physical sciences, the tendency seems to be toward the material, toward what we are pleased to call the "practical," there is special need of the spiritualizing influence of poetry. Macaulay says that "In the progress of nations toward refinement, the reasoning powers are improved at the expense of the imagination"; and that "As civilization advances, poetry almost necessarily declines." If this is true, we ought the more assiduously cultivate the poetic taste, that so noble a gift may not be wholly lost, and to appreciate the more highly those great bards who have already sung for us, since the probability of having others decrease as the centuries of civilization roll by. The tendency toward epicureanism, which the modern adaption of the results of the physical sciences to our bodily wants encourages, must not be allowed to strangle that religion of inner and spiritual things of which poetry is the apostle.

Men have at all times yielded to the sway of the seer. Originating as the poem did in the religious instinct, we are peculiarly rich in what may be termed "religious poems," many of them of great power and beauty. Combined with music, as vehicles of appeal they have been most effective. One heart may be open to conviction through the sermon, while another may be influenced more readily by the hymn. This is not due to the music alone: the words sung have also their weight. Who knows the power that has been wielded by "Rock of Ages" or "Nearer, my God to Thee?" Moody would never have had the marvelous success which has attended his efforts as evangelist had it not been for Sankey's services in connection with the work. The Psalms of the Bible and the inspired utterances of the Hebrew prophets take rank in the highest order of religious poetry.

Of songs on secular subjects there are many which have moved the hearts and influenced the lives of mankind. Thomas Moore immortalized Ireland by his patriotic lays, as did Scott his own native land. "Home, Sweet Home," is familiar, yet ever dear. The "Battle Hymn of the Republic" and the "Star-Spangled Banner" never fail to evoke the enthusiasm of American citizens. The antislavery poems of Whittier and Longfellow helped to break the chain which bound the slaves. Even the rude rhymes of the oppressed, sung amid the toil of the field, tended to ease the burden of pain at their hearts. Who can read "Evangeline" without being taught a lesson of patient love and resignation? or "Aurora Leigh" without gaining a nobler conception of womanhood? or "The Cotter's Saturday Night" without heightened sympathy with the domestic life of the poor?

Longfellow's fame may be said to rest chiefly upon Hiawatha, a romance of Indian life, but he has many minor pieces unsurpassed for melody and moral sweetness. Can any doubt the influence for good of such poems as the "Psalm of Life," "Excelsior," and "The Builders?" Burns, like the true bard that he is, recognizes that poetry lies in the sentiment, and not in loftiness of theme or pomp of language. He does not disdain such simple subjects as the "mountain daisy" and the "wee, cowering, timorous beastie." What of interest does the poetic mind find in a barefoot boy? Yet to Whittier, with his poet's perception of the nearness between the realms of reality and indeality, he is a source of inspiration.

> "Ah! that thou couldst know thy joy
> Ere it passes, barefoot boy!"

We quote from Tennyson lines which seem to us to contain the solution of the vexed question of the relative superiority or inferiority of man and woman:

> "For woman is not undeveloped man,
> But diverse; could we make her as the man,
> Sweet Love were slain; his dearest bond is this,
> Not like to like, but like in difference.
> Yet in the long years liker must they grow:
> The man be more of woman, she of man,
> He gain in sweetness and in moral height,
> Nor lose the wrestling thews that throw the world,
> Till at the last she set herself to man,
> Like perfect music unto noble words;
> And so this twain upon the skirts of Time
> Sit side by side, full-summed in all their powers,
> Dispensing harvest, sowing the To-be,
> Self-reverent each, and reverencing each.
> . . . . either sex alone
> Is half itself, and in true marriage lies
> Nor equal nor unequal; each fulfills
> Defect in each, and always thought in thought,
> Purpose in purpose, will in will, they grow,
> The single pure and perfect animal,
> The two-cell'd heart beating with one full stroke, Life."

Who is so lacking in patriotic feeling that he has not thrilled at these words of Scott?

> "Breathes there a man with soul so dead,
> Who never to himself hath said,
> This is my own, my native land!

Whose heart hath ne'er within him burned,
As home his footsteps he hath turned
   From wandering on a foreign strand."

What can be grander and more inspiring than this from
Holmes?

"Build thee more stately mansions,
   O my soul,
   As the swift seasons roll!
   Leave thy low-vaulted past!
   Let each new temple, nobler than the last,
   Shut thee from heaven with a dome more vast,
   Till thou at length art free,
   Leaving thine out-grown shell by life's unresting sea."

The following lines are characteristic of Wordsworth:

"Nature never did betray
   The heart that loved her. 'Tis her privilege
   Through all the years of this, our life, to lead
   From joy to joy! for she can so inform
   That is within us, so impress
   With quietness and beauty, and so feed
   With lofty thoughts, that neither evil tongues,
   Rash judgments, nor the sneers of selfish men,
   Nor greetings where no kindness is, nor all
   The dreary intercourse of daily life
   Shall e'er prevail against us, to disturb
   Our cheerful faith that all which we behold
   Is full of blessings."

Does not humanity owe something to the poet, to the high
priest of the beautiful, the lofty, the true? It has ever been slow
to pay its debt. Living, the world's heroes and benefactors are
neglected; dead, their dust is sacredly treasured. Thus it was
with the Christian apostles, with Socrates, Galileo, and Roger
Bacon. Burns spent his last days friendless and poverty-stricken;

but a splendid mausoleum marks his resting-place. Even the immortal Milton was little regarded as a poet by his contemporaries. "The old blind poet," says Waller, "hath published a tedious poem on the 'Fall of Man.' If its length be not considered as a merit, it hath no other." In the words of Carlyle, "Men of genius ask for bread and receive a stone."

There comes, however, a time of posthumous retribution, and he who was unappreciated by his own generation receives honor at the hands of posterity. Then every possible relic, every personal memento, every associated article becomes a priceless possession, and the old house at Stratford-on-Avon the Mecca of many a pilgrimage. Yet there are those who recognize the divine right of poets, whether living or dead, to the highest meed of honor. It is gratifying to note the widespread and enthusiastic celebration of recent birthdays of our own Whittier. Why not let the great ones of the earth know, while yet among us, the esteem in which they are held?

> "Blessings be with him and undying praise,
> Who gives us higher loves and nobler cares."

Milton calls a good book the life-blood of a master spirit. This is especially true of a good poem, for it comes directly from the heart, and is the very essence of being. We have only pity for those old days of Puritan rule when poets were styled the "Caterpillars of the Commonwealth," and indignation moved Sidney to write "The Defense of Poesy." Wolf had a true conception of the worth and dignity of the poetic art when he declared that he would rather have written the "Elegy" than to capture Quebec.

But if mankind owes much to the poet, does not the poet owe much also to mankind? He is made the instrument of a Divine message to the world. Woe betide him if he utter it not in clear and unmistakable tones. Given as he is a nature sensitive, intense and passionate, "dowered with the hate of hate, the scorn of scorn, the love of love," he may be peculiarly subject to temptations, but living so near the border-land of the spirit world, having communion with creatures bright and blest, he should be stronger than ordinary mortals to resist the evil. The waywardness characteristic of so many poets should not be attributed to the nature of their calling. On the other hand, probably poetry is a safety-valve for their excess of emotion, and they are the better men for being poets. The greatest punishment the erring seer can undergo is that agony of soul derived from his own clear perception of his deviation from his ideal. Yet there is a generous nobleness mingling even with the errors of the true poet. Amid all the excesses of Robert Burns, not one mean or petty action can be found.

The poet is but the mouthpiece of God, and should be modest in his highest flights. Mrs. Browning voices this thought when she says:

"Learn from hence, weak mortals, all ye poets that pursue
    Your way still onward up to eminence!
Ye are not great, because creation drew
    Large revelations round your earliest sense,
Nor bright, because God's glory shines for you."

Receiving true rays of light from the object, the faulty mirror may so distort them as to give back but an imperfect image. What an awful and yet sublime responsibility is his who is sent into the world to proclaim a message thereto! That grand and austere old poet, Milton, says: "He who would write heroic poems must make his whole life a heroic poem." It is small wonder that Rasselas, after listening to an enumeration of the qualities essential to the poetic character, exclaimed: "Who, then, can be a poet?"

"Needs of Our Newspapers: Some Reasons for Their Existence" (1889)

SOURCE: Josephine J. Turpin Washington, "Needs of Our Newspapers," *New York Age*, no. 2 (October 19, 1889).

Results of an Accomplished Woman Writer's Study of the Negro Press of the Country—Its Intrinsic and Extrinsic Requirements

That the Negro requires a press of his own, few will be found to deny. Were it simply that he desires news in general, this requirement would be much less urgent; for the long established and wealthy journals of other races are much better fitted to meet this demand than we can hope for a long time to be. But he wants besides general news, which any reliable and well-conducted organ can furnish, news of a special type, of such a kind as publications owned and controlled by white men will not give. He needs information of race doings; he needs to know how events appear seen through the eyes of leading colored men. He needs to conduct journalistic enterprises, that he may show to the world his ability in this direction.

You may say that this is drawing the color-line. Why not merge our interests in those of the community, subscribe for the best newspapers only and refuse support to those poor and struggling, irrespective of race or nationality? But why speak of our drawing the color-line? It is drawn and most persistently by the whites. For us to attempt to ignore the fact, would be like trying to walk through a stone wall by simply making up your mind it is not there. The wall stands and you have only a broken head for your pains. The best way to obliterate this color-line, which is contrary to both reason and Christianity, is not foolishly to ignore it, but to act in accordance with the existing facts, while at the same time protesting against the injustice of the situation, and to develop to the uttermost the powers within us, to prove ourselves worthy of equality of every sort, to "make by force our merit known."

Studying the Negro newspapers of the country, as any member of the race interested in its welfare must do, I have been struck with certain needs, both intrinsic and extrinsic, in drawing attention to which I hope I shall be understood. I had almost said "pardoned," but that would imply a fault of making criticism, which I do not admit.

In the first place the journalistic field is often entered with the wrong motive. Where motive is low and altogether lacking, there can be no high standard for the paper. Some become editors merely for the sake of notoriety, for the delight of being in print; some are simply political tools, hired to profess the principles they avow; others hope to make a fortune, a hope I hardly need add which has never been realized by a colored editor. Every paper should have an aim, and a high and lofty one, should devote itself to principles of right, and should be brave and outspoken in their advocacy.

A good motive is, however, not all sufficient. Journalistic ability is essential. It is true that not every one who can write a good magazine article or even a book, has the peculiar gift necessary to successfully conduct a newspaper. There are Negro editors, however, who cannot write a decent article of any kind, who cannot even speak good English. Such men have no business in the editorial chair. I have sometimes thought that were some of them to read an essay entitled "Writing for the Press," in Matthews' "Hours with Men and Books," they might lose some of that audacity which, after all, is but in accordance with the familiar quotation, "Fools rush in, where angels fear to tread."

The colored newspaper is too indifferent to the quality of its material. Editors seem to accept contributions through fear of losing subscribers or making enemies. Now, if people think that because they take a certain paper that paper ought to print any and all of their senseless effusions, the sooner they are disabused of this idea, the better for them individually and for the race collectively. Those who have control of newspaper columns should put forth efforts to secure the best writers and when able to do so should pay them for their services.

Many of our papers give too much space and prominence to letters containing the local and personal news of insignificant towns, which cannot be of any interest to the public at large.

We ought to have more original and less patent matter. There are few colored papers without a page or two of patent material. It would be better to have a smaller sheet and that original than one larger mostly patent. It would exact more time and money and brains but it would accomplish more for the race; and being more acceptable to the public would in the end be more profitable to its proprietors.

The original matter need not, however as is often the case, be personal abuse of a journalistic brother or some other disputant. If an opponent's reasoning cannot be confuted, it does not help the argument to impugn his motives or seek to destroy his reputation. Nor should the opposite error of giving fulsome and extravagant praise and bestowing titles where they do not belong, be indulged. Our newspaper encomiums are so generally in the superlative degree that one wonders if the authors of such meaningless panegyrics do not experience acute chagrin when something really great is achieved and they can find for its description no language more exalted than that in daily use. Every public man of any ability is a leader, every scribbler of verses a poet, every teacher a professor, every minister a doctor of divinity. All is splendid, grand, magnificent; by criticism praise is understood; and nothing which we do can be surpassed.

Another need is the improvement of the mechanical make-up of the paper. Many of our most talented writers are shy of the Negro press, because of the way in which they are unwittingly misrepresented. Articles appear with misspelt words, mistakes in grammar, sentences and parts of the sentences omitted or inserted in the wrong place. Greater care in the selection and superintendence of workmen would remedy this evil. The editors and managers of our newspapers should also manifest more interest in obtaining subscriptions and advertisements, and in securing active agents throughout the country. Mr. I. Garland Penn, in an able letter published in a recent issue of *The Age*, gives some pertinent suggestions on this point.

Among what I term the extrinsic needs of the Negro newspaper, one very conspicuous is need of support. This is why they "come to stay" and yet disappear after a fitful existence of a few weeks or months. Of course one reason why many lack support is because they are unworthy of support. The law of the "survival of the fittest" may be usually depended upon, yet there are reasons outside of the press itself why so many of our papers languish and die. Many colored people have a way of sneering at race enterprises. They are not colored men, they say; they are simply men. If the Negro newspaper ranks below white journals which can be bought for the same or a price even lower, they query why should they subscribe for the former. If they subscribe, they openly deride, and do the paper more harm with their tongue than they do good with their purse.

Those who are able ought to help the race by contributions to its literature; but the being able should mean not merely time and taste for writing but also something to say and a knowledge of how to say it. Too much sameness of subject is a fault to be deplored in our publications. Being Negroes does not prevent us from being also men and women, endowed with powers and inclinations similar to those of others. The race question is a very important question, but it is not the only one for us; nor are church affairs all that concern even church organs. There are political, social, moral, scientific, educational and economic problems which affect us as individuals and as a people. Why not show ourselves capable of aiding in their solution?

This is but one phase of an important subject, and our silence at this time as to the other is no indication that we are either blind or unappreciative. "The Achievements of Negro Newspapers" is a theme worthy of discussion and prolific material. My preference for this topic which I have chosen is due to the fact that we are already recipients of too much praise from our friends and too little honest criticism. That vile vituperation of which the race is every day the victim, comes from the enemies and, in no sense, can be considered criticism. The path of the editor, and especially the Negro editor is thorny and far from being a path of pleasantness and peace. The ideal newspaper can never be realized but he who works in steady contemplation and pursuit thereof, works more worthily and achieves greater results than those without an ideal. It is encouraging to note that we have newspapers that are striving for dignity and elevation of tone and general excellence of character. Prominent among these are *The Age,* Detroit *Plaindealer* and the Cleveland *Gazette*, while several others might be mentioned. Let the Negro editor who feels himself in his proper sphere grow not discouraged because of imperfections, but persevere in his efforts to work out the salvation of his people.

JOSEPHINE TURPIN WASHINGTON

"Anglo Saxon Supremacy" (1890)

SOURCE: Josephine J. Turpin Washington, "Anglo Saxon
Supremacy," *New York Age, no. 48* (August 23, 1890).

The Afro Americans attending the national Teacher's Association, at St. Paul Minn., heard at least one very unpalatable
address on the race problem.

Had it been that the simple truth was told, however unpleasant, it could have been received with a certain degree of equa-
nimity. It could have been swallowed as one takes bitter
medicine from the physician, who is not mistaken as an enemy
because his dose happens to be nauseous. From beginning to
end, the address was one mass of misrepresentation, distorted
facts and unjust assumptions with regard to the Negro. This is
all the more dangerous because the speaker, Mrs. Helen K. Ingram of Jacksonville, Fla., assumed the guise of friendliness.

Our Northern friends are not likely to be imposed upon by
the utterances of the avowed Negro hater, who expresses himself with violence and frequently makes no other attempt towards argument than the shotgun. His assertions are
disregarded or treated as the ravings of a rabid maniac. It is the
man or woman of acknowledged respectability, of high moral
and social standing, of expressed goodwill to the Negro, and of
apparent fairness to him, who can do us real harm with those
who are truly our friends, but who are not so situated as to
have an opportunity of knowing us well.

Such an enemy, in the garb of a friend, is evidently Mrs.
Helen K. Ingram. The fact that she was "born, brought up and
educated in New York State" and that for years her "nearest
neighbors were the intimate friends of Gerrit Smith and William Lloyd Garrison and active, earnest officials in that mysterious transit line—the underground railway," proves nothing.
Does she mention these facts in her personal history because
she thinks we must believe that one who lived so near to the
friends of the Negro must be necessarily herself his friend? Or
that one born and reared in a Northern State must perforce inspire confidence on this question? Mrs. Ingram is not the only

Northerner with Southern principles and ideas. The South teems, in some sections, with Northern men who came South and out-Herod Herod himself in injustice to the Negro. The fear of being ostracized in social and injured in business circles, acts as a potent influence. Perhaps the most prejudiced town in the State of Alabama—certainly the only one I know which has separate coaches on its dummy line for white and colored passengers—is the Magic City of Birmingham, built up almost altogether by Northern capitalists. Nor is unfairness to the Negro confined to Northern men who come South to live. We have a prominent example of this in the recent assault, in New York city, on T. Thos. Fortune of *The Age*. On the other hand Cable of Louisiana and Blair of Virginia are Southerners, and yet just and fair in their views on this race question. We cannot with surety classify either our friends or our enemies by sections, but we recognize them when we find them.

According to Mrs. Ingram, even the system of slavery itself cannot be deplored. The slave was happy, care-free, satisfied, "a slave in little but a name." He "was a picturesque feature in our country," "a favorite theme for poet romancers and song makers," a being invested with imaginary ills by soft-hearted romantic folks who were too far off from him to know his real delightful condition. It does seem to me that listening to such a representation of the barbarous system that reduced men to the level of brutes, that maltreated and mangled and killed when it would the body, that warped and distorted and degraded the soul, that disregarded the family relation and set a premium on vice, that tore husbands from wives and mothers from children, that perpetrated all the evil which can be conceived when one human being is placed entirely within the power of another—it does seem to me that we should feel justified in distrusting any statement coming from one who could so seek to palliate the crimes of slavery.

Nor is Mrs. Ingram's representation of the Negro's condition in freedom more reliable. She declares that "every avenue of trade is open to him;" that the South has given him "careful training in equal schools with her white population and she has given him equal opportunities for using that education;" that "not an occupation, trade profession, or business of any kind is barred to him." She cites as if they were common occurrence, two isolated instances of his employment in Jacksonville, in one case as a clerk in a shoe-store where "a white man and a colored man stand side by side behind the counter and in the other where "the young man whose hair kinks to the skin and whose eyes and teeth shine like stars in a midnight sky" will fill your prescription in one of the oldest and wealthiest drug stores in the city. "In groceries, hardware stores, anywhere you choose, the same equal chance is given." Can anything be farther from the truth? There was not one of those colored teachers who sat within hearing of his assertion that did not in his heart utter a denial; not one of the white people in the audience but knew it was false. There is no one so ignorant of the status of the negro in this country as not to be aware that neither North nor South are all employments open to him. A few remarkable exceptions only prove the rule of his general exclusion. Were his admission to all grades of employment for which he is fitted a matter of course, if would not excite such comment when it does occur.

The Negro is not given an equal chance, Mrs. Ingram and others of her class to the contrary notwithstanding. A colored photographer may be so fortunate as to have "a conspicuous gallery in a central location on the principle street in Jacksonville," but who does not know that colored professional men in the South, and to some extent in the North also, are daily refused offices in certain localities because neighboring white tenants would be offended? Who does not know that colored men of education, of refinements, of unimpeachable character, cannot rent or buy homes where they will? That colored photographer "cares not which race comes up his winding stair," but I venture to say his work lies principally among his own people. The colored dentist was admitted to practice, but how many white patients will he have? Jacksonville is indeed an exception if "the finest schoolhouses in the city are those built for the use of the colored race." Never having visited the city, I am not prepared to deny this. I must say, however, that I cannot believe in the statement that 52.3 per cent. of Florida's school fund goes to her colored pupils. If this is so, how is it that the colored schools are inferior to the white schools in number, in buildings, in educational appliances, and in the amount expended for teacher's salaries? This is undeniably true of Pensacola, with which I am well acquainted.

What has Mrs. Ingram to say of the refusal to the Negro of equal accommodations in hotels, theatres, and railway cars; of the race prejudice shown even in so-called Christian churches; of denials at soda water fountains, and proscriptions on the ocean beach? Then made the objects of such invidious distinctions, shown in these and a hundred other ways, are we given an "equal chance?"

"Ninety-five per cent. of our criminals are Negroes!" This may be a startling statement, but it is not altogether discouraging to one who knows anything of what goes on behind the scenes. How many of these alleged criminals are really guilty, can never be known. In most cases they are tried, without adequate counsel, by judge and jury alike prejudiced. The trial is opened with the assumption that the fellow is an abandoned wretch because he is a "nigger." The predominance of the accused's own color on the jury is, in case of the Negro, a very unusual occurrence. In some parts of the South colored men are never put on the jury. Their names happen never to be reached. The colored judge is a phenomenon—too rare a genus to be considered. Negroes are arrested for offenses which white men commit with impunity. When the white man is brought before the bar of justice (?) money and influence frequently secure him an acquittal, regardless of his guilt. I do not believe that an impartial administration of the law would give ninety-five per cent. of Negro criminals even if under present circumstance it is true; but were we to grant for the sakes of argument, that this is the correct proportion of Negro to white criminals, could we not find another explanation than natural and incurable depravity of the Negro? What of heredity, of the transmission of traits acquired under unfavorable environment, of the influence of two hundred and fifty years of slavery? In this there is nothing to warrant despair. There is no reason to believe that the stain of the deplorable past is not eradicable.

It matters little that Mrs. Ingram characterizes the Negro as "without dignity, sly, deceitful, improvident, simply imitative in small matters, self-sufficient and important," while the

Anglo-Saxons have always been "dignified, spirited, valiant, truthful, fearless, enterprising;" that she compares the one to the mule and the other to the horse in their respective capacities for improvement. Simple affirmations, from such a source and in such a cause are not convincing. We could speak of the Negro's patient and forgiving spirit, of his faithfulness and devotion even to the owners who oppressed him, of his loyalty to the union, of his remarkable progress since the acquisition of freedom, in education, in culture, in wealth, in morality, in all that go to make the man. We could contrast these virtues with the selfish and grasping natures of those who held him in bondage, with the cruelty and brutality with which they exercised their power, with the unjust and barbaric treatment they now accord him; but we would not say, "Behold, these men are Anglo Saxons: such must be the character of all Anglo-Saxons." Some Negroes are certainly what Mrs. Ingram says of the "the Negro," but the description fits some white men as well.

Apropos of this, soon after the late fruitless conference of able and learned white men who met to discuss the future of the Negro without having extended to any member of that race the courtesy of an invitation to be present and to participate in the discussion, the New York *World* published a short editorial in which it very pertinently remarks: "Negroes there are, but not 'the Negro,' a term which means, if it means anything, a certain type of persons, similarly circumstanced with identical characters and aspirations, whose case is to be dealt with by formulae, as is done with chemicals in the laboratory;" and adds further on, "The Negro race contains a great variety of individuals so unlike each other as to make generalization concerning them utterly absurd and misleading."

Mrs. Ingram says, furthermore, "All who have risen to any distinction among them (the Negroes) are nearly white." This was clearly and emphatically refuted in the person of the well-known Negro orator, J. C. Price, in attendance on that very convention and one of the invited speakers of the occasion. It is further refuted in the persons of New York's able counselor, T. McCants Stewart; Detroit's eminent lawyer, D. Augustus Straker; Dr. Alexander Crummell, a renowned scholar and theologian; Dr. Edward Wilmot Blyden, a celebrated linguist and scientist; Kelly Miller, Howard University's brilliant young professor of mathematics, and many others. Suppose we were to admit that the majority who have risen to distinction among us are of mixed blood. It would not prove the natural superiority of the Anglo Saxon. It could be explained very simply on the ground that blood relationship to the Anglo-Saxon race, as the race which has had the hundreds of years of training, of education, and of culture of which we have been deprived, is fraught with some intellectual benefit to the offspring; and on the further ground that the unnatural fathers were, in some cases, moved to give to these children of illegitimate birth educational advantages superior to those within the reach of the unmixed black. Would this justify the assumption that the whites are naturally superior and will always maintain supremacy? By no means. A mere statement of superiority amounts to nothing. It must be proven. The Afro-American is doing his part in schools and colleges, in business and in professional life to confound the advocates of white superiority. Clement Morgans will multiply as the years go by. Let the good work progress. Time will solve the problem; and it is my prediction that despite race prejudice, despite injustice, despite oppression, despite cavillings over race supremacy, the solving will result in the peopling of America with "the man of the new race," the "Minden Armais" of Dr. Jamieson.

JOSEPHINE TURPIN WASHINGTON

50

IDA B. WELLS-BARNETT

(1862–1931)

Ida B. Wells-Barnett is well known to most readers of this anthology. Born in Holly Springs, Mississippi, she had some of the least advantaged early years of the writers included here. Orphaned in 1878, she worked as a teacher to support five younger siblings left in her care. She moved with the two youngest to Memphis and briefly took classes at Fisk University in Nashville. In 1884 she refused to give up her seat to a white man on a Chesapeake and Ohio Railroad car and was physically removed. Wells sued the Railroad and won, though the ruling was later overturned by the Tennessee Supreme Court. Wells began to write and, in 1889, was invited to join the *Memphis Free Speech and Headlight*, a militant Memphis newspaper. After three friends were lynched, in 1892, her focus turned to anti-lynching efforts.

A year before her death, Wells ran for state legislature, making her the first black woman to run for public office in the United States.

The following selections showcase Wells's range as an activist. Though known mostly for her campaign against lynching, Wells advocated for racial justice on all fronts. In "Our Country's Lynching Record" and "Lynch Law and the Color Line," Wells's words meet their familiar target, while in "Our Women," "The Ordeal of the 'Solitary,'" and "The Requirements of Southern Journalism," her attention turns elsewhere. No matter Wells's subject, her rhetoric charges ahead, arguing for her audience's immediate effort. Every act Wells encountered that proliferated white supremacy was called what it was: violence. And the protection she sought for American blacks gained her recognition by her contemporaries.

"Our Women" (1887)

SOURCE: Ida B. Wells-Barnett, "Our Women," *New York Freeman* (January 1, 1887).

The Brilliant "Iola" Defends Them from the Memphis Scimiter

Among the many things that have transpired to dishearten the Negroes in their effort to attain a level in the status of civilized races, has been the wholesale contemptuous defamation of their women.

Unmindful of the fact that our enslavement with all the evils attendant thereon, was involuntary and that enforced poverty ignorance and immorality was our only dower at its close, there are writers who have nothing to give the world in their disquisitions on the Negroes, save a rehearsal of their worthlessness, immorality, etc.

While all these accusations, allowed as we usually are, no opportunity to refute them, are hurtful to and resented by us, none sting so deeply and keenly as the taunt of immorality; the jest and sneer with which our women are spoken of, and the utter incapacity or refusal to believe there are among us mothers, wives and maidens who have attained a true, noble, and refining womanhood. There are many such all over this Southland of ours, and in our own city they abound. It is this class who, learning of the eloquent plea in defense of, and the glowing tribute paid Negro womanhood, by G. P. M. Turner in the speech he delivered in the Bewden case, return him their heartfelt thanks and assure him that their gratitude and appreciation of him as a gentleman, a lawyer and a far seeing economist is inexpressible. Our race is no exception to the rest of humanity, in its susceptibility to weakness, nor is it any consolation for us to know that the nobility of England and the aristocratic circles of our own country furnish parallel examples of immorality. We only wish to be given the same credit for our virtues that others receive, and once the idea gains ground that worth is respected, from whatever source it may originate, a great incentive to good morals will have been given. For what you have done in that respect accept the sincere thanks of the virtuous colored women of this city.

IOLA

"The Requirements of Southern Journalism" (1893)

SOURCE: Ida B. Wells-Barnett, "The Requirements of Southern Journalism," *A.M.E. Zion Church Quarterly* (January 1893): 189–196.

Mr. President, Members of the National Press Association, Ladies and Gentlemen:

The conditions which led to a memorial to Congress and a visit to the President of the United States by this body still obtain in this country since last you met, the outrages which prompted that memorial have increased; the lyncher has become so bold, he has discarded his mask and the secrecy of night, has left the out-of-the-way village and invaded the jails and penitentiaries of our largest cities, and hung and tortured his victims on the public streets. Not content with this, Arkansas furnishes the spectacle of a woman vindicating her honor (?) by setting fire to a living being, who, as the flames lick his burning flesh, dies protesting his innocence to the crowd of 5000 that looked on and applauded the act in ghoulish glee. A fifteen year old girl in Rayville, Louisiana, suspected of poisoning a white family is promptly hung on that suspicion; three reputable citizens of Memphis, Tenn., were taken from the jail and shot to death for prospering too well in business and defending themselves and property; one of the journals which was a member of your organization has been silenced by the edict of the mob which declared there shall be no such thing as

"Free Speech" in the South. Within the past two weeks, honest, hardworking, land owning men and women of the race have been hung, shot, whipped and driven out of communities in Texas and Arkansas for no greater crime than that of too much prosperity. Indeed one almost fears to pick up the daily paper in which it is an unusual thing not to see recorded some tale of outrage or blood, with the Negro always the loser. The President of the United States announces himself unable to do anything to stay this "Reign of Terror," and the race in the localities in which these outrages occur are nearly always unable to protect themselves; the local authorities will not extend to them the protection they demand. The President and Congress have been petitioned, race indignation has vented itself in impassioned oratory and public meetings. But denouncing the flag as dirty and dishonored which does not protect its citizens, and repudiating the national hymn because it is a musical lie, has not stopped the outrages. Politics have been eschewed, civil rights given up, (rights which are dearer than life itself) and even life itself has been sacrificed on the altar of Southern hate, and still there is no peace. The assassin's bullet and ku-klux whip is still heard and the sight of the hangman's noose with an Afro-American dangling at the end, is becoming a familiar object to the eyes of young America.

If indeed "the pen is mightier than the sword," the time has come as never before that the wielders of the pen belonging to the race which is so tortured and outraged, should take serious thought and purposeful action. The blood, tears and groans of hundreds of the murdered cry to you for redress; the lamentations, distress and want, of numberless widows and orphans appeal to you to do the only thing which can be done—and which is the first step toward revolution of every kind—the creation of a healthy public sentiment.

In the creation of sentiment, the Southern newspaper can not do much, but it can do something. One of the first requirements then of Southern Journalism is to have, wherever practicable, an organ on the ground. Scattered throughout the South are journals which for lack of capital and good business management fail to do the good they might. Some have gone into the profession not always because of a love for it, or the desire to reach a high standard, but for personal aggrandizement or political preferment. Their weekly advent creates no ripples upon the body politic, disturbs no existing condition and if they can secure the wherewithal to feed the press—are permitted to exist, until they die a natural death. If it could be established, a fearlessly edited press is one of the crying necessities of the hour. Such a journal, edited in the midst of such conditions as exist in the South, can better give the facts, than out of it, or than the press dispatches will do. True, such a one might have to be on the hop, skip and jump but the seed planted even though the sower might not tarry to watch its growth, can never die. At present only one side of the atrocities against a defenseless people is given, and with all the smoothing over is a bad enough showing. The press dispatches of March 9, heralded to the country that "three negro toughs who kept a low dive, fired upon and wounded officers of the law who had gone to arrest one of their number, and as a consequence two nights afterward had been lynched." The *Free Speech* gave the facts in the case, exposing the rank injustice and connivance of the authorities with a white grocery keeper whose trade had been absorbed by these young colored men: how he set a trap into which they fell, and that although the wounded deputies were pronounced out of danger, these men were lynched in obedience to the unwritten law that an Afro-American should not shoot a white man, no matter what the provocation. Our paper showed the character of these men to be unblemished, gave the sketches and cuts of three as reputable and enterprising young men as the race afforded who were prospering in a legitimate grocery business; published a formal statement from our leading ministers addressed to the public; printed 2000 extra copies and mailed them to the leading dailies, public men and Congressmen of the United States. And so in part was counteracted the libel on these foully murdered men. How many such have gone down to a violent death without anything to chronicle the true facts in their case, will never be known. Besides, a respectful, yet firm demand for race rights is absolutely necessary among those whom they live, and through no agency can it so well be heard as the newspaper.

A prosecution of this work requires men and women who are

willing to sacrifice time, pleasure and property to a realization of it; who are above bribes and demagoguery; who seek not political preferment nor personal aggrandizement; whose moral courage is strong enough to tell the race plainly yet kindly of its failings and maintain a stand for truth, honor and virtue.

This is the greatest need of all among the masses of the South—the need of the press as an educator. Children of a larger growth, the masses of our people have never been taught the first rudiments of an education, much less the science of civil government. The vast army who make the industrial wealth of the South today have had neither the experience of slavery nor the training of the school-room, to teach them some valuable lessons, yet they are citizens in name, making history every day for the race. Some of them are seemingly content with their lot, but it is the contentment of ignorance in which the white landlord strives to keep them, by pandering in all ways to the most depraved instincts, and especially by the aid of liquor can exert the influence.

The Afro-American needs to be taught the power of union, to realize his own strength; how to utilize that strength to secure to himself his inherent rights as did the plebeians of Rome. He makes the money of the South, but has never been taught that a husbanding of resources will cease to enrich gigantic corporations at his own expense. Intelligently directed, by exercise of this power alone, the race can do much to bring about a change in race condition. The sudden withdrawal of the labor force of any one community, paralyzes the industry of that community. This is instanced in communities where preventive measures are used to keep the race, when outrages perpetrated have moved them to leave. The *Free Speech* advised the people of Memphis that if they could do nothing else, after the atrocious lynching there, they could save their money and get away from a city whose laws afforded no protection to a black man. They adhered so strictly to the advice that in six weeks the real estate dealers, rental agents, dry goods merchants complained—several firms went to the wall—and the superintendent, secretary and treasurer of the electric street railway company called on us at different times to know why colored people had stopped riding on the cars. They said they had recently spent half a million dollars to put in electricity, much of which had gone in colored people's pockets; that it was a matter of dollars and cents to them, because if they did not look after the company's income they would get somebody who would. "Then you acknowledge that the patronage of colored people keeps your business running?" "Yes, to a certain extent," was the reply, and then they voluntarily promised that there should be and was no discrimination on the cars; if such was reported it would be at once corrected, etc. For once in the history of Memphis, the colored people were united and the effect was wonderful. It was the silent forceful protest which was felt as nothing else had been felt.

The race as such must be taught the value of emigration, both to relieve the congested condition which obtains, and to better their own condition by coming in contact with newer ideas, higher standards and people who have the desire to be something. They must be led to go out in the boundless west where they will develop the manhood which lies dormant with nothing to call it into exercise. The Afro-American must be taught that there is one potent, never-failing method of dealing with prejudice; when you touch a white man's pocket, you touch his heart and his prejudices all melt away. Before the almighty dollar he worships as to no other deity, and through this weakness, a taking away of this idol, the Afro-American can effect a bloodless revolution. But he must be taught his power as an industrial and financial factor. He must be shown that the turning of his money into his own coffers strengthens himself; and that a religious staying off of the growing evil of the race—the excursion business—will do more to overthrow the odious Jim Crow laws of our statute books than all the railroad suits which are prosecuted. Who is to teach him this—line upon line, precept upon precept, example upon example? Neither the teacher whose work will not be discernable for years hence, nor the minister be he ever so able, for them it may be said as Franklin said of the Grecian and Roman orators—"they can only speak to the number of citizens capable of being assembled within reach of their voice—now by the press we can speak to the nations."

So great is the race need for instruction along the lines of education, of money-saving and character-making; of learning trades, cultivating self-dependence; of building good broad foundations upon which their citizenship is to stand; so imperative is the necessity for leading the race up to the clear heights of thought, then down into the valley of action, that if persecuted and driven from one place, we must set up the printing press in another and continue the great work till the evils we suffer are removed or the people better prepared to fight their own battles. Laboring to fill our columns with matter beneficial and calculated to stimulate thought, and cultivate race reading, the next move is to take all legitimate steps to circulate our journals among the people we hope to benefit. Many of our best journals adopt the first plan while ignoring the second. They do not seem to grasp the truth that they must not only champion race rights, but cultivate a taste for reading among the people whose champions they are.

As is well known, the requirements of Southern journalism make it impossible to always dwell in the section it hopes to represent, and show the true state of affairs. To read the white papers the Afro-American is a savage that is getting away from the restraint of the inherent fear of the white man which controlled his passions, and from whom women and children now flee as from a wild beast. This impression has gained ground from the white papers, and has blasted race reputation in many quarters. The Afro-American journal has not troubled itself to counteract that opinion—those of the South because they dare not in many cases, and those of other sections seeming to care not. But not only the reputation of individuals but that of the race is involved. The clearing of this odium attached to the race name is not only the duty of one section but belongs to all, and the National Press Association should no longer sit idly waiting for the garbled accounts of the Associated Press, which it in turn gives the world.

A white, not an Afro-American journal—the Chicago *Tribune*—kept sufficient tab of the lynchings of the past eight years, to be in position to say to the world that only one-third of the enormous lynching record of that time was for the crime of rape. Beyond a word or so of compliment to the writer, the exposure of the true inwardness of affairs in the South regarding this foul charge, which appeared in the *New York Age* of June 25, was almost unnoticed by race journals. Only one, the *Omaha Progress*, published the statement in full. It was not expected that Southern journals would, but there are many of them in other sections which could have done so. The writer thought until then that our journals only needed the facts to publish, and upon which to predicate a demand that public sentiment call a halt. That a matter of such vital race moment should be ignored by those whose duty it is to correct the growing impression so hurtful to the race's good name, was surprising, to say the least.

So frequent and serious has the grave charge of rape become, there should be full investigation of every such accusation which is considered sufficient excuse for the most diabolical outrage and torture. Afro-American Southern journalism cannot do it and hope to continue existence; but this united body as an association, can do something toward changing public opinion and molding public sentiment in our favor. This is *the* work of the association, as such, and while I was only expected to speak of the requirements of Southern journalism, I trust I may be pardoned for deviating long enough to implore this convention here assembled not to adjourn until some practical, tangible step to that end shall have been taken. For years this association has met and concentrated itself with talking, and we returned to our respective homes with no tangible or practical work in hand—until the thinking portion of the race has classed press conventions with all other race conventions which meet, resolve and dissolve. If in face of daily occurrences we can still do only this, the charge against us is not without foundation. The time for *action* has come. Let the association tax itself to hire a detective, who shall go to the scene of each lynching, get the facts *as they exist* in each case of outrage—especially where the charge of rape is made—furnish them to the different papers of the association and those so situated shall publish them to the world. Money should be placed in the treasury at this session for that purpose, and a tax assessed by which it shall be kept up. It will pay from every point of view. You are thus in the position, despite the connivance of press agents, telegraph operators, and civil authorities to secure correct information, and vindicate the race from the charge of bestiality which stands before the world to-day practically un-challenged. A correspondent of *The Age* did it in Paris, Texas, in the month of September, and uncovered a tale of cruelty, outrage and murder against the race which would make sick the heart of a savage. Our race papers since have used that ac-count extensively.

This could be done in every case, and for every garbled and slanderous dispatch sent out by the Associated Press, this asso-ciation would be in position to match with the true account of these race disturbances and lynchings.

Sheridan exclaimed on one occasion: "Give me a tyrant king, give me a hostile House of Lords, give me a corrupt House of Commons,—give me the press and I will overturn them all." Gentlemen of the National Press Association, you *have* the press—what will you do with it? Upon your answer depends the future welfare of your race. Can you stand in comparative idleness, in purposeless wrangling, when there is earnest, prac-tical, united work to be done?

"Lynch Law and the Color Line" (1893)

SOURCE: Ida B. Wells-Barnett, "Lynch Law and the Color
Line," *Washington Post* (July 7, 1893).

Reply of Miss Ida B. Wells to Editorial Comments in "The Post"

EDITOR POST: I have been shown the editorials of the daily papers of the country touching my recent visit to Great Britain and the addresses I delivered while there against "lynch law." With Southern journals abuse has over answered for argument, and so the Southern press has outdone itself in vile abuse of me. But the people of Great Britain did not consider that calling me "adventuress," "slanderer," and "liar" was any rebuttal of my statements nor explanation of the fact that scarcely a week passes without a lynching in the civilized parts of our country.

In THE POST of May 31 an editorial on the same subject also accuses me of misrepresenting my native country from a mercenary motive. Permit me to say that I went to Great Britain in response to an invitation from British people themselves. This invitation came unsolicited and unexpected. They could not understand why such lawlessness prevailed in the "land of the free and the home of the brave," and volunteered to pay my expenses to have me come and tell how my friends had been lynched in Memphis and my newspaper destroyed there because I denounced lynching and lynchers. This I did gladly, and received not a cent for the forty public addresses I made in Scotland and England. I felt that as they were interested enough to pay expenses, amounting to $500, to learn the truth, I was no less interested to tell them.

Your editorial says: "If Miss Wells had cared to confine herself to a strict portrayal and denunciation of the evil results of mob violence, it would have not been necessary to go to Great Britain for an audience." For six months before the invitation came to me to go to Great Britain I tried to get a hearing in the white press and before white audiences in this country, because they could do something to check this evil. Boston was the only city in which I succeeded in doing this, and on three of the occasions I spoke to white audiences there. I paid my own expenses there and back from Washington. I was glad of this opportunity in any way to appeal to them to bestir themselves in behalf of their country's good name. On only one of these occasions, Rev. Joseph Cook's Monday lecture at Tremont Temple, was any action taken or resolutions of protest passed. In Washington city special efforts were made to get the whites to attend the lecture, but few responded.

Every white minister in the city was notified, and it was well advertised in the papers. Besides this, hundreds of neat invitations were printed at extra expense and mailed to all the Congressmen and prominent citizens of the District of Columbia. On the night of the lecture, there were not more than a dozen whites in the house, while the President, Benjamin Harrison, was so little concerned he forgot (?) to send the letter of regrets he promised Hon. Frederick Douglass he would. The report of that lecture in THE POST the following morning, February 2, said the recital was enough to cause a blush of shame, to think that such things could be in a civilized country. I told that very same story in Great Britain. If it were not a "misrepresentation" in Washington city, how could it be so in Birmingham and London? (!)

That same issue of your paper contained a full account of the awful barbarity in Texas—burning alive of Henry Smith. If I misrepresented the case to my British audience THE POST also is guilty of the same offense, for the details of how Smith was tortured with red hot irons for fifty minutes, his tongue cooked, his eyes burned out, and his body thrown back into the flames when he crawled out, and how the mob fought over the ashes for buttons and bones as relics, were first taken from the columns of THE POST on the morning of February 22. It was when giving this account that English audiences cried "Shame," "Abominable," &c. THE POST editorial on this shocking affair the Sunday following, after denouncing alike the crime of Henry Smith and the Paris (Tex.) populace, says:

"Our correspondent, however, will find it very difficult to arouse any particularly strong feeling over the fate of Henry Smith. If he committed the unspeakable enormity of which he was accused, and it is just as easy to believe that as to accept the assertion that a collection of civilized men was temporarily transformed into a drove of pitiless wild beasts—if Henry Smith we say, were guilty as alleged, nobody is likely to concern himself very greatly as to what was done with him. Indeed, it is one of the worst effects of a frightful crime that it tends to dull men's minds to the almost equal enormity of its punishment.

"We hear a great deal nowadays of lynchings and the like, in truth, they are more frequent than any one could wish. But it is foolish, as well as untrue, to say that the negro is the especial victim of these extra judicial performances, and especially unwise of the colored people to think of it as a race affair. The vigilance committees of San Francisco, Vicksburg, New Orleans, and fifty other American towns in times gone by devoted themselves almost exclusively to white offenders. They sought to eradicate a special class of criminals, and that, no doubt is the object of the lynching parties to-day. The color of the victim is a mere incident. Neither is it fair to say that lynching belongs to any section more than another.

"Henry Smith would have been put to death in Ohio or New York or Massachusetts just as surely as he was in Texas, had he committed the same crime there and fallen into the hands of the populace. Human nature is very much the same all over this country, and in one part of it as much as in the other. You can argue from certain premises to their infallible results. No intelligent and observant person needs to be told that if lynching occurs oftener at the South than at the North it is because the crimes for which lynching is applied are committed oftener there, and for no other reason.

"Of course it would be better if the punishment of offense, no matter how heinous, were always left to the deliberate process of the law, but no one who lives in the District of Columbia should wonder at men's distrust of these processes elsewhere, or be too severe in their denunciation of people who at times, and under circumstances of peculiar enormity, refuse to wait upon their uncertain evolution."

The closing paragraph of this editorial destroys entirely the effect of the first third of it. If it were true that the law is uncertain in effect, the law makers and administrators should be punished for this. No law ever miscarries where a negro is concerned, and none others but negroes would have been or are being burned in this country. Since the appearance of the above condoning editorial in THE POST, the third negro was burned in the South April 24, and he was only charged with the murder of a white man, and, with no proof of guilt, was hurried away to a stake and burned.

The American press, with few exceptions, either by such editorials or silence, has encouraged mobs, and is responsible for the increasing wave of lawlessness which is sweeping over the States. Mobs may, and occasionally do, lynch white persons, but no white man has been burned alive by a white mob nor white woman hanged by one. The St. Louis Republic is authority for the statement that mobs draw the color line. In its issue the first week in February this year it says: "Of the nearly 7,000 homicides reported in 1892 236 were committed by mobs, this being an increase of 41 over the number reported for the previous year.*** Of the persons so murdered 231 were men and 5 were women; 80 were white and 135 were negroes, while only 1 Indian was reported."

Over fifty negroes have been lynched in this country since January 1, 1893, two of whom were burned at the stake with all the barbarity of savages. One man was under the protection of the governor of South Carolina, and he gave him up to the mob that promptly lynched him. A State senator was prominently mentioned in connection with the lynching. No concealment was attempted. One of these negroes was lynched almost in sight of Jackson Park the first of this month. In no case have the lynchers been punished, in few cases has the press said anything in favor of law and order, the religious and philanthropic bodies of the country utter no word of condemnation, nor demand the enforcement of the law, and still I am charged with misrepresenting my native country. If the pulpit and press of the country will inaugurate a crusade against this lawlessness, it will be no longer necessary to appeal to the Christian, moral, and humane forces of the outside world. And when they do so, not out of sympathy with criminals, but for the sake of their country's good name, they will have no more earnest helper than

IDA B. WELLS

"Our Country's Lynching Record" (1913)

SOURCE: Ida B. Wells-Barnett, "Our Country's Lynching Record," *Survey* (February 1, 1913): 573–574.

The closing month of the year 1912 witnessed an incident which probably could not happen in any other civilized country. The governor of one of the oldest states of the Union in an address before the Conference of Governors defended the practice of lynching, and declared that he would willingly lead a mob to lynch a Negro who had assaulted a white woman. Twenty years ago, another governor of the same state not only made a similar statement, but while he was in office actually delivered to a mob a Negro who had merely been charged with this offense—it was unproven—and who had taken refuge with the governor for protection.

It is gratifying to know that the governors' meeting formally condemned these expressions, and that a leading Georgia citizen has undertaken to refute the sentiment expressed by Governor Blease. However, while no other official has thus officially encouraged this form of lawlessness, yet, because of the widespread acquiescence in the practice, many governors have refused to deal sternly with the leaders of mobs or to enforce the law against lynchers.

To the civilized world, which has demanded an explanation as to why human beings have been put to death in this lawless fashion, the excuse given has been the same as that voiced by Governor Blease a short month ago. Yet statistics show that in none of the thirty years of lynching has more than one-fourth of the persons hung, shot and burned to death, been even charged with this crime. During 1912, sixty-five persons were lynched.

Up to November 15 the distribution among the states was as follows:

Alabama	5	Oregon	1
Arkansas	3	Oklahoma	1
Florida	3	South Carolina	5
Georgia	11	Tennessee	5
Louisiana	4	Texas	3
Mississippi	5	Virginia	1
Montana	1	West Virginia	1
North Carolina	1	Wyoming	1
North Dakota	1		

Fifty of these were Negroes; three were Negro women. They were charged with these offenses:

Murder	26	Insults to white women	3
Rape	10	Attempted rape	2
Murderous assault	2	Assault and robbery	1
Complicity in murder	3	Race prejudice	1
Arson	8	No cause assigned	1

Because the Negro has so little chance to be heard in his own defense and because those who have participated in the lynching have written most of the stories about them, the civilized world has accepted almost without question the excuse offered.

From this table it appears that less than a sixth of these persons were lynched because the mob believed them to be guilty of assaulting white women. In some cases the causes have been trivial. And it appears that the northern states have permitted this lawless practice to develop and the lives of hapless victims to be taken with as much brutality, if not as frequently, as those of the South—witness, Springfield, Ill., a few years ago, and Coatesville, Pa., only last year.

The lynching mania, so far as it affects Negroes, began in the South immediately after the Emancipation Proclamation fifty years ago. It manifested itself through what was known as the Klu Klux Klan, armed bodies of masked men, who during the period between 1865 and 1875, killed Negroes who tried to exercise the political rights conferred on them by the United States until by such terrorism the South regained political control. The aftermath of such practices is displayed in the following table giving the number of Negroes lynched in each year since 1885:

1885	184	1899	107
1886	138	1900	115
1887	122	1901	135
1888	142	1902	96
1889	176	1903	104
1890	127	1904	87
1891	192	1905	66
1892	235	1906	60
1893	200	1907	63
1894	190	1908	100
1895	171	1909	87
1896	131	1910	74
1897	106	1911	71
1898	127	1912	64

With the South in control of its political machinery, the new excuse was made that lynchings were necessary to protect the honor of white womanhood. Although black men had taken such good care of the white women of the South during the four years their masters were fighting to keep them in slavery, this calumny was published broadcast. The world believed it was necessary for white men in hundreds to lynch one defenseless Negro who had been accused of assaulting a white woman. In the thirty years in which lynching has been going on in the South, this falsehood has been universally accepted in all sections of our country, and has been offered by thousands as a reason why they do not speak out against these terrible outrages.

It is charged that a ceaseless propaganda has been going on in every northern state for years, with the result that not only is there no systematic denunciation of these horrible barbarisms, but northern cities and states have been known to follow the fashion of burning human beings alive. In no one thing is there more striking illustration of the North's surrender of its position on great moral ideas than in its lethargic attitude toward the lynching evil.

The belief is often expressed that if the North would stand as firmly for principle as the South does for prejudice, lynching and many other evils would be checked. It seems invariably true, however, that when principle and prejudice come into collision, principle retires and leaves prejudice the victor.

In the celebration of the fiftieth year of the Negro's freedom, does it seem too much to ask white civilization, Christianity and Democracy to be true to themselves on this as all other questions? They can not then be false to any man or race of men. Our democracy asserts that the people are fighting for the time when all men shall be brothers and the liberty of each shall be the concern of all. If this is true, the struggle is bound to take in the Negro. We cannot remain silent when the lives of men and women who are black are lawlessly taken, without imperiling the foundations of our government.

Civilization cannot burn human beings alive or justify others who do so; neither can it refuse a trial by jury for black men accused of crime, without making a mockery of the respect for law which is the safeguard of the liberties of white men. The nation cannot profess Christianity, which makes the golden rule its foundation stone, and continue to deny equal opportunity for life, liberty and the pursuit of happiness to the black race.

When our Christian and moral influences not only concede these principles theoretically but work for them practically, lynching will become a thing of the past, and no governor will again make a mockery of all the nation holds dear in the defense of lynching for any cause.

"The Ordeal of the 'Solitary': Mrs. Barnett Protests Against It" (1915)

SOURCE: Ida B. Wells-Barnett, "The Ordeal of the 'Solitary': Mrs. Barnett Protests Against It," *Chicago Defender* (July 26, 1915).

For more than fifty hours before he appeared before the coroner's jury Campbell had been in a "solitary" cell.

The "solitary" is this: There is a little whitewashed cell. It has two doors, the outer one of oak two inches thick, the inner of steel bars.

The man in "solitary" stands handcuffed to the steel door. The manacles are locked an inch or so higher than the arm extended from the shoulder. The prisoner looks directly in front of him at the blank oak door two feet ahead.

He stands in this way for two hours. A keeper than appears and the prisoner may rest for thirty minutes. Then he is shackled up again. From 6 o'clock in the morning until 8 at night this is kept up.

At night the man in "solitary" sleeps on a bare board six feet long and three wide.

Not a ray of light filters through to him day or night. He is in absolute darkness.

Bread and water is his fare three times a day.

Simpson, Cohn and George Edwards also have been undergoing this treatment. Several times they have been dragged at night from their fitful sleep to face inquisitors and volleys of sharp questions.

Back to their lonesome cells they go after each ordeal, there to be alone with their consciences.

Campbell has felt this grind more than the others, yet each time his stories have grown in strength.

Prison officials will not admit more stringent methods than the "solitary" have been used on "Chicken Joe." Physical force, they say, is taboo in the prison.

If Campbell has been physically mistreated his appearances belie it. Although pale from confinement in the dark, he appeared in good health. His answers, while given in an anxious manner, at times were almost defiant. Several times he started to take issue with his questioners.

Mrs. Barnett Protests

Editor of the Herald: In common with thousands who have read of the horrible murder committed in Joliet penitentiary Sunday last, I have followed the testimony given at the inquest now being held in an effort to find the murderer.

All shudder to think so terrible a deed could be committed within prison walls, but I write to ask if one more terrible is not now taking place there in the name of justice, and if there is not enough decent human feeling in the state to put a stop to it and give "Chicken Joe" a chance to prove whether he is innocent or guilty.

The papers say he has been confined in solitary fifty hours, hands chained straight out before him and then brought in to the inquest, sweated and tortured to make him confess a crime that he may not have committed. Is this justice? Is it humanity? Would we stand to see a dog treated in such fashion without protest? I know we would not. Then why will not the justice-loving, law-abiding citizens put a stop to this barbarism?

The Negro Fellowship League will send a lawyer there tomorrow and we ask that your powerful journal help us to see that he gets a chance to defend "Chicken Joe" and give him an opportunity to prove whether he is innocent.

IDA B. WELLS-BARNETT,

REPRESENTING NEGRO FELLOWSHIP LEAGUE.

WOMEN
MEMORIALIZING
WOMEN

51

S. ELIZABETH FRAZIER

(1864–1924)

Susan Elizabeth Frazier was born in New York City into a prominent black family. She graduated from Hunter College in 1888 and went on to become the first black public school teacher in a mixed school in New York. She was a notable member of New York City's black community and founded the Women's Auxiliary to the Old Fifteenth National Guard, an organization that aided black soldiers and their families during World War I. A tablet in her memory hangs in St. Philip's Protestant Episcopal Church in New York.

Frazier's "Some Afro-American Women of Mark" is a pointed response to Reverend William Simmons's *Men of Mark: Eminent, Progressive, and Rising* (1887), a list of one hundred and seventy-seven influential African American men. Frazier's essay was first read as a paper before the Brooklyn Literary Union on February 16, 1892. Frazier looks back at some of the writers whose work appears in this anthology (Frances Ellen Watkins Harper, Mary Ann Shadd Cary, Charlotte L. Forten Grimké, H. Cordelia Ray, and Fannie Jackson Coppin). The similarities among these women's biographies are worth noting. Nearly all of them grew up in privileged circumstances, allowing them to pursue intellectual endeavors outside contemporary gender norms. And, later in their lives, nearly all were challenged by racism and poverty, despite their accomplishments.

"Some Afro-American Women of Mark" (1892)

SOURCE: Susan Elizabeth Frazier, "Some Afro-American
Women of Mark," *African Methodist Episcopal Church
Review* 8, no. 4 (April 1892).

WE have heard and read much of men of mark of our race, but comparatively little is known of able Afro-American women. It is my delight to present brief sketches of the lives of "Some Afro-American Women of Mark," having gained my information concerning them from libraries, public and private, from correspondence and from personal knowledge.

Notwithstanding the obstacles that presented themselves to Afro-American women, some of them, self-prompted, and in some cases self-taught, have removed obstacles, lived down oppression and fought their way nobly on to achieve the accomplishment of their aim.

Slavery was the greatest barrier in the way of progress to the African race. History records the fact that slavery was introduced in America in 1620, in Virginia. The slave trade then began by bringing slaves from Africa. This trade continued to grow, and gradually spread throughout the Middle and New England States, except Vermont. Boston, Mass., held her slave markets in common with other cities. In the year 1761, a time when slavery had reached its zenith, was seen one of the most pitiable sights ever witnessed in the Boston slave market, that of eighty girls, of various ages, brought from Africa, each snatched from a mother's fond embrace by hands most cruel, taken to a slave vessel, huddled together like cattle, with but little clothing to cover their nude forms, a dearth of food and nowhere to rest their weary bodies.

The portion assigned them, the hold of the ship, has been described as having been a room thirteen by twenty-five and five feet eight inches high. Can we imagine the trials, the tortures of these poor innocent girls so situated? As soon as the vessel reached the port of Boston, these girls were taken to the market and advertised for sale, to which sale purchasers flocked.

Among the many attending this sale was a Mrs. Wheatley, wife of a Boston merchant. She, although in possession of a number of slaves, was desirous of finding a young slave girl with apparent docile qualities, in order that she might train her to be of service to her in her declining years.

Mrs. Wheatley carefully observed the various expressions of countenances, the many physical differences of this group, and was particularly moved by the meek and bright countenance of one half-sick, fatigued little girl about eight years old, who, to her mind, possessed the requisite qualities. She immediately purchased her, took her home, clothed and fed her, and gave her the name of Phillis Wheatley. Kind words, nourishment and warm clothing made such a marked change in the child that she was now a new being. Mrs. Wheatley, perceiving the child's improvement physically, still knew that by nature Phillis was unfit for heavy domestic work, and had her taught that which was lighter. Phillis knew no language save that of her native land, and so Mrs. Wheatley deemed it necessary for her welfare, as well as that of the child, to have her taught to speak the English language, and so requested her only daughter, Miss Mary Wheatley, to teach her to speak the English language and, what was most uncommon, to read it.

This was in opposition to the principles of slavery; but Mrs. Wheatley dared to do contrary to the slave owners of her time, doubtless through the Divine inspiration of the Almighty, for "God moves in a mysterious way His wonders to perform." Miss Wheatley kindly consented to teach Phillis. Much to her surprise, she found Phillis very apt and thirsting for knowledge. Daily she progressed, and in less than two years was able to read the most difficult portions of the Bible with accuracy. Most of her knowledge of writing she acquired through her own efforts, scrutinizing good writing and copying with rude materials upon rough surfaces when paper and pencil were beyond reach. Phillis, unlike other children of her years, sought pleasure in close application to study. Mrs. Wheatley and family determined not to curb the child's ambition, but to provide her with books and writing material, which were to Phillis the means to procure the end.

Four years from the time Phillis was purchased in the slave market, she was able to write on many subjects that were hardly expected of one double her years. Her correspondence with some friends of Mrs. Wheatley, in England and with Obour Tanner, a fellow-slave, in Newport (supposed to be one of the girls brought from Africa with Phillis, also intelligent), evinced, from her power of expression and originality of thought, a mind of more than ordinary vigor.

Feeling that she had acquired sufficient knowledge of the English language, being then in her seventeenth year, she directed her attention to the study of Latin. In this, as in English, her efforts were crowned with success. In a short time she translated one of Ovid's tales so admirably that the writing attracted the attention of the learned people of Boston and England, who sought her at the home of the Wheatleys, and, conversing with her, found she was indeed a literary prodigy. This production, coming from a member of an enslaved race, gave rise to so many comments that all America, as well as England, was in a ferment, for it should be remembered that this period did not witness general culture among the masses of white people, and certainly no facilities for the education of the Negroes. The learned people of Boston invited her to their homes, loaned her books and papers. It is safe for me to say, that contact with the great minds of the time constituted one of the best parts of her education. Phillis was sensitive, and understood the prejudice existing against her race, and, while enjoying many privileges denied her kind, still maintained that meek manner characteristic of her when first seen in the slave market, and treated her fellow-slaves with the utmost consideration, winning from all affection. The inquisitive mind of Phillis was continually prompting her to seek the best works; from her study of the muses she acquired a taste for poetry, and successfully wrote many poems, which were characterized by a spirit of gratitude, simplicity, chastity, Christianity. Early she devoted herself to the service of the Lord, and was received in the Old South Church, Boston. Thus we find many of her poems manifesting the power of faith and the efficiency of grace. The following poem reveals her sympathetic nature:

ON THE DEATH OF A YOUNG GIRL.

From dark abodes to fair ethereal light,
The enraptured soul has winged its flight;
On the kind bosom of eternal love
She finds unknown beatitudes above.
This know, ye parents, nor her love deplore—
She feels the iron hand of pain no more;
The dispensations of unerring grace
Should turn your sorrows into grateful praise.
Let, then, no tears for her henceforward flow,
Nor suffer grief in this dark vale below.
Her morning sun, which was divinely bright,
Was quickly mantled with the gloom of night.
But hear, in heaven's best bowers, your child so fair,
And learn to imitate her language there.
Then, Lord, whom I behold with glory crowned,
By what sweet name, and in what tuneful sound
Wilt thou be praised? Seraphic powers are faint,
Infinite love and majesty to paint.
To Thee let all their grateful voices raise,
And saints and angels join their songs of praise.

Perfect in bliss, now from her heavenly home
She looks, and, smiling, beckons you to come.
Why, then, fond parents, why these fruitless groans?
Restrain your tears and cease your plaintive moans.
Freed from a world of sin and snares and pain,
Why would ye wish your fair one back again?
Nay, bow resigned; let hope your grief control,
And check the rising tumult of the soul;
Calm in the prosperous and adverse day,
Adore the God who gives and takes away.
See Him in all; His holy name revere;
Upright your actions, and your heart sincere;
Till, having sailed through life's tempestuous sea,
And from its rocks and boisterous billows free,
Yourselves safe landed on the blissful shore,
Shall join your happy child, to part no more.

At the age of twenty Phillis was emancipated by her master. It was a source of great delight to her owners to see that, although Phillis had been declared free, she still remained the same, thanking God for His goodness in placing her in such considerate hands:

> 'Twas mercy brought me from my pagan land,
> Taught my benighted soul to understand
> That there's a God; that there's a Savior, too.
> Once I redemption neither sought nor knew.
>
> Some view our sable race with scornful eye:
> "Their color is a diabolic dye."
> Remember, Christians, Negroes black as Cain
> May be refined, and join the angelic train.

Signs of precarious health, probably superinduced by too close application to study, became more marked and caused her mistress to become anxious about her. Mrs. Wheatley consulted her physician, who prescribed for Phillis a sea-voyage. Mrs. Wheatley's only son was about to sail for England on mercantile business, and arrangements were made for Phillis to go with him.

Her poem, entitled "A Farewell to America," dated May 7, 1773, is the day on which she is supposed to have sailed. George Williams, in his renowned "History of the Negro Race," says, "She was heartily welcomed by the leaders of the British metropolis and treated with great consideration." Under all the trying circumstances of high social life among the nobility and rarest literary genius of London, this redeemed child of the desert coupled to a beautiful modesty the extraordinary powers of an incomparable conversationalist. She carried London by storm. Thoughtful people praised her, titled people dined her, and the press extolled the name of Phillis Wheatley, the African poetess.

In England, her book of poems was republished through the earnest solicitation of her friends, and dedicated to the Countess of Huntington, with a picture of Phillis, and a letter of recommendation from her master, signed by many of the leading citizens of Boston. This letter was to repress all doubts that might arise concerning the authorship of the poems. Before she had regained her strength she received a letter from home, telling of the illness of Mrs. Wheatley and requesting her to return. As soon as possible, she was at the bedside of her loved one. Mrs. Wheatley expressed her relief at the presence of Phillis, and seemed perfectly satisfied. Day by day Mrs. Wheatley grew worse; finally the end came, March 3, 1774. This was, indeed, a sad hour for Phillis, for she realized that her best, her dearest friend was gone. Phillis remained in the Wheatley household and resumed her literary work.

When George Washington was appointed by the grand Continental Congress, in 1775, to be Generalissimo of the Armies of North America, Phillis sent him a letter extolling his merits, and also a poem written in his honor, which brought forth the following reply from Washington:

Cambridge, February 28, 1776.

MISS PHILLIS:

I thank you most sincerely for your polite notice of me in the elegant lines you inclosed, and however undeserving I may be of such encomium and panegyric, the style and manner exhibit a striking proof of your poetical talents.

If you should ever come to Cambridge, or near headquarters, I shall be happy to see a person so favored by the muses, and to whom nature has been so liberal and beneficent in her dispensations.

I AM,
WITH GREAT RESPECT,
GEORGE WASHINGTON.

Another beautiful production of her pen is a poem "On the Capture of General Charles Lee by the British." In 1778 Phillis was again prostrated by the death of Mr. Wheatley. Some say she was compelled, after the death of Mr. Wheatley, to depend on her own resources for support. Be that as it may, Phillis had an offer of marriage, and decided to accept rather than be thrown at the mercy of the world. Phillis married John Peters, of Boston, a colored gentleman of considerable intelligence.

This marriage was not a happy one. Reverses came. Phillis had never endured hardship, but she knew that the little ones born to them had to be cared for, so she took up the cross and bore it with Christian fortitude. Disease laid its heavy hand upon her, and she sank beneath its weight at the age of thirty-one, a flower in her prime, when the promises of her youth were on the verge of their full accomplishment.

No woman of the race, since the death of Phillis Wheatley, has attracted more attention by her poetic productions than Frances Ellen Watkins Harper. To her is given the honor of being the ablest female lecturer of her race. Frances Ellen Watkins Harper was born in Batimore, of free parents, in 1825. She attended the school in Baltimore for free colored children, taught by her uncle, Rev. Peter Watkins, and continued there until her thirteenth year, at which time she was put out to work in a kind and respected family. Although free-born, she suffered much from the oppressive laws that bound her slave-brethren. Like Phillis Wheatley, she possessed an ardent thirst for knowledge. Before she had been employed in this family a year, her poetic productions, especially essays on "Christianity," attracted the attention of her employers, who encouraged her ambition by giving her the use of their library during her leisure moments. As a result of her communion with the best works, she was able to write many poems, as well as prose pieces, which she had published in a small volume called "Forest Leaves." This book attracted unusual attention as an earnest of what the writer could do. Feeling herself qualified, she took up teaching. In her own city the opposition was so bitter that she deemed it wise to go to a free State, and chose Ohio for her work.

Here she became dissatisfied and left for York, Penn., to resume her work. Blessed with a spirit of philanthropy, a generous mind and a sound judgment, understanding the wrongs perpetrated on her kind, she set to work to devise some means of ameliorating the condition of the race. In order that she might concentrate her efforts in this direction, she gave up teaching and found her way into the lecture field from the following circumstance: "About the year 1853, Maryland, her native State, had enacted a law forbidding free people of color from the North from coming into the State on pain of being imprisoned and sold into slavery. A free man, who had unwittingly violated this infamous statute, had recently been sold to Georgia, and had escaped thence by secreting himself behind the wheel-house of a boat bound northward; but before he reached the desired haven he was discovered and remanded to slavery. It was reported that he died soon after from exposure and suffering."

In a letter to a friend referring to this outrage, Mrs. Harper thus wrote: "Upon that grave I pledge myself to the anti-slavery cause." Soon after she left York and went to Philadelphia, then to Boston, to New Bedford. Here she was called upon to deliver an address on the "Education and Elevation of the Colored Race." In this address she poured forth a stream of eloquence that astonished all present. This occasion marks the beginning of her public career. On she has continued, fearless in her outspoken opinions. She has lectured on freedom in every Southern city except in Arkansas and Texas; has held the position of Superintendent of Colored Work in the Woman's Christian Temperance Union for nearly seven years, and has lectured and written many poems on temperance, exerting a widespread influence.

None felt more keenly the death of John Brown, the noble hero who planned and died for the cause of emancipation, than Mrs. Harper. Tenderly she expressed her sympathy for Mrs. Brown in her bereavement, beseeching God to sustain her in the hour of affliction.

Mrs. Harper was married to Fenton Harper in Cincinnati, November, 1860. She still labored in the literary field, never giving up unless compelled to do so by other duties. On May 23, 1864, occurred the death of Mr. Harper. Some of her best productions are "The Slave Mother," "To the Union Savers of Cleveland," "Fifteenth Amendment." "Moses," a story of the Nile, deals with the story of the Hebrew Moses, beautifully portrayed by her from his infancy, when exposed on the Nile, found and adopted by Pharaoh's daughter; his gratitude to the princess; his flight into Midian and his return into Egypt; his nomadic life, by means of which God prepared him to be the means of deliverance to His people; to his death on Monnt Nebo, and his burial in an unknown grave, following closely

the account of the Scriptures. Most pathetically are the death
and burial of Moses penned in the following lines:

His work was done; his blessing lay
Like precious ointment on his people's head,
And God's great peace was resting on his soul.
His life had been a lengthened sacrifice,
A thing of deep devotion to his race,
Since first he turned his eyes on Egypt's gild
And glow, and clasped their fortunes in his hands,
And held them with a firm and constant grasp.
But now his work was done; his charge was laid
In Joshua's hand, and men of younger blood
Were destined to possess the land and pass
Through Jordan to the other side. He, too,
Had hoped to enter there—to tread the soil
Made sacred by the memories of his kindred dead,
And rest till life's calm close beneath
The sheltering vines and stately palms of that
Fair land; that hope had colored all his life's
Young dreams and sent its mellow flushes o'er
His later years; but God's decree was otherwise,
And so he bowed his meekened soul in calm
Submission to the word, which bade him climb
To Nebo's highest peak, and view the pleasant land
From Jordan's swells unto the calmer ripples
Of the tideless sea, then die with all its
Loveliness in sight.
As he passed from Moab's grassy vale to climb
The rugged mount, the people stood in mournful groups,
Some with quivering lips and tearful eyes,
Reaching out unconscious hands as if to stay
His steps and keep him ever at their side, while
Others gazed with reverent awe upon
The calm and solemn beauty on his aged brow,
The look of loving trust and lofty faith
Still beaming from an eye that neither care
Nor time had dimmed. As he passed upward, tender

Blessings, earnest prayers and sad farewells rose
On each wave of air, then died in one sweet
Murmur of regretful love; and Moses stood
Alone on Nebo's mount.

Alone! Not one
Of all that mighty throng who had trod with him
In triumph through the parted flood was there.
Aaron had died in Hor, with son and brother
By his side. And Miriam, too, was gone.
But kindred hands had made her grave, and Kadesh
Held her dust. But he was all alone; nor wife
Nor child was there to clasp in death his hand,
And bind around their bleeding hearts the precious
Parting words. And yet he was not all alone,
For God's great presence flowed around his path,
And stayed him in that solemn hour.

He stood upon the highest peak of Nebo,
And saw the Jordan chafing through its gorges,
Its banks made bright by scarlet blooms
And purple blossoms. The placid lakes
And emerald meadows, the snowy crest
Of distant mountains, the ancient rocks
That dripped with honey, the hills all bathed
In light and beauty, the shady groves
And peaceful vistas, the vines oppress'd
With purple riches, the fig trees fruit-crowned,
Green and golden, the pomegranates with crimson
Blushes, the olives with their darker clusters,
Rose before him like a vision, full of beauty
And delight. Gazed he on the lovely landscape
Till it faded from his view, and the wing
Of death's sweet angel hovered o'er the mountain's
Crest, and he heard his garments rustle through
The watches of the night.

Then another, fairer vision
Broke upon his longing gaze; 'twas the land
Of crystal fountains, love and beauty, joy
And light, for the pearly gates flew open,

And his ransomed soul went in. And when morning
O'er that mountain fringed each crag and peak with light,
Cold and lifeless lay the leader. God had touched
His eyes with slumber, giving his beloved sleep.

Oh! never on that mountain
Was seen a lovelier sight
Than the troupe of fair young angels
That gathered round the dead.
With gentle hands they bore him,
That bright and shining train,
From Nebo's lonely mountain
To sleep in Moab's vale.
But they sang no mournful dirges,
No solemn requiems said,
And the soft wave of their pinions
Made music as they trod.
But no one heard them passing.
None saw their chosen grave.
It was the angels' secret
Where Moses should be laid.
And when the grave was finished
They trod with golden sandals
Above the sacred spot;
And the brightest, fairest flowers
Sprang up beneath their tread.
Nor broken turf nor hillock
Did e'er reveal that grave,
And truthful lips have never told,
We know where he is laid.

Mrs. Harper is now engaged in writing a book called "Iola,"
which is a work on the racial question. May we not hope that
the rising generation, at least, will take encouragement by her
example and find an argument of race force in favor of mental
and moral equality, and, above all, be awakened to see how
prejudice and difficulties may be surmounted by continual
struggles, intelligence and a virtuous character.

We also find in the lecture field, working for the best interest of her race, *Mary Ann Shadd Carey*, also an able writer and teacher. Mary Ann Shadd Carey was born in Delaware, and received a better education than was usually obtained by free colored people. As a speaker she ranks deservedly high; as a debater she is quick to take advantage of the weak points of her opponents, forcible in her illustrations, biting in her sarcasm.

The name of Charlotte L. Grimké, *nee* Forten, appears before me. A woman of rare intellectual gifts, a moral nature full of sympathy and benevolence for her race. Charlotte L. Grimké was born in Philadelphia. Like her predecessors, obstacles in the way of progress presented themselves to her. In her native city, then the most bitterly prejudiced of Northern cities, she was refused admission to institutions of learning, and was sent to school in New England—to Salem, Massachusetts. Here prejudice existed, but not so much as in Philadelphia. She was received into the grammar school at Salem. She was the only colored pupil in the school, and won the esteem of her teachers and fellow-pupils. A short time before graduation from this school, the principal requested each student of the graduating class, of which she was a member, to write a poem to be sung at the closing exercises, the successful competitor to be known only on that day. This proved a stimulus in drawing out the poetic genius of the young aspirants. The manuscripts were collected, each bearing a fictitious name. One of the many was selected and printed on the program. This was the poem, entitled

A PARTING HYMN.

When winter's royal robes of white
  From hill and vale are gone,
And the glad voices of the spring
  Upon the air are borne,
Friends, who have met with us before,
Within these walls shall meet no more.

Forth to a noble work they go,
  Oh! may their hearts keep pure;
And hopeful zeal and strength be thine

To labor and endure;
That they an earnest faith may prove
By words of truth and deeds of love.

May those whose holy task it is
        To guide impulsive youth,
Fail not to cherish in their souls
        A reverence for truth;
For teachings which the lips impart
Must have their source within the heart.

May all who suffer share their love—
        The poor and the oppressed—
So shall the blessings of our God
        Upon their labors rest;
And may we meet again, when all
Are blest and freed from every thrall.

To the surprise of all, this beautiful hymn was written by
Charlotte L. Forten, the only colored pupil of her class, the
only one of the school, convincing the prejudiced minds of the
possibilities of her race.

She next entered the Normal School, from which she graduated, and was offered a position to teach in one of the schools,
which offer she accepted, being the first colored woman to teach
in a white school. She continued to teach until her health became
impaired, and was advised, by her physician, to go South. After
recuperating in Philadelphia for a time, she went farther South to
teach the freedmen at Port Royal, on the coast of South Carolina,
a deeply interesting work to her, and the years spent in that work
the most delightful of her life; and while here, at the suggestion of
her beloved and life-long friend, Mr. Whittier, she wrote some articles about life there. She afterward resided in Boston and Cambridge, where she became assistant secretary of the Teacher's
Committee of the New England Freedmen's Aid Society. When
this society disbanded, she went to Washington to reside, and
there married Rev. Francis J. Grimké, who is well known to us as
an eloquent divine. To him she has been a true minister's wife, and
has done much to make his ministerial career successful. She has

contributed to the *Anti-Slavery Standard, Boston Common-wealth, Boston Christian Register.* She has made some translations from the French, among them one of the Eickmann Châtrien Novels, entitled "Madame Thérese," which was published by Scribner some years ago. Of late years Mrs. Grimké has been able to write but little, owing to her continued ill-health, which is the source of deep regret not only to herself, but to her many friends. One of her more recent writings, "A June Song," was read at the closing exercises of the "Monday Night Literary," at Cedar Hill, the residence of the Hon. Frederick Douglass:

We would sing a song to the fair young June,
To the rare and radiant June,
The lovely, laughing, fragrant June.
　How shall her praise be sung or said?
　Her cheek has caught the roses hue,
　Her eye the heaven's serenest blue.

And the gold of sunset crowns her head,
And her smile—ah! there's never a sweeter, I ween,
Than the smile of this fair young summer queen.
　What life, what hope her coming brings!
　What joy anew in the sad heart springs
　As her robe of beauty o'er all she flings.

Old earth grows young in her presence sweet,
And thrills at the touch of her gentle feet,
As the flowers spring forth her face to greet.
Hark, how the birds are singing her praise
In their gladdest, sweetest roundelays!
　O'er the lovely, peaceful river
　The golden lights of sunset quiver.

The trees on the hillside have caught the glow,
And heaven smiles down on the earth below.
　And our radiant June,
　Our lovely, joyous June,
　　Our summer queen
　Smiles, too, as she stands

With folded hands,
 And brow serene.

How shall we crown her bright young head?
Crown it with roses, rare and red;
 Crown it with roses, creamy white,
 As the lotus bloom that sweetens the night.
Crown it with roses pink as the shell
In which the voices of ocean dwell.
  And a fairer queen
  Shall ne'er be seen
 Than our lovely, laughing June.

We have crowned her now, but she will not stay,
The vision of beauty will steal away
And fade, as faded the fair young May.
 Ah, loveliest maiden, linger awhile!
 Pour into our hearts the warmth of thy smile,
The gloom of the winter will come too soon.
Stay with us, gladden us, beautiful June!
 Thou glidest away from our eager grasp,
 But our hearts will hold thee close in their clasp.
They will hold thee fast; and the days to be
Will be brighter and sweeter for thoughts of thee.
 Our song shall not be a song of farewell,
 As with words of love the chorus we swell
  In praise of the fair young June,
  Of the rare and radiant June,
  The lovely, laughing, fragrant June.

H. Cordelia Ray, daughter of the late Rev. Chas. B. Ray, is a woman full of *savoir-faire*, and stands among our able women writers, not only in poetry, but in prose, excelling in poetry in the sonnet, in prose critical literature. Miss Ray was born and educated in New York City, and began to weave verses at the age of ten years. Among her poems are "The Mist-maiden," "The Hermit of the Soul," "Dante," "Antigone and Epidus," "Reverie," "Hour's Glory," "Lincoln" (written by request and recited for the unveiling of the Freedmen's monument at

Washington in memory of Abraham Lincoln). This poem was quite widely copied in the papers.

Among the group of illustrative sonnets are, "Shakespeare, the Poet," "Raphael, the Artist," "Beethoven, the Musician," "Emerson, the Philosopher," "Sumner, the Statesman," "Toussaint L'Overture, the Patriot," "Wendell Phillips, the Philanthropist." Miss H. Cordelia Ray teaches in Grammar School No. 80, New York City, of which Professor Charles L. Reason is principal.

In June, 1891, the University of the City of New York held their commencement exercises. At this commencement, first in the history of education, university pedagogical degrees were conferred. An event of historic interest. Fourteen members of the University School of Pedagogy received the degree of Doctor of Pedagogy, and twelve the degree of Master of Pedagogy. Of the twelve, I am proud to say, three were colored—Miss H. Cordelia Ray, of whom I have just spoken, Miss Florence T. Ray and Miss Mary Eato. Miss J. Imogen Howard now attends the university, and will be the next to receive the degree of Master of Pedagogy.

Mrs. Sarah J. S. Garnet has proved herself the pioneer for the maintenance of colored schools, and an advocate of the higher education of women. Mrs. Garnet is a teacher of varied experience. She has filled the positions from the lowest primary grades. She was an assistant in Grammar School No. 1, Mulberry Street, New York, principal of Primary Department No. 3, Brooklyn, and afterward appointed principal of Grammar School No. 81, Seventeenth Street, New York, where she has served faithfully twenty-six years. Being a member of the National Teachers' Association for many years, and many times the only colored representative from this section of the country, she has enjoyed extensive travel over our own country and is well up in points of interest and information as regards the educational system and general development of our own country. As a philanthropist, nothing of interest to the race within her power and ability to be achieved has been lost. All opportunities are carefully watched and treasured for opportune development.

In Philadelphia, we find *Mrs. Fannie Jackson Coppin*, principal of the Philadelphia Institute for Colored Youth, an acute thinker, an eloquent speaker, a benefactress to her race. Mrs. Coppin was born in the District of Columbia about the year

1837, and was left an orphan when quite young. She was brought up by her aunt, Mrs. Clark. In Washington the opportunities for education were limited, that is to say for the race. Anxious to gain knowledge, she left and went to New Bedford, in her sixteenth year, where she began the studies of the higher branches. She entered Oberlin College and graduated with honor. Through her untiring efforts, the Philadelphia Institute for Colored Youth was founded for the purpose of giving Negro children an industrial as well as an intellectual education. This institution is a success. Says John Durham, now minister to Hayti, of Mrs. Coppin and her work: "Long before the industrial-training idea threatened to become a fad, she had introduced it into this institute for boys and girls. Had she been other than an American colored woman, or had she not had to struggle against the characteristic conservatism of the Society of Friends, she would have been one of the most famous of American's school reform instructors. As it is she works on modestly, indeed, too self-deprecating; eminent, but without notoriety."

It is said that the science of medicine has been regarded as ranking among the most intricate and delicate pursuits man could follow. Not long ago, woman began to feel that the science of medicine was not too intricate, not too delicate for her to follow, and so set herself to work to gain admission to some of the schools of medicine, that she, too, might become equipped with the necessary medical training, that would enable her to relieve the wants of suffering humanity. Nowhere was greater opposition to be found than in the profession and in the community.

It was doubted as to whether she was physically able to endure the hardships necessarily implied in an active practice. Slowly the portals of medicine opened to her, and earnestly she pursued her study. Afro-American women, best fitted by nature and education, have, like their white sisters, labored, although in the presence of more opposition, and met with success in the science of medicine. Those of mark are: Dr. Consuello Clark, Cincinnati; Dr. Caroline Anderson, Philadelphia; Dr. Hall Tanner and Dr. Susan McKinney. Dr. Susan McKinney leads the van in opening a sphere of usefulness. Dr. Susan McKinney, *nee* Smith, was born in Brooklyn, her father being the late Sylvanus Smith. The *Brooklyn Daily Eagle*, in mentioning and giving accounts of some able and noted colored people in Brooklyn, gave this interesting account of Dr. Susan McKinney:

"Dr. McKinney is a striking instance of force of character, conquering extraordinary, almost obdurate obstacles, and achieving success in the midst of difficulties that would dismay a giant. She not only had to overcome the prejudice against female practitioners, but those against her race. Her spirit was equal to the task, however, and at this moment her reputation is such that any woman, irrespective of color, might be proud of it. Dr. McKinney was a student in the Woman's Medical College, New York, under Dr. Clement Lozier, a professional woman of liberal ideas, a strong battler against the prejudice of caste, who first advocated the admission of colored women into the college. Shortly after Dr. McKinney's graduation she commenced to practice, an uphill course. Patients were slow in coming; her own race apparently mistrusted the skill of a colored medical woman. While she belongs to a class, that of Homeopathy, at that time discountenanced by the masses, she persevered and is now well established."

In former years she had sustained herself as a teacher in a public school, this city, out of the earnings of which position she defrayed her college expenses. That experience nerved her to struggle desperately for a standing in the medical profession at a juncture when to be courageous appeared foolish, so hopeless seemed the future. Dr. McKinney is one of the doctors on the medical staff of the Woman's Dispensary, on Classon Avenue, a member of the King's County and the New York Staff and City Society of Homeopathy, and a member of the Alumni Society. She has lectured on subjects bearing on her profession in several cities. One of the faculty of the college from which she graduated took the pains to look her up and engage her to attend a female member of his family, giving as his reason for so doing that she was, he thought, the brightest member of the class from which she was graduated. This was a high authority, and, therefore, complimentary to Dr. Susan McKinney.

The race points with pride to *Edmonia Lewis*, the greatest of her race in the art of sculpture. Her latent genius was stirred at the sight of a statue of Benjamin Franklin, in Boston. "I, too, can make a stone man," she said. She expressed her desire in this direction to William Lloyd Garrison, "that great Apostle of Human Liberty," and begged his advice. William Lloyd Garrison encouraged her and gave her a letter to the greatest sculptor of Boston, who, after reading the note, gave her a model of a human foot and some clay, and said, "Go home and make that; if there is anything in you it will come out." Delighted, she went, and worked out a copy. As soon as it was finished she returned to the sculptor. He was not pleased with it and broke it up, telling her to try again. She was not discouraged, for she was determined to achieve success in this art. Again she tried and obtained victory. "She has won a position as an artist, a studio in Rome, and a place in the admiration of lovers of art on two continents." Her studio in Rome is an object of interest to all European travelers. The most prominent of her works are, "Hagar in the Wilderness," a group of "Madonna with the Infant Christ and two adoring Angels," "Forever Free," "Hiawatha's Wooing," a bust of Longfellow the poet, a bust of John Brown, and a medallion portrait of Wendell Phillips. There are other Afro-American women of mark, brief accounts of whose lives I would be pleased to give, but the limited space will not permit.

We young women of the race have a great work to do. We have noble and brilliant examples of women, who, under all trying circumstances, have labored earnestly for the elevation of their race, their sex. Let us strive, with the advantages of a higher education, to carry out the aim of our noble predecessors—the success of the futurity of the race.

52

LUCY WILMOT SMITH

(1861–1890)

Lucy Wilmot Smith's essay "Women as Journalists: Portraits and Sketches of a Few of the Women Journalists of the Race," published in the *Freeman* on February 23, 1889, exemplifies the urge to canonize African American women writers at the end of the nineteenth century. Smith, like so many of the journalists in this anthology, was from the South, born in Lexington, Kentucky, in 1861. She was a teacher from the time she was sixteen years old. Her columns and sketches appeared in the *American Baptist*, *Journalism*, *Our Women and Children*, and the *Baptist Journal*.

Smith emphasizes her contemporaries' professionalism and hopes and that the work of these women should be seen as particularly extraordinary because of the obstacles faced throughout their careers.

"Women as Journalists: Portraits and Sketches of a Few of the Women Journalists of the Race" (1889)

SOURCE: Lucy Wilmot Smith, "Women as Journalists: Portraits and Sketches of a Few of the Women Journalists of the Race," *Freeman* (February 23, 1889).

The Negro woman's history is marvelously strange and pathetic. Unlike that of other races, her mental, moral, and physical status has not found a place in the archives of public libraries. From the womb of the future must come that poet or

author to glorify her womanhood by idealizing the various
phases of her character, by digging from the past examples of
faithfulness and sympathy, endurance and self-sacrifice and
displaying the achievements which were brightened by friction.
Born and bred under both the hindrance of slavery and the
limitations of her sex, the mothers of the race have kept pace
with the fathers. They stand at the head of the cultured, educated families whose daughters clasp arms with the sons. The
educated Negro woman occupies vantage found over the Caucasian woman of America, in that the former has had to contest with her brother every inch of the ground for recognition,
the Negro man, having had his sister by his side on plantations
and in rice swamps, keeps her there, now that he moves in
other spheres. As she wins laurels he accords her the royal
crown. This is especially true in journalism. Doors are opened
before we knock, and as well equipped young women emerged
from the class-room the brotherhood of the race, men whose
energies have been repressed and distorted by the interposition
of circumstances, give them opportunities to prove themselves;
and right well are they doing this by voice and pen. On matters
pertaining to women and the race, there is no better author
among our female writers than

Mrs. N. F. Mossell [Gertrude Bustill Mossell]

Her style is clear, compact and convincing. Seven years teaching in Camden, N.J. and Philadelphia, her present home, and
the solid reading matter, viz: The Bible, "Paradise Lost," The
Atlantic Monthly and The Public Ledger, which was her daily
food while under her father's roof, gave her a deep insight into
a human nature, and the clear mode of expression which makes
her articles so valuable to the press. Her career as a writer began many years ago, when Bishop Tanner—then editor of The
Christian Recorder—was attracted by an essay on "Influence"
which he requested for publication. Short stories followed, and
from then to the present, she has been engaged constantly on

race journals. "The Woman's Department" of the New York Freeman was edited by her with much tact and The Philadelphia Echo is always more readable when containing something from her pen. For three years she has been employed on the Philadelphia Times, The Independent, and Philadelphia Press Republican, following the particular lines of race literature and the "Woman's Question." Mrs. Mossell's experience in journalism is that editors are among the most patient of men, that the rejection of an article by no means proves that it is a failure, that sex is no bar to any line of literary work, that by speaking for themselves women can give the truth about themselves and thereby inspire the confidence of the people. Besides newspaper work her home life is a busy one, assisting her husband, a prominent physician of Philadelphia, whose own literary life has been an incentive to her. Spare moments are given to the completion of a book, on a race question, which will soon be launched on the current thought and society.

Mrs. Lucretia Newman Coleman

is a writer of rare ability. Discriminating and scholarly, she possesses to a high degree the poetic temperament and has acquired great facility in verse. Her last poem, "Lucille of Montana," ran through several numbers of the magazine Our Women and Children, and is full of ardor, eloquence and noble thought. Mrs. Coleman has contributed special scientific articles to the A.M.E. [African, Methodist Episcopal] Review and other journals, which were rich in minute comparisons, philosophic terms and scientific principles. She is a writer more for scholars than for the people. A novel entitled "Poor Ben," which is the epitome of the life of a prominent A.M.E. Bishop, is pronounced an excellent production. Mrs. Coleman is an accomplished woman and well prepared for a literary life. She was born in Dresden, Ontario, went with her missionary father to the West Indies where he labored a number of years, thence to Cincinnati, Oh., where he was pastor of a church, and after his death she went with her mother to Appleton, Wisconsin, to take advantage of the educational facilities. After graduating from the scientific course of Lawrence University she devoted her time to literary pursuits, and now ranks with the most painstaking writers.

Miss Ida B. Wells (Iola)

has been called the "Princess of the Press," and she has well earned the title. No writer, the male fraternity not excepted, has been more extensively quoted; none have struck harder blows at the wrongs and weakness of the race. T. T. Fortune (probably the "Prince" of the Negro press) wrote after meeting her at the Democratic Conference at Indianapolis: "She has become famous as one of the few of our women who handle a goose-quill with diamond point as easily as any man in the newspaper work. If Iola was a man, she would be a humming independent in politics. She has plenty of nerve and is as sharp as a steel trap."

Miss Wells' readers are equally divided between the sexes. She reaches the men by dealing with the political aspect of the race question, and the women, she meets around the fireside. She is an inspiration to the young writers and her success has lent an impetus to their ambition. When the National Press Convention, of which she was Assistant Secretary, met in Louisville, she read a splendidly written paper on "Women in Journalism or How I Would Edit." By the way, it is her ambition to edit a paper. She believes that there is no agency so potent as the press in reaching and elevating a people. Her contributions are distributed among the leading race journals. She made her debut with the Living Way, Memphis, Tenn., and has since written for the New York Age, Detroit Plaindealer, Indianapolis World, Gate City Press, Mo. Little Rock Sun, American Baptist, Ky. Memphis Watchman, Chattanooga Justice, Christian Index, and Fisk University Herald, Tenn., Our Women and Children Magazine, Ky., and the Memphis papers, weeklies and dailies. Miss Wells has attained much success as teacher in the public schools of the last named place.

Mrs. W. E. Mathews (Victoria Earle)

Ten years ago "Victoria Earle" began taking advantage of opportunities offered for acting as "sub" for reporters employed by many of the great dailies. She has reported for the New York Times, Herald, Mail and Express, Sunday Mercury, The Earth, The Photographic World, and is now New York correspondent to the National Leader, D.C., The Detroit Plaindealer, and the Southern Christian Recorder. Under various nom de plume she has written for the Boston Advocate, Washington Bee, Richmond Planet, Catholic Tribune, Cleveland Gazette, New York Age, New York Globe, and the New York Enterprise, besides editing three special departments. Reportorial work is her forte, yet her success in story writing has been great. She contributes to the story department of Waverly Magazine, The New York Weekly and Family Story Paper. "Victoria Earle" has written much; her dialect tidbits for the Associated Press are much in demand. She has ready several stories which will appear in one volume, and is also preparing a series of historical text books which will aim to develop a race pride in our youth. She is member of the Women's National Press Association and no writer of the race is kept busier.

Miss Mary V. Cook (Grace Ermine)

Whatever honors have come to Miss Cook are the results of persevering industry. She has edited the Woman's Department of the American Baptist, Ky. and the Educational Department of Our Women and Children in such a manner as to attract much attention to them. Her writings are lucid and logical and of such a character as will stand the test of time. Aside from journalistic work her life is a busy one. She has appeared on the platform of several national gatherings and her papers for research, elegance of diction, and sound reasoning were superior. She holds the professorship of Latin in the State University, her Alma Mater, yet however great her mental ability, it is overmatched by her character. Her life is the crystalization of womanly qualities. She moves her associates by a mighty power of sympathy which permeated her writings. She is a good news-gatherer and is much quoted, is a native of Bowling Green, Ky., where her mother, a generous hearted woman who sympa-thizes with her aspirations, still lives. Miss Cook is interested in all questions which affect the race.

Lillial Akbeeta Kewus (Bert Islew)

Those who know much about the newspapers of the race, know something of Bert Islew's Budget of Gossip in the spicy "They say Column" of The Boston Advocate. Bright, witty, sparkling, one would not think Bert Islew's career antedated only three years and that she was barely twenty when she caught the pub-lic ear. The early atmosphere she breathed may have developed a public spiritedness. Was born in the home of Hon. Lewis Hayden, that good man whose name is closely associated with the Crispus Attuck monument. When but thirteen years old and in the graduating class of the Bowdin Grammar school she entered a prize essay contest and carried off the third prize, al-though the other contestants were older High School pupils and graduates. This fired her ambition, and soon after gradua-tion she wrote a novel entitled "Idalene Van Therese," which, for lack of means, is unpublished. Then came her successful career with The [People's] Advocate. In addition to her newspa-per work, she has for several years been the private stenogra-pher and secretary to the widely known Max Eliot, of the Boston Herald. This position calls for proficiency, and Bert Islew's record for taking down copy verbatim is among the highest in New England. Then, too, her position in the Herald office calls for special articles and reportorial work, which she does creditably. She is recognized in all circles for her ability, and works side by side with editors and reporters without an iota of distinction being made.

Mrs. Amelia F. Johnson

In the mild countenance of Mrs. Amelia Johnson can be read the love and tenderness for children which was demonstrated last year by the publication of the Ivy, an eight-page journal devoted especially to the interests of our youth. It was a good paper filled with original stories and poems and information concerning the doings of the race. Mrs. Johnson is keen, imaginative, and critical, story writing is her forte. It is a part of her nature to weave her thoughts into pleasing imagery. Even when a child she would follow the scratches on her desk with a pencil and tell wonderful stories of them to her seatmate. She has written many of them at different times and is now engaged in writing a story book to be used in Sunday-school libraries. Many short stories from her pen find snug resting places in corners of weeklies. There is a vein of wit and humor in her sayings—a pith and transparency which makes her articles extremely readable. Of all the writers before the public, none of them possess in a higher degree the elements of a skillful critic. She has contributed to the Baptist Messenger, Md., The American Baptist, Ky., and Our Women and Children Magazine. Mrs. Johnson was educated in Canada—taking a thorough French course—and has taught both French and English branches in Baltimore, her present home.

Miss Mary E. Britton (Meb)

To the ready pen of Miss Mary E. Britton (Meb) is due many of the reformatory measures which have given the race equal facilities on railroads in Kentucky. The energy and resolute vim of her character is traced in her writings, especially when advocating woman's suffrage and the same moral standard for both sexes. She has studied language from the standard English and American authors and her diction is remarkably chaste. Miss Britton was editor of the "Women's Column" of the Lexington Herald, contributes special articles to the Courant—the Kentucky educational journal—the Cleveland Gazette, the American Catholic Tribune, the Indianapolis World and Our Women and Children Magazine. Her own ambition to excel prompts her to inspire others and nearly all her articles have this savor and was exhibited in those written for The Ivy, the children's paper. The local papers of Lexington, Ky., her home, and the Cincinnati Commercial have published and commented on her articles.

Miss Jane E. Wood

There is a dash of freshness, a breezyness in Miss Wood's writings, a clear, decided ring which will yet be heard in louder tones. She has pronounced views on total abstinence and is an enthusiastic member of the Woman's National Suffrage Association. She contributed several stories to The Ivy and now edits the Temperance Department of Our Women and Children magazine. Miss Wood will make a clever reporter. She is now tutor in Greek in the Kentucky State University.

Miss Kate D. Chapman

sends from her faraway Dakota home spritely poems and other contributions to racial journals. She is only eighteen, but the public is becoming familiar with her bright thoughts and unique expressions. She has read much and will write much. Her contributions have appeared principally in The Christian Recorder and Our Women and Children. Her ambition was stirred when but five years old by receiving a book as reward for committing a poem. She will devote her talent to juvenile literature.

Occasional Contributors—Among those who do special work and contribute valuable articles to weeklies and monthlies are Mesdames Francis E. W. Harper and L. F. Grimké [Angelina], Philadelphia. Cora C. Calhoun, former editor of the Woman's Department in the Chattanooga Justice; Olive B. Clanton, New Orleans; Lavinia E. Sneed, Ky.; Josephine Turpin Washington, Selma; Misses Georgia M. DeBaptiste, Ill.; Julia K. Mason, D.C.; Alice Henderson, Ark., and Meta Pelham, one of the essentials on the Plaindealer staff.

Editors—The Western Herald was edited by Mrs. Amos Johnson, Keokuk, Ia.; The Lancet, by Miss Carrie Bragg, Petersburg, Va.; The Musical Messenger by Miss Amelia L. Tighlman, Montgomery, Ala.; The St. Matthew's Lyceum, by Mrs. M. E. Lambert, Detroit, Mich.; The Ivy, by Mrs. A. E. Johnson, Baltimore, Md.; and Miss A. E. McEwen is Assistant Editor of the Herald, Montgomery, Ala.

This article includes only a few of our writers. When we remember the very difficult circumstances of the past, the trials and discomforts of the present, we are indeed cheered with the prospects. In the busy hum of life it is difficult to make one's way to the front, and this is true of all races, hence, we are not at all discouraged since our sisters have had such ready access to the great journals of the land. When the edge of prejudice shall have become rusted and worn out, the Negro woman shall be heard most potently in the realm of thought, till then shall we strive.

LUCY WILMOT SMITH
IN THE JOURNALIST.